D0905737

Martin Mordecai

The University of the West Indies Press

Jamaica • Barbados • Trinidad and Tobago

The University of the West Indies Press
7A Gibraltar Hall Road, Mona
Kingston 7, Jamaica
www.uwipress.com

A catalogue record of this book is available from the
National Library of Jamaica.

ISBN: 978-976-640-681-3 (paper)
978-976-640-682-0 (Kindle)
978-976-640-683-7 (ePub)

Cover image: Carol Crichton, *Roll Call* (photoprint composite on canvas, 39 × 59 inches); photographer unknown (photograph courtesy Archive Farms Inc.), extract list of names courtesy Joy Lumsden.

Cover and book design by Robert Harris
Set in Sabon 10.5/14.5
Printed in the United States of America

For Tony McNeil (1941–1996), fine poet, friend,
who started my journey.

For Kamau Brathwaite, fine poet, friend,
whose ideas and research sustained me.

For Pamela Mordecai, fine poet, friend, wife and grandmother of
Zoey Rita, whose love sustained and encouraged me.

Had nature intended negroes for slavery . . .
they would have been born without any sentiment for liberty.

—James Ramsay, *Essay on the Treatment and Conversion
of African Slaves* (1784)

Drum skin whip

lash, master sun's

cutting edge of

heat

—[Edward] Kamau Brathwaite, *Rights of Passage* (1967)

≈ Dramatis Personae ≈

GREENCASTLE ESTATE

Achilles, a slave, Anthony's son by Lucia, a slave
Angela, Squire's deceased first wife, mother of Anthony
Anna, Squire's daughter with Mathilde, his second wife
Anthony, heir, son of Squire's first wife, Angela
Balfour, slave, son of Lincoln
Bristol, slave, son of Tombo
Cherry, Jason's horse
Constancia, aka Miss Delphy, old slave
Cumberbatch, overseer succeeding John Wyckham
Creole Scotty, slave driver
Delores, aka Gatta, slave
Dollyboy, slave
George Pollard, aka Squire, deceased proprietor
Hector, slave, head driver
Hole-em, slave, works in the hothouse
Israel, slave
Jack, slave, personal servant to Jason
Jason, aka Kwesi, aka Jaze, Squire's first son by the slave Memba
John Wyckham, aka Backra, overseer
Juba Lilly, slave
Judith, slave, Pompey's woman
Lincoln, Muslim slave, saved Squire's life
Lucia, slave, Achilles's mother
Malachai, slave, personal servant to Anna
Mathilde, Squire's second wife
Marjorie, wife of M'sieu Jean Claude Richard

Memba, slave, deceased, mother of Jason
Miranda, slave, daughter of Prudence
M'sieu Jean-Claude Richard, in charge of the coffee plantation
Olive, slave
Pheba, slave, Pompey's daughter
Pompey, reinstated head driver (Jason lived in his hut as a child)
Portigee, slave, works in the hothouse
Prudence, slave, mother of Miranda
Reverend Sultzberger, Moravian missionary, house guest
Silas, slave
Simpson, bookkeeper
Tanti Glory, slave in charge of the hothouse
Teckford, slave driver
Tombo, aka Carpenter John, slave, father of Bristol
Zubia, slave, Hector's baby-mother

CASCADE ESTATE

Magnus Douglas, proprietor

BELLEFIELDS AND ENVIRONS

Adebeh Cameron, Maroon, come from Nova Scotia to find his
    sister, Baddhu
Arthur Hollyoak, free coloured, slave owner
Boynton, functionary at the courthouse
Brother Cephas, member of Zion Chapel
Brother Greenwich, member of Zion Chapel
Brother Theophilus Thomas, aka Uncle Teo, fisherman, carpenter,
    elder at Zion chapel
Courtney Waterman, Elorine's would-be suitor
Dr. Fenwell, Greencastle's doctor, owner of Fergus and his family
Fergus, aka Kekeré Bábà, Dr. Fenwell's slave and much-travelled
    sailor
Francine Beaumarchais, Elorine's best client
Joel Meyerlink, coloured Jew, slave owner
Jujube aka Juice, slave, daughter of Fergus and Murtella
Lawyer Alberga, Jew, Greencastle's attorney

Maas Thomas, official at the courthouse
Miss Clarissa Noughton, Ishmael's lady friend
Miss Meyerlink, shopkeeper, sister of Joel
Missa Cameron, government official
Missa Cavendish, member of the Vestry
Mrs. Grenville, tavern-keeper
Murtella, slave, Fergus's wife
Ralston Penninger, white slave owner
Trojan, Dr. Fenwell's horse

West Street
Christian, Mother Juba's grandson
Cyrus, Ishmael's helper and Jassy's babyfather
Elorine Livingstone, aka Elzie, daughter of Ishmael and Selina
   Livingstone
Ginger, family dog, Jumpy's offspring
Ishmael Livingstone, Elorine and Adam's father
Jassy, servant in the Livingstone household
Jumpy, family dog, mother of Ginger
Mother Juba, doctress, the Livingstones' neighbour
Quamina, Ishmael and Sel's second child, deceased as an infant
Selina, aka Mama Sel, deceased wife of Ishmael Livingstone

BUSH

Adam, Ishmael's runaway son
Adisa, Adam's wife
Baba Quaw, old runaway slave
Baby Selina, Adam and Adisa's daughter
Henry, Maroon, Adam's friend, Adebeh's first guide
Jabez, Adam and Adisa's son
Thomas, Adam and Adisa's son

ENGLAND

Caleb, Jason's son
Carla, Quaker, Jason's wife
Colin Warcastle, agent for Greencastle

Doctor Lushington, historical figure, abolitionist in London
Felix Warcastle, agent for Greencastle
Jeremy Cato, Jason's friend
Pastor Buxton, historical figure, abolitionist in London
Reverend Swithenbank, Jason's friend, abolitionist
William Wilberforce, leader of the abolitionists

MONTEGO BAY

Baddhu, aka Amarylis, Adebeh's sister
Delphis, aka One-Eye Sarah, obeah woman, Sister's guardian in
   Jamaica
Dove, a rebel; historical person
Petta, aka Amarylis, Baddhu's beloved
Kofi, a slave, Adebeh's friend and guide
Sam Sharpe, aka Daddy Sharpe, historical figure, Baptist preacher

NOVA SCOTIA

Eddie, Adebeh's brother
George Samuels, stay-behind Trelawney Maroon in Halifax
Georgia Marcy, Adebeh's woman
Kojo, Adebeh's deceased older brother
Maisie Foster, aka Mam, Adebeh's mother
Major Richard Maxwell, in militia, stamped Adebeh's free paper
Montague Cameron, aka Da, Adebeh's father
Precious, aka Sister, Adebeh's sister

OTHER CHARACTERS

Duncan, supposed messenger of Daddy Sharpe
Reverend Mr. Bridges, historical figure, anti-abolitionist, pen name
   Umbratus
Missis Victoria Schoeb, née Douglas, Magnus's sister

⇒ Prologue ⇐

Jason: Aboard the *Eagle*, Mid-Atlantic, September 1831

LAST NIGHT I DREAMED OF SQUIRE. The memory is of such vivid realness as to make the goings-on of yesterday the dream. I can still hear his voice, high-pitched and brusque, echoing around the oak beams of this cabin, and his laughter, rather like a dog's.

In the dream I was a child again. In fact, I became my father, when he himself was a child. I just knew this—that I was Jason aware that I was also young George. (And, as George, I was white!) He was leading me by the hand into the forest of Savernake, behind where the Evans live. I was aware that we were walking in Savernake Forest along paths that I, the adult Jason, have walked over many years. It was a damp winter's afternoon, and perhaps a Sunday, for we were dressed for visiting. The spongy paths we took—my father seemed, as fathers always do to little boys, to know where he was taking me—led to a grand white house with grey shutters, set far back from a tall iron fence that kept out the unknown, meaning us. In the dream the small boy, whether Jason or George, was seeing the house for the first time and was dazzled. The father had been here before.

"Who lives there?" the boy asked his father. The voice, curiously, was not mine, but of a boy grown in Wiltshire, with the coarse lilt of the Downs in it.

"Ah lad," sighed the man who was the father to my young George. "Great toffs they are, scarcely aware of the likes of us." It was Squire's voice, but his accent, like mine, was Wiltshire, so that he sounded like his brother Jeremy (whose rude dismissal of my "claim" to be his nephew resounds still in my head on dark nights). There was an edge to my father's voice. "Your grandfather lived here when he were a lad," he continued bitterly. Grandfather's station I did not have to ask about. (Squire's statements in the dream, not all of which I can correctly remember, were comprised partially of things he had told me in real life, or that I had learned from the Evans about the Pollards.)

Just then a pair of yellow mastiffs, huge and forbidding, appeared from nowhere and launched themselves at us, howling and snapping. My small face was pressed between the bars and would have been swallowed if I hadn't pulled back in terror. They came at us with such force as to rattle the sturdy iron, and from their purple throats issued sounds as truly belonged in a dream. Squire counterattacked with a stick he had picked up on the way, which impelled a greater frenzy of barking from the guardians of the gates.

"Get off with you, you bloody monsters," he shouted, and mocked their barking. This drove them quite mad, and they hurled themselves at the fence with demonic fury. Squire laughed, and jousted further at them with stick and voice, gripped by a cruel pleasure which I, shivering behind his legs, admired.

Suddenly there appeared a bearded giant of a man, waving a stout stick himself and shouting obscenities in a voice that blended into the yelping.

"Get away from there, Pollard, you bastard!" the man cried, rushing toward the fence. Squire, giving not an inch of ground, shouted back, "Begone with your beasts, Blackman. Threatening innocent passers-by like that."

"This is private property," returned the fellow, by now flush with the railing and not four feet from us.

"My arse it's private property," Squire mocked. "This side of your prison belongs to the King. And neither you nor those powdered ninnies that own you is the King." Blackman's face was quite purple, matching the mastiffs' open throats. He shouted further obscenities at us.

"Be off with you, Blackman," laughed Squire. "Take your bloody dogs with you and find the nearest water and bathe yourselves. All together, like you sleep." He made an obscene gesture.

Blackman reached through the fence and almost grabbed Squire's face in his hand. "Take yourself off, Pollard," he screamed, face distorted with fury. "You and your nigger spawn."

Squire cackled like a hen. "At least I can find something on *two* legs for spawning, Blackman." And at that he turned and took me away with him the way we had come. The yelping of Blackman and those dogs died away behind us.

I was too frightened even to speak. But Squire was laughing. "Never fear lad," he chuckled. "One day you will be the master of such a palace." "Master" and "nigger spawn" floated with me to the surface of consciousness. I was mildly curious (in the dream) at being called "nigger" when I was so obviously white.

Squire built his palace, and gave it a grander name: Greencastle. The first time I actually saw the Savernake great house entombed in that forest I thought it but a poor relation. By then, two years distant from last sight of it, Greencastle had begun to assume almost mythic proportions in my memory, my perspective reverting closer and closer to childhood, when the "big house," as everyone calls it, even those who live there, had loomed over my entire life.

When I saw Savernake and realized which house was built first, I gained that insight into Squire's central ambition which made many other aspects of his character—and of his relationship with me, his bastard son, his nigger spawn—fall into place.

Coming from a lineage of tenant farmers, virtual serfs—white slaves, he called his family and class, and I had seen the hovel in which he had grown—his only dream was a place of his own, with no one to order him about or demand tribute.

But in one important detail the dream was incorrect: Greencastle had not been built for me, and never would have been. The real white child in the dream was not me, but Anthony, who is no doubt by now the Maasa of Greencastle, de facto if not de jure. I am the nigger spawn.

≋ I ≋

Jason: Aboard the *Eagle*, Friday, October 28

EVERYTHING IS PACKED, APART FROM THE change of clothing for tomorrow morning and a few odds and ends that I will carry in my portmanteau. The little world of this ship, like a fairground, is about to close; tomorrow morning a new world will throw up its tents.

Earlier I was at the bow, from which I generally observe the day's ending. But it was not habit alone that drew me to that point this evening, and I remained there long after the evening star had appeared. While expecting nothing, I nonetheless peered intently into the gathering dark. But all the lights were celestial and I abandoned my position, returning here to put my things in order.

Three hours later I went to the bow again; the cabin was hot and airless, as now. As I approached what I had come to think of as my usual place I heard voices and saw two lumpish shapes outlined, leaning on the rail close together and staring out at the shimmering sea. I recognized the voice and the form of Fergus. The shape of the person beside him suggested the other Negro on the boat, whose name I still do not know and with whom I have had no conversation up to this time.

I came to rest next to Fergus, but keeping a polite distance, and bid him a quiet good evening. He shifted slightly away from me—a matter of inches, but it might as well have been a yard because I was not particularly close to them.

"Evening, sir," Fergus replied.

We gazed awhile into the blackness. His companion said nothing. I felt hesitant to disturb them further with conversation, for I was aware that it was as personal a moment for Fergus as for me. A long voyage creates its own world, one which is splendidly dissociative of all others; it makes the prospect of landfall, especially your own, disconcerting. And for Fergus at least, it also means a return to chatteldom.

But eventually I was impelled to ask, for his experienced seaman's eyes would be more perceptive than mine, whether he had seen anything.

"No, sir, we too far." Something in his tone, perhaps a hint of watchfulness, discomfited me somewhat; I remembered his shifting away from me earlier.

We all watched some more in silence, held there by mutual hope. But after a few minutes I bade them a good night and returned here.

The brief encounter brought me closer to Jamaica than the ship stands at this moment and less happily than I would have wanted. I recalled our earlier conversations in the days just after leaving London. These had sometimes been quite lengthy, and, after Fergus had surrendered most of his understandable suspicion, generally comfortable.

But this evening, in the few words we exchanged at the ship's rail, I detected an entirely new tone. He had seemed tense, as though wishing that at least one of us had been elsewhere on the boat. I realized, with a shock, that those same elements which had contrived to bond us together, however casually, during the voyage, were now creating a very personal distance between us. Jamaica has become not merely a place to journey, but a lens through which to view the world.

That same lens will soon be pressed to my own eye. It is the prism of history and it gives us a dreadfully distorted view of the world and, more terribly, of ourselves. Fergus has lived with this as his eyepiece all his life. I must now, perforce, place it against my own eye once again.

⇒ 2 ⇐

Narrative: Miss Abigail Walker,
Friday, October 28

MISS ABIGAIL WALKER STINKS. IT'S BEEN a couple months since her last fitting and Elorine had forgotten that detail. But now, in the shuttered bedroom where the plump young woman stands admiring her near-naked whiteness in the full-length mirror, Elorine, enveloped by a malodorous cocoon of powder, rosewater and sweat, wonders how she could have forgotten.

And, Elorine notes, the frilly pink underwear of Miss Abigail Walker is grubby. From habit Elorine had learned to ignore these unpleasant aspects of her work. And, to be fair, Miss Abigail Walker isn't the only customer to parade her grime in her sewing room. Elorine has long inured herself to the offence inherent in this occurrence, though seldom without reflecting that offenders have no excuse: any number of slaves are devoted purely to their comfort and cleanliness, if desired. She supposes that doctors are faced with the same realities, and worse, in their most exalted as in their humblest patients. For this reason she has always felt kinship—unspoken, of course—with Dr. St. John on Harbour Street; in their different dealings and purposes they share many a body. But those are philosophical points, whereas the powder-caked underarms and dirt-rimmed bloomers of Miss Abigail Walker are real.

As real as the oppressiveness of the mid-afternoon air in the room, which is barely stirred by Miss Abigail Walker's personal slave, a sulky girl of about thirteen, who sits on a stool in the corner of Elorine's little workroom, a small palm bough resting on her own bare dusty feet.

"Hortense! Y'asleep?! Chile, move y'self!"

At Miss Abigail Walker's screech, the slavegirl and palm uncoil languidly, the girl's eyes blazing momentarily beneath insolent lids. The palm fronds dip into the thick treacle for a few moments, raising the air like an impossible hope. Then, once her mistress becomes involved with Elorine again, the fronds and the eyes quieten, and the curtain of turgid air descends with the palm.

"I really should lose some weight," Miss Abigail Walker says to her preening reflection, which pulls in its belly and primps its large breasts and giggles. "You think I should, eh Elorine?"

"A few pounds perhaps," Elorine mumbles, her mouth clogged with pins as she takes the new dress off the hanger in her closet. "In this heat, maybe just a few."

Her customer's smile dies abruptly. She pinches her belly and draws a deep breath, launching her breasts like galleons on the heavy air. "I keep telling m'self—Y'need more exercise! Except, chile Elorine, a hour after you get up, the time so hot, you's exhausted." She giggles again, looking in the mirror for a response from Elorine, who carefully avoids her eyes.

It takes the efforts of Elorine and Hortense to wrestle the dress over Miss Abigail Walker's shoulders, bosom and stomach. She grunts and wriggles, squealing like a puppy when a pin sticks her.

"Hm, Elorine," Miss Abigail Walker scolds. "Y'seem to make it a little small this time. You measure me for this one? I can't remember."

Elorine had in fact measured her client with great care, but she has no intention of meeting the eyes that seek hers in the glass. "It can let out, Miss Walker," she mumbles around the pins. Her hands fly across the dress, marking with tailor's chalk the alterations made necessary by changes in her customer's figure. Miss Walker is now sweating profusely; the dress will have to be rinsed before Elorine does the changes.

Miss Abigail Walker hefts her besatined breasts, upon each of which a cluster of brilliant blue flowers floats. "I'm sure Captain Fletcher will be sorely tempted to pluck these, eh Elorine?"

Elorine chuckles politely. And no doubt succeed, she thinks to herself. The slavegirl snickers. "Y'dress pretty-pretty, Miss Abby."

Her mistress preens. "Tenky, Hortense." It's like two children play-ing, thinks Elorine, but, catching the mischief in the girl's eyes, she cannot help but smile.

Taking the dress off is somewhat easier, but still requires everybody.

"What Molly wearing, Elorine?" asks Miss Abigail Walker, trying for nonchalance in her voice and shrugging a damp shoulder. Elorine doesn't answer. "Molly Dawes," she says, tart now.

"A gown, Miss Abby," Elorine replies calmly as she hangs Miss Abigail Walker's dress on the rack. Hortense giggles yet again.

"I didn't think she was coming in her shimmy, Elorine." Miss Abigail Walker's laughter is edged with annoyance.

"Dressmaker is like pastor and doctor, Miss Walker," Elorine con-tinues placidly, her voice firm. "We have to keep we own counsel, or we soon find weself out on the street." Elorine broadens her speech for effect. "You would like it if I told everybody else what you is wearing tomorrow night?"

Hortense coughs this time. Her mistress silences her with a glance that promises retribution. "I suppose she'll be all in white, as usual," says Miss Abigail Walker; all effort at subtlety or teasing is aban-doned. "Still trying to convince us."

"You can send Hortense for the dress tomorrow morning," Elorine says, still calm. "It will be washed and pressed. As usual."

Bosom leading the way and her nose held high against the smells of burnt leather and hot iron wafting in from Ishmael's foundry outside, Miss Abigail Walker sweeps from the room, stirring the air more properly than Hortense managed. Elorine notices, as the slavegirl would too, two buttons open in the middle of Miss Abigail Walker's processional back; she doubts Hortense will point them out.

Moments later she hears the crack of a whip and horses' hoofs carrying a man's impatient cry down West Street.

With a huge sigh of irritation and relief Elorine moves quickly to the window and throws open the shutters, breathing so deeply of the rush of fresh air from the backyard that she feels momentarily giddy. Every fitting with Miss Abigail Walker is fraught, and leaves both of them scratchy and irritated. The wrangles are always, like this one, muted. There is sure to be another one over the bill; there always is. Miss Abigail Walker, whose father was one of Bellefields' richest merchants, is Elorine's most stingy customer. Always satisfied with her dress—until she hears the price. On price Elorine is unflinching.

Miss Abigail Walker probably thinks her uppity and rude, for a black, aware that she's talked about, and sniped at, when the white-ladies get together.

She breathes out the anger at Miss Abigail Walker and lets her blood settle. Times like this she wonders at herself: why not, like the other dressmakers, go to her customers' houses for the fittings? It's more convenient than having them come here, to this room that seems so spacious when she's working—until sweaty ladies and their body slaves, who always accompany them, and sometimes sisters or cousins too—crowd into its close semi-darkness. Many of them moan about the smell of the horses from Ishmael's yard outside, never mind the rosemary bush that she burns. The rooms in their houses, of course, are much bigger. Fittings would definitely have been easier, and they *were* easier, in the days when she had gone with Selina, her mother, and afterwards when she first set up for herself.

No one could understand why she'd stopped, and she can't explain. Not even to her father.

Especially not to Ishmael.

She feels a cold tickle in her belly-bottom and thighs, like she might pee-up herself.

≈ 3 ≈

Adebeh: Arrival, Friday, October 28

"ADEBEH CAMERON," THE WHITEMAN CALLS OUT. His voice comes through the cigar smoke like a fist, straight at my face. He's holding the paper I give him by one edge like it might have something for him to catch, and when I look at his finger, dirty like he just come from planting something, or worse, I's thinking, this man have a nerve. But I keep my thoughts lock-up, like Da say: "Talk with you head and not you heart."

I answer brisk. "Yes, sir!" I's speaking to him but watching the paper. First of all, whitepeople don't like when you look them in their eye, like you and them is equal. Second, that paper is my life! If the cigar touch it, or it slip through his dirty fingers into the big cup of something he have there on his table, my corner is dark as a rooster's batty. I will disappear! I will be like them old mash-down things you see people throw out on Gottingen Street, any old body passing can pick it up and take it home. And they will look at this Negro and see that I's worth something and take me home, because I won't have a paper to say that I belong to myself.

"Adebeh," the whiteman say again. "Cameron." The two words fall separate from his mouth like different-size seeds. He look up quick at me as if to catch me at something, but my eye was waiting for him already.

"Yes, sir," I say again. I let eye touch eye, but just a touch. Then I slide mine back to the paper he is holding.

"You are," he say, "from Halifax." A third seed, different shape, drop on the table in front of us both. The whiteman staring at me, waiting. He's not asking if I's from Halifax, he can see that plain on the paper. What he's asking, without saying it, is, *What the hell you doing here, nigger?*

"Yes, sir," I say for the third time, feeling stupid. I's trying to hear Da in my head at the same time as I's trying to figure the right thing to say to this whiteman, the thing that will get me back my paper. Da like to say, "Don't trouble trouble till trouble trouble you." So I say, "That is where I come on board, sir," as if is somebody else speaking for me. "I born in Boydville," I tell him.

"Boydville?" he say. "Where is that?" He let the paper down onto the desk, to one side of the teacup and the cigar, and I give thanks in myself for that.

"In Scotia too, sir," I say.

"Nova Scotia?"

"Yes, sir." I slip my eyes back into his.

"I said something funny?" he asks, sharp.

"No, sir," I say quick-quick. "We have plenty Negroes in Nova Scotia, sir."

He frown, like he's trying to figure something. "Negroes," he says, "in Nova Scotia." He look over my shoulder. "They have niggers in Nova Scotia, Fergus?"

"Yes, *Missa* Cameron, plenty Nayga in Scotia, sir."

Fergus and the whiteman know each other a long time, I can hear that in their voice.

I remember another thing Da is always telling me. That white-people don't like when blackpeople look like they think they're smarter than them. I's not playing smart, I just know what is what in this case; Scotia is where I's born and grow.

So I take wisdom from Fergus, who know more about sailing a boat than all the whiteman on the *Eagle* roll into one except the captain. But he don't ever let the others know it.

I look down on the floor at some scraps of crush-up paper. The whiteman grunt and shake his head. "But you sound like you come from here," he say, looking back at me with a sliver of a smile.

He wouldn't know, and I certainly can't tell him, how that please me. Da and Mam would be grinning. They wasn't to know

Fergus would be on the *Eagle*, but Da give me advice for when I reach Jamaica. Study them. So when I find Fergus on the boat, I study him, especially how he talk. I smile at the whiteman.

"So," he say, "they have Jamaican Negroes in Halifax and . . . Boydville?"

His words curl at me like the smoke from his cigar. And then I realize that I have nothing at all to be pleased about. If Da and Mam was here, they would box this head off my shoulder. I's not suppose to sound like Fergus at all! I's from far-far away. If I sound like Fergus, I's from Jamaica like him, so I am not the person the paper he's holding in his hand says. And if I's from Halifax, how come I sound . . . They don't have any Jamaicans in Nova Scotia without they be the few Trelawny people like us. And the Trelawny people, I hear Da and Ma explain over and over again, don't dare set foot back in Jamaica, upon pain of instant execution. That is what the law in Jamaica says about Trelawny Yenkunkun. And Jamaica is where I am now!

"You must be a secret amongst them," Mam says to me the night before I leave home for Halifax and the *Eagle*. But this man holding my paper can do anything he want with me. I hear Mam in my head: "Quick tongue cut you own mouth." This time it might cut my own throat.

I shake my head strong. "No, sir," I say. "They have plenty Nova Scotia niggers"—the word scrape my throat—"and some from the colonies who escape and settle there." I turn my tongue to sound like I'm talking to a whiteman in Halifax, and I talk fast.

He consider a moment, and then he ask, "So, what you doing so far from home?" Same time he pick up my paper again.

"The ship bring me here, sir." Right away him face start to make up, so I try again. "I join the ship in Halifax, sir, cause I need the work. I just work the ship, sir, and it bring me here. So I am here until the ship take me somewhere else, sir."

His face relax a little bit. "And what are you planning to do until the ship take you elsewhere?"

Before I can think what to say I hear Fergus voice from behind me. "I will response for him, Missa Cameron."

The whiteman turn his head to look at Fergus again. "How you's going to response for him?" he ask Fergus. "You is a slave. And Adebeh Cameron, according to this paper,"—and he wave my paper at Fergus—"is a free man."

I hold myself tight-tight. I feel like I am out on the yard arm of the *Eagle* balancing, and I could drop into the sea and drown, or drop back onto the deck and break something. I keep my body still and send my eyes out the window so I don't have to look at either white-man or Fergus. I don't want Fergus to see how I's nervous.

"Well, Maasa," I hear Fergus say, speaking slow, "I could bring a writing from Dr. Fenwell to you."

Quick as a fox whiteman say, "This Negro is known to Dr. Fen-well?" The word scratch my ears.

"No, Maasa," say Fergus. "Not yet."

I can't see him, but I think Fergus is directing his answer at the stone floor of this warehouse. Me, I's just watching the people on the wharf going about their business, like Fergus and whiteman is talking about somebody else. I's seeing Wainwright, the fat cook on the *Eagle*, in the shade of a big tree on the wharf, bellying up to a stout black woman who's laughing and holding out her hand for the canvas bag that Wainwright is carrying. I know it's stuffed with provisions from his kingdom on the boat. As he's handing it to her his other hand is feeling-up her bubbies. I's wondering if she know that on the *Eagle* it's the cabin boy Thickson who get his special tasties from the stove and keep Wainwright warm in the night.

Further up from Wainwright I recognize the back of Captain MacLurgh as he's walking toward the town between two men. The captain has his head down at the ground like when he's walking the deck of the *Eagle* and giving his officers orders.

"So," I hear the man say to Fergus, "how Dr. Fenwell is to write anything if he don't know this Negro, Adebeh Cameron?" I hardly recognize my own name in his mouth.

Fergus don't say anything. All the time on the ship Fergus is show-ing me how to do this and that, because I've never been on anything bigger than a cockle before. You have to say he look after me, getting between the white sailors and me, because they know that while he's black, he's sailing with the captain longer than all of them and has the captain's regard. But here is not the *Eagle*, and this whiteman, while he knows Fergus, is not the captain.

"You know Major Maxwell?" he ask. His voice sounds from far away. I's still looking out at the wharf, and the green-green hillside that leads right into it, with the town on either side. "Bwoy!" He bark like a dog, and I realize is me he's barking at.

Though I don't like it, I's custom to "nigger". But I stop being a bwoy long time, except in whitepeople's mouth, where it taste of ashes. I turn to him and say, quiet, "Yes, sir?"

"You know Major Maxwell?" He look down at my paper. "Major Richard Maxwell?"

"Yes, sir. Is he sign my paper."

"Describe him."

"Beg pardon, sir?"

"Tell me what him look like, bwoy," he say, loud and broad.

I shut out the voice, close my eye, and see Major Maxwell standing outside the stables at the regiment yard. I describe him out loud, down to the whip in his hand that he's always tap-tapping his leather boots with—and will blast your backside with, white or black, if you mistreat the horses. In my head I's back at Fort Nugent. When I open my eye the whiteman is looking at me as if he never see anything like me before. But something tell me that he knows Major Maxwell. As far as I know the major's never been in Jamaica. But is a small world.

He ask me back the same question, as to where I know the Major from. I tell him the militia. I have those papers in the bag at my feet but I don't tell him that, in case he want to look at what else I have in there.

"You do work for the major? Other than militia duty?" He looking right at me, and I don't allow my eye to stray.

"Sometimes, sir," I say. I tell him I look after the major's horses, the two he keep at his home.

"You like horses, Adebeh Cameron." That wasn't a question either, but he make it sound like something suspicious.

"You come here for horses?" He asks casual, but I feel Fergus tense behind me, like the air shift a little, and I spot the trick.

"No, sir," I tell him, "I don't come here to work, with horses or anything else, I just come with the ship." I make sure I still talking like he's a whitepeople in Halifax.

He listen to me leaning back in his chair, but all of a sudden he straighten up and bark again, "You have money?"

"Yes, sir," I tell him, "Captain pay us this morning."

He look at Fergus, who must be nod because the man's face relax. A little. He turn back to me. "And where will you sleep, Adebeh Cameron?"

"I will find somewhere, sir." Though I don't even raise that with Fergus yet. "I have money, sir."

He turn to look directly at Fergus, his face hard. "You," he say, "is responsible for this nigger." He look at me and point his cigar. "Anyhow this nigger doesn't show up for when the *Eagle* sails, you won't be sailing either. Ever again. You understand that?"

Fergus nod his head two times quick. "Yes, Maasa," he say. He hold himself straight and don't look at me. But I know what is running fast through his head cause it's going even faster through mine. Fergus keep himself to himself, don't talk much about his own affairs, but he tell me already that he will not be on the *Eagle* for the next sailing, that the doctorman he belong to is keeping him home for some other business. Captain MacLurgh knows that too.

I feel double bad because, while I tell Fergus many things about myself, when I was lonely and because the talking bring Boydville and Da and them closer, I don't tell him the most important thing—that I's not planning to sail out on the *Eagle* either.

BAM!

I jump. Then I see that whiteman bring down his stamp on my paper. Bam.

Everything's so quiet after, like the bang drive all sound out of the air, that I can hear his quill scrape something onto the paper back. He sprinkle powder on the ink and shake it off.

"Here, Adebeh Cameron from Halifax," he say, sounding official and British again. He look at me straight as he hold out my free paper. "You hear what I say to Fergus here?"

"Yes, sir," I tell him as I make two steps to his table and go to take back my paper.

"Tell me, Adebeh Cameron," he say, still holding on to the end of the paper in his hand while I have the other in mine. "How did you come by the name Cameron?" He have a little smile creasing his mouthcorner telling me it might be another trick question. Why this man is so interested in my name? Whitepeople like to wrap up salt with sugar, and then make it burst in your mouth.

But he still have my paper, so I fix me face and try not to smile when I say to him, "Is my father's name, sir."

"Adebeh is your father's name?"

"No, sir. Cameron."

He smile wider now, teeth in his mouth like black prickles. But he let go the paper, and I try not to hasten as I fold it up to put back in the pouch round my neck that it lives in all the time except when I's bathing.

"Passing strange," he say quietly. "Cameron is my father's name too. You think we could be related, Adebeh?" He looking up at me like he give a big joke and he waiting for me to laugh.

I could laugh, though it's not funny—to me at any rate. I could look at him like I don't hear him, which some whitepeople like from us, like we don't understand something really simple. Or I could tell him that the Cameron name was family name only for paperwork such as he just stamp and give back. That the names on paper is not how Yenkunkun know each other, only what they answer to when whitepeople call us.

So I just smile. I say, "Thank you, sir," and turn a little, to show him that I am going outside now. He don't say anything more or make any move to tell me otherwise, so I walk out of the little shed and leave Fergus to deal with him.

⇒ 4 ⇐

Jason: Homecoming, Friday, October 28

ISRAEL TELLS ME HE HAS BEEN waiting at the wharf with the curricle for several mornings. I recognize him, an old slave whom I remember for the empty socket of his right eye, gouged long before I was born, before he does me. He's delighted to be identified. Old slaves are excess baggage, left to fend for themselves or parked in the sickhouse until they die. Israel, the bulk that I remember squeezed out of him now, is pleased to be still useful. He chatters like a magpie for the first part of the journey taking us through Bellefields.

Because of the unfamiliarity of our respective accents, however, we cover the same ground several times, lobbing words with increasingly careful aim into each other's watchful intelligence. This consumes all my faculties; I hardly notice the buildings.

Then, as the roadway tilts up into the hills, Israel, after a long silence of searching for the right words, says simply, "Him gone, Missa Jason, sah. Nearly one month now."

Watching his knobby hands talking to the horse through the reins, I know instantly of whom he speaks. "Dem say that when you letter come to say you coming—is me carry it from the ship that bring it, sah—Maasa smile a big smile and put him head down on the pillow and sleep like pickni. Next morning him was stiff as a board. But him dead happy, sah." As if to emphasize that conclusion, Israel cackles briefly.

"That is good to hear," is all I can muster. I'm not much surprised, or even disappointed.

As I'd known from the start, my hope had been a foolish one.

He is like a child, says the letter from Anthony, in the portmanteau at my feet. I know it by heart. *Raging one minute & whining the next. Mathilde is resolute in following Dr. Fenwell's orders: no rum, no spiced meats. But the old brute browbeats & cajoles everyone & sometimes Lincoln, who has been with him before any of us were thought of, relents. Then his condition plunges again for the worst & Mathilde banishes old Lincoln to the quarters, the ultimate punishment. For a few days anyway, before Squire pleads for him & the maddening cycle begins again. At his lowest, when we are waiting for Dr. Fenwell to come, he calls for you. He thinks you are here at Greencastle, in the next room or out on the estate & demands you be brought at once, as only you understand & love him.* Anthony, surprisingly, makes no comment on this reported assertion by our father that raises the scab on an ancient wound.

We are about, perforce, to employ an overseer, but for some time now the everyday field duties for Greencastle have fallen on my shoulders. I do not complain, even here to you, because it is my inheritance. But as you also know, ends are barely meeting. We are all at our wits' end, even Anna, who despite her impulsive ways has a good head for figures & helps Lincoln with the books as best she can. Greencastle is withering like a cho-cho vine.

The letter was significant for being in Anthony's hand, which I scarcely recognized. Anna writes, and Squire, through Lincoln's quill, but almost never Anthony, until now. And he makes no clear proposal. On receiving it, however, I understood it to be more than a report about our father's condition, or the circumstances at Greencastle. Anthony wants something. But, true to form, instead of coming out and asking for it, he sets out the circumstances in such a way that giving it to him is an act of your own imperative, your own unasked generosity, and places no responsibility on Anthony.

He baits the trap with Squire, betting it would snare me.

For years now I had been resigned to never returning to Jamaica; certainly to never again seeing Squire. My own reports and infrequent letters seldom mention Jamaica except in questions. So, reports of Squire's illness and decline did not, at first, unduly alarm me. Bearing in mind the distance travelled by letters, the time elapsed—that while

I read that Squire was having a string of good days he could well already be dead—I tempered my prayers with resignation. Indeed, on being handed this rare letter from Anthony by Colin Warcastle, one of Greencastle's agents in London, I'd expected the worst.

Anthony's reference to Squire calling for me, however, catches on longing that I hadn't even been aware of. I hear his drunken voice as though coming from the pages in my hand. Voices, I'd learnt over the thirteen years I'd spent in England, can be a comfort and a torment.

On arrival I'd felt suddenly, profoundly, cut off from myself, understanding hardly anything anyone said, whether to me or among themselves; my words were incomprehensible to almost everyone I spoke to, even slowly; that first year, I said hardly anything. But in my head were the voices of those left behind—Squire himself, little Anna, Selina, Elorine, even Anthony, but especially of the slaves I'd grown with and felt most comfortable among. Those spoke in my language.

The voices were a comfort, of course. But their ethereality also deepened my isolation, my sense of hopelessness. Eventually a new voice emerged from within, my English voice. I was becoming a new person. Those voices from Bellefields, those people, sank slowly, emerging in occasional dreams or, later, in conversational scraps caught on the wind at the London Docks when I went there on Greencastle's business; by then they sounded quite alien.

Anthony's letter evoked all those voices in a whirlwind of clarity and wintry disaffection.

It was partly the moment: Caleb unwell, Carla consumed with him and distant from me; the courts about to recess for a cool sodden summer. The strangeness of England, before this as familiar as my hand, runs suddenly rampant in my thoughts. Greencastle—which I don't much think about between bi-monthly visits to Felix and Colin Warcastle to collect letters and do a reckoning of accounts—seems like a dream threatened by daylight.

A month later I find myself on the *Eagle*, feeling like a fugitive. I have said a fraught goodbye to Carla and little Caleb. She'd wanted to come with me; I was firm on going alone, and cruelly played our child's illness as the trump. In desperation I couched it as a scouting mission, one that could result in us all moving to Jamaica the following year. Besides, packing us all up would take several weeks, and I expressed an urgency about Squire. I knew the joust I was making, as did Carla, the Quaker stoic, against good sense that I should return to find Squire still able, however feebly, to call me, one last time, "Jaze."

Of peasant stock and proud of it, Squire had let the baronial gates erected by the previous owner of Greencastle—which he'd won in a now-legendary weekend of gambling—crumble. They could occasionally be glimpsed, cracked and mildewed through suffocating creepers of love bush. The real property marker, to be seen from all directions, is a towering guango tree on the hill-line that has watched over Greencastle from long before the property was cleared and named. Remembering many journeys past this ancient sentinel, I feel a ripple of excitement and dread. As if in reinforcement of the latter, a sudden puff of morning breeze brings a soup of burnt cane, molasses and sweat. And—in my imagination at least—blood. It teases a membranous layer of memory.

Journey's end. A new journey begun.

The tree and the roadway past it are visible from the house. A few moments after the curricle begins its descent, a cow horn flutters the air like a birdcall. At the same moment, as if summoned, Dollybwoy appears on the pathway coming toward us. With his ludicrous, utterly unique waltzing gait—one step sideways left, one step sideways right, one step forward, half-step back, one step sideways—all the while his arms swinging loosely across his emaciated body like the rag doll of his name, his tragic frozen face staring straight ahead—he appears as an omen and a reassurance. I was born knowing Dollybwoy, who has endured the taunts and pebbles of generations of Greencastle children and overcome them with his dark stone of a face that renders them insignificant: he has wandered the fields and pathways of the estate forever.

While managing to get out of the curricle's way just in time, he ignores the occupants as we squeeze past him. Squire is gone, but Dollybwoy is still part of Greencastle.

Nearer to the house, Israel and I find ourselves in a commotion of barking dogs and screaming children, dozens of each appearing to fight over holding the horse's reins, unloading my luggage and my person, all the while staring with a mixture of excitement and apprehension: I'm dressed like a white foreigner, but to the keen eye of a Creole, as these children are, I'm obviously not white.

Above the bedlam I hear my name. Looking up to the doorway between the brackets of curved stone stairs I see a young woman, large-limbed and red-haired, quivering with excitement on the topmost step. Anna. When I left she'd been but five years old, a wilful child overripened by her indulgent father and everyone else around, including me.

She comes rushing down the stone steps, almost tripping on her slippers, to launch herself at me even before reaching the bottom. Built more like her mother than her father, she is not a featherweight any more, and almost topples us to the ground, though our laughter would have been a cushion. I'm enveloped in wordless cries and kisses spiced with a mixture of food and early-morning frowziness.

She brushes away the children and animals like insects and drags me up the stairs. "Look what I have," she sings out two or three times as she leads me like a prize into the cool semi-darkness of the house. She's leading me back through time and memory, through the sitting room with the large stuffed chairs to the dining room with the long plain mahogany table that was Squire's favourite place when he wasn't in the fields. There are dishes on a sideboard against the nearest wall and the far end of the table is set with four places. Mathilde, somewhat stouter than I remember, rises from the place beside the head, next to Squire's empty chair. Eyes atwinkle, she steps lightly as she comes toward me, as if about to break into a dance.

"You iss home safe and sound, Jason," Mathilde says in her Dutch Indies–Jamaican chuckle, holding my hands and giving both cheeks in the European way that is still hers.

"Yes, Ma'am," I say, smiling.

"Yach, you iss a man now. I cannot be Ma'am any longer. I iss Mathilde."

"Yes. Ma—Mathilde."

She laughs. "Yah. Goot! Mathilde. It will get used to you."

She studies me as Anna dances beside. "Your Carla iss well? And da baby?"

"You shoulda bring them," Anna says petulantly, bringing to mind the excuses I'd made.

"Caleb wasn't well," I say, a little stiffly.

"So thiss iss not for goot?"

"Next visit," I answer, smiling but firm. She must have read my letter.

They have just finished breakfast. The first real meal on an estate, I remember, is taken mid-morning. Anthony has already returned to the fields, and a boy is sent to bring him back.

There was always an extra place set at table at Greencastle. "I've been a stranger in many strange places," Squire liked to say, "and a plate of food makes a friend." This morning the place is for me and Anna heaps it with more food than I've seen on one plate in my life, or so it seems. After three months of mouldy food made barely palatable by desperation and spices, the parade of fish and fowl and pig, of plantains and eddoes and sweet yams and guavas—their names returning to my tongue with their long-lost flavours—awaken long-dormant corners of delight in my stomach.

Throughout, Anna throws words at me like rice grains, and in accents little different from those of the picknis who had greeted me. I have to ask her, as with Israel, to repeat herself, slowly. But the meanings, like the sound and rhythm of the words, seep back into me in the way the sun does. An inner room in the house of my being that had been shut for a very long time creaks open.

The house itself grows warm around me: without looking I can sense its dimensions, spaces, furniture, shadows.

I'm so enmeshed in Anna's chattering and the food that it's some time before I become aware of a person standing beside the door that I remember as leading outside to the kitchen. It is a man, standing absolutely still to one side of a slab of mid-morning sunlight laid through the doorway.

Mathilde half turns and beckons the person with her head. "He iss vaiting a long time for you to come," she says merrily to me.

It's Lincoln. Briefly, after reading Squire's letters in Lincoln's flour-ishing hand, I would reflect on the strange relationship between the two men, which was such a dominant feature of life at Greencastle.

As I turn to the doorway it is as though I'd seen the old slave just the day before. The small barefooted figure, dressed in dark clothes that are a little shabby but, as always, clean and pressed, stops a few feet from my chair.

Lincoln had been such a colossal figure in my childhood that I'd forgotten his size.

Though sitting, I hardly need to raise my head to look into the old man's shining eyes and when I stand, automatically, at Lincoln's approach, I'm looking down on a thinly grizzled head like a tiny canefield at crop-over.

"Howdy-do, Missa Jason," Lincoln says formally, looking up. When certain visitors were expected, Lincoln's sepulchral voice and grave manner could be counted upon to provide a suitable presentation, Squire's one piece of baronial vanity apart from the name by which he liked to be called. The depth and resonance of that voice, so terrifying to a miscreant child, so tender to one cherished, rolls over me like a wave. It is—along with the silence of his moving about the house on floorboards that creak for everyone else—an inalienable aspect of Lincoln's hegemony at Greencastle.

"Howdy-do, Lincoln," I reply. For the blink of an eye Squire might have been alive and I the small boy again, negotiating access through this little man, as did everyone at Greencastle except his wife and full children. Lincoln takes my outstretched hand.

Few people still alive at Greencastle would have seen Lincoln, one of Squire's first purchases, do manual labour in the fields, but his left hand is still shaped by the handle of the cutlass—perfect for cuffing small heads.

"Welcome," he says formally. I bow slightly.

He holds the boy in his old eyes for a moment and says gently, "Maasa Squire gone over." Lincoln's tone has the aspect of a benediction.

"To a better place," I say.

"As Allah wills it," says Lincoln, reminding me of his Mohammedan faith.

Lincoln, long ago when they were both young, had saved Squire from drowning when the Blue River was in full flood. Everyone at

Greencastle and beyond knows the story. They were then, as they remained, master and slave, but that signal event transformed their relationship. "Your life belong to me!" I'd heard Lincoln rage at Squire to his face, the only Negro in the universe who dared to even raise his voice in that presence.

"And what you going to do with it?" Squire answered calmly.

"You going see!" the little man shouted, storming off like an overgrown child, his powerful chest and arms pumping. His owner never punished him or belittled him, and listened to his advice, whether sought or not, whether followed or ignored. Occasionally, deep in his jar of rum and irritated by the slave's presumption, my father would threaten to sell him to a possibly fictitious friend in Cuba. It was a challenge that Lincoln would decline to meet, because he knew that his master was perhaps even more irascible and intemperate than he and could possibly be goaded, especially when liquored, into acting on that threat.

This morning, however, there is a sense of abandonment about him. He seems even smaller than I remember him. He is bereft and my re-entering his life at this time makes that absence all the heavier.

Then the old face brightens and tells me-the-boy to follow him.

I walk through the door he'd been standing beside, through a splash of blinding sunlight in a small courtyard and then into the dark cauldron of the kitchen.

"Look what puss drag in, Miss Delphy," Lincoln bellows as he steps inside. It is as I remember, gloomy and fortress-like, but aromatic with promises to the stomach. A few rectangular spaces in the walls, small and windowless, give glimpses of outside, but all light seems to gather on the stove, which squats like a heavy-breathing monster in the middle of the room, steam and smoke coiling up into a black encrusted ceiling to escape into a circle of sky.

For as long as all but the oldest heads at Greencastle have known themselves, the kitchen has been the kingdom of Miss Delphy, Constancia, a Guinea woman. Outsiders, especially children, of whatever colour, are under her judgement, which can be arbitrary and harsh.

At first, recovering from the brightness outside, I can see only two or three girls attending to pots on the large stove like votive priestesses. Then I notice her at a table next to one of the rectangles of light: calm and methodical, Constancia is working a tiny peeling knife through a small heap of carrots on a rickety table in front of her, dropping them into a bowl held between her legs. She does not raise her eyes to the intruders, or pause in her work.

"Miss Delphy!" Lincoln calls out again.

"I not deaf, you old monkey!" Constancia snaps back, still stroking the carrot in her hand with the knife. "Me eye dark, but I not deaf yet."

I walk over and pick up one of the peeled carrots. Like a gust of wind her hand sweeps, the knife narrowly missing my fingers in their passage to my mouth.

"You was a tiefing little bwoy and you grow into a tiefing man," she says with a fierceness that would have chilled the blood, had one not known Constancia's way. Anna, who has followed us, laughs.

"And you are still a miserable woman," I chide.

Lincoln cackles. "And she worse now, like how she old."

She is as quick with her retaliation. "Anybody older than you, monkey man? Only the cotton tree-dem up the hill and I not sure 'bout some."

She finally favours me with a look full into my face. Hers is set, lips drawn into their unchanging firm line; but as they focus on me her eyes and voice soften. "You favour Backra Squire," she says, allowing a half-smile to escape.

"Fe true," Lincoln intones.

"You come at a sad time," Constancia says, still holding my face in her eyes. "Maas George woulda give him life to look on you now."

"He call out for you right up to the last," Lincoln says.

"Is true," Anna chimes in softly behind them. I don't know what to say, so say nothing.

"How are you keeping?" I ask Constancia, my voice sounding strange in my own ears.

She sniffs. "The old legs not working so good, and me eye-dem getting a little dark, but all in all I don't complain."

"Too much," Lincoln adds.

I bend over and kiss the top of her head—in fact a less-than-clean bandana. As with Lincoln, there is a lot less hair peeping out from under the cloth that Constancia has always worn, than when last I'd seen her. Her face, still plump as befits a cook, has fallen into creases and folds and there is a blue cataract in one eye.

"You're still cooking good, though," I tease her. "That breakfast was worth coming all this way from England for. Thank you." And I kiss her again, this time on her cheek. Her skin is damp and cool and tastes faintly of lime, as it always did.

A voice, recognized immediately, shouts my name from inside the house. The tone is peremptory and my instinct is to ignore it. But I feel the people around me quicken and so I appear unconcerned. Some part of me realizes, however, that as much as those moments at the table and in the kitchen are a coming home, so also is this voice, its challenging tone echoing down the years.

He waits in the doorway of the big house as I walk back from the kitchen, Anna behind. Anthony leans against one upright of the narrow doorway, filling the space. He shows, as I come forward, no sign of moving out of the way. Recognizing instantly that I have come back home in another important respect, I skip nimbly up the steps, my insistent forward pace forcing Anthony to stand aside. At the same time I reach out with my hands and take his right hand in both of mine. For an instant, we search each other's faces for a smile. The balance between us, in affection and behaviour, has always been fragile. Our whole history seems to tremble in the space between us: I the elder and, in Squire's oblique way, the more favoured by our father—but brown-skinned, my destiny implacably darkened by my Negro blood; he, new master of the inheritance to which he has been heir from birth, but nonetheless even more the orphan than I. His skin, his mother's early death and his position in the hierarchy of Greencastle have allowed him none of the ties of affection that have been my salvation and which I already feel reviving.

"You are well?" he asks.

I assure him that I am and that I could tell that he prospers.

"In health," he says, but laughs to dispel the serious tone. "It is good you are back."

I nod. We are stiff with each other. I don't even think it strange: the ambiguity of our feelings for each other is in the blood. But as I look into his face this morning I can see the etchings around his eyes and mouth that bespeak pain and hardship over a period long enough to leave permanent marks. Though I carry no clear image of my own face, I think that now, though almost two years the younger, Anthony looks the older of us.

"We will talk more when I come back," he says and wheels away back to the fields and his responsibilities.

⇒ 5 ⇐

Elorine: Kekeré Bábà, Friday, October 28

KEKERÉ BÁBÀ COME BACK! As I'm hanging out the window to clear my system of the Miss Abigail Walker, I hear Ginger bark twice, loud, and then he start to howl and sing, to say sorry and tell us is somebody he know well. And then Pappi call out. From his voice I know is only one person it could be.

My Kekeré Bábà, little father. They not related and they don't grow together. But their fathers was shipmates, which is closer than blood. When he come back from the sea this is the first place his foot find, before he even go to the doctorman who own him to hand over his wages.

I feel my chest swelling up but I wait, stay inside. That is proper. The liberty I can take with Pappi I cannot even think about with Kekeré Bábà. The respect due him, no matter that he is a slave, require me to wait until he come inside to me. So I hang up the Miss Abigail Walker dress to wash a little later, and turn to the one for Miss Veronica Birdsmith, the militia colonel wife, who suppose to come this afternoon, but I hear she may be sick again so I don't know. And then I have two frocks making for Mount Zion sisters, who will be coming for them later to wear Sunday morning. Is a full day ahead and I settle down to that.

All the time, though, I'm listening to Pappi and Fergus. I can't hear what they saying exactly, except for a word here and there, and I'm not really interested. They talking about what happen here while he gone, and Fergus is telling where his ship take him and what he see.

Every time Kekeré Bábà leave for one of his journeys I wonder if he will be coming back. The danger yes, cause sometimes fisher-men going just out into the bay don't come back, much less weeks and weeks on a whole big ocean. But that is in the hands of Maasa God—even though Fergus favour the old beliefs that their fathers bring over with them.

No, what I wonder about is if he's going to run away. He go all over the place, Bristol, Liverpool, London—plenty others he tell me about and more that he don't. He could just walk off the ship and disappear, because they have blackpeople in them places too—everywhere, it seem. Fergus could just become invisible, I hear him say that himself. And he would be free. But no, he walk right back onto the ship each time and come home and give the doctorman the money he earn. The man who own him like he own the fowls running up and down in the yard outside.

I don't dare ask him himself, that would be forward. But I always wonder.

And then I hear the floorboard in the dining room creak, and feel the doorway fill-up with him. But still I don't look up from my sewing.

He say softly, "Asabi," his Yoruba pet name for me. Then I look at him, and even though he is not a surprise my smile break free of respect and constraint and stretch my mouth wide. But I stay sitting down. "Bábà," is all I say, respectfully, "you come."

Then he smile and open his hands for me to get up and come to him. I put my two hands between his and he close on them. Like we is praying. "Káàbò," I say, welcome. "E kãarò," he reply, "good morning." It is our greeting that he teach me for each time he come back. He keep the old ways more than Pappi.

I feel the dead skin on his palm like the scales of a fish, and smell the sea on him. He bless my headtop with one hand and rest the other on my shoulder. Then he kiss my forehead and step back from me.

"You is well, daughter?"

"Yes, Bábà."

"I can see that," he say, and grin. "No man don't come to take you away still?"

"Not yet, Bábà. They know they have to ask you first, and

they fraid." It is a little joke we play from I know myself, before I even think about bwoy, much less man. But it is serious too. The old way, the uncle is the keeper of the family's children. Pappi have half-brothers here and there across St. Winifred parish and beyond, because Maasa was passing woman through grandfather's hut like they feed cane to the crusher, and he was a tallawah man, I hear, breed woman just to look at them. Pappi know some of them, and I know two, but I don't regard them like they is properly "uncle", not in the way that Kekeré Bábà is.

So any man want to take me off will have to get his permit, as well as from Pappi.

Everybody know that—at least everybody who might have ambition in that way. And that is all right by me.

Jassy appear, following her big belly into the room with a mug of fresh coffee for Bábà. He take it from her but before he even sip he hustle outside and come back with two packets wrap up in brown wax paper and tie with twine, one bigger than the other. I never ask him to bring me anything, that would be rude, but he never forget me. Even the time his ship catch up on some rocks somewhere off Cuba, he bring me back a big shell from the beach that they spend a week on. It sit on the windowsill behind me here, and when the breeze blow strong you can hear it sing. But since I grow big he mostly bring me cloth, because he know that it's a big thing in my line of work. When I can make a dress for a woman from cloth that she can be certain nobody else will be wearing, I can charge more—much more. The big parcel have three piece of cloth, and I thank him for them, thinking already what to make and for who.

The small parcel, though, is for me. "For your wedding dress," he say.

"The cloth going to get moth holes in it before it get to use as a wedding dress," I say.

"Is silk," he tell me, not listening. "From China."

"It look African to me," I say. He laugh and clap his hands like I give the right answer to a question. He know some African people in Liverpool, he say, who sell all kinds of things from Africa, and is there he get it from. Is silk, but from Africa.

"Very dear," he say with a smile of pleasure and mischief. The doctorman know from the captain how much money Fergus gets at the end of a sailing, and he would be a fool to not give that full amount to his owner. But—and only him and Maasa God know where from—Fergus always find money to bring back things for Murtella and the pickni-dem—and for me.

As I thank him for the cloth, though, I can't bring myself to look into Kekeré Bábà eyes. I feel a cloud of sadness like dust rise up from the cloth and surround me. Is a beautiful piece of cloth, wherever it come from, and it would be a shame if it never make something special. But, grateful as I am, I keep my eyes from his. What if he look in mine and see what I promise myself, that I not going to be marrying no man on God's earth. Ever. If I tell anybody, it would cause all kinds of palampam and upset. People, especially the men, would vex with me. And I would have to tell Pappi, and Kekeré Bábà, why. I couldn't lie to them about something like that. And I could not control what might happen after that.

So I give him tenky for the cloth, and ask if he want some bickle. For that I can look at him, and he smile. And then clap his forehead, hard. He call out a word softly, like he talking to himself, and disappear back outside.

Just then I hear a ruckus in the yard. Horse screaming and man-dem shouting. It sound like only one horse but is more than one man. Hardly a day go by without some excitement out there, what with the horses and the fire and smoke and the people always in a hurry. But this is early in the morning for that, so I quick follow after Kekeré Bábà.

I reach the door out to the backyard just behind Jassy, who have the cooking fork in her hand that she's frying something for breakfast with. I look over her shoulder into the yard. A well-dressed brown man is scrambling like a crab to get out of the way of a plunging black horse that is one moment walking on its hind legs and the next balancing on its front foot-dem to kick out viciously behind. Cyrus, eye big like a evening star, holding onto the lead rope like his foot plant in the ground, too frighten to simply let go, which is what any sensible person would do. Pappi and Fergus is dancing on either side of Cyrus, Pappi edging around the horse toward the man scrambling on the ground, Bábà meanwhile jigging from foot to foot in front of the furnace, to prevent man or beast from ending up in there.

The only quiet one in the yard is a stranger to me, a sturdy black man about the age of myself and wearing clothes of a unfamiliar cut. As Jassy body trembling against me I watch him carefully take the rope from Cyrus's stiff fingers, eyes never leaving the plunging horse. Cyrus, as though suddenly uprooted, back away fast-fast and come to rest on the kitchen steps, where Jassy collapse onto his shoulder, hot fork in her hand. I smelling something behind me like it's burning or about to, but my foot can't go anywhere just now.

The stranger change himself into a bird, flapping his arms slow and uneven like wings, bending and straightening, not letting go of the rope. Meanwhile he taking small, patient steps toward the horse. The horse's eye turn up in his head but you know he's seeing the young man still, because after a while every movement become a little less frantic than the one before, each kick a little less evil. The horse is snorting like Pappi's furnace, the man is singing deep in his throat to it, and is like the two of them speaking two different language but still understanding each other. They going round the yard in smaller circles, until both come to standstill, the horse with its front legs spread, its whole body trembling, eyes only half-white now as it wave its head to and fro, but still watching the man. Horse and man stare at each other for a long moment. The sunlight is polishing the horse's dark coat and picking out the silver sweat on the stranger's bare arms like he is wearing pearls.

I'm trembling too. Pappi know about horses, and they obey him, but that is because he is big like them and have a voice like thunder. But this young man—he don't even raise his voice to this animal, which is plenty bigger than him.

I feel something like a candle light in my belly.

The young man is speaking to the horse in a continuous low rumble, inching forward as he's gathering the rein with each step like a boatman pulling himself to shore, but slow-slow, crooning, like water talking soft to sand. Until he is a couple feet from the animal, and there he stop and stannup like a statue.

Everybody else, the whole yard, hold their breath, as though only the horse with its ragged breathing is alive. Then the brown man begin to puff himself up, vex with his horse, but Pappi hold on to his arm firm, and he settle. Bábà standing guard on the furnace relax, a little smile on his face—the young man impress him, I can tell that.

Then, as if the two of them agree on it, the man put out his hand, and the horse bow and rest his mouth in it. The man caress the jawbone or the horse rubbing his mouth against the man's hand, hard to tell which. The man is burbling all the time, like he's saying prayers, telling the horse a secret. The horse understand him. It snort and dance away a little, but only to release the tenseness in its own body. Then it sidle up again and butt the man on his shoulder, and I swear the two of them laugh at each other.

Just then, as I hear my own breath flare out of me with a sound like one of Pappi's bellows, a loud POW! crack the air behind me. POW! again, and a sizzling.

Something Jassy is cooking inside explode, and she bawl out for Jesus and almost stab Cyrus with her big fork as she scramble to stannup while her big pregnant belly swinging around, threatening to pitch her down into the yard. Everybody is wondering about the noise and watching Jassy. Except the man and the horse. Like they don't hear the excitement, they still playing with each other like two pickni. And I'm watching them, even while I'm listening to what's happening in the kitchen behind me, Jassy and the stove quarrelling with each other.

I watch as the man lead the horse to the far corner of the yard, where the big tub of water is for animals to drink from, and for Cyrus and Pappi to wash themselves when work is done. It take them pass the brown man that Pappi is still holding, and the horse dance away from him and curl his lip back over his teeth.

I take my toe and poke Cyrus on the step in front of me, ask him where the stranger come from.

"Maas Fergus bring him," Cyrus answer. "Him come back on the boat with him."

"What he name?" I ask, whispering.

"Adeh, or Adi," Cyrus say, "something like that I hear Fergus call him."

Funny name, I think to myself.

Cyrus say, in wonderment, "The horse know him, though."

That is true. A candle yes, something like that. Or a piece of coal burning in ashes.

≫ 6 ≪

Jason: The Gazebo, Friday, October 28

ANTHONY WORKS HARD. THAT WAS IMMEDIATELY obvious to me from the sweatiness of him when he came in from the fields to greet me this morning and the urgency with which he returned to his tasks. We did not see him again until we'd almost finished dinner, in the latter part of the afternoon. Mathilde says that many days are like that.

But after he expelled his frustrations—something overlooked by the overseer, Wyckham—he turned to me, whom he'd hardly noticed while eating. As if shedding a soiled garment, he smiled. "Welcome home, Jason," he said and raised his glass of Constancia's Seville orange wash, which we were all drinking. Everyone clinked glasses.

The edge of excitement over my arrival had faded somewhat and the conversation was almost casual as I answered those questions which Anna had not yet asked me about my time in England and the voyage back. I mentioned the slave Fergus being in the crew of the *Eagle* and was told by Anna, who apparently knows him, that he belongs to Dr. Fenwell, who is Greencastle's doctor for slaves and family and who is himself less than well at the moment.

"And how are your rabid friends in England?" Anthony asked with a broad grin.

From long experience I sensed a trap. "Which friends might these be?" I asked as calmly as I could, even managing a flicker of humour.

He put the fork down gently but his tone was caustic. "Mr. Wilberforce and Dr. Lushington and Pastor Buxton and all the saints," he said. "Who would loose the hounds of hell outside"—he gestured at the fields outside the house—"and have them at our throats."

"Only because you keep them leashed," I said, my voice flat.

"At your throat too, brother," he responded, his voice as sharp as the teeth of those putative hounds he was summoning. "Brother" in Anthony's mouth was generally ironic in its intent, or when he sought to draw me close—usually to my detriment.

"Perhaps so," I said. "But not necessarily."

"You think St. William will save you? Or the missionaries here? It is them who is training the dogs." Again he waved his hand toward outside.

I considered before answering. I do not know the extent to which my association with anti-slavery groups in England is known here. I have not included them in my letters home, and my activities for the most part are behind the scenes anyway: writing letters, petitions and speeches for the poobahs of the platform who pronounce my words while I am often elsewhere. But it could be that the world is smaller than I would have it; for a moment this afternoon, it seemed so.

"I don't know Mr. Wilberforce, nor he me. I can save myself," I ended curtly.

I was aware that the air from the other side of the table was cooler, whether because Mathilde and Anna shared Anthony's sentiment about the saints and the missionaries or simply from the change of temperature on our side. But my interest was in Anthony and in not letting his blade go any deeper without retort. I was poised for an argument, one of the terpsichorean rounds that he and I have danced from ever we had words to joust with.

But he looked away, almost in dismissal of me. "It's all doomed anyway," he said. For a moment it was Squire sitting there. In the same seat and even the sibilant breathing that pushed the despairing words into the silence. "Our blood will not nourish them either," Anthony whispered and shoved back his chair, food unfinished and forgotten.

The women rose as one, Anna hooking her brother's arm as though about to take him for a stroll, Mathilde calling out to Lincoln that we were finished. (Unlike every other house at which I have dined that has slaves or servants, here and in England and as far as Italy, Greencastle remains alone in not having them attend on family meals. The food is laid by them at the time appointed, then they withdraw. Squire was inflexible on this, even with Lincoln. They know all our business anyway, was his opinion, we shouldn't make it easy for them. And the white functionaries—maintained on estates to realize the legal requirement as between blacks and whites—usually ate in their own establishments.)

Anna steered us out onto the piazza. To ketch breeze, as she termed it, and there was indeed, as always at this time of day, I remember, a slight cooling.

In another of his abrupt changes of mood that I am getting used to again, Anthony turned to invite me to walk down the stairs into the yard. Once there he took me around the side of the house to the gazebo that our father had built for his mother and which, in my day, only her personal slaves and her husband and son were allowed to even approach. The slight rise on which it is built overlooks the river and the nearest canefields; in the distance there is a glimpse of sea. It is a peaceful spot, no doubt chosen to soothe the spirit of a woman I remember only slightly—I was five or six when she died—as the centre of a vortex of nervousness.

This was also the place, I remember, where Squire told me one evening of his plan to send me to England. The evening before, he'd told Anthony that he was being sent to Virginia. I was twelve years young, but growing to understand my place in the world and increasingly less than satisfied with it. I was showing signs of that dissatisfaction in ways that were disruptive to peace and order at Greencastle. My chagrin at life was much mollified by the news that I would be leaving also and particularly that we would be going in different directions. I can still see the twinkle in Squire's eyes as he gave me that information.

Anthony pointed to a shrub which, I could tell, had been recently planted.

"He's there," Anthony said, looking at me to make sure I understood whom he was talking about. "That's what he wanted, and Mathilde didn't object. She waters the tree and sits here with him some mornings."

Anthony's mother, Angela, is buried among her ancestors in

another parish; Squire lies here alone. But somehow that suits: Green-castle is his creation, almost entirely, she part of it for just a few years of frail health.

There is no marker on the grave other than the sapling. That was Squire's wish also: he was happy, Anthony said, simply to be part of the soil of his beloved Greencastle. I stood looking a while at the shrub: lignum vitae, Squire's favourite, of which there were dozens scattered across the acres of Greencastle—perhaps hundreds by now.

"He's left a mouldering bag of bones," Anthony said, looking from the scraggly little grave to the wider vista of Greencastle. "But you know that already, Jason, don't you."

Though I couldn't know the thoughts behind Anthony's despairing comment, I am familiar with their substratum. Less encumbered than many estates for which Warcastle and Sons are agents and creditors in London, nonetheless Greencastle has become a structure that could, at any moment, collapse and tip its owners into the desert of penury.

⇒ 7 ⇐

Adebeh: Bigi Pripri, Friday, October 28

DA SAYS THE ANCESTORS WILL WATCH out for me. Maybe so. I only have to hope they will know me. This is not the district where he and Mam come from, and I come from even further. So maybe none of the ancestors around these parts will know me. Da tells me they will. They will be on the boat with you, he tells me as I'm leaving.

Anyway, I feel home, in a way I don't even in Halifax. Almost every face I pass I can see myself somewhere in it. The people themselves is strangers to me, except for Fergus that I's walking beside, following him to his home. Some of them stare at my clothes, which are sweating me. But I feel to call out to some of them, cause they remind me of people I know in Boydville. They would laugh at me, I know. Or cuss me. No matter, is a good feeling inside.

Maybe is all because Elorine's food is sitting so nice in my belly-bottom. It remind me of home. The same smells come out of the kitchen there as I smell in Mam's from I know myself. And Elorine is sitting nice-nice in my head. I like a woman who listens, who don't ask plenty questions. Cause of that, as she's sitting across her table from me after the stupid man ride off with the horse (who will throw him again sooner or later) I almost tell her why I come here. I was on the edge of talking out. But I hear Da in my ears, Don't trust anybody. Anybody. That is the advice he and Mam give me over and over in the days before I leave, when I tell them I find a place on a ship. Not everybody who tell you howdy mean Maroon well, Mam says more than once. Never mind that you born in Scotia, I hearing Da say from I know myself, you is still Yenkunkun. One of the people.

Nothing can change that. And Mam says, the night before I leave,
If they ketch you, one of two things—they will make you a slave, or
they will heng you.

I feel in my soul I can trust Elorine, but I say nothing to her about
why I am here in this island, her island. Her eyes flash questions at
me, but that was all. When the time is right, I can speak to her.

Meantime, as I's walking back from her father's foundry I's feeling good. I know two people here already, three if I count her father,
though I don't tell him more than howdy and bye. And I know the
horse!

But it's still me-one to be doing this thing I's come here to do.
Thinking about that as I follow Fergus along the sea road on the edge
of the town, my head is full of Mam and Da's words, and the hope
in their eyes. But I really don't know where to turn. I's adrift here
except for Fergus. Never mind what Da say, I trust him, he don't deal
me wrong yet. I am the one who is going to misuse him. So, out of
a silence as we's walking along, I ask Fergus where Trelawny is. He
grunt and wave his arm at the mountains we's walking under.

"Far," he says. Then a few steps further on he ask, "How you
know bout Trelawny?" I's thinking from his voice that maybe Fergus
wasn't the person to ask about Trelawny. Maybe Elorine, if I ever see
her again, would be better. But is too late, I have to say something.
So I tell him that they have people from Trelawny in Scotia, which is
true but not the whole of the truth.

Fergus stop dead in the road and hold on to my shoulder. He look
at me and then swing like a clock to look both directions and then
back at me. "You is Maroon," he say, and he's not asking a question.
I hear Da say again, Don't trust anybody, even blackpeople. But is
too late now. I nod.

Fergus surprise me with a big laugh, right there in the middle of
the road. "I shoulda know," he say, slapping one hand with the other.
"You don't talk like the other Nayga in Scotia. So what you doing
here?"

And the words just tumble out of me, truth and story mix up so
that I don't even remember myself which is which. I listen to my voice
like it belong to somebody else, telling him about Da and Mam and

the other Trelawny Maroons who come to Scotia before I am born, and how all of them—almost all—get back on the ship and go off to Africa and that I come to be born in Boydville because my people didn't go. But I don't tell him why. The one thing I don't do is answer his question, why I am here. I don't tell him a lie, exactly, but I don't tell him the truth either, the simple truth. I begin and end with saying that I hear so much about Jamaica when I's growing that I think maybe I want to see it.

"They can hang you, you know," Fergus say. His voice is serious, reminding me that the whiteman Cameron put me in his charge.

"Only if they ketch me," I say, and look full into his face, so that he understand what I mean. He don't say anything, but something in his eye, the way he look at me before he turn again and resume walking, make me think that Mr. Fergus don't think very highly of Maroon. He don't say anything more, and I keep quiet too, empty of words.

By this time we's leaving the sea road behind us, nearing the edge of the town. The yards around the houses we's passing getting bigger. Everybody we pass know Fergus, greeting him with a wave or a smile or a clap on the shoulder, but he don't stop as he greet them back; he's anxious to reach home.

He stop in front of one of the houses and put me to sit on a big stone under a shade tree across the road. "Stay there till I come back," he tell me. Then he walk across the path to the big upstairs house, mostly white, with green shutters and a porch all around, top and bottom, and push the gate. He walk around to one side, where I can see mostly white sheets hanging on the line, and disappear round the back of the house.

Drowsiness set in from Elorine's food and the walking, and being awake most of the night watching for land.

And is like I fall into dreaming. I can hear people passing on the road between me and the house, but they is part of the dream too. I dream myself on Brunswick Street in front of the Citadel, leading some horses back to Fort Nugent. It's like I am underwater with my eyes open and the water is thick with shadows and movement. Some of the shapes is not people exactly, but they have faces. Some of them I recognize from Scotia, black and white both, including Major Maxwell, and George Samuels, the old stay-behind Trelawny in Halifax. But some is full strangers to me.

And then, clear-clear, I see a goat face in front of me, the jaw chewing, cracking something in its mouth, and I realize that I am really awake. It don't look like any goat in Scotia but it's a goat all the same.

Still, is not the goat that wake me, is the knowing. Da always say that goat, never mind how you see him here in this world, is part of the spirit world too. That is why Yenkunkun like to keep them. Goat-head soup give you courage for this world from the world over there.

Goatskin is sacred for the drums from Africa. And when you look in him eye, Da says, you know is not you he really seeing, is something beyond. It's true. This goat in front of me, the yellow eyes watching me, is looking right through me. Like it's seeing bigi pripri, the ancestors. Or is a ancestor itself.

I hear Da: "They will know you, you don't have to do anything."

There's a buzzing of laughter, children's voice, and somebody shake me. "You wake?" Fergus. His face bend over and block out the goat, who snort and move away. Fergus laugh at me. He has two pickni hanging on to him and dancing round us, talking at the same time like baby birds in a nest.

The yard is bigger than it look from the road, with a good piece of land running back behind the house. Plenty food things is planted there. I glimpse two women in between stalks of corn, skirts catch-up around their waist, weeding. Three more pickni are playing nearby, throwing something to each other. To the side as Fergus is leading me is a proper garden, bush and shrub and flowers, colours everywhere, and with a sort of order, stones painted with lime to mark the beds, and grass to walk on between.

Beside the planting is a paddock with two horses and a mule in it, and a donkey. They all lift they heads as we come past. Right away I's thinking I will like this place.

Coming inside the house out of the bright sun-hot turn my eyes dark. I bounce into things before I get back my eyesight. It's dark even then, but that is because we is right in the middle of the house, where they eat. A old whiteman is sitting at one end of a dark shiny table, his head in a cloud of cigar smoke. He's dressed in white, so he seems to glow, his reflection on the tabletop. His eyes fix on Fergus as he walk before me around the table and up to him.

Fergus nod at me. "This is him, Maasa. Him name Adebeh."

The whiteman rest his eyes on me a long time before he speak, and I's not sure he's seeing me; his head's pointing a little to one side of me like blind people's can. Then he say my name like it's something to taste. "Not from these parts, that name," he croak, like frog catch in his throat. And as my eyes get accustom to the place I can see Dr. Fenwell better. He's not as big as he look at first, is his shirt that's big, hanging on him like widow's weeds, as Mam would say. He's sick, I can see that too, something drawing him down. And he don't see too well either.

"No, sir," I say.

The doctorman take a pull on his cigar and his head disappear in a billow of smoke. "You can stay here then," he say. "Fergus speaks for you." It was hard to tell through the croaking but his voice like he's chewing the words. Born English.

I remember my manners. "Thank you, sir," I say. I offer to pay for my lodging.

He brush my words away like flies. "Just don't make Fergus a liar," he say. I answer quick-quick. "No, sir."

He turns his head away from me and draws breath. It rasps through his throat like Da's saw through wood. He press his hand to the table and make to get up. Fergus spring to life and grab him under his arms, while his foot hook a leg of the chair and pull it out of the way. Each of them turn, Dr. Fenwell as the pivot, until Fergus have him under one arm and he have his other arm around Fergus' neck. Fergus leads him away from me toward a room off the dining room. Fergus bark out something that sound like *juice*, and something red flash past me, a girl when I see her properly, into the room before them. I can't see inside the room but I hear the bedsprings creak and sigh when Fergus and the girl let the doctorman down into his rest. There's a little talking and laughing and sighing and creaking, and then the two of them come back out.

I look around, and things come to me clear. This is not a house of prosperity. Once, yes, but not now. It need paint on the walls, and the curtains have holes, some that look like the cloth just fall away from tiredness. Still, it is clean. The furniture and glass, they shine. But the doctorman is weary and sick. And when I see how gently Fergus lift him up and carry him into the room I come to answer a question I've been asking myself from I get to know Fergus on the *Eagle*: why he don't run away?

He go all over the place. He could just walk off the ship and disappear, because the cities big and have plenty blackpeople. Halifax have fugitives, and Dartmouth, and Sherbourne, they're on the sea. Some get catch, but only the careless. Fergus could just become invisible. Like I myself am going to try to do!

But no, he walks right back onto the ship each time, and come home and give the doctorman the money he earn. A man who own him, and probably the goat who dream me a little while ago. Own the people around too, Fergus and his whole family.

Is the family that bring him back, I think. But is also because, as much as the doctorman own him, in another way Fergus own the doctorman. He rely on Fergus. The way Fergus walk into the house, the way he speak to the whiteman, respectful but not like a puss, the way some blacks have, the way the doctorman regard him, taking Fergus's word for the way things are to go, and how the two of them walk each other through the doorway into the room for the man to lie down. In this house Fergus have respect. In Scotia or England, he would be just another nigger for people, including some blackpeople, to spit on.

In a certain kind of way, in this yard is Fergus free.

$\approx 8 \approx$

Jason: Letter to Carla (1), Saturday, October 29

Saturday, October 29, Greencastle

My Dearest Carla,

We parted unfortunately. That was my fault, and I apologize for the hurt I have caused to yourself, and through you to Caleb, who I hope is recovered to his bonny self. It could not have been otherwise: you wanted to come with me and I wanted to come alone. There was no middle ground possible, so I had to arrange my departure as I did, leaving the note with Mr. Warcastle and binding him to send it on only when the Eagle *had cast off and was in the estuary. It may seem to have been the leaving of a coward, but we will differ on that also.*

I am safely here and hasten to assure you that I am well, in the hope that in the intervening weeks of silence your animus will have subsided and your concern for my well-being have been restored. As you predicted, I arrived to find my father buried, though only three weeks ago. If the possibility of seeing him alive had been the only reason for the voyage, then I would have distressed you unnecessarily. But the real purpose was exactly what prevented me, as I explained to you, from bringing yourself and Caleb. In that regard it is too early for me to pronounce one way or the other. I have been here only one day, and have seen no one outside the actual household; I have not even ventured onto the estate.

Squire's death has transformed everything here—and nothing. His absence is, if you'll forgive the play with words, very present. He is hardly spoken of, but inhabits every conversation—even, I think, of the slaves in the house, particularly Lincoln, our major domo, who misses him perhaps more than those of us connected by blood.

But the pattern of the house is much as I remember, and I have fallen into it quite easily—to an extent your Quaker mother, and perhaps yourself, would almost certainly deplore. But it is difficult not to, with people to fulfil your every whim before you properly entertain it.

I had not given any thought on the voyage as to my particular accommodation in the house; there has always been, in memory at least, an adequate number of rooms for whoever might need to sleep a night or two. But in fact the house is smaller than I remembered, and there are only four bedrooms, the fourth one kept precisely for that unexpected guest. My own quarters, once I had finally become a member of the household, were a cubicle behind the dining room that became, after I left, Squire's office and now is Anthony's. Anthony and Mathilde tried to press me into setting up myself in the guest's room, but I declined, firmly, and Anna proposed the solution.

Now I find myself housed in two rooms, one commodious, the other more an anteroom, built onto the house when I was a child for the house slaves, at least the favoured ones. Since then, while I was in England, two further rooms were added on, in which some of the slaves now sleep.

It is, as I soon discovered and appreciated, an advantageous domicile: built at roof level on the slope behind the main house, and with windows on three sides giving vantage and breeze in equal measure. It offers a pleasing prospect of much of the estate and the distant sea, one not afforded by the bedrooms below. In addition, it gives a certain isolation and privacy from the rest of the household.

As the newcomer I am the object of especial attention: I have been assigned a boy, Jack, who first shadows me and then occupies the place to which I am headed before I can get there. He was waiting here for me this evening as I came upstairs to write this to you, and only left after the most stern instruction on my part, and without undressing and redressing me for sleep, as was his explicit intention. But I am gentle with him, because he is of an age and strength of body that, were he not in the house, would place him in a field gang *doing harsh manual labour. Were I to express any disfavour with him he might well end in the fields, where they can always use more hands and backs. But he sometimes tries my inconsiderable patience with his fawning.*

With that, I bid you goodnight with a tender kiss, and ask you to share it with Caleb. I will write again soon.

Your loving husband, who once more seeks your forgiveness,
Jason

⇒ 9 ⇐

Narrative: Prayers and Whispers,
Saturday, October 29

"WE ARE TROUBLED ON EVERY SIDE, yet not distressed; we are perplexed, but not in despair; persecuted, but not forsaken; cast down, but not destroyed." Ishmael's voice seems to issue from the belly against which his black Bible is cradled; the familiar words undulate on the lamplight of the dining room. "But though our outward man perish, yet the inward man is renewed day by day. For our light affliction, which is but for a moment, workest for us a far more exceeding and eternal weight of glory; while we look not at the things which are seen, but at the things which are not seen: for the things which are seen are temporal; but the things which are not seen are eternal."

It is a text known to them all, one of Ishmael's favourites. His tongue wraps the words with tender familiarity, making a present of them.

"For we know that, if our earthly house of this tabernacle be dissolved, we have a building of God, a house not made with hands, eternal in the heavens."

Head bowed, Elorine listens, her mind a toe playing in the puddle of her father's voice. She looks across the dining table at Cyrus and Jassy, who stand close together, still as statues, their eyes closed. Jassy's fingers, lightly plaited, support the mound of her belly. Of late Elorine finds herself noting the smallest change in Jassy's condition: the fingers and toes fattening into cucumbers, the ankles thickening, the once limber waist engorged with secrets, turning her girlish prancing walk to a shuffling waddle that easily tires her. She moves around the house, Elorine thinks but doesn't say, like an upright, turned-around snail, her belly leading her, eyes alternately opaque and shining, seeing nothing or bright with secrets. Tonight her skin throws back the lamp's glow as polished ebony.

Amid her father's words Elorine makes her own prayer: that mother and baby survive. Babies die quicker than puppies, sometimes the mothers too. It is worst on the estates, where women's bodies are already drawn down from incessant, punishing labour. But elsewhere, even in the great houses of the whites, as many babies die as live to their full strength; and not all of those become adults. Elorine's own mother Selina died in this house giving birth, neither mother nor child, a girl, living out its first day. Give them strength and life, she prays for the girl and her belly across the table.

"How long, Maasa God," Ishmael calls, closing and hugging the Bible, "must we wait upon you? For the wicked shall be cut off, but those who wait upon the Lord shall inherit the land. We are waiting, Lord, for our inheritance."

Her father's voice, rumbling with unease, perhaps even anger, pushes thoughts of babies to the side of Elorine's mind. Ishmael doesn't grovel before his Maker, or whine. Evening prayers is only one manifestation of the argument that Ishmael and Maasa God have been having from Elorine has known herself, and which sometimes threatens to break out into open altercation. It will probably continue until they meet face to face.

So far they keep faith with each other in large things and small.

"We wait, Maasa God, for the birthright of freedom that is rightfully ours, heralded by John your Baptist and sanctified by the blood of your Son. We know it is coming, Maasa Lord, and we know that those who hold your children in captivity and bondage also hold our freedom from us."

Maasa God is listening, of that Elorine is sure: Ishmael means "whom God hears." But she wonders who else might have ears turned to their little house, which sits almost on the street. Ishmael's voice can carry far, especially on the night's still air.

"We give thanks and praises for our own freedom, Lord," Ishmael continues, "but count it as a trinket against the chains of bondage that weigh down our brothers and sisters." His chin falls onto his chest. "We know, Lord, that you see what is done in secret, even done in the King's chamber. Reveal it to your people, Lord, who groan in waiting for their freedom. We pray for that freedom, Lord, which will lift from us all, slave and master, the crushing load of chatteldom." Ishmael raises his head and scans the room, his eyes briefly touching Elorine's, though she wonders whether he even recognizes her. "For this we now pray in the words of King David, a humble shepherd boy who became your champion, 'The Lord is my shepherd, I shall not want...'"

Elorine's amen at the end of the psalm is a sigh of relief. Cyrus and Jassy move like trees come to life. Ginger the dog, inured to the rumbling waves of Ishmael's petitions, sleeps; the people step around him. A cool breeze from the sea comes through the window, ruffling the lace curtains that need washing.

Ishmael rests his head against the back of the chair and closes his eyes. He is exhausted. Tonight the Spirit seized him, lifted him up and shook him in Maasa God's face. As usual, He had looked at Ishmael with kind, fatherly eyes, and listened. But He said nothing. On the other matters on which Ishmael seeks guidance—especially for the counselling of his flock in the Mount Zion Baptist chapel—Maasa God is usually responsive, if not always clear as water in His advice. But in the matter on which Ishmael has requested direction tonight, that of slavery's end, the Almighty, as He has always been, is fully understanding of the injustice but everlastingly silent as to the means of remedy. Higher than your ways, said Isaiah on His behalf, are my ways. Ishmael agrees. But sometimes a little too high.

After such intense staring into the abyss of Maasa God's love, the Spirit has brought Ishmael back to the little house on West Street wrung-out and exasperated, a pilgrim without peace. And tomorrow, in the chapel next door, the argument will be resumed at the main weekly service of the little flock he has charge of.

But it's not weariness alone that keeps his eyes closed. Elorine wants to speak to him. She has not said so, but Ishmael was aware of her restlessness at the supper table; the fact that she had not said anything to him over the food beyond their usual exchanges suggested

that it has something to do with Jassy, who was in and out bringing and clearing away the food she had cooked for them. Woman
business, he's sure. Baby coming. Selina never bothered him with
this, but Elorine is different. Is your house, she would say. As if she
was passing through, or moving out soon, though there is no sign of
that.

Perhaps if he opens his Bible, which is there in his lap. Or picks
up the knife and a bit of wood he amuses himself with from the box
under his chair.

"We have to talk, Pappi," Elorine says before her father can do
either.

Ishmael sighs. "'Bout what?"

Elorine feels guilt for not allowing him his peace after a long day.
But she is determined.

"You have to careful how you talk, Pappi."

"Talk 'bout what?"

"Freedom and them things. Emancipation and the like."

"Why? I was talking to Maasa God."

"That is true," Elorine agrees, "but Maasa man might be listening."

"So what?"

"They can say you talking rebellion."

"Everybody talking rebellion. On every estate, on street corner . . ."

She cuts him off. "Them is slave already. Backra cyaant do
anything worse to them. Backra can stop you preaching at Zion.
Him can tear-up your free paper and send you to workhouse. And
me with you."

"Not since law pass last year. Them cyaant just tear up people
paper as dem like any more."

"That law is for the brown people and Jew-dem. Black is still
black. No matter if you free, even if you born free, you is still black.
And you don't born free, you born a slave."

"And who going fix them horse and bridle and sugar kettle when
I gone to workhouse?" He is alert and aggressive again.

"You think they studying that?" Elorine had not set out to quarrel
with her father, but his dismissive response to her caution riles her.
"They fraid for rebellion worse than obeah. And they don't care

which law the people in Spanish Town pass or don't pass, Bellefields is a far ways from Spanish Town. If they even think you talking rebellion, magistrate will deal with you. That Magnus Douglas-one is magistrate now, him would be happy to send you to workhouse."

Elorine shudders inwardly at her own words, but her fervour sweeps away her distaste. It's several years since she's seen the pieces of paper testifying to her freedom, and that of her father and mother. They are kept in a small iron box Ishmael made to safeguard them from the earthly corruption of moth and dust, as well as from Maasa God's natural scourges.

Elorine always thinks of the markings on the papers with a slight unease: they remind her too much of the lists, also kept in the iron box, of tools and other foundry equipment to support Ishmael's ownership in case of theft. Her freedom is like the anvil, or a pair of tongs. Whitepeople have no need of a paper to testify to being persons. They just have to get up in the morning and draw breath.

The new law that Ishmael puts so much faith in—more black markings on paper—gives Elorine little comfort. The law is for those who have the power and money to use it, and blackpeople, slave or free, have little of either. A lot of blackpeople go into courthouse believing Maasa Jesus when He says, *The truth shall make you free*. But it doesn't work like that in magistrate's court. The truth is whatever Backra says it is, and you mightn't be free at the end of it. Truth and freedom can change like the wind.

Elorine can't remember having had this kind of argument with Ishmael before. Her father irritates her frequently, and she's not afraid to say what she feels back to him. Usually she remains in the house and listens to the men in the foundry—when no whites or rich browns are around—chewing on their anger and fears like spicy food. Tonight, surprised at her own assertiveness, she wants reassurance against her fears.

Ishmael seems to sense that. He laughs suddenly and reaches across the space between the chairs to pat his daughter's knee. "Right, Miss Pepper," he teases gently. "I will talk softer."

Elorine feels for a moment as a part of her has wanted to feel all evening—like Pappi's little girl. She thinks of the numberless nights over how many years that they have sat like this. As a child she had sometimes fallen asleep on the floor between the feet of her parents, Ishmael in the chair he occupies now, her mother in the chair that is now Elorine's, doing the same thing, sewing. Elorine slipped into the routine like her feet had grown into some of her mother's old shoes, a pair of which she has on right now.

"Shwimps! Shwimps here! Buy you nice pepper shwimps!" Samson's screech startles her, never mind that it comes most nights around this time. Old when Elorine was a child, he has a wavering voice, metallic as a nail scraping against old iron.

This is his last trip around Bellefields before going home with his takings to Madame Deschamps, his mulatto owner. Elorine or Ishmael would sometimes cry out and stop him to buy a portion that he scoops out of the basket that smells the same as his coppery body. But tonight Ishmael, chewing on Elorine's questions and his own thoughts, shows no interest in the old man's fare, and Elorine cannot afford to let the spices that make Samson's food so delicious anywhere near the dress she's sewing.

"Not tonight, Samson," she calls out. "Walk good."

Just after Samson's cries die there's a knock on the back door, the entrance only a few people use. "Hold dawg!" a man's voice calls, before old Ginger can even summon a bark. Jassy and Cyrus have gone home right after prayers, so Elorine, irritated, goes to the door. Brother Theophilus Thomas, Uncle Teo, is outside. She's wondering what it is that can't wait until service tomorrow morning, when she sees a shadow move behind him.

"Beg pardon for disturbing you, Miss Elorine, at such a hour," the old man says, bowing slightly so his bald black head flashes silver for a second.

Elorine doesn't respond. Her attention is on the shifting darkness beyond Uncle Teo that becomes the shape of a man. A stranger—she knows that instantly, and is uneasy. Brother Thomas notices too and says, "I thought it meet to talk to Deacon tonight, Miss Elly. He's in, I hope."

"Yes, Uncle Teo." Elorine finds her voice and opens the door wider, standing back and slightly behind to allow space for the stranger to enter also and not pass too close to her. She doesn't know everyone in Bellefields but something—perhaps the pieces of grass in his hair—tells her he's not from these parts.

As slight a man as Uncle Teo but younger, more vigorous, he does not seem to see Elorine as he passes her into the house, which irritates her further. A rude stranger, the worst kind.

"Deacon," Uncle Teo says as Pappi rises to his feet, "I ask pardon for disturbing you household at this late hour, but I feel I had was to do it."

"You know you is always welcome in this house, Brother Teo," Ishmael says, though Elorine can hear the caution in his voice, as he adds, "Who this you bring with you?"

"He have a message," Uncle Teo begins, shaking Pappi's hand and then turning to the man behind him.

But before he can perform the formalities, the stranger says, "A message from God, Brother Ishmael," and Elorine's irritation hardens.

She sees her father catch himself for a moment and then smile. "We don't get many of those round here," he says. "Mostly people is listening out for Maasa God. Or Him for dem."

The man, Elorine notices, is smart enough to take Ishmael's rebuke. "I beg pardon too, Brother Ishmael," he says more pleasantly. "I bring important message from a messenger, and I come a long way to bring it."

"Who is the messenger?" Ishmael asks, "and what is the message?" He towers over the two men and fills the intimate space of his own house. Elorine eases around the newcomers to stand beside her chair, close to her father.

"For he that is called in the Lord, being a servant, is the Lord's freeman," the stranger says, his voice urgent. "Likewise also he that is called, being free, is Christ's servant."

"Ye are bought with a price," Ishmael intones, finishing the injunction from Paul to the Corinthians that he himself has preached on at Mount Zion more than once.

"Be not ye the servants of men."

He pauses and looks sternly at the stranger. "That is an old message, Brother . . ." And he cocks his head to receive the man's name.

"Duncan," the outsider says, and Elorine's dislike congeals further. Duncan is a slave name, and not uncommon up and down the land; she knows three or four Duncans just around Bellefields. Everyone has another name, the name they know themselves by, and which they give to their friends, or when they want trust, or help.

"Welcome, Duncan," Ishmael says, his voice flat. "Who you bring that message from?"

Elorine is watching Duncan closely and is relieved when he doesn't hesitate before saying, "Daddy Sharpe."

Elorine has heard people at Zion talk about this Daddy Sharpe. He's a leader in the Baptist community. But what she hears is that he's a deacon in the missionary church. He preaches when the white pastor is elsewhere, and helps to prepare the candidates for baptism. During the week on the estate he belongs to, he's like a missionary himself, leading prayers, teaching slaves to read and write. But it is his preaching that carries his reputation as far as Bellefields and probably beyond. Even the whites sometimes come to hear him, they say.

"He send you?" Ishmael sounds doubtful.

This time Duncan does pause. "Not directly," he says with a quick smile.

Ishmael looks at Brother Teo and then back at Duncan.

"So how you find youself to Brother Teo here? Who send you to him—directly?"

Uncle Teo's eyes flash at the stranger. "Who you belong to?" His voice pecks at the man.

Elorine wonders if Duncan gave Uncle Teo a different story.

Uncle Teo has been part of the Livingstones' lives for a long time. He appeared out of nowhere, an itinerant preacher, just after Selina died and while Ishmael was struggling with his grief and his foundry. The white blacksmith that Ishmael had apprenticed to after buying his freedom from Cascade had finally succumbed to the rum and syphilis of his misspent life, and his widow, anxious to get back to England with her children, had offered the black man a share in the foundry and, as importantly, the house. Uncle Teo is a carpenter, among many other useful skills, and set about turning the shed that the Livingstones had lived in to that point into the chapel it is now. He also preaches there sometimes.

But he's a man of mystery. Sometimes for months he's simply not around. He disappears and comes back without warning or explanation. Perhaps he's a runaway, Elorine surmises, changing location on the wings of his preaching and skills (he goes out with the fishermen sometimes) and to keep himself a little ahead of the authorities. And perhaps it's those pathways he makes to other places that have brought this uppity stranger to him, and to the Livingstone house this night. The walls of the little house draw closer around Elorine's anxiety.

"Kensington," Duncan says in answer to Uncle Teo's spiked question.

"Is that where Daddy belong to?" Ishmael asks.

Duncan shakes his head. "He is on Croydon. But sometimes he is in town with Backra. The Bay."

Duncan is a runaway. Montego Bay is far to the west of Bellefields, and it will have taken this stranger three or four days to get here, perhaps more if he's stopped elsewhere to give Daddy Sharpe's message. Kensington's Backra will know he's missing and may have put up posters by now and sent out slave hunters. Anyone harbouring him is liable for punishment too. Elorine's dislike of the man hardens, even as she listens more keenly to noises coming from the street.

"So if Daddy Sharpe don't send you directly," Uncle Teo says, "and you and he not even belonging on the same property, what you doing clear in Bellefields in the middle night? Look how far Bellefields is from the Bay."

The man looks at Elorine and then back at Ishmael.

"We don't keep secret in this family," Pappi says. Which they both know is not true, but Elorine is glad for the declaration. "You can speak what you come to say to everybody here."

Betraying nothing on his face, Ishmael wonders silently whether Maasa God is making joke with him. After all the earlier exhortations, this man out of the darkness of night is His answer? Maybe it is so in truth, because the ways of God are never straightforward and this Duncan seems unable to give a direct answer to a simple question.

But there is something there. Although Duncan may or may not be his name, he isn't from these parts. He talks quite different to the Creoles around here, and he isn't a Guinea either. Maybe he really knows Daddy Sharpe. Ishmael has never seen Sharpe or heard his preachment but he knows people who have, and the awe in which they hold his fervour and wisdom is plain in this stranger's voice also. Sharpe is part of the white missionary church that Ishmael has left behind, but as there are many rooms in Maasa God's mansion so are there many earthly paths to salvation.

A black American preacher brought Ishmael into the arms of Jesus and dipped him in the pool of conviction. But it was a white Baptist missionary who taught him and Selina to read the Word and the newspapers. And Pastor Goldworthy out there in Riverside still brings his horses to Ishmael for shoeing, and Ishmael never thinks to charge him.

Sharpe—so this Duncan says—is apparently planning something. It's not an uprising. He says that over and over. "Is a siddown," he says finally.

"What you mean?" Teo asks, suspicious still. Ishmael can see the old man is caught between two concerns. Duncan hasn't mentioned anyone that Teo knows, so far. So how does he find himself to Teo's shack, which Ishmael hears is all by itself on a little hillside that shoots right down into the sea? But Teo is also intrigued by the prospect of rebellion and freedom. All blacks, even those already free, are.

"After Christmas," Duncan says, "when the conch blow, nobody is going to walk out in the field." It was the first direct response they'd got to a simple question. But this time they didn't understand the answer.

King William has given the slaves their free paper, Duncan says, and the planters in Spanish Town have burnt it. Ishmael and Elorine and Teo have heard versions of this story many times, over many months. But now, Duncan says, one of the white missionaries, a Baptist like Daddy Sharpe, has gone to England to get another paper. He is returning to Montego Bay with the free paper around Christmas. So Duncan says that Sharpe says, and many other people in those parts believe. But in any case, Daddy Sharpe says the slaves, no longer being slaves, should rightfully be paid for their work on estates and elsewhere. The new system is to begin after Christmas. Otherwise, no work.

"And when Backra and the driver-dem bring out dem whip and lash Nayga raw—what your Daddy Sharpe going to do?" Brother Teo's voice is like a driver's whip.

"Daddy say we must just siddown still," Duncan says, sitting forward in his chair. "But some people say that if that happen, if they bring violence to Nayga, then Nayga will bring violence to dem."

Ishmael sighs.

West, where Daddy Sharpe is and Duncan says he comes from, is a faraway world of flat fertile land with huge estates, several hundreds of slaves on each. Many of them are African: Akan and Kongo—men and women who remember well the villages of their childhood and their ceremonies, who make rebellion not only for their own freedom but to honour the spirits of those who did not make it across the doomed water. They plot ceaselessly. As soon as they are betrayed, the ringleaders executed or transported, new leaders arise and the conspiring begins again.

In Bellefields, though there are more Creoles, fewer Africans, and the mountains carve the land into pockets of smaller estates with fewer slaves, conspiracies still bloom like love bush. In his time as a slave on Cascade estate Ishmael had known of every conspiracy and sympathized with all of them. Every pulse in his blood pushed him toward the plotters, whose machetes and hoes he had made and kept sharp; some of them were the children of his father's shipmates.

But while Ishmael didn't carry tales to anyone, not even Selina, he kept his distance from the rebels. He plotted and nurtured a quiet rebellion of his own: the purchase of freedom from Maasa Douglas—father of the magistrate Magnus, whom Elorine has just mentioned—who owns Cascade and whose blacksmith he was then. Freedom for himself, and then for Selina.

Adam, a child, would have to wait his turn. Their Christmas gifts to themselves did not come from on high, as the white missionaries taught, but from themselves: money earned from special jobs on the quiet for his fellow slaves, or that Selina brought back from Sunday market and from making clothes for slaves who could pay. In dead of night he would bury the coins in a hole created beneath the anvil, scraping ever more space to accept more pieces, until he had enough to buy his own freedom from Maasa Douglas.

As he listens with half a mind to Duncan arguing with Brother Teo about what should be done and what would be done, Ishmael discerns the real message being brought, whether from Daddy Sharpe or just from Duncan himself: an island-wide siddown, or uprising—whichever Maasa God willed. Duncan hints that he has visited other places, spoken with other elders with influence, like Ishmael, and that other slaves from West are doing the same elsewhere.

He does not make a direct request of them, and for that Ishmael at least is grateful.

Backra is suspicious of all free men who are not white, thinking that they are part of the roiling ground beneath their feet that would consume them. Free blacks worst of all, for some like Ishmael were once in their rightful place: yoked.

The stranger asks for a prayer to end the night, turning to Brother Teo, and keeps his head bowed as Teo prays for Maasa God's blessing on their several endeavours. Meantime Ishmael finds himself recalling the injunction of Maasa Jesus to the disciples as he sent them forth: *Be ye therefore wise as serpents and harmless as doves.* This man and even Daddy Sharpe are sheep in the midst of wolves, but whether they are wise or harmless only the Lord knows for sure.

Finally Brother Teo, somewhat mollified by Duncan's request for a prayer and in any case bound by the unspoken laws of hospitality, takes the stranger back out into the night, to his own house. As he latches the door behind them Ishmael reflects on a injunction of Paul to the Hebrews: *Be not forgetful to entertain strangers, for thereby some have entertained angels unawares.*

Or devils.

❧ IO ❧

Jason: Butterfly Spirits, Sunday, October 30

THE COOING OF DOVES WOKE ME this morning, the second of my return. From my cot in the middle of the room I could see two of them, smudges against the pearly light that filled the window above the table on which I write. The birds tugged at my consciousness like a worm in soil, but I resisted and slipped into a reverie.

Squire was gone in person, but as I'd written to Carla, his presence—his duppy, as the Negroes would say—haunts the place. He liked the world at this time of day also, when, other than a few kitchen slaves, he was often the first riser in the house. He'd put a chair outside on the top step of the stairway to the house and sit there, surveying his kingdom, smoking his small pipe of jackass rope tobacco. Its pungent smell would reach into my fusty sleeping cove, tickling me into wakefulness.

It was in that time that the bond with Squire was forged, if that is not too heavy a word for so delicate a process. My first few months in the big house, aged five or six, I'd be as quiet as a mouse—mus-mus, as we'd call them in the quarters. I started at shadows, jumped at loud noises, scuttled back to my cove at the crash of crockery. Anthony, having known no other life but that of darker pickni, even older ones, as I was by more than a year, bound to his will, established his suzerainty early. But Squire would not allow him full rein. Our father never expressed what Anthony came to convince himself was his partiality for me. Still, once I could bring myself to come physically close to him, Squire's regard for me was something I could feel, like the warmth of the stove in Constancia's kitchen—another place where I felt safe and welcome.

For myself, I've never shared Anthony's resentful conviction, nor acted on it. But once I lost a persisting fear of being sent back to the quarters I was able to address the imbalance in our status. Here also Squire did not allow full freedom to our fractious passions, commanding, when necessary, peace and a practised amity. Thereby was laid the groundwork for the complex interplay of feeling between Anthony and myself, which has persisted to this day.

My relationship with Squire began on those front steps at the very break of day. Like a mus-mus I'd settle my bottom on the warm wooden floor of the house, my feet on the cool stone of the broad final step beside where Squire sat in his chair that lived in the sitting room the rest of the day.

Lying in my cot this morning I could summon the feel of his large hand—quite small in reality—coming to rest on my head-top.

Occasionally he would go down into the yard, me his shadow, often to the gazebo he'd built for Anthony's mother. Bringing from the quarters the omen of disaster that enclouded the place, I would hang back. But Squire would summon me to sit beside him on one of the two iron benches he'd had rooted there.

It was on one of those dawn expeditions that I discovered the butterfly spirits that surround lignum vitae trees, plentiful on the estate and much loved by Squire, as his own grave attests. With the delight of a child himself he walked us to several of the nearest trees, each of them seemingly alive, wearing a nimbus of small white butterflies in flight.

Nayga have it to say, Squire explained, them is spirits. I remember the explanation, and the kisses of the butterflies on my skin as we moved among them. Squire, a man largely indifferent to creatures, made no move to dismiss the butterflies.

The next morning, excited by the prospect, I ran past Squire in his chair, down the steps and to the nearest tree. The clouds of butterflies were nowhere in sight, just a few desultory ones that seemed heavier and slightly larger than yesterday's miracle. Squire explained, to my deepening disappointment, that it was a seasonal thing, not predictable by any calendar except the earth's. And so it went. You awaken one morning and there they are, infesting your own spirit with rapture; the next day, they're gone, like a happy dream.

Fully roused from my reverie of Squire and the butterflies I stared at the ceiling, listening to the quiet of daybreak—the doves, having hopped onto my desk and found nothing of interest, had flown off to begin their day. I found myself reaching into my portmanteau for *The Life of Olaudah Equiano, Or Gustavus Vassa, the African.* The pages fell open at his evocation of his childhood in Africa, a mixture of idealization and the poignancy of hindsight and loss. As always, I thought of my mother, which would provoke, in some unexpected corner of England, its own vortex of melancholy.

She was a Guinea African named Memba. This much I learned as a child from Constancia—a Creole herself but from Guinea parents—who has been the secret source of the little that I know about my mother. Thus I am, by blood, as much African as English, and by upbringing . . . both . . . and neither.

The vagaries of history and lust brought the bloodlines together in a third place. This makes me, despite the smooth blend of my brown skin, a creature of hostile histories. It is a conflict I've been aware of all my life, even in England, where one part of me was subjugated to the other as a matter of expediency. But the African was never entirely forgotten; it was what set me apart from everyone around me. I can no doubt continue to live in England without too great discomfort, as many like myself are doing. I am not alone in being married to a white native, and Carla's family and Quaker friends are charmed by Caleb's irrepressible spirit, ignoring the mahogany hew of his unknown grandmother's pigmentary gift.

It's an irony of fate—the more so of my own choosing—that has brought me back to this triangle of heritages, existing in their shifting disequilibria.

I was somewhat solemn at breakfast, and declined, politely but firmly, Mathilde's invitation to accompany her to the service in Belle-fields. It is All Souls' Day and, she was thinking of Squire—as perhaps I should have been—and so accompanied Anthony, Anna and herself. But I was embroiled in my own consideration of souls lost.

Much of my life at Greencastle was lived in a penumbra of double meanings and half-silences. I was the master's son, yes, his firstborn (who survived, anyway); but my mother was invisible. Born a slave myself, raised to the great house table—except when important visitors came, when I ate in the kitchen—I was the cargo borne by a ship that cast anchor in a certain harbour, one that happened to be nearest that day.

Memba is a pebble beneath the surface of the stream of my life. I have no feelings for her and regret that. But there is nothing on which to build such feelings.

A peaceful quiet descended on the house after the carriage and horses left. I lay on my bed, somewhat dulled by Constancia's breakfast, and dozed, perhaps searching for Memba's face. Jack came in and interrupted me, eager to be of help. I sent him away, deciding it was time to venture away from my morbid fancies, out onto the estate where I'd been born. Downstairs, Lincoln, seeing my intent, insisted I take a floppy wide-brimmed hat that had belonged to Squire.

As I stepped down from the piazza onto the ground proper, something flashed at the edge of my sight and then touched my nose, quivering there. A pale butterfly. I brushed it off and my eyes followed it. To Squire's sapling. Which had four or five dancing around it.

I walked away from the little gazebo, looking. And soon found it: an old tree, squat and rooted and scarred, that I had climbed into the arms of many times as a child. It seemed now to dance in the air amid the corona of butterflies that it wore. I stood in a trance of happiness.

It was the season and on All Souls' Day, no less.

The sense of awe was easily maintained because the fields themselves were deserted. Sunday is the one day the slaves get for their own endeavours. For many of them it is another day of backbreaking labour but it is in their own behalf, on the hillsides that crouch around the more fertile sugar lands. There, on what the Negroes call the "what leff", they cultivate whatever they need to augment what little the estate provides in the way of food—which is usually the bare minimum that the law demands, if that.

There were few people abroad; most would have set out for their grounds at first light. One little group, however, two women and three children, not dressed for field work, was coming up the path that had been created over the decades from the slave quarters to the boundary of Greencastle. The children especially were turned out prettily as could be; I found myself smiling as they drew closer to where I stood. One of the women, walking at the head of the group, cradled a book, a sufficiently remarkable occurrence to draw my attention. We stopped a few yards apart. I looked from the book—I guessed it to be a Bible—to her face: a large smiling face whose bright intelligent eyes knew me.

I bid her a good morning, resisting the impulse to touch my hat-brim.

"I did hear you come home, Kwesi." Her smile broadened. "You favour Maasa Squire in dat hat." She didn't quite laugh aloud, but her voice lifted toward it. "Ehnglan suit you good."

I reconstructed her other words afterward. For that moment my thoughts swirled around just one of them, "Kwesi." Who was coming home? From England? I had brought a Kwesi?

The woman saw the confusion on my face and this time laughed out loud.

"He don't remember we," she said, turning slightly to the woman behind her without really looking away from me. I glanced at the other woman—also a stranger—and back to the one with the Bible. She pat her own chest and smiled. "Judith daughter. You don't remember? Pheba!" She almost shouted the word and then giggled.

And slowly, through the buzzing of "Kwesi" in my head like a persistent fly, and the distraction of the pale butterflies around us, the vault of memory opened. I found myself, to my own relief and that of the women, smiling. Pheba, slightly older, and her younger brother, Silas, who was my age, were my closest companions during the sojourn in Pompey's household before Angela's death, when man-umission brought my ascension to the big house.

As circumstance had moved me out of their ambit, they had faded from my awareness.

We all looked at each other, the three adults and the three children momentarily dumbed by understanding. All waited for me to speak.

"Is Judith well?" I heard myself ask.

That gave Pheba back her voice. She laughed. "She better than you and me."

I was about to ask to be commended to her mother when the other woman spoke for the first time. "She gone over. Some time since."

Pheba laughed again. "Beg pardon, I forget my manners. That is Olive." I nodded at the other woman.

"We going to chapel," Pheba said, her chin lifting a little with what looked like pride. "We is Christian."

I said the first thing that came to mind: that that was good. I also asked whether Maas Anthony knew about the chapel-going, because it was an article of faith among some abolitionists in England that the planters forbade attendance at worship.

"Maas Squire give ticket to all who want to go the missionary-dem," Pheba said. "Him say Nayga who is Christian work better than the pagan-dem. Since Squire get sick, Maas Anthony don't stop we. Him even ask we to pray for him sometimes." That brought a smile.

"Backra Wyckham don't like it," Olive said, her voice dry. "But he don't try and stop us yet."

"And you can read," I commented to Pheba, nodding at the Bible she held against her. Her chin lifted again. "Long time now. Missus Missionary teach we, Olive too. And we is teaching others. We read newspaper too, when we get it."

This tumble of information was delivered with an enthusiasm that made it easier for me to recover the child Pheba from the adult woman before me.

"You remember Gatta?" she asked. When she saw that clearly I didn't, she said, with emphasis, "Delores. She used to drive the pickni gang."

Instantly I remembered. A small scrawny woman with quick hands that slapped and pinched without mercy.

"She dead last week," Pheba said. "We having wake for her tonight."

Pheba then lost interest in her accomplishments, in Delores, and myself, and rounded up the children like a sheepdog, setting them in front of her.

"Olive, we going late for chapel. Beg excuse, M . . ." She hesitated, tossed between thoughts of how to address me.

"Pray for me, Pheba," I said to relieve her. She nodded and smiled as the little party moved off.

But as my eyes and thoughts swivelled between Pheba and the butterflies like a silent choir around me, the word "Kwesi" was a strangely shaped key to a door I had not even been aware of, and I tumbled into a chamber whose dimensions were, at that moment, infinite.

Feeling suddenly weak, I found a low-hanging bough of the venerable lignum vitae and rested against it. Ignoring the radiant butterflies—whether Squire or my slave ancestors—I reflected on the distance that I had travelled, from Judith and Pompey's hut with Pheba and Silas, when I had been Kwesi, to what I still call the big house. Where I am now.

II

Adebeh: Sunday, October 30

BLACKPEOPLE'S SUNDAY IS AS LONG IN Jamaica as in Scotia. The Bible (and Mam) say, *By the sweat of thy brow shalt thou eat bread*. And lickle bread for plenty sweat, Da would rejoin. That is a true word, and you see it on a Sunday, in both places.

Murtella, Fergus' babymother, has everybody up before light to go to market. Market have to finish by eleven o'clock, when the law says it is to finish so that the slaves can go to their worship, though not a lot of them go. They can only go to worship if the whiteman who owns them gives them leave—a ticket, they call it here. And most of them won't, Murtella says. So it's a stupid law. But it's the same in Scotia, without a law. The whitepeople there believe that if only blackpeople would go to church and be baptized, and go to school and learn to read and write and sing "God Save the King," we will be saved, and good.

But that doesn't mean we will become people. We will still be niggers, only saved and good niggers. When Crown land is to be divided for saved white and saved black, the saved white will get a hundred acres or more, according to how many pickni he have, and the saved black, no matter how many pickni, will get twenty—and the twenty is a stubborn twenty, believe me.

So the sun rise to find us stringing along the track into town. Fergus says I don't have to come with them, I can stay and groom the horses and maybe take the doctorman into town for church or anywhere else he might want to go, which is what Fergus would do in any case. But the Dr. Fenwell says he's too poorly for church, and asks Murtella to pray for him when she goes to her church.

So Fergus decides he better stay at the house, in case. Murtella, Jujube their daughter—Juice as everybody but me calls her—and two smaller pickni head to market as the light is bleeding the darkness, we three big ones carrying baskets with things they grow behind the house, where I discover as we's picking things this morning that the land goes further back than it look. The pickni, whose names I still don't know, each carry a live fowl by the legs.

As we're walking I start to feel myself breathing hard. Is not the basket, I accustomed to that from I's younger than Jujube, going with Mam and Eddie and Precious to sell in Sackville. It is the green of this place that is coming out of the morning, like it is wanting to choke me. I feel it filling up my eyes and throat and nostril like water that I fall into, sweet and stifling.

I's following the road, but I's watching the dancing backside of Jujube. I don't call her Juice because she and me is not friend, I didn't even know her before yesterday. But Juice is her name and Juice her nature. I feel to bite her, and you know, even her sweat would taste sweet.

But I's careful even in my thoughts. I know that the quickest way to turn Fergus against me, and the doctorman whose roof I am under, would be to make the slightest move toward that girl. Besides, Murtella would just take that big knife she uses for everything, from cooking to digging ground, and peel me like something they call breadfruit here, except that it's white.

⇒ 12 ⇐

Elorine: Mule, Sunday, October 30

I KNOW THEY CALL ME MULE. Woman my age should breed a long time ago, they say. And should have a man, furthermore. I see them more than hear them, and I understand from how they look at me what they thinking, because I grow up hearing it, that woman born to breed and if not them is mule, which is the worst thing, not really a woman. Mule in truth, when you see how the man-dem ride them. Black and white alike. No man is to ride me like that, so I stay far from all of them.

I know I can breed. At least, I used to able. I don't know about now and I have no mind to find out! When I was younger, just getting custom to my monthlies and beginning to understand what they mean, I think a lot about babies. I had a dolly, rags of Mama Sel's leave-over cloth stuff that she make for me when I'm small. I find myself carrying Venus everywhere I going in the house, and Mama have to stop me taking it out on the street with me. "You too big for dolly," she say, "you will soon be a woman." Like, as I growing up, going forward, I'm looking back too, and holding on to the child I is leaving behind. I get big so I put it aside, like Apostle Paul say to put away childish things.

But I wasn't sure I want to be a woman. I see all around me how woman have a hard life of rockstone and baaj. Even Mama Sel. She work like a slave (which she was born and grow to a woman as) from I know her until the day before she dead. She work through pregnant, when baby born, when baby die—one die before me, one die after me, then the one that kill her—and she just have to keep on, no matter. Is not Pappi driving her, he is a good man in general. Is life.

Times hard, Mama say all the time when I beg her to slow down a little. I grow to learn early that life is hard for a woman. Always.

Still, I cherish Venus. When I was in private, sometimes I slip off my blouse and put her mouth to my bubby—I have to laugh at that now, cause they was little like june plum, and don't have any juice to feed even a dolly.

But even as I'm thinking that I know it is foolishness. On the estate, and here in town too, there is plenty young girl twelve and thirteen years who get fling down somewhere and them legs prise open like pliers for a man—white, black and brown—to drive into them like Pappi's bellows, except is not air they filling them up with. And the girls, who is really pickni, blow up like bladder and, whether they ready for it or not, a baby come.

Sometimes the baby live, sometimes it die. If it live, sometimes bubby have milk for it, sometimes is nurse that have to keep it alive, somebody whose own baby dead and leave all that milk in her bubby. I give thanks to the Risen Lord that nothing like that happen to me. You learn a lot of things when you small, is just you don't always know what they mean at the time. Understanding is the breath of God that He breathe into you little by little as you grow in His wisdom.

But even when you know all this, you have to cherish a baby. Life is rockstone, cerasee tea and civil orange. But baby is a sweet syrup that Maasa God pour over your life like balm, and it never ask to born.

Jehovah! Forgive me for killing mine.

⇝ 13 ⇜

Jason: McKinley's, Monday, October 31

WITH A HINT OF DISPARAGEMENT THAT I had lolled too long inside, Anthony invited me to ride out into the fields this morning. But last night's events were too fresh in my mind—and in my dreams, during a fitful night. I had not the stomach for the fields, where I would likely encounter Pheba, old London, and the others who had brought Kwesi back from the dead. For me to be galloping behind Maasa, looking down at them from a horse, would unravel the association, however transient—and perhaps illusory—that my presence had created.

I saw the irritation forming like a cloud in Anthony's eyes as I hesitated, searching for words. And then instinctual memory came to my rescue. I would visit the Livingstones.

"Tomorrow," I said, forcing a smile. "I'd like to go into town today. See what's changed and all that."

"Nothing has, brother." His smile was as grim as mine.

"Nor on the estate," I returned.

We were both correct. Coming down from Greencastle, the slope of the low hills that surround Bellefields presents a pretty view of buildings and towering trees set in a curve of sea like a smile. From closer, the smile is gap-toothed. One comes first to the upstairs town homes of the wealthiest of our citizens, planter and merchant, taking what breeze is to be had on the slopes. Some of them are quite splendid, but on the flat their promise leeches away in the shabbiness of more modest homes and shops, which need repairs or even just a paintbrush. I've seen some of the great cities of England and Europe—more to the point, I've seen some of the small towns, the Bellefields of

Wiltshire and elsewhere, which aspire to the great squares of London and Manchester. Bellefields' square, with its courthouse and vestry offices, and its dolorous workhouse and scaffold, is all pretense without ambition.

And then the beggars! Anyone of light skin or on horseback is fair game. I even seem, after thirteen years, to recognize some of them! Having no largesse to distribute I spurred the horse Israel had found for me past them.

I was brought up short, however, at McKinley's across the square from the official buildings. The mere sight of the sign over the entrance to it caused something to communicate itself through the reins to the horse, which stopped opposite the smaller entrance to the establishment.

I forget what sent Squire into Bellefields but he decided that Anthony and I should come with him. We needed haircuts. There may have been some occasion in the offing, because usually one of the house slaves was the barber, for Squire as well. Anthony rode us both in on his pony, following Squire's stallion. I did my best to balance behind Anthony without holding on more than was necessary.

Squire appeared to enjoy his torture of clipping and shaving and patting administered by a wizened old man of colour who seems in memory to have requested permission before every snip and touch. The barber ushered Anthony into the chair that his father had vacated to disappear through the connecting doorway into McKinley's. As the boisterous converse from the other side revealed, it was a place for men—white men. Presenting itself as a "Men's Club," McKinley's admits women, in a separate room that serves fruit drinks and various infusions; the claim on its facade is to keep out non-whites of both sexes. White boys were apparently allowed also, for Anthony disappeared through the connecting doors when his trim was completed. As I got to my feet to take Anthony's place in the chair, a boy entered from the street, looked at me as though I was an unpleasant smell and sat himself in the chair. The old man bowed and began his clipping.

Saturday morning was popular for barbering. I sat there for a very long time as men and boys, all of them white, all of them glancing askance at me, succeeded each other in the chair.

Finally Squire, Anthony following, returned. "You ready to go home?" I couldn't speak, for anger and shame. He understood. I can see his face flushing as he turned to the chair where a white boy about my age squirmed under the old man's ministrations. With the energy of fury held in polite check, Squire went over to the barber chair and, with a muttered "Excuse me, bwoy," lifted him clear and deposited him in the chair beside me. In continuation of the gesture he lifted and deposited me in front of the startled, jibbering barber. "Cut his hair." And to ensure his meaning Squire stood right beside me as the old man—I can hear still the hissing terror in his breathing—snipped and combed my unruly Negro hair.

When all our business was completed, Squire put me in front of himself on the saddle.

Anthony, I remember, raced ahead of us back to Greencastle, perhaps to avoid having to observe my enthronement from behind.

The adjoining doors of McKinley's bar and barbershop are probably still there. And I would receive the same treatment were I to dare to venture through either one. One of the pernicious effects of slavery is the reduction of the already powerless. At that moment a man, I was a child again, anxious for the succour of Squire's presence.

But I kicked my horse forward and shook off those morbid thoughts. My destination was elsewhere.

⇒ 14 ⇐

Elorine: Jason, Monday, October 31

PAPPI LAUGH AT ME AFTERWARDS, nearly choke himself. I hear this voice outside talking to him. I can only hear it because Pappi stop working, and he only do that for somebody important. I not doing anything much myself, so I let my fastness simmer a little and then I go behind the curtain and look out into the workshop.

Is a strange man, dress-up like a Englishman just arrive off the ship, but he don't look like a whiteman and . . .

Is Jason!

I feel my chest tighten and my feet feel to move in two directions at once—outside to the workshop, and back into my bedroom right under the bed. Is like I find something I looking for this long time—but I confuse about what to do with it. So I grab hold of myself and walk through the kitchen to the back steps. "Jason Pollard," I cry out, before even looking properly at him, "you leave you manners inna Englan!"

He talking to Pappi, his back to me. He turn, and I feel so stupid. Is a stranger in truth. I never see this man before in my life. I feel the blood drain from my face down to my foot. I want to run inside but is too late.

"Hello, Elorine," the man say, quiet and smiling at me. "I was just coming inside to you." His voice is so proper, sound like Reverend Ogilvie. Is only when Pappi laugh out loud that I come back to myself. Is the same eyes. That is what tell me who it is. And he know me, I can see that in the eyes too.

Is somebody I know from I know myself, and he turn into somebody else now. But me too. Two strangers who know each other all we life. Imagine.

I find my normal voice. "Howdy, Jason. You come."

He laugh. "Of course. You thought I wouldn't?"

I couldn't answer him truthfully on that so I turn away and say, "Come inside," in my softest voice.

He was easier with the talking than me, though. He's staring at me, but all the time he's smiling too. Not at me, he just seem happy to be here. Yes, he talk funny. Sometimes it was all I could manage to stop myself from laughing out loud when he say some little thing. And I realize soon enough that is not just that he was away in foreign, England, and come back sounding like a Englishman, but that he see things and do things and have to think about things that poor me can't even imagine in this little corner of the world, behind Maasa God back. It put a distance between him and me that wasn't there before. But only in my own mind, cause is not him make it, I have to say that. He soon talking, except for the accent, just like when we was younger. Is only when I think of him as lawyerman that I feel the dust on my bare footbottom, and my toes curl.

Still, it was easy enough to talk, when I forget all that and how he sound. The bwoy Jason begin to appear as if the sun rise on him from behind. He have the same crooked smile, except now he have a little moustache shading it. And his puss-eye, moving around a little nervous-like same way. Like he's watching for something to ketch him.

And I see a day, almost evening, when he was maybe nine, so I was just six, barely knowing myself, when Jason arrive here on his mule, both of them sweating, looking decrepit. Jason nose was bleeding. Looking careful now, I can see on his nostril a tiny ridge of skin on the curve.

Nothing was wrong with the mule, it just needed water. Jason needed cooling down too, and, after a thorough wiping by Selina, he join us around the table for supper. It wasn't the first time he sit around the table but it was the first time he come by himself. Usually is Squire leave him while he go into town on his own business—I'm so custom to Jason when I'm growing that I never wonder, even now, how he come to be almost part of this family. I can still see his eyes, bruised and furious, looking at me across the food. He want me to know something he couldn't find words for, but I didn't understand. Nobody at the table ask him anything, but is so many different ways he could come by that cut nose. From Maasa Squire, who could be wicked when he drink, Pappi say. From Anthony, who none of us like and treat Jason like a slave sometimes, he tell Pappi. Anything and anybody. But I can still see his eyes burning at me.

"I can stay here?" Jason ask, smart enough to look at Selina rather than Ishmael. "Tonight. Just tonight," he say quickly.

"No," say Ishmael.

At the same time as Selina ask, "Why?"

He probably know how Pappi would answer before he ask. But Selina, without testing her husband, scrape the answer to her own question out of him. Anthony demand that Jason call him Maasa Pollard. "Only one Maasa at Greencastle," Jason say, staring at his food, tight and red with remembering. "And is not Anthony. Not yet. And I am not no slave, to call him Maasa."

Mama prevail in the end, and Jason bed down on a pallet under the dining table, with Ginger's grandmother for company. There was nowhere else for him except my room and the kitchen.

Next morning, daybreak, Pappi put him on his mule and send him home with a piece of paper for his father.

They didn't even send anybody to look for him.

⇒ 15 ⇐

Narrative: Politics, Monday, October 31

BEHIND STUTTERING EYELIDS HE HEARS pickni voices and sees Caleb, his son left behind in England, playing with them, Carla hovering near like a white bird. Among them is Elorine Livingstone—the ten-year-old girl he left to go to England, not the woman he visited this morning. Elorine the child is playing alone: the woman Elorine has no children, which he doesn't understand but didn't ask about.

The whisper of bare feet stirs the soup of images and sounds. As he struggles to the surface something flat and soft is placed in his lap. A shadowy figure moves away. He opens his eyes fully. A girl, better dressed than the generality of slaves in the house, is moving quickly toward the doorway back inside. "Stop," he calls out, and she does. The piazza's louvred light dances around her. He glances down at his lap and sees some newspapers, and then looks up at the girl again. Her back is to him.

"Who sent these?"

"Missa Lincoln say to bring them, Maasa." Her voice is husky, substantial for such a slender body.

"Turn around," he says, "let me see you." His own voice sounds heavy, burdened by dozing and the effect of her dark limbs gleaming through the light-filled frock.

She is new to him. Not pretty, her nose a little too large, her lips a little thin, but her eyes clear and intelligent. The colour of a fawn, her limbs as she awaits dismissal are at once indolent and aggressive. Like a wild animal caught between impulses.

He asks her name.

"Miranda, Maasa," she says, her eyes suddenly as flat as her voice. Put in immediate mind of Shakespeare's wild thing, he considers this girl—for she is little more than that—well named, and wonders by whom.

"I am not Maasa," he says, sounding pompous. "Maas Anthony is Maasa."

"Yes, Maasa," she answers, predictably, and bolts into the house before he can think to say anything else. He could summon her back, and she would come. But he has nothing really to say to her, and the strength of a desire to just look at her, to watch her limbs as they move in the striped sunlight of the piazza, startles him.

But once he turns to the newspapers in his lap, thoughts of the girl fade quickly.

In themselves they aren't strange to him: they'd found themselves to the parish halls and coffee houses he'd frequented in London. But it's been some months since he's seen anything even notionally current.

With a sigh of relief mixed with not a little irritation he notices that the names of the principal actors in the stories on the front page of the first journal consulted, the *Jamaica Courant*, are familiar. He'd come to know these people by reading about them in England, and they were saying the same things yet. There was even still the vile Reverend Mr. Bridges, Lucifer in the costume of a priest.

Such a situation is ours: even the priests of the most high God must become militants in the combat. What were the adverse Gauls of Rome, compared to the barbarous, treacherous foes with whom we shall have to contend? The first fought for honour and empire with a nation who were their natural rivals. Whom have we to contend with? Our unnatural enemies in the mother country, to whom, till now, we have been warmly and beneficially attached. Their object is strife, confusion, blood, and massacre; to oppose them is the duty of all: and let me conjure you, fellow-sufferers, to join in the sacred cause with heart and hand, body and soul, with all your might. In such a cause, the cause of honour, truth, justice, and humanity, we ought to have no fear.

Disgusted, and wide-awake now, he throws the papers to the floor.

He dispenses poison as communion bread and wine, Jason writes later in his diary, instigating hatred against the missionaries and their converts—though his own church doesn't seek any among the slaves. The canvas he paints, with some of the planters his eager assistants, is lurid and blood-soaked: Hayti and the Bastille all rolled together. An odious man, but a hero to many who do not darken a church door from one year's end to the next.

And the public meetings have continued from parish to parish, resulting in the same splenetic resolutions of outrage and idle threats to discard the Mother Country which is, as they feel, abandoning them to the missionaries and their niggers. The island is their property to dispose of as they will, like their slaves and other chattels.

These men feed on their own delusions. Can they not feel their insubstantiality? When will the Negro become tired of this depredation on his person and labour and move to fulfil the reverend gentleman's nightmares? I cannot but wonder whether their dire prophesies will not, in fact, cause their fulfilment, for the slaves are well aware of the fulminations and plans of their owners. They cannot themselves but guard against such measures—and in the process, perhaps decide on pre-emptive strokes of their own.

I feel myself sinking into a darkness deeper than the night outside this window. The only light is the guttering flame of the child Miranda. Before embarking on this venture I had not given thought to managing my intimate physical needs without Carla. I am sworn to her by oath, but as much by common intelligence—the clap is everywhere, as available as the pleasures of the bed but longer lasting. Miranda is little more than a child and I am not a monster for my musings. The image of her, though, a brown forest creature shimmering among the piazza's blades of light, quickens disturbing impulses, while at the same time leaving a patina of sadness.

≈ 16 ≈

Jason: Blood Tree, Wednesday, November 2

THE IDYLL OF RETURN, SO PALPABLE up to last night, ended brutally this morning as I saw the runaway Zubia whipped raw, virtually rendered for the charnel house. In the cool grey dusk as I write this, her screams are as raucous in my head as the flight of parrots that passed a few minutes ago on their way home to their night trees.

Soaking up the green light like a walking plant, I had not intended being the witness and incidental player that I became. I was on my way to Angel Hole for a bath, Jack following with cerasee bush to scrub with and a large piece of towelling. In his other hand was a change of clothes. The Hole, as it's called by everyone, through which Bamboo River runs, is where the whites soak themselves in the day, protected and shielded from dark eyes by their personal slaves, but where at night—as I remember from my days among them—the slaves frolic and hold assignations.

Although it was still early, we encountered, not very distant from the house, Anthony, on his way back from the fields. He was leading a little procession: himself angrily striding back toward the house, matched step for step behind by Hector, the head driver, whom I recognized from his early-morning consultations with Maas Anthony. A powerful bare-chested brown man, he hauled a woman, Zubia, by a truss of ropes that pulled her by underarm and groin a short length behind him. A bushy tail of spectators, come to see the dreadful sport they knew would ensue, followed. Bringing up the rear was the overseer, Wyckham, a scrawny jackal of a man to whom I'd taken an instant aversion upon meeting.

"Morning, Jason," Anthony barked at me as he passed, waving his arm as if throwing air in the direction he was headed. "Come see what we wretched colonials have to do to support the easy pleasures of you Londoners."

Immediately I recognized the Anthony of old. The Anthony of the last few days—the generally cheerful host, the ambivalent brother— had been chewed up and spat out somewhere on the path behind him.

Almost before I realized, I had joined the ragtag procession going back toward the house, noting somewhere in my shaken-up mind that Anthony had not even turned to see if I had changed course. Why did I? My own diffidence, the historic uncertainty as to my status here—that was surely a part of it. As it dawned on me what was about to happen, the hope grew in me that Anthony's own resolve would ultimately be consumed, as often happened in the past, in his own fury of indecision. This time, however, he drew fortitude from the salivatory anticipation of the overseer and Hector, who jerked the woman's harness with relish.

It was overcast and grey this morning, but I will remember always that shaft of sunlight like the eye of God illuminating the open space in front of the house, an open courtyard of flagstones and bare earth polished and melded by generations of feet, animal and human. It was the stage upon which our straggly group made its entrance, observed by a growing audience from within the big house, drawn there by the commotion. There was grim expectation in the crowd's eyes, knowing well the dramatic piece about to be performed. There were no white faces outside on the steps, but I noticed a pale flicker in a louvred piazza window: Anna. Our eyes met, hers flat, inscrutable. I looked away quickly, embarrassed.

As our little procession reached what everyone else had known to be its destination a moment of sudden stillness passed over us all, like a johncrow's shadow. "She a-go hug-up de tree," I heard a woman's voice nearby say in a hoarse whisper and it was though a sudden gust of wind blew away the curtain of my jumbled thoughts.

And there stood the tree. It thrust itself out of the ground in ironic testimony to its name—lignum vitae, tree of life. The same tree whose tender shoot Squire had had planted beside his grave. Whose several

specimens across Greencastle had worn the garlands of white butterflies so joyfully just days before.

But not this tree. Raised on its own little mound, like a diabolical
crucifix on an altar, it seemed never to have lived or borne leaves and
flowers and seeds. Despite its name there was not the least promise of
resurrection. And it seemed, with its stark, torn limbs unblessed by
even a vestige of growth, to more belong in the bare wintry landscape
of the Wiltshire downs I know well.

Within, I feel like the tree itself, which is cursed of the gods, African and Christian, from leafing and flowering because of the purpose
to which it has lent itself. Trees are living entities, spirits themselves
and the abode of spirits—so the Negroes believe and so I believed my
whole childhood; even now, vestiges of such ideas remain. With its
durability and dark foliage the lignum vitae is easy to conceive of as
an abode of spirits or, when alive with butterflies, a spirit itself. But
this particular tree, which has embraced the bodies of the brutalized
for decades, drinking their blood as nourishment, is damned. The
drenched wood has borrowed the lustre and colour of the skin of
those whom it has held helpless.

I wondered if Memba my mother had hugged the bloody tree of life
and death in this yard. And if so, who had applied the lash. Squire?

Meantime, without my intending it, I had found myself in the front
rank of the gathering, directly across from Anthony, who had not
looked at me since my summoning. He carried the riding crop that
had been an increment of Squire's arm of authority and nervously
tapped his calf with it, revealing the Anthony of yore—the fire of
anger suddenly chilled, scattered like embers by an older instinct,
which our father scorned as weakness, but which I preferred to think
of as a disposition to gentleness, which he had sometimes showed,
even to me. I could see those forces wrestling like demons in his mud-
died eyes for a few seconds before Hector's shout of triumph belled
the air.

"I ketch you now, you bitch!"

As indeed he had: Zubia was bound tight to the runted wood by
ropes threaded through the iron hoops embedded atop its truncated
arms, her feet tied tight where tree and earth meet. The tightened

sinews of her sturdy back could have been an outgrowth of the wood's musculature.

The trussing had been done with effortless efficiency born of practice, the head driver often being the direct instrument of punishment on an estate. But in this case, as it evolved, there was an intimate factor that lent a dreadful light to Hector's eyes. They splashed the helpless woman with a venomous fire, reinforcing the malice of his tone and posture. It was intensely personal—business between Hector and the woman who, I learned after from Anna, had borne him a child which she had taken with her in her attempted escape. Anthony was there as mere licensor, the rest of us as hapless bystanders to Hector's intense drama of power and revenge.

But as Hector stepped back to regard his handiwork, Zubia turned her head, the only movement the ropes allowed. And spat. The acid of her hate scorched Hector's eyes and he drew back with a dog's yelp, wiping the spittle with one hand at the same time as he flung up the arm that bore a thick bamboo cane as a monstrous extension.

Anthony shouted, "Hector!" in a voice as fierce as the slash which the huge Negro would have delivered, and he froze, quivering, both arms raised like the tree. He shrieked with fury, his voice raw, his body coiled with frustration and rage. Then he twirled the air with his whip and sent forth a chilling, triumphal burst of laughter, which then sent ripples of disquiet through the crowd of onlookers. Hector's whip, his driver's badge of authority and the source of his fearsome power, was likely his only friend at Greencastle, including Anthony. And I heard a woman's voice behind me, clear as a klingkling's cry overhead and as cold, say, with no attempt at concealment or soft speaking, "Christmas for him."

I was a jumble of sensation and alarm, nothing so formed as thought. The word NO! kept pounding like a pulse in my head. I saw the fingers of my brothers and sisters in the anti-slavery campaign pointed at me, their eyes asking me, What now? But I was immobilized in horrified fascination.

"The law say," Anthony shouted, slapping his boot loudly with his crop to get attention back to himself, "you can be whipped thirty-nine times, since I am present." He was speaking to Zubia but not looking at her; indeed, not looking at anyone. "For running away," he continued. "For taking my chattel with you." He suddenly looked fiercely at the driver. "Your son, Hector." He threw the word at the Negro like a stone, slapping his thigh for emphasis.

Hector received it as a body blow—and then smiled, as if Anthony had in fact given him a gift. His right arm, the one bearing his whip, twitched, as did his lips, parting in a parody of pleasure on broken teeth and purple gums. "Yes, Maasa," he grunted. "My son."

His cane sketched the air as his eyes laced its target with malice. The woman Zubia was standing still as the tree to which she was tied, but her eyes never left Hector's; she was not even listening to Anthony, her master.

Do something, the voices in my head shouted. But I was thinking of Memba. Should she come to me now as I write, in her person, I would be impelled to ask her business, for she has no face for me: Squire sold her quite soon after my weaning. I was looked after by Pompey, the then head driver (he who would probably have lashed Memba) and Judith, his wife. Of those two I have memories, not all of them pleasant, for Pompey was a violent man. While he dared not lay a hand on me, the general air of menace and threat in his household, which encompassed Judith and their children as well, was like a dark mantle around my early years. I was seldom allowed into or near the big house, unlike the pickni of house slaves, many of whom enjoyed almost complete freedom there.

Particular care was taken to keep me out of sight of Squire's wife, Anthony's mother, whom I remember mostly as a thin carrying voice calling one or other minder, for she was often poorly. It was only after she died, when I was about six, that I was brought to the main house, upon my father's decision to establish me then in a state of freedom.

"But," Anthony continued, his smile at that moment disturbingly like Hector's, "I feeling generous this morning. Our brother, Maas Jason, whom some of you will remember but not recognize now, has returned to us from across the big water." I flinched at the honorific and at the disdainful illumination suddenly thrown upon me. "To show that we are not the savages that fine Englishmen like Maas Jason think us . . . only . . . nineteen lashes, Hector!" He shouted out the number and for a moment I thought he was going to bow to the driver or the crowd, so much like a carnival barker had he suddenly become.

Aware as I was of eyes coming at me like arrows from the crowd that Anthony's words had plucked me from, I was more conscious of his eyes: glittering with anger and with a little mania.

Hector fell to his task like a bloodhound unleashed. I knew not where to look but it didn't matter: wherever I might have looked, even up into the sky, I would, between memory and sound, have seen everything. Unable to make myself blind, to not see the flashing snake, or deaf, to not hear its whistling at and cutting of the woman's flesh where it landed, like the pop of a roasted chestnut, I felt my skin creep as if a thousand jiggers were burrowing into it. I was sick and felt to vomit. God Himself withdrew His sunlight in an abrupt closure of clouds that rendered the air fraught with darkness and the prospect of pestilential rain that can descend on these parts in a moment.

The Negroes, however, especially the women, grunting with each bite of the whip and stamping their feet in contra-rhythm, bore up Zubia with rhythmic, obvious defiance of the rampaging driver and of Anthony himself. She hugged the tree indeed—but in her own way. On the pivot of her tied hands she twisted this way and that, in an evasive dance of her own to Hector's lashings, so as to soften—if such a notion can be credited—the vicious effect of his blows. The measure of her success was the driver's gradual uncoordination, as he attempted to counter Zubia's wriggling and catch her at the moment of greatest exposure. A few children giggled at his discombobulation, which drove him to greater ferocity. But, of course, the impact of his rage was regrettably stark and streaming redly from the stripes across her back. At the fifteenth or sixteenth lash Zubia, finally, screamed. She screamed as though her voice was being torn out of her body and thrown up into the dimmed sky, where it disappeared in a trail of silence that silenced the onlookers too.

As if made fanatical by the woman's shriek, the driver's lips drew back, his teeth bared like a rabid beast's. He stepped back to give himself space.

"Hector!" Anthony shouted. His own whip was raised on high

as if threatening the driver, his face twisted. The whole scene was a grotesque frieze.

"Maasa," Hector pleaded, whip-arm shaping the air.

"Enough," said Anthony and lowered his crop as if drawing down a curtain. He pointed to Zubia, who now sagged against the glistening tree like a sack of blood. "Take her to the sickhouse," he commanded.

As he turned without looking at me and walked toward the house, I vomited. Fortunately, I had felt the surge and in an instinctual reaction thrust myself free of the crowd surrounding. I made it over to a bed of impatiens—just in time. I decorated the colourful little blooms with the fried flour cakes and the strong coffee which Constancia had prepared and I had eaten not an hour before. I felt such shame, peppered as I was with giggles from unseen mockers dispersing to their daily tasks, that I did not dare look up. A silence swelled around me until it seemed absolute, everything reduced to my burning eyes and bitter mouth.

≈ 17 ≈

Adebeh: Wandering, Wednesday, November 2

I'M WANDERING IN THE WILDERNESS LIKE one of the Israelites, lost and fearful. The time for the *Eagle* to leave is coming closer and closer. I've made a decision that if I don't find any trace of Sister, then when the time come I would go back on board and face the music from Da and Mam when I get back to Boydville. I see the captain one time in my travels around the town. I look him straight in his eye and tell him I'm coming back with him. But in myself I know that if I find something to give me hope then I will disappear, and take my chances in this place. There's always another ship.

I go down to the wharf two times since I come, and they's always looking for hands. I could've get a berth going to Liverpool already. You have whitemen that leave ships just like I's planning to, with no plans like I have except thinking they's going to make a fortune here and go back where they come from, rich like a lord. I hear Fergus and the doctorman talking bout them, laughing quiet at the stupidness that greedy people will always believe. A few of them will make it, Doctor say, but only a few. Luck and connections, he say, that is what will make the difference. Rum and pussy will doom the rest, Fergus say.

I's thinking of late that rum and pussy might doom me too, and I's not even white. The one is too easy to find in this place, the other is scarce like good news.

Well, not that scarce. I see it. I just can't touch it. Juice, for one. Right here in the same yard, but is more than my little life is worth that I even look at her more than passing, cause her mother is watching me, the Murtella one, like a hawk. Somewhere else, I would visit her.

I visit the Elorine-one, though. Follow Fergus. Something to do while I's waiting and wandering. I go back there once already with Fergus. She was busy with a whitelady. (I get to find out she is a seamstress like Belle Compton in Boydville.) After the whitelady leave she come out looking for Fergus, cause she hear his voice, and then she see me, sitting quiet in the corner of her Da's workshop, talking with his apprentice. She smile when she see me. That was nice. Is like when that first warm breeze of the spring blow off St. George's Bay across the ice of the world just before winter really finish: it lift your spirit out of the grey.

I feel the breeze in my belly that was frozen over through the long waiting to touch the softness of a woman these many months since I leave Georgia Marcy in Halifax. The whore in Bristol—who was bones and grunting and necessity—don't count.

There wasn't hardly any time to talk then, cause Fergus was on another mission. He wasn't coming back this way and there was no reason for me to stay at her. But she tell me to make sure and come back before the ship sail. I catch a look from her father, and afterward on the way Fergus tell me to watch myself. He have a sound in his voice that I know from the ship: don't give me any trouble. I don't know what the two of them think I am up to, or want to do with their precious girlchild. But I know better than to say anything: they will look down my throat and think they know what I am thinking.

But I want to go back there and talk to her, that I know. About what, it doesn't hardly matter. It might even be that she knows something that can help me to get closer to finding Sister. I feel I can talk to her about that, now, and that if she knows anything she will tell me.

Betimes though, as Mam would say, it looks like I will have to wait a bit longer for a little ease in other matters.

⇒ 18 ⇐

Elorine: Jason Come Back, Thursday, November 3

JASON SPEND ALMOST THE WHOLE DAY here today. I didn't even know when he come. He was outside in the workshop a long time before he reach in to me. Pappi say he sit in the same corner he used to as a bwoy, just watching him and Cyrus. And is like Pappi go back into himself also, cause he say he don't ask Jason anything, they just smile at each other when their eyes meet.

He arrive in my doorway like a duppy. I was sewing by the window when the light around me change and I look up, frighten. For a second I think it was Squire, cause Jason was wearing the hat Squire used to wear. Not one like it, the same one—he say Lincoln give him to wear. Not that Squire would ever darken the inside of this house, much less my room. But I know how he stay from seeing him in the yard and workshop from I'm small. Jason grow like him in his body. He favour Squire in more than his body too. He was pale like a flour sack.

When he see me busy he step back and turn away. I call him back. I don't like anybody in my room, especially when I'm working, but Jason is not anybody. I'm barefoot and wearing old clothes, but even so. Is Jason.

"So soon again?" I say, bright like new money. "What bring you?"

He smile that smile that bounce between eyes and mouth and the wall, but he don't say anything for a time.

"I was passing," he say, but that wasn't what he mean either. His face was like he was playing Jonkanoo at Christmas, a mask. But he's looking also into himself, and what he see there don't seem to have any words to talk it out.

I find myself playing like Mama Selina used to. "You hungry? Is almost lunchtime." He shake his head, but whether is to tell me no or to clear cobwebs I couldn't say. So I get up and lead him out into the sitting area, where he take Pappi chair and I sit down in mine. And I call Jassy for some wash for both of us. After he tell her tenky with his little smile, I turn back to the dress in my lap. I don't pay any mind to anything else for a time cause Miss Francis is coming for it this evening. Something catch my eye-corner and I turn. Is the hat that fall from Jason head, which is back against the chair. He's sleeping. Poor thing.

And not a restful sleep neither. The banging from the workshop never trouble him, but his face was twitching the whole time with whatever was going on in his dream. I keep myself as quiet as mus-mus. He struggle up from his darkness like he's coming from under the sea and look around, eyes wide, until he see me. I make sure to smile, though he frighten me a little. I don't know this Jason.

"I should not have come." His voice is a old man.

Right away I vex. And he see it. He smile.

"Not here, Elzie," he say. Is the first time I hear that name for thirteen years. He wave his hand. So I quiet down. I know exactly what he mean, and I couldn't help but say, "So why you come back?"

I never ask him that the first time, though from first I hear he return I been thinking it. But is not my business, and him is a man now, to go and come as he please. When he turn back to me is like I'm looking through his eyes into a dark dusty room with some old mash-down furniture.

He shrug. "Well, I'm here."

"Ship come and ship go," I say. I feel myself bubbling-up, vex again. I bite my tongue. Even as a bwoy Jason had a way to wait for things to happen to him. You can't entirely blame him for this because of how he grow, and where. Any little status he have is Squire give him. Anthony make his life a misery when they was bwoy together. I don't know if things change now, but probably not. Anthony don't find himself here like his father used to sometimes; he send the slaves with the horse-dem. But he don't own any of his pickni the way Squire own Jason, and unless Anthony is a Sodomite—and I never hear that—one or two little Anthonys bound to be running up and down Greencastle or elsewhere.

While my mind is wandering here and there, Jason is staring at the floor like he lose something. Maybe he looking for the answer to what I say to him about ships. But I don't think so. I think he's looking for himself.

≈ 19 ≈

Jason: Droit du Seigneur, Thursday, November 3

IT IS THE PLACE HERE WHERE I feel most myself. The Livingstone yard at West Street has been, like the Evans's Long Barn when I was at school in Savernake, a refuge. And it is less the places—both very modest establishments—than the people. Even without Miss Selina, who passed shortly before I left for England, I have felt myself slipping back into the comfort of the regard of Mr. Livingstone and now Elorine, a woman of quiet intelligence who takes me as I am. And this morning, after the whipping yesterday, I needed to feel returned to a whole self. One who doesn't inhabit Greencastle.

I left the Livingstones refreshed and calm, having divided my time between Elorine and the workshop where I found myself in the corner I'd favoured as a youngster. I was hardly spoken to by either of them. Even a petulant outburst was returned to me by Elorine for further thought: I can go back to Carla with the next sailing of the *Eagle*. Perhaps I will.

Jack was waiting on the steps, springing to his feet as I rode into view and practically pulling me off the horse in his agitation.

"Where you was, Maasa? Everybody looking for you, send to town to find you."

Fresh from the democracy of West Street I answered him as I had the girl Miranda, that I was not Maasa. To which he responded as she did.

Inside, there was a lone setting on the table at the place that had become mine. Everything else, including the sideboard of food, had been cleared. But I'd shared some soup with Elorine and was not hungry, so made to go upstairs to my room.

I'd only gone a few steps when I was caught by a sound. A soft bark. I thought perhaps one of the dogs, always lying around on the floor, had been kicked. But it was a human voice, a man's. Anthony's—I recognized it immediately. The alcove that had been my childhood bedroom and was now his office was sequestered behind an elaborately carved mahogany screen that had once afforded Squire and Mathilde privacy when using their bedroom chimmeys. My elevated position afforded me sight over the top of the screen, sufficient to see Anthony, standing straight and close against a bare brown back that was lying across his desk and shuddering from his rhythmic piston thrusts.

I did not get any sense of intruding on a private act; rather, my vantage point merely afforded observation of a quotidian activity such as polishing the wooden floor, a daily task for a gang of house slaves. There was no intimacy surrounding the act, even within the ambit of the screen: the two actors were connected only at the hip, and that was soon ended in a quivering frenzy in Anthony that was almost comical. He backed out of the woman as I've seen dogs do, and—Maasa to the last—required her to wipe his equipment with her dress; indeed she did it automatically, and then continued on in the direction of the kitchen, perhaps her original destination.

Something about her was familiar but as I didn't yet know many of the slaves by name a further element of anonymity was added to the deed. Anthony himself pulled the chair that had been pushed aside for space and sat down at his desk; in a few moments his head was bent over papers.

I unstuck my feet with some difficulty and walked up the stairs, unaware of whether my presence was noted. I was scarcely aware of my own person. When Jack, on not finding me downstairs, arrived with a plate of food from Constancia, I couldn't even look at it. Rather than sending it back, however, I invited Jack to eat it himself. He protested, but only briefly, and then fell to with his fingers, laying the cutlery he'd brought on the floor beside him. The sounds coming from behind me—as I looked out through the window over the yard and fields—were not dissimilar to those I'd just heard downstairs.

⇒ 20 ⇐

Jason: The Will, Friday, November 4

SQUIRE'S WILL WAS READ TODAY AND I am returned to the windstorm of feelings that was my childhood. My life has been recaptured, so to speak, through stealth and duplicity and is no longer my own. But mixed in with the deep personal anger of betrayal, directed at others, is a self-directed fury at my own gullibility. It's an old feeling that I'd gradually lost in England. Now it's returned, and I am once more immersed in the maelstrom of animus that so fed my growing. The worst part, now as then, is to have to play the civilized naïf!

I'd assumed the will done and executed before my arrival, so hadn't even asked on the matter. Besides, Squire's last letter to me, almost two years ago—the last one to which he'd affixed his own scrawl to Lincoln's pen—is beside me. *You are my firstborn, and although others have followed you, not all of whom you know, or perhaps I, there is something always exclusive between a man and his first whelp.* This was Squire's word for children, slave or free, others or his own; with regard to the latter, it was generally said with affection. *It pains me, therefore, to send the news which this letter brings to you, no less so because you will already have figured it.*

The news was that there would be no provision for me in his will, which Squire thought it best to make now, while generally sound of mind, as Lincoln wrote for him. At the time, I wrote tenderly in reply to reassure that he had provided for me perhaps most generously of all his whelps by affording the opportunity to be educated in a good school and acquire a profession through which, in some small way, I was making recompense to him by being his agent in England.

In truth I was relieved at the news, since I did not relish the prospect of Squire providing for me out of the fragile patrimony that was, by right of law and custom, Anthony's, and would thereby provide yet another element of my brother's umbrage.

I had given no further thought to the question of an inheritance, considering that I already possessed an abundance. Besides, I had no idea of returning to Greencastle, or indeed to Jamaica. And my main concern, following Zubia's punishment and up to the moment this morning that Anthony spoke to me, has been to remove myself as soon and as far as possible from Greencastle, perhaps even to London on the *Eagle*, as Elorine had hinted. Yesterday, indeed, I went back into Bellefields to the wharves: it sails in ten days. All my consideration has been of a stratagem to fill the time without drawing undue attention.

My acceptance of Anthony's almost nonchalant invitation was from a sense of the politics of my situation. To have declined would have created interest as to the reasons and I did not want to share with Anthony any aspect of the correspondence between Squire and myself.

We made a little caravan into Bellefields, Anthony driving Mathilde in the landau, Anna and I following on horses, Jack and another slave sharing a mule behind us.

After expressing his condolences to me, Alberga asked us all to sit down. Expecting no real part in the morning's affair, I settled at the end of a semicircle and relaxed. In the old lawyer's voice, as he read the will, I heard Squire's as an echo, as though he was there among us. It's a very short will and there were no apparent surprises to the other Pollards present.

Everything, by and large, is left to Anthony—*with regret that I could not leave him a sturdier inheritance but with confidence that he will succeed where I have largely failed.*

Lincoln is to be freed. *He saved my life, and, perhaps to his surprise, I am returning him what remains of his.* A one-time sum of one hundred pounds is to be settled on Lincoln to provide him wherewithal. Everyone but myself knew about the manumission but the money was a surprise: Anthony grunted as if poked. It is indeed a princely sum to devolve on a Negro, one that affords Lincoln a very strong start in his new estate. But no one, not even his owner pro tem, could challenge the merit of the bequest.

There's an annuity for Mathilde—*my invaluable & understanding companion & helpmeet,* and a smaller one for Anna—*in hope that it will afford her, with her native skills & spirit, a measure of timely independence.* Lawyer Alberga paused then, and at the time I supposed us all to be considering the implications of her father's vain hopes for Anna, whose meagre endowment would be subsumed into those of a husband and placed under his sole control—such are the laws and custom. Anna's smile conveyed an added sense of irony, she having been for some time now involved in the keeping of Greencastle's books and thereby knowing the exact value of her legacy.

But then the old lawyer sought my eyes.

"There is one last thing," he said gravely and looked down at the paper. *To Jason, a fine son, if he returns to these shores, a gesture of thanks & of assistance to establish himself appropriately, namely, a bequest of One Hundred Guineas & two slaves, the personages of which are to be decided with the approval of my other son and heir. And without interfering unduly from the grave I would ask, should he return, that he assist his brother as* locum tenens *in illness and pestilence should such dire need arise.*

A dark cloud of redness enveloped me. The word *slaves* pounded my head like a hammer, drowning out whatever else the old lawyer said. My mind refused to believe what my ears had heard: Jason Pollard, stalwart of the anti-slavery movement, charged, albeit unofficially, with furthering its aims as best he could in His Majesty's prime slave-holding colony; Jason Pollard, the son of a slave—a slave owner!

Some aspect of my frenzied thoughts must have communicated itself to the others, because when my eyes sought theirs, each in turn was looking elsewhere. Even Anna would not meet my eye. That was the moment that I began to suspect the workings of a conspiracy seeking to draw me deeper into the cesspool in which they all lived. Hindsight only confirms the validity of those suspicions.

When Alberga indicated closure, all the others rose. I continued to sit like a church statue, staring out the window behind Alberga's chair. In his yard two little boys were chasing a frantic chicken, their cries and the fowl's threading through the open window. I was in sympathy with the chicken. Mathilde called out to me that they were going over to a Miss Grenville's establishment across the road to have some food—did I wish to join them? Alberga was also invited, but declined graciously. At that moment I wished to be anywhere else but in the company of this family.

But my lawyer's experience has instilled in me a healthy caution on the hidden motives of man: I could only see to my own interests if present. I sensed an urgency about Anthony that was nothing to do with food, about which he has been indifferent from childhood.

Mrs. Grenville, a light-skinned Negress of mature years, had eyes of a grey-green that sparkled with the liveliness of her personality, one that bespoke good humour and cordiality, essential attributes for an innkeeper, as well as energy and forthrightness. She was not, I learned later, a native of these parts, but from Kingston; strange in itself, because people in her profession tended, I would have thought, to move to the larger towns for their greater custom. By all appearances, however, her move had been a smart one: her eating space was crowded, and by prosperous-looking customers. But there was an anomaly: the patrons seemed overdressed for their surroundings, which were, to be kind, plain. I could hardly credit the claim, which I heard from Mathilde before tasting a morsel of it, that the best food in Bellefields was served here.

The place was really an enlarged fisherman's shack, twenty yards back from the shoreline. A strong wind would probably be sufficient to demolish it, but at the moment a gentle breeze cooled the space. The flooring had gaps that allowed you easy recognition of the sand beneath; the tables and chairs were obvious castoffs and did not always match. But it was spotlessly clean, with brightly checkered oilcloths and a pot of fresh flowers on each table. The food, served on wooden platters, was excellent, and the atmosphere of ramshackle grace enhanced the spirits of the diner.

In any case, the lady's premier establishment—this eating place being referred to as Molly's Shack—was to be found across the road and a few doors from Alberga's. The Grenville Arms, which lodged travellers, was a sturdy upstairs building of cut stone, with, I am told, mahogany furniture throughout and in its dining room, everything of crystal and china and silver.

This, again, is reconstruction and comment after the event. Anthony was already at the table when I reached it, the oilcloth packet of letters that Alberga had given him opened and its contents spread about. He was scrutinizing the envelopes, one after the other; my arrival was unnoticed by him. Anna, however, greeted me with serious eyes. She knew of things that I did not and was anxious. I handled the chair roughly in my sitting down, thereby securing Anthony's attention. Without pause I told him of my determination: I did not wish to become a slaveholder and therefore would respectfully decline Squire's bequest. In response he swept the letters on the table together and placed them on the open oilcloth, tidying them as he absorbed my declaration. Finally, he looked up at me.

"It is too late, brother, for your outraged sensitivity to have any effect. I have already set in motion the transfer of property and it has gone beyond the point where even Lawyer Alberga can rescind it. The guineas have been placed in Alberga's keeping. Is that not so, Anna?" He turned to his sister, who had kept her eyes on me; she nodded to his question. "As a legal person," he continued, "and no doubt a good one, you can no doubt undo what I have done, in due course. But for the moment I, at least, have been a dutiful son."

His tone and manner were disparaging; he was wrapped tight and concentrated, waiting for me as if in physical ambush. I brushed his disdain aside with mine. He scoffed, asserting that I had had no objection to profiting from the fruits of his iniquity.

"It was Squire's choice," I responded. "I did not ask to be favoured."

He pounced on the word. "Favoured you were," he growled at me, like a terrier finally getting at a desired object. "Richly favoured, I would say!"

I did not flinch, but breathed deeply before speaking.

"Richly," I agreed, modulating my voice. "And I have tried to make recompense," I pointed out, through being of service to our father and to him, Anthony, in London. I rested matters there and waited for Anthony to calm himself also. Even without looking around, I sensed that we were being attended to from adjoining tables, all of whose occupants would know Anthony and would quickly determine my identity. I longed for the anonymity of London.

By visible effort Anthony dampened his own fire. "There is further service you can render," he said soberly. "To all of us," he corrected himself, including with a glance Anna and Mathilde, who had quietly joined us from a chat with Mrs. Grenville. I waited, anxious within but holding fast to a façade of calm.

"You recall the provision for yourself as *locum tenens* at Greencastle." I nodded, observing dryly that he seemed in the best of health. He agreed that his health was good and then paused. It was in that interval that I experienced what common wisdom has as the final moments of a life about to end on the scaffold, but with a reversal: instead of seeing my whole past life flash before my eyes, I saw my future. And just then death would indeed have been welcomed. Without even glancing down I became aware of the oilskin packet the old lawyer had handed to Anthony and knew its purpose. That insight shattered my patina, and Anthony, vigilant eyes unwavering on my face, noticed.

"Yes," he said quietly.

That was all he said for a while. For one thing, one of Mrs. Grenville's pretty young serving girls brought our first course, a bowl of green soup—pepperpot, Anna reminded me, trying to lighten the mood. But they were all waiting for me to speak.

I did not bother with the pretense of ignorance. "Where are you going?" I asked him. "England?" I now looked at the reassembled pile of documents, tidied and tied once more to make space for the food.

He paused, as much for effect as to take a large swallow of his soup. He patted his lips delicately, as if having tea with a duchess, before replacing his spoon.

"England don't have nothing for me," he said. His descent into the common parlance was abrupt and unexpected. It was how he spoke to the slaves. "England see us as cane trash. All the juice squeeze out already and what leave is only good for burning. They will burn us one day, sooner or later. If the slaves don't burn us up first." With that he resumed eating his soup.

I declined the invitation of his silence to engage him on these matters and pressed him as to his destination, intrigued despite my anger.

"Virginia," he answered simply.

Anthony, who had never been to England, knew Virginia: he'd been to school there. While I was in England he'd gone to Hillyard, an establishment known even in England. The story came out piecemeal, around mouthfuls of Mrs. Grenville's repast. As it unfolded I realized that I knew next to nothing about my half-brother's life, or of the life of Greencastle and its white inhabitants; I knew more, in a sense, about the lives of the slaves.

At Hillyard he'd become fast friends with one Edward Townsend, whose father was a well-connected figure in Washington with links to politics and the army. The friendship had been nurtured, after Hillyard, by visits to and fro, and by business; this traffic I had been occasionally made aware of in Squire's letters.

Between the mouthfuls of food and history, I was also learning that Greencastle, as an economic concern, was kept afloat—waterlogged, but not yet sinking, in Anthony's turn of phrase—not by sugar or rum but by coffee and logwood, both grown in the hills behind the canefields. I realized that I had no real grasp of the layout of the estate as it stands today; indeed, my memories from earlier years were so formless as to be completely unreliable.

There was another world in the high hills behind the canefields: a coffee plantation and a grove of mahogany and other trees that was being cut one tree at a time and shipped, piece by piece, to Norfolk for the making of fine furniture for the houses of wealthy officials and socialites there, whom Townsend connected with. It had become very profitable business. Listening, I formed the sense of another Greencastle, a remote place of abundance away from the house that had always been the centre of my world.

"So why are you going to Virginia?" I asked pointedly. "Could this not be done by letter?"

Again a fussy wiping of his lips and a swallowing of food before he spoke. "Fresh money," he said with a swift smile. He had dropped his voice and brushed his fingers across his mouth to indicate that I should speak softly also.

What was there to be said? Greencastle was now his property, to do with entirely as he wished; my concern was far more limited and immediate, which he had not addressed. It seemed to me that the American colonists had ample opportunities to invest their capital at home, in the vast and expanding enterprise their country was becoming, rather than risk it in a venture under a British dominion that they had gone to such bloody effort to separate themselves from. I asked him for an assessment of his chances of finding new capital. Besides, what had he to offer as surety?

"Coffee," Anthony said confidently. "The Americans can't get enough of it. They buy everything we can send them, other growers too." His friend Townsend had lined up potential investors for Anthony to meet with. "They need to meet the man," he said with a smarmy smile. I could imagine Anthony at his charming best, brilliantined and coiffed, fluffing his words to a shine with the English accent he could summon in a blink, to smoothly reach into beguiled colonial pockets.

"So Greencastle is to be a coffee plantation?" I asked. As our conversation had progressed, the silence of the women confirmed to me that nothing new was being said.

"It would mek us more money," said Anna the bookkeeper. "And it need less niggers." I saw Anna anew, today: no longer the wild child or frivolous girl, but a young woman with the crusty earthiness of her blood—Squire and Mathilde well combined.

Anthony seemed to consider that a sufficient answer, for he busied himself anew with his food. But I wondered also if there were other reasons for this trip, for which long preparation had obviously been made. I thought, first off, of a wife. It was a time-worn practice for young scions here to make alliances with families abroad—to deepen the blood pool, so to speak; also to deepen the resources available to the family. Such could be Anthony's mission. But I doubted that event would be kept secret—or could be with Anna in the middle of it! She took as lively an interest in her brother's recreational activities as she did in expenditures at Greencastle. I could not bring myself to report my own witness to Anna.

Another idea formed. This one was more substantial and, potentially at least, portentous. The measures forced by the abolitionists upon the parliament at Westminster to ameliorate the most brutal violations of the slaves' humanity had been resisted from the first by the Assembly in Jamaica. It had come to the point, and this was well-known in England, where there was talk of throwing off the suffocating mantle of the King for the lighter and more congenial protection of the United States; but not so much the government of these states—a fractious and fragile construct still in the process of being determined—but of those states which were formed and sustained by slavery. States like Virginia! Was even a part of Anthony's efforts to be directed to the end of securing a place for the family of which he had recently become the head?

There were questions in the air, as many as the flies that buzzed around us as we ate. But for me, at that moment, only one question mattered. No one dared utter it and I gave no outward indication of even thinking it. But it was like a wind blowing around our table.

I made my decision quickly, asked their pardon and pushed my chair back. As evenly as I could I said that there was much I needed to think about, and stood up. Anna made to rise also, but Mathilde pressed her back down. I turned away, and then, remembering my manners, turned back to proffer my thanks for the meal. It gave me no satisfaction to see on their faces, as they finally looked up at me, something akin to trepidation.

"I will meet you back at Greencastle," I said, more gently, and walked away from the table. I had sufficient presence of mind to seek out the patrone on the way out, and thank her for an enjoyable meal.

≈ 21 ≈

Elorine: Jason's Problem, Friday, December 4

JASON IS FALLING BACK INTO A old habit now. Whenever life don't suit him he find himself here. And it certainly don't suit him now. After not seeing him all these years I'm very glad to see him—but still and all . . .

And he smell of rum too. On a Friday, barely past lunchtime. I look at his face. It red.

Either from the sun or the rum inside. Is him I looking at when I call out, "Jassy?"

She answer me from the kitchen behind him. "Yes, Miss Ellie?"

"You give Missa Pollard rum to drink?"

"No, Miss Ellie! Wash."

Jason lift the mug he's holding and show me some teeth.

"You drunk?"

"Not yet," Jason say, and flash some more teeth. From he was small he could be a sweet-bwoy when he put his mind to it, but he pick the wrong person at the wrong time. A drinking man don't get no sympathy from me, especially a young one.

"I hope you don't come here to get drunk," I say, my voice cold as river water. "Is the middle of the afternoon."

He stiffen. "I haven't come here to get drunk, Elzie. I wouldn't do that. If I wanted to get drunk the saloon where I was has more rum than I can buy." He still sounding very formal, English, even though the words round-off a bit from the rum. "I came here to talk to you," he say, softness creeping into his voice.

"You need rum to talk to me?"

"Maybe," he say, serious now.

"I listening," I say. My voice is still flat.

From small Jason is a serious one, and I couldn't hardly blame him for that. His mix-up blood run through his life like dirty water. High colour can have benefits, but it can hold you down too. In this place it may be better than black, but even then, not all the time. So when his father send him to England, I was glad for him. I figure that his high colour would give him a chance to just disappear into England so he could find out how to be his own self.

Truth to tell, I never expect to see Jason again. Anthony come back from Virginia, and plenty others who get send over the sea for a education, like the Magnus-one. Still, Anthony don't have nowhere else where life can take him as high as in Jamaica, moreso now since Squire dead. But Jason—what he's coming back for? I glad to see him, I have to say that. And he seem glad to see me, which please me.

He chewing his tongue, just like when he was a little boy and he anxious about something. Finally the words he bring here to tell me come out. "I have become a slave owner," he say, his voice tight. In my ears is like the words is completely new to me. His eyes flick at mine and then fall on the floor between us. I find myself drawing my dusty feet as far under the chair as they go, even though he probably not even noticing them. I wait for him to say something more, but he sit absolutely still, as though he's alone in the room.

From somewhere inside me a giggle bubble up. Before it can break out I say, "You buy somebody?" The whole idea, when I put the words together again, sound like a joke.

He shake his head. "Squire." Is like he clear his throat with the word. "In his will." I wait, and he start to talk.

He talk slow, as if he not sure he himself understand what he's saying, so it take him a while, but I don't rush him. He never expect his father to leave him anything when he dead, and instead he end up with two slaves. He don't know which slaves yet, Anthony will decide. But it don't matter who they be. He sound like he's getting angry, and I notice that the Englishman begin to sound a little like the rest of us now. "I don't want any slaves," he say, looking at me as though I am the one pushing them on him.

"You can don't take them," I say to him.

He snort. "It's worse than that."

And as he's telling me what Anthony want him to do, I'm seeing Anthony's face like it is right behind Jason shoulder looking over at me and laughing at the both of us. Jason and he have almost the same eyes from Backra Squire, puss-eye. Except that in Anthony the eyes is hard as glass even if he's laughing. Just like Jason eyes is always dancing to find light somewhere. Anthony looking into darkness, Jason looking out of it. Because Anthony, he is white, so he is on top of everything in this world. Jason, he is more fortunate than most, yes, especially the seeds plenty Backra leave in black woman belly and allow to grow like weeds. As I'm listening to Jason it's like Squire, while he leave two slaves to Jason, really leave Jason to his brother.

"And you see, Elzie," Jason finish, "what makes me so angry is that I have no one to blame but myself." He look at me with a sad little smile. "He sent me this letter, the first one I had received from him in years, many years."

I ask him, "The letter tell you to come home?"

He bristle. "Anthony knows that he cannot tell me to do anything, those days are over." He pause and give another little smile, looking into himself this time. "But perhaps not."

"Duppy know who to frighten," I say quick.

He smile, looking sad. "Anthony doesn't frighten me."

"Maybe is Maasa Squire then."

"Maybe," he say.

"You could go back to England. The ship that bring you is still there in the harbour. Or another will soon come."

He smile. "I sat in a saloon near the wharf this afternoon for an hour or more before I came here, watching the harbour. Thinking about just what you say."

"It would fix Anthony business." I hear the venom in my own voice, but it's too late to call it back.

"It would fix everybody's business." His voice is quiet as mine, but bitter.

"Well then. And too besides, you don't know the first thing about estate and how it is to manage."

He laugh out loud at that. "You are absolutely right there," he say, and sound like Backra Englishman again.

"The estate will run you."

"Right again," he say, and then his face freeze-up.

"And if the ship sink, or Anthony dead or something, what happen then?"

"Anna," he say. "If Anthony has no children, it is to go to Anna." He sounding like a real lawyerman now.

"I sure Anthony have children," I say, "but he cyaant leave it to none of them."

"Yes, I notice at least one little boy playing out in the yard that could be his."

That is himself Jason could be talking about also, when Squire was Backra Maasa.

"If he had asked," Jason say, looking past me out the window. He's talking with himself again, I just have to listen. "Just *asked* me what he wanted me to do."

"You would do it?"

"No," he say, "that matter settle long time. But I wouldn't have left everything in England and come back." He is confuse in himself, I can see. He don't tell me what the letter from Anthony say, and I don't want to know. But is clear he feel the letter trick him. And maybe cause him to trick himself into thinking that is a visit he is coming for.

From I know him Jason trust people too much. Me? I don't trust a soul further than I can see them. Maybe Jason mix-up with decent people since he is in England, and forget about the old tief they have here. Including in his own family. St. Paul can say to put away childish things when you become a man, but is not easy. When I'm by myself and my spirit is dark, I still suck my thumb. Anthony, he still playing tricks on his brother. Except now is big-man tricks.

I remind Jason that he don't owe Anthony anything. "I owe Squire," he say, serious. "And Anthony knows how I feel about Squire. He knows I have a hard time saying no to what he proposes."

"You make it sound like he more than propose it," I say, and he shrug.

Just then Pappi come in through the door. I never even hear his heavy boots. Jason stand up. Pappi see right away that something is wrong.

"Howdy again, young man," he say. "You dress up like you coming from church." I know he is joking but Jason look confused.

"No, sir," he stammer out, "I just come to talk to Elorine." Pappi know he hardly ever call me that, so figure it must be something serious we talking about. He turn to go back out but Jason stop him. "I would like to talk to you too, sir," he say, "if you have the time to spare."

"It sound like something serious," Pappi say, "so I will make time."

I make to get up out of his chair but he wave me back down and lift a chair from around the dining table to sit down opposite the two of us.

Jason tell him. He know not to waste time with Pappi, so he don't take long. Funny thing is, he tell about managing the estate for Anthony, but he don't breathe a word about the two slaves that his father say he is to get. When he finish he don't exactly ask Pappi what he think he should do, but the question is plain in the telling, and hang in the air. While he talking, Pappi is looking at the floor, elbow on his knee, chin in his hand. That is how he is when the Mount Zion brethren come to talk over things with him, or when he's leading the worship and considering what to say to God and the rest of us. He can be so still you think he's sleeping.

But this time instead of answering Jason's unasked question he half turn toward the door in the kitchen and call Jassy.

"Yes, Maas Livvy?"

"Me throat dry, you have any wash?"

"Yes, Maas Livvy, just make some."

"Bring some for me, please. And for these young people here." He don't even ask if we thirsty, but that is Pappi sometimes.

"Yes, Maas Livvy."

He turn back to Jason then, and surprise both of us with a smile. "Two days ago when you was here and I ask you what you intend to do, you say you don't know." He's teasing Jason, but not unkindly. "You seem to know now."

"No, sir," Jason say, quick before that thought can settle into Pappi head. "Not at all." Pappi turn serious then, and look at Jason, who don't move his eye from him. "I have not given Anthony an answer."

"But he make his arrangements already." Jason nod. "Is either he don't care what happen to his property or he sure you will say yes." Pappi speak matter-of-fact, like he's adding up sums. "Pardon for asking, but Maas Squire leave anything for you?"

"A little money," Jason say, his gaze breaking but not looking at me neither. "He and I had agreed for some time that he'd done more than enough for me already. I was his agent in London."

"I hear that," Pappi say. "I hear that is not plenty much here to leave either. Except for the Anthony one."

Jason shrug. I can see he's glad Pappi is talking us away from the matter of the slaves.

Then Pappi turn to me and ask what I think Jason should do. By now I calm down somewhat, but what I think don't change. I tell him I think Jason should tell Anthony to look after his property and leave Jason to look after his own business. I almost say look after his own property but then remember that the only property Jason have, apart from whatever things he bring back with him, is the two slaves that Squire gift him with.

"You think," Pappi ask Jason, "that Maas Squire know about what Anthony was planning before he dead?"

Before he cyan answer, Jassy come inside with a tray balance on her belly that have three mugs, and she hand them around, collect the ones Jason and me was using, and disappear back, tenkys following her into the kitchen.

"This was a new will," Jason say. "The date was almost the same as the letter that Anthony sent telling me how poorly Squire was. But everyone has said he was quite alert and aware until the day before he died."

"I hear that too," Pappi say. "We know he was poorly, but it was still a shock." He and me wait before we say anything else.

"You know anything about estate business?" Pappi ask eventually, and Jason shake his head.

"All the same, all kind of people running estate now. All you have to know is how to lash people like you lash cow or mule to drive them." Pappi voice turn hard then, the words like they have a smell. "And you have Nayga on the estate will do that for you."

Jason pull back into his chair like Pappi lash him! "I can't do that," he say, his voice small, eyes staring straight ahead. "I *won't* do that."

Pappi let that settle in a while. We two talk about this more than once, whether there is any other way to get Nayga to do estate work. Pappi was a slave and he know the whip. What burn him more than the whip self is that is another black man who lash him with it. As he say more than once, "Only Backra give thanks for sugar cane. No Nayga ever get up in the morning and sing a hymn to sugar cane except to sweeten him cocoa tea."

But Jason is new. When he leave here for England, nobody except crazy people was talking about freedom, or wages for slaves, or anything of that sort. Things change now. Some slaves believe that freedom will soon come, and that Backra must start to pay them to cut cane and to cook him food and look after him pickni. It don't have no other way to get all that work done, we agree, cause nobody is going to do it willingly. Either pay them or lash them.

Jason is holding the mug of wash on his leg and looking out the window at the sour orange tree in the yard. Pappi giving him time to think. Then Pappi get to his feet, and the little chair creak with relief. The quiet in the room make him look even bigger than he is.

"You is a man now, Jason," he say. "You name Pollard, same as Anthony, but you is not him. You is Jason Pollard. You have to decide, and nobody can tell you what to decide."

"I know, Missa Ishmael," Jason look up and say, his voice like he is apologizing.

"The Good Book say to honour you father and you mother," Pappi go on. "I don't know if you is a man who consult you Lord and Maker, even sometimes." Jason go to answer but Pappi pay him no mind. "But Moses say, you father *and* you mother."

Little later, watching Jason riding off, I could only see young Jaze, heading back to Greencastle to face his comeuppance. Is like nothing change. Only everything is bigger now, and dead serious.

⇒ 22 ⇐

Jason: New Maasa, Saturday, November 5

THIS MORNING I KNEW SOMEWHAT of how Jacob felt after wrestling all night with the man who turned out to be, according to Genesis, an angel. There are differences between us, of course. My thigh is not shrunken as a result. On the other hand, I have not been blessed by my angel—if angel it was. The forces were often malevolent and could as readily be called Lucifer, that most radiant of angels. Jacob and I are alike in one respect, however, albeit a small one: our names have been changed. He was renamed Israel and promised power with God and over men and a nation of descendants; his name is still remembered, and blessed. I, on the other hand, will shortly be known as Maasa, and within this small world that I will be ruling over, cursed. I will have power over men and women and many things that crawl on the earth. When I say come, they will come and when I say go, they will go; I hope so, at least. That power—despite the assertions of many planters and their toadies here and in England—will not have been given me by God but by law and barbaric custom.

The angel I wrestled with had a host of arms and faces and harangued me in a discordant chorus of voices. One belonged to the Reverend Swithenbank—a man who could be as pompous as his name is long, but is rigorous, especially on the subject of slavery. A stalwart of the Abolition movement, I have spent many hours in his chapel, more of them at meetings than at services, to be sure, but as many in his study also, reading the newspapers from Jamaica and some of the missionary reports from the field to the headquarters in London.

My thinking was also attended throughout by the watchful eyes of my Carla, occasionally frowning as I veered toward a sympathetic consideration of Anthony's predicament.

With dawn came exhaustion and a decision. I was far from happy with it, but would not have been any happier with its opposite. The course was chosen because the other course would have incurred anger, further disruption to a greater number of lives and once I were returned to England, a divorce from the Pollard family whose name I bear and of which I am a part.

Beyond that, however—and beyond the anger that ignites still at the memory of his bequest to me, and his probable connivance at Anthony's cunning—I felt a sense of obligation to Squire. He, more importantly than giving me life, likely a casual act with unconsidered consequences, gave me freedom. Verily, it was that freedom which brought me to this fulcrum of dreadful choices on which the long night teetered. Indeed it has brought me little joy. But the alternative fate has always been, for a certain, manifestly worse.

I made sure to be waiting for Anthony at the bottom of the stairs when he came from his room to begin his day, and invited him to step outside with me. He led me through the kitchen to retrieve his mug of strong coffee. Constancia herself handed me a mug, practically a jug, of orange juice, my own preference for early beverage, as she remembers.

I led him over to Squire's grave. We sat within his mother's gazebo, which added its own sense of irony. I allowed a silence to establish itself, daring Anthony to break it. He tried once to hold my eyes but failed. He was very anxious about what I was likely to say, and far more nervous than I.

I started speaking, his nervousness calming me. I did not allow him to interrupt. I first told him my decision, at which there was an audible sigh of relief, and then my reasons: I felt obliged to honour our father and to assist as I could in at least preserving the family's property. I emphasized to him that I did not, by my reasoning or resultant actions, lay claim to any part of either. I took the opportunity to chide him for his artfully guileless letter, by which, I said, I felt somewhat manipulated.

"I did not seek to deceive you," he protested. "I had thought to go north for money, that had been an idea for several months before the letter. Squire was sickly but his mind was still clear, and we had an overseer then. A drinking man, and not very useful, but here, so able to lend a hand." He smiled in sour recollection of the man. "I discussed my idea with Squire and Mathilde. It was they who felt that you would be the best person to leave Greencastle in the hands of."

"And you did not," I challenged him, affronted despite my earlier disclaimers.

"I did not think you would be interested," he shot back. This time he did hold my eyes. "I sent the letter while still undecided about the whole venture," he concluded.

I wanted to believe Anthony but my experience, as sibling and as lawyer, bade caution.

Furthermore, such concerns were beside the point at this stage: I had made my decision.

"Would you have come?" he asked me.

"Probably not," I replied promptly.

"Not even with the chance to see your father before he died?"

"I had already reconciled myself to not seeing him again," I replied and gave an involuntary glance at the nearby mound which seemed more covered with grass and weeds than just a few days before. "And I did not come in time anyway," I reminded.

"Not to see him," Anthony said, "but to save me." Our eyes, serious, flickering with uncertainty, held each other's for a moment, dancing like awkward partners.

I told him that I would act as his attorney for six months from the day the documents of attorneyship are signed.

"I expect to be back before then," implying that in six months his inheritance would be ruined by me. His tone was provocative, the Anthony I was becoming re-acquainted with. "Unless the ship sinks," he continued, "or I die of some disease contracted in one of their foul cities. Or I elope with a rich American heiress." He gave a lopsided grin at this, and I could not help but join him.

"Then I shall put Greencastle and everything else up for auction," I said soberly, erasing his smile. "Mathilde and Anna can pay off your creditors as best they are able. I shall be done with it." My firmness gave him more than pause; he also looked at Squire's mound, as if for inspiration.

"I will return," he said firmly, leaning forward. "This is mine. And nowhere else."

I did not think his statement required a response, so gave none. I swallowed the last of the orange wash and made to rise.

"What will be your fee?" he asked suddenly, and the question startled me. I had not thought of money even once, and told him so. I still have no sense of what it costs to live at a decent level in this society, and such funds as returned with me from England are still largely intact. Besides, there is the bequest of Squire; that I will accept. I asked Anthony to propose a sum.

"Two hundred guineas," he said straightaway. "The money is already in Alberga's safe," he hurried on when I hesitated, and I could not help but smile, as he did. It seemed a fair amount, given that I was not doing this for the money. So we shook hands on it.

Mathilde was on the piazza, in one of the peculiar semi-reclining chairs she had brought with her from Suriname that had spawned several copies around the house. She watched us keenly as we came up the stairs, stirring her morning cup of chocolate with a cinnamon stick.

Rising as if pulled by an unseen string as we reached the top, her face pinched and expectant, she looked from one face to the other and back. She must have found what she sought, for she was transformed into a radiance of teeth and sparkling eyes. She came toward us and enveloped me in the warm morning frowsiness that I remembered from her occasional childhood intimacies.

"Goot," she said loudly. And then, in a whisper into my ear: "Tank you, Jason."

Mathilde's voice crystallized in my mind the thoughts that had swirled around in my head all night and even after I had decided my mind about the family's request: that I was doing the wrong thing for the right reasons.

☙ 23 ☙

Elorine: Prayers, Sunday, November 6

I GET UP EARLY THIS MORNING to pray for Jason. And I pray for him again in chapel. That he do the right thing. Only Maasa God can tell him what that is. And to hear Maasa God you have to listen. Jehovah don't just throw out words, like those man-dem at the rumshop babble-babbling to hear their own voice. To hear Him you have to listen with your heart, and be ready to receive His Word.

Cause is no right thing to decide when it have anything to do about slavery. Except to destroy it. Is an evil canker in the soul of all of us. All. Slave and free, black and white and in between, like Jason. But even when that day come and the Jericho walls come tumbling down, when Maasa God wipe that abomination of desolation from the face of the earth, slavery business will still be there inside us, like yaws, like junju in a dark corner of our soul, all of us that ever have anything to do with it. All.

⇒ 24 ⇐

Adebeh: Yenkunkun, Sunday, November 6

MAYBE DA IS RIGHT AND THE bigi pripri find me. I don't know. I was in the market with Jujube when I hear a man and a woman talking. I wasn't listening to the words, was the voices that catch me. They's familiar, like I know them all my life. But when I look at the people speaking, a man and a woman, both much older than me, I never see them before. But something about them is familiar, some little thing in their voice.

I's trying to figure it out when I hear the man say, rough: "We have something for you here?" And I realize that I was looking at them, staring, which I know from Mam is rude. But I also realize that he ask me in English—Fergus kind of English anyway. And that what he was speaking before, when I overhear them, was not English of any kind save for a word here and there. It is then that my ears really open.

What I was hearing, the way they's talking and catching their breath with the words take me right back to when Da and Mam and the other stay-behind Maroons in Scotia get together to talk the old stories. Some of the stories come from Jamaica, but some bring through Jamaica from all the way in Africa, where the first Yenkunkun come from. They do this every few months, and it's a very important thing for the old ones. In between time, they live for those days and nights. Mam and Da insist we come with them, even Eddie and Precious, who is too little to understand much. The other Maroons bring their pickni too.

Those of us born in Scotia, we don't always see the use of it, to listen to the old people, some of them close to ancestors themself, just talking and talking, all the while drinking the Scotia screech that is not what they'd prefer, but it's rum, and it have to be rum for the proper observance. The food is worth going for, especially the pig.

I bring my mind back from all of that to see the two people in the market staring at me, waiting for me to say something. Remembering the sharp question from the man, I shake my head.

"No, sir," I say. "Nothing."

But I realize, like the sun rise in my mind, that he and the woman, who also is staring back at me, is Yenkunkun! Maroon. No one else look at you like that. Always watching for an ambush. I watch people like that myself.

Is the bigi pripri who bring me to them!

My head feel like when you push a stick into a ant nest. But I keep still, looking down at them on the ground as they's looking up at me, and trying the hardest to keep my face straight.

The man frowns. "Where you be coming from?" he ask me. He remind me of Maas Clarence back in Preston. The same way his forehead bulge over his eyes, the same way his nostrils flare out like a horse, the same piercing voice like it want to open up your head. I's trying to hide from this man, so I pull down the shades in my eyes.

"Nyuman, onti yu prandes?" Where are you from? His voice drops low, like a secret message.

"Scotia," I say in English, without thinking enough. And the game is lost! The man clap his hands together once like when you break stones, and cackle. He shoot a stream of Akan at the woman and she laugh like is the best joke in her life. I can only stand there like a fool-fool little bwoy. They's squatting on the ground below me, behind a pile of fruit and vegetables that surround a clay kettle covered with a white cloth.

I feel like a stupid little pickni. But I am glad too, eh. Is like just when you think you's going to stifle, then a door blow open, and a breeze come through to give you another breath. I squat down to them. What is under that cloth kiss my nose sweet-sweet.

"Scotia is far?" the man ask, but his eyes know the answer already. I nod, still smelling the pot between us.

"And you is Yenkunkun?"

I have in mind what the old ones in Scotia tell when they's in their screech, that the other Maroons didn't rise up against the soldiers when they march into Trelawny Town. I give them only half. "Me mother."

"What she name?"

I tell them the truth. Their eyes wander inside their heads and catch onto something.

They look at me suspicious. "What you doing here?"

"Waiting for the ship that bring me to ready again." I can be suspicious too. They might be Yenkunkun. But maybe is not the ancestors send them after all.

Jujube find me just in time, before the questions I see in the man's eyes can find the words to ask. I's so glad to see her I jump up without excusing myself in the proper way and walk off with her, holding onto her arm like she belong to me, even though I know she doesn't like that. I let go of her before she can say anything or pull herself away.

"You buy any pork?"

I ask her what pork. She says the Maroons I was talking to sell the best jerk pork in the market, so how I didn't buy any? I remember my nose, and beg her pardon.

Apparently the doctorman send to buy pork every market day, and anyway she herself is hungry now, so if I have any money. I give her some and she go back to the two Yenkunkun. But I stay there, looking at the baskets and cloths spread with different things, which remind me of the market in Halifax. I'm looking anywhere except where Jujube has gone. And I tell myself not to look at her when she's walking back to where I am, even though the first thing that catch my eye about Jujube is the way she walk, like she's just bouncing the air aside as she pass through it.

The pork is sweet for true, and remind me of the Treaty feasts in Scotia. Jujube stop again and buy a piece of yam right off the fire, and we's blowing and eating that and the pork as we walking home, laughing and sucking the sweetness down into our belly. I see her looking at me, and I feel my belly filling up with more than the food.

≈ 25 ≈

Jason: Into the Field, Thursday, November 10

THOSE FIRST YEARS IN ENGLAND I carried Greencastle—its very name—like a torch, or a muffler to keep my soul warm through each dark winter. The cold I tolerated and the snow was a delight when it was fresh. But the absence of colours, especially of green, squeezed my spirit.

But now that I am returned to it, I feel entombed in a green vault. Everything is green: the pale green of the bamboo down by the river, the dark green of the breadfruit trees, which were new and small when I left, and now form a grove running down the hillside, providing much-needed food for everyone on the estate and wood for furniture, such as the table at which I sit. And of course the green of the cane, a quilt of it, the paths between the fields like stitching. The very light seems green. It is so overwhelming.

The feeling of interment has no doubt been abetted by tiredness such as I have not felt for many a moon. When left alone I fall asleep wherever I've come to rest. When awake, I ache. But I do not complain, for it follows from the decision I alone made.

Looking back to Monday morning, Anthony, with cheerful busyness, hauled me out into my new domain bright and early. I had bound him to silence about his plans and my part in them until I judged it meet to reveal them. Undertakings from Anthony, so freely given, so unpredictably held, are fraught with the potential for disappointment, but I had no choice but to seek his complicity. I was and am still easing into this decisive turn that my life has taken; I wished, if you like, to be a spectator in it for a little longer.

We traversed the different fields, four of them, each of which has its name and is in the charge of a driver, whose names I am learning. One of them—pro tem, according to Anthony—is Pompey, the erstwhile guardian of my slave childhood. He's older, of course, with fewer teeth and whatever hair remains entirely grey. But there is still about him the menace of the ruthless man that so terrified my childhood. His greeting was circumspect—a doffing of the hat that is as much a driver's badge of office as his whip; a nod that could have been equally respect and dismissal. "Judith gone over long time, sah," he said. I told him I knew that from Pheba; his eyes gave no indication of mourning.

Anthony made clear to me that Hector, Zubia's tormentor, was head driver, over Pompey and the others. I wonder how that sits with Pompey, who was that once, and for a long time, up to when I left for England. He is older than Hector, and much more experienced in the ways of Greencastle. But it is a prize that the Maasa plays politics with, bestowing and withdrawing at will, and sometimes on a whim.

I have heard it argued that this enhances control by preventing the accumulation of favours and loyalties of the subordinate slaves to the driver, focusing both on the master, or the overseer, who is also the source of much largesse. It strikes me as a sure recipe for coalescing discontent among people who evince qualities of leadership and a kind of courage. They are invariably, and necessarily, physically powerful men of uncertain temperament. On the other hand, though Hector is half the age of Pompey, I would not lay odds against the old man in a fight.

Hector was waiting for us, in a crossroad where the corners of three fields meet. His eyes, as Anthony and I approached, were steady on mine and mine on his. I had not seen him since his whipping of Zubia and I did not want that traumatic episode, much less my pathetic response, to gain too much substance in his mind. At the same time I did not myself have any authority over him.

Hector's black eyes were pregnant with contempt for me. In answer I felt a surge of abhorrence and a wave of anticipation for the time soon to come when my authority over him could not be challenged.

It was a curiously exhilarating set of feelings that I did not, on examination afterwards, find exemplary in myself. It is a precursor of the interplay of power and submission that characterizes every relationship on an estate, awakening memories of my own feelings of helplessness: Pompey, Squire, even Anthony.

The head driver was all obsequy and teeth, bowing from the back of his mule. But our eyes took the true measure of each other and I sat still on my mount until making sure that he was first to look away. I found a crude resolve to my undertaking, a nascent steeliness that frightened me a little.

From the fields we went next to the boiler house and sugar mill, the heart of every estate.

One could well say the soul too, for there are contained all the evil spirits of slavery crystallized in one place in the hogsheads of sugar that are produced there. As we approached, the childhood images of the place in crop time flooded my eyes: the booming noise and clatter, the shouts and screams of animals and humans, indistinguishable in a cacophony of exertion and pain, of dismemberment and death. At crop time it was Dante's workshop. The rollers and boilers ate cane and people indiscriminately, each crop marked in new scars, lost limbs, missing people. Blood sugar, we had called it then. It was also the life's blood of the planters.

But this morning the place was quiet as a church. Five or six people were at work, men and women and a naked boy pickni, sweeping and cleaning a place already swept yesterday. For all but field hands there is a lot of make-work on an estate.

As we entered the darkened portals Anthony shouted a word into the vault and was briskly answered from the silence above us.

"Yes, Maasa."

The voice, of indeterminate gender, echoed around the space like a trapped bird.

Moments later, whispers of movement came from above and every head on the ground turned upward. Separating itself from the dark shadows, a patchwork doll of a figure came limbering down like a monkey I had once seen in a menagerie in Hertfordshire.

It presented itself before us, a mallet dangling from one misshapen hand as if grafted to it. The figure seemed put together of twigs and branches, hardly a straight limb or feature. Even the eyes, which peered questioningly at me, were of different sizes and unevenly placed in a crumpled face, the smaller eye higher by an inch, the larger one nearer the mouth. A gnome from a child's storybook, no taller than my navel, who would have frightened anyone—but for a brilliant smile, more lips than teeth, that seemed to light up the whole sugarhouse.

"Kwesi-bwoy," the troll croaked at me, voice as broken as his body. "You come back."

There was nothing in that misshapen assemblage of skin, bones and torn cloth that struck a chord anywhere in my memory. I had no idea, except that it was a man—a good-sized penis peeped from the ragged trousers. The disparate eyes held me, however, as surely as the claw-like hands would have. Because they knew me and seemed happy to see me.

"He don't remember us, Maas Anthony," the man said, a shoulder shrugging with laughter. "He go to foreign and turn white man and forget all him old Nayga friend-dem."

Anthony sat on his horse silently enjoying the operetta; the small audience of cleaners had stopped work to watch intently. The little man leaned toward my mount and, as if he thought I might be deaf, shouted suddenly, "Carpenter John!"

I was on the verge of responding that I was not that person, when illumination, dim at first, opened the previously dark cavern of my memory. The smile that I felt overtaking my face was mixed in equal parts of remembrance and bewilderment. This was not the Carpenter John of my childhood. I wondered if a monstrous joke, arranged beforehand by this gargoyle and Anthony, was being played on the gullible foreigner who spoke proper and vomited at the sight of blood. Anger bubbled in my throat, pressing to be released against these mockers.

He dispersed my conflict by taking a step back and bowing elaborately. It was, in one so far removed from the parlours of England or indeed of Bellefields, at once a parody and an imitation so perfect as to be genuine in itself.

"What leave of John, Kwesi," he said as he straightened. "Not much leave, but at your service."

And somehow, in that mismatched agglomeration of features and mannerisms I found, like a whole object glimpsed in scattered fragments, the Carpenter John of my childhood.

The setting undoubtedly helped. The Carpenter John of childhood had ruled this domain where we stood, in charge of ensuring that every mechanical thing here worked properly. To a child involved, albeit tangentially, in the apocalyptic drama of the sugar works at crop time, Carpenter John, with hammer or mallet or saw in hand, was a figure of awe—and calm. We pickni were afraid of him, of course, but not in the way we feared some of the others who could be cheerfully cruel to things and persons smaller and weaker than them. More than once or twice Carpenter John, though himself a strong believer that sparing the rod spoiled the child, had protected picknis from such capricious treatment.

I found myself asking for Bristol, a name surfacing from some dark well of memory. That was preferable to asking the little man what had reduced him to this pass. He cackled like a yard fowl, at the same time as moisture brightened his eyes, accentuating their oddness.

"If you did see Bristol in front of you now, Kwesi, you wouldn't be seeing me." He gave his little bow again.

Anthony spoke for the first time. "Dem call John 'Not My Time'," he said, and explained. Bristol, one of my chief playmates when circumstance permitted, had grown strong enough to take his place in the second gang in the field after my departure, which brought him into the sugarhouse at crop time. A recalcitrant mule kicked him into the mill, then grinding at full tilt. In the bedlam of the moment no one noticed—except his father, who happened to be nearby. John threw himself at the wheels, trying to stop them with his body. Which he did.

With some difficulty the wheels were slowed and reversed. Just enough to get the two bodies out. Everyone thought they were both dead. But then John's tongue moved.

Bristol was summarily buried. What was left of his sacrificial father was patched by Dr. Fenwell, the estate doctor, assisted over time by several doctresses in the sickhouse, using their greater knowledge of herbs and barks, baths and unguents. He refused to die. Three crops later he was back on his feet, the only part of his body to emerge unscathed; by the fourth season he was back being Carpenter John.

"Not my time yet, Kwesi," he said in commentary on Anthony's report.

And no one had thought, in the letters that went back and forth from Greencastle to England, to tell me of this tragedy. Except, of course, that it was not a tragedy for Greencastle, only for Bristol, and John. They had brought in, Anthony said as an aside, jobbing carpenters from here and there while John mended.

"So you come back, Kwesi," John said. His tone and moreso his eyes—which seemed to belong to two separate people, one to Bristol of memory and dust, one to his father in front of me—were a silent challenge: Why?

Indeed.

I could not answer John directly, especially so with Anthony at my shoulder. So I offered my regrets about Bristol, which were heart-felt but sounded paltry in my own ears. He cackled again in that genderless voice that had emerged from his ordeal. "He gone home," he sighed. "We still here, leave behind."

There, I think, is the eternal dilemma of the slave: the desire to escape a brutal life and to return to Africa, as some believe, coun-tered by a life-force that surges from within. Carpenter John's life-force, perhaps to his own dismay, had proven extremely strong, perhaps even absorbing that of his son, as some blacks believe. But that had left him trapped in his own bereft condition—which Bristol had escaped.

≈ 26 ≈

Narrative: In Bellefields, Saturday, November 12

ELORINE LIKES TO BE OUT AND about early on a Saturday, get her business in town done before the stream into Bellefields thickens, and be back home by midday. But this morning she is late. She had a restless night. Woken from sleep by whimpering that she thought first was Ginger dreaming, she quickly realized that it came from Jassy's room at the back. When Elorine gets to her she is holding one side of her belly and staring into the moonlight with crazy eyes. Elorine panics, thinking the girl's time has come, a month earlier than Mother Juba said. She considers sending for Mother Juba across the road, who has birthed seven children and helped many more into the world.

But it's not Jassy's time yet, and after some strong cerasee tea the pain, from gas, evaporates and Jassy subsides into a stony sleep. Not so Elorine, who remains a little frightened. What if the baby had come? Finally, at first light, exhausted, she rests.

But she can't stay home. Francine Beaumarchais is coming bright and early Monday morning to look at the trimmings for her Queen of the Sets gown for the day after Christmas. The Christmas ball that the custos gives every year is coming too, with the ladies outdoing each other with fanciful imitations of what's in London. What she'll need can only be had from Miss Meyerlink in town.

As she sponges herself down with khus-khus water and scrubs underarms and crotch with sweet orange, never mind it stings a little, it occurs to her that Jassy's baby and the final fittings of Francine's gown—both likely to be tumultuous events—might arrive together. She puts those thoughts to one side as she finds her best Saturday clothes to put on, knowing that even her Sunday best would still not be good enough for the whiteladies she'll encounter in town, in their padded shoulders threatening to bounce her off the walkway and their elaborate hats, getting in one another's way but fortunately passing clear over her tidily coiled headwrap.

She almost doesn't enter Miss Meyerlink's shop on Charles Street when she sees through the glass doorway a face that she knows: Missis Victoria Douglas. It's changed from when last seen some years ago, but there's no mistaking the Douglas jaw. Missis Douglas is looking out into the street, but straight through Elorine. Who, after a moment of pause, continues into the shop and past Victoria Douglas, wishing Miss Meyerlink a quiet howdy as she goes to the back of the store where she'll find what she's come for.

There are three other whiteladies there. The majority of Belle-fields's whiteladies patronize Miss Meyerlink's establishment because it has much greater choice and better quality goods than the shop run by Missis Timberton. A dry-up spinster sister of the Maasa of Glendale in Blue River Valley, Missis Timberton was given the shop and put to live upstairs in order to keep an eye on Maasa's coloured lady, Viona Fleetwood, who resides in the cottage in back of the property. For her brother, the shop and its merchandise are of far less concern than knowing who, especially wearing trousers, visits his baby-mother—now, after a lifetime of idleness and bearing several children for him, no longer the slim buttermilk beauty of their youth but still the object of Backra's tender and possessive affection.

Missis Timberton is deserving of the town's sympathy but not too much of its patronage.

The virtues of Miss Meyerlink's shop are obvious to all, even the coloured and black women like Elorine who, because they make their livings from using the goods that Miss Meyerlink sells, are the back-bone of the business.

So that those among the whiteladies sashaying through the aisles and around the shelves touching this or that bauble, feeling-up the latest bolts of fashionable London cloth, and who do not come from estates or town homes prosperous enough to have in-house seam-stresses, might well find themselves on a Saturday rubbing shoulders with the people who make their clothes. Indeed, Elorine made two of the dresses being worn in Miss Meyerlink's shop today. The blue and white gingham frock on Missis Parchment, a regular customer for whom there is also a dress in her workroom for the custos's Christmas ball. And the red cambric with the frilly white sleeves on Missis Patterson.

Elorine knows they've seen her. But neither acknowledges her presence. For which she's relieved.

And—Elorine knows also, from long observation—if they purchase anything they'll be barely civil to Missis Meyerlink when time comes. It's almost as though some of the whiteladies resent doing business with her. Because though she is light-skinned, and wears long-sleeved blouses to keep her arms pearly, there is no getting around the wide freckled nostrils and generous lips that are a family stamp. Unmistakably, Nayga blood is in there somewhere. Plus, she's Jewish. The lips seldom smile as they serve, and the nostrils can flare eloquently.

Miss Meyerlink owns the building that has the shop and a dry goods store next door. And now, since caving in to pressure from London, the assemblymen in Spanish Town have made browns as one with the whites, legally at least. So the brother and sister cannot be ignored and can only be privately scoffed at.

Victoria Douglas, having grown in Bellefields, knows the stories and would have joined in spreading them. But she doesn't live here any more, and is in the shop as company for her friend, the fourth whitelady, whom Elorine doesn't know. Missis Douglas too was Elorine's customer. Once upon a time.

Mama Selina had sewn for the whole Douglas family on Cascade, which had elevated the price Ishmael eventually paid to buy her freedom. And though someone took her place in the sewing room in the big house, the Douglas women still sent her special dresses and repairs. When Elorine began making clothes three or four years after her mother's death, the Cascade whiteladies resumed sending work to West Street. Missis Douglas, as she had for Selina on occasion, would even send a buggy to bring her to Cascade and take her back home after a fitting.

The last time Elorine had been there was such an occasion. A dress for Missis Victoria's sixteenth birthday party. There were only a few alterations and she'd made them on the spot, eagerly, because all Missis Victoria's white friends from the district round would be there the next night to admire her pretty dress and to ask her who made it. It was also the biggest money Elorine had earned on her own.

She had found her way back to West Street that evening. On foot and empty-handed.

Both choices were her own.

Looking up into space to better picture Francine's naseberry skin beneath the lace spread over her own black fingers, Elorine is staring straight into the eyes of Victoria Douglas on the other side of the display table. They gleam like marbles under the broad brim of her hat. But Elorine knows Missis Douglas is really seeing the bonnets and hats displayed on the wall behind Elorine. She herself is invisible.

It is a comfort of sorts. She can go about her business like a mus-mus, careful only about not getting underfoot. Bouncing into one of the whiteladies, even by accident, would provoke shrieks, as if she were a real mouse. Words would fly through the air as nasty as what their tone purported to describe: doo-doo, stinking toe. Elorine would still be invisible, still unacknowledged. But she would be properly demeaned and, worst of all, unable to say anything for herself. Except "Sorry." A talking mus-mus.

Miss Meyerlink's shop, thankfully, is spacious enough and Elorine knows it intimately.

By opening the eyes in the back and sides of her head Elorine can keep out of the way. Still, Elorine feels crowded by Missis Douglas. She drapes the lace she's thinking about over her shoulder and moves to the very back of the shop, to the cases with buttons.

Just then Miss Meyerlink's door opens, ringing the overhead bell to alert her when she is around the back.

"You will have to learn, and I can teach you some." The voice is unmistakable: Anna Pollard, who blows in from the bright dusty street and, as Elorine looks up, Jason, holding the door for her. "Howdy, Miss Meyer," Anna calls out as though in continuation of whatever she was saying to Jason, "You shop nice and cool." As usual Anna is swaddled in a long-sleeved blouse under a big planter's hat to protect her freckled skin and is sweaty, in contrast to the other whiteladies in the shop, whose fans have been out and working from they left home.

"Howdy, Eunice chile," she calls to Missis Patterson, "how you do?" and Elorine knows right away that they are some sort of friends. "Good afternoon, Missis Schoeb," she continues, "I hear you are visiting with your family here. I hope everybody is hearty, and you also." The use of Victoria's married name and Anna's tangle of language and accent tells Elorine that they are not fond of each other. As Victoria is about to respond, Anna notices Elorine.

"Miss Elly, how you doing, look who I bring?"

Elorine smiles. "Howdy, Miss Anna. Howdy, Jason." Anna has always been able to make her smile, and she is glad to see Jason, whom she has wondered and prayed about since his visit. But she senses an indrawn breath at the tone of friendship between herself and Anna, and her relaxed greeting to Jason, whose lineage everyone in the store would know. Elorine feels as if she's breathing through the lace she's holding.

Anna comes right past Victoria and touches Elorine's shoulder. "What you doing here, Miss Elly?"

"Looking for some lace for a dress. What bring you?" Her response is spontaneous—it's the way she has always spoken to Anna in her workroom at West Street. But she also knows that their familiarity contributes, like dasheen in soup, to thickening the air around them.

Anna laughs from her belly. "Idleness. And Jason want to come in to get cloth."

"Here?" Elorine asks.

Another rumble of laughter from Anna, and Jason smiling behind her. "Good morning, Miss Elly," he says. But she is grateful for the courtesy, grateful too that he didn't use his long-time pet name for her, which would have been tainted by the ears that heard it.

But she looks him over and smirks. "You still wearing those funny clothes?" His face is ruddier from being out in the sun every day now, but his awkwardness at her remark is visible in his cheeks.

"Prudence been fixing some of Pappa old clothes, but she say is not righted that Maasa should walk round looking like poor-ting, with patch-up clothes." Anna cackles at her own teasing, and Jason's blush deepens. "So we just come from Morais to buy some cloth for him. Malachai and Jack gone back home with it already, cause Prudence waiting on it, she and her daughter measure him up already. Next time you see him, Miss Elly, he will look a proper Backra. You won't know him."

Elorine feels she needs to say something to comfort Jason. "He looking hearty now, Miss Anna, the sun agree with him. And you feeding him up."

"Not me," the young woman cackles. "Constancia fattening him up like a Sunday chicken."

"That is true," Jason says. "But I'm learning to say no."

"Nobody say no to Constancia," says Anna. "Only Mama."

"And Lincoln," Jason adds.

Ignoring the whiteladies, even Anna, Elorine searches Jason's face, swift and keen-eyed as when she inspects a dress before final delivery. She sees the tiredness that has crept in since Monday, stretching his skin. While still cloaked in his English manner, as though his clothes are choking his movements, he also seems to glow. Which pleases Elorine, but also makes her anxious. Maybe he's looking forward to being Maasa. Not just for his father's sake, or his family's, but because he's a brownman, and enjoys shouting at Nayga and telling them what to do. With the whip, if needs be.

Elorine tries to ignore the anger that sparks for a moment like a flint. Not Jason, she tells herself over and over. He is not Backra. He's Jaze.

"We come for some buttons," Anna begins, but another voice bites through her words.

"Trust that Anna Pollard," Elorine hears. Victoria Douglas has turned from her contemplation of hats to address her companion in a voice she knows will be heard by all. They giggle with each other. Then Victoria Douglas turns to Jason. "Don't I remember you?"

Jason's eyes narrow, and then widen with light. He's about to speak when Victoria Douglas says, "You come to Cascade when you was a bwoy. With Anthony?" She smiles, answering herself. "You's one of Squire Pollard's bastards. The one he send to England to become a gentleman." Her voice and eyebrows lift the last word an inch.

Elorine, embarrassed for Jason and Anna both, stares at the row of buttons in the slanted glass case beside her.

"Good afternoon, Missis Douglas." Jason's voice behind her, crisp and correct as his English clothes, turns her around.

"Hark, Belinda chile," says the Missis Douglas. "It even sounds like a gentleman." They giggle together.

Elorine can see that Jason is livid, but he still smiles. "I'm flattered that you even bother to remember me, Missis Douglas."

"Remember you?" Missis Douglas laughs as if the idea was outrageous, but she's not as composed now.

"I am indeed one of Squire's bastards. And I remember you." He nods for emphasis, his smile now more relaxed.

"You do?" the Missis Douglas voice prickles.

"Very clearly. I did come to Cascade with Anthony. And once we shared a glass of wash." He's painfully, unremittingly polite. And Elorine, though anxious for her childhood friend adrift in the vicious cross-currents of this pool to which he's now returned, knows from one quick glance at Missis Douglas's face that she remembers too. Whatever there is to remember floods her fat cheeks.

Elorine feels a sudden chill. That Jason and Victoria Douglas— whatever her name now—should know each other is not strange. Anthony and Magnus were visiting friends from childhood, she'd known that from Jason himself. The bwoy Jason disliked the slightly older bwoy Magnus intensely, and Elorine cannot imagine the Jason she knew sipping wash at Cascade, except at the back door. Certainly not with Magnus's sister.

But his smile suggests to Elorine something more . . . private. She hugs herself as if cold and looks back down at the button case.

"Come, Belinda, Helen, let us get some fresh air. Is a little musty in here, don't you think?" Her companions giggle their agreement and the three of them rustle their way through the jangling door, ignoring Miss Meyerlink, since they've bought nothing.

Elorine helps Jason and Anna choose buttons for Jason's clothes, and they pay. Miss Meyerlink keeps an account book for Elorine that is settled monthly.

They have just stepped down from the walkway outside the shop onto the street, when a man's voice calls out, "You there. Nigger." It comes from further down the street toward the courthouse square. Jason and Anna keep walking up the street, where their horses are. Elorine turns to see a fat whiteman who is strange to her waddling up the street toward them, holding a riding crop in one hand while dragging a leg swollen with gout, red-faced and sweating.

He's obviously come out of McKinley's Men's Club at the corner across the square. Elorine glimpses, standing on the steps of the club, Missis Victoria, watching the progress of the tubby man up the street.

"Nigger," the man cries out again, his voice as grating as a kling-kling's.

Elorine grips her package of lace in its brown paper so that it won't fall to the ground, and braces herself for trouble. But the whiteman wobbles past without even looking at her.

"You!" It's a screech now. Elorine turns.

Jason and Anna are now walking backwards, but still moving toward Grayson's stables where they'd have left their buggy.

"Stop right there!"

Jason pauses. Anna grabs his sleeve and pulls him onward. But he resists and turns square to the figure approaching them.

And Elorine suddenly remembers a moment from their childhood. Jason and Anthony had come to West Street with Squire, and were waiting for their father to finish his business with Ishmael. Anthony had been provoking Jason—Elorine can't remember about what—with Jason refusing to rise to the bait. Until finally, when a frustrated Anthony had kicked dust onto Jason's bare legs, he'd turned and spread his scrawny legs. Just as he was doing now as the overweight whiteman came nearer. He'd hit Anthony a solid blow on the shoulder, spinning him around and onto his knees in the dirt. They'd wrestled furiously, Squire watching with amused interest but not interfering, until Jason was sitting on Anthony's chest, both of them in tears.

The whiteman totters up to Jason, both arms raised as if appealing to the younger man for support, and brings the riding crop down on

Jason's shoulder. He's aimed at his face but at the last moment Jason turns away. And then turns back, grabs the man's neck and pulls him to the ground in a fury of arms, legs and shouts. They tumble into the gutter of sewerage that neither had noticed.

Almost instantly spectators appear in every doorway on the street and seeping out from McKinley's. "Give it to the nigger, Stephen," a man calls out from behind Elorine.

Jason disentangles himself and staggers to his feet, filthy and spitting shit, but holding the riding crop high above the clutching hands of the man still thrashing in the gutter, unable to rise because of his swollen leg. Jason, suddenly calm again, hands the crop to Anna and then stretches a hand out to the man in the dirt.

For a moment Elorine wonders if the man is going to spit on the offered hand. But he thinks better of it. Jason pulls him to his feet and steps back.

"Who are you?" Jason's voice is tight, his legs spread.

"You insult my wife," the man says, balancing with difficulty as he tries to brush the dust and shit from his clothes.

"Who is your wife?"

"You know who she is, nigger." He's regained some of his bluster.

"I have no idea," says Jason, "about your wife or about you, sir."

"Vicky," the man begins, and is totally disarmed by Jason's reaction, a brilliant smile that melts into a chuckle.

"You are married to Victoria Douglas?"

The man, Stephen, takes a step toward Jason, his face crumpling with renewed fury.

"How dare you."

"How dare you!" Jason shouts at him, stepping forward. "You don't even know me."

Spectators have formed a loose circle around the two men, but not too close because of the smell. Elorine notices Victoria Douglas across from her, several yards from her husband and making no effort to get closer, watching like everyone else. Elorine senses the anxiety of the whites in the group, and the uneasy helplessness of the few coloureds and blacks, servants and slaves, who are, like herself, on the fringes, seeing and hearing everything. Some of them belong to whites in the group and none, excepting herself and Anna, would know Jason except to know that, despite his light skin and strange clothes, he is not white. So the fight is not so much about the woman, Victoria. It's about skin.

Jason: Evasions—Victoria–Miranda,
Sunday, November 13

I DIDN'T REMEMBER HER RIGHT AWAY. She's now almost fat, nothing of the girl remaining. Except that crow's voice, which brought everything suddenly close again: the shadowy room in which the pale filaments of hair dusting her thighs glowed, her rum and orange breath, my own musk congealing with the afternoon heat, where Time slowed for the hour or so, balanced on my fulcrum of fear.

But no one noticed anything, or asked. Surprising me and perhaps Victoria also. Not even when her brother and Anthony had returned from their mysterious mission into the reaches of Cascade, leaving me, inexplicably, in Victoria's company. We were there, Anthony boasted on our way home, for a farewell fuck of his favourite Cascade slave before we left the next day, he to Virginia, me onward to England.

The smell of her—toddy and sour orange, the mustiness of her skin—went with me onto the Atlantic until the salt wind in my nostrils diluted it, and my hands became so encrusted with spume they could not have felt the softness of her spiked breasts.

Eventually, she leeched away almost beyond recall. Every so often, in some back-lane of Swindon or London I'd hear a snatch of children's singing that prickled memory:

When yu see a pretty
bwoy When yu see a
pretty bwoy When yu
see a pretty bwoy
You tek yu finger call
him.

It was a ditty that slave children sang, a game. That afternoon, on her scratchy voice and moist lips, it was the siren song of doom. But those evocations too would subside without trace into the dark memories of a faraway life.

Until yesterday.

She knew me. I could tell that.

I could not set this out for Carla. She knows I've not been a saint, but how could I explain the intricacies? And the anger. That which remains now, as I write, is directed mostly at myself. I am angry and ashamed—not so much of dissembling to my wife as of taking advantage of Victoria's fool of a husband. And why am I, beneath the anger, flattered that she remembered, as she obviously did? I've asked myself that question all day. And the only answer is: because she's white. I'm a brown man misled by himself, as we all are.

As I fell into sleep through the words I'd written to Carla, I dreamt of the slave girl Miranda. I was a young brown buck, about to go off to England. I was riding through a forest that might have been Savernake or the woods surrounding Greencastle, filled with a feeling of anticipation. A dark shape flashed across my path: prey. Spurring the horse I gave chase to a girl who flicked smiles over her naked shoulder as she escaped through hidden passageways she obviously knew while at the same time enticing me to follow and catch her. A wild creature at home in the wild.

She disappeared, falling into Angel Hole with a splash and a shriek. I reined in hard and looked down at the girl, as emergent from childhood as myself, and now as fully naked as I suddenly found myself, and already easing off the horse to join her. But before my eyes Miranda's dark luminescence melted like candlewax and re-formed in Victoria's whiteness, her guava nipples paling to rose, ochre pubis suddenly jet.

As suddenly, from the other side of Angel Hole, came two plump furious white men on horses, one flourishing a whip, the other a cane-field cutlass—Victoria's husband and brother, with murder in their hearts and eyes. The eyes of this strange Miranda–Victoria girl still sparkled with enticement, drawing me into the pool. I woke, shaken and jabbering in the darkness that seemed, for the first few moments, pregnant with menace. I ached, cock by now resplendent in dream and reality, for the comfort and oblivion that seemed to beckon from sparkling thighs. But within a few moments, as my breath settled and my mind unfurled itself, I saw again in my mind's eye the fat woman encountered in the milliner's shop, and the fat husband in the square.

The slavegirl Miranda, however, remains in consciousness as a bright russet light burning in my flesh.

≋ 28 ≋

Adebeh: In Town, Monday, November 14

WALKING ALONG THE MAIN STREET in the town this morning minding our business. We's going slowly because Trojan don't have on any shoes. He get up this morning with a shoe that is loose, and the hoof is not in a good way either. Trojan is doctorman's regular horse, but Fergus send him off on another one. I tell him I can fix the hoofs with a sharp knife and a file, but he don't know my knowledge of horses and don't have a file, so he tell me to take Trojan to Elorine's father. I am happy to hear that. I's been looking for excuse to visit her.

I's making myself useful around the doctorman's house and trying to stay clear from Juice. She leave herself careless many times, and I'd only have to blink at her. Besides, Juice is pickni. Elorine is a woman.

So me and Trojan walking easy, slow, but going along easy. I's hoping Elorine's father will take a long time to put on the shoes so that I can spend time with her. I's wondering if she'll be glad for my company, when I hear this man's voice from behind: "Stop in the name of the law!" I don't pay it any mind cause I don't think it could be me he is talking to. Trojan and me keep walking.

The shout come again, "You! Nigger with the horse! I say to stop in the name of the law! Stop!" I look round now and see a small red man in a ragged uniform pointing his gun at me. It is almost bigger than him. I's not a fool, the damn thing might go off, so I stop. Trojan bounce into me, almost send me flat. But Trojan don't understand what the ragged man says and he's not in a good mood anyway for his bare feet must be sore. So he bounce my shoulder to keep me walking. But by then the red man is wobbling toward me following the gun and I am trying to keep my face straight.

"Who is you?" he bark at me. So I tell him my name. "Who is the horse?"

"Trojan," I tell him, though I know what he mean.

He wave the gun at me. "I mean who he belong to, bwoy."

I tell him I am not a bwoy.

"Who you belong to?"

"Myself."

"Who is you?"

So we start again, until his hand get real tired from the big gun and it come to point at the ground between us. Meanwhile Trojan start walking around me so I have to keep turning with him, and the red man is turning with me and people are stopping in the street watching the three of us like we's playing a ring game or performing on a stage.

When I get Trojan to stop at last the man shout, "Nigger, you is under arrest. You and the horse you tief." He wave the gun at me again and say, "Go over there," and he point to a big building that look just like the courthouse in Preston.

But as I turn to go over there Trojan find himself next to the man and butt him. The big gun let off with a BOOM! right behind me, blow a whole lot of dust and stones onto the back of my legs, and everybody scream and run like chickens, including the red man and Trojan, who drag me down and cause my shirt to tear before I could get him back under control. But is not Trojan I's vex with. The damn fool man don't know his arse from his neck-back about guns.

I's calming Trojan, talking to him soft-soft, getting his eyes to come back down into his head, when I see a whiteman under a big hat come out from under the courthouse and walk toward us. His mouth is moving like a fish before I even hear any words—a string of cussing—English and Jamaican ones mix-up together. But is like he don't see me—his eyes and voice are burning the red man, who seems to name Boynton or something like that. He is struggling to reload the gun and everybody is moving further and further away from him in case it go off again. Me and Trojan is the nearest ones to him and I am backing the horse away slowly, when the whiteman pass me and goes right up to Boynton and cuff him hard in his head, almost box him down.

He shouts at the ragged man, "You stupid nigger, who give you that gun?" Before Boynton can answer the whiteman cuff him again. Boynton is still trying to reload the firearm and the blows throw him off balance. He drops the gun and staggers back from the whiteman, who steps after him as if to hit him a third time. The little crowd re-gather—mostly blacks but some brownpeople—and I glimpse one whitelady just stepping out from a shop. Meantime, Trojan and me are edging away. Which was a mistake. Boynton catch us in his eye-corner and shoot out his hand.

"Stand still, bwoy!" My tongue lift to tell him I'm no bwoy, but I bite it in time. And I have the sense to stop, though Trojan take three or four steps more.

"He is a tief, Maasa," Boynton shout. "I is arresting him!" So of course everybody turn to look at me.

The whiteman's eyes open wide. Still looking at me he ask Boynton, "What him tief?"

"I don't steal anything, sir," I say in my best voice.

"The horse-deh, Maasa," Boynton say, picking up his gun now that the whiteman turn his back.

"Who you is, bwoy?" the whiteman say. "I never see you around these parts."

I not fraid for him, but it would be putting my head in the mouth of a grizzly to answer him like I answer Boynton. So I stay calm and say, "I's Adebeh Cameron, sir, and I did not steal this horse. You can ask Dr. Fenwell. Is his horse."

"You have a paper from the Doctor?" Right away, as I clap my hand to my neck I see the pouch hanging like a bird on the tree outside the zinc box where I wash myself this morning. And I remember Fergus. At the wharf when we land, he warn me to never leave behind the leather pouch with my paper from Major Maxwell in Halifax that testify to my status. The one the man Cameron stamp. "They can lock you up without it," Fergus tell me more than once. I's seeing that come to pass in front of my eyes now.

"You are one of Doctor's slave," says the whiteman, and it wasn't a question.

"No, sir. I am not the doctorman slave. I am a free man."

"Free," he say, like I tell him I am a tree or a fish. "You know him, Boynton?" He not taking his eyes from me, only turn his head a little.

"No, Maasa, him is a stranger to me, Maas Thomas."

The whiteman Thomas look away from me at last and turn around to look at the little gathering. "Anybody know this free man?"

I turn and look with him. About fifteen people, give or take, and the sun is behind some of them so I can't see their eyes, but not one is familiar to me. As the two of us turn again, our eyes come into range of each other like two cannon. The whiteman's eyes is serious, but his mouth is smiling. He look like when puss find mus-mus in a corner.

"What you say you name again?"

I tell him, trying to sound like Reverend teach us to speak in Baptist school in Boydville. But the words scrape my throat like a fishbone.

"And you is free, eh?" His eyes and mouth is dancing.

"Yes, sir." I was not going to call him more than sir. I don't do it for Dr. Fenwell or the captain of the *Eagle*, and I's not putting myself alongside the likes of Boynton.

"You don't sound like a slave, bwoy." He wipe his lips with the last word. "But last week we catch a bwoy who speak good just like you. He tell me he is free and we find out he was running all the way from Port Antonio. Where are you running from, bwoy?" He wave his hand at me to come closer. "Come. Let we go talk to him. Maybe he know you." His voice is soft but his eyes are flint. "Boynton!" he shout.

"Yes, Maasa!"

"Bring him over to the workhouse!"

"Yes, Maasa!"

Just like the one in Preston, the courthouse raise itself up over the square on a set of steps, to remind you, as if blackpeople didn't know from they's born, who is fire and who is trash. Underneath is the jail and beside it, like in Preston, is the workhouse, where many enter and few leave.

I's seeing my pouch hanging on the tree at the doctorman's place, and trying not to let my knees knock together.

"Move, bwoy." Boynton have his gun ready in hand, and he's smiling as he point it at me.

"I tell you already," I say, wrath now stronger than fear of him or his gun, "I's not a bwoy."

"We will see," he say with a laugh, greedy now to shame me.

We walk toward the courthouse, the whiteman in front and Boynton behind me and Trojan, with a tail of people following to see what will happen next.

As we's passing the courthouse Boynton tell me to tie up the horse on a railing beside the steps. I protest at that. "Them will steal him," I say, holding the rein tighter and watching the straggle of mostly men behind him. Lame as he is, Trojan is a sweet piece of horse, and them niggers would steal him to sell in a blink.

The red man laugh, show me his rotten teeth. "Tief from tief," he say.

Right away I come back at him. "Well, shoot me then. I's not leaving the horse."

That stop him on the spot. He don't know whether to show me more teeth or shoot me. He wave the gun at me and I don't move. The people behind me shift in case any more shots fly at them.

"Maas Thomas!" he call out. His throat is dry, like the words hurt him.

The whiteman stop and turn around. His face is red enough for a tomato. And it get redder when he shouts at Boynton, "What?"

"Him say I must shoot him, Maasa."

"He wants you to shoot him?" Whiteman Thomas don't even glance at me, he's so surprised.

"Yes, Maasa. He say he not leaving the horse for somebody to tief, and I must shoot him."

"Well, shoot him then." He's still looking at Boynton, as if he don't know who they's talking about.

"Maasa . . ." the little red man bawl, like a pickni begging.

That is when whiteman Thomas bless me with his eye. They's still shining like puss, but he know now that I am not a mus-mus for him to play with, not just yet. He don't know that inside I am trembling that the damn fool with the big gun might decide to shoot me so the whiteman won't cuff him again and give the people behind him a story to laugh at him with.

None of them know that I am Yenkunkun, who will dead before him step back from his word. I don't want to dead, but I don't want to go back to Fergus and the doctorman and tell them that somebody steal Trojan. You have to dead some time, and for some thing.

Whiteman Thomas study me. I hold my eyes steady on him even though I really want to see what Boynton behind me is up to. He laugh. "I should make the red nigger shoot you, bwoy." He turns away from us like is something he's throwing off his shoulder. "Bring the fucking horse."

As we get closer to the workhouse the little crowd behind us falls away. The big iron gates rear up like the gates of Sheol, and it takes three men wearing tear-up clothes like Boynton to open them from inside for whiteman Thomas. Boynton behind us is saying all the time, "Move up, move up, bwoy." I's hoping Trojan will let go a big splat of shit on him.

When we pass through, the first thing I notice is the screams—may be a man, but really it sound like a animal that you want to put out of its pain. He is in a corner of the yard we are walking into, tied to a post by his neck and his ankles, naked in between, and a big brown man in a uniform that is sweated blacker than his skin is laying into the wretch with a switch. The screams fly out of the man like birds. My belly-bottom tickle me as though I eat something rotten. But no one else is paying this any mind at all. Normal business.

The whipping post is in one corner of the yard. In the other corner is the scaffold. The scaffold is empty today.

Then the smell hits you with a fist. Shit and piss and misery mixed-up in a soup from the rain last night, and dawg and pigs and chickens and pickni running up and down in it, spreading it around the open ground in the middle of the place. On both sides of it is more misery, rows of cells with bars for doors on most of them and a few with doors of solid iron. You can see hands waving through the little box windows cut into the iron, though you only notice it because the hands are moving—they's all black.

I look back and see the big gates closing behind us. I wonder if whiteman Thomas and Boynton behind me intend to leave me here. Same time, I promise myself and the ancestors that I's not sleeping here tonight. They will have to shoot me, or hang me, or let me go.

Five or six men dressed like Boynton are in the yard, couple of them with guns too. They're watching us, especially whiteman Thomas, who calls out two names. Two of them jump to attention and answer. "Bring so-and-so," he shout, and they run over to one of the cells and disappear inside. They come out with two men joined at the neck with collar and chain. One is lame, dragging his foot behind the other man, who is younger and walking in time with the guards. The lame man is wheezing and whimpering from the collar that is strangling him. But nobody's paying him mind either, especially not the man yoked to him. The guards march them up to the whiteman, who by this time is over next to me and Boynton.

The old man's neck is raw from the collar, blood running down his scrawny chest. He looks like a mangy black dawg. But it's him that Thomas speaks to.

"Fippence," Thomas say, "you still here? I thought Backra Gayle come for you."

"He send Busha, Maasa. But when Busha hear what he have to pay for me he say I too old now. He say you must keep me." The old man give what could well be a laugh, three teeth showing.

Whiteman Thomas laugh too, like they's sharing a joke. Then he bounce his head at me. "You know this nigger?"

The man can barely raise his head but he take his time to study me. "No, Maasa," he whisper, serious again.

Whiteman Thomas laugh. "He say he is a free man."

Fippence raise a shoulder. "Maybe, Maasa. If he say so."

"Or he could be a slave like you, trying to pass for free."

"Yes, Maasa," Fippence say, without any expression in voice or face.

"He wearing good clothes. Just like you when Boynton stop you."

When I look at him, in truth the old man's clothes look like they were good once. Now they's just smelly rags.

"Yes, Maasa," he say again.

The whiteman look around and shout, "Anybody know this nigger?" A big silence swallows his words.

Then I hear a voice call out from behind me, "Maas Thomas!"

Whiteman Thomas hear it too, and Boynton, and the two of them spin around. It's a big brown man, one of the guards, the only one who look like himself and the gun belong together.

"I don't know the man, but that is the doctorman horse from down Robert Street," the man say, and I feel the two of them beside me stiffen. "He name Trojan," the guard say. The horse recognize his name and whinny. I had to smile, but swallow it just before whiteman Thomas put his eye back on me.

"So how you come to have the doctor horse, bwoy?" he say, the words scratching the inside of his nose.

I fix my mind on getting away from here and decide to let the *bwoy* and the *nigger* pass again, even from Boynton. "I taking it to get shoes."

The whiteman makes a move like he want to pick up one of Trojan's legs but the horse don't like that and dance sideways, clearing his throat and turning his eyes up into his head. Thomas see that and pull back. "He don't look lame to me," he say, accusing me.

I bend over and pick up the two front legs one after the other. Trojan stand steady as a tree as I'm doing that. "He not lame, sir, but he need shoes and some repairs to his hoof."

"So you belong to the doctor," Thomas say, again not a question.

"No, sir," I say. "The horse belong to the doctor. I belong to myself."

He laugh again. "But nobody know you, bwoy."

"The doctorman know me, sir." Mam always tell us, "It don't shorten you one inch to show respect. Especially when they don't respect you." So I keep my voice calm.

"But the doctorman not here." Thomas make a big show of looking around the stinking yard.

"You know the doctor, sir?" I ask.

He spin around and raise his hand to me. "Is not for you to ask questions of me, nigger."

He was going to cuff me but I didn't even blink, and I see the thought drain from his face. He must be see in my face that I would have to cuff him back, come what will. He shout for Boynton and another one, tell them to take me up to the courthouse. As they come forward I wrap the reins tight around my fist and bring Trojan close, so none of them can get between us as we walk behind whiteman Thomas. He doesn't say another word to me or even look my way when we go back through the gates, then he disappear into a room they have under the courthouse, some sort of office with desk and chair, from what I can see.

Boynton hand his rifle to the other guard.

"Shoot him if he move, Brisket," he say, and follow Thomas inside. Trojan and me stand up at the bottom of the steps in the sun. I never get into the habit to wear something on my head, even when it is bitter cold in Scotia, and I regret that now. Brisket has a floppy old hat at least. He's a older man than me, and a little bigger in his body, but like plenty of the blackpeople I see everywhere, from Boydville and Halifax to Liverpool and now here, he look like his food always finish before his belly is finished with hungry. But at least he don't make up his face like Boynton, looking fierce to try and frighten me.

We talk a little. I don't tell him much of my business, because Scotia Maroons are not to be in Jamaica any at all, on pain of death— and the scaffold is next door! So I tell him my father was a Black Loyalist from Virginia who reach to Scotia and settle there, and I tell him about the boat and Fergus. He knows Fergus—everybody knows Fergus.

Brisket listens well, especially about Scotia.

But me and Trojan are standing out in the sun frying our heads, and Trojan don't like that at all. He's snuffling and growling and dancing on his bare toes, and I's talking quiet and loving to him in between the words with Brisket, who says after a long time of watching the two of us, "Come."

He get up with his gun and step off in front of us, he who is supposed to be our guard. Trojan and me follow him round to the back of the building, where they have a big stone trough with water. Trojan smell the water long before we reach it. He's not listening to my hands on the rein, but I follow him, glad for the water myself.

Brisket in his hat and his uniform take up a position like he is guarding us, but I know is only a pose if somebody pass by, and I give him silent thanks for that. The trough have leaves and cockroach floating in it but I sweep them out with my hand and Trojan and me drink our fill, side by side.

But by the time we get back to the courthouse steps whiteman Thomas is standing there looking up and down the street for us. He's not alone. Another whiteman is standing beside him, a step above. Just standing. He is wearing the same kind of white clothes as Thomas but his clothes look somehow better, so maybe he is higher up. He fix his eye on us as we're coming from round the back. As we get closer I see a little smile creep into his face.

"Mr. Cameron!"

I recognize him more from his voice. The whiteman from the wharf, when Fergus and me land from the *Eagle*. The one who signed the paper that should be around my neck.

"You still here." He's smiling broad now, like we's friends, but he's telling me serious things as well.

"Yes, sir," I say as Trojan and I come closer to him. "The boat not ready to leave yet."

Thomas's mouth is open to catch flies. You would think I drop from heaven the way he's looking from me to Cameron and back.

"And you find yourself a horse, I see," Cameron say, not even looking at Thomas.

"Yes, sir," I say again. "But I don't find it. Is not mine."

"You steal it?" He looking for a joke.

"No, sir!" My voice come out loud, but I don't care.

"So where you get it?"

I couldn't help but look at Thomas and the puss smile on his mouth. Then I look back at Cameron, serious. "Dr. Fenwell send me with it to the blacksmith, sir. It need new shoes."

Cameron hold me in his eyes like I'm a fish on a hook, considering what to do. "Make sure you is on the ship next week when it sail."

"Yes, sir."

Right away Thomas start to argue with him, but Cameron ignore him and disappear into the courthouse. Thomas look back at me as if he's thinking to do me something. I can't imagine what, but white-people don't have to have reasons when they deal with us. Is for us to decide whether to put up with it. And Thomas knows by now that I won't.

So, like earlier with Boynton, the fucking man haul back and cuff Brisket in his head and shout at him to get back to his post. A part of me is hoping the guard would plant the gun in his head. But Brisket is not the fool that I am. Thomas stomp off back under the courthouse while Brisket get himself straight again and march off toward the stinking workhouse place inside the walls. But as he's going through the gates he turn around, give a little wave.

I take that as blessing. The whole morning is a blessing, a offering from the bigi pripri.

They's telling what I must do and not do.

Trojan butt me with his big head and show me his teeth. We have things to do, he's telling me. Sometimes a horse have more sense than a man.

≈ 29 ≈

Narrative: Adam, Monday, November 21

GINGER'S BARKING IS PART OF THE cacophonous background of night that usually ensures Elorine a sound sleep. The large yellow mongrel is suited to its task of watchdog. It sleeps all day, when all manner of people and horses of various temperaments come through the yard of the Livingstone foundry and dressmaking establishments; an excitable dog would be a cross. But after prayers he moves without reluctance through the door into the yard of his kingdom, to establish his despotic rule. No one passes the gate without acknowledgement, and no one enters more than two steps into the yard without being pinned to the spot by a stiff quivering shadow, bristling with outrage and menace.

Tonight is different. Ginger's explosive challenge is ignored. The gate's squeak more than the barking wakes Elorine. And when Ginger's hoarse woof turns to a yowl and then quickly to a whimper, Elorine opens her eyes and sits up, stiff with apprehension. She can tell from the slash of moonlight across her bed that it's middle-night, too late for one of Ishmael's flock. The gate squeaks again as it's closed, and then a man's voice speaks softly to Ginger. The old dog moans with pleasure. Elorine, anxiety and anger churning in her stomach, can almost see the man, whoever he is, bending over to tickle the stupid mongrel behind his ears, which he loves.

Then silence, from both of them. Broken, eventually, by clicking: Ginger's nails against the hard-packed earth. Coming closer. Mind racing crazily, Elorine's hand moves by itself to the floor beneath the bed and grasps the handle of the small cutlass there.

"Ellie." The voice, close, soft but not whispering, could have come from inside the room.

She yelps.

"Jesus!"

A chuckle answers her. "Is not Jesus this time," says the voice, calm, amused. "Only me."

When Ishmael bought his freedom from Maasa Douglas at Cascade estate he'd left behind a family: his wife Selina, Adam, who had seen five Christmases, and Quamina, who didn't live to see her first. Every month-end Ishmael carried money made from his blacksmithing to Cascade to Maasa Douglas to put toward a free-price for Selina. Adam was in his twelfth year when his mother, bought and paid for by her husband, left him on Cascade in care of a friend. Ishmael continued his monthly visits, now with the portion for Adam's free-price. They saw him on some holidays—Christmas, Crop-over—and the occasional weekend when he was given a pass to spend a night, two nights at Christmas, at the little house on West Street.

Elorine had gathered this information from overheard conversations: Ishmael and Selina, Ishmael and Fergus, Selina and those of her friends, slaves from Cascade, who visited from time to time. Elorine herself was born the year after Selina came free to West Street. And the year after that, everything changed.

Adam didn't wait around for the full price of his freedom to be paid. One Christmas, his thirteenth, escorted to within sight of Cascade's boundary by his father after a bawling farewell from his mother, he just kept walking. Three days later the Cascade overseer arrived at West Street, demanding that Adam, who by then was in charge of the pickni gang, return with him. No one on Cascade or at West Street saw him again for five years. Ishmael had to continue paying for his freedom—a higher price than agreed because there was no further labour to be had from Adam. It was that or supply the labour himself as a slave again. An eye for an eye, Maasa Douglas said.

One night, just as prayers were ending, Ginger's mother Jumpy barked, startling them, and skittered out of the house. Everyone lifted their heads and looked nervously at each other. But Jumpy's barking quickly calmed to whining and then squeals of delight. Someone she knew. But no one recognized the muscular young man who suddenly filled the doorway between the kitchen and living area, his eyes scanning the room. Then his thick lips twitched nervously into a smile, and Selina screamed. Elorine still remembers the scream, and the river of tears darkening Adam's shirt as Selina sobbed against her son, now almost as big as his father. She remembers also the cuff Selina delivered to the side of Adam's head—affectionate, but hard.

"We pray for you every night," she said, joy and anger mixed in her voice. "How you could do us that?"

"Mama," Adam began, the powerfully grown man like a little bwoy, flicking his glance away from her stern searching eyes.

"You father had was to go to Slave Court," Selina continued, inhaling outrage from the air. "Little most they lock up you father. Or worse."

"I sorry." He looked at his father, uncertainty crossing his face.

"Sorry?" Selina's anger rose again.

"Yes," Ishmael interrupted, abrupt and imperious. "The bwoy say he sorry. What more you want?"

"What more I want?" Selina had turned away from her son to confront her husband. But she couldn't find the words to express the blazing anger in her eyes. She crumpled onto a chair that was right beside her and held her head in her hands.

Elorine would remember the powerful sobs rippling against her bony six-year-old chest folded in futile comfort over the bent back of her mother, and her father's hand, spreading easily across her shoulder blades, petting them both.

She remembered too Ishmael's voice above her, full of forgiveness and thanksgiving. "The prodigal son has returned. Where you been, Son-son?"

"Round and about," said Adam, his voice, like his body now, an echo of his father's.

Elorine felt rather than heard her mother ask, "Where is that?"

The men laughed, and then Selina too.

Eventually, over a big plate of food his mother set before him, he told them his story. But not, Elorine sensed even then, everything.

Through his words, Adam grew into a man before their eyes. But he also retreated deeper into the shadowy world of mystery and unanswered questions, into which he disappeared before daybreak the next morning.

Adam's visits punctuated Elorine's growing. They were always at night, usually after prayers. He had to come through Bellefields at night for fear of recognition by someone from Cascade estate, or of being challenged for the papers required by law of every roaming black.

Elorine was fascinated by this stranger, a younger version of Ishmael to look at, with the same big voice and warm smile. He would come to her room to say goodnight—and to answer her questions. She was the first to know, two visits before Ishmael and Selina, that Adam had a woman, Adisa, also a runaway; but they did not actually meet her for a long time. She wild, Adam would say in explanation.

Elorine was twelve when Adam arrived one night to tell her that she had a niece, born just a couple weeks before and named for her grandmother. He had not been there for several months, and so had no way of knowing that his mother was three months into her own pregnancy. After that visits were sometimes only a month apart. He brought little gifts for his mother: yellow yam freshly dug from his own ground, star apples which he knew she loved, breadfruit that grew wild in the wet mountains where he and Adisa and baby Selina lived. He was as excited as Elorine about the two babies.

But he wasn't there when Selina was taken suddenly one night, a month before her time. He arrived with his basket of presents, bright-eyed and lively, a few days after Ishmael and Fergus had buried his mother, the tiny bundle who would have been their brother placed on her chest.

Elorine would remember always his stricken face after Ishmael, who stumbled over the words, answered his question as to her whereabouts. He who had spoken softly at all times screamed to the roof like a dog baying at the night's shadows. The little house trembled. His large frame collapsed into the nearest chair, Selina's. He put his head in his hands and bawled like a child. On and on, tears falling on the floor like shiny beads. Elorine went over and hugged his head to her scrawny belly, crooning "Hush, hush" like she did with her dollies, patting his springy, less than clean hair that trembled against her, inhaling his smell of earth and leaves and jackass-rope tobacco, that had now become part of her sense of him.

They didn't see him again for three months. Then he arrived just before dark, with baby Selina and Adisa, whom they were meeting for the first time. Her stringy brown body fit well in the men's clothing she wore to disguise herself from the police, and when she opened her shirt to calm the restless baby she revealed a chest and shoulders intricately patterned like a piece of fabric. Elorine had seen such patterns in the market: Guineamen, irrespective of gender or which part of Africa they or their parents came from. Adisa was Creole but her parents had raised her in the old ways as best they could on the estate she'd run away from.

She didn't say much that first time, or smile, except at the baby at her breast. But that didn't matter. Selina, just a few weeks old, took their numb spirits in her tiny hands and blew laughter back into their lives. Her very name, which Ishmael in particular found difficult to mouth, became a talisman, a guzu against the darkness into which the other Selina had disappeared. Between their visits to West Street, Elorine's thoughts of the girl-baby were like smooth river stones in her mouth, springing water in her soul.

She is not a baby now, nor even an only child: Thomas, a dreamer, came a couple years later, and then Jabez, now five, lame from birth and sturdily independent in his ways. Elorine longs for them, and feels light and free as a butterfly, when they are on one of their rare visits to West Street.

So as she pads through the shadowy house to let Adam in, Elorine prays that even one of the children is with him. But the space around his bulky form, his smiling eyes and teeth in the foreday like a cluster of peenie-wallies, is empty except for the adoring Ginger.

The disappointment passes quickly as she rubs her hand up and down his arm as he passes her into the house, and feels his rough fingers squeezing hers. She's glad to see him; it's been more than two months.

He pads silently into the front room, Ginger clicking behind him to sprawl at his feet as Adam sits heavily in Elorine's chair.

"How the pickni?"

He sighs. "Is that why I come."

A cold finger pokes Elorine's belly.

≈ 30 ≈

Jason: Entertainments, Monday, November 14

THE PICTURE OF THE WEST INDIAN planter that is widely purveyed in England, to the point of caricature, sets the man in his capacious drawing room surrounded by others of his kind, all of them almost comatose from food and drink; or puts him on an Arabian steed prancing upon the backs of cowering but somehow grinning, thankful Negroes. It is something I soon noted in him and have come to admire despite the other aspects of his character, that Anthony does not fit that stencil. The second morning after my return he'd said to me:

"I probably don't need to remind you and you'll be reminded soon enough for yourself, but the Pollards are looked upon in the district as eccentric, because we do almost everything for ourselves except digging the fields."

There was a gleam of pride in his eyes and smile as he said it; he looked and sounded much like our father.

Another aspect of the Pollard eccentricity was with regard to entertainments. I had forgotten the extent to which the drear of estate life is relieved by social get-togethers. It was not an activity given much credence by Squire, though I distantly recall some grand affaires at Greencastle when Anthony's mother was the missis. She came from old planter stock; it was in her blood. But Squire, with a foreign pedigree, was not comfortable playing the potentate; he had too keen a sense of how much such posturing cost his pocket.

Visitations, which involve huge dinners and entertainments almost every night, is a traditional way of life in the colony. For some indeed and not only those of the fairer sex—who may be excused, since there is so little that they are required to do on an estate—socials could seem the very purpose of existence.

In a caravan of equines and carriages of all sorts, travelling as one understands the caliphs of the Arabian Desert to move, one estate descends, often with scant notice, upon another, expecting a warm welcome and munificent provision for their stay, which may be for several days before they move on.

It is a custom that Squire endured with ill grace. I recall him saying after one such invasion, "They are like a swarm of locusts, picking the leaves from every bush in sight."

He did not indulge in such frivolities himself, though he occasionally visited friends in the distant reaches of the island, with just Lincoln and another slave for company.

It appeared, from talking to Anna and Mathilde anyway, that in this regard Anthony embodied more his father's blood than his mother's. His attention to his inheritance was not trifling or whimsical. Greencastle was not so small that he could see to every detail himself, but not so large either that he could afford to leave things—as many of our neighbours do quite happily—to overseers, bookkeepers and other sundry whites. Earnestness such as Anthony's leaves little time or energy for entertainments. Besides, he does not have a wife to organize such things. Mathilde, while convivial with such visitors as find their way here, is well aware (though uncaring) of her status as a soon-come in this environment that fancies itself as anciently planted in the soil of its arguable provenance.

So Anthony's announcement on Saturday evening of a dinner for Tuesday, two nights before he departs for Virginia, was received with some surprise. Not least by Constancia and Lincoln, who would do much of the work for it. Israel and other couriers were sent on mounts to the various invitees in the district, twenty of them. It was to be his opportunity, Anthony said, to say farewell to some friends to whom he had not vouchsafed his plans and to pay a few social and political debts as well. We all understood, without any mention made, that it would also be my coming-out to Bellefields society in my prospective role as Maasa pro tem.

To that point Anthony had been, so far as I could tell, faithful to his word regarding letting people outside the family know about his own plans and my position in Greencastle's future operations. The documents giving me power of attorney had been prepared and properly registered; Lawyer Alberga sent them to the house last night and I have them on the table beside me as I write.

I had also demanded Anthony's agreement that the matter of the slaves left to me in our father's bequest would be put in abeyance until his return and I had myself carried the letter by which he so instructed Lawyer Alberga. But, ever the conniver, Anthony had driven a counter-demand: that he would inform Lincoln of his freedom at a time of his choosing. As it stands, only three days remain for that task and it is not beyond the pale of possibility that Anthony will resile from that commitment, so leaving Mathilde and to a lesser extent myself with the complicated task of rearranging an order that has been fixed in this household from long before any of us now here had arrived.

≋ 31 ≋

Elorine: Into the Bush, Monday, November 14

IS JEHOVAH THAT SEND ADEBEH TO US.

Adisa is sick. From he tell me, Adam and me been arguing about what to do, cause he don't know, that's why he come to me. He swear somebody obeah her, say he see the signs. A dead lizard hanging in a noose in the calabash tree outside their hut. Stones raining down on the roof in the middle day out of a clear sky, and when they run outside to look, not a soul nor a sign of man. And Adisa, out of that clear sky, she just start to have running belly. The only one of them, though they all eat the same food and drink the same water. He worrying that it is maybe something the pickni can catch, cause is the three of them looking after her now that he is here. Same time as he is asking me what he's to do he's thumping himself that he shouldn leave them alone in the bush.

Right away I want to help Adam, and Adisa. She's not somebody that give much of herself to other people—but then I am like that too, so I cyaant hold her up. And she is Adam's babymother. That is all I need to know.

But I would have to go with him to bush. Adam himself don't know what he might find. By the time we get there it will be four whole days since he leave them. And then what? If Adam cyaant leave again, who would bring me back?

We been trying to keep our voice down, but Pappi wake up and come out. He's happy to see his firstborn but the joy soak right back inside his face when he hear why Adam is here. He insist that I must go, of course, but he himself don't have an answer for how I am to come back.

"Cyrus?" he say.

"Jassy can drop the baby any day now," I answer. "Is his baby, he should be here."

"Fergus?"

"You would know."

He shake his head at himself. "Doctor not too hearty. And he have things for Fergus to do why he's not sailing now."

He and Adam looking at each other like they're holding each other up. I'm so custom to Pappi iron and fire out there in the workshop, or full of the spirit at chapel or prayers. Big like one of them guango trees in the courthouse square that hold up the sky. This morning, though, they look like firewood, ready to break, or turn into ashes.

Pappi put his hand on his son shoulder and give it a little squeeze. "Lemme consider it," he say. His voice sound like he have a stone in his throat. He go outside to start his day.

Adam stand up. "Till next time, Ellie," he croak. He sound old like his father, but his face tell me he's ready to go back to his woman and pickni, whether or not I'm coming with him. I want to cry. I can't imagine what is going through his head, but I gather my feet to stannup, to tell him I will come with him and find my own way back. Somehow.

Is then that the Adebeh-one walk through the doorway from the kitchen.

I turn to stone with surprise. Adam have his back to the door, but he notice when my eyes bounce past him. He turn. But the foreigner don't notice Adam at all. He smile at me and say, "Morning, Miss Elorine."

Is a blessing when a man look at you like that. Like he seeing you, not a plate of food to lick his lips over. The light in his eyes touch me like sunlight and I am glad for my blackness, else I would look like tomato with the warming inside that I feel in my skin. I now understand the horse, that first morning he come here with Kekeré Bábà.

Adam tense-up, ready for trouble. Even with his pickni running in and out of the house when he bring them, Adam mostly stay inside the house. Because hardly anybody else come inside but whoever we have working in the kitchen. When I'm expecting a customer I tell him and he gather the pickni-dem and find himself to Pappi room for the duration, all of them quiet as mus-mus. That is how, all these years, he keep themself safe and free. Everybody, even Nayga, could be a messenger of the Devil.

So quick-quick after I smile back at Adebeh I call out to Jassy, "Bring some more coffee, Jass," and move around the table to touch Adam, rub his arm that is tight as a board to tell him is alright.

"Howdy," I say to the newcomer. I smile broader this time, which wasn't hard, but the real purpose was to hold his eyes on my face cause the clothes I had on was barely decent and I don't want him studying me. To tell truth, though, I don't mind. I feel my skin colour some more but it wasn't for shame.

"You come back," I say to him, as if him and me had a arrangement. He was here last week with doctorman's horse for shoes, and we had a nice visit. "Another horse lame?" I ask him.

"Missa Livingstone said I could wait inside. I's sorry for coming so early but Fergus said it's alright to bring the horse now." He almost sound like Jason, so formal. But a nice round voice like cocoa-tea.

And I feel Adam, when he hear a familiar name, ease himself down a little. He was behind me but I could feel it.

Just then Jassy blow past Adebeh like a fresh breeze with a tray of coffee and juice and journey cakes she been frying that was itching my nose. I use the busyness of Jassy to get the stranger to the table and Adam back to his chair. The two of them watching each other like dawg over a bone. I almost break a laugh out loud—each of them is protecting me from the other one!

"Miss Murtella send three breadfruit for you, Miss Elly," Jassy say. "I must roast them?"

I smile to myself. The breadfruit is to soften the earliness of the hour.

"Yes," I tell Jassy, "roast all of them." Adam and me can carry one into the bush. And some of these same journey cakes on the table.

"You not from these parts," I hear Adam say. Is not a question.

"No. I come on the ship with Fergus."

"From where?" He is leaning at the other man.

"All over. You from these parts?" He turn the talk onto Adam gently, taking a long draught from his mug to give them both time.

I feel I had to get into it. "Is my brother, Adam," I say. That get a smile from Adebeh, who put down his mug and hold out his hand across the table, saying his name. Adam hold back awhile before he take the hand.

And my woman-brain get to working! I excuse myself and go into my room. I change into something respectable. I'm not sure if Adam will countenance what I want to do, but I am not about to ask him permission. I go out through the back door to Pappi in the workshop. Fortunately Cyrus is still building up the furnace. Ishmael is talking to a big redman—Missa Roseberry I think is his name. And a black-man that I don't know is waiting nearby. I smile pardon as I ease behind him round to where Pappi can glimpse me. Not to interrupt, just for him to know I am there.

When he finally finish with redman Roseberry, he beg the black-man pardon and turn to me. The sadness settle back into his eyes as he look at me, but I can't pay any mind to that, so I just draw in a big breath and talk it out as quickly and quietly as I can because even the trees have ears.

He crinkle his eyes like when smoke from the foundry fire get into them. A bad sign. I don't like to go down the street with a young man I know, much less clear into the bush with a stranger. He look into me for a reason. And to tell truth I don't know it myself. So I tell him the only thing in my head.

"Is the only thing we can do. We can't send Adam away by himself in daylight." And I find my feet taking me back toward the house. Not vex. More to show that I'm not pushing him. Waiting for Maasa God who send the man to tell Ishmael what to do.

Before I reach the steps he call me back to him.

"Tell the bwoy to come here to me." His face don't tie-up any more.

"Him is not a bwoy," I say right back. "I wouldn't be going into bush with a bwoy."

He frown. Then he laugh. "Please tell the young man I wants to have words with him, if he so incline himself." And he give a little bow. I couldn't help but laugh. I feel light of a sudden.

Still, the harder part is to come.

Inside, Adebeh is sitting by himself. With his eyes he tell me that Adam is in the outhouse. I'm glad for that as I siddown opposite. As I settle into the chair I start to talk it out. Adam's whole story. Everything except the obeah and my own feelings, because I don't know the words for that and is none of his business. I frighten in myself as I'm listening to myself, that he will find me forward and presuming. But I can't consider that either, I'm desperate. I'm watching his eyes as I talk, hurrying myself along.

He's a good listener, I have to say that. Better than Adam or Ishmael, who always ready for the next thing you have to say. Adebeh listen. His eyes get smaller when I talk about Adisa and how I'm afraid cause of the pickni.

"So what you want me to do?" he ask when I finish. He know where I am leading him, but his voice is still calm.

"Come with me," I say. I'm fighting my toes so they stay flat on the ground. From I know myself that is how I show my worry. But I'm determined not to have him think I am begging him a favour, so my voice is flat.

Adam come thumping up the steps from outside and look at me. "The girl could fix some bickle for me to take? I will tell Paps I'm going," and he turn to go back outside.

"Adam." The foreigner call to him, not loud, but enough to stop him.

"What?" I don't know what they was saying to each other when I was outside with Pappi but Adam sound like he ready for a fight.

Adebeh push his chair away from the table. "We will come with you. If you want."

➢ 32 ➣

Jason: Dinner Party, Wednesday, November 16

MAGNUS DOUGLAS WAS ONE OF THE early arrivals, followed by a hugely pregnant wife who should have stayed at home. She looked as though the journey back to Cascade later, not a long one but on rough tracks more suited to a patient horse than an unwieldy carriage, especially in the dark, might accomplish what the pregnancy promised. Magnus left her with Mathilde and Anna, greeted Anthony in passing as he hurried over to me. His face made it clear what was on his mind, and brought back to my own mind the last time we had seen each other, thirteen years before. Had it not been for Saturday's events in Belle-fields I would merely have noted that, always plump, he had grown corpulent. But those events, linked as they are by Victoria—who has returned home with her husband—revived my long-standing dislike for the man, and his for me, which was plain in the jut of his jaw and his headlong progress.

"How dare you!" he began, stopping a yard distant.

"How dare I what?"

"Strike a white man."

"I'll strike any man who strikes me first."

"He was defending his wife."

"Whom I had not attacked. I had merely spoken to her. Respect-fully. As befits a lady. Any lady. Of any colour." As I spoke my gorge was rising, frustrating my voice. But I managed to hold it level—this was not a time for shouting. Not yet.

"Those Frenchy ideas don't belong here," he said, his own voice climbing, and calming me. "Nor do you, Pollard."

Knowing what I did—and he did not, apparently, not yet—I could not suppress a smile.

Which was too much for Douglas.

"You will be sent back whence you come!" His voice soared above the soft clamour around.

"I am whence I come," I replied, holding his eyes.

"Not here," he scoffed, waving his hand to encompass the room and the house. "You's a coloured bastard from the quarters. That is where you belong."

I inclined my head to mockingly acknowledge my status. "An accident of birth, Douglas, but not any more."

From his eyes I knew immediately that my omission of the honorific "Mister" had taken our exchange, our relationship into new, bleak terrain. My comments to Carla were prescient.

With deliberately formal courtesy I half turned away to beckon a slavegirl—"Get Missa Douglas something to drink, Zilla"—and then stepped away, childishly pleased at remembering the girl's name, and for snubbing Douglas.

Every doorway and louvre was open to catch what breeze was to be gleaned from the cooling late afternoon, but the place was still stifling, increasingly so as more guests arrived. I was thankful for the ingenuity and efficiency of Prudence and her daughter Miranda who had, in two days, fitted me up with new clothes that allowed my fretted skin to breathe.

I glimpsed Miranda in the crowd of slaves on the fringe of the gathering—Lincoln had brought almost all hands on deck for the occasion—and felt a flash of embarrassment for my dream of a few nights ago, and my evanescent recollection of her hands on my legs, measuring the trouser seams.

I was brought back to myself by a glimpse of the overseer Wyckham arriving. In England it is inconceivable that an overseer would grace a proprietor's table with family and guests. An exception might have been made for M. Jean-Claude Richard, overseer at Flambouyant, the coffee planting "up so", as everyone refers to it, a white refugee from the eruptions in what is now Hayti.

But here, as this quickly reminded, the commonality of skin was sufficient to elevate the lowest to the level of any other member of the white caste. Outside the vast domain of blackness and its variants, whiteness was, socially, something of a republic. Coming so recently from England, where social class determined all other protocols, from invitation lists to the way a teacup is lifted, the democratic mixture around the table was very welcome—but for Wyckham.

He has been overseer since the beginning of the year, Anthony says, which is a lengthy tenure for Greencastle. Squire in his more active days kept as few whites as he could on the estate, preferring to pay the deficiency tax than to wrangle with the myriad of complications that such folk often cause. Besides, he didn't have to pay those slaves who did the skilled jobs and much of the supervision, and who didn't drink as much rum as the whites. Squire having been abed since Christmas, however, Anthony has found it necessary to employ assistance; there is also a bookkeeper about, Simpson, little more than a lad.

It was a fraught evening in many ways, not all of them to do with Douglas, or Wyckham. But it also exemplified the changes that have taken place in the years I've been away from Greencastle. I cannot remember an occasion in Squire's time when brown faces, my own excepting, were entertained as guests here. Occasional Jews—Alberga prominent among them—but no coloureds. The reasons for the change are several, but the prime one not difficult to grasp.

Income from sugar is declining. Owners who live in England, a significant portion of the whole, have no incentive. Their properties are in the hands of local managers in *locum tenens*. Of late years, the preponderance of these attorneys, so called (for very few are of the law) are men of colour. Through diligence, connivance and luck, some of them are among the wealthiest in the island of any colour.

Both Arthur Hollyoak and Joel Mayerlink are married, and to women lighter complexioned than themselves. "Dem could muster," as Anna put it to me. And M. Richard has a properly churched coloured wife—also absent. The white women will not sit at table with them, it seems. Not even Mathilde, who otherwise plays the democrat convincingly.

Indeed some of the liveliest conversations at table danced, turbulently at times, around skin colour. Over the weekend an unmarried young woman had given birth to a baby who was indubitably the offshoot of a man of colour, possibly a slave on her father's estate. As Anna had explained it to me earlier, the disapproval expressed once her pregnancy became obvious was mild, given that the occurrence itself was not unknown. But what eventuated was very far outside the realm of even possibility. In otherwise normal circumstances, her parents would not have been short of likely suspects: the stud sons of their fellow planters, the soldiers from Fort George and sailors from His Majesty's passing ships—even, at the very lowest rung of desirability, an overseer or bookkeeper. The usual expediency, a hasty, and, if need be, forced marriage, would have been resorted to and the pond of convention thus left unrippled. Except that the young lady refused to name the culprit.

Nor—another common resort—had they been able to send her to England to construct a new life for herself because, Anna says, the pregnancy was rife with illness from the beginning, making travel impossible. Even without those cloaks to respectability, the clucking of hen's tongues would soon have stilled in due course—had the baby been white, as expected. The little brown pickni made such recourse impossible, however, merely by its skin, thereby opening the floodgates of heaven's disapproval on its mother and, by extension of negligence, her parents.

Perhaps inevitably, it was Magnus's wife—so bountifully pregnant she sat a foot away from table but yet managed a steady transfer of food to her mouth—who led the charge into a silence in the conversation.

"Lickle bitch, her poopa shoulda lock her up." Her husband spluttered as if poked, and food flew from his mouth. "I would drive her like cow from one end of George Street to the other."

Indeed the men—the white men, that is—were even more indignant than their womenfolk, their comments the more ferocious in condemnation. They wouldn't stoop to say it, but they felt their manhood betrayed, and their deepest sexual dread, that their black animal chattels hold a greater desirability in the eyes of their sainted women, exposed like bones on a beach.

I could not but be aware of the large number of dark bodies, accustomed to invisibility, flitting silently around and about with food and drink, plates and cloths, Greencastle's augmented by those brought by some guests. Some of these, making use of the subterranean network that crosses estate and tribal boundaries, would already know the identity of the offending progenitor.

The Devil in me enjoyed the discomfort that was like a stiff breeze blowing around the table. Constancia's excellent food grew cold as the whites tumbled over each other like unruly children to give word to their sense of personal assault. M. Richard, to be fair, was not among them; for whatever reason he kept a cool distance, merely allowing that things like that had happened in St. Domingue. But Magnus Douglas and Ralston Penninger, proprietor of a large estate in the Blue River valley and a long-time member of the Assembly in Spanish Town, seemed to joust over insults to the young woman, of which *whore* and *slag* were among the mildest.

I remember Penninger a more robust figure from Squire's days; he's now bent over and semi-blind, but his tongue is not as feeble as the rest of him. Nor his hands. Zilla, a plain sturdy girl with lively eyes, bent over from behind to offer him a platter of chicken and suddenly wobbled, almost depositing it on the table. I saw Penninger's shoulder rising and falling as the girl found her balance and moved away. Blatant and casual, he'd goosed her, as he might have stroked a pet dog.

To this point Anna, the youngest person at table and the recipient of cautionary glances—the fallen young woman is about her age—had kept her peace. Then, into a moment of silence she opined, "Maybe she just did want a baby."

That was a flint applied to a fire that had almost run its course. It flared again with greater ferocity. Even Mathilde, whose opprobrium of the errant girl had been fairly mild, was re-energized, now that her own daughter had raised the most dreaded spectre of all.

"She vas raped," Mathilde said, with uncharacteristic primness in the set of her mouth.

To which there were grunts of agreement from some of the men. Anthony, charged as he was by the prospect of his new adventures and the soul of wit and jollity so far, gave his sister a poisonous look.

The vigour of engagement must have tired them, and conversation afterwards was desultory. Compliments on the food were paid to Mathilde and Anthony, as if they themselves had prepared the dishes. Then, as Mathilde made to lead the five ladies out to the piazza, Anthony gestured her back into her seat, tapped his glass and stood. It was the moment I'd been dreading. But he carried it gracefully enough.

"Friends," he began, looking around. "To speak as our reverend pastor Mr. Ogilvie, who unfortunately could not join us, would have it . . . 'a little while and you shall see me, and then again a little while and you shall not see me'."

Anthony's declamations, such few as I can remember, did not usually run to flights of fancy, much less Biblical allusions. My first thought was that he was drunk. But there was no other sign: his voice was crisp, his face no more flushed than after a day in the sun, and his arm as he held his glass at half-mast was steady. "For I goeth to Virginia with the goodly captain on the morning tide after tomorrow's," he announced, motioning toward Captain Bosworth down the table.

In the murmuring pause that followed I looked around the table to see what the effect would be, and on whom. Only one person apart from the Pollards received the news without affect: Magnus Douglas. Anthony must've told him of his own plans. I wondered at the safety of my own secret.

"And then again a little while," Anthony resumed with an almost boyish grin, "and I shall be restored to you." There was laughter mixed with renewed conjecture, but he didn't pause. "And while I am away my living and my fortune, such as it is, will be in the capable hands . . . at least I trust that they are capable . . . of . . ."—and here he did pause for dramatic effect, long enough to command silence— ". . . my brother Jason."

Up to that point everyone had been looking at Anthony, no one at me. Magnus Douglas's head whipped around from across the table and his mouth fell open. Our eyes touched. He looked away quickly and closed his lips. I noted also a grunt from further down the table on my side: Wyckham.

Other eyes eventually found me; I probably blushed but can only remember feeling exposed as on a hillside. Apart from M. Richard, who from his seat beside Anna raised his glass at me, I sensed that most of the others shared Douglas's surprise at my appointment. His was personal, I think. Aside from his historical dislike of me, so recently revived, he may have expected his friend to give over Greencastle into his keeping. But the others' wonder was likely based on the presence at the table of two other people who, in the normal course of events, would have been prime candidates for Anthony's trust.

Arthur Hollyoak, by the report of Anthony earlier today, is one of the most prosperous free coloureds, as we are called. The son, it is variously said, of a sea captain or a boatswain, a visiting Earl or a transported bankrupt, he was sponsored to Wolmer's School in Kingston and then became clerk in a law firm there, from which he spread his skills and services, building his fortune as he went. He originally settled in Bellefields for the convenience of some attorney-ships. He has since become outright proprietor of two estates in the next parish, where he now himself employs attorneys. Rather small, unremarkable in presentation, he was, except for a few of the slaves serving us, the darkest man in the gathering last night. He was also likely the richest, including Magnus Douglas and Penninger.

Joel Meyerlink represents another arm of coloured wealth, responsible for two estates in the Blue River valley as well as owning shipping vessels that ply the coastal trade and several commercial properties, in Bellefields and elsewhere. His sister owns the milliner's shop Anna and I had visited on Saturday.

Despite their riches and background, these men and those of their ilk have limited influence in the affairs of the island. The colour of their skin places them outside the sphere of power occupied by men who are not only their inferiors in accomplishment but are also, in many cases, their debtors.

Both men were reserved in their demeanour throughout the evening. As indeed, in retrospect, was I. It's in our blood, the natural order of things, for a brown man to be docile in the company of whites, especially when outnumbered.

After the toasts (one for the King; one for Anthony's safe passage and return; and, led by M. Richard and subscribed to less enthusiastically, one for my own success in the interval) Mathilde led the women out to the enclosed part of the piazza for their secluded conversation. There was now, with Anthony's double announcement, added grist for that mill.

The men had hardly resumed their seats when Douglas lowered his lance.

"That is, Anthony," he said, "if there is any fortune for you to return to."

Every eye, mine included, was upon him, as he'd intended with his affected casualness.

Anthony scowled and asked, crossly, his friend's meaning.

"Well," Douglas continued as if the thought were hardly worth the effort of expression, "they might all be gone into the hills around us clutching their pieces of free paper." His gaze wandered around the table as he spoke but ended locked onto me. "Signed by your brother."

"And why would he do that?" Anthony turned in his chair to look more directly at his friend.

Douglas smiled with feigned insouciance. "Your brother fancies himself an abolitionist. He consorts with them in England, he's married into Quakers. He'd be a hero when he returns there, gathered into the bosom of the saints of Westminster and Clapham. He could start a newspaper, like that nigger-loving *Garrison* in Boston. The *Jamaican Liberator.* Tender tales of Christianized nigger families at worship, stirring odes to black rebels drinking the blood of their master's wives and children. Why not?"

He looked around the table for supportive comment. I quenched my burning impulse to respond, hearing Carla's gentle chastening in my ears. But I held his eyes, marbles in twin pools of rum, which tried to keep their scorn bright but could not, and eventually looked away.

Silence settled and stretched itself like a cat along the table. I sensed that in this gathering, except by the host, Douglas was not particularly liked. Feared, perhaps—he's a magistrate, and on the vestry— but not regarded fondly as a man.

"Will you give away your brother's niggers, Mr. Pollard?" The voice quietly rumbling at me was Penninger's.

"They're not mine to give away," I replied. "And I will not have to."

"Why not?" the old man asked.

I was remembering his fondling of Zilla, and her flaring eyes, as I said, "They'll take their freedom for themselves."

"Not here they won't." That was Wyckham, thankfully seated on the same side of the table, so I did not have to look at him.

The overseer's bluster was swept away in an eruption of outrage over my comment. The loudest voices were white but the greater discomfort belonged to Hollyoak and Meyerlink.

Coloureds—this discerned from experience, and from within—occupy a fretful place in this little world: struggling to maintain and improve ourselves while despised and suspected by whites *and* blacks of being agents of the other. My two tablemates have much to lose materially in an upheaval of freedom—they're owners themselves.

The "fucking missionaries" were boiled in coconut oil several times over. So were the "fucking bastards" at Westminster for encouraging both the slaves and the missionaries in their notion of a misconceived "freedom."

"The Reformers," Penninger intoned, all but spitting, "want to destroy our whole basis of government. They want everybody with a lickle piece of land to vote in the Parliament. And the next step, if that happens, is to free the slaves. You abolitionists stir-up bad-minded people."

"The stupid niggers think it happen already," said Douglas, sweating. His eyes found mine. "Your friends," he said.

"I know no missionaries here, Douglas," I replied, noting him flinch again at my presumption. "And I only read about the people in the Commons; they're not friends of mine. People believe all sorts of strange things, I find."

I held his eyes as I said that. Once again, Carla's voice within stilled my inclination to argue, and I heeded it.

"King William," Penninger began, diverting me from Magnus,

"tell them already that they's not free. He tell them that he don't send out no orders for them to be free. It was in the papers."

In England too. It was a piece of political sleight of hand by the government to cosset the West India lobby in the Commons and Lords.

"I can't understand," Penninger continued, shaking his head, "what that fool-governor Belmore is waiting for to proclaim it here."

It wouldn't make any difference here either, I was thinking to myself. The slaves already know of the King's proclamation—they've read it in a local paper or heard it discussed at table by their Maasas. But those who believe they're free are, in a certain way, already free.

I became aware of a rising tide of port and rum and brandy in the room as a carafe of something dark appeared over my shoulder. I placed my hand over my glass; the evening was not one for untidy thoughts or heavy tongues.

"But you think the niggers should be free," Penninger came back, leaning forward like a dog about to pounce.

"Yes," I replied. "I think they should be. And they will be."

From across the table Douglas gave a theatrical sigh. "What can a savage know of freedom? Eh, Lincoln?" He half turned his head and shouted into the dimness behind.

"Nothing, Maasa Douglas," came Lincoln's prompt response. I looked sternly at Anthony, who understood my question and shook his head.

"What about you, Ragabag?" Douglas turned his head to the other side. "You think you free?"

"No, Maasa," came back the equally quick reply from a tall freckled brown slave, liveried, who hovered behind Magnus's wife.

And I thought to myself: idiot! Surrounded all his life by people more intelligent than himself, and learning nothing from them.

"Dem is pickni, Missa Jason," said Penninger, as if appealing to me. "Dem would dead without Backra to feed dem and look after dem, dem so stupid."

His voice sounded tender. But I could restrain myself no longer. "So. Why do you let savage stupid pickni raise your own pickni?" My voice was scathing, uncaring of consequence. "And cook your food, and look after you when you are sick. You should employ civilized adult people for that."

Neither Douglas nor Penninger could hold his gaze steady in the flame of my anger.

"Might I ask, Mr. Pollard, whether you'll be staying here among us? After Mr. Pollard returns." Arthur Hollyoak's tone was teasing, but serious too, and intended for more than soothing feathers. "You would be handy in Spanish Town."

I understood his meaning immediately, and could not help but smile as I replied that I'd seen enough of politics, both here and there, to stay well clear of it. Besides, I have no property that would qualify me even to vote. I avoided a full answer to his question since I had not told Anthony or anyone else of my resolve to leave once he returns.

As I settled into a self-willed silence, I longed for the quiet reasonableness of the Livingstone house. The law that Elorine's father warned me about is the backdrop for what was being said. And not said. The vituperative disapproval of the planters on both sides of the sea had been given a good airing, not least in the House of Lords, where efforts to even ameliorate slave conditions have met a turgid grave. But with no thought at the time about my returning to Jamaica, a law according free persons of colour and Jews legal equality with whites was peripheral to my life and I'd paid it little mind. At last night's table, however, it was very current business.

"There been change enough," Penninger growled. "You people have two member in the Assembly a'ready! What more you want?" The trampling of proper English underlined the intent of his remark.

The silence into which it fell had a deep bottom.

"If you do not dig it out from the root now," said M. Richard, who'd added very little to that point, "it will overgrow you. Like ze bush."

His voice had sufficient passion, albeit contained, to command attention. St. Domingue's revolution, which created the Haytian republic, is a sore that has not healed in near thirty years. I could not help but remember Elorine's father's prognosis: Slavery will abolish itself.

I was framing a clarifying question in my mind when Mathilde brought the women back inside. The conversation resolved itself once more into generalities and gossip. Eventually, after an extended leave-taking as multiple carriages and slaves and horses were marshalled, the evening ended with good wishes all around—some even flung in my direction, though not by Douglas. Meyerlink and Hollyoak assured me of their concern for my well being and success, and offered their availability for advice at my pleasure, for which I thanked them.

The house quieted as Lincoln directed his minions in clearing the table and sideboards. Anna, and then Mathilde, found their weary way to bed. I loitered with intent, as the law puts it: that of pressing Anthony to speak to Lincoln. My demeanour must have conveyed my purpose to him because in due course he summoned Lincoln away from his duties and they walked outside into the piazza.

I did not remain behind to see or hear the outcome, being very weary myself. In part, at least, I was removing myself from the torches of the slaves' eyes. They are now, as I write this morning, assessing their individual fortunes under a dispensation that changed radically during last evening. And I am, for all of them except Lincoln and Constancia, a wholly unknown quantity.

Nothing like this, even Squire's death, has happened in their lives before last night. Nor in mine.

⇒ 33 ⇐

Narrative: Stories, Wednesday, November 16

THAT FIRST NIGHT IN THE BUSH, Elorine hears many stories.

They are perched in the earhole of a mountain that Adam has brought them to after most of a day wandering lost in the wilderness like the tribe of Judah. Bellefields is several worlds away, like one of the stars in the sky.

They leave West Street separately, Elorine and Adebeh going first to Dr. Fenwell to buy medicine, bringing two live chickens in payment for Murtella to cook for him. And for Adebeh to assure Fergus, first regarding Elorine's safety, then that he'll be returning in time for the *Eagle*'s departure. Adam's way out of town, in the unchosen and dangerous situation of daylight, was a mystery she didn't enquire about. But before leaving West Street he'd told them how to locate a tree, a giant guango that stands out on the brow of a hill like a finger. That was to be their signpost. He'd meet them there.

And he does. Through the day's trekking through the bush—hell for her, a cheerful adventure for her whistling escort—Elorine senses Adam's proximity. The sound of Patoo, owl. Who sleeps in the daytime, of course, so his soft call coming from different directions cannot be a real owl.

And then he is there, sitting against the trunk of the hoary old tree as they climb up the slope to it.

He leads them, Elorine between the men, up the hillside, which soon becomes a precipice that they're edging along, back scraping stone, feet trembling on the lip of disaster. Later—the first story—Adam tells them he'd found it on the third night he'd walked away from Cascade while escaping a pursuing Maroon who'd have taken him back to Cascade for the reward. Ducking into the cave, Adam watched the man hurry by and then heard his screams as he made a misstep and plunged onto the trees and rocks below.

Elorine knows little about her brother's life. His rare visits are spent talking about her nephews and niece. Perhaps he tells his father things like this, out in the workshop where he spends time when there aren't customers, but if so Ishmael keeps these stories to himself.

Adam has a fish that he stole in Bellefields on his way out. She cleans the fish at the opening of the cave, using Adebeh's knife to scrape the scales and guts into the darkness and washing the flesh in the sudden downpour of rain that is like a waterfall at its mouth. Behind her Adebeh starts a fire with the makings that Adam travels with. He does it expertly, Elorine notes.

Elorine hears the men behind her talking, their words indistinct in the roaring rain, the voices calm and conversational. This morning's tension between them is washed away. She feels content. She's fearful about tomorrow, as she knows Adam is, but for the moment all is in Jehovah's hands, and He seems at ease.

A cooking spot is already there in the cave, with wooden skewers and blackened stones for resting pots. This is Adam's cave that he uses on his way to and from West Street. He says he's never seen sign of anyone else coming here between his visits, and before the meal gives thanks to Eshu and the dead Maroon for leading him here.

Elorine skewers the fish and places it over the flames; the bread-fruit from Jassy's kitchen is wrapped in plantain leaves at the edge of the fire to warm. The fire and a torch-bottle that Adam keeps here provide a dancing light. They stare into the fire as if cooking the food with their eyes. If this were town, Elorine thinks, there would be rum. But if this were town Adam wouldn't be here and it wouldn't be as agreeable as it is.

"What bring you here?" Adam looks up at Adebeh. "Other than the ship." He smiles—the stranger has answered this already.

Adebeh smiles too, accepting the gentle rebuke, and looks at Elorine. "I looking for my sister," he says simply.

"Here?"

"Not in this place," as he looks around their little space. "But she is somewhere in this island."

"How . . .?" Elorine's eyes flick between Adebeh and the fish. "You . . ."

"I's Yenkunkun," he says, looking first at her and then Adam.

Elorine keeps her eyes on the fire. "What is . . .?"

"Maroon," says Adam.

Not noticing her brother, Elorine asks, "Maroon? In . . .?"

Adebeh smiles and nods. "I born and grow there, but I is Maroon."

Just in time she lifts the fish above a sudden eruption of flames. "How?"

Adam, his face opening in understanding, says, "Preston?"

The men smile at each other in a new way, eyes flickering from within memory.

"No," Adebeh says, "Boydville. But I know Preston. Well. You too?"

Elorine feels her head spinning. The men's words pop in the air around her like fat in Jassy's skillet. Adam is suddenly a bigger stranger than the foreigner.

"Yes." Adam is grinning at Adebeh, the stranger who is making more sense.

Elorine concentrates on playing the sizzling fish in the flames. Her brother's words create a silence in her head filled with peculiar shapes that shift in unruly winds. She holds tight to the skewered fish. It's the truest thing in the little cave perched on the edge of a mountainside in the middle of a bush full of mystery and revelation. Adam in Scotia! A place she only knows about because Kekeré Bábà mentions it in stories of his travels. If the seven angels of the Book of Revelation had appeared in this smoky little space she could not have been more astonished.

"How?" Adebeh asks. Perhaps the most confusing thing for Elorine is that Adebeh is not surprised at Adam's disclosure, as if he is always meeting people, even in Jamaica, who'd been to Scotia.

"I had to leave here to save my life," Adam says calmly. "Then I had to leave there to save my life." He laughs at the memory, Adebeh joining with a smile. Elorine is ignored.

"Food ready," she says, sharp as the edge of the plantain leaves they'll eat off.

And while eating—after the men have thrown pieces into the fire for the ancestors—the men share their stories, Elorine thirsty and silent. Later, as she's dozing into sleep, their words come to be one story: of a world outside her life as vast as the night sky. The men have been there, to distant stars named Boydville and Preston and Halifax and Groningen Street, while this is the furthest Elorine has ever been from Bellefields.

In the story Maroons, Yenkunkun, are everywhere, slave hunters and protectors, exiles and settlers, here and in that distant star-place of Scotia. As well as the one who chased him to this cave, Adam saved the life of another the next day from a rampaging wild pig, then had to flee from yet another who pursued him across the island to the far coast. Where a ship took him to Scotia across distances he never imagined. At the end of that voyage he'd found another form of bondage, a lot of blackpeople and among them Maroons. Just a few. And not Adebeh, though he was there, a bwoy then, and not in Halifax or Preston, not yet.

But as they talk and talk and grow easier with each other, they find a person they know in common. George Samuels, an old Trelawny who, like Adebeh's parents and a few other Trelawnys, had stayed behind when the tribe went on to Africa. He'd saved Adam's life. And Adebeh had rented a room from him in the place called Halifax. Before meeting Kekeré Bábà and coming here on the ship.

Adebeh tells his story, of the Trelawny Maroons provoked into war with the British, deceived into surrender and then betrayed by the governor into exile in Scotia and then, after protests and trouble-making there, sent to Sierra Leone to fight down other blackpeople on behalf of the whites. But a few didn't go. Like Adebeh's people. Like George Samuels.

"They never explain why they don't go," he says, relaxing his tongue a little, "and I don't ask them. But I figure is because Scotia is closer to Jamaica than Africa." A dozen questions are buzzing in Elorine's head, but she waits. "The family is not complete," Adebeh says. "Sister is still here." Adebeh's voice thickens, pushing out the words. Her irritation at him is seeping away. "They have three pickni in Scotia. Me, Precious and Eddie. The other wife, Fushabah and her pickni-dem, they gone to Africa. They is kin too, but only through Da. We don't talk much about them."

Elorine has heard that the Maroon men have more than one wife, living together in the same village. She thanks Maasa Jesus she's not Maroon.

"Sister here is a full sister," Adebeh concludes, pausing to drink from his gourd of rainwater.

"You know where she is?"

That is the question Elorine wants to ask, but Adam speaks first.

Looking down into the flames Adebeh shakes his head. "She could be anywhere." His voice is a whisper, scratching the air of the whole island.

"Henry cyan find her," Adam says.

Elorine finds her voice. "Who is Henry?"

"Yenkunkun. I save his life, he save mine. We is bredda." Adam looks from one to the other smiling, pleased with himself. "He cyan find anybody. I will send fe Henry. He will find you sister."

He is chattering like a child and Elorine feels for him: the thought of his friend Henry is a crumb of hope that he can give to this stranger who is going with him into his own darkness. It's a sort of exchange, and Adebeh lifts his shoulders .

In the comfort that settles around them, Elorine asks her question. "How come you sister is here?"

A smile from Adebeh looking into the coals, giving Elorine a glimpse of what he looked like as a bwoy. He takes a deep breath, ageing from it. "They give her to somebody."

Elorine knows stories of mothers—not all of them out of their heads—who poison or smother their baby to save it from slavery. On estates and in town the people who raise children are not always their born parents. Sometimes the minders, especially slaves, are compelled to do it. But even on estates, where every extra mouth to feed means less of the little there is for you, there are other reasons—shipmates, aunties or uncles, half-sisters or half-brothers. She waits for Adebeh to say more.

"Somebody?" asks Adam. "Who?"

Adebeh shrugs, eyes still on the fading fire, and smiles at what he knows is silly. "She name One-Eye Sarah. That's what Mam tell me." He's spoken of Mam to Elorine as they wrestled their way through the bush. Sister is the real reason he's here.

"Where?" Elorine hears herself asking.

"A place call St. Ann's Bay," he answers. "They have a map, don't ask me where they get it from in Scotia. Maybe Mam bring it from here; she have some learning and can read. Sometimes she teach us from the map. Falmouth. Accompong. Dromilly. Maria Bueno. Port Royal." He smiles at Elorine like he's repeating homework.

Adam's laugh cracks the silence. "Bueno is where I get the ship that take me to Scotia. Is a few days to walk from here."

Adebeh acknowledges that fact and tells his story to the glowing fire, his soft words clear now that the rain has stopped.

The duped Maroons were being marched from Montego Bay to Kingston. "We thought they was taking us back to Trelawny Town," Da told, and his son repeats. "But once they take us pass Falmouth and don't turn up into the hills, we know we going into big trouble. Mam was his first wife, the girl their first together who survived. There was, in the Yenkunkun way, another wife, younger, and two children."

"I learn this later," Adebeh says with a shy smile at Elorine. "They gone to Sierra Leone before I am born." Another place for her to find space for in her crowded head. "The march was along the seacoast, with the tempting hills close by, sometimes coming almost down to the water. Some Trelawnys escaped. Mam and the baby got away but Da's second wife alerted the soldiers. She got beaten, her wrist broken protecting the baby. Is still crooked," Adebeh says.

"So Da and Mam decided. The baby would stay here, a root planted to grow in freedom."

On the edge of the soldiers' encampment in St. Ann's Bay a strange young woman with an eyepatch appeared the second morning, selling food and ornaments even the Yenkunkun hadn't seen before. She seemed to live within the roots, or even in the trunk, of a huge cotton tree full of duppies. The soldiers couldn't manage to tumble her, as many wanted: she defied them with a piercing look from her one blue eye (though her skin was very dark) and silence. They became afraid of her, tried to drive her away. One of them fired a pistol at her. The Maroons who saw it swore afterwards that her hand flashed and she caught the bullet. She put it in her mouth and chewed it like plantain, they said, and then spat it out with a grin at the trembling soldier.

The camp followers—prostitutes and higglers from nearby settlements who changed with the progress of the march—were terrified of her too. Obeahwoman.

On the third evening there, a Sunday, Mam said, Da took the sleeping child through the darkness and returned alone. "I promise her I will come back for her. I cut me hand-middle and swear to Olodumare. One day." That was how Da always ended the story.

"He come back?" Adam wanted to know, like the stranger's tale is a bedtime story.

"No," says Adebeh. "He still in Scotia. I come back."

≋ 34 ≋

Elorine: Too Late, Wednesday, November 16

JEHOVAH GIVETH AND HE TAKETH AWAY. Blessed be His Glorious Name from everlasting to everlasting. Amen.

For all Adam rush us through the bush yesterday morning, with his big knife swishing left and right through everything like it is no more than licorice stick, we reach too late. He give his Patoo call when we get near, and Baby Selina come running between the trees. Her little face is painted with dirty tears, dust and salt drying. When she see her father she just stop and wait for him, eyes like seeds, until he gather her up onto his chest. I glimpse a little smile like a hummingbird, and then the sadness swallow it.

Adisa couldn't wait any longer, Selina explain to us as Adam put her down and she lead him to the hut. She travel quietly last night. The other two pickni is sitting inside the hut when we reach, holding on to each other. They have a piece of bush brushing flies off their mother. More bush is burning in three spots in the hut. She don't start to ripen yet, but whatever kill her run through her belly and soak into the cloths she's lying on. You can smell it from you reach into the little yard. The hut smell like a outhouse. Calabash with water is all around Adisa's body, with lime and sour orange cut up into them, and petals and berries, to give a little freshness to the air inside. That and the smoky bush help, I suppose.

She is lying on her back like she is sleeping, and is later we learn that the three pickni take off her dead clothes themselves, wipe her down with lime and water, and put on something clean on their mother so she will go decent into her next life. They not crying, but all their faces marked with tracks from earlier. They don't look like they change their clothes for days.

Adam, he start to cry. He stand up there like a tree holding up the hut, looking down at Adisa, his cutlass like a long-long finger pointing at the ground, pointing deep into his misery. His shoulders just shake like the ground under is shaking him. I ease up beside and hold him round his waist. I'm a sapling beside him but I feel him settle against me a little. The children too, they get up from the ground, serious as parson, and hug up his legs. I feel some fingers like caterpillar wriggling on my legs. The Adebeh-one stand still behind us, barely breathing. He is not family but he was hoping, just like Adam and myself. I cyan feel his sorrow in the hut, and find comfort in his presence. He may not be family, but the two days trekking through the bush make a bond.

Adam loose himself and gather his pickni like him harvesting them with his arms. "You do good," he say into their heads, voice burbling like water over river stones. And that start them crying, like they was waiting for him to come before they could start their own grieving.

I look around for Adebeh, and he is gone. Outside, he is sitting in a lignum vitae tree that is on the edge of Adam's clearing, a branch like a bench low to the ground that everybody must be sit on, it's so smooth. He have a hoe with him. He watch me walking toward him but I don't mind that. I find myself making a little joke. "You going to dig ground?" A smile flitter across his mouth. He nod his head toward the hut behind me. I understand: he's ready to dig Adisa's grave because Adam can't. The tree-bench is broad enough so I sit on it, not too close. Bush cyan be a noisy place but right then is like the birds and insects know the sadness and they're keeping vigil with us. I only hear the little stream we cross over to get here like it is whispering prayers for Adisa.

Adam and the pickni come out, still holding on to each other. Everybody's face draw down. Then Selina let go of her brothers and walk past us into the bush. Is only a few months, but she look so much older than the last time she's in town. Poor ting. She have to be mooma for the other two now. Thomas run after her.

"Where they going?" I ask Adam.

"To tell people."

I don't wonder at what he mean. All the time we was making our way here, I had in mind to find Adam's little hut all by itself in the middle of nowhere. But from we come down off the mountain this morning, I start to notice little huts here and there, and pieces of ground growing food, even a few people that Adam hail and wave to as we pass by. I know that Adam and Adisa have a ground for their provisions, he tell me that, and when he come to Bellefields he usually bring some yam or callalloo. Adisa even plant a flowers garden on the slope down from the hut to the river. You would have to say that Adam and his family is part of a settlement, right out here in the bush. And nobody don't even know.

Backra probably looking for most of these people, like Maasa Douglas was looking for Adam for a while, and her Maasa was looking for Adisa.

Funny when you think about it—Selina and the other pickni is slaves, cause they born from slaves. That is what the law say. But they don't belong to anybody, they don't have no Maasa that can claim them. You have to wonder what *slave* and *free* really mean, and who is the real Maasa of who.

While I'm considering these things I notice that Adam get another hoe from inside, and him and Adebeh go a little way down the bankside, near to where Adisa plant her flowers.

Little Jabez make to follow his father but I call him back. Time enough for him to know why they're digging the hole. When he is at West Street he's always playing with a wooden ball his grandfather carve for Thomas, so I find a orange and we play catch, and I soon have him laughing, cause in spite of his twist-foot he's a happy pickni.

The two of them digging in a rhythm, bum-bum, bum-bum . . . bum-bum, bum-bum.

Like a drum. But it sound like it's coming from inside the ground. Like somebody or something is trying to get out! I feel a chill, of a sudden. They say that is when somebody step over your grave. But that spot is not a grave yet, and not mine.

We bury her in the cool of the day. A woman, Syl, who come out of the bush with Selina and Thomas before the others, bring a big cloth, yellow and blue and green, and she and me carry water from the river and wash Adisa again, and wrap her in it. The men is not to touch her, so while we doing it Adam and the men make a palette with branches and twine. Syl and me and two other women bring her outside. Poor thing, she light like a pickni. A big woman she was, but maybe her spirit was the weight of her.

We lay her down beside the grave. Pointing toward Africa, Adebeh tell me, but who's to know? Is the same way we dig our graves in Scotia, he say, pointing in the same direction.

Adisa was a Guinea woman, so that make sense.

Is a dozen or so people standing around the yard, plus a few pickni who find themselves naturally to stand with Selina and Thomas and Jabez, next to Adam. Poor Adam barely notice them, his eyes staring down into the space they just dig. Is like he don't see the two women who jump down into it as Syl and me take the whole burden of Adisa—not very much—and hand it down, then help them back out.

A drum start. A old man I get to know later as Kente, sitting a little apart on the other side of the clearing. He's looking up into the trees around us, looking to where Adisa has gone, beating her there with a quiet drumming that make you know it won't stop for now. And then things just appear in hands, and people walk over to put them on Adisa's belly. Yam, and plantain, and other provisions, janga from the river, and a half a chicken, cook already. That is so she won't be hungry on the journey, for is a far way she have to go.

Syl start a singing, and I lift my eyes to see that Adebeh is smiling to himself as he is watching the people putting things down for Adisa. Is a smile of understanding—maybe they do that in his country also. It happen when we bury people from Mount Zion. The more proper Baptist missionaries don't allow it, they call it heathen and ungodly, but Ishmael, even though he don't too follow the old ways any more, let it pass. Jehovah don't strike anybody down dead for that. Maasa God say there is many rooms in his mansion, enough for Nayga and whiteman, heathen and Christian.

Soon the other women join in, and then a few men, then a shak-shak, and soon everybody, even the pickni, even Adam, is swaying and moving their feet, circling around Adisa. Is not a dance, really.

Still, is a celebration. She gone from us, but the place she's gone to is a better one than here could ever be for her—and for us. We know that in our blood. The pickni-dem born knowing.

And the missionaries—Baptist, Moravian, all of them—don't like this kinda singing neither. They don't understand so they don't approve. Fe-dem funerals is mostly about the living, who is wondering how to manage without that wife or that friend or that pickni. It is a selfish grieving. But we is glad for the body who's gone over, even though we is left behind. Their happiness is more important than our own.

Jason: Taking the Reins, Friday, November 18

ONCE BACK AT GREENCASTLE FROM SEEING Anthony onto the boat I went out to the fields directly. I turned aside the assumption by Israel that now that I am Maasa I'd take Anthony's horse Charlie, a magnificent black; I retained Cherry, a small but sturdy roan aptly named in colour and temperament.

I set out with a feeling of authority and power that was alcoholic, like a draught of good old rum. At the time I did not recognize it for what it was, a base set of feelings no different to those of the men around the dinner table two nights before, and founded on baser metal. I felt obscenely optimistic, confident of success in my venture to change Greencastle while pleasing the shade of my father and remaining true to the principles I had espoused and argued from these many years. Alcoholic indeed: drunk with power. The slaves that I encountered in those first minutes on my own seemed, in my own delusional vision, a transported tribe of Rousseau's noble savages given into my keeping for their own improvement.

But that air of spacious benevolence did not last—it couldn't. Waiting at the beginning of the fields was Wyckham, the overseer. Cherry slowed, perhaps in answer to an unconscious restraint on my part, and brought me to a halt a few yards from him. I'd given him little thought since the dinner, but he'd obviously given me more. His flat eyes measured me, as they had since I had left the house, and it was a second or two before his lips thinned in a smile that was almost a rictus.

"Maasa get off safe?" On my assurance that he had Wyckham,

who had not previously addressed me by name, continued somewhat formally, "I'd thought, Mr. Pollard, that I could show you how things are progressing at the moment."

My immediate impulse was to reject his invitation, which had no warmth nor interest in it. But I was spared having to answer by something or someone rushing toward us from over Wyckham's shoulder, so to speak. It was the bwoy Achilles, whom I'd encountered before and not forgotten. He ignored the overseer and came straight to me, tugging at my stirrup.

"Maasa!" he cried out, gasping for new breath. I waited, Cherry dancing in place. Then he called out imperiously, "Come," and bolted in the direction from which he had just arrived. I had no difficulty in running him down and blocking his progress with the horse's intimidating bulk.

"What is wrong?" I asked him, as calmly as I could.

The words tumbled out of his mouth like water thrown from a washpan. I picked out "Hector" and "Tombo" and "sugarhouse" before the bwoy ducked under Cherry's belly and darted away again. At the same time Wyckham galloped past me and overtook Achilles, the two of them disappearing into the path between canefields. I spurred Cherry to catch up.

Without looking full around, I was aware of growing a tail behind Cherry's, a rider and then people running. I was tempted to stop and order them back into the fields, but I too was caught between duty and curiosity.

I came upon Wyckham, horse abandoned, kneeling over a person writhing on the ground, a group of five or six others having drawn back in a small semicircle. They withdrew a few feet more as I arrived.

I dismounted and went over. Hector, the head driver, was on the ground, holding his own arm against his torso and screaming with pain and rage, his heels thudding the ground in an excess of fury. That fury was in his eyes as they registered my arrival. Meanwhile Wyckham's back, and his keening voice, spoke only of tenderness. Until I spoke and asked the matter.

"That fucking nigger, John," Wyckham began, and then his own rage boiled over in a torrent of expletive abuse scarcely more comprehensible than Achilles' chattering. But I understood that he intended to strip bare Carpenter John's bones with his whip.

Work around us had been brought to a halt by my arrival. There was a sense of expectation in the air, but it was directed at me: Wyckham's performance they were accustomed to, as a few smiles behind hands told me.

To briefly put it: On his way to his sugarhouse tasks, Carpenter John had, not an hour before, come upon Hector deploying his privilege as head driver across the back of Zubia, his whip raising fresh blood from the barely healed wounds. John had, after shouting a warning to Hector that was mockingly discarded, leapt upon the driver from behind, pulling him down from the mule and slashing the offending arm deep enough to expose ligaments, before absconding at surprising speed into the sugarhouse. From whence John had repelled all comers—and there'd been several, apparently—with mallet and knife.

Zubia stood a few yards apart from the circle of slaves, a mix of men and women, one of them comforting her. Her arms and shoulders were scored with bloody lashes, some of them embroidered with cloth from her upper garment, driven into her flesh by the driver's whip. I felt pity for the woman and also—in my new dispensation—outrage at Hector's effrontery. He'd assaulted my proprietorship on the first day of it! She gazed upon the felled, reduced brute now whimpering in pain, as at an insect. But her hand, holding a cutlass, twitched. Thankfully, before she could act on her thoughts, she flung herself away and disappeared into the cane.

I heard Wyckham say to the fallen driver, almost affectionately, "I will get him." Then he turned to me, voice cold and calm. "The only thing to bring that little nigger down is to shoot him." His proposed course was also, we both knew, a challenge. Such matters are normally in the charge of overseers. Theirs—his on Greencastle—was the primary responsibility for punishment, administered by themselves or delegated, usually to the head driver. Had I shown him the slightest hesitation he'd have proceeded with his plan forthwith.

I held his eye and spoke loudly enough for the slaves to hear. "There will be no shooting today, Mr. Wyckham. The kitchen is

not in need of birds. Take Hector to the sickhouse. I will bring John
down."

For a brief moment his challenge flared anew, but my eyes didn't
waver; his did. He became his blustery self, ordering the nearest men
to lift his driver. I could see Zubia's face watching them through the
cane, her eyes expressionless.

This time I tailed Wyckham. The five men carrying Hector on a
makeshift support of cloth and rope had a hard time of it. Progress
was slow, with several pauses. But we had to pass the sugarhouse to
get to the sickhouse and I wanted to make sure that the overseer did
not change the plan I'd given him. As we got closer to the mill he
turned in the saddle but my eyes were ready for his, and he turned
back and kept going. I watched him a minute longer, hearing the murmuring behind me of my human tail. I then turned toward my task.

Much of estate life is lived out in the public sphere; there are no
secrets in this amphitheatre. As Maasa, one is always in performance
and there is always an audience, a well-experienced, judgemental
audience. The ambience was enhanced by the sugarhouse being raised
above its surroundings for ease of access at crop time. I had sufficient
wit about me to realize that my best chance of success, before this
jaded audience, lay in seclusion, in dealing with John entirely on
my own. So, before even entering I ordered the extras away. That
required much shouting and imperious gesticulation on my part—a
parody of the planter magisterium. There were protesting murmurs,
but eventually they dispersed to the edge of the cobblestoned mound
on which the structure stands.

The sugarhouse was like a church. The same silence, the same fur-
tive noises that have no apparent source, the same mustiness (mould
in a church, muscovado here), the same vibrant sense of timelessness.
As a child this was a place of terror that we were warned to stay away
from by those who minded us. I wondered whether Carpenter John
continued to work here, in the belly of the beast that had eaten his
son alive, in order to be close to the spirit of a child who had become,
by an inversion of fate, his ancestor.

Deliberate in my movements, I dismounted from Cherry, tied her
to a post near a trough that held water, and entered. I sat casually on

a discarded hogshead, as though pausing in a meander of the estate. By an effort of will I deterred my strong instinct to look upward into the rafters—and waited.

"Maas Jason." It was a stage whisper by the time it reached my ears. I answered but still did not look up.

"Yes, John."

"You come for me." It was not a question.

"Yes, John."

"For the hothouse."

I did not answer: he knew.

"Where Backra Wyckham?"

"You want me to send him for you?"

"No, Maas Jason."

John's cackle floated down like feathers, and I could not help but laugh. We lapsed back into a silence that was almost companionable.

"What Zubia is to you?" I called out. The question had been nagging at me. But what surprised me—even before he gave his answer—was the form of my words, of my own intonation. My voice sounded strange to me . . . Jamaican, a deeper echo of the child that lived within. Where had Kwesi arrived from, I wondered.

His voice reached me from a long way off but it was crystalline with pride. "She to call me uncle, Maas Jason."

"A lot of people around here call you uncle," I said.

"Her modder and me was shipmate," he explained. "When her modder dead from giving birth to the next one, I promise her to look after this one. I did beg Maas Squire to take her away, give her back to Cambridge, she have two pickni for him. I beg Maas Anthony too. But the driver one did fill him eye with her. That man is a animal, Maas Jason. A animal!"

I could not but reflect on the numberless times in my life that I had heard the word applied to Negroes, all Negroes. I had resented it silently, or objected to it vocally. On this occasion, however, I couldn't but agree—perforce, silently.

Our silence spread as each waited for the other to break it. Finally, I looked up.

"Come down, John."

"Yes, Maas Jason."

In the syrupy brown air above, I detected movement more than form. Eventually there was rustling above me, like large wings wafting the air. A skittering from Cherry told me when John had landed, somewhere behind me.

The moment of John's descent was pivotal to the whole endeavour that I had undertaken for Anthony. As well as the many moral dilemmas that his request had posed, there was also a very stark matter about which he and I had not needed to talk. It's an incalculable factor that informs all actions, all decisions, here at Greencastle and at all other estates: personal safety. It is the chimera that haunts every aspect of life in this lovely, bloodied island. I recall a snippet of conversation between Squire and Lincoln, in many ways his closest confidant. I do not remember the exact occasion or context, or even how I came to be within hearing of their exchange; but it has remained with me ever since.

SQUIRE: The problem, Maas Lincoln, is in the numbers. There are so few of us.

LINCOLN: Maas Squire.

SQUIRE: And so many of you lot.

LINCOLN: Yes, Maas Squire.

SQUIRE: And our few are such a bloody sorry bunch, on the whole.

LINCOLN: If you say so, Maas Squire.

SQUIRE: You could slaughter us all before first bickle.

LINCOLN: Yes, Maas Squire.

Lincoln's tone, I remember, was flat as a plank; my father was perhaps in his cups at the time, and Lincoln knew to keep a measured distance between them at such times.

SQUIRE: So why don't you, Maas Lincoln?

I cannot remember my age at the time, but even then I knew what Squire was fishing for: the archetype of the happy slave that planters and their partisans produce like a playing card in any argument about slavery. But as Squire would have known well, it was not one that Lincoln had ever played.

LINCOLN: I don't want to dead yet, Maas Squire.

The sense of that conversation hovered in my mind as I heard the soft landing of John behind me. I knew not to turn around, rather, to wait for him, even if he had his mallet and I only a ragged woman's crop that Anna had presented me like a badge of office that first morning I rode out into the fields with Anthony.

I heard the uneven whisper of his approaching feet as, I confess, the murmur of fate. Then he appeared from behind me, his shadow preceding him. His mallet dangled from one hand; I glimpsed a knife handle in his belt.

"Ready now, Maas Jason." His voice was impassive.

I looked up, prepared for anything. His large eye was unwavering on me. But it was not a challenge, more a signal; as was his shoulder, which was inclined toward the archway that led out of the sugar-house. As I rose he turned ahead of me, and we processed out of the dark shelter into the light of the afternoon yard. As he passed Cherry, tethered to a post quietly cropping whatever she could reach, John untied her, and Cherry allowed herself to be led in our peculiar procession, with John on one side of the horse and myself on the other, to the hothouse.

As we got close Wyckham passed on his way back to the fields. He glared at us both.

"Settled him in, Mr. Wyckham?" My question was a taunt, as he understood perfectly.

He took out his fury on his poor nag, and disappeared toward the fields.

The hospital—or, as the slaves and I have always called it, the hothouse—is supposed to be for the care and restoration of slaves who fall ill, are injured or need delivery of their babies. In fact, it is a place of mingled comfort and terror. Many slaves will not set foot there except on pain of death—which sometimes eventuates. Even when seriously ill they prefer the dubious ministrations of their own men and women of medicine. But slaves also use it as a blind from the crushing labour in the fields—and who can blame them. The slightest scratch, bruise, gripe or ache is routinely parlayed into an imminent demise. At the same time genuine illnesses, which are legion and constant, many of them highly contagious to the ignorant or unwary, abide there also, like mire waiting to suck them down.

Malefactors and recalcitrants are housed there, either in the cellars beneath its raised flooring, or in the stocks and bilboes that are built into its outer walls. Between the delinquents and the sickly, genuine or not, the hothouse is always well patronized, full of medieval humours.

As Cherry brought herself to a halt in the yard facing the steps into the building, a voice called out, "Tombo! You old monkey. Is you use knife pon that one?"

John looked up and smiled.

"Fix him up, Glory. For next time . . ." He grinned at the prospect.

Pausing at the bottom of the steps long enough to hitch Cherry's rein to a nearby post, he limped up the steps. A tiny old woman, almost as misshapen as himself, blocked John's way into the building, holding out a hand, palm up.

"Gimme, Tombo," she said, her voice thin but commanding.

John looked down at his hand as though making a discovery of the mallet. For a moment his fingers flexed on the handle; then he handed it to the stern little crone. Without asking permission she reached into his belt and retrieved the knife, then ushered him inside the dark kingdom that was obviously hers.

That was my introduction to Tanti Glory, doctoress and warden of the hothouse. Coming out of the sunlight the small vestibule was like a threshold to the underworld. The people within, most of them lying on wooden pallets placed on the floor and covered with cloth or straw, seemed to float in a green ether barely contained by the dank stone walls of the place, a large room with shuttered windows on two sides.

This was the men's section. On the other side of the building were discrete spaces for the women who were sick and those who were lying in or had just birthed. The heat, saturated with a Biblical odour of dung and bodily corruption, was intense, choking. And the groaning voices, whose pitch and volume rose as I entered the room, were a perfect complement in this portico of Sheol. The gurgle of a baby fell like a drop of water in the semi-darkness.

John turned of his own accord toward the section where he must needs wait for a decision about his punishment.

A thin voice scraped the air. "Over here, Kwesi."

Glory was beckoning me with a spidery arm. Propped against a wall, bound across the chest with only one arm free of swathes of dirty cloth, was Hector. He was unmoving, his eyes closed.

A tinny cackle came from Glory. "If I never tie it on it would drop off already."

Then she turned her sparrow's eyes on me. "You turn big man, Kwesi. Come back to rule over us in place of you fahder."

A rumbling sound from behind her distracted me from the old woman. Tanti Glory turned also. "It wake up."

Hector seemed in the green half-light to be wrestling with himself. "I goin to kill him," he barked, a wounded brown dog. His left arm, his whipping arm, the arm John must have slashed, was strapped to his chest; his other arm hammered the hot air. His eyes seized on me like teeth. "Kill him," he repeated. Then the pain stuck him from within, crumpling his face.

Tanti Glory's giggle sounded sinister. "If him don't kill you first," she said.

I spoke sternly. "Keep John safe," I said. "He will be punished tomorrow."

"Yes, Maas Kwesi," she said, bobbing a curtsy.

"And this one too."

"I will do me best, Maas Kwesi." Her voice was flat, promising nothing.

≈ 36 ≈

Elorine: Going Back, Friday, November 18

WE HAD TO LEAVE. ADEBEH HIMSELF didn't want to. The children get used to him, the Jabez one in particular. He limping around everywhere after Adebeh, even when he go to relieve himself. The two of them stand at the end of the bush with backs to us, peeing. You had to laugh.

Adam and Adebeh settle down with each other also. But he have a promise to keep, to Fergus. Not only that he will bring me back safe, but that he will be there for the ship when it's leaving to sail back, because Fergus give his sure word to the government man at the wharf.

It's when, on the way back to Bellefields, we're sitting around the fire in the cave we were in before that he tell me his plan. At Adam, after the burial and celebration finish, I notice Adebeh and the Henry-one talking. Henry is who Adam save from the pig when he run away, so they is close as shipmates, even though some of Henry's Maroon people wanted to take Adam back to Maasa Douglas for the money. For myself, I have to ask why they wouldn't keep him, since they themself have slaves!

But I don't say anything.

"I's not going all the way back with you," he announce.

"What you mean?" I ask him, feeling cold of a sudden.

"I coming back here to find my sister," he say. "Henry say I am to come back to Adam, and he will take me."

"To you sister?" I ask.

He laugh a little laugh. "To a old man, Henry say. Who know everybody."

Adebeh looking at me all the time he's talking, and I like that. His sister is the guiding star for him now, but I can see in his face that I am not a pane of glass neither.

I ask him, "The old man will know where to find her?"

He shrug. "Is the first little sign I get."

"Suppose you find her?" I ask.

He shrug again, but a smile tell me the answer, that it won't matter after that. I don't have the heart to ask him what if he *don't* find her.

Is funny. I hardly notice him when we was at Adam. We was both so busy with what we needed to do. And all day yesterday as we was walking back to Bellefields, my mind leave behind there, worrying about the pickni, about Adam. But it catch up with me in the cave last night. I realize that for the whole time since we leave West Street until then, four days and nights, we been breathing the same air a few feet from each other. And that on the morrow all of that would be done and finish with.

The cave is so quiet I can hear the firewood singing as it burn itself. I frighten for myself.

Is me look away from him.

We don't say much more. He will take me as far as Dr. Fenwell, he say. He have to tell Kekeré Bábà to his face what he's doing, because he might be making a lot of trouble for him. The whiteman Cameron will try to find a way to lock up Fergus. If that is the case, he say, then he will just have to leave on the ship, as he promise. But he want to find Sister, too. I see the two promise that he make—to his parents and to Fergus—fighting in his face.

Still, like a flint somebody strike in the dark, I find myself hoping that Kekeré Bábà will tell Adebeh he must stay here. I snuff out that thought, though, quick-quick. We settle down on the ground across from each other, the fire between.

I was awake a long time. Him too. Our back was turned, but his breathing didn't change. I was still frighten. One time I almost get up and go over to him, for him to hold me. Just hold me safe. Calm me like he calm the horse that morning. But I know the calm wouldn't last long and I wasn't ready for the excitement that would follow. That make me more fraid. But then by-and-by, listening to him breathe was calming enough, and I sleep.

Next morning we're hurrying, and hardly talk going down to Bellefields. Adam give him a old cutlass when we leave. "Mark you way going," Adam says to him, "so you can find it back here," and from we leave Adam, Adebeh's been busy notching trees every few yards. From the big cotton tree near the cave, where Adam meet-up with us, we use the St. Agnes church steeple to take us to the edge of town, where the doctorman live.

Just before we come out of the bush I hang back to make him turn. He come some steps toward me. I'm frighten again, my chest stretch tight.

"I wish you God's blessings on you journey," I say. My voice sound like a croaking lizard.

"Thank you," he say, serious. "And on yours."

So as not to think whether or not, I simply step up and put my arms round him and hold on. It feel so good I couldn't but wonder why I wait so long to do it. But I know, and I know why I wait until then. He feel and smell like a tree, and when his hand come around me on both sides and meet in my waist I was content that it should be only so, nothing more. That is enough for now. I feel his root grow against my leg but that don't frighten me. I don't care if he feel my nipple-dem like plum-seed in his chest. That is how man and woman is to be with each other, I realize. Not like the only other time I get so close to a man. I didn't choose that time, or that man. This time is different.

I let go slowly. Then quick and brisk I lead us out of the bush and down to the doctorman house. Juice is outside in the front yard digging the flower bed. She look up and cut her eye at me. I know Juice from she born, and she never once show me bad face—until now. I couldn't help but say to myself, *You not getting him either, you little force-ripe gyal, him have bigger things to do.*

I don't look back or dawdle, and go on my way into the town, walking slow to show Juice I don't care. And for Adebeh to linger his eye on me.

$$\rightsquigarrow 37 \leftsquigarrow$$

Adebeh: The Search Begins,
Saturday, November 19

BY NOW THEY MUST BE HAVING snow in Scotia. The water in the rivers don't freeze over yet, maybe, but it'll be cold. In the day too, but especially at night when the breeze come off the water. Mam and Da is shivering. Neither of them get used to the cold, even after twenty-something winters. Is a good thing they have each other for when the breeze is ready to just walk through the little house as it please, like a bailiff. Here, is the heat I have to fight with.

You don't have to search to put on every scrap of clothes you own, but sometimes the little clothes you have on burn your body and you want to tear it off and go naked. Except if you do that the bush have a million teeth just waiting to bite you every step you take, every time you move. Clothes hardly matter. Here, they have every kind of flying and crawling thing, plenty more than Scotia, and it's always summer. The best thing to do is get into the river, like we do in Boydville when it's warm. Henry laugh at me when I throw myself into the water but I don't care. He's used to this dry heat.

We don't take to each other right off, Henry and me. It may be the place where Adam put us to talk, his hut, to make sure the wrong ears don't listen. Adisa was in the yard outside, buried in the ground, but her spirit was still alive in the place. It's like our skins was still feeling her. Yenkunkun skins, both of us. We honour Death, cause it comes for all of us. But we honour Life more, cause that is all we have. And this place, Adam's hut, smells of death. The shit smell that greeted Elorine and me, and the lime juice that little Selina sprinkled to drive away the shit smell, both still here.

"I need help," I said to Henry as soon as Adam leave us alone.

Henry chew on his own thoughts. "Why I should help you?" he say at last. "Adam say you is Yenkunkun, but how I to know?"

My time to be silent. My mind raced over all the stories I'd heard from Da and Mam, and from the old people when they get together and mix stories with screech to comfort each other in their cold exile by talking about this island.

"Montague James," I say, looking straight at him.

Yenkunkun know our history. Every battle, every betrayal, every ambush, every leader, from Juan de Bolas to the bastard Balcarres who tricked us and cause me to be Scotian.

Henry look back into my face. "What about him?" I can tell that he know who I am talking about.

"He is my father's cousin."

"You name James?" Careful.

"No. I name Cameron."

"So how you can be Montague James cousin?"

"My father name Montague Cameron. His mother name James."

"Ah." He withdraw back into himself to chew some more. Then look down at the ground, and as if he find the words there, says, "You is Trelawny."

I nod. He nods back, relaxes a little.

"What is the favour?" His voice is rounder, eyes also.

Henry take me to his home settlement. I's made welcome, I could never complain, after he speak for me, that I am Yenkunkun. They welcome me with food and drink and old-time story, some of which I know from the celebrations in Scotia, word for word. And the Yenkunkun at the market in Bellefields that I went to with Juice, they are Henry's people.

As I's sitting with Henry and his uncle, the colonel, the woman in the market come over and smile at me. But the man who was with her, and the questions some of them ask, polite as you please but their eyes cutting, tell me that some here have two set of thoughts about Trelawnys. They raise their glass to us, hail our courage and skill, and spit at the betrayal of Balcarres, to send us into exile in such a cold far place.

Amid the stories one old man speak another truth. When I subtract my years from how he looks to me, he would've been in his full nature at the time of the Trelawny war. "Your people was unfortunate," he say at me across the fire they made in the centre. "But your misfortune rain on us also a heavy rain. De guvment start to take more interest in us than before. Everywhere we turn we find guvment man watching us, with gun and dog. Dey pass law in Spanish Town to take away we guns and powder. Even we slaves!" He didn't have to say it: Is you Trelawnys cause all that. And I could see from the faces around the fire, hanging there like masks in the darkness, that some agree with him.

Since it was me one, and plenty of them, I didn't even think to give any version of the story the old men and women tell at the feastings in Scotia. That not a single Maroon from anywhere else lift a finger or bring a gun to help the Trelawnys when the English soldiers bring war to us and destroy Trelawny Town.

I sleep in Henry's hut. Meet Gattu and their four or five pickni, I don't even remember how many or their names. The girl remind me of Precious, about the same age. Next morning, without mention of it the night before, Henry shake me up while it's still dark. I thought it was Da getting me up to go fishing in Feely Lake. We leave quiet as mus-mus, back into the bush. Gattu, she watch us leave and throw a little smile at me like a piece of cloth. She want me to know I am welcome back in their hut.

We walk into the daylight, me barely keeping up. Up and down we go, turning here or there, as though breeze is blowing us. But Henry don't hesitate.

As we go I's learning that as much as the whiteman thinks he control everything that happen in the world, that is only true for where he can see, and only for the Negroes that live around him. Bush is a world completely outside what the whiteman knows or could understand. Bush belongs to Yenkunkun. Is why they had to trick us to get us to surrender.

But Yenkunkun is not the only blackpeople out here. Henry and me, we don't directly meet anyone on the paths we're going on, but you see things that tell you people is around. I am glad, because out here it's easy to think that you's the only people alive in the world. But Henry don't show the slightest interest, he don't change neither step nor direction. And the ancestors tell me already that I must leave it all to him.

By-and-by he bring us to a spot beside a stream where we roast some roots we dig up on the way, under some ashes that somebody else leave there. Henry's been here before. It's for everybody, he says. Bones big and small decorate the edges, and stones black from fire in the centre. You use it and leave it for the next person, to use your ashes and any pieces of wood you don't use, as a courtesy.

As I's going forward with Henry, I's thinking about Sister, but I's also thinking back, to Bellefields. One set of thoughts drive me deeper into bush, the other draw me back toward the town.

"Careful who you talk to, and what you say." That was Fergus yesterday. After he quiet down from my telling him that I will miss the *Eagle* sailing. After I tell him he put a knife on his tongue: "Why you bother to come back to tell me that, you should stay in the bush!" I tell him that I know he's given surety for me to the whiteman Cameron so I feel obliged not to lie to him. Is like I tell him a joke. "Him!" He laugh. "A good thing I not going out the next sailing anyway," he say. "As for Cameron, he don't remember you already, rum-up half the time." I don't tell him the full story of the day me and Trojan walk through town, that white Cameron, rum-up or not, certainly remember black Cameron.

Still, he's not vex with me. In some measure he understands, and he can see in my face that I's not about to change my mind. "Careful where you walk," he say finally. Is a kind of blessing in his voice. "Go quick-quick," he say, looking at the gate. "I will tell Doctor. And Murtella." Then he laugh again. "Juice not best please with you, this will make it worse." He put the cutlass he was holding in my hand. "Don't fraid to use it."

It's Elorine I's thinking about more. That night in the cave she listened so careful, and didn't say anything until I finish telling her that I's coming back to meet-up with Henry. Then she smile her little smile, remind me of Mam when I tell her something she know already. Elorine ask me what I will do when I find Sister. I like that, when. I had to shrug, cause I don't think that far yet. When I find her it's the bigi pripri who will tell me what to do, it's them who's brought me this far.

But Elorine don't ask me what if I *don't* find Sister, and I like that too. And just before we come out of the bush, how she come right up and hold me. Not with any calculating as to what might happen. She must be feel me rising against her. Just because.

Baba Quaw lives in the bush by himself, in a hut that my breath could blow down. He's brown and mawga like the trees around. Henry is leaning in calling his name inside, and after he make Henry call a few times, Baba Quaw answer from behind us. And when we turn we didn't see him at first. He is nearly invisible. "Come out of the bush a little way and stand up"—we must come to him. I see one hand tighten on the stick he's leaning on and the other hand tilt the cutlass it's holding, ready.

Henry, me behind him, take three steps toward the old man and then stop. He drop the cutlass he's been carrying all day and I do the same with mine. I feel the watchfulness of Baba Quaw's eyes like a tight string between him and us.

"We bring food, Baba," Henry say. He hold up the tied-up cloth that he's been carrying all day.

The old scrawn don't move a muscle except his mouth. "Why you bring food for me? We is stranger to each other."

"We need help, Baba," Henry say.

Baba Quaw cackle like the goose on the water at Boydville. "You far from ground, Maroon. Maybe you come for old Baba."

Now it's Henry's turn to laugh. "Backra forget bout you, Baba, you gone so long. Nobody going pay fippance for you now. You want the food or not?"

He wasn't going to move, Henry. He just hold up the food, and eventually it's Baba who come to him. The two of them watch each other like puss. I could see Baba's fingers tighten on the cutlass. Henry don't reach down for his, but I can feel him thinking about it.

After he take the cloth from Henry the old man rest it inside the doorway and turn back to us, his big knife still at the ready. Henry move his legs apart, tense.

"What help you need?" Baba ask. He's looking at Henry, he don't notice me at all. And I can see we's not getting a tenky for the food.

"I come from over Green River," Henry begins. "I looking for somebody. Maybe up this side."

Baba bark like a dog. "Who?"

"They call her One-Eye Sarah. You know her?"

Baba shake his head, but too quick for thought and too slow to hide the flash in his eyes.

To try and hide it deeper he turns and looks at me for the first time since we come into his yard. "And who you is?"

Before I can summon a word Henry speak. "He is Trelawny."

The old man cackle like a hen. "I old, but I don't dead yet, Maroon. I still have some lickle sense."

Henry turn to look at me. My time to talk. "You may not believe it, old man, but I's Trelawny, as Henry say."

Is a funny thing, but as I start to talk, immediately I know what to say and how to say it, so that Baba Quaw will know exactly who is talking to him. In Scotia, you don't have to say you is Trelawny. Everybody, black and white, slave and free, know who you is. Even though I been listening out for it from other people since I come here, the word itself taste rusty in my mouth. But not for long. Maybe it's the ancestors, maybe Montague James, dead over in Africa this long time. The stay-behind old-people in Scotia, when they get word that Colonel James is dead, they drink a barrel of screech to honour him. Could be him, or someone else I don't even know about that anoint my tongue. Bigi pripri do as they please.

As I's speaking I feel the words like food in my spirit, making me grow. Behind me I can feel Da and Mam, and feel the sorrow of their waiting from before I was born for the least scrap of a word about Sister. But I don't tell the old man about Sister. I just say that my father send me to look for One-Eye Sarah because she have something for him.

The dog bark again. "What?"

I don't answer him, and how I look him in the eye should tell him I am not going to.

"Is family matters, Baba," Henry say, voice softer than before, and

I realize that I am on the road to anger with the old man for nothing that is his fault, or mine. So I temper the edge of my tongue and tell him the old people in Scotia will put his name in their stories when I tell them of his help. "You and she is fambily?"

"In a sort of way," I tell him. But from the question and his voice I can tell that he know who we's looking for. So I relax a little.

≈ 38 ≈

Elorine: Reporting, Saturday, November 19

HARDLY A WORD PASS BETWEEN US today. He's not vex with me, I know that. And is not that we's both so busy. Christmas is coming and everybody seem to remember that while I'm in the bush. And Saturday is always as busy for me as for him. But it's not that either. Is like there is a great silence around him. It draw everybody around him into it too.

Yesterday afternoon when I reach back he was glad to see me, but mostly relieve that I'm sound in body and spirit. Right away he ask about Adam, soft, his back to the shop. I look behind him to see his customers, some of who know me and I know them, but nobody I could speak in front of. Later, I tell him, and I go inside.

While I'm inside getting back into my work I hear Pappi and Cyrus outside working, hurrying, for him to hear what happen in the bush.

At the supper table I tell him everything. Well, not everything. When I say that we get there too late, and find the babies minding Adisa's body, he stop eating. His whole body get still as a stone. I didn't tell him about the state the hut was in, or the smell. But I couldn't keep the pity from my voice when I tell him about the pickni, how brave and quiet they were. His face crumble, as he listen to me, and his eye get bright. I'm frighten to look, in case I see a tear roll down his face. Even when Mama Sel die, dreadful as that was, Pappi never cry. Maybe in his bed at night, since she wasn't there with him any more, maybe then. He come close to it today, though. I didn't tell him that Adam feel that somebody obeah Adisa. Since he turn a Christian he put all that behind him as the works of the Prince of Darkness.

I tell him about Adebeh enough to say that he maybe is not back at the doctorman's house with Fergus, and I tell him a little of why, keeping my voice normal. I tell him about how Adam, when we didn't hear from him in the bush all those years, was in Scotia, where Adebeh come from. This was news to Pappi too, but he smile for the first time, to see that his son could have such adventures in his life, and can take care of himself. Ishmael don't linger any further on the Maroon, he want to hear about Adam.

So I tell him everything I can remember, and he listen without interrupting. But as I speak it's like he grow smaller. Like his chair become bigger than him. It frighten me, and I begin to stumble over the words. To help myself and to make him laugh, I tell him how I ask Adam to send the three pickni back with me. And he laugh, the first time I see his teeth.

"Backra would just grab them up like chickenhawk," he say.

Then he soften his voice as he look directly at me. "He take care of you?"

I know right away who he mean, and I straighten my face but laugh with my eye. "He don't put a finger on me except to help me round a bush or cross a river."

"Good," he say.

Neither of us finish everything on the plates but I call Jassy to clear, making sure to tell her the food was tasty. She laugh: "Ginger will eat well tonight."

While she's clearing, Ishmael move over to his chair in the sitting room and settle into his own thoughts. I don't know what to say to comfort him, so I sink into mine too.

"What him going do?" Pappi voice squeeze the words out.

I catch myself in time. Cause I was thinking just then about Adebeh, who Pappi forget long time. What he mean to say is: What we cyan do for Adam. And the answer is—nothing. Pappi know that as well as me.

Or maybe was really to Maasa God he's talking, in the way they have with each other. Cause a little later he reach under his chair to the shelf he build into it and pull out his Bible. He open the Book to where Maasa God lead his fingers. I'm watching him from my eye-corner as a finger float over the page and then stop. From how the Bible fall open it look to be somewhere in the Old Testament, maybe one of them prophets who preach brimstone and fire, plague and destruction. I'm waiting for him to read it out to me, but he don't say a word. He smile to himself and put his head back on the chair. Maasa God show him something.

Little while, my own head back down in the sewing, I hear a snort from Pappi. Fast asleep.

Maybe that is what's on his mind all day today, whatever God show him last night. Maybe it's the Word for his preachment tomorrow. I don't have time to consider any of that, cause a string of people coming through the gate from early morning, for this and that. And everything is to be ready for Christmas, of course. I tell all of them, white and otherwise, that I'll try my best but I'm not promising. The Miss Francine-one have the gall to send one of her little slavegirls to say she's coming this afternoon for a fitting. I turn the pickni right around to tell her mistress that nothing is here yet for her to fit. Which is not the entire truth, but the woman is facety! Always want her things to come before anybody else's. Still, is my friend, and a big money will come from that frock, so I tell myself I will visit her later. Not to fit clothes, just to chat and keep the peace.

By time I begin to see a little ease in the early afternoon I hear water splashing outside from the stall in the back where we bathe weself. The Ishmael-one lock down his workshop and is getting ready to go out.

The Miss Clarissa Naughton! Nothing more nor less than that. Most Saturday afternoons he shut down the furnace early. Most Saturday afternoons he meet up with Uncle Teo or others of his Saturday afternoon combolo at Miss MacMorris shack, to drink rum and eat the fish that her companion Wilbert catch that morning. If his destination is only Miss MacMorris old shack, he will wash-up and change from his work clothes but he don't generally bathe until tomorrow morning for chapel. So I wait to see what he's going to do next, the old goat.

He and me don't talk about Miss Clarissa Naughton. Maybe he think I don't know about her. Or maybe that I'm fraid of him on this private matter. Is his private business yes, cause he's a big man and I am not his wife. But I get to learn about it from just after he start to visit her, almost three years now. In due time we will have to have words about Miss Clarissa Naughton, he and I both know that.

But he don't slip off like a shadow, he call me out of my workroom. "I going into town," he say, "you need anything?" Like him was just going down the road. Like he wasn't wearing that white linen shirt Selina make for him just before she leave us, and that he don't even wear to Zion. Like he didn't have on one of the two pants he wear for Sunday chapel. Like his sampatta on his foot wasn't still wet from washing them clean. But his eye was steady on mine, and his head was a little back, like he daring me to say something. So I smile—which he wasn't expecting—and shake my head and go back inside to Miss Vendryes who was there for a fitting.

After she leave I don't have the energy to visit Francine Beaumar-chais, so I send Jassy over to Mother Juba to send her grandson Christian to Francine, to tell her to expect me tomorrow instead, after chapel. I sit back down in my chair, thinking I should really go outside and bathe my skin, like Ishmael, though I don't have anywhere going. But the afternoon silence, me one in the house, is like a shroud that cover everything.

Then I hear a horse passing on the street snort, and the world just fall down inside me. It bring Adebeh right in front of me, and Adam behind him. They just come crashing into my head like a big wave on the beach. I hug myself tight as though my belly would run out onto the ground if I let go.

The pickni-dem! Baby Selina turn woman before her time, poor thing. Now she have to look about the two little ones and her father. I say to Adam that he should send them to town with me. He smile a sad little smile and shake his head. I was so anxious to help him I didn't really think how I would explain to anybody how I suddenly come by three pickni, like Maasa Jesus just shape them with His hand and put them down here in West Street, like one of his miracle. Adam understand that is only by looking far ahead that he can hope to stay free. In no time police would hear about it, and they would be gone to workhouse until somebody buy them. Magnus Douglas would just wipe his lips with that.

Cascade people come to Ishmael on the quiet and tell him the Magnus-one feel that Adam still owe him for all the years of labour on the estate since he run away. If they was to end up in workhouse he could seize Selina and the pickni for himself, with no one to stop him or claim them. They wouldn't think twice to beat Selina until she tell them where Adam is living. And then Magnus would send the Maroons to find him.

When I think of Adam and the pickni-dem out there in the bush with those people, all of them having to hide themselves every time a shadow fall in front of them, it burn me.

I fraid for Adam. He have plenty friends out in the bush. But he believe he also have an enemy nearby. He have his father's temper, slow to anger but quick to wrath. *He that is hasty of spirit exalteth folly*, says the Lord, and I fraid for the folly that Adam might do in that place behind Maasa God back.

All of that rise up in my throat like rancid bread. I cry out aloud, not screaming but not caring who hear me either, and a waterfall of eyewater just overflow. How long for, I don't know. Maybe I even doze, when every last drop is gone.

When I come back to myself it's almost dark. I manage to stagger outside and bathe my skin. Then I sleep till morning. I wake up when Pappi come in, but he don't bounce into anything so I know he is not in his rum. Which, with everything he have on his mind, maybe he'd have a right to be.

So maybe Miss Clarissa Naughton is a balm for him.

≈ 39 ≈

Narrative: Sunday School, Sunday, November 20

"I AM THE LORD THY GOD, which have brought thee out of the land of Egypt, out of the house of bondage. Thou shalt have no other gods before me."

Elorine looks up from the Bible on her lap at the group of four men and three women in front of her. "Who know how to spell *brought*?" They are sitting on benches a few feet away. Between Elorine and the group is a rectangle of sand held in shape by a frame of wood. Beside Elorine on her own bench is a small lignum vitae branch with a bushy head. The men and women each have short sticks in hand. "*Brought*," Elorine repeats, sweeping them with her eyes. "Who know how to spell it?"

The men and women are all older than Elorine, a couple of them as old as Ishmael, whom Elorine hears moving around inside the house behind her, gathering his energies for the service in the shed at the bottom of the yard, in an hour's time. But they are like children, avoiding Elorine's eyes or looking at her sideways, smiling sheepishly. She softens her voice. "Mama Claris? You always know the words."

A burnt stick of a woman in the middle of the group cackles, deftly catching the little red-tipped cigar as it drops from her lips and twiddling the fire out of harm's way. "That is big word, Miss Elly," she says. "Backra word dat," and cackles again.

"I know what it mean," says the man next to Mama Claris, leaning forward. "Maasa God carry the Israelite-dem on his shoulder through the Red Sea and put them in the promised land." He is older than the woman, sturdier in frame and voice.

"Like he will brought us," says the youngest woman in the group, just a few years older than Elorine.

"Maybe so, Lissy," says Elorine, "but only if you can read and write."

"Say what?" Mama Claris's voice cracks like a whip at her young teacher. "Maasa God only coming for Backra?"

"No, Mama. He coming for all. I was running a little joke."

"Backra too?" Lissy's smile is curled, cunning.

"Who can know the mind of Maasa God?" Elorine proclaims, and claps her hands. "Come. *Brought.* Who can spell it for me? What it start with?"

Lissy leans forward with her stick poised over the rectangle of smooth sand. The tip of her tongue peers from a mouth-corner. Then her stick, as if with a life of its own, slashes the sand. Elorine looks and smiles. "Good, Lissy. Go on."

Gradually they all become involved in writing in the sand, Elorine's erasing brush guiding them to completion of each word. Once spelled correctly, the word is transferred by charcoal to a sheet of brown paper that wrapped cloth from Miss Meyerlink's store. At the end of the session they will review their progress, as they will again next week before embarking on new words. It is how Elorine learned to read and write herself, sitting across the box of sand from her mother, a child among much older adults, slave and free, who found their way here by various routes, singly, not attracting attention from anyone except the whitelady in the house and her children. It was her idea to begin with.

At that time the Livingstones lived in the shed that is now Mount Zion chapel. Elorine was born there. Accommodation was part of Ishmael's wages from the white man who had taken him on after he'd bought his freedom; most of the rest, a meagre amount of actual money, had gone to Maasa Douglas for Selina's purchase. Ishmael had done most of the foundry work. The white man, a terrifying figure in Elorine's earliest life, and in his own children's, was often too liquored up to lift the hammers or hold the tongs steady. His drunken roaring could be like the wind through the trees that bordered the property.

Then, suddenly, the storm had ceased: choking on his own vomit one night, his heart had given out.

His wife and children—Elorine couldn't remember their names—had held on for a couple years, Ishmael in full charge now, with an apprentice of his own. Now, every quarter, as he had done for nearly twenty years, Ishmael takes his black ledger and leather pouch of money down to Lawyer Alberga and they work out the widow's portion. The lawyer sends it to her in some far place, not England. It was bondage of sorts, but one that Ishmael counted himself fortunate to bear.

Her legacy—as well as the house, which the Livingstones moved into—was the little reading and writing class that Selina, then Ishmael, and now for these past ten years Elorine, taught every other Sunday morning.

While Elorine is going over the words on the brown paper the yard slowly yields, as if from the air or the ground, for they are all black and brown, more people, men and women, the occasional child or young person. Elorine pays no attention. Except for the children, the newcomers are silent: they know serious business when they see it, and some of them have been around the sandbox themselves. Besides, this is a sort of secret. Backra knows they are there, and they know that Backra knows, but even infants are good at keeping secrets like these.

As Elorine gathers the implements of learning together to put inside the house, greeting regulars with a smile, a touch, kisses for the children, she notices a yellow man, light enough for freckles to show on his skin, even his arms, and for the grey-green of his eyes not to seem unusual. There is something familiar about him, and she's not sure it has to do with Zion. He's in conversation with Uncle Teo, so maybe it does; the old man seems to know him—but Uncle Teo knows everybody. As she goes past them into the house the stranger turns toward her.

"Good morning, Miss Livingstone," he says with a little bow.

His teeth, she notices, are good, plentiful. If he is a slave he is at least in the house. Or a driver in the field.

"Good morning," Elorine says and brushes past him.

With getting herself ready for worship there is no chance to ask Uncle Teo or anyone else about the man before Ishmael appears at the top of the steps leading from the house. "Brothers and sisters," he says, his voice as clear as his anvil, or the bell of St. Agnes in town, to hush the little crowd of murmuring congregants. "Let us gather to praise Maasa God."

Some Sundays he raises a hymn, and leads them singing into the little shed that seems to swell from the joyful voices. This morning, though, he opens his arms that are like tree limbs, one of them holding the large Bible as if it were a piece of paper, and waves them forward, falling in behind Uncle Teo, who is the other elder, to bring up the rear.

The procession is a silent one.

⋟ 40 ⋞

Jason: Hector and Tombo and Pompey, Monday, November 21

THIS MORNING, A ROUGH HAND SHOOK me out of sleep. "Wake up," a woman says. "Wyckham downstairs. He vex like pepper."

Anna.

Restless for much of the night, I'd finally fallen into a deep rest. I came to the surface confused and irritated. Anna stood over me, large but insubstantial in her flimsy nightclothes.

"Him say Hector dead."

The words cut through my fog. "Good," I say immediately. I remember Carpenter John: "Him is a animal." Carla's husband, however, regrets his savagery.

"And Tombo run way."

"Who?" I ask.

"Carpenter John."

"Ran away?"

"Yes."

Misty through the mosquito netting, she's bending over me. Glancing up, I'm looking at her dangling breasts, freckled, their pink eyes a foot from mine. I look away quickly but inhale her frowsy-sweet bed scent and remember Carla's morning-warm body in a surge of melancholy lust. The images and smells linger like smoke the whole day.

She steps back as I push the netting away. "You better go talk to Wyckham, he waking up the house."

I'm grateful for her not sending a slave to wake me, but before I can thank her she's flung out of the room, in a bad mood, as this is long before her usual time for arising. The stairs creak loudly as she stomps back downstairs.

To dispel the last cobwebs I splash my face with cool water from the calabash on the night-table and push my feet into a pair of Squire's old boots that have become mine. It's Sunday, the house is very quiet. On my way downstairs I can hear Wyckham's pacing before I see him from the steps. I do see Jack, hovering by the door out to the kitchen and watching the overseer with an expression of disdain.

Wyckham senses me and turns, barking. "Your bwoy's done it."

Prepared by Anna's succinct report I'm able to turn to Jack and give it full theatrical rein.

"Jack, what have you done now?"

"Nothing, Maasa!" Jack responds as if coached.

Wyckham is a kettle about to boil. "Not him." His outflung hand would have demolished Jack if he'd been near. He shouts, "Hector is dead!"

"I know," I reply.

"That nigger kill him."

I am the spirit of calm. "He was alive yesterday," I say. "After John's attack. I told Glory to look after him. What happened?"

"He's dead!"

"I know, Mr. Wyckham. We'll have to find a new head driver."

"The cripple run way."

"So I've been told. He'll be back, he can't get far."

"I'll drag him back by breakfast. Dead as a field rat."

"No, you won't," I say.

He looked at me as though I'd said something in the Abyssinian tongue.

"What you say?"

"Have you sent after John?" My indirect response gives him further pause.

"As soon as I hear I send for Pritchard and his dawgs."

"Well," I said firmly, "you can send back to Pritchard and tell him to stay home with his dogs. There'll be no hunting today. And not the Maroons either."

He burns me with his eyes for a long moment and then says, "Missa Douglas was right."

"What was he right about?"

"You's a fool," he barked and turned on his heels toward the door.

I called after him. He stopped. I waited for him to turn back to face me.

"I might be a fool, Wyckham," I said, "but, just so we are clear, you and I, there will be no dogs, or Maroons, sent to look for John. He'll be back in short order."

He gave a chilly smile. "It's out of your hands now. Hector's death will be reported to the authorities. Including Missa Douglas. They will tell the Maroon. They will find the cripple. And he will hang." His relish in the prospect was flung at me like a glove.

"Perhaps, Wyckham," I said. "But you will do nothing to find John."

"Either way we have to find somebody for the boiler house," he said. "As you know crop soon start to take off."

Wyckham's leer was exultant.

A half-hour later, dressed and fortified by Constancia's bracing coffee, Cherry and I are at the hospital. The odour of the place surrounds it like a protective nimbus, and my stomach heaves as I walk up the steps. But with Zubia's whipping still fresh in mind, I was determined not to show any sign that could be interpreted as queasiness.

Tanti Glory must have known the reason for my visit but expressed humorous surprise.

"You up early, Maas Jason." Her eyes were shrewd, waiting for my questions.

"You all right, Tanti?" I ask, casual.

"Yes, tenky, Maas Jason."

"Plenty excitement here last night," I continue.

"Yes, sir! But Tanti miss it all." She laughed and clapped her hands together.

"How so?" I ask, my tone tighter.

"Old Tanti sleep like piece of wood."

"That's not what I hear," I say, feigning a smile. "I hear that Tanti is like a owl, eyes open all night." (I've heard no such thing, but I wasn't going to give the crone advantage.)

She waits for me to speak. "Tell me what Tanti hear when she wake up." My smile, genuine now, invites confidence.

Zubia arrived after dark with food. For both of them, Tanti exclaims, clapping her hands again. She feed her brute first. He start to quarrel with her from she come, Tanti says, but Zubia shut him up with the threat to give his food to Silver, the old man beside him who is just waiting to go home, according to Glory, and from her tone I understand Africa.

"That shut him mout! Him nyam de food like hungry dawg." Her shrieking laughter was spontaneous and self-satisfying. "Zubia tell him she will see him with more food tomorrow."

Zubia left and came back, this time with food for Carpenter John. "I did give him lickle vittles already," says Glory with a glint of pride.

"She sit with Tombo a while, Maas Jason," her tone tender. "She tell me g'night when she leaving, and I tell Tombo the same. Then Portigee lock the door and I go lie down, Maas Jason."

"And then what happened?" I ask her calmly.

"Nothing, Maas Jason. Kwesi." Her use of my child's name is coquettish, giving me a glimpse of the young woman she must have been then.

"When did Hector die?" I ask, my voice even but not stern. I know she'll retreat behind shrugs and feints if I play Maasa.

She gives me the courtesy of a calm stare, and then half turns inside. "Portigee! Maasa calling you."

From the interior a huge figure emerges, an albino, his face pocked as though a score of raisins had been driven into it. One massive leg shows lesions that could be the beginning of yaws. He's easily Hector's equal in size, and while apparently fat—an unusual enough attribute—conveys such a quality of power that only a fool would challenge.

"Tell Maasa what you tell me," she commands.

Along with his other misfortunes, Portigee has a cleft palette, and is a little simple, though by no means stupid: his pale eyes are canny in weighing me as he gives his report. Glory has to do a fair amount of translation.

The night was quiet. Nothing happen, according to Portigee–Glory, though there was a long recitation of the nothing. Until morning, just before daybreak, when Portigee hears a choking sound. He finds Hector "spewing out his gizzard", as Tanti reports it. Green and slimy, according to them both.

"She set pison for him." I hear Portigee quite clearly on that, and his eyes are the dancing stones of a child who's been satisfied in some way; for whatever reason, he clearly hated Hector.

I cannot deny a sense of relief rising within at his information. Poison. Not John's attack.

"You want to see him, Maas Jason?" Glory's eyes glint maliciously up into mine, anticipating my revulsion at the gory corpse.

Portigee speaks again, clearly. "He outside, Maasa. Stink baaad." The albino's screwed-up face is comic, but I resist a smile. With the deliberateness of a justice I tell Glory to send someone for Dr. Fenwell, to examine the corpse. "And bring Zubia here," I say sternly.

But Portigee isn't finished with his story. Doing his morning rounds after finding Hector, he comes upon the empty restraints in the place where John bedded down last night. The other prisoners slept through the night like logs.

Prisoners are manacled at all times, by hands and feet, sometimes (though I forbade it for John) around the neck; there are bolts and screws closing these devices which cannot be opened except deliberately and with some effort and noise.

I look from Glory to Portigee and back to Glory. I ask her, stern now, who is in charge of the prisoners at night. She repeats the screeching that summoned the albino: "Hole-em! Maasa want you."

Hole-em doesn't obviously look the part of jailor. He's small and wiry, fine-featured and precise in his gestures. But his eyes are dark burning seeds of distrust, and his left hand seems welded to the leather strap around his waist from which hang his instruments of authority: keys, strangely shaped devices and levers, and a mallet, not unlike John's but smeared with blood.

"Is the woman do it," he spits out before I can ask him anything.

"Which woman?" I ask.

"The cow for Hector." Malice curls his tongue.

"She let him loose?" I ask. He hesitates a second. And I pounce. "You were sleeping too!" That brings them all to attention.

"Is she, Maasa," he whines, looking askance at Glory as though she might've betrayed him.

But there was no betrayal, except of the truth. And no one, as they all studied me, offered any further assistance toward that end. I felt myself entombed in a netherworld of dark mirrors and fetid air; the singing of horseflies, unrelenting and close, was oppressive. But more oppressive by far was the silence, polluted as the air.

I clung to Portigee's analysis of the driver's death as a prophylactic, and brushed them aside on my way out into the sunlight. But even there the horror pursued me: Hector's corpse. It was in the shade of the steps, and had already begun to smell, from decomposition and the damp, fly-strewn patches of vomit that Portigee had mentioned. He'd died in terrifying pain, the poison as it rose in his body and consciousness stringing his muscles as tight as rope and popping his eyes like marbles.

I turned away and went looking for Wyckham. In fact he found me, galloping from behind to block my progress. A sour smile transformed his face. "The bitch gone too," he announced, sounding so much like Hole-em that I almost laughed.

"Who?" I asked. "Gone where?" Somehow I knew the answer to both my questions, but advantage is important.

"Hector's bitch run away." He spat out the words but his eyes on mine were gleeful. "Both of dem will hang."

Without responding directly, and concealing my pleasure, I announced that I'd sent for Dr. Fenwell.

"For what?"

"To examine the driver's corpse," I said.

"For what?" He was becoming shrill.

"Poison," I said, as calmly as I could.

"Poison?" He shouted the word like an accusation.

I replied archly that I had not poisoned the driver, and then in succinct terms told him Portigee and Glory's story. I invited him to go and look for himself, averring that my limited knowledge of medicine was sufficient to convince me that Hector had not died from his wound, serious though it was. For a moment I thought he might attack me, but instead he kicked his heels hard into his poor horse and tore back the way he'd come, toward the hospital.

As I was pondering the events of the morning, and my stomach anticipating Constancia's breakfast, Pompey came by. Inspiration hit like a kick from his mule. But I said nothing to him, or to anyone else, until after I'd eaten.

I sent Israel to request Mr. Wyckham's presence at the house. Wyckham slouched up the front steps and only removed his hat when Mathilde passed, bidding him good morning.

I went straight to the point: "I think Pompey should be head driver."

His mouth could have caught a sparrow. Then he laughed, shrill as a monkey. But his eyes, which never left my face, saw that I was serious, and he stopped himself by coughing.

"Pompey!" He spat out the word as though he'd choked on it.

"Why not?" I asked, playing the innocent. "He was head driver once, and is a driver now. He knows what's required."

"He's old," Wyckham shouted, that being sufficient explanation for him. "I was going to send him out to pasture next month. The slaves won't listen to him."

"They listen now," I said.

"And the young drivers will eat him like cornmeal."

"I'd back Pompey against any of them." He was surprised at my certainty, doubted it, and sneered.

"You don't know them like I do."

"Perhaps," I conceded. "But you don't know Pompey like I do."

That shook him, but only for a moment. "Drivers and such are my business. You said so this morning."

I nodded admission of his charge. "I did," I said. "But I must also do what I feel is best for the estate."

"I don't agree with you," he said, glaring.

"You don't have to," I pointed out.

He seemed to weigh several conflicting thoughts for a few moments, and then marched out of the house.

I was about to follow the overseer when a movement on the piazza caught me. Lincoln, ostensibly dusting the chairs out there. A task for a minion, as we both acknowledged with our eyes. He was there to listen, plain and simple; we acknowledged that too. I beckoned him over.

"Not a word," I said, tilting my head toward the outside world. "I will tell Pompey." The old knave nodded and threw me a bleak smile that could have meant anything.

He's free now. My new authority is meaningless unless he willingly accedes to it.

≋ 41 ≋

Narrative: Maasa God Requireth

ISHMAEL CONTINUES TO SIT, HEAD DOWN, even after the hymning voices fade away into the leaves praying outside with the breeze. Usually, he sings with the rest of his flock, lustily if a little off-key, and approaches the lectern with light steps and a smile to match the good news of salvation in his heart. This morning, not even mouthing the words of the hymn, "All Hail the Power of Jesus Name," one of his favourites, he is solid-faced. Sits down with the congregation and as they settle, stares at the floor. Usually he stands patiently. Brother Teo looks nervously across the space the two of them occupy at the front of the chapel, and then studies the floor himself, silent, anxious. Ishmael is a stone.

Finally, with a sigh that Elorine can hear at the back of the chapel, her accustomed seat, her father gets to his feet and takes the two steps to the lectern, which he made himself when she was a child. He rests his Bible on it, opened to the place his finger was marking, and takes out his kerchief, one of three that Elorine folds into the top pocket of his shirt on Sunday mornings. His solemn eyes sweep the twenty or so people in front of him as he says, softly, "Set a watch, O Lord, before my mouth, and keep the door of my lips." It's an invocation he uses, sometimes testifying entirely on just that prayer, on the importance of listening and looking before speaking, especially about certain matters. It's advice he doesn't always heed himself, and Elorine wonders if he's cautioning himself against his own thoughts.

Ishmael looks down at his Bible and reads, "All flesh is as grass, and all the glory of man as the flower of grass. The grass withereth, and the flower thereof falleth away. But the word of the Lord, the most high Jehovah, endureth for ever." Elorine hears a few voices say Amen, quietly. She is aching for her father up there on his pulpit. Not even Uncle Teo knows he's brooding on Adisa, on Adam, his distant grandchildren. Part of Ishmael's mind, she knows, is in the bush.

"Proverbs say, 'The fining pot is for silver, and the furnace is for gold, but the Lord trieth the heart.' Amen." He smiles for the first time this morning, a small one, quickly gone. "I myself don't work with silver or gold, I work with iron. But I know about the furnace. I know that"—he taps his chest—"we is the silver and gold, and life itself is the furnace. The wood in that furnace"—he pauses again—"is slavery." Amen, Daddy. "That furnace burn up we flesh like charcoal, and down into ash.

"But that same furnace burn up Backra, too. Is Backra same one that make slavery. And slavery is sinful. Nayga don't say, 'I want to be a slave, please Missa Backra.' Nayga say, 'I want to be a free man, Missa Backra. I want to be like you, Missa Backra.' That is what Nayga say. And Backra say back to Nayga, 'You cyaant be like me, God make you black and make me white as snow.' He say, 'I cyan buy you and sell you like goat and sheep.'"

Elorine feels the unease of a congregation being led into perilous waters. But Ishmael's gentle mockery of Backra's tone raises smiles to some lips, even, reluctantly, her own. Arms across her chest, she finds her fingertips digging into her elbows as she watches her father gather the soaring pieces of his grief and anger back within the confines of their chapel. He swallows, fans his face with the yellow kerchief, looks at his people, smiles.

"But we know we are bought with a great price," he says gently, returning them to familiar ground. "Not by Backra. By the blood of Jesus, who tell us through Paul, 'Be ye not servants of men.' We is not goat or sheep. We don't walk on four foot." "No, Daddy. We is man and woman." His voice rises. "Woe unto you, scribes and Pharisees, hypocrites! For ye are like unto whited sepulchres, which appear beautiful outside, but within are full of dead men's bones."

He drops his voice again. "Is our bones," he says conversationally. "Nayga bones." He takes out a fresh kerchief and wipes his face.

"The Lord trieth our hearts, day by day by day in the furnace of slavery. Backra furnace burn us up like cane trash. But Maasa God word will never burn up. Backra burn up we body but him cyaant burn up we spirit, cause that is filled with the word of God."

Elorine presses her shoulders back against the sturdy wall of the chapel, all that protects her, protects Ishmael, from the wrath of the world, the world of Backra's vengeance that she expects to descend upon the shed at any moment.

"Backra look around and all that he see belong to him. Everything! Every puss and dawg, every pickni and granny, every cow and goat, every stone and tree." He gives his audience his most gracious and all-encompassing smile as he leans on his lectern and says to them, "And Maasa God make Nayga." *Yes, Daddy, Nayga.* "And him don't make Nayga for Backra to own. Jehovah make Nayga for himself to own."

Elorine feels the cold hand of dread squeeze her throat. "'I am the Lord God of the whole earth, every creeping thing and everything that fly in the air and walk on my earth.' My earth, not Backra earth." Ishmael's is the voice of Jehovah Himself. "Nayga purpose"—his chest is a drum as he slaps it—"is not to be a beast of burden. Not to be horse or mule or donkey for Backra to ride, especially the woman-dem." *Amen, Daddy.* "Not to hunt we down the same as wild pig when we run way from the whip." Ishmael is looking in the direction of Brother Cephas, a frequent runaway in his young days. But Elorine knows who he is thinking about, and she waits anxiously for her father's next words.

But he surprises her again, stepping back from the lectern and looking through the space in the wall beside him into the backyard of their house. When he speaks again, back in front of his Bible and looking down at it, there is the stillness of pond water in his voice. "And Maasa God requireth that which hath been and that which is to come." As if calmed, no one responds. "We know what is to come when we come face to face with Maasa God. Judgement Day. When the lame shall walk and the sick shall be well, and all our wounds will be healed. But there is another Judgement Day coming, Brethren. One that Maasa God may be pleased to let us see while we is alive. Noah saw the rainbow. I see the fire." His words are so simple, his tone so composed, so sober, even Elorine relaxes a little more as Ishmael looks down at his big Bible, turns a few pages, and reads: "Through the wrath of the Lord of hosts is the land darkened, and the people shall be as the fuel of the fire. For wickedness burneth as the fire. It shall devour the briars and thorns, and shall kindle in the thickets of the forest. Amen."

Without even looking up at them Ishmael closes his book, tucks it under his arm and sits down.

Adebeh: First Scent, Wednesday, November 23

MAM SHOULD BE SEEING ME now—she would laugh. She always calling me town bwoy, say I don't like the bush. That at least is true. Nothing in that bush for me except toil and frustration. Look at Da. Look at Mam. Their whole life spend in the bush, here in Jamaica and now in Scotia, and what they have to show for it? I want something more for myself.

But right now is bush I's in, like it or not. It's not that different to the bush in Scotia. The trees and shrubs are different, and thicker, cause they don't have winter here to purge things. And it's hotter. But the ground is just as tough, and even where you find some cultivation, whatever is growing look so poorly, it remind me of the land the government in Scotia give to blackpeople. They don't play favourite. They treat Loyalist and Maroon the same. Bad. Sometimes you think that slaves are better off. Their owner have to take care of them, though some of them is wicked in that regard too. But we other blackpeople are out on our own, like crows.

They have crows here, call them John. They's different to ours. The ones here don't have feathers on their heads, and have a beak like a hawk. They fly around looking for dead meat. Yesterday they find some.

Henry and me just set out from where we stop and roast some roots. We come out of the bush on a hillside that looks out over a stretch of ground with some yam hills and other vines, meaning somebody lives around here. We see some birds flying, about a dozen of them, circling around in a spiral wind. And we catch this awful rotten smell. My belly heave like on the ship in a storm. Henry, he mumble something and then set off down the hillside, fast. I had no choice but to follow as best I could. He know the bush and he never lose us once in four days and nights.

We don't see any of the people responsible for the yam hills and vines, but as we go along the crows is getting thicker, and closer to the ground. And then we come from behind a big tree to find about ten of them hopping and fighting each other and tearing at something. Henry right away rush at them, slashing his cutlass right and left to drive them off a bundle on the ground. I's right behind him, and recognize it the same time as he stop and I bounce into him.

Pickni. A little girl. And you only know it's a girl pickni because they's just starting on her little star-apple. Her eyes and mouth and cheeks are gone already, her little teeth in a horrible, horrible grin.

I think of Precious, and the food and me part company. I stagger back just in time to avoid bringing up all over Henry and the little pickni. I double up with pain, but is not my body that's hurting me. I run at the crows that settle in a circle nearby. They jump straight up in the air and take off, but one of them wasn't fast enough and my cutlass catch it and chop off one wing clean, and as it drop on the ground I swoop, like a crow myself. I didn't know until I stop myself that I was screaming as I chop it up into pieces, blood and feathers flying everywhere until I come back to myself on my knees on the bloody ground.

All I hear for a little while is my own breathing like waves coming and going on a beach, and the wings of the crows, who's flying a little higher now that they see what can happen. And then I hear singing, and I quiet my breath to listen.

Is Henry. I turn to see him bending over the little pickni, his hand making a shape in the air over her, and he's singing something like words, but not really. It's maybe that he's trying to say what is in his heart, like I just finish doing. When he's done he says to me, "Keep them off," and stare at the crows.

He start digging next to the little girl with his cutlass and stick. I stand up and start waving my cutlass at the birds to make sure they don't even think to set down again. And I's glad for the job, because then I don't have to look at Henry, and the child lying beside him. She was in a little hollow, that is what Henry is digging deeper. Stones are around it. So maybe she was buried before and something dig her up. Not the crows, big as they is they can't move stones.

Henry's made a grave for the pickni, with heavier stones on top, and bush, plenty bush. "They won't trouble that," he say, satisfied with himself. The bush has some red and green berries on it. "The pig-dem won't come either." When I look down I notice two or three marks in between the bird claws and Henry's feet that could well be from pigs.

It's like the crows know, because after Henry finished his work they don't come any closer. Most of them fly off. But Henry hasn't finished. He take out his dram-bottle from inside his shirt and pour a small libation on the grave, mumbling.

Then he turn and set his face in the direction we were going before this. Like he's putting all this behind him now. Because the day is going fast. This morning when we set out Henry said we'd reach where we're going by dark. But now, maybe not. So as we's going along, we's also looking for shelter, some cave or leave-alone shack. They have many of those. That is where we spend last night after we leave Baba Quaw.

Henry is hurrying and I know why. I's keeping up with him but a little piece of me is lagging behind. Because Henry tell me this morning that the day after tomorrow he'll have to turn back to his home, he's gone long enough. I will be on my own then.

But just as I's thinking about that, in fact not thinking about it, we hear shouting. Just voices at first, far away. Men. Then a squeal, a animal could be. And coming closer. Henry bend forward and raise his cutlass, I grip mine tighter too. "Hoi!" and "Hole him!" come through the leaves to us, and we hear things crashing through the bush, getting closer. Without thinking I find myself behind a tree, Henry behind another one. Neither hides us, but we's not looking to really hide, more to protect weself from whatever is coming, man or animal or the two in one.

A pig bursts through just where we were about to walk and comes charging past Henry's tree toward mine. I chop at it and feel my blade sink in, almost wrenching the cutlass from my hand. Same time two men and then a bwoy with sticks come into what I see is a little clearing. I put this all together in my mind afterwards, because right then I run over to where the pig fetch up against another tree. I stick the cutlass into the throat. The blood like a fountain just shoot out all over me including me eye.

So I wasn't seeing the two men and the bwoy good, only hear when one of them say, "Who you?" and the other man say, "You kill we pig." I smell trouble in the air. I can feel them closing around me as I hear Henry say, "Is him kill it, is fe-him pig."

When I can see properly, the bwoy is the closest to us, the men behind him pointing two long sticks, spears, and one of them have a cutlass in his waist. The three of them are watching Henry and me like johncrow.

"Who you is?" the biggest one say. And the other one, the one with the cutlass, look at Henry and say, "Maroon," like it's a dirty word. Everybody is breathing hard except Henry beside me, who is holding in his breath. The big man raise his stick a little, meanwhile I'm feeling blood from the pig crawling across my foot.

I say, "I's Maroon, too." So it's two and two now. (I's keeping the bwoy in the corner of my eye though, cause he's not that small and he has a knife himself.) They look at me funny and then look back at Henry. I know that my face doesn't have Guinea markings like Henry's and some of the others in his village, and my clothes is different, ragged.

But what I say stopped them. That give me a chance to say the right thing, cause there was no chance we were going to have the pig for ourselves, just Henry and me.

"You drive the pig to us, so we will share it with you." In my head I hear Da, who is not a man to run from a fight: *A kind word turneth away wrath.* There's plenty wrath to turn away just then.

That satisfy them, and things fall into their place. In no time Henry and the bush-man with the machete, Darby by name, was side by side slicing up the pig and cleaning it for the fire. Sam the bwoy put himself to work building a fire, while myself and the bigger bush-man, name of Pembroke, look around and chop wood from certain trees and shrubs for Sam to set under the pig. And while the pig is cooking, Sam in charge of seeing it doesn't burn, we talk. We don't laugh like friends, cause Henry and me know by now what Maroon means to bush-people. But Henry tells them right away that we're not here looking for anybody to take back to Busha. They relax a little.

They ask if I am a real Maroon.

"True-true Maroon," I say.

"Which Maroon?" Darby want to know, and I tell them, "Trelawny."

Darby open his eyes wide but Pembroke laugh as if I's giving him a joke. "I did know," he say, like to himself.

"Know what?" Henry asks.

Pembroke laugh again. "Backra think every Trelawny gone over the sea, even back to Guinea. But Nayga know otherwise." Da like to say, "Sometimes you must play fool to catch wise," so I take a deep breath before I ask him what Nayga know. "Some Trelawny never make it onto the ship," Pembroke say. "They still here." I say that everybody know that, that some dead beforehand. "Not only the dead," he say. "Look at you."

"Don't worry bout me," I say quickly.

Just then Sam call out that the pig is ready, so nobody give an answer. But I could see that the both of them was holding secrets from us. Henry see it also, because as soon as the pig is divide-up and put on four big plantain leaves and everybody start eating and saying how good the pig is, he come at it from another direction.

"We going on the way to Golden River," Henry say. "Which way we must take from here?"

Everything get still again. You can hear jaws chewing as loud as the flies singing over the entrails that Henry and Darby bury further down the slope.

Henry laugh just once, more a bark than a joke. "If you think that I looking to take you in to the magistrate, you can kill me right here," he say. He open his arms to show that he don't even have his cutlass nearby, whereas Pembroke and Darby don't move two feet without the sharp sticks being close. "I not trying to trick you," Henry say, "I trying to find me way." They still don't say anything.

"You know who they call Sarah?" I's looking at Darby as I ask—he is older and may know more. "One-Eye Sarah?"

Darby look away from me, and I know from how he avoid Pembroke that both of them know something, something I want to know.

Da like to say, when he want to start a quarrel with me, that I am my mother's child, cause Mam have a way to just flare up out of a silence like gunpowder. That was me now.

Before I even think I get up straight and say to Henry, "Is time to go. It getting late."

I speak like I am the one in charge. Henry, he get up right away, scooping up his leaf with the pieces of pig. I bend for mine as well, and eye what is left in the middle between all of us.

"We not going away without our share of that." The two of them stay on their haunches, eating and watching us. Sam is looking from them to us but no one is paying him mind. By this time Henry has his cutlass in hand, and carefully divide the pig that is left. No one is going to argue with his sharing, which is fair. Then he untie the oilskin bag at his waist and put our portion into it.

"I bid you good day," he say with a nod.

Pembroke say, "Don't come back through these parts, Maroon."

But as I turn to follow Henry, Darby call out, "Ask for Sarah on the way. They will know her."

My foot pause for half a step, but then I keep going, and call out tenky, like Mam teach me. I step into the bush behind Henry.

I's tired and vex, but I's stepping a little lighter.

⇒ 43 ⇐

Jason: The New Order, Thursday, November 24

"ISS DIS A NEW IDEA FROM one of dose books you bring home from England? So many many books!"

Mathilde, who usually greets even serious matters with a twinkle, looked at me with suspicion this morning.

I shook my head and tapped it. "From in here," I said.

"Widdout de whip, eh? You trying to make dem love you?"

I shook my head again.

"I don't care if they love me or not," I said, "as long as they work." We were sharing an early-morning coffee on the piazza, something of a routine.

"But dey iss working now," she said.

I agreed, but said they weren't working hard enough.

"You expec dem to work harder widdout de whip?" She laughed out loud.

"Yes, I do," I said, refusing to laugh with her.

"Dey need de whip. Everybody know dat."

"They're not horses," I said. "They're people."

"Some of dem," she said carefully. "Some iss like horses. Dose need de whip."

"They're also hungry," I averred, "all of them. And they'll stay hungry until Christmas, when the law says we have to give them food. I don't know how much food that will be, and that is some weeks off. We cannot afford to feed them any better right now. They will work to fill their own bellies."

"If dey belly iss full dey will sleep."

"If they sleep, I will put them in the stocks," I said, quick and firm, though I had not in fact thought about that, I'm so confident in my scheme.

"Dey can't work in the stocks."

"They won't eat in the stocks either," I said.

"You can't starve dem, dey'll make complaint to the magistrate."

I pointed out that they are close to starving now, but that I don't expect them to continue doing so if they have a choice.

"You tink we iss starving dem?"

I saw immediately that I had touched a sensitive spot. Mathilde is not a cruel person by nature. She spends a lot of time with slaves, so must surely see that they're mostly, even those in the house, as scrawny as chickens.

Softening my tone, I said that it was not a matter of food, but of production. In the same way as a well-fed horse runs farther and faster than a nag, so with a slave and work. The analogy, as I used it, cinched my stomach with self-reproach. I repeated that Greencastle could not afford feeding them more than was already the case, which was a bare minimum. That is not enough, I said. They need to be strong for the crop after Christmas.

"Well," she said, beginning to puff a little, "we can make de food ground bigger, I suppose."

"We could," I agreed, "but the same number of people would have to work that ground, I can't afford any more field hands. Besides," I said, "the slaves—and not only those who work the food ground— would probably steal more than they already do, since there would be more food to steal."

"Dey will not come back from their ground, dey will run away," Mathilde said, challenging me.

"Maybe so," I conceded. "But most of them come back now."

"Wyckham will never agree to this," she said, as if that was the end of our discussion.

And, of course, he didn't. Cherry and I bearded him in his lair, so to speak, arriving outside his cottage before he'd arisen. Pleasant, his "housekeeper" du jour glimpsed me through the open door as she passed from the living area toward the kitchen and turned back to alert Wyckham. (It is customary, indeed expected, that overseers and bookkeepers make their own concupiscent arrangements on an estate. But I confess to a certain resentment that this detestable man should be free to tamper at will with Greencastle's females.)

I remained seated on Cherry. He came out of the house stuffing shirt-tails into his trousers and then paused on the porch. We looked at each other for a steady quarter-minute before he stepped off the porch, because neither Cherry nor myself was moving.

"G'morning," he said, stopping far enough away so he didn't have to look too steeply at my face. I nodded and showed some teeth.

"Will you come in?" The tone was more rounded than in the greeting.

"No," I told him, but I got off the horse, which I hadn't planned. I asked him if he had his targets for the day set.

"I always start knowing where I want to finish," he said with a little smile of self-congratulation.

"Could your tasks be done by mid-afternoon?" I asked, attempting innocence.

"No," he said simply. But he'd sensed something in my manner or voice and raised an eyebrow.

There was nothing for it but to go straight ahead. His eyebrow remained at half-mast as I began to explain the new order of things.

Before I'd properly finished he exploded, rearing back as if I had insulted or threatened him. "Time off? You're crazy!" Anger rose like a tide into his face. "They'll drink and fuck and sleep the whole fucking day. You might as well declare a holiday." He was almost screaming.

"I might do that, too," I told him. "In due course. But in the meantime, if they drink and fuck and sleep, they'll starve. Such rations as they get will not be increased."

I had one more firecracker to set off.

"And there will be no whipping," I told him.

As knives, Wyckham's eyes would've carved me like a Sunday roast.

"No whipping?" His astonishment expressed itself as a giggle. "You expect them to work harder with no one behind them?"

"Pompey will be behind them," I pointed out. "Pompey and the other drivers."

Now he laughed out loud. "Pompey? I tell you already that they don't fraid for Pompey. And without a whip . . ."

"They don't have to be afraid of Pompey," I said, advancing my gambit as calmly as I could manage. "They have to be afraid of me."

"You?" His scorn was out in the air before he could scotch its flight.

"Yes, Mr. Wyckham. Me." I couldn't squelch the smile.

I remounted Cherry. Polite but firm, I requested he show me the extent of the tasks he would set the slaves for the day. From the first morning he'd resented my close interest in his quotidian duties. With Anthony he'd meekly appear at the bottom of the steps for his instructions. Since Friday, pointedly, he had met me as I was riding out for the day, to inform me of what would be done.

As it happened, Pompey was awaiting instructions at the edge of Hope Come Over, the field nearest to the big house. I'd been the one to inform Pompey of his elevation, for the simple political reason that I wanted him to be in no doubt as to its source. The old dog recognized right away the neat inversion that history has played on our relationship. But I'd kept myself away from both himself and Wyckham after that, visible but distant. Wyckham had had three days to get used to the idea of Pompey as his lieutenant.

When I saw the head driver, I let Wyckham go past.

"Maasa Jason tek way you whip, old man," he began, flattening his voice for Pompey's benefit.

Pompey—true to the form of slaves, who know their lives are not theirs to order—said nothing; he didn't even shift on his mule.

Wyckham laughed. "Maasa Jason say nigger will work harder if you don't beat him. You think so old man?"

By this time I'd manoeuvred Cherry into a clear sight of Pompey. Whose eyes flicked mine and returned like an arrow to the overseer.

"Maybe, Maas Wyckham," he said, shrugging. "It depend on how Nayga feel, Backra."

"Maasa Jason say nigger feel hungry. That is why nigger will work without you whip him. You hungry, old nigger?"

Wyckham's voice and posture demanded the answer he didn't receive.

Pompey laughed. "I old, Maas Wyckham," he said, still ignoring me. "Meself don't need plenty food. But Nayga need food to work. That is for certain."

Having been around Negroes for his many years in Jamaica at least, the overseer should have understood the seriousness behind Pompey's chuckling retort.

"Well, Maasa Jason here say that nigger don't need food to work, and he don't need whip. Nigger can do as he like now. Not so Maasa?"

He turned to me. But before my rising anger could respond, Pompey's laughter, openly mocking now, showered us both.

"Backra a-play fool fe ketch wise, sah. Dat is foolishness. Maas Jason couldn't say dat." The old fox's mockery tempered my ire.

"You're quite right, Pompey," I said, ignoring Wyckham. "That is foolishness. But Mr. Wyckham is right about the whip."

"Yes, sah?" The watchful stillness of the slave expecting a trick returned to his eyes.

"Yes," I said firmly. "You won't need it."

I felt more than heard Wyckham's derision as I explained the new scheme to Pompey. The old man's eyes remained suspicious as I spoke, but he had the presence of mind to ignore the overseer's snuffling until I turned to Wyckham and asked him to set out the tasks for the day. I didn't understand all the references and terms, but listened with manifest attention, watching Pompey more. His face betrayed little, but his eyes were calculating: could it be done without the whip. But he didn't seem frightened—which I realized, on reflection, had been Wyckham's first reaction.

"Well, Maas Jason,"—he shrugged, shoulders eloquent with scepticism—"me will try it, sah. Nayga will decide."

Which was true. I could propound, as I had, the most reasonable and progressive scheme, with grand objectives born of noble convictions. But Wyckham's niggers would decide whether those objectives were to their liking and, more important, their benefit. The banning of the whip they would welcome. But if they deemed the rest not to their profit, then even the whip would not accomplish my purpose. And once banished, that whip could not be reintroduced. I suddenly felt myself exposed on a cliff's edge.

But I'd already jumped. Pride alone would not allow me to withdraw: the overseer's scorn would have been like a rain of arrows, and far more corrosive of my authority than any slacking off or open rebellion could be.

"Me will haffe tell Scotty and Teckford," Pompey said, turning his mule as he tipped the brim of the ancient hat that had adorned his head from I was a child and he was head driver the first time. He was grateful to be rescued from the ranks of the useless, I imagine, but only to a point: he'd more see it as having been restored to his rightful place in the scheme of things.

I declared that I'd do the telling of the other drivers. This drew a flash of the resentful Pompey of old into his eyes, but he busied himself with sending a nearby slave to tell Scotty and Teckford to meet us at Old Man, an ancient guango where the three main fields of Greencastle intersected.

The three of us, Pompey leading, me bringing up the rear, traipsed past the puzzled glances of the slaves to Old Man. This time, however, Wyckham knew better than to speak first; instead he pushed me to the forefront with ill-concealed condescension: "Maasa want talk to you," he said, the honorific sour in his mouth.

Ignoring him, I pitched my voice so that at least the nearest slaves could hear. And, knowing as I did the genius of Negroes to exploit ambiguity that could be lawyerly in its acumen, I spoke slowly, in simple words.

When I'd finished there was silence, a stillness that extended past those who had heard the words to those beyond, who instinctively grasped that something unusual was afoot. Work stopped in all but the most distant parts of the fields.

The response of Teckford, who had the casual brutality of Hector in his freckled face and would very likely have been appointed by Wyckham, at whom he glanced before speaking, was the reflexive Negro reaction, especially when something seemed to their benefit: to smell a trap.

"You expect dem to work fe demself, sah?" He looked again at the overseer as if seeking guidance.

"Exactly that," I responded with a smile. "If you work harder, you will eat more. If you don't work, we'll go back to the old system."

Creole Scotty, a burly mahogany man of perhaps forty years whom I didn't remember from before, grinned at me.

"Dem will work, Maasa. We don't love to hungry." His opinion was cheerfully given. I nodded at him, still ignoring Wyckham. But the sub-driver himself looked up at the overseer.

"What we to do now, Maas Wyckham?" asked Creole Scotty.

"Get back to your work," Wyckham roared, raising his own whip, at which Creole Scotty, instead of flinching or dodging away, stood still and looked up into the overseer's roiling face. His quiet defiance and my presence quelled Wyckham's fury.

"You know what to do," he yapped with as much dignity as he could scrape together.

Touching their hats with their now useless whips the new head driver and his two subs departed. I watched Pompey and Scotty talking to the men and women at Tankwell, the nearest field to Old Man. The slaves divided their attention between the drivers and the two of us some distance off. There were murmurs and laughter and then men and women disappeared into the canes back to their tasks, with—I'd like to think—greater alacrity than I'd seen before. Pompey set out with Teckford for Breadfruit Tree to spread the strange news.

"Next you'll be offering to pay them," Wyckham said from behind me.

I assured him promptly, without bothering to turn, that if I could afford to, I would.

"God help us if that happens." He spat, with exaggerated loudness.

At that point I brought Cherry about. "God help us if that doesn't happen soon, Wyckham. God help all of us."

Our eyes locked for a moment, then he jerked his horse's head around and galloped off.

The man's hatred of me was so radiant that I wondered what might cause it to erupt into physical assault.

This mid-afternoon, as I'm coming down the steps after a light lunch and rest, anxious to view the success of my project, I'm distracted from Cherry, being held by Jack, by a rider galloping out of the cane toward the house, waving and shouting and whipping his donkey. Creole Scotty. He begins to jabber before coming close enough to be understood.

"Maas Jason," he calls out more than once, waving his arms as though I were not looking straight at him. He throws himself off the ass and bends double to catch his breath. Cherry, impatient to be off, dances around the rein in Jack's hand.

I ask Scotty what he's doing here. I attempt sternness in my voice and demeanour but really I'm intensely curious. He and his gang can't possibly have finished their work.

"Problem, Maas Jason." He's panting but coming back to himself. "Big problem." His manner is agitated but his eyes are also watching for my reaction to his sudden appearance. As calmly as I can, I wait, my mind flying into the dark realms of disastrous possibility.

And as I listen to his story I realize that Creole Scotty is describing a subconscious dread, or more accurately a premonition, that had been in my mind since broaching my plan to Wyckham this morning. Yesterday, Scotty said, at the end of work the overseer had given Pompey and the drivers their instructions for the next day, as is the custom. "Nayga day begin plenty sooner than Backra get up," as Scotty put it, "so we haffe know what to do."

The gangs had been well into their assigned work this morning when Wyckham, Pompey and myself had appeared. "Everybody hear what you say, Maas Jason. About how things to go from now onward. An dem work like you light fire under dem tail. Me never haffe say a word to dem except to stop dem fe eat when Pompey blow de conch. And dem start back after break long before he blow it again. Dem finish quick after dat. When we reach where Pompey put de post to say dat is our work for de day, everybody laugh and step out on de path now, ready wid dem cutlass and stick to head out to dem provision ground now like you say we cyan do.

"Is right den dat Backra Wyckham come riding up the path," Scotty continues, his voice icy with contempt. "And when he see

Nayga, he lick de horse and come pelting up to us swinging de whip he just use pon de horse. So I run quick and stannup between Backra and Nayga. Him haul up de horse nearly pitch the both of dem over pon de ground, an look down pon me like if him did have him gun wid him, him wudda shoot me dead. Him shout at me, "What you niggers doing out here in the middle day?' Except him never say it like dat, Maas Jason, he use a whole heap of nasty word mix up in it besides.

"So I explain to Backra as respectful as I can that I hear what Maasa say this morning, and that Maasa say when we finish we work we can go and do some digging in we own provision ground. I tek me courage in me hand, Maas Jason, and ask Backra if dat was not what he understan from what you say.

"Well, Maas Jason, is like I spit in Backra face, the way he go on. Him shout at me dat nigger don't take order from Maasa, Maasa too busy to worry bout what nigger doing in the canefield, dat is why Maasa have Backra, so nigger will do what Backra say. And Backra say dat we is to find we monkey tail over into de next field and get to work dere, because crop time is coming sooner dan we tink. Except him use plenty odder word, Maas Jason, dat I won't say to you because I have respect.

"Nayga looking at me, Maas Jason, to see what I going do. Right then I not sure, Maas Jason, cause I custom to do what Backra say and den tell Nayga what to do. But I know what I hear you say, Maas Jason, and plenty Nayga hear you as well."

And then, unexpectedly, Scotty cackles. "Is a good ting I am looking into him face, Maas Jason, cause Backra hand fly back wid de whip and lash it after me, and if I wasn't watching, it wudda strip me face. But I throw up me hand and block it. See it here, Maas Jason."

Scotty stretches out his arm, and indeed skin and shirt are slashed. But I'm silent, because I can see in Scotty's eyes and hear in his tone that the story isn't finished.

He laughs again, reflective. "Backra know that he cyaant do dat any more. I don't have to tell him. He give the poor horse the lick he want to give me and pelt off like gun fire." Scotty shakes his head and sighs as he looks at me. His story has flowed out of him in an unbroken rush of words and now he's exhausted, seeming smaller somehow.

He ends by saying, "De Nayga-dem don't trust me, Maas Jason."

He doesn't have to spell it out for me, the situation is clear in his voice and eyes: *The slaves don't trust you, Maas Jason.*

My dander was up by this time anyway. If Cherry had been a sturdier beast or Creole Scotty less weighty himself, I'd have had him mount up behind me as I took the reins from Jack and set off. Cherry, so long quiet, was unable to keep herself to a walk at all times, and Scotty had a punishing time trying to keep up. But I was grateful for the slower pace forced upon me: with each minute my fury weakened and my head gained ascendancy over my emotions.

Once I spotted the overseer—more correctly his hat over a breadth of cane—I sent Scotty off to his ground. Wyckham, a choleric man, I'd long decided, was remonstrating with Pompey, who sat calmly on his mule watching Backra make a nuisance of himself. It was a posture I knew well from childhood, when nothing that Judith or anyone else said, except possibly Squire, could penetrate his iron assurance. Wyckham was half turned away from me, and the rattle of wind in the cane tops obscured the sound of Cherry's approach. Pompey, without betraying evidence of it to Wyckham, saw me, and nudged his mount backward a step. At that Wyckham turned. His argument with Pompey ceased abruptly; indeed the head driver disappeared from his concern.

"I was just telling Pompey here that your idea is a good one, Mr. Pollard, but won't work with these niggers without we use the whip. Wasn't I, Pompey?" So sure was he in his self-satisfied smirking that he didn't even bother to wait for the driver to speak up but went on, "A pity, really, it would be nice if . . ." When Pompey's voice broke over his.

"It cyan work, Maas Jason. Widdout de whip. It work today. It cyan work."

I had the good sense to hold my own tongue, whose impulse was to lash the condescending overseer. But Pompey's words had already done that far better. Wyckham's smile slipped in the way a queen's tiara might, and he was, for a moment, ludicrous.

And then the sound and fury resumed. He berated Pompey with all the words that Creole Scotty would not repeat out of respect, challenging the driver to repeat the lie he had just uttered. Pompey did not address the ranting man in front of him, but looked at me instead.

"It work today, Maas Jason. An widdout anybody use de whip."

He saw in my eyes that I already knew what had happened in my absence from the fields. But he was in no way hesitant about stating his case.

Still, that case was a challenge. I could not indicate my agreement in the slightest way in front of the overseer, with the old slave's circumspect eyes on us both. Fortunately, the intemperate Wyckham eased the point with another explosion of ire such as I was becoming used to, once more applied his heels to the hindquarters of his poor horse, which almost tipped him over as they bolted away from us.

I shouted his name at my loudest pitch. He heard it and stopped. I did him the unwilling courtesy of jogging Cherry part of the distance between us and waited for him to come back; I did not want Pompey further involved. Wyckham's face was puce, his eyes about to dissolve. I waited until he and his horse were still, and then told him that he was to dismiss those gangs who had completed their original tasks, or he was to dismiss himself. Strangely, what followed was not, as expected, further alarums and excursions but a sudden paleness, and silence.

But his eyes were as thin-edged as the slaves' machetes, and I knew, looking into them, that I am in far greater danger, physical danger, from the overseer than from the most rebellious or deranged slave.

≈ 44 ≈

Jason: Wyckham, Friday, November 20

HA! I DID NOT EVEN HAVE TO RELEASE Wyckham: he's left of his own accord. And the wretch allowed his own splenetic bad humour to cost him wages. Had he waited just until tomorrow I would have been required, under the terms on which Anthony engaged him, to give him two weeks of wages in lieu of notice—which I was determined to do. There was never any question of notice. I had reached the decision that I would terminate his tenure tomorrow, without consultation with Mathilde or anyone else. I had written the necessary letters, to Wyckham himself and to Lawyer Alberga, the latter's authorizing Alberga to release the requisite sums—after Anna had assured me that there was sufficient cash in hand.

When I went down the front steps to begin my day I found Pompey come to tell me that he'd gone to the overseer's house for his instructions to find Pleasant sitting on the steps weeping. Wyckham had left the property—and now, without his favour, she would have to return to the field. According to Pleasant as reported by Pompey, "Him gone at first light." I could see a smile behind his eyes, but he raised an eyebrow instead.

"What we to do, Maas Jason?" But the old man wasn't really asking for specific direction. What he wanted, really, was endorsement of his own enhanced authority.

Perforce, I've learnt a lot about the estate, and very swiftly. The antagonism of Wyckham to my involvement quickened my interest and my determination to learn. Based on where they'd stopped the day before, it didn't take me long to set Pompey the targets for the day for the different gangs, and he did not demur, for they were reasonable enough. After the first day's contretemps with our erstwhile overseer the targets had been met by mid-afternoon.

As much if not more work is being done at Greencastle than was the case two weeks ago, and there is less obvious disgruntlement about. Not everyone takes advantage of the time for themselves by going to their provision ground. Some go home to sleep, but not in the numbers that Mathilde predicted; and who can blame them. I'm exhausted from just riding up and down in the sun, my most strenuous labour being to control Cherry's lively personality.

Often, after returning to the house for a jug of wash and one of Constancia's bakes, I doze for an hour in Mathilde's Suriname chair on the piazza before returning to the fields.

I was there this afternoon when—as if knowing that his greatest enemy was now gone from the place—who should appear but Carpenter John, Tombo, as I've come to calling him. I was dozing when a commotion of people and dogs in the courtyard below roused me; the inside slaves gravitated toward the louvres also.

John was standing just back from the bottom of the steps, some yards ahead of a small crowd of people, who fell silent as I appeared above them. He was almost naked and looked even more mangled than before, visibly thinner than when we'd last seen each other. His mallet, though, his badge of office, still dangled from his fingers, and the knife with which he'd slashed Hector was pushed into the belt of plaited vines that held up his shredded trousers. Tanti Glory had disarmed him of both when he'd arrived at the hothouse—someone must've given them back to him.

John walked with a stick taller than himself but would not allow himself to wilt against it, and his good eye was plumb on mine.

"You come back to us," I said, resisting a smile of relief.

"Yes, Maas Jason. I come back fe me punishment." There was, however, not a tinge of contrition in his voice or stance. The thought came to me that his real reason for return, as was often the case, was hunger. But I did not wish to humiliate the man any further than the bush had done.

"You bring back Zubia?"

"No, Maas Jason. She will bring back herself. When she ready."

It was, as with so many of John's attitudes and words, a quiet defiance. He knew where Zubia was, what she had done, and what was in store for her when she returned. From his long experience he knew that despite the principle of slaves being chattel like pigs and cows, the penalty for killing one was death. He knew too that he could be punished—not only by myself but by the authorities—for aiding in the escape of a slave and, by his silence, harbouring her, as Magistrate Douglas would no doubt see it.

In the end, however, none of us could do anything to John that would radically affect his life beyond what had happened to him already. Death—from the whipping that I or Magnus Douglas could prescribe, and which would in his present state almost certainly eventuate—would be a release. That, it seems to me, is the irreducible core of the most worthy slave: his or her condition is already so demeaned that his spirit is untouchable. That spirit, like a bird, hovered in John's carbuncle of an eye gazing up at me in his muted insolence.

The slaves' workday, by their own efforts, was over, so there were sufficient numbers about to add to those who had followed John to form quite a tail as I led him, myself on horseback this time, back to the hothouse. As I listened to the scuffling feet and murmuring voices behind me, I pondered the question of countervailing forces. Not as a question of physics but of life and death. Most of the men and many of the women behind us had machetes in their hands. There was nothing tangible preventing them—indeed preventing John with his mallet, bloodied knife and stick—from dispatching me to the regions of the netherworld reserved for those who mightily oppress God's children.

The hairs on my head prickled from the thoughts beneath them.

≈ 45 ≈

Narrative: Called to Order, Saturday, November 26

MATHILDE: What iss you going to do, Jason?

JASON: About what?

MATHILDE: About Wyckham.

JASON: I intend to ask Lincoln to bring out that jug of best rum that Squire kept for special occasions and have at least two shots from it.

MATHILDE: Iss no laughing business. I iss serious.

JASON: So am I. At least two shots.

MATHILDE: So. You iss happy to see him leave us.

JASON: Delighted.

ANNA: Me glad too. The man is a croaking lizard.

MATHILDE: How you mean?

ANNA: Him eye undress me every time they ketch me.

MATHILDE: I didn know.

ANNA: I tell Anthony more than once, but is like he don't notice. Or maybe he glad for Wyckham to help out. Dadda woulda shoot him.

MATHILDE: I didn know, Petal.

JASON: And he saved us some money!

MATHILDE: How?

JASON: Anna knows how. I was going to give him notice today, with two weeks' wages. But as he left of his own accord yesterday, we don't owe him anything.

ANNA: He will bad-mouth you up and down the district.

JASON: Maybe. Wyckham and Magnus can sing a chorus.

MATHILDE: And what iss you going to do now?

JASON: About what?

MATHILDE: About Greencastle.

JASON: Wyckham wasn't running Greencastle. He was the overseer. A bad one.

MATHILDE: But he know about estate. And how to get niggers to work.

JASON: With a whip. I have got them to work without a whip.

ANNA: You going get them to take off the crop without a whip?

JASON: Why not?

ANNA: Nayga don't like to work. And crop is the worse work.

JASON: They don't like to be hungry either.

MATHILDE: You know about ze crop?

JASON: Not yet. But it's a month from now, Pompey tells me. Maybe more.

MATHILDE: Pompey!

ANNA: Pompey old like a cotton tree.

JASON: He knows more about growing cane than I know about the law.

MATHILDE: He iss a nigger.

JASON: That's why he knows.

MATHILDE: So now you make Pompey overseer? Or Lincoln? Iss still here, that one. And I hear you iss paying him. A nigger?

JASON: He's a free man, and he's working. I must pay him.

MATHILDE: Iss living here. And eating here too.

JASON: And working here. He's helping me.

MATHILDE: Helping you with your crazy ideas. Perhaps he put them into your head, eh?

JASON: No. You think my ideas are crazy, I know. But I am not crazy. The crop will be taken off, I promise you. I gave Anthony my word.

ANNA: Anthony far away.

JASON: Yes. The crop will be taken off and on the wharf by the time he comes back.

MATHILDE: Iss better be, Jason.

≈ 46 ≈

Jason: Letter to Carla (2), Sunday, November 27

Greencastle
Sunday, November 27, 1831

My Dearest Carla,

It seems a very long time since I wrote last, but so much has been happening that I am not in fact sure when that was. Forgive me.

Anthony has gone to Virginia & I am now, de jure, attorney & Maasa for the property.

As such my changes to the estate have made Greencastle notorious in the district & possibly further afield. At the Anglican church service this morning Anna heard a planter aver that I had driven off all the whites, proclaimed the slaves free & given them run of the place. I could not but laugh at Anna's report. The white man, an overseer, whom I've driven away, left of his own accord—though just before I'd have sent him packing. There is another white man around, really a youth, whom I hardly see, so in actuality, the slaves are running the place.

What sticks in everyone's craw, however, is that I've banned the use of the whip. By the day after that three slaves had run away. I did not bother to send after them because most runaways come back of their own accord, hungry & torn by thorns & rocks, or worse. These did. I had them put in the bilboes to consider their ways & they thanked me for the food they were fed while there. None has run again since.

The other boiling contention among the planters & attorneys is the system of piece-work that I've instituted, & which, taken together with the whip, proved too much for the odious overseer. It's not unknown in the island, but is not widespread, or favoured. At the beginning goals were set for the day that were too easily & joyously achieved. But as I've come to better understand the workings of the estate, I've made a harder bargain between the challenge & the reward, which is time to work for themselves, or sleep if they so choose. It pleases me that a decreasing number seem to take the indolent option, perhaps because there is no profit in it.

The reason for this—& a prime cause of our notoriety hereabouts—is the ubiquitous Lincoln, who is still in situ despite being a free man. As well as keeping the books, which he has done since time immemorial, Lincoln is now in charge of the expanded plot near the house by means of which we feed the slaves. Some of them call him Nayga Maasa. I've given him a free hand (except with the whip, of which he has no need anyway) to augment the gang of a dozen or so that labour there with as many as he likes—but not from the field, where we can spare no one at this time. So he finds new hands from within the house, probably settling old scores from that time of his ascendancy there. I could have put our remaining white, Simpson, a young Scot, in charge of that project, but the slaves don't much respect him, as he's recently off the ship. They have a lively fear of Lincoln, whom all know well, house & field.

To Simpson I've given responsibility for the hospital & jail, familiarly termed the hothouse. He too is unhappy to be unwhipped, but he is fortunate in that: those slaves who run that charnel house would have his guts for garters if he whipped them.

Everyone here, myself included, is slightly uncomfortable at the presence of a free black man within the household. It's a radical idea. Though always a little bit above the ebb & flow of Greencastle life & occupying his own niche in relation to Squire & therefore to everyone else, Lincoln was a slave, always. Now, with this new distinction thrust so suddenly on him & on us, an imbalance has been created, like a dining table that tilts with each slice of a knife.

Adding complexity is the fact that he is still, in the eyes of the law, a slave. His "free paper" is with Lawyer Alberga, awaiting the next court session to be duly recorded & stamped; at that point his guineas will also be handed over. But there is nowhere for Lincoln to go: he has no domicile that we know of other than the hut at the end of the quarters nearest to the house, which has been his from memory begins. And too besides none of us would dare think to turn him out onto the road, for fear of Banquo's ghost (in this case Squire's).

That I've not seen Lincoln off the property is a particular irritant to Mathilde, who never fully accepted the old rogue's insidious authority. As soon as Anthony left she elevated Balfour, Lincoln's son, to the post of maître d'hôtel, but is still not happy, because from long habit Balfour still defers to his father.

So with all those reasons we are pariahs in the district—but also curiosities. Mathilde had a visit yesterday from the mistress of a nearby estate whose talk was all about rumours of insurrection while, in Anna's words, "looking around for Nayga". She'd brought with her two enormous Negroes who hovered nearby, cutlasses prominent, to protect her from Greencastle's rampaging slaves. And this morning at the church Mathilde was the centre of attention for men & women who were surprised at her normal liveliness.

Mathilde herself is not comfortable with the changes I've wrought, as I was reminded yesterday at dinner. However, she's shrewd enough to understand that she was part of the scheme to bring me here for the purpose I'm now fulfilling. Her innate cheerfulness remains her shield & buckler & I silently thank her for it. Anna, also part of the stratagem, teases me mercilessly for my "softness" but, thankfully, has not tried to interfere. She runs her corner of the house—the seamstresses, & aspects of the bookkeeping—& leaves the rest to her mother. The estate itself has been left to me. But only, I sense strongly, for as long as it does not transgress the laws of nature any farther than my measures have already threatened.

I am weary, my precious one. The unwavering pressures of quasi-proprietorship, quite apart from the physical rigours, send me reeling into my lonely bed at nightfall, which comes early here. I sleep most nights through. But on those nights that I don't, my restless thoughts are mostly of you & Caleb & of this place, which is & is not my home. Much of my previous life at Greencastle, before England, was lived in a penumbra of double meanings & half-silences: I was the master's son, his firstborn, slave like the others & then free. I was the same colour & lineage as some of the slaves but I ate at the master's table. And now I am returned into this penumbraic existence, wherein everywhere I go on Greencastle I encounter myself, my doppelgänger. I awaken charged with the determination to do my best but, even after a full night of sleep, wary of the relentless scrutiny in which my life is lived & judged. To think that I once envied the privacy afforded the slaves who occupied the eyrie where I now am lodged!

But I do not complain, having made my own choice, which could have been otherwise. And it is, at least, a healthy life: I am trimmer than I came & burnt almost to my original colour. Caleb will not recognize his Poppi when the time comes. That time cannot come soon enough for your loving, lonely & ardent husband,

Jason

≫ 47 ≪

Narrative: Alone, Sunday, November 27

HENRY LEAVES ADEBEH ON A HILLSIDE above the town of St. Ann's Bay and he is completely alone for the first time in this place.

"I gone too far from home already," Henry said last night, almost in apology. "Ground need to clear and plant. If I not there, when crop grow I will lose out when it share out." They are communal fields, of course, the Yenkunkun way, the way that was lost in Scotia when the Trelawny community left for Africa. The few Yenkunkun left behind are separated, unable to plant the same ground and share the crop. So most of them is hungry.

Adebeh has known this moment was coming from they set out. Now that it's here he feels numb. But his spirit is also filled with gratitude. He doesn't know what to say to Henry except tenky. Henry says, "You can manage good enough now," as a sort of commendation. He points his cutlass ahead. "That way to Golden River. Remember." Then he squeezes Adebeh's shoulder. "Eshu walk with you."

That brings Adebeh's voice back to him. "You also," he says and touches Henry's shoulder as the man is turning away. As he watches, unease rising, Henry melts into the weave of leaves and branches behind. "Tenk you," Adebeh shouts at the green air, and hears the man's voice throw a word back to him. He turns quickly away from the bush.

Henry pointed to the west, which the last person they'd spoken to this morning, no more than an hour before, had said was the direction for Golden River estate. He was a man of Henry's age, and scrawny like all the people they'd met in the bush, underfed, suspicious. And he knew of One-Eye Sarah. Adebeh could read that in his eyes. But he has learned that too many questions, and especially a wrong question, can slam a window shut. So he says nothing as the man tells Henry and himself how to get to Golden River. Which has brought them to this hillside overlooking St. Ann's Bay. Where Adebeh is now totally alone.

Always, even when he first went to Halifax, there was somebody. In Boydville there was Mam and Da and the others. When Adebeh had decided to go to Halifax, Da had sent him to George Seymour, Yenkunkun from Trelawny, who had been in jail when the ship *Asia* left for Africa. Through Seymour he had got to know other people. On the *Eagle*, thanks be, there was Fergus. And all the people since coming to Jamaica, in Bellefields, and in the bush with Henry, now gone. The Elorine-one seems as far away as Georgia Marcy in Halifax. He remembers them together on the way back from Adam, her strong arms shining with sweat, the smell of her when he walked behind her. It floats in his nostrils like a dream. Her strong fingers making the fire, her bubbies like dark fruit in the soft basket of her bodice as she bends over the pot. He can taste the yearning in his loin, the same now as then. A hunger for the oblivion of fucking, but more than that for the consolation of nearness.

But there is no one. He doesn't really know where he is. No sign of the ancestors. Eshu walk with you, Henry said, and then himself walked away. Maybe Henry was really Eshu.

Then he hears something. A bird. No. A bell. A church bell. Like St. Winifred's in Boydville. Da never went, but sometimes Mam would dress herself in the one frock she has without holes and take Adebeh and the other children and go. She was grateful to the white parson for teaching her children to read and write. The bell in the middle of his thoughts of being alone is, he decides, Eshu calling him. Not to go to the church. He looks like a vagabond, they wouldn't allow him in. But instead of going west to Golden River, where One-Eye Sarah might or might not be, he will go to the town below him. Eshu will show him what to do there.

From the hillside he can see, far beyond and below, the curved harbour that the town embraces, a few ships studding the dark sea.

He aligns the sound of the bell with a matchstick steeple, and sets off. Very quickly the trees swallow him. As he is walking he combs his hair with his fingers, removing all the leaves and twigs he can feel, so he doesn't look like a bush-man and stand out. Following the slope of the land leads him to a smooth pathway, winding down through the trees like a brown snake. People come out of the trees onto the path like streams joining a river. Some of them are carrying baskets on their heads or shoulders, others hold chickens tied with grass around legs and wings. One man in front of him has two piglets, slaughtered, gutted and split, strapped across his naked back. He looks like he's bleeding to death. No one speaks to Adebeh, or seems to notice him.

The path broadens into a roadway, with more tributaries, more people feeding it. A few buildings, people in doorways, looking out of windows. Adebeh feels their eyes on him now but he keeps walking like he knows where he's going. And there's only one way to go, down. On a flat ledge of land is a paddock, the horses scrawny but for one big roan on higher ground, sleek and brilliant as a jewel. The buildings get bigger, wooden uppers built on a stone foundation, reminding him of the merchant's houses in Preston. The bell has long since died, but a slight breeze brings voices on the air sighing tiredly, a hymn vaguely familiar.

The sun is almost overhead, burning. The town's smell, of rotten food and shit, chokes him after the freshness of the bush. Between houses and crossing streets Adebeh glimpses the sea, the masts of cutters and sloops, canoes and barges dancing in the liquid light. Then he smells it, a whisper in his nostrils. He inhales the briny smell deeply, feels a little giddy. Hunger perhaps; he'd sent Henry back with what remained of the pig. The sea always smells the same. Blackpeople, horses, the sea. He doesn't know where he is exactly, but he doesn't feel lost.

Only to find Sarah now.

The stream of people he's in carries him to the edge of the market. Which is where he wants to be. The market is where food and news are to be found. Adebeh needs both. He taps the leather pouch flapping against his chest, to reassure himself with the clink of coins and the rustle of his free paper. Nobody knows Major Maxwell here, and the whiteman Cameron may already have reported him. But at least he can buy food.

Under and around a huge spreading tree, the largest Adebeh has ever seen anywhere, is the market. Between its knuckled roots little groups of people sit or stand behind clumps of produce. Like disembodied spirits, pieces of clothing for sale hang on some of the lower branches. The cries of children playing in the dust, splashing in the fringe of sea, the laughter and calls of the vendors swallow him as he walks toward a slender column of smoke, led by his nostrils and stomach. Adebeh remembers the market in Bellefields where he went with Juice and found the two Yenkunkun. But he doesn't expect to find any here.

An old man squats on his haunches behind a mound of hot coals, ashes and bricks, from which protrude thick blackened roots like babies' limbs. On a wire grate a few strips of something dance and sizzle in the heat. Meat or fish, Adebeh is not certain until he looks closely, bending over. Codfish. Perhaps from Scotia. A message?

"Mind you spit on me food," the old man snaps, his sunken eyes bright.

But Adebeh is in such a good mood, suddenly, that he laughs at the old man and addresses him tenderly. "No, Dada," he says, "I not going to spit on you food. I want to buy some."

The man, who looks as though he's been roasted himself over a slow fire, flashes a toothless grin. "So why you never say so, bwoy?"

In a minute Adebeh is sitting on one of the roots of the ancient tree, knowing he's been overcharged because the old buzzard had spotted him as a stranger, but happily on his way to a full stomach. He is balancing a square of banana leaf with a thick wedge of roasted yellow yam moistened with fragrant oil, and a palm-sized piece of salted cod. Carefully, before eating, he places a chunk of yam on a hollow in the root as an offering of thanks to Eshu for bringing him here. The burnt food seems to melt on his tongue. He belches and farts and sighs with content.

He recognizes the man with the two pigs, now clean from washing in the sea and selling pink chunks of pig at a brisk pace. It seems to Adebeh that generally, the blackpeople here are less woebegone than those in Tracadie, or at the market in Halifax. There is a liveliness here that is missing at home. Perhaps, he thinks, because there are more of us here. This market, and much more so than in Scotia, is a world in which whitepeople hardly figure.

Adebeh goes back to the old man, waits patiently until he serves a customer and then approaches, smiling.

"You want more food?" The man's tone is softer.

"No, Dada. It is very good, but my belly is full now."

"So what you want?" A hint of watchfulness is back.

"One-Eye Sarah," Adebeh says casually, as if it's the most natural thing to say.

The old man pounces. "What you want with her?" His eyes on Adebeh withdraw deeper into the leather face.

Adebeh keeps his voice kindly. "You know her, Dada?"

"What you is to her?"

"Nothing, Dada. But she knows somebody who is somebody to me. I want to talk with her."

The old man's eyes, quick as a bird's, flick past Adebeh's left arm and back to his face. Adebeh turns. Twenty yards away, at the edge of the pool of shadow under the tree, a tall woman stands in silhouette, in a flour bag dress with embroidery around the neck and sleeves that looks made for church. She is presiding over a bazaar of similar dresses hanging from the tree, and bracelets and necklaces made of beads and shells, several of which adorn her stringy neck and arms. She has a patch over her right eye. Her left is looking at Adebeh, steady as a beam.

He feels suddenly cold, afraid. But the woman's stillness, flames of daylight dancing behind her, pulls him toward her. She is expecting him. Or maybe he was expecting her to be here. Eshu.

Adebeh stops a few feet from her. Her gaunt cheeks bear the faded scorings of Africa. A red emblem that resembles an eye is etched on her black leather eye-patch.

"You come back fe her," the woman says.

⇒ 48 ⇐

Jason: Zubia Returns, Monday, November 28

TWO DAYS AFTER TOMBO, ZUBIA RETURNED. I was in the midst of an argument with Pompey and Teckford, a freckled blowhard whose authority over the slaves was floundering without the whip, a problem that Creole Scotty and Pompey himself did not have, being by nature cheerfully violent, self-preserving men. Teckford was likely as violent but without Wyckham he was rudderless. I was already studying the field slaves for likely candidates for sub-driver for Breadfruit Tree.

One of his Breadfruit Tree gang, a woman, had refused an order from him and he was trying to keep her back after the rest of the gang had been dismissed for the afternoon. She'd sucked her teeth at him, according to Pompey, and walked off. Whereupon he'd ridden her down and hit her. With his whip, which they all still carry. She'd sought out Pompey as a court of appeal.

So soon after its implementation, that breach of my policy on whipping was a serious matter and presented a dilemma. I could not simply dismiss or demote the fool or every field hand would provoke their driver to distraction, and the balance of ascendancy would, ineluctably, reverse—to my own detriment also. But something had to be done. Old devil Pompey, growing more secure in his pre-eminence by the day, awaited my Solomonic judgement with guarded eyes.

I was spared the necessity for immediate wisdom by a figure appearing, weaving a crazy path along the roadway between Breadfruit Tree and Hope Come Over. It formed into a woman, almost naked, and cradling something against her chest—a baby, which seemed attached to one bare teat. She howled like a demon, one who had no knowledge of words, only screams; meantime, her free arm waved for our attention, which she already had. Eventually, beneath the dusty grime and leaves that pockmarked her skin, and the baby's, I recognized her.

Teckford urged his donkey toward the running woman, but she ran straight past him to me. Even Cherry, normally the most placid of beasts, was turned to dancing by Zubia's baying approach. Jibbering, her wild eyes fixed on mine, she held her bundle up to me like an offering. When I looked down at the baby, a boy, flies were crawling in and out of its mouth and across its eyes. Not something unusual in itself. But this baby's eyes and mouth were making no effort to repel the insects, and its little black body was still as a sculpted board. It was dead.

It was as though my eyes' acknowledgement of that fact set off a renewed eruption of wordless fury, an abuse of the air itself.

At the back of my mind was the ultimate fate of this presumed murderess, as Dr. Fenwell had found her to be. But I was also, again, faced with my current problem: Teckford, and maintaining discipline and efficient work. I beckoned Teckford closer and told him, with an anger that was easy to summon, that another such use of the whip would get him returned to the gang, where he knew that his former subordinates would exact their own punishments with, as the Negroes say, a "brawta," something extra.

I then turned to Pompey and made him personally responsible for Zubia's well-being. The baby was to be buried immediately. Zubia was not to be punished—yet—but should be returned to her hut and given food. He was to bring her to me in the morning.

An hour or so later, before dark, he was at the foot of the steps. Zubia had hanged herself.

The driver's report was brusque, as though he felt personally affronted by the runaway's action. "Me do what you say, sah. Me tek her to Hector hut and get some food for her. She tek the food but she wudden give me the pickni. She mek to bite me like mad dawg. So me leave the food wid her and go bout me business. Little more time her big pickni Rupert come run after me, tell me to come quick. But quick wasn in time, sah. She still warm, sah, but she dead as the pickni in her han, the same one she show we just now."

I asked him where.

"Head driver hut, Maas Jason. I don't get to even clear Hector tings out yet."

I could understand Pompey's truculence. His inheritance, perhaps the most meaningful appurtenance of office, is now tainted. Death abounds in the quarters, of course, but violent death and particularly suicide leave restless, malevolent duppies. Propitiation has to be elaborate.

For myself I could envision the scene he'd just described with chilling clarity. That large hut with its tall conical roof is where I'd come to first know myself on Greencastle, during Pompey's first regime as head driver. Many memories remain with me, few of them worth dwelling on.

I think he expected me to come with him, in keeping with the attentive attorneyship I'd established. But I told him to alert our bookkeeper, Simpson, and have him deal with it. I went back up the stairs into the cool silence of the house. There was no peace for me there, however. Conversation with Anna about Zubia's return and death articulated my unspoken fear.

"Better Tombo did stay in the bush," she said. "Is Cascade that Hector come to us from. Him bredda is a driver there now. Magnus will want blood for Hector. Mark my words, he going to send for Tombo."

I marked them.

≈ 49 ≈

Elorine: Missing Adam, Monday, November 28

THE FIRST CHRISTMAS BREEZE CATCH ME this foreday, as I was going to the outhouse to do my morning business. It frighten me at first, like somebody spring from behind a bush and grab me. But then I feel my bubbies tighten and the tips crinkle like shame-me-lady, and I had to smile. When I realize what it is, I feel like a little pickni.

But today is not to smile about. Not after the preachment yesterday. I'm seeing a different Pappi since Adisa. I'm getting to understand how much he is missing Adam all this time, these years and years that I thought only I was missing him so. He know better than me that, hard as Adam have life out in the bush, is better than it would be on Cascade. Far better. But he is still missing his son, and the granpickni, such as I don't give him yet. If I did, maybe it would be easier for him.

After I heat-up the food that Jassy leave for us, I ask him about the preachment. I know he's empty as a drain and looking to just go inside and sleep till evening, and I feel for him. But my own insides was fulling-up of more than food.

"You challenging Backra," I say.

His mouth was still full, so he wait until he chew and swallow.

"Challenge how?" He still looking at his plate, his voice steady.

"You say God's word will burn Backra."

Now he look at me, his eyes as still as his voice. "And you think it won't?"

"Yes, but is not in our place to tell Backra that. Backra have his own preacher to . . ."

"I wasn't telling Backra, I was telling Nayga."

"But Backra listen to what Nayga tell Nayga." I feel the annoyance lifting in me like oil.

"I can't be response for what and who Backra listen to." His voice get prickly. "I must preach the word as Maasa God tell me to, and to who Him send to me."

"Backra think his word, his law, come from Maasa God too."

"I can't be response for that either," he say, sounding tired, and he put some food into his mouth and look away from me.

We finish eating in silence.

As he's wiping up the last gravy with his bread crust, though, and belching his big belch you can hear out in West Street, he turn to me and smile, like he's come back from far away.

"I know you think I think I am Maasa God. And you think that I think that Maasa God will keep me from harm wid Backra." He chew a little on the gravy bread, and I don't even think to argue because he is right about what I think. "I render to Caesar what is his. But on Sunday the only body I have to render anything to is Maasa God, and He tell me what to render, and how." He chew some more and swallow, belch again. When he resume talking his voice is calm, but it's deeper, as in chapel when he's wanting us to pay close attention.

"Maasa God don't create man in his own image so we can live like the animal-dem. We is man, in the image of Maasa God Jehovah. We don't walk on four foot and we don't crawl and creep on the ground. And we is not to make other man-dem crawl and creep on the ground like dem is animal!" His voice lift itself on the last word, and then it settle back into a croak. "That is a abomination onto the Lord. 'It were better for him that a millstone were hanged about his neck, and he cast into the sea, than that he should offend one of My little ones.' That is what Jehovah say. I wasn't talking anything but Maasa God's truth this morning."

I don't say anything. I have no words. We sit there a while longer listening to our thoughts and to the birds outside. I hear Miss Evelyn out in her backyard next door feeding her fowl-dem. Eventually Pappi sigh and get up. He go inside to his room.

He sleep like a iron bar until morning. He open the workshop same as always and everything proceed as normal. People and horses come and go. There wasn't anything different, except he's very quiet all day.

So far, Backra don't seem to hear about the preachment, or he would come for him already. But that is no comfort.

Backra have plenty ears. Some of them is black.

≈ 50 ≈

Adebeh: One-Eye Sarah (Delphis),
Monday, November 28

ONE-EYE SARAH IS NOT THE FIRST person to tell me I favour Da. Both of us is proud of that. But even as I's trying to convince Sarah—or Delphis, as some call her—that I's not Montague Cameron but his son, and the son of Maisie Fowler, who left a girl-baby with her thirty-five years ago, she's looking at me as if there's more to the story than I's telling her. Not suspicious, really, but seeing more than you and me would see.

Her eyes is the first strange thing. They see a different world from the rest of us. Not the same world looking different—a completely different world! And you don't know really what she's seeing with those eyes. One is real, one is not. But which is which, that is the question.

And which sees what—another question. The real eye, the one that moves around, is blue as a marble, and cock-eye. But the red eye painted on the patch over her other eye seems to look more directly at you. You only really know where she's looking from where her nose is pointing. And she's seeing the people and things and colours and animals around her, yes, same as the rest of us. But as well, she seems to see things that nobody else see. You sense that in her voice—she's speaking to you but maybe other people is listening. But she's not crazy-mad, definitely not.

"I looking for oonu this long time," she say, as if it's my fault why I just reach. "I see you get on the ship and come cross the water. You tek long."

"I didn't know where you is," I say to her. "The only place they tell me is Golden River. This is Golden River?"

"I is always here," she answer, without answering my question.

I look around beyond the tree at the rest of the market. "She is here with you?" I ask her.

"She gone back home." That tone again, as though she's talking to somebody else.

That word stop me. Home? Cause that one word can mean plenty things, not all of them good. Sister could be dead, her spirit gone to Africa, where we all come from. I have to think that Eshu and the bigi pripri bring me this far. But maybe this is where the journey stop.

"I send to call her," Delphis say with a little smile, as if she knows what is inside my head.

By then I's wondering whether Da and Mam knew that they hand over Sister to a obeahwoman, and if they knew all this time and didn't tell me. Maybe what Delphis really mean is that Sister is dead and she's sent to call her spirit.

I hear myself ask, sounding like a little boy, "She will come?"

"She will tell us."

And before I could ponder that properly, she stretch out her arm at me. "Buy a little something, nuh? For the woman over the water. Very cheap." Her nose is pointing at me. "She will like it."

So how the hell she know about Georgia Marcy?

"And the Miss in Town will like this one," she say. Another smile, holding out her other arm.

I feel the chill again. The old people have it to say, when that happen, that somebody walk on you grave, and I never pay that much mind. Until now. Is like this woman with her two funny eyes is looking in front and behind, from on top and from under. I feel naked. The shiver inside is melting into anger.

"Come tomorrow," she say, turning her nose to look for the next customer. I'm invisible.

"Here?"

She sounds vex. "No market tomorrow, bwoy." I bristle at the *bwoy* but bite my tongue. "Ferris will tell you where to find me." The hand with the bangles points to the old man whose roast yam and codfish I just enjoyed.

So here I's today, sitting on a sailboat that is bobbing in the water amongst a heap of bags and boxes with all kinds of goods and all kinds of smells, including blood and entrails—a whole cow slaughtered, without the head but with every other part on board. That is our first stop, thank God, to hand over the carcass to three slaves on a little jetty in the bush. Cheaper and quicker than driving the one animal, says Headley, the captain and steersman of this little boat. Two other men are with us, for lifting and rowing in case the wind fail—me too, if it came to that.

I sleep at Ferris, who belong to a brown woman who run a inn further along the shore road. She have four slaves sleeping in a shed out the back, so one more body, especially since I come in with Ferris well after dark, wouldn't notice. The oldest one remember the Trelawny war, and some of the Maroons marching through here with the white soldiers and brown militia guarding them, on the way to Port Royal and Halifax. I don't mention Sister.

This morning before day Ferris wake me, and I follow him through the silent town and a little way up the hillside into mist, and to a hut in the corner of a field. As I see the young cotton tree growing over it I know in my bones that this is where Delphis lives. Mam has told me about this cotton tree. No other blackperson would live so close to one.

Ferris call like a owl and Delphis come out. I can feel that he's fraid for her. She hardly notice him; her nose point to me. Her painted red eye is misty, but the blue eye is like a lighthouse beacon in the mist.

"She say you is to come."

At least I know—at least I think I know—that Sister is alive.

"To come where?" I ask, but she doesn't answer me directly.

"Headley will take him," she say to Ferris, and hand something to him. "Give Headley this."

"How I will know her?" I's getting a little vex now. I's not a slave like Ferris.

"She will know you. Here." She step toward me, same time taking something from around her neck, lifting it over her head. It's a necklace of beads and stones and seeds, with a little feather at the bottom. Mam, who is not a full-time Christian, would still call it obeah, but I don't have time to think of words.

"Bend down you head," Sarah say. "Give her when you reach."

When it touch my skin, even though it's just come from resting against Sarah's, it feel icy, like when snow get into your clothes and is dripping down your back. I don't know if it's obeah, but it's something.

She turn without another word and go back into her hut.

Ferris, he doesn't waste time, scamper over the wall around the field and back down toward the town. As we's going, the sun's waking up behind some far hills and soon is peeping over into the town. Ferris take me down to the wharfs, to Headley, a short light-brown man with a body like a tree and eyes red from rum or from staring at the sea, maybe both. I don't her what they say but Headley look at me and nod. And I see that when Ferris hand him what Delphis give him, Headley's face tighten. It's a bangle, like the ones I bought from her yesterday for Georgia Marcy and Elorine. He put it on his wrist. He don't have any other thing on his arms.

"Come," he say to me, turning away from Ferris. "Help me load."

Coming along the coast I's thinking of Scotia and the sailboats taking people and goods to little coves and inlets along the shoreline. Just like here, it seem. And what my eyes are seeing now is new. The island is like a dawg, sleeping on the sea. One of those mongrels you can count every bone leading up to a spine of mountains, higher than the Scotia hills. At the same time, though, I feel like I's been feeling since I come off the *Eagle*. This place is new, but it is as if I know it in some part of me. It's not strange.

I's also thinking that maybe Da and Mam find the right person to leave Sister with.

≈ 51 ≈

Jason: Knob Hill, Tuesday, November 29

FROM KNOB HILL THE WHOLE OF Greencastle is beneath you. And it is a knob, rising from the slope going away beside the big house like a thumb under a green cloth of hillside. All the fields and works and quarters of Greencastle are visible from there—and the big house, appearing quite modest.

Squire made it his lookout on his kingdom. Often, when he was not down in the fields or the works himself, he was on Knob Hill, watching. I can remember him there, still as a statue on his big black horse whose name I've now forgotten, then suddenly galloping headlong down into the cane, shouting and swinging his riding crop angrily at all who were near, to correct by brute force and presence some piece of the vast human machinery that had gone awry. Looking out from here, he must have felt pride of ownership and achievement; at a remove, I can sympathize with such feelings. But Greencastle was his. It isn't, and I would not wish it to be, mine. I am caretaker to a legacy I did not seek, and in some measure abhor.

There are two views from Knob Hill. One is Olympian, of the bowl of the estate, including the approach to Flambouyant and the smoke from its barbeque rising through the trees. The other is quite the opposite, a view inward. You are aware of being exposed, a target. The events of the past few days sharpen that facet. Any number of people on Greencastle might wish me harm. Acts of violence can seem, from the safety of England, the vigorous strivings of an unfree spirit, the unquenchable flame of everyman's inherent birthright. The aspect is quite different here, when it becomes very personal.

For the moment things run tolerably smooth; I feel quite pleased with my considerable labours. Pompey and his sub-drivers and the other artisans keep the estate true to its quotidian rhythms; and to be fair to the bookkeeper Simpson, he does his job and keeps out of the way. But there may be those who wish me harm, either personally, as Hector probably did, or as a symbol of their condition. There is talk of rebellion for Christmas; everyone has heard it. In times past such rumours were exchanged between whites like children trying to mock at what frightened them. It is an annual rite that I am familiar with.

This year, however, appears different. I have not heard such talk myself—and to ask Lincoln would be gauche in the extreme—but have been assured that the slaves speak of it among themselves, not at secret meetings as in times past but in the field and in the town. As Mr. Livingstone has explained it to me, many think they would already be free but for the devilish trickery of the assemblymen in Spanish Town, who have placed their fat arses on the instructions of King William and the English parliament, of whose workings, especially in respect of the effort to abolish slavery, the slaves diligently inform themselves through the newspapers and the excitable table talk of their masters.

Among themselves and in their prayer meetings, they sing songs to Mr. Wilberforce. For their part the whites dare them to make themselves free. It is a fraught situation, perhaps the more easily grasped from the distance and height of Knob Hill.

I have been both now, so I can affirm that there can be no tender feeling between master and slave. At the same time, an estate is a world of fierce complexities. There are ties that weave like vines through the lives of all who dwell on it, that could pass for love in another kind of place. But such ties would not exist in some other place, or they would be crucially different.

The mixture of power and fear, brute force, dependency, and dread exists nowhere else but in the peculiar crucible that is an estate. It is a world of masks and mirrors, because the power and dread has two sides: the near-absolute power of life and death that Maasa enjoys over his chattel, and the dread within whites at the obliterative power that large numbers of slaves could summon at will or whimsy. I feel the seeds of it now in myself, that blight of white apprehension. But I feel also the instinct to lash out and cut down, like clearing the canefields for milling. And I cannot convince myself, as many, white and brown, manage with apparent ease, that their own proclivity for violence is actually the will of God in His majestic dispensation for an inferior people.

Such musings come naturally atop Knob Hill.

But they are brushed away like spiders' webs upon return to the flats and the quotidian. This morning it was to get a report from Pompey, confirmed by Simpson, of more runaways. Three of them were absent from this morning's count, Simpson says: a woman and baby, and two men. All of them have gone before, but not lately; the woman was released from the sickhouse just yesterday and didn't even bother to go back to her hut.

Their names brought no faces to mind, but I was concerned about the woman and baby. Simpson indicated two rough-looking men a little way off, each holding a large dog that looked very hungry (they are kept so, Anthony had advised me) and eager: the regular search party. I instructed Simpson to leave the dogs behind and go with the men to find the woman and child.

"What about the two men?"

"After you find the woman," I said. "They'll come back when they're hungry. Or the Maroons will get them and bring them back."

"You'll have to pay the Maroons," Simpson said. "The usual way is cheaper."

I concede the principle with a nod. "But your dogs may kill them," I said, "and they look hungry enough to eat the baby. They are Greencastle property."

I blanched inwardly to hear myself, and asked forgiveness of God and Carla. But it sufficed the occasion. The bookkeeper sent the men to kennel the dogs and meet him at the edge of Breadfruit Tree field for the search.

The woman had not gone far. She managed to climb a tree but the baby gave away their hiding place. I happened to glimpse the two hunters dragging the woman, the baby still squawling and Simpson behind, toward the stocks. I headed them off. Simpson's displeasure was palpable. Perhaps he thought to impress upon me his suitability for Wyckham's job, but if so he's driven that prospect further away.

The woman, Belva by name, was mildly grateful—if that is what her nod meant—for my sparing her the stocks. The dismissed hunters, when they were a little way off, taunted her with dire promises for the next time she ran. She was unmoved and unmoving, holding my eye with an appraising gaze.

"You want to fuck me?" Her flat rasping tone pinioned me in mid-thought: I had the notion to tell Constancia to send Jack to the woman with some pap for the child, who looked all sticks and string. "Is dat why you send to find me?"

I was about to answer her harshly when her eyes suddenly melted into pools of what could've appeared as calculation but was fever. The poor thing was still drawn and fraught from the birthing bed that she'd left only last evening. There were sores around her mouth and the sign of yaws in her thickened legs. I was disgusted. Far less at her, or by the momentary flash of myself in congress with so pitiable a creature, as at myself for presiding over such a cesspool of degeneracy as would bring a young woman, any young woman, to this pass.

It is a traffic as old as time that women would use their charms to favour themselves and change their circumstances, especially in respect of their children, for the better. I have not yet had any open offers, but I've been evaluated by several pairs of eyes in the field and the big house; the offers will no doubt come.

I was transported right back to one of those meetings in Reverend Swithenbank's little study when the reports from the missionaries or the latest outrage printed in the *Anti-Slavery Reporter* was read aloud, the air claustrophobic with our puffed-up superiority to the people being lampooned and denounced.

Am I becoming one of those people?

As odious evidence of this—or perhaps of destiny—I found myself, upon return to the house, in accidental proximity to the girl Miranda, she coming down the stairs that I was ascending to my room. I knew Jack, sedulous as always about my comfort, was waiting there to change my sweaty clothes, sponge me down and lay out fresh togs, which the Miranda child has helped her mother to make, in which I would dress for the dinner that was already being laid out by Balfour and his minions behind me.

She saw me first, and like the startled forest creature she'd reminded me of in our first encounter, she paused on the steps, halfway down, undecided whether to flee. The slave in her prevailed and I saw just the pink of her heels as she turned to escape. I recognized her from a scar on the back of her leg, a livid gash. I felt a small frisson of pleasure at the mere sight of her, something luminous and unsullied by the morass I had just traversed. A spirit thing. That was the first response. One that came from behind my eyes, one might say. But as I recall it now in recording the encounter, the dominant sense was not sight, but touch. The desire to touch that spirit child. And overarching that was the knowledge of my own authority, the power that was in my voice as it called out "No!" Not loud enough to be heard behind me in the dining room, where Balfour was fussing around, but firm enough to command Miranda's stillness on the steps. And I cannot but confess that my loins proposed the course of ordering Miranda to my room to perform Jack's duties. I could have done. And almost did. The thought alone gave a sheer electricity to the moment.

"Yes, Maasa?" It was a whisper from above, a scratch on the air. I looked up. She had turned; her bare toes gripped the edge of the stair. Above in the shadow her face seemed like a lamp. But it was, I recognized immediately, the face of a girl. Not a creature, not a thing. And not, though maturing in body as I could see plainly in the flimsy frock she wore, a proper subject, if such there be, of lust for any but the most depraved character.

In subsumed shame I stepped back and said to her, loud and gruff like the Maasa she'd called me, "Hurry up, pickni." I could not even look at her hurried descent as she shuffled quickly down and disappeared behind me.

≈ 52 ≈

Adebeh: Trelawny, Wednesday, November 30

HEADLEY TAKE ME ALMOST TO FALMOUTH by evening. He hand me over to a woman, Jacinth, who is one of those who help us to unload the things that his little ship brings. It's a busy port. Big ships like the *Eagle* in a big harbour, and small ones like ours at a jetty to one side. So nobody pay any mind when Jacinth and myself walk off the pier carrying a roll-up carpet on our shoulders and into the town. She is a strapping woman, big as me, and walk easily under the carpet. We don't talk much.

She take me through some streets to the house where her owner live. I have to say, Falmouth have plenty buildings the likes of which we only have a few in Halifax. Money is washing around this town. But it's not a healthy place, I can feel it in the air. The merchant who owns Jacinth, while he has a house in town that she takes me to, sleep in a house on a hill outside. The house in town, which is not small either, is in the charge of his mulatto son, Jacinth tell me, a man who look like a ginger root.

I only glimpse him from underneath the house where Jacinth lead me to store the carpet we bring, which is really three carpets roll into one. They are for her owner's house, the one outside town, not this one, which I can see from outside is not well tended. I learn what he care about under the house. Jacinth put me in a corner as she go upstairs to tell the son she's back. He follow her back down to inspect it, and she don't roll it out properly before he put his foot behind hers and fall her down on the carpet and drop on top of her. He's a big brute, and it take but a moment for him to rip her dress and peel her open from titty to toes like a plantain, and then open his trousers and plug her right there, never mind she must be dry. She's not making a sound nor moving a finger, before, during or after. Only her eyes are looking to the corner where she hide me, telling me not to move. This happen often, her eyes tell me also.

Later, she bring back two plates of food and we sit on some boxes and eat. We don't talk because people are moving around above us in the house. I notice something on her wrist. The same bangle that Ferris gave to Headley. A token. And I am a token passing from hand to hand along the pumpkin vine of One-Eye Sarah.

Four other slaves sleep down there with us. In the bottle lamps, I can only see that it's three women and a man. The man and one of the women sleep together in one space, one sleep close to Jacinth, and the other woman off by herself. I's in another corner. Jacinth must be explain to the others about me because more than to nod and look at me a few times they don't pay me any mind.

As we settle I hear more than one person moving around upstairs. Maybe the ginger man have a wife or woman up there, but I don't ask. The space under the house is cool and musty, but not only because of the air. This is one of those houses that is dark on the brightest day, dark with pain and fear. I can feel it heavy around all of us.

In the middle night somebody crawl onto my pallet. From the smell and the size I know it's Jacinth. She's crying, mewling like a puss. She wriggle right up against me but her two arms cross against her chest between us. So I put a arm round her shoulder and we sleep as best we can. Before first light she shake me and we go outside quiet into the street. She have to be back before Missus wake, she whisper, so she can't take me too far.

We's not the only people on the street, but everybody else is black so we's like duppies gliding through each other.

"Why you don't run away?" I ask Jacinth.

"Run where?"

"Come with me," I say before I even think it.

She don't say anything for a long while. And then she start to talk. One of the slaves who come down to sleep under the house is her daughter. She big like her Mumma, Jacinth say, but she is a gyal.

"Her first blood come just last Christmas. Him been trying to get at her from before that, I have to watch him like hawk. When I see him circling round I put myself in his way and he grab me instead. Sometimes twice in a day, and not only me, Clover too."

She walk a little more.

"If I was to come with you now, by tomorrow he have Kamla on her back and into her. By next Christmas him would mash her up wid that donkey something him have between him foot. And she would breed for him. Better me."

I can't think of anything to say.

The sky open up as we walk. It's still mostly black and a few brown people about in the streets. We's walking out of the town, toward the mountains I begin to see in the distance. We cross a road that carts and mules with riders are already travelling, both ways. People greet each other, but don't have time to stop and talk. The busyness and the light tell me that Jacinth has to leave me soon.

She stop us, point up at a little peak in the rim of mountains like a nipple on a dark young bubby.

"That is where you going," she say, her voice strong again. "Up to there, don't tell anybody you business. But you can ask for her on the other side, them will know her. Tell her Franky send howdy."

We look at each other. Her broad face is soft in this morning's light. Her eyes tell you a person lives there who know what she is about on this earth. I forget what I heard this morning and remember how she felt last night. I tell her tenky. I put my hand in my pouch to give her money but she wave it away and step back.

"Keep you cutlass close," she say, turning away.

"You too," I call after her. She laugh, and keep walking back toward town and that dark household.

I watch her a long time as she gets smaller, but she doesn't turn her head, so I turn mine.

⇒ 53 ⇐

Jason: Arresting Tombo, Thursday, December 1

MAGNUS DOUGLAS POUNCED THIS MORNING LIKE one of those chicken hawks that circle continuously above the fields like evil thoughts. His prey was Tombo, now charged with murder. He didn't come himself, of course. But Thomas, the fat white official who brought two armed men in uniform with him, made sure to tell me who'd sent him. The satisfaction in his voice no doubt was an echo of the voice of his master.

I followed them to the hothouse and watched them barge into the dark maw of the place, banging and shouting like devils. A few minutes later they emerged, Tombo dangled between the two guards like a broken mannequin, Thomas behind, pleased with himself.

But once I saw their intent—to tie John to one of the guard's mules and drag him the three miles to Bellefields—I urged Cherry into their midst and confronted Thomas.

"You'll not take him like that!" I shouted. "He's a cripple!"

"He got far enough into the bush when he was away," Thomas replied.

"But not on a rope behind a galloping mule."

"He's a murderer. Murderers don't ride."

"He's not a murderer," I said. "The driver was poisoned."

"That's not my business, the magistrates will decide." He took comfort in his lowly position of simply following orders and spurred his horse at me. I didn't move, so suddenly angry was I, and his horse reared and threw him. He yelled in terror and fell on his side to the hard ground, knocking out what Squire would've called his stuffing.

The commotion brought faces to the open spaces of the hothouse, and Portigee and Tanti Glory to the front steps. I took advantage of the confusion to send Jack for a mount, quick. One of Thomas's guards let go of Tombo to tend to his wheezing master; the other had the presence of mind to hold on to his prisoner but made no move to attach him to either mule.

Jack came back with a sorry-looking donkey just as Thomas, with the help of the guard, regained his feet and his breath.

"You can be sure Missa Douglas will hear of this," he puffed, brushing himself off.

"Here's a mount for your prisoner," I said, ignoring his fury and implied threat.

The man shouted, "He'll walk!" his face regaining its puce colour.

"Not on this estate," I replied, "and I'll follow you to town."

Thomas spun around at the guards. "Tie the nigger!"

By then Portigee and Hole-em were halfway down the steps, Portigee carrying a machete that looked like a toothpick in his hand, Hole-em's slight stature given heft by the jangling accoutrements of his office. From the top step Tanti Glory presided over them all like a dark witch, holding the sceptre of Tombo's bush staff that was taller than herself.

It was an untenable situation: had Thomas been on his horse he could've simply ridden away and there would've been nothing I could do except to physically assault him—with dire consequences for all of us. But he was surrounded by hostile black people and his own guards were clearly intimidated. The matter was settled by Portigee lifting Tombo like a sack and placing him on the donkey Jack was holding. With an inane smile, the giant jailer handed the rope tying the old man's hands to a guard. Another slave had caught the white man's horse and now brought it to him.

"They're right about you," he growled at me, once re-seated on his horse. "Pussy nigger." I smiled briefly and inclined my head in a nod, but said nothing. A verbal fight would've eroded the momentary advantage that had been won.

Myself and Jack followed them all the way to the jail in Bellefields.

⇒ 54 ⇐

Adebeh: Climbing to Sister, Thursday, December 1

AFTER LEAVING JACINTH, OR FRANKY AS she know herself, it take me the whole day to reach the hilltop. I see a lot of people on the way but I make sure they don't see me.

The first thing was to get around a big sugar estate that spread out on the flat and up into the hills I's heading for. That take me until the middle day, but I find myself in a provision ground just when I's hungry. I feel a little bad for tiefing from slaves, but only a little, man must live. I only take a sweet yam and two plantains. I go further up and then find a hollow by a stream to roast them in a small fire that doesn't make much smoke, like Henry teach me.

As I get closer the body of mountains flatten themself, as if they's taking a deep breath. But the bubby is still standing up and I keep it in view. From time to time I hear noises that tell me somebody is nearby, and when that happen I find a tree or rock to stand against, still as them. One time a gun fire not twenty yards away. I drop on the ground like I's dead, and watch through the leaves to see a black man with a gun, followed by another man with a bag that is dripping blood. They's hunting for food to carry back to Backra on the estate. But they could as easy turn and hunt me.

And then night tumbles down the mountains like God throw a sheet over the world. I's been following a little stream, so I look for the nearest big tree to lay down against. Give thanks to Henry and the bigi pripri, I's not afraid to be alone in this bush. I give thanks also for the heavy linen clothes that Mam insist I wear. They draw attention to me, but at night they keep me warm. I bless the pieces of plantain and yam that leave over from midday, and leave some pinches on the roots. By the time I finish eating, I have just enough mind to bring out my cutlass and rest it across my lap. In case. And then God's dark sheet swallow me too.

What wake me is something trying to take that cutlass from me. My hand tighten of itself on the handle, and my legs come under to get me up, but I bounce something hard and alive, and end up rolling down into the river. The wetness shock me awake, but I still hold onto the cutlass handle. I steady myself and face two men standing on the bankside where I was sleeping. It's bright morning. I's slept late.

Like with Pembroke and Darby, one man is bigger than the other, very big and dark.

They step apart to flank me. I keep the big one in the corner of my eye but I focus on the smaller one, who put me in mind of a ferret. Neither of them have a weapon that I can see, but he look the more dangerous.

The big one ask me who I am, but I's looking still at the other as I answer that it's none of his fucking business. They laugh.

"Is the magistrate business," the small one say, and the tone of his voice tell me I am right to watch him, he is the leader.

"I will tell the magistrate then," I say. "You is not a magistrate."

The big one step into the water and I turn the cutlass toward him while I keep my eye on the other. I can't keep them off forever, I realize, and they's not going away. I will have to do something with the cutlass to one of them. They know that also.

"Which one of you want to dead?" I say, and look quickly at both and then back at the smaller one.

"Who you belong to?" that one ask.

"Myself."

"What you doing here?"

"My business, not yours."

"Maybe is more of us behind," the small one says with a little grin.

"One of you will still dead," I say. I point the cutlass at him. "Maybe you."

He blink at that. The big one scoop water from the river suddenly and throw it at me. It fling me off-balance, and as I's struggling not to fall I feel my shirt tear open. I's about to slash at the big one first cause he is nearest, when they both stop dead. They's both looking at me, but not at my face. At my chest.

The necklace that One-Eye Sarah give me for Sister holds those two men like a hand. While they's staring at it I steady myself in the water and step to the other bank, keeping the cutlass ready. But they's not going to rush me, even together. They frighten.

The small one speak first, still not looking in my face. "You passing through?" I's still trying to settle my breath so I just nod.

The big one step back onto the bank where they'd surprised me. His eye don't leave the necklace. The smaller one, his face melting into a oily smile, ask, "Where?"

I was about to answer him when I hear Da in my head like he was right there beside me. *Stupid like monkey, wise as snake.* So I speak with my cutlass, waving him onto the far bank beside his friend. When he don't move I step toward him and he jump back to where I want him to be. Now I's looking down at them. I step back half a step, over and over, backing myself away from them into the shrubs and trees, looking to get away and hide.

And then all of a sudden the small brown one reach behind him and pull out something from his waist and rush across the river pointing it at me, screaming. But as he's scrambling onto my bank he trip, and fall right at my feet. I bring down the cutlass right away and juk it right through him until it stop in the ground. He scream and scream and the blood burst in a fountain. I don't feel it. I's looking into his eyes.

The green light in them flare and then dribble away like dirty water into the ground he is lying on. What he has in his hand is a short planting stick, smooth and shine from use. We have them in Boydville. The dark point that fire has made hard and deadly could kill me as easily as my cutlass killed him.

The sunlight overhead catch the blood and riverwater on his skin and set it alight. It's almost pretty. But by then he is dead.

As I's looking down at him I hear more splashing, and I glance up to notice the big black one scrambling into the bush away from us.

I hear him crashing through the leaves for a little, and then nothing more.

"Why you do it? I just want to go on my way and find Sister. I wasn't troubling you, is you trouble me."

I's never killed a man before in my life. I had to, or he would kill me, pure murder was in his eye. But my stomach heave and I spin away just in time to puke onto the ground behind me. Then I start to shiver and shake like a winter breeze is blowing round me. Then I feel hot like a fire is in my skin. I stumble over to the river to wash out my mouth and the water feels scalding.

I barely know what I's doing and don't have two thoughts straight in my head until I come to myself sitting between two toes of a big cotton tree, as far in as I can go. Hiding. From what I don't know, myself maybe. My right hand is burning, and it's not until I let go of the cutlass that I realize that I's been holding it tight since last night. I can't barely feel my fingers.

I sit there a long time. I don't even wonder about the duppies that Mam say live in those trees. I don't think about the ancestors who might be round about. All I can think is, Why he do it? And the only answer I find is the necklace that I am to give to Sister.

One-Eye Sarah is a blessing and a curse both. She's turned me into a killer. The necklace, which I didn't even remember until the fall into the river showed it to the men, hang heavy round my neck now. Like a rope. I feel to tear it off and dash it into the bush. But when I lift my hand to remove it, my fingers start to tremble. It's clinging to my chest like a magnet.

≈ 55 ≈

Jason: Fallen, Friday, December 2

IN THE DARKEST MOMENTS OF LAST NIGHT I heard Isaiah cry out in Reverend Swithenbank's sepulchral voice: *Woe is me! I am undone! I am a man of unclean lips and dwell among a people of unclean lips.*

I've now fully joined the people I dwell amongst, and am indeed undone. But I cannot blame any agent beyond my own will and permit. My lips are unclean by the pieties they've uttered on historical occasions. I am the steersman, put on the rocks by my own cravings.

I can try to blame my fall from dubious grace on the demon rum, but that would be sophistry. I'd returned from the expedition into Bellefields with Tombo and Thomas exhausted, despondent, and deeply angry. After a meal for which I had no appetite, and whose silences and silly chatter revealed the women's incomprehension of my action in the affair of Tombo's arrest, I sent Jack for a flask—an unusual enough occurrence to silence them—and retired to my eyrie.

Seated at my desk reading, I'd had but two shots when I heard the door open behind me and turned to see Lucia's speculative eye. I'd noticed it before as she'd pass me downstairs about whatever business was hers in the household. She's Israel's daughter, I'd learnt from him, and I don't put it past the old rascal to support the ambitions quite evident in her appraising glances.

I knew at once the evening's possible course and, by saying nothing, chose it. She'd assayed her case before in just such a manner and at such a time of day. I'd rebuked it with a frown and a turning of my back. Tonight I did neither. I waited for her entry and her closing of the door, serious as the proverbial judge, but one whose gravitas was compromised in secret by his cock, rising as the equally proverbial morning rooster.

The prettiest women serve in the house, and retain their looks far longer than those in the field, from better and more food and easier tasks. Lucia's pretty, with lively eyes that mirror her name. She's by no means a girl, though, with a belly that's been ploughed, sown, and has cropped more than once, I'd think. She's brown, as almost all the house slaves are, and pockmarked, though not badly.

The habitual everyday clothing of slaves, even those in the house, is economical. Bellies and breasts may not be on deliberate display but are not always sequestered. There are exceptions, however. One token of favour by one or other white in the big house is clothing. Lincoln, for instance, could unnerve my childhood eyes when seen from the back, seeming a shorter version of Squire, whose clothes he inherited and had adjusted.

And Lucia had attracted my notice for being the most stylishly dressed of the female house slaves. That remembrance also brought recognition: hers was the naked brown back laid across Anthony's desk that afternoon when he'd slaked his thirst.

I'd seen it in the eyes of even Mathilde, but especially Anna: the wonder that I've not yet fallen into the practice of actively expressing my presumed concupiscence, licence being in the very air and the means of satisfaction effortlessly to hand. It'd be an easy enough habit to develop, and it's expected of me as Maasa. But I've withheld any show of interest, both in the house and the field, where the overseers and bookkeepers, even some of the drivers, are known to fuck the females in situ, as a prerogative. And Anthony, as I'd been made aware, is not exempt.

My ambiguous position in the household while I grew gave me a close perspective on the politics of it, one that I came to a fuller understanding of as I grew older. An estate is a bubbling cauldron of jealousies and struggles for the attention that equates, however fleetingly, to power. And in no part of an estate is that wrangle more aggressive as in the big house.

There, a favourite of the couch is expected, almost an institution. In Squire's time, in the interregnum between Anthony's mother and marriage to Mathilde—indeed even when Mathilde was in residence as "housekeeper"—there were several, serially. Here was Lucia, come this evening to both show her hand and claim her rightful place with the new Maasa.

In the specious calm of this morning's recollection, however, the most heinous of all the several aspects of this matter is that throughout the tumbling and heaving with Lucia my mind's eye—my loin's eye, I should more honestly say—was filled with images of the girl Miranda. I don't often see her in the house; she's hidden away in a cubicle behind Anna's room with her mother Prudence and another girl, where they work at making and mending clothes for Mathilde and Anna, and more recently myself.

Anna, determined to naturalize me, regularly commands me to them for fittings. I go willingly, though having no interest in the clothing. It is Prudence who always attends to me while telling me, with a lift of pride, that her daughter is responsible for making whatever I happen to be wearing. My compliments and thanks, however, always find the back of the girl's head. I know not whether it is modesty or aversion but now—as my feelings have developed in complexity and force—I have not the gall, as at our first meeting on the piazza, to command her face. She is always turned to the window for the light, which dances on her needle and allows her eyes and fingers surety in their purpose. At least so I tell myself.

The eyes of Lucia as I passed her in the house today were bright and greedy. I felt everyone else's on me: nothing remains hidden long in this house of glass. While such behaviour is expected of the Maasa, I blush with shame at myself for being that much the Maasa. And at the thought of facing Carla, however distant that prospect. The blush is deeper for the fact that at the same time as I deplore the event, I sense it will happen again. With Lucia most likely, and possibly also with others. Whatever the squirmings of my conscience, the bodily signs are all there.

Consideration of this presents a sere prospect that puts me in mind of Mr. Shelley's Ozymandias, King of Kings, and the toppled ruins that surrounded his remains on the lone and level sands stretching far away. Anthony's return seems immeasurably distant, and I can easily imagine my broken self sinking into such a wasteland.

As countervail and sop against the darkness I hold up the girl Miranda's so-far untouched radiance—even as it melts my loins.

≈ 56 ≈

Elorine: Ishmael Arrested, Friday, December 2

THEY COME FOR HIM THIS MORNING.

Cyrus was just getting the furnace going, Ishmael still inside finishing his bickle. The sweet stinging smoke is filling the yard and mixing with the smells of Jassy's cooking when the gate burst open and three black men in uniforms that could do with a sew and a wash ride into the yard on some mules that look as woeful as them. I'm inside at the table with Pappi, but Cyrus tell me afterward that they look around like hungry dawg for a scrap. After them the chief scavenger himself, Johncrow Thomas, ride in. His horse is a horse, but is only barely not a mule. Living here, I get to know horse almost like I know cloth, and you can tell where in society a man stand, especially a whiteman, from what he ride.

This one is lowly. He is a mongoose looking for flesh, down to his face, which sit on top of a big body and is small and pointy-nose, with his chin running straight into his neck.

Just then Pappi present himself on the steps from the house, setting off to start his day's toil.

"Livingstone?" Thomas shout at him. He know full well who Pappi is.

He nod at the whiteman, and say "Good morning," like he say friendly to everybody, black, brown or white, if he see them come in. He's thinking is business, I can stay inside and hear that in his voice. But is another business the scavengers come about.

"I am arresting you," Thomas continue in the same loud voice as if he want to shout down in advance anybody who might have a thought to talk back to him. That bring me outside, in time to hear Ishmael say, still polite, "For what, sir?"

"The magistrate will tell you for what!" the Backra bawl-out.

"You don't know, sir?" Ishmael ask, raising his voice a little but still polite.

That is when the slimy red snail Boynton, puffing himself up like a frog, screech, "Silence!" as he get down from his mule, the other two Nayga also. The three of them walk toward Pappi, Boynton pulling irons from his waist to clamp on Pappi. Irons that for all I know make right here, cause Pappi do work for the courthouse sometimes.

Pappi look down at Boynton like the worm that he is and tell him, "Don't form the ass, Cully." Ishmael speak quiet, to him alone like is a personal conversation, and the fool have enough sense to realize that he's looking into trouble's very face. His hand leave the irons where they are.

"Cuff him up, nigger!" Mongoose Thomas shout at Boynton like he's telling a dawg to sit.

Boynton deflate like you juk him. Backra behind him with his big voice and power, Ishmael in front threatening him with his eyes. He look like he might doo-doo himself. Pappi save him.

"I will go with you, sir," he says to Thomas, firm and level. "But you don't have to cuff me." What his voice is telling the rodent is that nobody would dare to cuff him and take him through the streets.

For a moment I see the thought fly through his eyes that this facety Nayga must be beaten down like Boynton. But Ishmael, never mind his hair is grey, he's the biggest man in that yard and the heavy work he's been doing all his life show on his arms and shoulder. Mongoose understand that right enough. He hold himself back and bark at his Nayga-dem, "Bring him!" then wheel himself out of the yard.

As if they're not there Pappi turn to me. His eye have a deep fury in them, but also a softness for me to melt in.

"My help cometh from the Lord, who made heaven and earth," he say like he's telling me goodnight. "Be of good courage, and He shall strengthen your heart."

As he's walking out he turn to where Cyrus is standing in the workshop door with his mouth open and call out, "Cyrus, hold firm. And close the gate."

None of us that leave behind move for another minute. My head was spinning and Jassy start to bawl loud-loud as soon as Cyrus close the gate. But he had to open it back a little later as customers start to come. Poor Cyrus. He don't know what to tell them why Ishmael isn't there, and there is only some things he can do by himself. So Pappi lose business that day, and who knows when he will come back? Backra is like Jehovah, mysterious in his ways.

As I'm trying to calm myself to think what to do, I also feel the anger rising inside me.

Backra might be mysterious but Maasa God is not vicious. They will keep him there for all kinds of make-up reason, or for no reason at all. He's black, but he don't bend his knee to them. That is reason enough for Backra.

I couldn't but be mindful of the week before last Sunday's preachment, though. Something tell me that that have something to do with this.

But I couldn't think what to do. I send Jassy over to Mother Juba across the street for Christian, her grandson. When he was a pickni I teach him to read and write Sunday mornings, and he run errands for me sometimes. I send him up to Greencastle for Jason.

Jason: Visiting Prison, Friday, December 2

RIGHT AFTER BREAKING MY FAST, I set off for Bellefields to see the situation with Carpenter John. I'd promised him yesterday. I alerted Pompey, with whom the tasks for the day had been agreed the evening before, and Simpson, the bookkeeper and senior white on the estate. Not in my hearing, but Simpson had expressed disapproval of my decision to banish the whip, and of my programme of task work. He'd found himself to Greencastle straight off the ship from Bristol, and the overworked Anthony had taken him on; he was here before Wyckham. Without a reference from Anthony (or now myself), he has nowhere else to go except back to the wharf. And though he is young he's not stupid. I'm determined, however, that he's going no further on Greencastle—not during my hegemony anyway. He has the look of a Cassius, lean and hungry, but not for food. No doubt he's one of the general pack of brutal civilizers. When I told him where I was going his eyes betrayed the same incredulity as Mathilde's—that I should be bothering about a slave, and such a pitiful one at that, soon ready for superannuation and in any case, if accused by the authorities, likely guilty of something.

I was uncertain myself as to my true motives. Perhaps I was being sentimental about Bristol his son, a playmate of my childhood whom I'd honestly forgotten until returning and encountering his broken father. Was I grateful in some dubious way for Tombo's part in the dispatch of Hector—who would've been a nemesis, as driver or field hand? Was I seeking to balance the scales of conscience: Tombo for Lucia? Whatever the reason, I knew I could not live with myself if I merely let the law and custom of this place take its course. And I'd promised.

It was, as often after rain the night before, a cool blue morning, and Cherry and I were in fine animal spirits despite our serious purpose. I thought to visit the Livingstones but deemed it too early—on the way back, I thought, to cheer myself against the almost certain embroilment, physical and mental, that lay ahead.

As it turned out a visit was made, but at the jail!

It was sufficiently difficult, and testing of my patience and manners, to gain admission to Tombo. The florid, fat white man Thomas, who'd taken Tombo away the day before, simply refused me pass.

"He's my slave," I said, firm in voice while flinching inwardly at my emphasis. "You cannot deny me access to my property."

"You're merely an attorney," he said with a smug smile. "Not the owner."

"I act for the owner," I replied with some heat, "with all his rights and privileges."

"He's a murderer!" said Thomas, who reeked of stale rum and fresh sweat.

"He's not," I said, "and that's not for the likes of you to decide." The insult had the same effect as my defiance yesterday: a flare of fury quickly quenched. He would've heard by now that I'm a legal person, which he is not. While out on the street a white skin trumps a brown, in the confines of a courthouse slightly different conventions apply.

"I'll hang him myself," he said, attempting a mocking laugh as I walked past into the shadowy regions behind him.

There, an enormous fetid cage comprised the jail, relieved only by the bars that allow air to reach the occupants from within, there being only slits in the three walls. There were thirty or forty of them in various postures of despair and shame, almost all of them dark-skinned. Women and children were mixed among the men like differently shaped bundles, the whole a restless mass made urgent by my unexpected presence. Arms and voices reached out to me as I looked for Tombo. I'd just sighted him when I heard my name called. I turned to the voice and came face to face with Ishmael Livingstone.

I don't know who was the more startled. He smiled as if my presence were a private joke; my mouth probably hung open.

"Elly send you?" He said it as though that was part of his joke. I could only shake my head. "So what bring you to this place?"

My gaze flickered away to Tombo, whose cyclopean eye was fixed on me. That gave me back my voice. "Someone from Greencastle," I said, my tone hushed. "And what are you doing here?" I managed to ask. The bars between us widened the small space, a few feet at most, that separated our persons, a monstrous cleavage in the world.

He laughed, himself again. "They say I'm preaching without a licence."

It's a serious charge under a law used, by denial or withdrawal, to persecute Wesleyan and Baptist missionaries who are not lapdogs of the planters; particularly virulent in their hounding are the Anglican pastors like Umbratus, he of the vituperative letters to the papers. To our meetings in his home, Reverend Swithenbank read aloud many reports from Wesleyan preachers thus harassed and silenced.

The lawyer in me asserted itself to ask, "Do you need a licence? I thought it was only for foreign preachers."

"It depend on who you ask," he said, still smiling.

That was puzzling enough, but when I asked him if he had one, I was confounded by his shrug. What exactly did that mean?

He saw my confusion and said, with an odd formality, "I'd count it a favour if you go and see Missa Cavendish at the vestry and ask him to stop by here." He was, in his way, answering my unasked question. I promised that I would.

The sense of abandoning Mr. Livingstone trailed me over to Tombo, who smiled a greeting worth riding all the distance for. He'd been punched and battered, I saw this immediately on his face and almost bare shoulders. But he smiled and said through his few teeth, "They setting to hang me, Kwesi," his use of my childhood name conveying an incongruous intimacy in the dreadful ambiance.

"I won't let them do that, John." I spoke with more confidence than I felt, and pushed out a little smile to match his.

The courage of the slave, the black, is based as much on despair as on personal bravery. Life, law, and custom have reduced him to a thing, a beast, a speck of dust. The world can grind him no smaller than it's already done. His cackle of laughter, his shrug of a shoulder, his quiet mockery of authority and circumstance is his claim to humanity, a comfort that only death can expunge.

"I'll get the doctor to speak in court," I said.

Tombo's fuller shoulder shrugged as if of its own accord. "Yes, Maas Jason." His lopsided smile was him patting my shoulder in consolation.

It was too early for the clerk of the court to be at his desk. So I rode out to the far side of town where I understood Dr. Fenwell to live. Would he testify for Carpenter John?

The doctor was on his front porch in a large rattan chair puffed with cushions that all but swallowed him. He was out there for the blazing sun, which pierced him like a sword but was surely life-giving. When suddenly, while we spoke, a cloud blocked the brightness, it was as though the man wilted, like a plant we children called shame-old-lady that we could make shrivel by touching. I didn't yet know when Tombo's trial would take place and wondered whether the man would survive for it.

His old yellow eyes roamed my face speculatively for several seconds. I thought he was deciding on his answer. Instead, his first words to me with a brief sad smile were, "You favour your father."

I blushed, but drove past it in my anxiety about my mission. With far less grace than his, I said, "So I've been told."

He halted me again. "I didn't know who had sent for me, at first. 'Maas Jason', Israel said." The doctor's eyes searched my face. "I remember you now. Anthony was a torment in your life. Squire missed you."

His voice was quite strong but he spoke in long breaths, beneath which a dark silence lurked. "Somebody poison the driver." The broadening of his speech lifted my spirit.

I asked specifically about the wound: could that have killed him?

"Eventually, maybe, if it wasn't treated. But that old doctress was treating it." He chuckled with respect for Tanti Glory's skills, which were known far and wide in the district. "Somebody get him with his food. Doubtless cassava. Nice for cakes and pone, but certain death if you know what to do with it. From what Fergus tell me, he deserve it."

I considered letting him know the likely source of the poison but as quickly decided to spare the old man that tragic story.

"And you'll come to court?" I heard myself, anxious as a child at Christmas.

"If God spare life," he sighed. "When?"

My worry renewed itself. "I'll let you know," I told him, thinking to myself that I'd get an affidavit also, in case.

To show me out the doctor called the said Fergus, who was familiar to me from the *Eagle*. Back on home turf he'd regained some of the ease I remembered in our earlier encounters on the ship. The memory of the awkwardness of our final shipboard meeting, however, inhibited my tongue, so I sought a generality.

"Do you know the Livingstones?" I asked him.

He grinned, a little patronizingly. "Yes, sah."

My news of Ishmael's arrest wiped his smile clean away.

"Do you know where I can find Mr. Cavendish?" I asked him, and told him why.

"Yes, sah. At the vestry. But he won't reach there yet; you'd better find him at his warehouse down by the wharf."

Cavendish, when I found him in the dusty reaches of an odorous cavern, knew immediately who I was—it was my morning for favouring Squire. He knew too, I'm sure, of the unusual practices at Greencastle.

"As long as the peace is kept," he said, a severe gaze fixed on me—an occupational attribute, I suppose, a vestryman being a powerful political broker in our system, accustomed to being heeded. His obvious prosperity gave authority to his admonition.

I assured him that it was not my intention to disturb anyone's peace. I then, before he could figuratively pat me on the head, told him that someone else's peace had been unduly disturbed, and reported about Mr. Livingstone.

He laughed quietly and shook his head as if at the thought of a recalcitrant child. Such is the sense of power seeming to inhere in the man that, despite what might be called my republican reservations about him, I was comforted on Mr. Livingstone's behalf.

"I will make surety for him," I said, "and will speak for his character."

"It's not his character that is in dispute," Cavendish said, stern again. "Everyone involved in his prosecution know him well. There's something else at work against him." He looked thoughtful but said no more.

I asked if he would visit the jail, as requested.

Still caught in the tangle of his own thoughts he nodded. "For what good it'll do," he said. "Yours is the more useful part. Tell Byfield I support your application."

"Byfield?"

"The clerk of the court. A fool, but you must be nice to him. For Ishmael's sake."

That proved difficult. The clerk of the courts is a mixture of oil and vinegar. The former was in full flow as I stood in the doorway of his office and heard him greasing the spirit of a white man who apparently had a matter before the court that had not reached hearing as speedily as the man would have liked.

"I will do my utmost, Mr. Harricks. A word in the ear, you know?" Byfield tapped his nose and beamed at Harricks in collusion with the power they both shared by virtue of their skin, hinting at his own place in the hierarchy of influence. Harricks wasted no more words but turned and brushed past me in a cloud of rancid sweat. Which brought Byfield's eyes, following him, to mine. His narrowed immediately.

"Yes?"

As I told him the first part of my business, to pledge surety for Ishmael Livingstone, the vinegar appeared.

"And who are you?" His tone was addressed to my skin-colour, and its place in the scheme of things.

I told him my name, which did not affect his expression. Then I told him that Vestryman Cavendish would be along to support my application for surety.

The oil returned. "Well, in that case . . ." His voice smarmed me, but without the slightest brightening of the eyes. "The magistrate will set it when the time comes."

"When will that be?" I asked.

"Later today," Byfield said, his curt, dismissive self again. And then his eyes did catch a light as he looked up at me. "Or he might keep the prisoner confined," he said with something close to satisfaction.

That struck a blow, and he saw it.

"The charge is a minor offence," I said. I kept my voice determinedly firm so as not to give even a hint of pleading.

"Not at all," he said, and fiddled with the papers on his desk. He lifted his head to throw me a malicious grin before bending it to read: "Preaching rebellion, it says here." His studied casualness fully conveyed his malice.

I heard the vestryman's voice in my head: *There's something else at work against him.* And that's when the charge was a minor one!

"That's preposterous," I heard myself say. The voice conveyed indignation but my body and mind were numb. Preaching rebellion is a capital offence.

My outrage had no effect on Byfield except to tighten his lips. "We cannot tolerate rebellion," he said. "Or those who encourage it."

But his eyes, and an involuntary lift of his shoulder like a spasm, betrayed something more than official determination. Fear.

And that set off a strange internal conversation, as though my memory grew ears and I listened for the first time to words I'd heard before. Mathilde and Anna are my conduit to the world beyond Greencastle—I hardly go beyond its gates except for specific purposes and the too-few visits to the Livingstones. Anna in particular is about the district like a horsefly, visiting her age-mates in town and country. It's not all frivolous time-filling: sometimes she has estate business with Lawyer Alberga or others. Whatever her purpose, she brings back bon-bons of gossip and news with which to regale us at table. I've learnt the most scurrilous and intimate details of men and women, free and slave, whom I've never met nor am likely to meet—and hope I don't. A young woman raised by and with slaves, she offers her most scandalous information with the phrase they use: So me get it, so me give it.

But for all her flippancy about some matters, Anna is astute about other kinds of information gathered on her jaunts. And—inwardly trembling for Elorine's father in front of this self-important man—I recognized that I'd paid insufficient attention to Anna's chattering. The Negroes have a saying: "One-one pebble fill-up de ribber." What Anna brought back were the pebbles of unrest. Mathilde would gently scoff that it was part of the Christmas-season gossip, every year. Anna would demur.

"This is not su-su, Mama. They planning something out west. Everybody say so. And our Nayga in the district know about it." She'd drop her voice and look in the direction of the kitchen, where she knew Balfour hovered just out of sight. "If something happen there, it might happen here," she'd whisper hoarsely.

I'd ride back out into the fields worrying about rows dug or ratoons planted for the next crop, brushing Anna's words like dust from my shoulder. I'd comfort myself with Mathilde's disbelief.

Standing in front of Byfield, I understood the change in charge against Ishmael. What was up, in Vestryman Cavendish's phrase, was the old nostrum at work: prevention is better than cure. Whose was the guiding hand I did not know, though I thought of Magnus Douglas, the justice of the peace and magistrate, before whom Ishmael could well appear later in the day. In any case, white officialdom, knowing Ishmael's place in the Bellefields community, of all colours and conditions, would seek to make an example of him, light a beacon to match the rumours of (and possibly plans for) rebellion smouldering around them.

In Biblical terms, Ishmael is to be the offering whose sacrificial smoke would appease the whites—as well as cleanse rebellious thoughts from the minds of the blacks.

≫ 58 ≪

Elorine: Hope in the Lord, Friday, December 2

COURTHOUSE IS FULL. THIS IS BLACKPEOPLE'S amusement. The entertainments they put on in St. Agnes church hall is for whitepeople—the money, for one thing. Our festivities is free. Funeral, and courthouse. Dead serious matters, but we laugh nonetheless. We have to laugh. It's how we stop from killing those same whitepeople. And weself, though some do that.

It's not a big courthouse we have in Bellefields. I hear they have big ones in Spanish Town and Montego Bay and Kingston, but that might be because they have so many wicked people there.

Everybody is sitting close, me and Jason squeeze-up together on a piece of bench. The smell of Nayga around you is strong as syrup. You can see the sweat on the magistrates' face.

They sitting there like johncrow, the two of them, waiting for Pappi. They's fat and shining from the goodness that they suck every day from us. It's no wonder blackpeople is so mawga.

When Jason arrive to tell me what they're planning to charge him with, it didn't come as any surprise. I keep warning him to be careful in what he say, in the chapel and otherwise. He like to tell me, *I must be about my Father's business*, but I tell him back that his earthly father wasn't a preacher, and whiteman can't lay hand on his heavenly Father.

Well, now they have him. And I can't do better than he teach me from small: *Trust in the Lord, He will recompense you.* Cause to tell truth, I'm frighten. Jason say he will speak up for him and give a surety so they will let Pappi come home tonight. Missa Cavendish will speak for him also, though he don't reach the courthouse yet. Jason say he will get Lawyer Alberga to be in court for Pappi if a trial comes, this is only a hearing. But I'm still frighten. I don't put anything past that Magnus. His is the evil hand behind this palampam, I know it in my footbottom. I don't give chapter and verse to Jason when he wonder aloud what cause them to change the charge, and I don't say anything at all about me and the Magnus-one. Time enough for that in due course.

And he is the chief johncrow today, sitting in the middle of the table even though he's younger than the one beside him. That one is nearly sleeping already, though is only three little matters they hear so far, the woman next to me say.

I reach just in time for them to finish off with one little old man. I hear him tell Magnus he eat the chicken but he didn't steal it, cause he belong to Maasa, the chicken likewise. So is like Maasa dawg eat Maasa chicken, he say, and that cannot be stealing. Poor wretch, he still get himself three days in the bilboes and one hundred lashes. And the Magnus-one, he have the gall to pronounce, "Go thou and steal no more," a big smile on his face. I feel Jason squirm beside me. Maasa Jesus will not be mocked. Judgement will reach Magnus. And for more than what he do as magistrate.

Then the fat little whiteman that sit under the magistrate table call out "Bring in Ishmael Livingstone!" like his mouth full of hot food and nowhere to spit it.

People in the courthouse know him, of course, and everybody but those up front surprise to see him here. A whispering breeze run through them as he come out. Everything hold breath for a second. Me too. But I let it out when I see him. He look exactly like when they take him away this morning. Even though Jason assure me that he look his usual self when he see him, I was expecting them to do something to him downstairs in the jail, beat him up or something, cause they didn't get to abuse him in the yard when they arrest him.

His eye catch on me and Jason and he smile a big smile. My stomach unclench a little as he turn to face the two whiteman.

But I only have to look around Pappi broad back at Magnus face to understand that this is nothing to smile about.

"Clerk," Magnus announce, his face like he's hungry, "read the charge."

Jason say that when he went back down into the jail to tell Pappi that they change the charge, Pappi didn't say anything, just get still-still. All the way through the fat little whiteman reading out book and receipt of what-and-what Pappi say to be inciting rebellion, I don't see a muscle move in his back as he listen to the words that could hang him. The Magnus-one is watching him close, looking for something in Pappi face, but he don't know Ishmael Livingstone. He'd drop dead right there before he show any concern to the likes of Magnus or the old man beside him.

"Do you understand the charge?" He's still trying to provoke Pappi.

I can see from how his ear move that he's smiling as he say, "Yes, sir." His voice is his render-onto-Caesar voice that he use in the shop with his white customers, but the smile vex Magnus.

"And how do you plead?" Is the old man croaking, his voice full of the mucus in his throat.

"Not guilty, sir," say Pappi quick and brisk.

"The prisoner is bound over on the capital charge of rebellion until trial at the Assizes at a date to be set."

"Next week," say the croaking lizard beside Magnus, before clearing his throat.

"Take him below," Magnus announce and bang-down his hammer.

Is like he lick Jason with it. He jump-up and say, "May it please the court, I'll pledge surety for Mr. Livingstone, for him to be released until trial."

Well, it didn't please the court at all, not the three whiteman that Jason was talking at. The little fat one that read out the charge turn whiter, like he see duppy, and the old one choke on the slime in his throat. The Magnus-one lower his eyelids and throw a look at Jason that could cut wood. "You're out of order, Pollard," he say, "I should find you in contempt."

"I'm not in contempt," Jason say, bright as a new coin. "Intemperate perhaps, Mr. Douglas, but not in contempt. Not yet. And I apologize to the court for my intemperateness, but I wanted to assure the court that they could release Mr. Livingstone and be assured he will return for trial."

"This is a matter of preaching rebellion. Bail cannot apply."

"It can, Mr. Douglas. Bail can always apply." Jason give a little nod. "At the pleasure of the court, of course."

"Is that so, Pollard? And what if the court does not pleasure?" He look around as if expecting somebody to clap him for making a joke.

"Then, Mr. Douglas," Jason say, cool as water, "the business of the town will be severely disrupted. There was considerable confusion at Mr. Livingstone's foundry when I visited there an hour ago."

"They can go to Brashfield," the old croaking lizard say.

"They can, and some of them will. But not all, and most of those will be back at Mr. Livingstone's in a few days."

The people in the courthouse, Nayga and otherwise, don't know Jason, though when they hear Pollard they sure to guess who he is connected to. What they know, and like, is that he talk back to the whiteman. Give them something hard to chew on. Nayga know from his own life that after everything, Backra might spit you out and go on with what he intended from the start. I give Jason a silent tenky.

But I also feel the steel between him and the Magnus-one. I remember they don't like each other from time. And since Jason come back maybe, they have words about that sister of his. They can take care of themselves, they are big man both. I am worried about what Magnus can do to Pappi. He have the handle and Jason, for all his fine lawyer talk, is holding the blade.

Then I notice the Byfield-one looking like he's choking on whatever he's thinking when Magnus and Jason are exchanging words. He turn his back to us and bend over to whisper to Magnus and the old man. The three of them back and forth a little, then Magnus bang his hammer again.

The two other whiteman jump, causing Nayga to laugh and giggle, causing Magnus to bang down again and call out, "Order in the court!" That is a joke you hear pickni with when they playing Court with each other. The one who is Judge find a piece of wood or metal and make the most noise he can with it, and call out, "Order in the court, you noisy niggers!" and everybody cackle like yard fowl.

But Magnus is serious. Nayga settle themself. "Bail is set at five hundred guineas." People draw breath—is plenty money that! "The prisoner will report to the courthouse every day, including Saturday and Sunday, and he is not allowed to preach in public at any time between now and his trial. Is that understood, nigger?" Is Pappi he talking to.

"Yes, sir," he say. His voice is flat like the table between them.

Magnus look at Ishmael and hold his breath. He waiting for Pappi to bend his knee and tell him tenky like the poor old man who Magnus send out for the hundred lashes. He don't know his man. He should talk to his Daddy, who know Ishmael good-good.

When he realize he not getting anything from Pappi, he address himself to Jason. "You is responsible for the prisoner. If he doesn't report every day, or if he says a word of preaching, you will be held in contempt and taken to the same Assizes. Do you understand, Pollard?"

Jason give his little bow. "If it please the court."

But everybody could see that it don't please the court at all, at all.

Narrative: Sister, Saturday, December 3

TWO WOMEN ARE DIGGING BELOW A SHACK perched on the hillside. But Adebeh knows Sister right away. She is built like their Mam. And with Da's hawk nose, which he says comes from the First People, who were here before the whites or the blacks, and which causes the Mi'Kmaq in Scotia to call Da one of their own.

Sister is a black eagle guarding the shack as he approaches; they spot each other the moment Adebeh comes round the clump of trees a few hundred yards back. He doesn't hesitate, taking his eyes from hers only to navigate around roots and big stones in the twisting path between them.

His parents could not possibly know what is built on the spot now, but the land's contours and landmarks are in their blood. Once he'd gone beyond the bubby that Franky pointed him to, he started looking for the outcrop of rock, square like a house, Da says. There are many outcrops, sudden and strange. Some covered in green, some half-naked. This is where the bigi pripri, when they were alive, evaded and ambushed their invaders. "Look for the one with two big tree hanging out one side," Da tells him. "Like two flag." Adebeh feels the welcoming presence of the ancestors around him as he treks, calming him from the trauma of his attack. Bringing him to this end of journeying.

"Who you is?" she demands when he stops about ten yards below her. She lifts her arms slightly to show that she has a cutlass and a pointed stick, one in each hand. She's as big as he is and on a rise above him. He keeps his own cutlass limp.

But he smiles. The long journey is over.

"You is Baddu," he says, still smiling. "I's you bredda. Adebeh. And you is Baddu." Her eyes flare. "They call you Amarylis, but your real name is Baddu." He isn't asking her. "And I's you bredda."

He taps his own chest.

"My bredda dead long time. Who you is?" Her voice is rough and angry. And a little afraid.

Adebeh is suddenly aware of the frightening spectacle he presents to her, clothes and legs and face bloodstained, an iguana that he'd killed, as a gift, hanging from his belt, burrs and twigs and leaves in his hair that hasn't been combed in a week. Maybe even Mam would not recognize him.

The other woman edges away from her digging and into the shack, and stands in the doorway. Two pairs of hostile eyes are watching him.

He speaks gently and slow. "I am you brother."

She peers as if he is far away. "You is Kojo?" She is hopeful, and afraid.

"No." He softens his voice further. "Kojo is dead."

"Say who?" Her arms twitch the weapons.

"Say me. I am brother to him too."

"And he dead?" Her voice is so close to breaking, and so suddenly, that he doesn't trust himself to more than nod.

As quickly, she gathers herself. "You see him dead?"

"No. He dead before I born. He dead on the ship before it reach Halifax."

"So how you know he dead if you don't see him?"

"Because they tell me."

"Who?"

"Mam and Da."

"Who them is?"

"You mother and father. He name Montague Cameron."

"I never hear of no Montague Cameron." Her voice is not as firm as before.

"He know you, though. Is he tell me you name Baddu, though is Delphis that tell me Amarylis is your slave name."

"Delphis?"

"Who raise you," he explains patiently. "And tell me she tell you everything about Mam and Da that they tell her. So you know Montague Cameron and Maisie Fowler. You know their name at least. I am Adebeh Cameron. You brother." He understands the suspicion in her eyes, and doesn't want to irritate her. But he also wants her to know that she is playing "fool fe ketch wise", as Mam would say.

"I don't name Cameron." She is breathing heavily, as though she has run up the hill that Adebeh has just walked. But her breath is laced with anger and fear.

He calls to her softly, first her Yenkunkun name, Baddu. Then her secret name. The one only her uncle should know but that Mam whispered to him on his final visit home before the *Eagle*.

Her eyes open wide in echo of a scream. "How you know that? You is a obeahman?"

He smiles. "No, bigi pripri bring me here. And Mam send the name with me. When Uncle Morgan was leaving for Africa he give her your name to keep safe. He wouldn't see you again, but he think maybe Mam might see you, so he tell her. And she tell me."

"Africa? Uncle in Africa? How he get to Africa from here?"

Adebeh relaxes. Delphis has told Sister everything she knew, everything Mam and Da told her about herself and her family. And Sister remembers.

"The same way he get from here to Halifax. On a ship." He smiles, but carefully, so as not to seem mocking.

"So how you get here?" Her arms flex again.

"Ship too," he says.

"Ship from where?"

"Halifax. And then I walk."

She relaxes, but only a little. "How you find me?"

He remembers the necklace and reaches for it. "Delphis tell me to give you this." Now it is easy for him to touch it and take it off. It's not burning, or cold. Just a pretty necklace of beads and stones and wire.

She looks down at him a long while before holding out the stick. He inches slowly up the incline and puts the necklace on her digging stick, which is long enough to be a spear too. She lifts the stick to slide the band down onto her wrist. To put it on she'll have to let go of her weapons. Reluctantly, glaring at him, she puts them down.

But her whole being is changed by touching the ornament. As she's fixing it around her own neck, he's unsure she even sees him there. Looking at Sister's face Adebeh feels as though he is peering through a parted curtain at her nakedness.

"What you staring at?"

"You put me in mind of Mam."

She preens like a little girl. "I favour her?"

He nods, his mouth too full to speak. "You favour each other."

Her companion smiles at them from the doorway. Adebeh smiles at both of them.

He lifts the lizard. "I bring this," he says.

He doesn't tell them that the lizard, headless and now drained of blood from hanging behind him as he'd walked here, is also stained with human blood from the cutlass that killed it. The two killings are linked in his mind with the necessity of them: to defend himself; to feed himself, and now Sister and her friend.

"Long time since I eat meat," she says, smiling.

She sends him off to the river, possibly the same one where he slept last night, to wash away the blood. When he returns, she and her companion, whose name she tells him is Petta, have skinned the lizard and laid it out wrapped in leaves in the cooking pit, covering it with small stones around which fragrant smoke coils.

She takes his fouled garments and gives him clothes from a bag inside the hut. Men's clothes. "He not here," she says.

They're big for Adebeh. He'll have to get some clothes of his own now. He should have asked Elorine to make some for him in Belle-fields. Or bought some in the market in St. Ann's Bay—One-Eye Sarah maybe had some selling, or one of the other vendors. But he's grateful: he doesn't stand out any more, the funny clothes and the necklace are both gone. He's invisible again.

They talk, cautiously at first, offering words in handfuls like pieces of food. Delphis's necklace has persuaded her he is not an enemy.

"You wouldn't live to reach this far," she said simply. "It would strangle you." But she's still getting used to him as brother.

Adebeh tells her about the Yenkunkun in Scotia, the few that are left. He was born the year that all the rest went on the ships to Africa, including the woman whose name is no longer spoken in the house, and her two children by Da: Adebeh and Sister's half-siblings. She remembers the woman. More a girl, she says, the children tiny and sickly; she is surprised they made it to Halifax and survived the cold-cold winters he's told her about.

He tells her about Eddie and Precious, and of the ones born between himself and Eddie who didn't survive the winters on the little bit of food, all of them always hungry, the babies always crying.

"The spirits come back for them," says Sister, face suddenly a mask. He thinks of Da, who doesn't go to the Christian services.

He has known about her all his life, he tells her, almost from he knew himself. They talk about her, Mama praying in church that she was alive and free. Most of all, free. Not free like she would have been in Scotia if she had come with them. Free like they had been before the exile. Like she is now. He gives thanks to the ancestors.

As he listens to himself Adebeh understands, as though he is on a hillside overlooking a long valley unfolding in the melting mist, the full extent of the exile his parents have endured for longer than the thirty years of Adebeh's life. An exile that has drained their strength from them into the unyielding soil that barely feeds them. Sister, planted still in Jamaica, is the seed of themselves, all of them, even their half-siblings in Africa. A testimony.

≈ 60 ≈

Narrative: Decisions, Saturday, December 3

ANNA: You decide who yet?

JASON: Decide what? Who?

MATHILDE: Ze slaves your father leaves you.

JASON: What about them?

ANNA: Who them is?

MATHILDE: Who you will give their free paper to?

JASON: I don't know. I haven't given it any thought.

ANNA: Maybe it don't need thinking. Just acting.

JASON: It's an important decision. And I've been very busy.

ANNA: Is not that kind of acting I was talking bout.

JASON: What kind were you talking about?

ANNA: Maybe is the Lucia-one, like how you and she is combolo now.

MATHILDE: And Achilles iss ze odder one.

JASON: Achilles?

ANNA: Her pickni.

MATHILDE: Your nephew.

JASON: Nephew?

ANNA: Anthony.

JASON: Ah.

MATHILDE: She will expect.

JASON: Expect what?

ANNA: Her free paper.

JASON: Well, she can ask Anthony when he comes back. Squire left it up to me.

ANNA: And Anthony.

MATHILDE: Well, who?

JASON: As Anna points out, I don't have to decide until Anthony comes back.

MATHILDE: You should decide before. You and Anthony does not agree about things, you know that. You should at least decide in your head, who.

ANNA: And decide which head you thinking with.

Jason: Letter to Carla (3), Sunday, December 4

Sunday, December 4

My darling Carlita,

I am demolished, as though a team of your father's quarter horses had walked slowly over me. Of all the events that have presented themselves in this benighted place this one, for some reason I have not understood entirely, has affected me the most severely. Perhaps I am simply tired and overwhelmed by the plethora of things that present themselves and seem to relentlessly pursue me, day after day after day. There hasn't been a day since Anthony's departure that I have not been out on the estate. Even on a Sunday like this one, which I know you wouldn't approve of. Though I confess, but only to you, that the stillness of the place, when the Negroes are sleeping, some themselves at church—as Anna & Mathilde generally are— or at their provision grounds, gives me opportunity and space for reflection not afforded me during the week. I ride out as I please, almost like a visitor.

But I digress, and deliberately, in one sense. What is uppermost in my mind, and the reason for this gloomy start to my long overdue letter is a small matter in the scheme of things. But in another sense it encapsulates that scheme and exposes its putrid core. I cannot now remember whether it was to you in a letter or to myself in my intermittently inscribed diary that I spoke of Carpenter John, an important figure on Greencastle both for his role (a crucial figure in the sugarhouse during the grinding, monarch in the off-season) and for the respect and affection in which he is held by the Negroes, as an ancient Guineaman who has belonged to Greencastle as long as

Lincoln. And by myself. He's no angel—for angels cannot live in the foul air of a sugar estate—but he is not a monster.

He is now convicted of a murder that he did not commit and for which, but for a successful appeal for clemency now made to the Governor, he will certainly hang. The victim, the former head driver Hector, was a monster, whom John wounded severely, and deliberately, but who was dispatched to his fate by separately administered poisoning. Probably administered by his wife (though so hated was he that there could be many other culprits) who is herself now dead, a pitiful suicide. The situational sequence was given to the court by me. The medical facts were all stated in court by the doctor whom I'd called to examine the corpse of the man poisoned, a medic well-known in the district who testifies in many cases of all sorts. He left his very sick bed to make his appearance in person, when he could have sworn an affidavit.

None of this availed John. I felt his fate in peril the moment I saw that that odious man Magnus Douglas was one of the magistrates. But I placed some faith in the jury—though, of course, they were not a jury of John's peers. Misplaced, as it turned out. Evidence mattered little or not at all. Magnus allowed the obnoxious clerk of the court, acting as prosecutor, to have at Dr. Fenwell, suggesting that the bile in which Hector's body was covered could have been gangrenous—turning the argument back to the wounding by John.

The whole proceeding, like a tragedy written by an unseen, unknown hand, moved inexorably toward an end that even John knew. As Magnus, with pompous solemnity and a smug glance at me, announced the verdict, John chuckled. Not loudly, more to himself, but that unnerved the bastard. So he added, for good measure, fifty lashes before hanging. There were gasps even from some jurors, and the other magistrate, who had taken little part in the proceedings, shook his head, recognizing the additional penalty for what it is. But people like Magnus feel that this kind of wilful cruelty, which underpins the very institution of slavery, promotes fear and ensures a respect that is entirely specious.

And then Elorine Livingstone's father, Ishmael, a blacksmith and preacher of whom Rev. Swithenbank would approve, has also been *charged with a hanging offence: rebellion. With some difficulty I managed to get him released after pledging what amounts to my whole inheritance from Squire as the deposit on his bail. Fortunately, Magnus Douglas—to whose estate Ishmael belonged long before I knew them—will have nothing to do with the trial. Officially at least. But white authority is indivisible in a way that undermines the very concept of justice that they all hold up to the world, including the Negroes, as sacred.*

All of the above, and much else I'll not bore you with, is taking place in the circumstance of Christmas and rebellion, which both approach in seeming lockstep. The preparations for both have begun, it would seem. By the time you read this letter at least one of them will have passed. The rumour of rebellion is and has been, from I was a child, a seasonal thing, like the Christmas breeze. That is understandable in some degree because it is, whites feel, the organic outcome of the three days of idleness, keenly anticipated by the slaves from late November, when preparations by everyone of every colour and station begin. It is, in a deeper sense, an admission of the irrepressible desire for freedom that only the most ignorant or wilfully blind can deny.

There is talk of it on Greencastle also. Lincoln, with whom I have periodic consultations on this and that, warns of a breeze blowing in from West, which is some distance from here but close enough for influence. West is where rebellion seems to grow from the soil of the huge estates they have there, much larger than our topography would allow. Lincoln says that he hears su-su even on Greencastle, but he mentions no names and I do not ask. In that regard I am perhaps remiss, perhaps even cowardly. But Lincoln himself is in a doubly ambiguous position because of his manumission. The slaves who were in fear of his authority are suspicious that he is now on the side of Backra, the worst accusation that can be entertained in a Negro breast.

So now we wait, in no preordained sequence, for Christmas, rebellion and the Governor's mercy.

And I await, keenly, my own return to your loving arms.

Jason

⇒ 62 ⇐

Adebeh: Amarylis, Sunday, December 4

"YOU CALL HER MAM. I DON'T remember what I used to call her, but I remember her. I remember how she smell . . . And she was big. Strong . . . When she lift me up I cyan see far-far. Like a bird . . . I remember she did say she would send for me. I remember that. . . And Delphis tell me that. All the time, that she would send for me . . . And Delphis tell me that I am Maroon, not a slave. Even when I was on Red Pond and getting lash and grind like a mare. I am Maroon. I tell meself that every night and morning. As I wake up."

Sister is talking softly. If the fire she's staring into was any louder I'd have to strain for the words.

"And is some Maroon-dem from Accompong that hold onto me and sell me to Maasa Pritchard on Lima. I was on me way here from Delphis when they ketch me. She bring me up to know I am Maroon, but she is not Maroon, so she don't know the language to teach me to talk. So when dem hold onto me, all the telling them I is Maroon like them, they only laughing at me, and drop licks on me to make me behave."

"Once I realize how the slavery business go, though, I start to run away. Still trying to get to here." She waves at the air around us, summoning spirits. "Dem send Nayga to catch me and bring me back. And to bruck me spirit, Maasa tell dem to breed me. Cause I am strong. So mi pickni will be strong too. To be slave in the Maasa field. Driver and overseer, bookkeeper, black and white. Even Maasa Pritchard bwoy-pickni. Him barely have anything to tickle a woman with. All of dem. Like me was a ground for dem to dig . . . Trying to bruck me spirit and body so I wouldn't run again. But as dem put a seed in me I wash it out. I am not borning no pickni to be slave."

"Time come at the last when the only thing that would stay in me belly was food. I turn from mare into mule." She spit a bitter smile into the fire.

I am silent, listening. Petta, knowing all that is new to me, is chewing quietly, her eyes on Sister tender as fireflies.

"Dem think I was a obeahwoman. Fraid for me. One time the bookkeeper-him, him fall down into the copper pot in the millhouse and bwoil-up with the juice. One minute he is standing normal, shouting at Nayga to do this and do that. Next minute, braps, him is in the copper pot. Dem had to stop the whole mill to clean it out. Maasa vex. I wasn't even dere, but dem say is me do it. Everybody know him was pestering me, and that I hate him."

She laugh like a lime is in her throat. "Next time I run, nobody don't send Nayga or dawg to look for me. I go to Delphis this time. Dem think she's obeahwoman too, so they leave her alone. And then more time, I find meself here. The ones you call Mam and Da tell Delphis when they leave me how I was to find it, and she been telling me over and over from I was small. After I leave her the second time, I had to be careful on the way, but it wasn't hard to find. You have to know who to ask." She smile at us, pleased.

It's the same stories I'd heard, the same directions given me by Mam and Da when I was leaving Halifax, the same landmarks to look out for, the same advice given and lesson learned.

With my own journey fresh in mind I remember, and convey a Howdy from Franky in Falmouth. Sister smile in acknowledgement. Likely she came the same route as I did, from Delphis in St. Ann's Bay to Jacinth in Falmouth. I still don't tell her about the man I kill between Franky and here. Time enough for that, if I have to.

Evening is staining the sky. Sister gather the food into a wire cage and hang it in the ceiling of the shack, away from animals; the pepper she's laced the meat with in the Maroon way will keep the insects at bay. She return to where we was eating, a flat clear space between two tree trunks worn smooth with sitting, and throw dirt on the fire. Her cheeks and eyes is shining.

She scream suddenly into the sky, "Why they leave me?" She's throwing the words at me.

Taken aback, I try to explain. About the freedom that Mam and Da wanted for her. About the hard unresponsive land they'd been given in Scotia. About whitepeople spitting on blackpeople, Loyalist or Maroon. About reports from Africa. War and starvation there too. And this time of year in Scotia, the cold is like a knife in your gut, I tell her.

I run out of words and stare mutely into eyes that are now drained of anger.

As unexpectedly as she shouted she erupt into laughter. "It sound like this place. Except the cold. I wouldn't like that at all."

I smile nervously, waiting for another sudden change of mood.

"I glad you find me." Her voice is soft as she looks away into the crouching darkness, acknowledging the ancestors who brought me here. Then she hug herself against a sudden cool breeze. "Is very alone here. Even with Petta." She beam a smile at the girl. "She is not Maroon. I glad you come."

⇒ 63 ⇐

Jason: A New Overseer, Monday, December 5

I NOW SIT A HORSE, PARTICULARLY Cherry, as comfortably as a chair; that is how much my life has turned. I am proud of the accomplishment—I who resolutely refused invitations to the hunt in England because, slave son of a slave, the concept of quarry was in my blood. Nonetheless I was in awe of those who leapt over hedges and pelted across fields, at one with their powerful other-halves. I do not aspire to that level of achievement, but Cherry and I can now canter with ease and dignity, and change direction without temerity or drastic reduction of pace. That, for me, is sufficient, certainly for the tasks to hand. Clara, a country girl herself, would be amused.

This reflection brings me to the point of this entry: a new overseer. Cumberbatch is a better horseman than I, and quite proud of it. Not difficult in the circumstances and a benefit to add to the very few that he does possess. I suppose the slaves will automatically hold him in some regard simply by virtue of his position over them and his white skin. And he is a large presence, as big as Pompey in his prime and, standing or sitting still, impressive. But as he moves, the imposing picture shifts and rearranges itself into that of an actor playing a role he has perhaps seen in a theatre but does not entirely believe in. He is delighted to be playing this role at all, but somewhat bewildered; he has been off the stage altogether for some time. This has created in him—or perhaps it is inbred—an unctuous desire to please that in another situation would infuriate me and pull to the surface all the latent instincts to humiliate and demean whites. But, first, I could not do that in front of the slaves, and second, I have no desire so to do.

Cumberbatch has one overriding virtue as an overseer, in contrast to Wyckham: he has absolutely no ambition to be Maasa. Indeed, he regrets the day he ever set foot on this island. His whole endeavour now is to find his way off. To that end he has foresworn spirits, which have swallowed the largest part of his emoluments these many years. He confessed this himself, which commended him to me. I found him at Mrs. Grenville's establishment, sipping tea and discreetly importuning every customer who seemed more prosperous than himself for a job. His references were both more than a year old, and from estates on the other side of the island, so were impossible to check. Both spoke of his cheerfulness and discretion.

To his credit he has already put in place with Mathilde, to whom he took a liking from first sight, a plan whereby I will deposit his wages with her, with only a very small disbursement to himself. To the eventual end of his rehabilitation also, I have already, again at his request, given instruction to Lincoln, eternal keeper of the still, to let me know whenever Cumberbatch makes a request for rum, even so much as a toddy. It is difficult to resist the efforts of a man so intent on self-redemption in this unredeemed place. And so intent on leaving, as I myself intend to do (though at this time only Carla and this diary know).

The presence of Cumberbatch is comforting for two reasons. The routine of the estate is unrelenting. Were it not a grotesque usage, I could term myself a slave to the place. And having begun as I hope to continue, I cannot, too obviously, relax my vigilance and exertions.

The task work practice is now firmly established in the minds and rhythms of the slaves—the majority, Pompey asserts. But he also testifies to the several who regard it as "Backra (me!) working Nayga harder so he don't have to feed us." Which is, of course, correct—about the feeding at least. I have let it be known that they may take me to the magistrates if they wish, in hope of enforcing their legal entitlement. But I doubt there is judgement in precedence on this matter as all estates have had to live with this conundrum, almost as a condition of their survival. It is particularly pronounced in times of drought, like now. The general solution is simply to drive the slaves even harder; I'm taking a different route, allowing them to drive themselves, as I see it.

I do not pretend that a system of task work absolves the taskmaster of all his responsibilities. But it is the least absolute of the conditions of their labour, of that I am convinced. Absent paying them wages, which I have overheard mooted in snatches of conversation among them, or driving the estate further into debt, there is no other road I can see that combines continued production and political calm.

The other reason for relief at Cumberbatch's presence follows on the first: that between Tombo and Mr. Livingstone I shall be busy in Bellefields over the next few days at least.

Uncertain of how Pompey and Simpson will react to this new dispensation, and uncertain of Cumberbatch himself, I'd have preferred to be here. But it cannot be helped.

Mathilde and Anna, at least, are somewhat assuaged in their concerns over their patrimony.

≈ 64 ≈

Elorine: Pitchy-Patchy, Monday, December 5

YOU KNOW THAT CHRISTMAS IS REALLY coming when Kekeré Bábà come for his Pitchy-Patchy scraps. I hear Jassy cry out from the kitchen and then a funny kind of music sounding in the house. A thumping like a drum and a strange whistling like a body out of breath. Is nothing more than Kekeré Bábà playing Jonkanoo early, coming through the house with his chest as a drum and whistling through his teeth like a pennywhistle. Then his head pop around the doorway into my workroom.

"Is only me," he say with a grin on his old face that allow you to see the bwoy.

Fergus been playing Pitchy-Patchy in the same Jonkanoo band from Jesus was a bwoy. As a pickni I come to know Christmas through him coming to Selina for the bag of old cloth and pieces she's been keeping since the new year. Since she dead, I've been following along.

When he take the bag home, Murtella and Jujube will make his costume. If Fergus is on the sea at Christmas everybody know, because nobody else in that band would dare to play Pitchy-Patchy. They have other bands in town and the district, and other Pitchy-Patchy, but his band is the favourite, and his Pitchy-Patchy is the most frightening. At least for the pickni-dem.

They tell me that one time, every estate have a Jonkanoo band at Christmas, and three or four play in Bellefields alone. Those days, Ishmael tell me, he was Horsehead in the Cascade band, the leader. But after he hear the Word and become a Christian, he leave those things behind. He call anything like that devilish. Never mind that, or that Fergus look to Ogun and the old gods and play Jonkanoo when Christmas come, he and Fergus is still closer than brothers. And his band always come onto West Street just as chapel is over. They come into the yard and the old people get lively with them to the fife and drum and pennywhistle. Even Ishmael can't help moving his feet with a little secret smile on his face.

Not these last few years, though. The vestry—never mind that Missa Cavendish speak up for Pappi in court yesterday to help him get bail—start to send people like that cockroach Boynton to try and break up the bands and arrest the people. Since the troubles a few years ago, whitepeople is saying that Jonkanoo is making rebellion behind the masks. So you start to hear of arrests and punishment, especially on the estates. But somehow the band with Fergus is still playing every Christmas, sure as Christmas breeze.

So far, at least. What will happen this year only Maasa God is to know. Nayga and Backra both is saying that something is to happen this Christmas. They say that every year, and mostly what happen is that everybody get drunk. Somebody might get extra drunk and settle some old matters that bring them up before the magistrate. But generally, by the time they get their two days at Christmas, everybody on the estate is too tired to think bout rebellion.

This year, though, from even before that Nicodemus Duncan come to us in the night, I've been hearing whispers in the market, and now it's louder than whispers. And Backra know, Jason say. That is why they come for Pappi, and are out to hang him if they can, Lord God! A offering and warning to Nayga. Nayga have it to say that what is to happen is a siddown, nothing more than that. Backra say that whatever name you want to call it by, its name is rebellion, and he's setting for it with fire and brimstone, same as always.

When Jason bring Pappi back from jail yesterday it was like Christmas all by itself. But now, as I'm listening to him and Kekeré Bábà laughing outside in the workshop, the Christmas breeze is a cold wind blowing right through me. Assizes start next week Wednesday, and Ishmael is to present himself there to hear when his trial is to start. It is a comfort that Jason says he will be there, and will represent him if that is allowed. If not he will get Lawyer Alberga to speak for him. But I still tremble with fraid just to think about it.

Still, life must go on. Kekeré Bábà come for his scraps and I promise I'll bring them for him. So I pick up the bag from where it live in the corner, put a few more strips from the floor into it, and take it out outside to him.

To tell truth, though, what is on my mind, even with the concern about Pappi, is to find out anything from Kekeré Bábà about Adebeh. I realize as I'm walking out there that I should've ask him that when he was in my workroom, just the two of us. I don't want Pappi nose in this.

Is like Kekeré Bábà look at me and know what is in my mind. As he take the bag he turn me around a little and step us out into the yard.

"The bwoy gone back into the bush," he says, looking hard at me. That make me flare up.

"Is not me send him."

He smile. "I know," he say, like he trick me. "If it was you he would stay. Not so?"

"Maybe." I feel like a little girl again and couldn't help but smile back.

I ask him about the ship.

"It not ready to sail till Wednesday next," he say. "I take time and don't walk near the wharf, so nobody don't get to ask me anything about Scotia. Not yet." He grin.

"And if they ask?"

Fergus shrug. "Nobody going to ask before Wednesday."

I couldn't let it go. "And what you going to tell them on Wednesday?"

He's a little vex with me now. "I will tell them the truth. That he disappear."

I feel myself chilling.

"Backra will put money on him and send the Maroons after him."

"Well, don't him is Maroon too?" Fergus laugh a bitter little laugh. "Him will know what to say to them."

Something else to frighten for. And on the same day that Pappi is going back to courthouse. Is like my life is leading me to courthouse.

I don't know who most to frighten for. Pappi, when they start to twist the words of God inside out to look for a little mote of rebellion in his eye. Or Adebeh, when they set the bounty hunters and their dawg after him, plus the Maroons. Or Kekeré Bábà, looking at me now easy and smiling, when they decide to send that mongoose Thomas to the doctorman yard to hold him to the promise he make to bring Adebeh back to the ship.

≥ 65 ≤

Jason: Up So, Tuesday, December 6

FLAMBEAU IS ANOTHER COUNTRY FROM GREENCASTLE. When I'd left for England, there were a few dozen bushes grown up so for provision of coffee for the big house. The overseer, if there was one, or the bookkeeper, kept an eye, sending small gangs up there from time to time to bush and clean and reap. Many estates hereabouts use their mountainous back lands similarly.

But as I could see from the moment Cherry and I rounded the huge rock face that was the boundary between up so and down here, M. Richard had turned Flambeau into a well laid-out and productive enterprise. As I rode through the tidy red-berried rows toward the courtyard and cottage ahead, I could appreciate Anthony's enthusiasm for finding capital for Flambeau in Virginia.

Up here, vistas are either inconsolably distant—of Greencastle below, and the hazy sea, and behind of mountains retreating into veils of mist and dripping leaves—or intimate as breath. The coffee bushes are human-sized, the trees that offer shade sufficiently large for their purpose, but neither as majestic nor overwhelming as the gargantuans of Greencastle. And everything is soaked, like a crust of morning bread, in the sumptuous aroma of coffee.

Jean-Claude Richard—though I never used his Christian name and addressed him always as M'sieu—was awaiting me. Yesterday a note had arrived by a handsome bwoy who reminded me of the slave Achilles: Would I join M. Richard and his wife for lunch at noon. Early for most folk down here, but perhaps the routines of coffee are different.

As I breasted the last rise and came into a courtyard with mossy cobblestones that thudded under Cherry's hoofs, M. Richard stood in comfortable proprietorship before the house, an L-shaped bungalow around which all other attributes, even the sky, seemed to arrange themselves. He's of no more than average height, like myself, but even from my perch on Cherry he appeared tall, perhaps because of the trimness of his figure and the straightness with which he held himself. His posture suggested that he knew the importance of Flambeau in the scheme of things. And he had an implement in one hand, longer than a riding crop but short of being a whip, that somehow added to his stature.

"Welcome, M'sieu Pollard," he said, with just enough warmth and show of teeth. I was being guardedly welcomed into his world. But the fragrance of the approach to Flambouyant—to give the plantation its formal name, called Flambeau colloquially—may have sweetened my disposition toward the man, already favourable from our exchanges at Anthony's dinner party.

A horde of pickni appeared before I had even brought Cherry to a halt, dancing around us and crying out words that flew past me like insects. It all seemed, at the time, quite magical: the tidy establishment floating in an extravagance of mountains and clouds, Richard's almost military attentiveness upon my arrival, the children swarming, the narcotic smells. It seemed a secret I had discovered for myself.

Before speaking a word he made me welcome by taking Cherry's reins himself, a task usually performed by a slave. There was no deference in it, merely politeness toward an invited guest.

"You've come, then." His tone was formal but not unfriendly. His dark, serious eyes were set in a face that had weathered many storms. I sensed that he was not yet fifty years old.

"I've come," I said, summoning a smile as I dismounted and we shook hands. "Anna has told me many times how beautiful it is up here." She comes up here from time to time to copy M. Richard's accounts into the big ledger that she and Lincoln keep.

"That sister is a clever girl," he said, admiration colouring his voice. "Not like those other ones, oiseaux. I hope she find un bon époux."

I was spared the need to answer by a voice calling, turning M. Richard like a vane toward the house behind us. In the doorway with a smile like a flower was a butter-skinned woman in a white floor-length robe; she shimmered in the liquid green shadows of the court-yard. From behind him, I could feel Richard's smile open as he walked us toward the woman, tucking his little leather whip under his arm.

He caressed the word as he introduced his wife Marjorie—Mahjie. I couldn't help but think, as I inclined my head to her in a bow, that her mere presence at Anthony's dinner—had convention permitted it—would've transformed the whole evening's conversation. Not by her own words so much as by the effect of her loveliness on the men—and the women.

"Welcome, M'sieu Pollard." Her voice was in contrast to her smile, which showed a full mouth of white teeth; it was almost gravelly, like a boy's when his voice is breaking.

The admonitory words of the ninth commandment rang simul-taneously in my ears and my loins. A flush slowly stained my face; I felt exposed. But if she noticed, three of the children from the throng in the courtyard throwing themselves into the folds of her gown diverted her. She folded herself over them, reminding me of Carla with Caleb.

"Entrez, M'sieu," she said.

As we entered the dark cool house Mme Richard—Anna assured me they were properly churched—excused herself and herded the children through a door in the far wall. Her husband, tapping his near-whip against his boot, called out. The boy appeared who had brought the original invitation from M. Richard. He bore a tray and two mugs, and came first to me. He was a near copy of Achilles, whose parentage I now knew.

"A little refreshment," Richard said genially, waving me to a chair, taking the other mug and a seat himself. He rested his leather imple-ment, which was assuming an ominous air to me, on the arm of his chair, and covered it with his own.

There was a fire in the stone fireplace. Thankfully, for away from it the room was chilly.

M. Richard lit himself a pipe after offering me a cheroot. I declined, never having taken to the habit.

"So, M'sieu Pollard, how are tings going? You seem very busy when I pass." From time to time he rode through Greencastle on his way into Bellefields, but we'd not more than waved at each other across the canetops, or exchanged any but shouted greetings.

I confessed my continued, though diminishing, ignorance about growing sugar.

He laughed. "There is a lot of tings to go wrong. But now you have a overseer it should be better, eh? De slaves mostly run de place anyway. Not so much with café."

I inclined my head in a question.

"We have very busy time," he began. "Den," he shrugged, "nothing. Den busy again. Dere is always something to do, and it must be done"—he held thumb and forefinger almost touching—"exactement."

"I understand what you want to do in the field down there"—he gestured almost dismissively—"but we have task work here already." He smiled briefly. "When we is busy it is like crop time for you. Everybody must be here, everybody working. Hard." His voice itself hardened. "We cannot have some sleeping and some off digging yam or cutting plantain."

I saw immediately where his words were leading us, and attempted an interjection. But he swept on. "Dere is only one way to make sure of dat, M'sieu Pollard: M'sieu Jacques." To my astonishment, he again tapped the little leather whip beside him. "Without M'sieu Jacques we have no coffee growing, no coffee reaped, no coffee roasted, no coffee sold. M'sieu Jacques, he's not a nice person, oui, but he is necessary." His smile chilled my bones.

The challenge was more in his tone than his words. Instead of rebutting him, I resorted to the role of legalist. I extended my confession of ignorance into the area of coffee, where it was as dark as the brew, I said. Therefore I would not, I told him, presume to instruct him in matters relating to the management of the slaves, even though—as I softened my voice to make the point—they are Greencastle's property. I explained the practical reasons for my resort to piecework. Perhaps, I suggested disingenuously, your people are fat and healthy.

He laughed, but not with his eyes. "They work hard, they eat," he said. "But a good dog must be a little hungry, oui? Or he sleep."

I tried to keep my dismay within, but it leaked into my eyes, for M. Richard laughed again, mocking this time.

"Dis shock you, M'sieu. I do not treat dem like dog. Some people . . ." He shrugged. "But dey is not happy to be slave, so dey will not work without M'sieu Jacques to tell them." He shrugged again. "Is so it is, oui?"

I pointed out that they are working on Greencastle.

"So far," he said. "Dey will understand soon dat you can do nothing to dem if dey don't work. What den, M'sieu?"

"They understand already," I replied. "They also understand they will starve. No one wants to be hungry."

Mention of hunger was a cue for him to stand and invite me to his table. "You are popular with your slaves, M'sieu Pollard. Perhaps. But not with de odder planters, oui."

It was my turn to shrug. "At this point I really don't care," I said.

The meal was almost austere by Constancia's standards, but very tasty. I complimented Marjorie, who had rejoined us, and remarked in particular on the spicy pork.

"From the mawon," she said.

"We have entente." He threw me a conspiratorial smile across the table like a condiment. He gestured. "Our neg do not disappear in the bush."

The Maroons are beacons and villains to the Negroes, especially the runaways, whom they may hunt and return for profit, or keep for their own use.

The undemonstrative authority with which Marjorie presided over our table belied her barefooted casualness, which itself imparted a kind of intimacy to the setting. She ate enthusiastically, employing both finger and fork, and watched me closely. I was aware, however, of wanting her to like me—far more than her husband—and tried to be as witty as I could.

Mahjie, he called her, voice as tender as a feather. Her cheeks flushed each time, with embarrassment, but also with pleasure.

That would be her name in the thoughts I would carry down with me. But beyond her luscious fruit-like beauty, the more persistent image of my visit up so would be, I knew, of M'sieu Jacques.

≋ 66 ≋

Elorine: Palampam, Wednesday, December 7

THE DAY START SO QUIET. I ease myself out of the house, stepping over the boards that will creak, and giving a sharp look to Ginger. Then out into the yard and under Jassy window into West Street, toward the beach. As always, Mother Juba is outside her little hut across the way, sweeping. I never get up yet and Mother is not outside before daylight, schwupsing her broom. I tell her the softest howdy as I pass, cause everything around us is quiet and blue, no one else is moving on the street. I reach the beach in a right frame of mind.

I go down there sometimes to restore myself. To start the day right. True, I just wake up so my body at least should be rested, but the body is not everything. Besides, I didn't sleep good last night. I dream Adisa, and Adam, and the pickni, as fresh as when I am awake and seeing them in front of me. And then the Magnus-one come riding down on them and scatter them like birds. But is really Pappi he's looking for. I wake myself up before he can catch him.

Going to bush with Adebeh seem a long-long time ago now. Myself, I don't expect to see that one again. My heart is heavy in a way I don't remember even after Jason leave. He and me don't have any under-standing—we don't know each other long enough for that. Still, it's as if we know each other well enough in ourself. When I count it up is just the four days in bush, and the first morning when he come here with Kekeré Bábà, and that morning he bring the doctorman horse.

It must be the dreaming of Adisa that make me think of the Scotia man. I hope she is happily arrived in Guinea and united with her people. She leave plenty sorrows behind.

I don't reach properly down to the beach, about to undress to my shimmy and go into the water, when I feel the ground thudding under me. Du-du-dum du-du-dum. Horses. Which mean whiteman-dem. Something is up. Excitement. Maybe trouble, cause Backra don't leave his bed this early just to ride up and down. Trouble for somebody. More often than not, that mean trouble for Nayga.

So I draw back into the bush where I usually hang my clothes and watch. A line of horses, and not only Backra is riding, I see coloured and black too, behind them. Everybody is in uniform. All going in the same direction. Courthouse square. They going to muster. Which mean that something serious happen. Palampam. Either invasion or rebellion, one or t'other.

When they finish passing and disappear like duppy, I dress quick-quick and hustle myself back home. In the short time I'm away Pappi get up. Moreover Uncle Teo is there with him, I can smell the coffee they drinking. Must be Pappi fix it for them, cause poor big Jassy is still snoring in her little room as I pass. That alone tell me something important happen. Outside of Sunday, and not every one, Uncle Teo mostly keep to himself. Uncle Teo can sound like a Haytian when he's ready, or a Cuban. And he will disappear for weeks. When you ask you hear that Backra was asking for him just before. He is a fisherman, so is easy for him to fade away like the mist.

The two of them stop what they're talking about as I come through from the kitchen. Uncle Teo throw me a little smile like one of the sweeties he used to bring for me when I was small. I nod back. I know better than to say a word, just take time ease myself into my regular chair, make myself small, and listen.

PAPPI: Backra pickni?

UNCLE: And the nurse.

PAPPI: All of them?

Uncle Teo nod, solemn as chapel.

PAPPI: And Backra run away?

UNCLE: Disappear into de bush like smoke. Bout a dozen of dem, counting house slaves.

PAPPI: So what going on in the big house? Plenty dancing and drunkenness, bet you.

UNCLE: Maybe. But Backra pickni dead. Plenty Nayga have to dead to pay for that one pickni.

PAPPI: They have a leader?

UNCLE: Must be, but I don't hear.

Is always a surprise to me how a fisherman can stay out at sea, sometimes for several days, and know so much of what is happening on land. But I take my courage in my hand and offer them what I have, about the horses and the mustering. Which was news to them, but not a surprise.

Everybody put everything into the pot now. Excitement last night up at Rickhambone. Which is a name I know but I'm not too sure where it is. Next to Cascade, Pappi say. Nayga fire the trash house and then fire the roof of the big house to distract the house Nayga-dem from running to help put out the trash house. Next thing you know, piece of the roof in the big house, over where Backra have the nursery for his one pickni, fall down on the pickni and the wet nurse that sleep there with it. Roast them like chicken. When it come to a fire, and especially when even one Backra get dead, even a pickni, that is rebellion.

On top of that, as if to spit in the eye of Backra, Nayga-dem move into the big house and drive Backra into bush like him is Nayga.

"Them will say is you preach it, Elder," Uncle Teo say as he drain his cup and get up.

Pappi grunt. "Nobody from Rickhambone come to Zion that I know bout. How they can blame me?"

"That will stop Backra?" Uncle Teo laugh like he give himself a little joke. "Maybe I should give the preachment on Sunday."

"You will have to," Pappi say, and get up with Teo.

"Tenky for the coffee, Elder, sorry to wake you so early. Good day, Miss Elorine." He give me a little bow, as always, and walk through the house to outside, Pappi following. When Pappi come back, he get himself ready to work because he know what the day will bring.

≋ 67 ≋

Jason: Alarums and Premonitions,
Wednesday, December 7

I AM NOT SO EASILY RID of Wyckham, it appears. His musk precedes him, and follows me.

In the early hours of yesterday, on an estate on the far side of the parish, Richambeau, which I had never heard of before, a trash house was burned down and the roof of the big house set afire. The piece over the nursery collapsed and the baby and its wet nurse were burnt up. The family in residence—according to a young brown man from the militia office who came pelting in here last evening with a proclamation—have fled into the hinterlands of the estate, and rebels are now in residence in the big house at Rick-ham-bone (as he announced it). All able-bodied members of the militia are required to muster at dawn tomorrow in the town square, for exercises to be conducted against the rebels.

The young man, a clerk of Mr. Meyerlink I learned afterward, and his son by one of his slaves, was visibly irritated when told that there are no able-bodied members of the militia in this house. He rode off in a greater flurry than had attended his arrival.

Mathilde and Anna were shaken. The demise of the infant was given a few minutes' remorse, more for the circumstance than the death itself: early mortality is common as yaws. Their shock and fury were reserved for "dem Nayga", the rebels. We were sitting in the cool of the piazza, so *our* Nayga were all about.

I kept my counsel—there was no space for my words. In truth I was troubled. The image of the infant burned to death brought to my mind's eye, instantly, Caleb in that easily imagined agony. But the unease went deeper. Were the prophecies, not least my own, of the slaves liberating themselves, coming true? Had the uprising rumoured for Christmas, now just two weeks away, arrived? When would it reach Greencastle?

My mind went to the sturdy mahogany chest in Anthony's office in which were stored a few rifles and muskets, his militia uniforms, and a few extra items. The key was on one of Mathilde's bunches at her waist; perhaps unconsciously, she was fingering them now.

I passed—we all did, even Anna who sleeps like a stone—a restless night. But I'd planned to go into Bellefields anyway, so this morning, after my conference with Cumberbatch, Pompey and the drivers, I let Cherry take me into town at her own pace. I am required by law to enroll in the militia no later than three months after my arrival in the island.

The first thing I saw as Cherry and I arrived at the open space across from the courthouse was Wyckham doing what he enjoys most: haranguing a group of subordinates. These were not slaves, but they weren't white, so his tone and manner was irritatingly familiar. He was sitting atop the horse he'd ridden off on, shouting at a ragged platoon of brown men trying without enthusiasm to march in step in the already broiling sun. Wyckham himself, with a similar uniform to theirs but with epaulettes and strings of braid across his chest, looked like something from the stage of a farce in a cheap London taproom. He is some kind of officer, and the thought made me blanch inwardly, because I will almost certainly become one of those miserable men—a few of whose faces I recognized—when I find myself mustered. I felt my stomach tighten.

This drilling, at this time, would be particularly severe. Whites believe that coloureds are congenitally sympathetic to rebellious slaves and surreptitiously promote rebellion. I doubt that, as most people of any colour and status are too busy maintaining or advancing their own positions on the slippery incline that is this society; besides, many despise the blacks as much as the whites do, and take every opportunity to buy slaves, whom they treat worse than Backra.

But I can understand the belief in our villainy. At base, just below that sense of superiority that energizes scum like Wyckham, is an insidious realization. Of their numerical insignificance but also—in the very existence of a mulatto, or octoroon, or any of the other classifications they've sliced us into—a recognition that they have stooped to conquer. They've dipped the most cherished aspect of whiteness in the dark ooze around them. They hate themselves, but hate us more for being their indulgence made visible.

Wyckham himself may even have left spawn at Greencastle, or on some other estate before coming to us, and he was making the twenty or so men under his temporary command pay for his misdeeds. The sins of the fathers are indeed visited on the children.

He tried to visit this anger on me. Cherry and I had entered the square from behind his shoulder, so it was not until he was returning from the far end of the clearing, shouting at the marchers, that he spotted me. We stopped at the same moment.

"Pollard!" he shouted. I did not answer. The marching men noticed right away, and their lines became even more ragged. Ignoring them, Wyckham dug his heels into his mount's flanks and came pelting across, fetching up a few yards away.

"Why aren't you in uniform, Pollard?" His face was as red as I remembered it.

"I don't have a uniform, Wyckham." My tone was deliberately conversational.

"A uniform, *sir*!" he shouted. Wyckham had been with the regiment here, at Fort George, and remained after his time-in to make his fortune. Many soldiers do that, beginning as overseers in the hope of becoming, eventually, proprietors.

No doubt, his service recommends him for this position of authority, that and his natural avocation for despotism. I ignored his livid face, looking instead, with pointed indifference, to his ragged troop that was now clustered behind him, guns askew.

Cherry and his horse, I also noticed, nuzzled each other familiarly. Which gave me my cue.

"We have unfinished business, Wyckham." My tone hardened. The men noticed. For a moment he was puzzled, and I took advantage of the moment. "Your horse," I said, nodding at the beast.

He yanked the reins on the poor creature's head as if he would've wheeled it away, but it yanked back, unwilling to give up its newly rediscovered mate. There was a cascade of giggles from the men behind him.

"What about the fucking horse?" he shrilled.

"It belongs to Greencastle."

"You owe me wages!"

But his slightly muted tone acknowledged, as the men around recognized instantly, the true contour of our relationship in the broader world.

"I don't," I said, firm and flat. "You left. Without a word. I didn't give you notice or fire you. You *left*."

My firmness and the restlessness of his men rattled him. But his white God smiled on him, for just then, his podgy body squeezed into a better-sewn theatrical uniform, who should appear but Magnus Douglas on a handsome chestnut, plump and sweating from exertion and his own self-importance.

"There you are, Pollard," he called out as he approached, as though we had an appointment for which I was tardy. "Welcome."

I refrained from responding, except to raise my riding crop in token greeting.

"You come to join us." He continued to look pleased with himself while ignoring Wyckham.

"Afraid not," I said, sounding stuffily English in my own ear, but also enjoying his puzzled reaction.

"Oh?"

I turned to the erstwhile overseer with a bleak smile. "I came to settle unfinished matters with Wyckham here."

I could feel Magnus's chagrin. "This is a muster!" he shouted.

I turned back to him and calmed myself. "I know. But I cannot be mustered yet. Three months, remember?"

"There are rebels!" he yelled. "Killing babies and living in the big house. God knows what . . . We need every man we . . ."

"I'm sure Wyckham and these worthy citizens will deal with them," I said, waving my arm at the cluster of brown faces.

The word *citizens* was a provocation: it rings the bells of bitter memory for whites, of the revolution in France and its consequences closer to home, in Hayti. It was not deliberate on my part but I didn't regret it.

Douglas flushed a deeper shade and shouted, "I can arrest you!"

"On what charge?"

"Insubordination!"

"As I've already pointed out, and as you know, Douglas, I am not yet under your command."

"Assisting the rebels!"

"How?"

It was a farce, and I waited patiently on Cherry for that to sink into his engorged brain.

Eventually, spurred perhaps by the keen interest of the coloureds surrounding us, it did.

"I wish you good fortune in capturing them," I said calmly, and bid him a polite good morning as I rode away.

As I heard the business of the muster resume behind me I thought, there will be a reckoning. And I realized when it would likely come.

≈ 68 ≈

Elorine: Muster Day, Wednesday, December 7

THE WHOLE DAY, FROM JUST AFTER Uncle Teo leave until almost dark, whiteman and brownman and a few blackman come streaming into the yard, one after the other, sometimes three of them at once. Naturally, when that happen, the coloured man have to wait until Backra get through, even if he come before him, and the blackman wait on the brownman. The darkest get serve last of all. Sometimes I tease Pappi to say that if he was his own customer he wouldn get serve at all, he is so black.

I get out his uniform and put it in the yard to air-out. Just in case. He won't have to muster today, and maybe not tomorrow. When excitement like this happen, he get excused from the vestry, cause how else Town Backra would get his saddle and gear ready? Estate Backra have people to do these things for them, but in town here they find themself to West Street.

Every month-end the law say free man must go to the square by the courthouse to march up and down. Selina make sure, and I continue it, that Ishmael go off looking better than the Backra officers. Some of them look like they use their uniform to sleep in. And he come back in a worse mood than when he leave, cause on the parade ground the same people who owe him money and have to wait on his pleasure in the shop can give him orders and make him run around in the hot sun like bwoy. And they do it for spite!

But if this Rickhambone ruckus last beyond tomorrow, they will expect him to report.

After supper, Ishmael say the shortest prayers for a long time. He too tired to argue with Maasa God, which was relief of a sort. And after that he just go into his bedroom. In two-twos, I hear him snoring like when river come down. I go to bed early myself, though I don't sleep as good as him.

When something like this happen every Nayga is conflicted. Our head know what is likely to happen. Is what always happen. But a part of our very self is with the slaves, burning down everything we can, and running until we cyaant run any more. That is what our heart feel. Even me, who is free already. Cause as Pappi say, Maasa God make us all in his own image and likeness. Man born free. Is man who make some people to be slave.

≋ 69 ≋

Jason: Memba, Thursday, December 8

THE RECKONING CAME EXACTLY AS I'D FEARED.

A week had gone by since Lawyer Alberga's appeal for clemency had been sent to Spanish Town. We'd not expected any response until after Christmas. But even in the busyness of the estate—which increases as we get closer to crop—John was often in my thoughts; indeed John is part of the busyness, as Cumberbatch needs to hire someone to fill his role once the frenzy begins.

It was Lincoln who brought me news last night.

Unusually, we had guests at table: Reverend Sultzberger, a Moravian missionary from the next parish who will be here for a few days at least, with his pregnant wife.

The morning after the firing at Richambeau they were burnt out by whites in their district, men they know, and who didn't even bother to conceal their identities. They were looking for scapegoats, even though the Sultzbergers are miles from Richambeau and have no connection to that estate.

Missionaries are easy targets. According to planters and white merchants, niggers were happy until they came with their Bibles to minister to the monkeys' souls, thereby, it seems, implanting notions of freedom. It's a charge laid as far away as London, and impossible to answer to the accusers' satisfaction.

But nothing exposes the fissures in this society as violence by slaves. Whatever their professed sympathies, it terrifies whites into a state where violence becomes an expressed preference even among the otherwise pacific. Reverend Sultzberger was circumspect about events at Richambeau, even though victimized by them. Not so his wife.

"Zey kill ze baby," she said, holding her belly, her ferocity a surprise from a small, scrawny woman who'd hardly said a word. "Zey had no cause to."

Her husband tried to mollify her. "I'm sure zey didn't set out . . ."

"May be zey did, may be not," she said, truculent as a child. "But zere is blood in their hands. I vill never leave my babies vith a nigger." The word exploded from her mouth like phlegm. "Vee are in God's hands. But my babies are mine." She thumped her own chest.

We learned later that they've buried two children of their own since coming to Jamaica just a few years past. But they will go back to their parish, and their mission.

"We are ze clay in ze potter's hands," said the reverend, as if pronouncing a blessing—or a committal.

In truth, their faith presents them with a quandary. With a deep and personal knowledge of conditions on an estate, they understand the slaves' natural desire to be free. And they know that, as individuals bobbing like corks on a black sea, their white skin is not an impregnable shield. Despite all that, they remain committed to the lost and found, as they term our Negroes. They do not, like many whites, call them children, which is a commendation of sorts.

As his son supervised the clearing of the table and ushered us out onto the piazza for coffee and the promise of coconut cakes from Constancia, I noticed Lincoln hovering in the doorway to the kitchen, ignoring Balfour as he looked fixedly at me. It was, so to speak, a cypher between us, and five minutes later I was seated in his little office.

It adjoins the kitchen-house under an ancient tree whose spreading branches provide an almost perpetual shade, fashioning a courtyard of bare earth hardened by decades of feet. It's an area that from time immemorial all knew to be for the use of Lincoln and Constancia. Two rickety chairs were there, probably the same ones from when I was a child. It is a place that had become increasingly familiar to me.

"I hear something, Maas Jason," he began. For more than a moment I was the little boy again squirming inwardly in the gaze of those dark judicial eyes.

I waited; Lincoln does not like to be rushed.

"Paper come for Missa Alberga."

"Here?" I felt a momentary flare of anger at Balfour that he'd said nothing to me about a paper, but Lincoln's shaking head waved that away.

"Courthouse, Maas Jason." His tone was at once patronizing and soothing. "Your name is on it too."

I was brought up short. But I waited.

"I don't hear what the paper say, sir. But is from Spanish Town."

The nigger-breeze had blown by; that is the term that whites use for the transmission of information between blacks. It's a breeze—invisible, insidious—that chills their bones. They know their most intimate secrets are coinage in the blacks' private discourse, and are blown far and wide.

I waited for more information, but Lincoln had transferred his attention to a cup he'd brought outside. I was rising to thank him when he looked back at me.

"May Allah the merciful grant you peace, Maas Jason." Our eyes rested in each other's for a moment, and then I walked away, going out to the piazza to resume my familial duties.

I excused myself early from the gathering, to work.

But I did nothing related to Greencastle. Surrounded by the paraphernalia of estate business I could only hear Lincoln's sonorous voice, and wonder about Tombo's fate, contained in the paper waiting at the courthouse in Bellefields. I tried to comfort myself with the thought that it was a bureaucratic acknowledgement of our appeal. My stomach told me otherwise.

There was still light in the day, so I called Jack and sent him with a note asking the old lawyer to meet me at the courthouse at nine o'clock next morning, when the office opened.

Alberga was late. Instead, Magnus Douglas was sitting on his horse outside the courthouse. I don't think it's my fevered imagination that believed him waiting for me. He knew the contents of the paper. I could tell it from his smug, toady face.

"You come to say goodbye?" he asked, affecting a sober demeanour as his muddy eyes danced with amusement.

Now I knew the contents of the paper. But I held my dread and anger leashed.

"You're travelling, Douglas?"

The affected lightness of my tone wiped the light from his eyes. "Not me, Pollard. Your cripple! Today-self!"

If he'd held a glass instead of the reins of his horse, he'd have raised it in a mocking toast. But words and thought itself were trapped within my lips. I felt such a fool! Felt and saw John's gentle Cyclops's eye winking sadly at me, justified in his quiet despair. Felt the clarity of the colonial's—this colonial's—gullible belief, as he'd been taught, in the majesty of the law and the blindness of Madame Justice.

Finally I found words.

"He's innocent," I said. "You know that."

"No, I don't, Pollard. He was found guilty. The governor . . ."

"On your advice, no doubt."

He smiled and bowed, as if receiving a compliment. "Is my duty . . ."

"Your duty to distort the truth? The evidence?"

His eyes clouded again. "Dr. Fenwell is a old sick man who sleep with niggers. We had was to dispense with his services."

"I heard that he dispensed with Cascade," I said acidly, "because your Negroes were so badly treated, his ministrations were useless. And you wouldn't pay him."

He recovered his good humour. "As you lawyerman say, I rest my case."

I repeated: "There's no evidence, Douglas." My voice sounded strangled.

He grinned contentedly. "The evidence is right behind you," pointing over my shoulder at the courthouse and jail.

Once again, old Carpenter John, long in his life of slavery, had caught the ball before it had even been flung. They had him. No need to look any further, especially for someone already dead. Truth was dead, Justice to hand.

My inner churning was stirred further by Douglas's voice. "He worth much less than Hector. But you could petition for compensation. I would consider it. Hector born on Cascade. Is me sell him to Anthony." He smiled with something like pride.

"There'll be no more petitions," I said, curt and stern. "I'd be loath to profit from an injustice."

"Suit youself, Pollard. I looking for this in the *Watchman* next week." He was jesting with me like a puppy with a rag. But I couldn't leave.

"What happens now?" I asked, as calmly as I could.

He pulled an ornate timepiece from his fob and glanced at it.

"I shouldn't take more than an hour to get everything ready," he said, casual as a breeze.

I heard Squire's cockiness in me as I said, taking a step forward, "Well, I'd better go see John now."

"No, Pollard." His voice was peremptory, gilded with a smirk. "You have no right to. Unless I say so."

"He is Greencastle's property," I reminded him tersely. "I do have a right." I continued walking past him.

"I can arrest you, Pollard!"

I dismissed his shouted threat with a wave and continued into the dark building. Thomas, already sweating out last night's rum, rose behind his desk and prepared to block my way but I bounced him aside and plunged into the pool of foul air behind him. My eyes and trajectory dared the two guards, on either side of the passage, to stop me. Wisely they stood aside, batons down.

The whitemen's voices died away behind me in the gloom. I saw John's eye gleaming like a pearl, drawing me forward to my unhappy task.

He sensed it from my face. "You don't come to take me back, Kwesi."

His gothic calm deserted him when I replied, "No, Tombo, I'm sorry." His face around that single eye became a yawning cavern of terror that threatened to swallow us both. But only for a moment. Then he blinked, and sighed it away.

"Don't fret, Kwesi. Is home I going. And I will see Bristol—I will tell him howdy for you." It was said with the beginnings of a smile, which broadened. "And I will tell Memba how you turn out good."

The word gonged in my head, shattering every other thought or feeling. Tombo cackled like a fowl. "By rights you is to call me Uncle,

Kwesi. Memba modder and me was shipmate—you never know?" He mimed surprise and then went on to answer his own question, his teasing smile disappearing into his words.

"Maas Squire eye did fill-up with Memba. From she first bleed, him was toopsing her, busy as you please. Pickni drop out of her before you, but once you ketch in Memba belly Maas Squire had was to send her away. Missus—that is Maas Anthony modder—would surely get to know and she would kill him. She was a lickle sicky-sicky lady, look like she couldn't mash ants, but she have a temper on her like a cutlass. So Maas Squire sell Memba to him friend Douglas on Cascade. Not the young one who going to heng me, the fahder, who I hear is a decent man; Squire and him was friend. They agree that when Memba time come, Maas Douglas was to send her back to Greencastle for the pickni to born there as Maas Squire property. I hear say they write it down in front of the lawyerman, Backra Alberga.

"But Memba tek-in sudden, and dead from birthing you, before dem could send her anywhere. You born on Cascade." John's humour revived. "Don't tell the Douglas-one out there, but by rights you is to belong to him. Even now!"

He sniggered at his own thought, drawing puzzled glances from his fellow prisoners.

"So far as I know," he chuckled, "his fahder don't free you yet, Kwesi. And this one would dead before he do that. If he only know!" He laughed again, baring his few teeth.

I could not help but smile with Tombo. The peril of his situation, and the mystery of mine, complemented each other in a strange and ironic way: we would never speak again. About Memba—or anything else.

But he gave me a last bouquet, tendered with a sad smile. "Is me Lincoln send to sneak over to Cascade and bring you back." His eye peered into my face as if looking for the baby he'd smuggled onto Greencastle. I came within a breath of telling him Tenky, Uncle Tombo, but his face was clouding.

"G'waan, Maas Jason." His scratchy voice was suddenly sombre, and firm, dismissing me like the little bwoy I was at that moment.

"You have things to do, go do dem. Remember me to Lincoln. I don't sorry for nothing I do or cause to happen, except to you. That Hector-one was a animal, Maas Jason. De Zubia-gyal fix him business as him deserve. I will manage. Bristol and him modder waiting for me."

His powerful fingers, the colour of ancient mahogany, held the bars between us. I rested my hand on his, but could find no words; nor could I match his sad smile with anything but a frozen face, eyes smarting. His eyes and thoughts were already moving beyond the present, or the past.

70

Elorine: Fire fe Fire, Thursday, December 8

WHERE NAYGA AND REBELLION IS CONCERNED, Backra fight fire with fire. And as soon as you hear that the soldier-dem from Fort George come into it, you know blood will flow, and not dem-own.

Courtney Waterman say that they march through the night, with torch and moonlight showing the way, until they reach near to Rickhambone. Not a word cyan be spoken, you don't dare cough or sneeze, his friend Royston tell him. Two platoon of militia arrange at the back, and a set of soldiers at the front.

When they reach, the big house was quiet, nothing was moving but puss, Royston say. The white officer-dem say the slaves sleeping off Backra rum that they plunder and drink out. Backra think that is all Nayga would do with freedom, get drunk and sleep it off. He never consider the Nayga-dem who is free already, and going around sober as a tree.

The militia start a fire behind the house, the soldier-dem was waiting in front for when the slaves wake up and run out for their lives. The big house burn so bright it was like daylight outside, Royston tell Courtney. The soldier just pick them off as they fly out like blackbird through door and window—man and woman it don't make a difference to the soldier-dem. And when some of the slave-dem run round the back to escape the bullets in front, militia and the officers was waiting for them. They shoot some and hold others, man and woman again.

Thirteen dead and they hold seven to bring to trial. Royston say he was surprise is only that small number.

And when the excitement is over, they notice a whole heap of

Nayga gathering in front of the big house, which is still burning. The rest of the Rickhambone slaves. They was peacefully sleeping in their quarters, waiting to see what would happen. No doubt when the palampam start two days ago, some of them take opportunity to scarper off into the bush. But plenty of them just take time going on with their life. The next day they went out into the field same as always, and do what they was doing the day before. And maybe they are out there today as well. They don't know what else to do, except to make sure keep themself from making Backra even think they is rebels.

Courtney, as he telling me what Royston say, is laughing at the "stupid Nayga-dem," as he call them, cause they don't take the chance to melt into the bush. I bring him up short and tell him that bush is not a easy place if you don't custom to it.

"You know?" he ask, and laugh again like I am one of his stupid Nayga.

"I do," I answer, brisk and serious. And Courtney know better than to ask.

He's a nice enough brownman, Courtney, but too soft. Good, but not strong. He's not in the militia because his leg cripple from he was small, horse trample him. He can walk and run in his way, and everybody so custom to him now they don't laugh like when he was a pickni. But he is a lost soul. Don't know his father, who must be white or high-colour, and that mother of his, Miss Delcie, a washerwoman, don't give no quarter to the clothes she wash, nor to her pickni, three of them living, of which the Courtney-one is the first. She work him like a slave, carrying and picking up clothes until he get big enough to tell her off and runway. Is then his troubles really begin. Sometimes he sleep in the street, and drunkard pee-pee on him. He sweep out store and wash horse and even clean out pit latrine when they full-up. Until Uncle Teo bring him to Zion one Sunday morning to learn to read and write.

From that day Courtney take set on me. He learn to read and write quick and brisk, but that is not me, that is him, cause he is keen. And he study his Bible and take the Word to the sick and the hard-up all over Bellefields and beyond. He's a good man in his way.

Poor me. I don't know how to tell him he's wasting his time. First of all, I not looking a man, but you can't tell any man that, cause he think he is the one to make you change you mind. Either that or you funny. Second, Courtney don't have two coin in his pocket to rub together. But is not even that, because silver and gold is not everything for man to live on. Or woman. But what this woman want to live on she don't find yet in any man. Except maybe the Adebeh-one. And him I might never see again.

Rebellion always frighten Backra. This one moreso because Nayga move into the big house and live there for two days. Like him is Backra-self. Nobody ever hear of that before. So now every Jack-man is in their militia uniform patrolling. They send to tell Pappi to show his face tomorrow morning. Courtney say two platoons are at different estates, or nearby: Cascade (cause the Magnus-one is Officer and can tell them where to go) and another estate in the other direction. Soldier from Fort Dallas walking up and down the town. All to show Nayga who is in charge.

Maybe is what Uncle Teo say: the Rickhambone slaves couldn't wait for the Christmas plan.

71

Jason: The Hanging of Tombo, Thursday, December 8

NO ONE LOOKED ME IN THE EYE as I passed through the office to the square outside. Thomas and another functionary I didn't know pretended busyness at their desks; the guards were resolutely polishing their batons, the ones outside their rifles. Mercifully, I didn't see Magnus: I wouldn't have known whether to curse or laugh.

But I didn't go back to Greencastle, as Tombo recommended. I waited with Cherry under an old guango tree that dominated that part of the courthouse square, around which the vestrymen had placed a few benches and a trough for the horses. I sat on the edge of the trough while Cherry refreshed herself. My own throat was too tight to even consider drink. My thoughts were not really thoughts, they were images and words and memories, none of them coherent, rather squeezed into the restricted space of the moment as though they were clothing for a month to be folded into a weekend valise.

I was aware of the area around the courthouse coming alive with people having business there, and of the drays that trundled past me to deliver goods to the commercial establishments on the other side of the square. The town was rousing itself.

Knowing what was to come, I recalled the only hanging I'd ever witnessed, at the instruction of old Benton, to whom I was articled at the time. You must know the ultimate consequence of indifferent work, he'd said sternly, though I had had nothing to do with this particular case.

My eyes never left the stone arch at the entrance to the jail, and eventually two guards with rifles emerged, followed by Thomas, with Tombo behind, flanked by two more guards who were superfluous: John was in shackles, and showed not the least protest at his fate.

Behind John came the hangman. One knew him less by his accoutrements (rope, hammer, pliers) than by his bearing: prancing like a thoroughbred on race day, swivelling his head from side to side with the intent of attracting eyes; for a moment I was minded of Hector. All the more so when Magnus stepped out into the broiling sunlight from the imperious height of the courthouse balcony. His eyes searched too—for me. Unconsciously, I'd risen to my feet when John appeared; thankfully so, as I wouldn't have wanted Magnus to think I was giving a mark of respect to him.

As the procession turned away from me to the left, heading to the walled compound that was workhouse, punishment site and execution place in one, I mounted Cherry: it's the only way I would see any of the events within the compound, as I was determined.

Seeing the procession—its destination and purpose clear—people paused in the street and on the raised board pavements. Some blacks formed a ragged tail, a few others mounted the roots of a cotton tree beside the wall for a grandstand view. A couple of them knew Tombo and called out to him.

"Go easy, bwoy," one said in a kind of blessing, or prayer. As I came closer I heard a woman say to the man beside her, "Poor ting, look how him winjy. Him going tek long fe dead."

He did.

The entrance of the hanging party gave a pause to the everyday business of the workhouse compound. Two floggings on opposite sides of the walled yard—a man, and a girl who looked just out of childhood, both with bloodied backs—were halted; no doubt they continued after. Stick-like figures, like marionettes, appeared in the open doorways of the cells that defined the stone walls: runaways waiting for claim or punishment; incorrigibles whose owners had parked them there and paid for the guards to break their spirits; one white wretch who was probably a seaman working off a debt of some sort.

John was given a sort of distinction: from the scaffold Thomas read his warrant in booming voice. An uncommon practice, I was told after, one designed on this occasion (with the Richambeau rebels still afoot) to let those niggers with thoughts of violence know their certain fate. By then the shackles had been removed and the noose placed around his winjy neck. John stood unmoving beside the white-man, indifferent to his words or the attention of others. His good eye looked out into the world, a beacon of resignation. And a magnet for my two. I was numb with horror, dreaming while awake. If he were seeing anything, John could not have helped but notice me: I'd chivvied Cherry right up to the wall, could've stepped from horseback onto it, and was basted by the sun's bright light.

Then he disappeared—his body did. His head remained above the flooring of the scaffold, now monstrously tilted by the rope and thereby his deformed features attenuated. A further grotesquerie was added by the visibility of the rest of John below the scaffold: dancing. Frantic, deranged like a demon having no connection to the head above. Except that I realized what John was doing. Every time a foot encountered a foothold it reflexively pushed him back up, so that he would drop again—and thereby hopefully end his strangulating pain.

As the woman in the crowd had discerned, it took long.

The gathering was silent witness to Tombo's agonizing, extended passing over. When his body was finally still, they released a collective sigh like a puff of breeze. With a conscious effort I released my hold on Cherry's reins; my fingers were cramped, burning. My heartbeat came back with a rush, thumping like an animal within me.

The hangman was left on the scaffold gathering up his tools for the next job.

The grim procession reversed itself to the courthouse, Thomas lead-ing, the guards straggling behind. No one gave John any attention.

I intercepted Thomas just outside the workhouse gates. His face was grey beneath its sweaty sheen, his eyes turned in on himself.

"I will take his body," I said.

"Where?" He spoke as though waking, the word slurred.

"To Greencastle," I said. "He belongs to Greencastle."

Thomas was awake now. "He belongs to the Crown, Pollard. The Crown will bury him. Eventually." He jabbed me with the word.

"I'll get an injunction," I said, my voice rising. "He belongs to us."

"The Crown will compensate you for your loss of property. Eventually."

"I don't want compensation, Thomas, I want his body. For a decent burial." I was close to shouting: the guards and people around had paused to watch us.

My last comment gave him the fillip that he needed. Repeating it, he straightened in the saddle and laughed mockingly. "And you will be shouting and dancing with the niggers tonight, won't you, Mr. Pollard."

I didn't move a muscle; Cherry stood still. "Can I have his body, Thomas?" I asked, though not asking.

He smiled a cat's smile, and shrugged. "Is not me you's to ask, Pollard." He threw his red-veined eyes upwards and to his right: the courthouse. Magnus.

I kept my posture and face straight as Thomas and his gang continued on to their places under the courthouse. Magnus could—perhaps would—dispose of me as peremptorily as he and the governor had disposed of Tombo. But I would not surrender without trying, albeit preparing myself for further mortification.

Normally, I'd have gone up the courthouse steps and waited there for Magnus, who was likely presiding over cases inside. But to compose myself I returned to the bench under the tree where I'd waited for John's execution. There I sat down and let Cherry wander over to the trough where another horse was also watering. When she'd drunk, I tied her to a stake in the trunk and we waited in the shade. My eyes were drawn occasionally toward the workhouse walls, but mercifully they obscured John's dangling body.

It was at least an hour before a guard—not one of those who had walked with Tombo—came hustling out from the archway underneath the courthouse to inform me that Maasa Douglas would see me. As I passed her, I touched Cherry's flank for reassurance and luck.

Magnus was sitting behind his magistrate's table, alone in the empty courtroom, writing. I took—without invitation—one of the chairs across the table from him.

"Thomas tell me you want the boilerhouse man body." He tilted his head. "Why?"

"For burial," I said, having promised myself only to answer as asked, and cogently, in a calm voice.

"We will bury him."

"Yes. But he belongs to us. He deserves a decent burial."

His expression told me I was introducing a new thought—one of dubious provenance—to his world.

"He's a murderer. And a slave." In his world, murderous slaves—indeed slaves in general—were not accorded decent burials.

"He's a slave," I agreed, not pressing the other point. "He's Greencastle's slave."

We looked at each other for a few moments, much history flowing through our eyes. Then he made his decision with a glare.

"You can tell Anthony tenky for this." He scratched his quill across a piece of paper and pushed it to the edge of the table. "Give it to Thomas downstairs."

My impulse was to take the paper and go on my way, but I caught myself.

"Thank you," I said, my voice held as evenly as I could, before picking up the paper.

With an effort I directed my eyes to his face, but his had turned away: perhaps he was already regretting his action.

But Magnus had the last word after all, and it was a hard one. "Pollard," he called out as I turned toward the door. "You have another matter in the court." He meant, of course, Ishmael Livingstone. He gave that bleak mocking smile of his. "Take care it don't end up the same way as the cripple."

"He's innocent also," I said icily.

Magnus's smile broadened as he shrugged his fat shoulders. "You say so."

I left before my good temper could fade, and hurried down the stairs to Thomas, silently pushing the paper at him.

He read the scrawl with a deepening frown. After yapping at a guard to go cut down John, he looked at me and said with obvious pleasure, "You will have to go with him and take the body youself, Pollard. Since you say you want it."

I caught up with the young guard at the bottom of the courthouse steps, relieved to see him with a pushcart; I'd thought it possible, from Thomas's bald words, that I'd be handed John's corpse directly.

But I did have to follow him, on foot, into the workhouse compound, an outdoor form of Dante's Inferno, replete with lashings, screams, moans, screeching children—children!—tugging at my clothes like rabid animals; the manic tableau vivant taking place, despite its outdoor setting, in the foulest potpourri. I grabbed shallow breaths and strode purposefully forward. But the prospect ahead was as horrible as the passage.

John's neck had stretched even further in the hour since his expiration. He reminded me of nothing more than one of Constancia's plucked chickens. Except that his skin was now grey, leeched of the blood that had settled into and swollen his feet. My empty stomach heaved, but I was able to swallow the bile that seared my mouth.

The young guard, not yet in his twenties and by all appearances a recent recruit, spat to left and right of the body as he stood on a crook of scaffolding and sawed with a dull cutlass at the noose, John swaying in an unfelt breeze. He fell like a sack, with a clacking of limbs, into the cart below, his grey misshapen head coming to rest in a corner of the cart, as though sleeping. His large dark eye, filmed with the same grey coating as his flesh, stared defiantly at the sky.

The guard and I walked the gauntlet back to the gates; but it was different. No one wanted to be too close to death; the children gave us a wide berth and the sounds of anguish seemed muted. In a place redolent of bodily torture and corruption of the flesh, death itself, especially by hanging, was somehow prophylactic.

With heavy steps I followed the young man as he headed in a straight line to Cherry.

What would he do with John's body? What would *I* do with it?

A beneficent fate intervened in the person of a tall grizzled black man who'd been watering a mule at the communal trough; beside them was an untethered dray cart, its shafts resting on the ground. Both man and mule were chewing.

"Me will tek him, sah," he said briskly as I approached, the anxiety I felt no doubt showing on my face. "Me know him, Tombo," he continued. "Not good, but I bring tings up to Maas Squire estate from time to time, to the sugarhouse. Dem young bwoy who born-ya fraid fe touch dead, say him duppy will reach out and hold him. Stupid!" He laughed and spat, not even deigning to notice the young guard.

I could see the old man, Fortitude by name and character, would be quite happy to bend my ear for the rest of the afternoon, so, as mildly as I could, I interrupted him with the mention of money. We agreed on the price and I paid him half immediately.

Fortitude hoisted John with ease from the guard's small cart, laying him gently down on his dray. He took the cleanest of his cloths and covered the body before tying it to both sides so that it wouldn't slip in passage; then re-harnessed the mule as I mounted Cherry.

I considered sending them on ahead while I went first to West Street to tell the Livingstones how the appeal had turned out, and in some way warn of the hovering threat from Magnus. But I didn't want John to arrive before me—which might happen if I got involved talking with Elorine and her father—so I led us straight home. Fortitude, with scant encouragement from me, kept up a lively chatter behind me that was mercifully dimmed by the noise of his dray and the hoofs of our mounts, becoming one with the birds and the wind.

As we passed the marker tree and entered Greencastle proper, Dollybwoy appeared out of the bush, swinging his arms across himself. I knew better than to bother to greet him.

Fortitude hooted with laughter—and was likewise ignored; Dollybwoy kept such thoughts as he had to himself. His jerky dance, though, reminded me plangently of Carpenter John's final moments. I muttered a prayer under my breath, for John, for Dollybwoy, for myself.

Jack must have sighted us from the big house and came running, waving frantically. Before he could interrogate me about events in Bellefields, or Fortitude, or the load on the cart, I sent him to the field for Pheba.

We waited—Fortitude, after I'd paid him the rest of his fee, thankfully silent—at the edge of Hope Come Over, though only because it was nearest. I had no idea where Pheba was working that day, I'd last noticed her in Tankwell. And that is the field she came out of, hurrying, with Jack close behind. I saw Judith, her dead mother, striding toward me as if I'd never left Greencastle: a powerful woman soaked to the skin with sweat that outlined her teats and plum nipples like a breastplate.

"Yes, Maas Jason." Her tone was conversational but her eyes were wary—not the slightly amused condescension of her general demeanour.

"I have Tombo here," I said. "He needs a decent burial."

The mention of burial made her swallow, but she recovered quickly. "Tombo is not a Christian." She wasn't the playful older sister of my childhood, nor the tender-if-stern reincarnation of her mother: she was a newly minted Christian, righteous and exclusive.

I adopted my maasa voice, albeit slightly softened for her benefit.

"I didn't say I wanted him to have a Christian burial, Pheba, I said a decent burial. Get the people who can give him that, and tell your father to allow it."

"You have to talk to Busha," she challenged me. "He watching me like chickenhawk."

"You're giving Busha trouble?" I couldn't help a smile escaping, in token of Pheba's ingrained talent for nuisance.

"I do me work as best I cyan," she said. "He must know why he pick on me."

I asked her if Cumberbatch was pestering her. It's a common situation, an almost automatic use of Busha's power. Her answer astonished me.

"Him don't pester we," she said, patting her chest. "Him is a Sod-omite. Is the lickle bwoy-dem that he pester." Her scorn was like lye.

Knowing me well, Pheba could see from my face that this was new information.

"Now you know," she said cryptically. "But tell him to stop pick-ing on me. I work as good as anybody else."

I assured her I would.

"Tell Pompey to excuse Juba Lilly and Cubba to help me. Where him is?"

"I have him, Miss," Fortitude announced.

I sent Jack to the house to prepare a bath for me, and went to find Pompey and Cumberbatch.

Elorine: Frighten for Zion, Friday, December 9

WHEN WE HEAR THE HORSES THIS morning from the breakfast table we look at each other. Is so the previous morning of troubles did start.

From outside we hear a rough voice I don't know asking for "Livingstone". Right away you know is Backra, who only give Mister to other Backra-dem. By the time Cyrus put his head in the doorway, Pappi is standing up and heading out, but taking his time. I go to the window looking out on the yard but stay behind the curtain, where I can hear but not be seen. I'm not able to have Backra facety to me in my own house. And too besides, I'm still in my sleeping clothes.

"You know a nigger name Cornelius Douglas?" Backra growl at Pappi as soon as he step outside. As often as not you don't get a greeting from them, but Ishmael is always polite in return.

"Good morning, Missa Cameron," he say. "Is who you enquiring about, sir?" Molasses is thick in his mouth.

"Don't play the fool with me, Livingstone," Backra bark again. "We are looking for that quadroon Cornelius Douglas."

"I think I hear you say Nayga, Missa Cameron. What him do?"

"So you know him?" Backra voice sharpen, and I hold my breath.

"If is the one I think you mean, Missa Cameron, I know who him is. I don't know him directly, but I know who him is."

"You see him?" Backra sound ready to jump down into Ishmael throat.

"No, sir."

"Don't he come to your chapel?" another voice shout out. Richardson. A brown wretch that work with the vestry. Always happy to bring trouble to blackpeople, slave or free.

"Plenty different people come to Zion," Pappi say, addressing Backra still, "as you well know, sir."

"To plan rebellion." Backra snarl like dawg again, and I make a quick prayer that Pappi keep his own temper.

"No, Missa Cameron," he say, reasonable but not altogether calm. "You know that is not true. Richardson know that also. If anyone was planning rebellion, you would know."

"How we would know?" Richardson say. Him is we-ing himself into importance, when him is just a messenger bwoy for the vestry. Backra Cameron work for Spanish Town at least. And him is white.

"The same way you know that the person you looking for come to our chapel the one time."

"So you know him." Richardson, barking like the dawg he is.

"I know who he is, Missa Cameron. Because I born on Cascade and he born on Cascade. Me and Cascade don't have anything to do with each other this long time. And he was still a pickni when I leave there. He name Douglas. You ask for him on Cascade, sir?" Pappi is respectful, but they know he's turning argument back on them. And they don't like it.

"It's not your business where we ask questions, Livingstone."

"No, sir," Pappi say, polite but not frighten.

Richardson begin to say something, but Backra cut him off with a last bark at Ishmael. "We're looking for that murderer, and we'll find him, and hang him up by his balls. And we are watching you, Livingstone. Make sure your nigger balls don't get caught in the same noose."

He ride out, with Richardson puffing-up himself like a bullfrog behind him. In the silence they leave behind I don't know if the swelling in the air is Pappi's anger or mine. Black as him is, he don't like anyone to call him nigger. Nigger is not in the Bible, he say, only in whiteman mouth when he want you to feel like the dirt he walk on. For me, I listen to the voice more than the word.

But I'm frighten. You know they watch you, you know that in your blood. They watch every blackman and blackwoman who's trying to take themselves up a little further than the ground. But when they come right out and tell you, almost like a promise! Cameron—funny that he have the same name as the Adebeh-one—didn't even have to mention courthouse or the charge against Pappi. It was there in his voice. He is hoping Pappi slip up. They come here to trick him, so they cyan have excuse to throw him back into jail—for good.

So before he even start the workday Ishmael march down to courthouse to show himself to Mongoose Thomas, as the bail arrangement require.

I'm frighten for Zion also. From now on they're watching all of us. Is only when I talk to Cyrus while Pappi is at the courthouse that I get a picture of the Cornelius Douglas-one in my mind. He was at the Sunday worship after I come back from the bush with Adebeh, talking to Uncle Teo. I hardly paid him any mind at the time, but now I will have to.

He must be involve in that kas-kas up at Rickhambone and the dead white pickni. How he come to find himself clear from Rickhambone, which is behind Maasa God back, down to Bellefields, and to Zion?

≈ 73 ≈

Adebeh: With Sister, Saturday, December 10

SHE CALLS ME ADE. NOBODY IN Scotia, even Boydville, calls me anything but my full name. Mam and Da call me Son-Son, cause I am their eldest there. Unless they's vex, with each other or with me. Then I's Adebeh.

And Georgia Marcy calls me Ade. In the night, after loving, when we's both draining like water into sleep. When I hear it from Sister I smile at her. She is taking me into herself. Even though she don't know it, she's stretching the distance to Scotia as well. And from me to Elorine in Bellefields. The bangles for them, both, is in the goat-skin pouch that Delphis sell me to carry them. "To whoever you heart take you to first," she said. I make sure it's never far from me. That and the pouch around my neck with my papers. I even bathe with that.

When we's out in the field in Boydville, digging the hard ground as best we can, Mam like to remind us, *In the sweat of thy face shalt thou eat bread, till thou return unto the ground; for dust thou art, and unto dust shalt thou return.* She make it like a song, digging and singing, the hoe or the axe that she swings breaking up the merciless ground and the words into something we can feel in our body. Even Precious with her little digging stick, doing the best she can.

The people in Scotia is very much in my mind. This is where we all come from, even those of us born in Boydville. It's a harsh place, for the most. Maybe that is why the stay-behind Maroons in Scotia manage well enough, better than the Loyalists, who are custom to the good land that their owners had in the old states below. When

they come to Scotia, though, things turn upside down. Their owners
don't own them any longer, and don't have any responsibility to give
them land to feed themself. White owners always get the good land.
Blackman, including Yenkunkun, get what is left.

Sister have a piece of ground for herself, some ways from her hut,
and we work it every day, she and me and Petta. She grows yam
and eddoe there, and plantain, just like all the other runaways I get
to know in the trek with Henry. It's good enough ground, down in
what they call cockpits. You have to pass between the big rock piles
that God drop there and allow trees and shrub to cover them like old
clothes on nakedness.

Still, as I say, is here we all come from. Mam and Da, Maas George
Seymour, all the stay-behind geezers sinking into their stories as they's
falling asleep from the pork and the screech rum. Even those in Sierra
Leone. All come from here. I count myself blessed that the bigi pripri
led me here.

So I don't mind the digging and sweat. I am just happy to find
Sister and this place. To have her right beside in this place that I been
hearing about from I know myself. She's happy too. "Is like I find
meself," she say one time when we stop to draw breath. And I had to
say, "Me too." Her smile show me Mam when she was young.

I's here with them a week, working beside Sister and Petta. We
sweat like horses in the day, every day. Well, the woman-dem sweat
more than me, because I am responsible for the food, especially the
meat-kind. The iguana I bring with me the day that I found Sister,
both of them still lick their lips to remember it.

But Scotia has more plentiful meat-kind on foot to catch than here.
And there's no fish here. You can see the sea from the highest point
behind Sister's hut, where the English build a tower with a flagstaff
after they tricked us down to the coast to surrender. But it's very far.
For food there's only birds, or something I learn from Henry that
they call coney, like a big rat. Both is plentiful, but I only bother with
the pigeons.

Every now and then I hear a pig, but when I think of the last set of
crosses the pig that we killed cause me and Henry, I forget about the
sweetness of the meat. I just let it go along.

Still, I catch two lizards. As we finish eating one, I catch another. The women count me for that, which is good.

When we's finished digging and weeding, we go to a little stream close to Sister's ground, and there we bathe weself. The woman-dem go one way and I go another. I hear them like pickni together, laughing and splashing, and I feel lonesome, far from everything and everybody.

Petta doesn't talk much, and I don't ask anything of her, or of Sister about her. She must be a runaway like Baddu, but I don't know where from. Maybe Lima, like Sister. I don't ask. Listening to them in the river they's like sisters, reminding me of when Eddie and Precious are out in the yard playing catch. Happy. But in the night, from the other side of Sister's shack, I can hear they's more than sisters to each other.

We's leaving tomorrow, Sister says. When people see Nayga walking about on a Sunday it doesn't come strange, that is our day off. If they see us abroad the rest of the week, though, then they sniff at us like dawg, as Sister says it, to find out who we belong to and where we's going.

Jason: Letter to Carla (4), Sunday, December 11

My Dearest Carla,
I'm at my lowest ebb since returning to this awful place. I long for
your arms of comfort, and Caleb's tinkling voice to lift me closer
to the sky. The sky here is oppressive. I cower from it in my room.
Today, for the first in a long time, I did not venture outside at all; I
hardly left my room except for the necessary ablutions, and avoided
even the most trivial conversation downstairs.

They hanged Carpenter John yesterday. I was witness to it, an
atrocity that chills and boils my very bones anew at the memory of
it. Everyone involved in this outrage knew that they were executing
an innocent man but they didn't care about that little technicality:
Justice was being enacted—as a tragic farce! A man convicted and
sentenced and appealed and denied was being hanged for an act
everyone knew was not his. Well, I spit on Madame Justice—she is
indeed blind! It gave scant comfort, but the Governor, while uphold-
ing the sentence, did at least prohibit the fifty lashes the monster
Magnus had decreed, and which we had specifically protested.

On the way back to Greencastle it was as if from a clear blinding
sky a dark cloud descended that seeped into my spirit, my very limbs.
I have never felt like this ever before, my dearest one, and am a little
concerned for my state of mind. It is fire and then darkness following
swiftly; but mostly the darkness. It's taken me an hour to pen these
few lines to you, and, as you must notice, my hand is very uneven.

His heartfelt feelings for you and Caleb are firm, but believe your
loving husband who says that his hold on sanity is daily loosening.
Jason

Narrative: Cornelius Douglas, Tuesday, December 13

"Pappi."

"Yes, chile."

"You sleeping?"

"Not now."

"Sorry. I know you tired."

"Is alright. I should be in my bed. You too."

"Soon."

"So what you want?"

"People quiet in prayer meeting this evening."

"Hmmm."

"You too."

"Whoso keepeth his mouth and his tongue keepeth his soul from troubles."

"You weren't keeping them last week, though. And look where it land you!"

"'Our lips are our own. Who is Lord over us?' Except Jehovah."

"Backra is lord over you now. You have to report to him every day, remember?"

"Hmmm."

"Who is this Douglas bwoy them ketch yesterday? You know him?"

"Not really."

"But you know who him is."

"Yes."

"Him is a real Douglas?"

"I know him is a Douglas from I look at him that day with Teo."

"Yes. But who is him father? Not the Magnus-one."

"No. That one have pickni running up and down Cascade, but Cornelius is almost Magnus age."

"So is old Maasa Douglas?"

"And not old Maasa either. I don't rightly think old Maasa have any pickni on Cascade. Elsewhere maybe, him was a devil when him young. But Missus would neuter him."

"So is who?"

"Old Maasa Douglas brother. Come from England for a visit. Christmas time."

"I never hear bout a brother before."

"Cause him wouldn't dare come back. People would be setting for him even now."

"Why?"

"Him was a goat, that one. I hear say that he didn't land in the house good from the ship before he start touch-touch the woman-dem, even the gyal-pickni. They run from him. As him wife turn her back him is after them."

"You remember it?"

"Yes. Me and you mother was still on Cascade. The whole family come, pickni and all."

"So how the brother come get at the woman-dem?"

"They had a bookkeeper, I forget his name. Him was little more than a bwoy himself. The brother used to get old Maasa to send him to town when he want to enjoy himself, in the bookkeeper house. After he get him to bring woman to him too. Cloris did take set to poison him, cause he tamper with Cloris daughter Ivy and give her a belly. But he leave go back to England before she could get to do it."

"So who is the Cornelius mother?"

"Who could know? Three pickni born in the August month, I remember that. But I don't remember from who, and I don't remember which one was Cornelius. The other two dead early. And maybe the mother dead too, or sell off. Missus didn't joke about that. But the man was old Maasa big brother, so he never say anything to control him. But the brother don't come back this way again."

"So how the Cornelius-one come to belong to Rickhambone?"

"One of the Douglas-dem must be sell him there."

"And how he find himself to chapel? Uncle Teo bring him?"

"I don't rightly know if anyone bring him. Maybe he just find himself here. That mean he have a ticket."

"Maybe."

"But how he find himself *here*? Plenty chapel between Rickhambone and Zion for him to worship at. If worship is what he come to do."

"What you mean?"

"Maybe somebody send him."

"Send him?"

"Yes. To listen to you."

"He was listening, I could see that. But so what?"

"The wicked watch the righteous and seek to slay him."

"Why?"

"Him is a Douglas. Magnus feel you still owe them for Adam."

"I pay them for Adam."

"You pay old Maasa. Young Maasa think you should pay more. You say so more than once."

"I had a agreement withold Maasa and I pay him in full after Adam run away. Adam is a free man. If anything is me him belong to."

"You don't have a free paper for him, though."

"I have paper to say that I pay what was asked and agreed. Me and old Maasa exchange paper."

"But the paper at Cascade might say something different by now. Magnus is a magistrate. He cyan make a paper say anything he please."

≈ 76 ≈

Jason: The First Crack, Wednesday, December 14

I AM A MAN OF AUTHORITY. I say to this man, Go, and he goeth, and to another, Come, and she cometh.

I send Jack for her and fuck the black gyal till she bawl out.

Not a soul pay it any mind.

Elorine: Maasa Indeed, Wednesday, December 15

ANNA POLLARD COME TO CALL THIS morning. First I thought she was bringing me something for Christmas that she want back quick-quick—that would be just like Anna. As always, she enter like she's rushing to somewhere else. But I always find time for Anna, even when I'm busy like this morning with Francine's Queenie gown that she's coming to fit this afternoon.

"I don't know what get into the bwoy head, Elorine, must be the sun he ride up and down in all day, it fry-up his brain."

The other whiteladies, when they come for a fitting, they stay in the front room and send their slavegirl to tell you to come. Anna always call out herself, to let you know who is there, then she come and knock on the outside of the door even if it is open, and ask pardon for interrupting. From she was small, never mind that she's like a white Nayga, rawchaw, she have manners and respect for people. I don't know how she treat her Nayga-dem up on Greencastle, but I don't have cause for complaint.

From she open her mouth I know who she bring story about. But I ask her nonetheless. "I don't know whether to say he tun Nayga, or tun Maasa," she say.

I remind myself that Anna is a white Nayga in how she talk, but she is still white. Jason is not. But I keep my counsel.

"You should hear the way he talking now." She drop her voice to sound like man. "'Bwoy!' is Jack he talking to, 'you stink like a goat, go wash yourself.' I never hear him talk to Jack in that voice before. Nor anybody!" Anna cackle, and I couldn't help but to smile myself.

"He did talk so nice when he just come back, he make me feel shame for how I was talking. But now!"

And then she look straight into my face and turn serious. Talking soft, like she frighten, or might frighten me, she say, "And Elorine? He start on the gyal-dem now."

I wasn't expecting that. After Anna leave, I think to myself: Him is man. Man must live. And bumbo is life for them. But at the moment when Anna open her eye wide and say it, I couldn't help myself, my face freeze.

"The only thing left is for him to turn drunk-a-ready on us. And maybe that would be better to bear." Anna sigh like a old woman, and I feel for her.

From Jason leave her as a baby she was missing him. Lincoln learn her to read and write so she could read his letter-dem to her. When she get bigger and start to come here from time to time she do nothing but talk about Jason, and I was happy to listen to her. I would try in my own little way to caution her that he wasn't Maasa Jesus come to ground, but even when she bring him here that first time the light in her face was like the oil lamp beside me when I sew at night, bright-bright.

Well, that lamp blow-out now. And it dim for me too.

"That Lucia-one," Anna say with her mouth turn down. "Israel daughter. Him is a good old nigger, but him must be lie down with a dawg to get that bitch. After Anthony leave I see her set her eye on Jason. And she ketch him too. Next thing you know, when he gone back to England a little Jason-nigger pickni will be running around in the big house."

My heart just shrink inside me. I was thinking bout his wife, I don't even remember her name. And his pickni for her. Caleb—him I remember. But then I shake myself. For all I know I have brother and sister other than Adam running around Bellefields. Pappi wasn't always a preacher, or even a Christian. And he name man!

I had to ask Anna. "What cause this?"

She shrug and knot-up her face. "I was wondering the same thing myself. Mama say that is from when they arrest your Daddy. She say he start getting irritable at the slightest little thing." I know that that upset Jason, but I wasn't expecting anyone else to notice. It please me.

"And then they go and hang the cripple. Carpenter John. You shoulda see him the night, after he come back from the workhouse with the body. I tell you, the man take-up some serious puncheon, and it fly straight up in his head. The bwoy go on bad!" Anna clap her hands and laugh. "He cuss everybody he could think of except me and Mama and Lincoln. He cuss even Hector, who dead already. Magnus he cuss up and down the hillside, through the trees and over the river. He start out cussing the way he normally talk, but is like he couldn't find the words he want there, and some slave words start jumping off his tongue like spit. Mama and I trying to calm him down, telling him is only a old nigger, who due for superannuation anyway, after this crop. That seem to just make him worse vex, and the words-dem bounce off each other like flint, English and slave talk, slave talk and English. You could barely understand him, same time you had to laugh. Next day, Elorine-chile, he calm down. But he's not been himself since then."

Myself, I keep my silence on that, looking out the window. Carpenter John is a piece of dry wood to Miss Anna and them. But I remember Jason, when he was a bwoy coming here, talking about Bristol his friend, and his father, who wasn't broken then. And since he come back I hear him talk with respect for the cripple. From what I pick up here and there, it's certain that is cassava poison that kill the brute Hector, and good riddance.

But Backra, and especially the Magnus-one, don't care about a dry wood Nayga, guilty or not guilty. They shaping now to cut down a tree, and that tree name Ishmael Livingstone.

≈ 78 ≈

Elorine: Johncrow, Thursday, December 15

BACKRA POUNCE ON NAYGA LIKE A set of mad dawg on a old puss. Courtney say they catch ten of the Rickhambone slaves yesterday and hang five of them by breakfast this morning. Court usually start at ten o'clock, but this morning it was in session by nine. The trial for each Nayga last five minutes. No defence. Charge and sentence before they had time to draw two breaths. And in a hour they was hanging by their necks. Three more this afternoon, Courtney say.

And this afternoon was when I had to go right past the hanging place.

I couldn't put it off. I tell Francine that I'm coming later on with her crown, which wasn't ready yesterday. That was before Courtney come to sweep the chapel, for which he get a big lunch from Jassy and a few macaroni from Ishmael. He come twice a week for that, and always bring me something. This morning it was two lovely breadfruit. I don't ask is whose tree they come off, but as I'm telling him tenky the news just tumble out of his mouth.

Rickhambone shake-up the Backra in this district. He was expecting something coming from out West, not his own backyard. From what I hear from Uncle Teo, who was here last night, the slaves in West still planning a siddown after Christmas. Maybe that is why they jump down on Rickhambone so quick and hard, think they can stop the siddown. Not if Daddy Sharpe is the serious man everybody say him is!

But as I'm walking past the poorhouse this afternoon on the way to Francine, is Pappi I'm worrying about in all of this. He find himself

ketch-up in the middle of this palampam, and all because he grieving for his son who is in exile like the Israelites, and for a daughter
and grandchildren that he hardly know. Backra is out to make him
a example, just like the slave-dem on Rickhambone that they ketch.
Being as everybody far and wide know Ishmael Livingstone, he would
be a bigger example than even the Cornelius-one, who nobody would
know. Family with black blood don't count for anything with whitepeople—Magnus himself would put the noose round his cousin neck.
I count Squire for his regard for Jason.

I reach into the square at the wrong time.

They have only the one gallows in the workhouse yard. But they
have a big guango tree near to the wall that provide the only little
shade in the place. That serve them just as good to string up a person.
The stringing-up stretch your neck, and you dead slow, fighting for
the last little scraps of life.

Try hard as anything, I couldn't help but look over when I reach
the square. I hear a big set of coughing. They was hoisting two, a
man and a woman, the three biggest guards they could find on one
end of each rope from behind the tree-limb. I see them heave like the
sailor-dem when they're pulling in the anchor, but what come up out
of these depths is two bodies, like fish. But it's like they think about
things beforehand, and they didn't fight. Tenky God, they let themself
drop, and in two twos there was no movement from them. They was
ready to dead.

I praise them in myself, they're strong like the tree they're hanging
from. But all I could see, as I'm watching, was Pappi! Gallows or tree
is the same dreadful thing.

By the time I reach to Francine I was in no mood for her nose-
in-the-air ways. She must be see my face when I come in, there was
none of her usual foolishness concerning if I find a man yet, and
nothing about her slaves that she is always bad-mouthing to everybody who'll listen. I wasn't listening this afternoon. I just roll out
the lace and other things I bring for her consideration on her dining
table—which the same terrible slaves keep spotless, like they keep
her whole house—and stand up over them until she tell me what she
want where on her costume.

As I'm folding up the things I bring into my bag she say, in her sweetest voice, "It will ready for Christmas Eve, cherie?" Francine only call anybody *cherie* when she want something extra from them.

"I trying my best, Francine." I fling that over my shoulder as I'm going to the door. "Plenty dress to ready for Christmas." I can feel her bad-eye on me, so I turn and soften my voice a little. "I trying." I like Francine, and she make sure Missa Penninger send the money right away. But sometimes she can make a soul walk and talk to herself.

Thunder greet me as I step outside. And then a swift burst of rain that soak me to the skin. That cancel the route I was going to take home, by South Street on the harbour. It would be mud up to my ankles by the time I reach there. So I had to go by the square again.

They was still there, hanging in the rain like rotten fruit. I was expecting it, cause Backra want everybody to learn the lesson. But I couldn't look away. And I couldn't but notice a johncrow, perch as comfortable as you please on the woman's head, waiting. When I was watching them hang I was frighten and tighten-up, but give thanks my stomach hold on to itself.

Narrative: Cries in the Night, Thursday, December 15

HE CRIES OUT IN THE NIGHT like a mewling baby. Though sometimes he shouts. Barks like a dog, or howls like they say wolves do. Sometimes it is from fucking the bitch, when he comes. And sometimes it's frighten; he's frighten of the very dark itself. The dark around and the dark inside.

He can remember—every night now he remembers—the pickni Jason-who-used-to-be-Kwesi. Lying on the pallet in Maas Squire's office after he put up the screen at the end of the day to make it a bedroom. He lies there restlessly, listening for the voices crying out like birds or dogs. His father's and, mostly, Creole Dido's when Maasa is pumping her like an engine. Mathilde—still the housekeeper, not yet the wife and mother—is two bedrooms away.

Jason knows what is going on because Kwesi used to hear Pompey fucking Judith, almost on top of where he and Pheba and Silas huddled together so as to get as far away as they could from the flying feet. Up in the big house he's further away, but it's the same as when he was close.

Now Squire's big room downstairs, which has become Anthony's, is shadowy and quiet even in the day. Anna and Mathilde sleep across the hallway, Anna in the little cubicle that held her crib, now expanded into a room. Creole Dido used to sleep there when she was in favour. Until Maasa kicked her back upstairs to the slave quarters, where she slept on whoever's pallet was empty. Whoever was in Maasa's bed downstairs.

He can see Dido now. A pretty bright-eye brown gyal. Supposed to help Constancia in the kitchen but nobody could find her when the yams needed to peel, she'd be skylarking in some other part of the big house. Missus Angela's girl she was, brought into the marriage from her parish. Missus Angela left her for Squire in her will, he was told. And perhaps in her bed. To be remembered.

Before Dido—even before Missus Angela's death—there would have been Memba, according to Tombo. Not fucked in the big bed, or even the cubicle. Perhaps bending over the desk like he'd seen Anthony that afternoon. Unless—he thinks suddenly—it was right here in this room, which used to be part of the house slave quarters. Maybe here, where he is now doing his Maasa fucking.

He has no idea where Creole Dido might be now, and doesn't ask. She might be any one of the mostly brown women, scoured by time, shuffling around the big house. In due course, Lucia will be too.

But for now she's the pump-engine that peels his voice from him, flinging it into his dreaming darkness. From just down the hallway in the quarters, she slips into his room like a duppy. Practised and proficient, she disappears again after, though she does hold him with something like tenderness when he awakes whimpering in the dark.

She doesn't know the limbs he wants coiled through his. The hands he wants soothing his terror back to sleep. She doesn't care anyway. She's right where she wants to be: Maasa's bed.

⇒ 80 ⇐

Adebeh: Setting Out, Thursday, December 15

IT'S GOOD TO BE BACK IN THE BUSH. The quiet is the best part. When you grow in a place like Boydville, atop Maroon Hill, as the white people call it, quiet is the soul of it.

Which put me in mind of Peter, and when we used to go into the bush around Beaver Bank, sometimes as far as Webber Lake. Others would come with us, but neither of us would go if the other wasn't coming. I think about him a lot since I leave Halifax, wondering where he is now. He gone to sea before me, now two years, so he could be anywhere, because he's not coming back to Scotia. Is not his home, he says from we are boys, even though he'd born and grown there. I can't fault him for that. Maybe worse than to be black in Scotia is to be Mi'kmaq. And Peter is both. His Mi'kmaq people send his mother to live with his father, a leave-behind Maroon like Da and Mam. So Peter was born to hunt from both sides, and that is what we do every chance we get.

But Scotia bush has better hunting, more things to eat that you can trap and kill, and lake water where you can fish. In these mountains you have rivers, but they run too fast for a pool to form and fish to live in and wait for you. The river through the Cameron ground behind us in Kojo Town is better.

Despite what Sister say about travelling on a Sunday it passed in idleness, me mostly thinking between Elorine and Georgia Marcy. In the quietness sometimes I hear something that could be a bird or a church bell, and I think of the church Georgia Marcy takes me to on Gottingen Street with the other Black Loyalist families like hers.

I's seeing her father's eyes like fish hooks on me before and after the service. He don't forgive me for taking his first and favourite daughter out of his house and to Campbell Road with the other low-life Negroes, as he call them to my face. He includes me with them, of course, since even when I scrub and scrub with carbolic and pumice stone beforehand, I can't get the smell of horse off myself. Even Mrs. Belknap—who like me just a little more than Georgia Marcy's father—I can see the little birdwing flutter in her nostrils.

Meantime that I's remembering, I's wondering whether the worship at Elorine father's chapel is as lively as the service in Africville, and whether she sing as lovely as Georgia Marcy in the hymns. Georgia Marcy has a voice like molasses. Never mind she's small and trim like her father, her voice come from her bubbies that she inherited from her mother—and that I like to rest between.

The idleness give time for thinking too. The three of us is lounging outside, me lying against the tree stump with a hat on my head that Sister lend me, Baddu and Petta gone to the ground to bring back provisions and plantain to cook.

I's not sure how to read what's between Baddu and Petta. I's not in any agreement with the thundering pastors at Georgia Marcy's church, both of them the same. They hammer Leviticus into your head like nails, the different prohibitions of who can sleep with who—or what—and what you can eat and not. Meantime, Georgia Marcy tells me, they themself is touching up some of the choir women.

Myself, I don't believe in judgement by one man of another. Reverend Smythe like to preach that Jehovah is Judge, fear Him. And I don't have certainty as to what Jesus means when he say you must love everybody. I can tell that Baddu and Petta love each other. Not just in the pleasuring I can't help but hear in the darkness. When I'm in their company I feel like a shadow in their sun.

Before we even know it, the day slip into the ground like water and night begin a slide into the cockpit from the mountains behind. Belly is full and idleness sweet, so when too many mosquito and fly bite us, we just go inside and crawl onto our pallets. Tomorrow is another day.

But Monday we don't leave either. We finish the food we have on

Sunday, and it take us most of the day to find food and cook what we need for that day. Same thing on Tuesday. Wednesday, we make sure to get up early to find and cook things to eat for the day and something to put by for the journey tomorrow.

So today we have a lizard from yesterday, and the bush has a lot of juicy fruit things to eat that I don't know the names of, and some roots that I know from when Henry and I was trekking. But otherwise food is scarce.

The fact is that blackpeople have to steal from blackpeople to survive here—not so different from Scotia when times are tight. Sister lead us away from the estates, which is where there might otherwise be food, but is blackpeople who grow that also. Today we don't need any food, but by tomorrow we will. We'll either have to kill it or steal it. Or starve.

But I give thanks. In Scotia now I'd be following my breath through snow looking for deer tracks. Or coons. Which, if you can stew it a long time with a lot of salt and pepper and onion, will taste tolerable. Lizard is not as meaty but you can roast it right off, whereas roast coon will break your teeth.

And no flowers is blooming in the Scotia bush at this time, or too many birds singing. So I can't complain. And I's with Sister. She know this bush better than me, of course, and is teaching me as we go along. I's far away from any place or person that I know, but you could say I's happy.

It's not a easy country, though. And it don't forgive fools. Petta was bouncing along between Baddu in front and myself in back when I notice like she get shorter of a sudden. I only notice because she have a nice backside that I was watching, it remind me of Georgia Marcy. She cry out and pitch sideways and turn, and I had the presence of mind to grab the hand she fling out to find something to save herself. When we look down, there was a sinkhole big enough to swallow both of us.

"I did tell you before we set out," Baddu says, her voice rough, "step where I step. Not so?"

Petta and me had to nod, cause it's true. Petta was close against me, trembling. A nice tremble, I have to admit, she smell like grass on a hot day. I was trembling too, inside.

Baddu turn away, vex, and set off again. But her strides is not so long, and her eyes is just a few yards ahead. Petta and myself take every zig that she zag, like our feet is tied to hers. But I couldn't help myself—my eyes returned to hitch a ride on the two halves of Petta's backside, bouncing on them like a fly.

We're following Sister. I know we's going to meet up with her man Bryden, but that is all I know. Petta maybe knows where Bryden is, cause I learn in the lazy time we spend at Baddu's shack that Petta is Bryden's sister. But how Baddu come to find herself among the two of them is a mystery, to me at least. And what will happen when we find this Bryden, whoever and wherever he is, that is mystery also.

≈ 81 ≈

Elorine: Missus Justice, Friday, December 16

PAPPI LIKE TO LEAVE HERE QUITE EARLY to show himself, as Backra require. To get to courthouse just when they open the doors, and to get back here for when his customers start to arrive. This morning was the same. Only different. Backra get up extra early to hang the Cornelius-one. To make sure that when the townpeople start to go about their business, the whitepeople will be calmed and the rest will know who is truly Maasa in the place.

The mongoose Thomas say to him, "You next, Livingstone." Pappi say he had to bridle his tongue and his fist before he could find the quiet to say, "I don't convict yet, Missa Thomas."

"I am respectful," Pappi say to me afterwards, "but he surely understand what I mean, stupid as he is." Pappi snort, near to spitting, which is not something he generally do outside of the shop.

Backra have a way to say that Madame Justice, as they call it inside the courthouse, is blind. A picture of a whitelady with her eyes tie-up is on the wall behind where the magistrate-dem sit, and they like to point at her and tell you that they is just instruments of her truth, or some other big talk. Like is Maasa God Himself up there on the wall.

Nayga know better. First, Missus Justice peep from under her bandage to see if you is white or black. Then she decide on which truth she is going to deliver that day.

I wonder what Missus Justice will decide about Pappi.

"Trust in the Lord, chile. And pray." I do, both. But I worry too, in case Jehovah blink.

Pappi must have it in his mind that Assizes start next week Tuesday. He will get a date then for his trial. That will be Christmas week. I don't follow these things but Backra don't usually have anything official like court in Christmas week. If I'm right, then what it might mean is that they're setting for him specially.

To hang him!

From yesterday I feel myself smalling up inside. I don't want to think about what I see in the courthouse square on the way to Francine. So everything inside me screw up like the cloth I knot around the blue-cake when I'm washing the white clothes for customers. That make them pretty-pretty, white as snow, like the Bible say.

But right now is not snow I'm thinking about. The only thing white in my mind is Magnus Douglas and Missus Justice. And when I put my mind to that, everything seem black.

Adebeh: Captive, Saturday, December 17

THE BIGI PRIPRI ABANDONED ME. Me and Baddu, and Petta, though she is not Yenkunkun.

Mam when she's telling us stories always calls the Cockpits "the duppy place", because of the cotton trees. Not so many of them here-abouts like in Adam's bush, but there's some. The recently dead and the ancestors, the bigi pripri, live in these trees, waiting for the right ceremonies that will release them back to Africa. Mam say that some of them are the people who came here before the whiteman even. Wherever they came from they made canoes from these same trees—don't ask me how, cause they's huge and tough—and rowed or sailed here. And now they's waiting here to go back home, though is a different home from Africa, Mam say.

Maybe it's those duppy who deliver us over.

It was afternoon, just after we eat. We's bone tired and stop to rest. A cotton tree was near. We settle between the roots like is dolly-house we're playing. Baddu and Petta in the biggest space, me in the next space.

Under the tree was dry enough, but it rained last night on Baddu's hillside, and all the way here the ground is soft.

Must be that why we didn't hear them.

The dawg was the first sign, and is me it comes to. I was dozing, my hand wrapped around the cloth with what leave of the food, which is tangled with Delphis's leather pouch. I feel something tugging at it. I's thinking is one of the women come to wake me. I open one eye. To see this big brown and grey dawg-head over me, moving for my hand. The mouth is open, pink and black with a big tongue hanging out, sniffling.

When I pull my hand back, though, without even thinking, the sniffling change to a growl, like far-off thundering—is a big dawg. I know more about horses than dawg but I see right away, even though I's not fully awake, that this one is trouble. Big trouble.

Again without thinking, I pull the food cloth and the pouch closer, to protect it. And that was a trigger for the dawg to open his mouth and shout at me. As if to say: "Who the fuck you think you is?" Well, from habit with Henry in the bush, and even at Baddu's hut, I get accustom to sleep with Fergus's cutlass in my other hand. It was going to come for me next, I could see, and the teeth was dripping with drool.

Is only the one shout the damn dawg get to shout, before I swing the cutlass at its head.

A geyser of blood colour the air as the dawg seem to throw itself at me and land in my lap, screeching like something sent from Beelzebub. The head is hanging on by a strip of skin, and everything inside it is oozing out into my crotch.

But I didn't have time to think of that. The world explode into noise and pain. I hear the women in the next root-cave cry out, but before I see them, three men appear from nowhere, like the dawg, whose head is still quarrelling. They block out the light over me. And just stand there, studying what to do about this blood-soaked man with their dawg dying in his lap. Is their dawg—one of them even have a strap coiled around his wrist like I have my pouch. That one's face screw-up with vex. The dawg belong to him. The other two is almost smiling. Like I's a meal to them.

Just then Baddu appear from over her root. The men move fast, back away three steps to give the two women space to come to me. And then they step in again.

I's still holding my cutlass, but it's as though the biggest one of them read my thinking. He reach behind his waist and pull out a pistol that he wave at the three of us. I push the damn dawg off my lap and start to get up, which make him point the pistol directly at me.

There was a whole lot of shouting and pushing and cuffing, back and forth between us and them. The dawg man use the leash as a whip and beat us all with it while the pistol man was pointing at whosomever was talking loudest.

The short story from long is that the three of us find ourselves hands tied behind our backs, and then tied to each other by the neck.

I's in front, Baddu at back. The dawg man put the collar around my neck and is pulling me on his leash. He set a brisk pace that we have trouble to keep, but at the back is the pistol man. He is the leader, I figure, cause the others don't have any kind of gun, and he's the one who tell the dawg man which way to turn, and also threaten to shoot us if we make a move, as he call it. We all understand him.

The third man, the smallest of them, is dancing between the three of us cackling like a monkey, "Step lively, nigger." He have a sharp stick that he's poking at whichever of us is nearest.

We all understand what is happening, but we don't know who is responsible. Is not Yenkunkun. Between Baddu furious at them and myself shouting in the little Akan I can muster, we come to thinking that they's not Yenkunkun.

Still, we's their captives. That is the important thing that we all know.

⇒ 83 ⇐

Jason: Letter to Reverend Swithenbank, Sunday, December 18

Dear Rev. Swithenbank,

When I review my thoughts over the last little while, something I do compulsively, & concurrent with the thoughts themselves, I am forced to wonder at my own sanity. I could say that the world has changed around me, but I do not make so bold a charge. Such claims are generally made by those unfortunates who have loosed the bounds of reason. I thank the Father of us all—Maasa God, as the Negroes address Him—that I am still bound. In some degree.

It is perhaps the question of degree that gives me cause for concern about myself. You could say that I no longer recognize myself, even in the looking-glass above this table from which I write. The eyes looking back at me are not always my own as I've known them. But to whom they belong I know not, either.

When I am among the older slaves, or abroad in the district, I am often told that I favour Squire, my father. They remark on the similarity of build & also the eyes. The eyes staring back at me in the looking glass are indeed those of my father. The eyes of Maasa, the mammon who plays at Godness in the slaves' lives.

Mr. Cowper's popular poem is directly to the point:

I am monarch of all I survey,
My right there is none to dispute,
From the centre all round to the sea,
I am lord of the fowl and the brute.

It is a monarchy that has corrupted me utterly. You'd not recognize the man you think you know; your goodly, godly wife & your sweet children, who are all, I earnestly pray, in good health & spirits, would flee from sight of me. My clothes are dishevelled—not casual, as is the popular style in hot climes, but untidy and grimy. I smell. Not unusual for the tropics but as easily remedied; I care not any longer. And my language! Over-listening, you would not understand three words in ten.

I find myself slipping back into the language of the Anglican observances, in order to cogently express my present concerns. I have erred and strayed from His ways like a lost sheep & have followed too much the devices & desires of my own heart. And indeed, my reverend & esteemed friend, the desires of my heart augment those of my flesh, making them doubly hideous.

In some wise, the practical work of my charge, Greencastle estate, proceeds in fairly good order. I am, outwardly at least, as sedulous in my responsibilities as before, and take some satisfaction from that. Since writing last I have banished the whip & changed the nature of required work from dawn-to-dusk to piece-work. Thereafter they're free to do what they will. Most work in their own behalf, a few lounge or sleep. The slaves at least appreciate the changes, though they still run away as if from habit; but they come back. Some still put themselves in the sickhouse with sham complaints.

But I am an empty vessel, a sounding brass & tinkling cymbal. I crave the indulgence of your prayers that I may turn from my wickedness and live in God's good grace. Especially so at this time, as the Birth of the Christ Child approaches, heralding salvation for all sinners, however wretched. This missive will reach you after the Christmas season has passed, but my prayer tonight is for your prayers for that salvation.

In wretched sinfulness I remain.
Your unworthy friend and servant,
Jason Pollard.

P.S. Please, Reverend, if you encounter my dear Carla in one of her visits to your fair wife, I beg you to say nothing of this letter. I do not of course ask you, in such a circumstance, to dissemble. I ask merely, and humbly, for your forbearance. And, once more, for your prayers.

≈ 84 ≈

Elorine: Teo's Preachment, Sunday, December 18

ZION FULL UP THIS MORNING. A lot of faces I don't see in a long time present themself. I'm glad to see them, Pappi too. He stand at the doorway greeting everybody like they're coming into his home, not to worship.

Me, I'm happy to see the old faces, but what I'm looking for is anybody new! Like the Cornelius Douglas-one who just appear that morning. I cyaant say for certain that is him carry story to Backra, it could as well be one of these same faces grinning up with Deacon, as some call him. As the prophet say, *The heart of man is deceitful above all things, and desperately wicked.*

Still, is Maasa God bring them here this morning, like he carry them in his hand. They all know what the day after tomorrow signify for Ishmael. Most would also know that he cannot preach a word until his trial, and with Pappi that is like telling him he cannot eat or drink or have a rum!

But they come nonetheless. They come to bear witness. To Backra and whoever else say that Nayga is savages. These people, pickni and grands and in between, not fraid for anybody but Maasa God Himself. But they is anxious, you can feel it in their eyes. Anything could happen on Tuesday, because when it come to matters concerning Nayga, Backra is like the wind that bloweth where it listeth. Who can know the reasoning?

Uncle Teo is a different kind of preachment from Pappi. If you want to talk clothes, Pappi is gown and button shoes and ruffle and long sleeve, when Uncle Teo is bodice and slippers. But a lot of them like his preachment. Ishmael can be heavy sometimes, like too much yam in your belly-bottom. Uncle Teo is more like good wash when you's thirsty.

He was a good drink this morning, and people was thirsty.

Usually, Uncle Teo begin his preachments with a story, often something funny that he see or hear on his rounds. Pappi too, sometimes. Both of them take the joke into something from the Good Book to show a serious point.

This morning, though, after the first hymn and people sit down, Teo start right in. "I will lift up mine eyes unto the hills," he say, looking out over our heads, though you can't see hills from Zion chapel. "From whence cometh my help. My help cometh from the Lord, which made heaven and earth. He will not suffer thy foot to be moved, he that keepeth thee will not slumber." Everybody there know this Psalm, it's a favourite of Ishmael. I don't know if Teo can read and write his own name, but he know his Bible, he don't even open the one he's holding. He recite the whole Psalm in his scratchy sing-song voice, and eventually bring his eyes down to look at Pappi, sitting in the front row. I am in my usual place at the back, one ear still listening for sounds from West Street, for someone leaning against the fence, listening.

As Uncle Teo is going along I see heads in front of me bowing like they is in prayer. A hanky or three come out and dab at the eyes. I understand, cause my own is burning me too.

I can see from the tilt of Pappi head that him and Teo is looking at each other as Teo is speaking. "The Lord shall preserve thee from all evil, he shall preserve thy soul. The Lord shall preserve thy going out and thy coming in from this time forth, and for evermore."

In Teo's mouth the Psalm is a prayer for this morning, this particular day. And he is not only praying for Pappi, he's praying for all of us. That we be strong in the days ahead, whatever they may bring. That we *be not afraid for the terror of night nor for the arrow that flieth by day*, because we is under the shadow of Maasa God's wings. Always.

Teo sit down and look at the floor in front of him. That is his whole preachment.

Pappi stannup slowly and raise a hymn for us. His voice start with a croak—he was maybe tearing up too. But by the second verse he's leading us in full voice, and slightly off as usual. He's telling Teo tenky.

≋ 85 ≋

Adebeh: Pain, Sunday, December 18

I DREAM PRECIOUS. SHE AND ME was racing down Maroon Hill to the chestnut tree that herself and Eddie is always raiding this time of year, bringing baskets home for Mam to roast. My foot trip on something and I tumble over and over and fetch up against something hard that blow out my lights. And I wake up.

There's a fire raging inside my body. It start at my neck and then flare out into every part, even into my toes. The neck pain, raw on the outside, flame on the inside, bring remembering.

We're in the mountains. Not Cockpits, where we started out from. They capture us on the edge of that. Since they're not Yenkunkun, I figure they may be bounty catchers. We have some in Scotia. So I was surprise when, instead of turning down toward the sea where the towns are, and the sugar estates, they turn up further into the mountains.

Baddu and Petta keep asking them where they's taking us. But that only get them poked by the monkey man so they soon stop. And I realize that the dawg man is likely to kill me for the least excuse in revenge for his monster dawg. People can be funny like that. They would rather you tamper with their wife or their daughter than you harm their dawg. So I keep my words to myself and do the best I can to stay upright. Easy in one way, cause we's going uphill, but not always, because of his pace and the collar around my neck.

By and by we come to a sort of road. It has plenty holes and big stones, but somebody put some muscle, probably slaves' muscle, into making it something going through the bush. We're walking through some bushes with berries. Coffee. Henry showed me in the bush. He'd pick off a few berries and chew them. It gives him energy, he say. They's bitter, I find, and I's not sure about the energy. And with the dawg man in front and the monkey man beside I's not going to even touch them.

Is almost dark, and still we're going up. There's a house up ahead but that is not where they're going. The dawg man pull me vicious to the right and I see up ahead a smaller building, part wood, part stone, no light outside or in.

We're dragged up the steps and thrown inside a dark hole where we fall hard on a dirty stone floor. I must be pass out cause I don't remember anything until I dream Precious. I stay there just awake, not moving, thinking of Precious and Scotia behind my lids. Not for long, though. Remembering yesterday bring me wide awake, and force my eyes open.

That is worse!

I's on my back, looking up into a shadowy thatch ceiling I don't know. From the light it's nearly morning. Something is playing with my fingers. I know it's not Precious, who do that sometimes for attention. I fling my hand away. Only a few inches before something stop it. I kick my leg. A few more inches than my hand, but not much.

And I understand the reason for dreaming Precious and me running free down Maroon Hill. That is dream. Here, now, I'm tied. Hand and foot. The only part of me I can move as I please is my head. I turn, and my eyes drop like stones straight into Baddu's. I turn the other way and Petta is staring at me, big eyes frighten.

We is all naked. Like the rabbits hanging up in the butchers' at Halifax Market. I'm not really thinking about my own, but am ashamed to be seeing Sister's body naked. To see her spread out like a pig on a barbeque.

As I's looking away from her up into the ceiling, I see something dropping down. It land right on my belly. And start to crawl. Slow. It's cold, and my blood run cold from it. I remember the doctorman's house in Bellefields. Croaking lizard, the folks there call it, because of the noise it makes, like scraping a piece of old iron pipe. It live behind things, so don't have any colour like the other geckos here. Murtella is fierce when she see one, swatting it off the wall and slamming it with whatever come to hand. I would have her swat my belly now, I tell you.

I hear a whinnying like a horse, and realize it's in my belly. Not from the lizard, but from everything that happen since yesterday lunch. It just curl up inside me in a big tight ball. The only way to get it out of myself before I choke on it is to scream. So I scream. And scream. And scream. I feel my throat shredding like paper, and the scream is like a wild animal tearing around the space we is in. Which, I notice as I's twisting myself in fury to get the damn lizard off me and get out of my ropes, is a stone place, not very big. And we three isn't the only people here.

"Shuddup!" A man's voice from behind. Not loud, but harsh—a warning.

I fight the ropes and struggle my head around to look. A scrawny old man is staring at me, eyes bright as mica.

"Who you?" he ask. His voice is softer, but no more friendly. I'm still angry.

"Who is asking?"

The old man cackle. "Dat is for me to know and you to find out. Nigger."

That is Mam, when she teasing us. The anger in me just evaporate like it's spit on a hot stone. I feel naked and alone. Helpless. I look across at Sister. She's not smiling, but there's comfort in her eyes. It's like she knows my feeling.

Then a shadow fall across us. I lift my head and am looking at a doorway to the blue-grey outside. A big man's filling it. The one yesterday with the gun. He's still carrying the gun.

His eyes pass over the three of us with no more interest than the croaking lizard. Then he step aside and another figure fill the doorway. A smaller man, well-fed, plump. With a whip around his neck like a garland, and a thin curved branch in one hand, the other hand in his trouser pocket. Look us over too. And as his eye light on Petta, you can see him quicken. She see it too. I feel her stiffen beside me. That bring a grin to the man's face as he come over toward her, his eyes not even blessing Baddu or me.

He look down at her like breakfast. The thin switch in his hand, smooth dark wood, find her pussy hair and play in it like a finger. Petta wriggle as best she can and quarrel behind her teeth. The man's grin broaden over her. Is all he can do to stop his other hand playing with himself through the trouser pocket. Might as well he just go ahead, cause his eyes are bright with it. Clear glittering eyes in a brown face. The face of a glutton and a drunk.

My eyes are used to the shadows now, and the day is brightening as he turn to look at the gun man by the door. They don't say a word to each other. The brown man step back, and in half-a-dozen big strides the black man is over us. I flinch as he reach into his waist and pull a knife.

But it's not for me, or Sister. Quick-quick he slice the ropes on Petta and pull her to her feet like a dolly. The brown man lead the way through the doorway.

"That is first bickle for Busha," I hear. The old man behind me is chuckling. A nasty kind of chuckle. Scrawny and old as he is, he'd like Petta for his bickle.

My stomach turns. Instead of saying anything, though, I look at Baddu. Her eyes are wet. If I could, I would hold her, naked as she is, for comfort. She's with Petta wherever she is, knowing what is going on and knowing how it feel. A big tear roll out of one eye, across the bridge of her nose, run through the other eye and into the dirt we's lying on.

I look away as best I'm able. My own eyes spring water.

☙ 86 ❧

Jason: Diseased, Monday, December 19

FOR MY LOINS ARE FILLED *with a loathsome disease, and there is no soundness in my flesh. I am David the Psalmist.*

Is not only in my flesh, though.

⇝ 87 ⇜

Elorine: Closed for the Day, Tuesday, December 20

THE MORNING START OUT FINE. He eat a hearty breakfast, asking Jassy for two extra fry dumpling with the corn pork. When Cyrus arrive at the kitchen steps to report for work, he call out to tell him not to light the fire today, to go home.

"You sick, Maas Ishy?"

Pappi laugh. "No, Cyrus," he call out, "go home and pray."

"Yes, Maas Ishy." I hear a few words to Jassy and then the gate creaking.

As we's leaving, Pappi pull out a piece of board that he must be write on from yesterday, and hang it over the gate: CLOSED FOR THE DAY.

Pappi step off like he marching at muster, but as we turn into Charles Street that lead you into the square, I feel him take my hand. He is still walking strong, but it feel strange for me, cause is not something that ever happen the few times we find weself walking in town together. He is disquieted in himself. He's not trembling, nothing like that. Ishmael is the one who Maasa God hear, and who hear Maasa God. He is a tree, and Jehovah pour down His strength into that tree, and that strength run down into the roots that bear us all up, me and the whole Zion congregation.

So when I feel his hand take mine and hold it, not to just touch but to hold on to, I know that today will be different—he want me to be the strong one. To tell truth, I am barely holding up. I barely sleep last night. At bickle, I was watching him downing the pork and dumpling and coffee and could barely force one dumpling pass my throat.

But I squeeze his hand and he squeeze back and we walk on. For strength I'm hearing Uncle Teo's preachment on Sunday. And then, after the final hymn and everybody is getting themself together for home, Mama Claris stannup and give a shy little bow, and sing. "Why art thou cast down, O my soul? and why art thou disquieted in me? Hope thou in God, for I shall yet praise him for the help of his countenance." Claris is maybe the oldest of us, knowing Ishmael from before Zion. Her voice crackle as she start, but then everybody join in as if to bear her up. Is really ourself we's holding up, cause nobody know what will happen in the days ahead.

As we get closer to courthouse I feel Pappi's hand in mine strengthen and his step get strong and regular again. He is not letting Backra see him anything but upright and firm. And he's wearing—the both of us—Sunday best. Court make a rule of the clothes. We's not giving them cause to look down on this and this Nayga.

Missa Alberga arrive same time as us, from the opposite direction. He raise his hand and Ishmael wave back. But they can't get to each other right away because a parade is going on. Soldiers from Fort George making two lines, and the three Assizes judge-dem one behind the other walking between the lines like they's looking for something in the soldier-dem face. Back of them two drummers and a bwoy between them blowing a pennywhistle. So close to Christmas morning, this coming Sunday, it could sound like Jonkanoo. But is a different rhythm, and nobody dancing except some little bwoy-dem on the fringe of the crowd of Nayga who stop to watch the free show.

When the judge-dem finish and walk back to the courthouse steps, they stand on the middle step and look out. The man in charge of the soldier-dem shout two time at them and they spin around and raise their rifle into the sky and fire. Is one big sound and Nayga jump, even Pappi. Everybody know is not bird they aiming at, cause the target is not up above. They's looking for another way to make Nayga know who is in charge. As if we don't born knowing that.

Eventually the free show finish and Nayga drift away about their business. Drums and pennywhistle behind them, the soldiers from Fort George march out of the square with a left-right-left from the shouting man in front.

When they meet up, Ishmael right away say a tenky to Missa Alberga. I know my father: he tell him tenky already, last week when he send for Pappi and he spend a whole morning answering the lawyerman questions about his preachment that Sunday.

"The man to thank," the lawyerman say with a nod, "is Jason Pollard." The look on his face is as though he doing Pappi a favour because of Jason. I feel Pappi draw back into himself. But he don't say nothing or let anything show on his face but the same tenky. As the Good Book say and Pappi teach me from small, *A fool's mouth is his destruction*. His face too, sometimes.

And they is not strangers. You would think that twenty-plus years of seeing Pappi bring the rent money for the widow-woman—never miss a quarter, never short—the Jewman would have a little more respect. Backra funny in truth.

He barely nod at me as he take hold of Ishmael and lead him over to the underneath of the courthouse where Pappi go every morning to report. I don't want to go in there with them, to see whiteman Thomas try to shame him. So I find myself over to the big guango tree to one side of the steps going up to the courthouse. Is a busy place. The public water trough is there so Nayga and horse contending for the same water. Between the beggars and the higglers selling sweetie and roast yam, and the bwoy-dem hustling money to hold horse or carriage, nobody don't notice little me come to kotch against a bruck-down piece of wall that look older than courthouse itself.

Is there that Jason find me. To tell truth, is me find him, cause when he ride up and get off the horse he's clearly in a hurry and looking all around, eye wild. He couldn't see anybody except whosomever he looking for. Must be Missa Alberga. He draw out a watch from the fob pocket in his pants and then look around some more, even more fretful now. He fling the reins to a bwoy and was about to run over to courthouse when I take pity on him and call out.

He stop and look round, slow this time, he never expect to hear his name. I push off from the wall and walk through the busyness toward him, waving like I'm crazy. When I reach close, I see him look me up and down, and I feel myself flush. Jason not custom to see me dress up, but he seem to like what he see, so I relax myself.

"They inside," I say, and he let out a big breath he was holding. But my next words fly out before I could stop them. "You alright, Jason?" Cause his wild-eye wasn't just when he come and looking for Missa Alberga. Now that he settle down I notice not just his eye but his spirit is all over the place like a bird, and his eye themself is red, like he don't sleep or he been drinking. Not this morning—for days. "You don't seem youself," I make bold to say.

Now he look into my face. "I'm fine, Elzie." And then, as if he don't sure that I hear him, louder, "Fine."

Which make me know for a certain that he is not. But what am I to do? He's a big man and I am not Selina. Not yet, anyway.

⇒ 88 ⇐

Jason: Ishmael's Trial, Tuesday, December 20

LOOK AT HIM! BULLFROG. ALL MISSING is the drool. His frog eyes hardly leave Mr. Livingstone, like he's measuring him for a slurp and swallow. Every now and then they swing round, slow, to find me. Measuring too. My skin crawl. And then they slide over to look at Elorine sitting beside me. Something slimy there. I wouldn't think he'd know her but it's clear that he does.

Even though he's not presiding, his stamp is all over this matter, exorcising some ancient animus. Magnus was a bwoy when Ishmael left Cascade, left it legally and square. Why the reckoning so long after?

But the preacher is holding his own. "I cannot response for what others do," he says, firm in voice and look.

The prosecutor is trying to tie him into the affair at Richambeau last week, says that the one Cornelius was acting on his orders. Mr. Livingstone laugh a mocking laugh, and Lawyer Alberga jump to his feet to cut him off, cause that is trouble, when a blackman laugh at a white.

"You have no proof of that," Alberga says, abrasive.

"The slave confessed," the prosecutor shouts.

"And then you hanged him," Alberga counters. "You should've thought to keep him alive to confess to this court."

Mr. Livingstone bestow a smile on his lawyer.

But then I look at the jury. All white freeholders, except for Meyerlink. Some of them, maybe even the half-Jew, might take their horses and metalwork to Ishmael's foundry. At this time, though, with rebellion in the air, that won't count.

Alberga wasn't keen to take the case. I offered money but he tell me I don't have enough. It's when I tell him of the change of charge, from preaching without a licence to sedition, that the lawyer in him wake up. Had I been a barrister, I'd have done it myself, I told him, but he brushed that aside.

"You not been here long enough," he says. "They want blood." We both know who he mean.

Every now and then I remember Alberga is a Jew. A Christ-killer, as Squire would mock him from the bottom of their shared cups—Squire the atheist, though he wouldn't recognize the word. Alberga's white skin and position don't protect him from the legal strictures against those of his faith or the accompanying taint. Those laws are now gone, but no doubt the stain remains, part of the air of this place. For me too.

So perhaps that play a part in his taking the case, and his aggressiveness. He and his client is well-suited. Ishmael's a man reconciled to the worst that life can throw at him. He was born a slave—no lower gutter to fall into. Some never leave that sludge behind, but he do that long ago. His faith in God make him free, more than the paper he has from Magnus's father.

Today, all can see clear that he's not giving up that freedom without a fight.

"As Maasa God is my witness, Missa Judge," he says, slapping the rail of the witness box for emphasis, "that fool Douglas could not take anything he hear me say and make rebellion from it. He fool himself. And, begging your pardon, Your Honour, he fool the court."

They don't like that. "No talking back by blacks" could be as well a rule of the court as how to dress. Ishmael observe the one but not the other. And mention of the Douglas name quicken the eyes of the bullfrog. Lincoln tell me Cornelius is a cousin his father sell to Richambeau to get him out of sight. But not out of mind, it seem.

Again, while the judges and prosecutor catching their breath Lawyer Alberga jump up.

"If it please the court, the said rebel Douglas didn't mention Mr. Livingstone at all in this courtroom."

"You were here?" one judge ask.

"No, sir. But my informant is absolutely reliable."

"So you do not believe the prosecutor on the matter of the confession?"

"I do not disbelieve my learned friend, Your Honour, that a confession was made. But everyone knows niggers will say what they think Backra want them to say. Especially when some persuasion is brought to bear."

Alberga's smirk is sphinxlike. One couldn't tell whether he was mocking the prosecutor gently, or simply speaking the commonly held truth—held even by blacks themselves.

"So, Mr. Alberga," says another judge, peering at the lawyer as though Ishmael beside him is invisible, "is Livingstone telling us what he thinks we want to hear?"

"I'm telling you the truth, Your Honour." Ishmael's voice booms like a cannon in the court. "And I'm not a nigger, Your Honour, I'm a free man. Bought and paid for by myself."

Ishmael bangs his own chest, a cue for many people in the courtroom to pop a laugh, just loud enough to let Backra know that the defendant is not alone. Which is not necessarily a good thing. I've seen it in England: a well-liked defendant can be sentenced for the crime of popularity. Here, and in these times of fear and anger, that could cost Ishmael his neck.

Bullfrog Magnus burps and beams a chill smile at his former property. I feel the wet towel of a noose on my own neck-back.

"Call the slave, Cephas," the prosecutor announce, and the call goes through the clerk of the court to one of the scruffy guards, who plunge into a cluster of blacks at the back of the courtroom.

A wizened old man, seemingly as thin as the stick he's walking with, emerges, making his way past Ishmael, to whom he gives a solemn nod, to the witness stand. There he mutters impatiently when asked if he understands an oath, and swears from memory.

He's the first in a parade of witnesses, some ancient, some quite young, that the prosecution calls and, with rising frustration, dismisses. They are members of Ishmael's Zion congregation, who all swear to having been there when, as they call him in testimony, Deacon give his preachment that Backra is asking about. In this case, however, the niggers don't tell Backra what he want to hear. They tell him what they want to tell him.

"What you hear the defendant say to you?" The prosecutor broaden his voice and is gently conversational, inviting intimacy with Cephas. He's young and recently out from England, you can tell from his colour.

"Deacon say we is silver and gold," the old man croak, "that Maasa God mek us for His own purpose."

"And what is that purpose?"

"That is for Maasa God to know and we to find out, sir."

Cephas face is plumb, but you hear a few giggles, and the young prosecutor's lips twitch.

"Did you see Cornelius Douglas there that morning?" He drop the friendly now, become the hunting lawyer.

"Who he be, sir? I doesn't know that name or that person."

The prosecutor seems about to say something, and then he throw up his hands and go back to his seat.

Lawyer Alberga waves his hands too. He doesn't have any questions to ask Cephas.

And that is the way it goes through the morning. The young prosecutor hunt and hunt through the witnesses for damning words that Ishmael said, and for mention of Cornelius Douglas, whom they're now regretting they was so hasty to hang. In the end he finds neither.

A moment come late in the morning that quickened him, and that juk Elorine and myself like a macca prickle. A slave named Pomelia who, Elorine whisper, belong to a mulatto tavern-keeper, said she remember Cornelius at Zion chapel.

To which Elorine mutters angrily beside me, "She holding grudge for Pappi cause she didn't get select to baptize last January."

Her testimony is undercut—under single-minded questioning by Alberga—by her uncertainty as to exactly when the Richambeau slave had been present, and demolished by the next witness, Mama Claris. A freewoman who cooks for a member of vestry, she's adamant that Cornelius Douglas has not darkened the doors of Zion.

"I never miss a Sunday, sir, and I never see anybody like that yet. Strangers come and go, for Deacon give the word of the Lord as manna to the afflicted, but he don't have no truck with people like that."

"So what manna did the defendant offer that day?" The young prosecutor lean close and harden his voice. "Did he speak of fire?"

Her plump face opened in a smile. "Daddy always talking bout fire, sir."

"Yes?" He sniff like a dawg.

"Him is a blacksmith, Maasa." Mama Claris show her dimples. "Deacon is always talking bout fire. The fire from above, that will rain on sinful man-dem."

"Any particular man?"

"All of we, sir. We is all sinners." Her tone is instructive, and she let her serene gaze traverse as much of the courtroom as she could.

Alberga waved away Mama Claris also. When, after her departure, the prosecutor remained seated, staring at the table in front of him, Alberga rose.

"Your honours, my worthy friend has not produced a scrap of evidence against Mr. Livingstone that would allow the word *sedition* to enter the court's mind. I could in turn adduce several instances of the defendant's acting to calm troubled waters between men and women in this town, and I could bring forward witnesses to attest to them. But I feel I needn't bother, as Mr. Livingstone is well known at all levels in this town for the peaceable person that he is. I therefore move for a dismissal of the charge."

He sat down to scattered but firm murmurs of approval.

In the corner of my eye, I'd notice movement while Alberga was addressing the court, and turn my head to see Magnus, having left his seat close by the dock, in conference with the prosecutor, who is perked by what the bullfrog tell him.

Magnus saunter back to his seat, from which he once again fix his humid eye on Ishmael, and then swivel them onto Elorine and myself. He has sown the seeds of mischief in the young man's ear.

At the bench the three judges huddle in conference. Is a political decision as much as judicial. Of late the Colonial Office has been vigilant about abuse of colonial courts' powers. A case like this could well end up in London, and the Assembly and governor put under pressure.

That is in the minds of the judges too as they huddle in their dark robes like crows.

Lawyer Alberga, meanwhile, is concentrating on some papers he have on his table, paying no mind to the deliberations in front of him, or to the prosecutor. He appear indifferent to the outcome of his case.

The coven of judges break up and turn to face us. The one in the middle clear his throat and tap his gavel. Lawyer Alberga put down his papers and take off his glasses. Ishmael straighten up and look at Elorine and me.

"The charge of sedition is set aside for lack of evidence," the judge say. You can taste the disappointment in his voice. "The jury is dismissed."

A big noise erupt from the public benches, people laughing and patting each other—Nayga, of course. Elorine and me bounce arms into each other to hug up. Her face is a lamp. I look over her shoulder at Mr. Livingstone. His head bow, his lips is moving in prayer.

So much happiness and noise is around that nobody notice the young prosecutor, who jump to his feet and rush to the bench and say something urgently to the judges who lean around him.

When they straighten up, the chief judge hammer his gavel several times to bring quiet. The bailiff and clerk shout for silence too. Eventually it come about, and the three of them look over to the prosecutor, who is back standing behind his table.

"If it please the court," he starts, governing his smile, "there is another matter concerning the defendant which is still to be heard."

"And what matter is that, Mr. Paxton?" the chief judge asks, though he already knows the answer.

"The defendant was first charged with preaching without a licence, which Your Honours know to be a serious offence, one committed in many parts of this island by men far more distinguished than the defendant. Nevertheless it is an offence under the law. I beg your Lordships to recall the jury . . ."

"Surely not at this time, Your Honours. Neither Mr. Livingstone nor myself are prepared in this matter."

"I am prepared, Your Honour," Ishmael calls out. "I have nothing to fear."

Alberga is vex with Ishmael. Everybody can see that it cross his face to pack up his papers and go about his business. But eventually he siddown.

Better to be here, he thinks. But I feel a chill like the Wiltshire breeze that blow all the way down from Yorkshire squeezing me inside.

89

Elorine: Licence, Tuesday, December 20

THE MAGNUS-ONE IS THE FIRST WITNESS they call against him. He nearly trip over himself to get to the witness box, and give himself the oath before the brown man with the Bible could even stannup.

"You are . . ." the prosecutor begin.

"Magnus Aloysius Douglas the Second," he jump in quick. Like he is King George—everybody else who name after their father is junior to the older man senior.

"And are you a member of the vestry for this parish?" The hungry-belly prosecutor-dawg was so glad to see him.

Magnus draw his belly up into his chest. "For the past eight years I've been privileged to serve the people of this parish in that capacity, sir."

So the rest of us is not people! The vestry do some useful things. Is them arrange to fix roads, and some charity work in the town. But they don't serve Nayga!

"And is it the business of the vestry to license people who preach in churches and chapels?"

"Strictly speaking," Magnus say, trying to look like he's wise, "it is the magistrates who grant licence to preach. Under the law."

"But aren't magistrates like yourself members of the vestry?"

"Yes. Several magistrates is members of vestry."

"Has the defendant been granted a licence to preach, Mr. Douglas? Either by the vestry or any of the magistrates?"

"No, he has not," Magnus say, tasting the words like sweetie.

"Is there a reason for that?" The dawg for certain know the answer to that already.

"He has not applied." He trying to keep his voice flat but you can hear the satisfaction bubbling in it.

"But isn't the defendant a preacher?"

"You have just tried him for preaching, Mr. Paxton."

Missa Alberga is back on his feet again. "Your Honours, you just dismissed those charges." He's vex now, and staring hard at Magnus. "The prosecutor . . ."

"He preached sedition, Alberga." The Paxton-one is barking now. "And without a licence. That charge has not been tried."

He turn his back on Alberga and look back at Magnus, his mouth sweet again.

"Doesn't the law require a preacher to have a licence to preach?"

"It does, Mr. Paxton."

Meanwhile Ishmael is paying them no mind whatsoever. He have his eye closed and I know from how his jaw is twitching that him and Maasa God is deep in conversation. I hope it's about what is happening in the courtroom, because the way things is headed Pappi is going to need Maasa God help very shortly.

"And he hasn't applied."

"No."

"Thank you, Mr. Douglas. You are excused."

The two of them, like two bwoy playing, bow at each other and Magnus waddle back to his seat.

The prosecutor-one pull in his belly and call out, "Ishmael Livingstone to the stand."

Pappi, he still talking to God, so don't hear his name right away. It have to call out a second time, louder, before Pappi ease himself back into the courtroom, and you can see it's like when somebody wake him up early.

He walk slowly to the witness stand, nodding at me and Jason as he pass. Missa Alberga face is a picture—he look almost frighten as Pappi settle himself on the witness stand and look at the prosecutor-dawg. He's a short bantam-rooster of a man, so Pappi is looking down at him as he put his hand on the Bible and take the oath that the brown clerk recite at him.

"Are you a preacher?" the prosecutor start right away

"I am a blacksmith, sir."

"But you were just tried for preaching sedition," the man bark.

"So you claim, sir," Pappi reply, polite as ever.

"Your Honour." Lawyerman jump to his feet.

"Sit down, Mr. Alberga," the head judge tell him, and he sit, but working his mouth.

"You were preaching sedition," the man repeat, coming down on preaching.

"The judge just say I wasn't, sir."

"But you were preaching. And Mr. Magnus Douglas just said you are a preacher."

"I have never see Mr. Douglas at Zion, sir. To know whether I preach or not."

Magnus not pleased with that at all. He turn to look at the judge-dem, as if he want them to silence Ishmael.

"What I do at Zion is I teach the Word of God, sir. Other than a blacksmith, I am a teacher."

"So you have a school?"

"No, sir," Pappi laugh. "I am a blacksmith."

The head judge speak up. "Don't play games with the court, Livingstone."

"I not playing, Your Honour. I am a blacksmith. Everybody in Bellefields know."

"You were first arrested and charged with preaching without a licence. How do you plead, guilty or not guilty?"

"Not guilty, sir."

"Are you saying, Livingstone, that Magistrate Douglas and the whole panoply of the law that brought the original charge is wrong?" The judge speak as though Pappi was talking a different language to him.

"Is Missa Douglas that bring the charge, sir?" Pappi sharpen his eye at the judge.

"That is no concern of yours."

Lawyerman is back on his feet and even more vex. "With respect, Your Honours, the defendant should know who his accusers are."

"In this matter, Alberga, the law is his accuser. He's broken the law." His voice is clear: Blackman and Jewman cannot prevail against Missus Justice.

"The court has decided that, Your Honour?"

Maybe I did misjudge the man. He's a Backra like them, but his quiet way is just as facety as Ishmael when he's being mannerly. A few Nayga behind give sounds of appreciation.

It don't fool the judge, though. "One more question like that and you'll be in contempt," he say like a blunt knife.

Missa Alberga bow deep at the three of them and sit down, same time the prosecutor get up.

"Your client," he announce, making the word sound like spit in his mouth, "is charged under the laws requiring preachers to have a licence from the magistrate. Which, as we have heard from a member of the magistracy, he does not."

"Those laws were meant for missionaries, foreigners," Missa Alberga call out without even getting up.

"They were meant for preachers, Counsel. All preachers, foreign or otherwise." The *otherwise* make Pappi sound like the creatures in the Book of Genesis that creep and crawl on their belly.

He turn to Pappi. "Do you have a licence, Livingstone?"

"No, sir."

"And yet you plead not guilty to the charge. Your Honours . . ."

He starting to turn to the judge-dem when Pappi beat him to it. "Ask Missa Cavendish why I don't have a licence," he say, looking up at the three judge-dem. Then he turn to look at where Missa Cavendish is sitting.

Poor Missa Cavendish. When he get onto the stand and swear his oath, the young-dawg prosecutor rough him up good! He is a decent man, Missa Cavendish. I know his wife better because I sew for her. Sake of Pappi, she is one of the two or three Backra ladies that I take their clothes to. Is him ask me to do it, and he don't ask those kinds of favours often. Sometimes Missa Cavendish is there when I go, and cause he know I am Ishmael daughter he is civil to me. And now, in the courthouse, I understand why Pappi ask me.

Even the Nayga-dem that he own say he is a decent man. Even though he is a Anglican, and a churchwarden on the vestry, he give ticket to who want to come to Zion. Philadelphia is in charge of the warehouse for the haberdashery and check everything that come from the wharf. Also Mary Bees. They call her that because is she look after the hives Missa Cavendish keep behind his house, and sell the honey at market come weekend.

He have the regard of whitepeople also, otherwise he couldn't get himself elect onto the vestry, and be there for so many years.

But is nothing to do with the warehouse or the bees that have him in court this day.

"Does the defendant, Ishmael Livingstone, have a licence to preach in this parish?"

Missa Cavendish could be father to the Backra bwoy, except that he wouldn't raise such a unmannersable pickni. He's so anxious to ketch Pappi after he get away from the first charge, you can hear him panting. Dawg.

Missa Cavendish say, "No."

"Do you know why he doesn't? You and the defendant seem to know each other." He make it sound like something shameful.

"He didn't ask for one, Your Honour." Missa Cavendish is now getting fed-up with the Backra-bwoy and incline himself sideways the better to talk to the judge-dem. "Until recently, Your Honours, he didn't need one."

"Why not?" one judge ask him.

"Because he is a foundryman, a blacksmith, if you like. He's a preacher on the weekend, and he doesn't have a set-up like the missionaries. The missionaries need licences. Other preachers don't."

"But he preaches," the prosecutor-dawg bark, "you just said so."

"Yes, but . . ."

"The law is the law, Mr. Cavendish," another judge say, "and the law says preachers need licences for each parish. Are you challenging the law, Mr. Cavendish?"

"No, Your Honour. But the law also gives some discretion in interpreting the law."

"Which is why we have courts, sir." That is the head judge. "Your interpretation is being put to the test."

The same as most Nayga, I like to see when Backra-dem fight

amongst themself. But not this time. When Nayga is concern in that
kind of fight, is him going to suffer in the end. And this fight is over
Ishmael.

Missa Cavendish incline his head. "Of course, Your Honour. I
didn't mean to suggest otherwise. But our young friend here seems to
have decided the judgment already."

Wrong move. The young-bwoy don't want to be his friend. He
want Pappi for his lunch and Missa Cavendish is in his way.

"How would you define preaching for us, Mr. Cavendish?" He
playing like he making conversation, only curious.

"I've never had to define it, Mr. Paxton."

"You don't know what preaching is, Mr. Cavendish?"

Missa Cavendish turn to the judge-dem again. "Your Honours, I
find the tone of the prosecutor offensive."

"Answer the question," the head judge say, and he beginning to
sound like the young dawg. Which make me anxious. The judge-dem
may be looking for blood too.

I feel Jason quicken beside me. I make a quick look at Pappi. He
catch my eye and smile. Trust in the Lord.

"Well, try to define preaching, Mr. Cavendish." He want to smile,
I can see it, cause he know he have Missa Cavendish in his hand now.

"Is someone stanning up in front of a crowd of people and talking
about God and such things." Missa Cavendish is born here. Not in
Bellefields but close. But mostly, even when he's talking to his slaves,
he talk proper. When you hear Backra like him begin to sound like
us, you know he's either vex or anxious.

"And does Livingstone stannup in front of a crowd of people and
talk about God and such things?" He's openly mocking him now.

"I wouldn't know, I have not been to his chapel."

"So he has a chapel?" He say it like he just discover blackpeople
walk on two foot, but that don't fool anybody. He's building a wall
around Missa Cavendish—and Pappi.

"So I've heard it called."

"But isn't chapel another name for church, Mr. Cavendish?"

He don't answer.

"Do you go to church, Mr. Cavendish?"

"Do you?" Missa Cavendish vex now.

"I am not the one on the witness stand, Mr. Cavendish. Please answer my question." He's not a dawg anymore, he sound like a puss, playing with a mouse until he can raise-up and nyam him.

"I am a member of the chancellery of the Established Church in this island." Missa Cavendish find his proper voice again.

"Does the person who preaches to you on Sunday have a licence?"

"Of course."

"So why doesn't Livingstone have a licence?"

Is like Missa Cavendish wake up now. He realize that the dawg have his teeth right at his neck, and is about to bite-down. Missa Cavendish turn to look at Ishmael as if to beg his pardon. Pappi throw a smile back at him. Trust in the Lord, you high-up Church person. Like he's comforting the Backra.

"He hasn't applied for one."

"So he doesn't have one from a magistrate or the vestry."

"No. He took the Oath of Allegiance, and I told him he need not apply." He not looking hang-down any more. He look straight in the prosecutor eye as he talk. "I discussed it with Custos Morgan. He agreed with me."

"In what capacity did you take that decision, Mr. Cavendish?" This is the chief judge.

"In the capacity as acting chairman of the vestry. Custos Morgan was away at the time that Mr. Livingstone first came to me, and I was acting chairman."

Something whisper in my ear to look over at the Magnus-one. He's smiling, and I understand now the play that him and the young-dawg was playing before. They not only setting to get Pappi, they's trying for Missa Cavendish too!

Of a sudden the prosecutor-one lose interest in Missa Cavendish. He walk over to his table and sit down. "I have no more questions for the witness, Your Honours."

You could hear feather drop in the courthouse. Everybody understand what is going on, where this will end-up. I feel cold-cold. I couldn't move if fire was to break out.

And Pappi is not smiling anymore. I think maybe now he understand. He would know that Maasa God don't desert him, but that He find another way to teach him something, and he looking for what that something is. That is what I see on his face anyway. Higher than your ways are my ways, he like to preach. Now he's going to find out how high. Me, my thoughts are not high at all. They's low and boiling and bitter as baaj. They is the arrows of Jehovah, pointing at the prosecutor-dawg and the judge-johncrows. And a special one is for Magnus.

But it is fated. The prosecutor get up and tell the court the case is cut and dry. The law say a preacher must have a licence, and Ishmael Livingstone don't have one from anybody. It don't matter that Lawyerman Alberga jump up to say that is not Pappi that is wrong, is Missa Cavendish. Nobody is listening to that but Nayga.

When the two of them done talking, everything get quiet. Head judge clear his throat and tap the desk once with his gavel. "Has the jury reached a decision on this charge?"

I been concentrating so much on what is happening right in front of me that I didn't even remember the jury, seven whiteman and Missa Meyerlink, sitting to one side. Maybe because I know his sister, and because he come to West Street from time to time to Ishmael, I stare at him, praying. His face is stone. He don't even look at the whiteman at the end of the bench, who get up and bow to the judge-dem.

"We find the defendant guilty as charged, Your Honour." His voice is brisk—he have more important things to get on with.

Head judge return the bow, like this is a tea party. "Thank you, Mr. Quimby, and members of the jury. You are discharged."

The three judge-dem put heads together and whisper to each other. But not for long.

Head judge clear his throat and tap the desk again with his gavel.

"You have been found guilty, Livingstone, of the charge of preaching without a licence. The punishment for that is two years in prison."

I stop myself just in time from pee-pee up myself, right then and there. Then the judge give a funny little smile. Nayga know right away that worse is to come.

"But the court is generous. The sentence is hereby suspended."

I relax my stomach, and hear Jason draw breath beside me.

"But you have broken the law, and the court cannot allow such disregard to go unpunished, especially at a time such as this." The lizard smile again. "You will not have to go to the workhouse," he say, and pull-up his chest. "But the sentence of this court is"—and he pause for breath—"twenty-one lashes."

A woman scream out in the court loud-loud, like the judge put his hand into her belly and is tearing out her tripe. The pigeon-dem that roost in the ceiling to watch the proceedings scatter, and drop doo-doo on a few people. Everybody is looking around for who it is.

Is me.

≋ 90 ≋

Narrative: (Ishmael), Tuesday, December 20

"The Lord is my SHEPherd
I shall not wANT
He maketh me to lie down in green PAStures
He leadeth me beside STILL waters
He resTOReth my soul
He LEADeth me in paths of righteousness
For his name SAKE
Yea though I WALK through the valley of the SHADOw of death
I shall fear NO evil
For thou are WITH me
Thy rod and THY staff
They comFORT me
Thou preparest a TAble before me
In the presence of MINE enemies
Thou anointest my head with OIL
My cup runneth oVER
Surely goodness and MERcy
Shall follow me all the DAYS
of my life and I shall DWELL
in the house of the LORD forever."

"Thank you, Brother Greenwich. Maasa God will bless you."

Jason: The Colour of God, Tuesday, December 20

TODAY I HAVE TO WONDER WHETHER the Almighty is black or white. He don't have a colour, of course, Reverend Swithenbank would reproach me for even thinking that. But it seems so natural in this place to assault the very foothills of heaven and ask unanswerable questions. I'm not saying Mr. Livingstone isn't guilty under the law, but is a stupid law, made, as Alberga said, against missionaries trying to teach the slaves to be men and not cattle.

And the punishment! Pure wickedness. Bullfrog Magnus lick his lips when the chief judge announce it. And to make it worse, the man they select to administer the whipping, so Elorine tell me, is a member of the Zion congregation. He lay on with a vengeance. He had to, or himself would end up tied to that same post in the open workhouse courtyard with the whole town watching. Magnus watch too, from the courthouse steps to get a better view.

Because that was the objective of this whole travesty. The humiliation of Ishmael and the cowing of the blacks. Rebellion rumours intensify over the weekend. The native deacon in the flock of Reverend Sultzberger—who is still with us, his wife is no better—come to advise him against return. The chapel and their home is not yet rebuilt but that's not the main reason for his caution, which, he made clear, come from the whole congregation.

"Trouble coming, Missa Reverend," he say. When pressed by the Sultzbergers and Mathilde, he was circumspect. Emissaries from West, where a large siddown is planned for the day after Christmas, have linked up with those Rickhambone rebels still free. The congregation, who come from all bout, are aware of this, and fear possible violence.

"Trouble coming," he repeat to us. "Stay where you is, Missa Reverend, Missus. There shall be war and pestilence in divers places," he say. "You don't want to be in midst of that."

I'm thinking of all that in the courthouse with Elorine, watching Ishmael's followers and Alberga destroy the veil of lies against him for sedition. After that, and when Magnus and prosecutor Paxton resurrect the first charge of the licence, he don't stand a chance of fairness or mercy.

He challenge them again out there in the workhouse yard. Loud-loud he recite the Psalm that people like Reverend Swithenbank think is a prayer for peace. He never falter. Even when the whip lash him, he only pray louder, his voice bite-down on that word. But he never waver in his prayer. And the people watching hear him, and understand.

Mostly I was concern with Elorine, who turn her face into my shoulder and holding me tight-tight so as not to see what's happening over the wall. But the spectators understand. Those who stop to see a entertainment become quiet as a rock. I feel Elorine, though she still can't turn her head to look, draw strength from the crowd, which slowly gets bigger and bigger. The Whites who pause to witness and gloat soon slip away.

Tied to the whipping-pole Ishmael is preaching to us, you could say. His courage is a defiant sermon.

So maybe God is black. If He can raise up a man like Ishmael.

≈ 92 ≈

Adebeh: Belvedere, Wednesday, December 21

THIS PLACE IS A MADHOUSE! I realize that the first morning.

Cummings, the one who is in charge here, is the maddest one of all. I never lay eyes on the man before this, nor him on me, but he swears that I's Billy, who run away week before last. No matter how much I's telling him Adebeh, shouting sometimes from frustration. When I shout, he box me. And I have to take it because the pistol man, who I come to know is named Mandeville, and who bring me to Cummings from where Sister and me was tied up, is never far away. Cummings play with the leather snake around his neck, daring me to even look like I might hit back. So I only look hard at him. He smile.

"You is a naughty bwoy, Billy," he say, and caress the cheek he just box.

He's up close, looking into my eyes. I smell coffee on his breath. His tongue and teeth is black from chewing it all the time. He spit his dregs onto the floor and a little pickni scamper behind him to wipe it up.

"I should let Mandy tie you outside in the yard and tear you." He giggle at the thought. "But you find the bitch for me, so I will forgive you. She fuck sweet you see?" He lick his purple mouth. "You fuck her in the bush, don't she sweet?"

I don't answer the brute. But inside, I's a tangle. When I picture the fat slug crawling over Petta, I feel to vomit. But I's remembering my own thoughts about her when I's listening to the night sounds in Sister's hut, and following her backside through the bush.

"You don't fuck her?" My head shake itself.

He laugh out loud. "Oh, I forget. You prefer them big like Cubba. So you was fucking the big one in the bush."

He has to know just from looking in my eyes that I will kill him one day. "Who is Cubba?" I ask.

The man box me.

This time, I box him back. Right away, without thinking.

And lightning explode in my head. Prison arms grab me from behind and pitch me to the ground. All in silence. Until I hear Cummings: "No, Mandy!" When I turn and look, the big black's naked footbottom is a foot from my head, about to squash it into the floor like a cockroach.

I will kill him one day also.

Cummings look down at me and shake his head. "You turn wild, Billy. The bush turn you wild." He tut-tut like Mam at Precious when she's bad. Then he turn to Mandeville and dismiss me with voice and hand. "Billy don't deserve to stay in the house any more. Put him out with Penzance." That one smile down at me as he grab me upright.

Soon, I understand why. Mandeville take me up and down hillsides of coffee bushes planted in between with pumpkin and provisions, with blacks bent over working, men and women. My eye was skinned for Baddu, but I didn't see her. We walk in silence. After a while, Mandeville call out, "Penzance!"

He walks me up to a man who is half turned away and standing apart from the ones among the bushes. He looks like he's leaning on a stick.

"Maasa say to bring him to you," Mandeville announce to the man, who turn.

Penzance is the man from the day before in the bush. Not the monkey, the one whose dawg I killed. When he see me he smiles also—like Mandeville has brought his lunch. And he has another dawg, on the end of a leash that I thought was a stick.

For the next two days I's his meat and drink. He doesn't take his eye off me, and I get the hardest tasks in the shortest time. I dig, I plant, I prune, I pick, I carry. And when it doesn't please him, he lets the dawg's leash out enough for it to catch at my clothes. Or I feel the tip of a whip that he has over his shoulder.

What stop me from killing him—because I can't do any of those things he tell me without a hard digging stick or a knife—is Sister. The first day he had me working directly for him, say he's teaching me. The second afternoon he take me to join a group that was working on another hillside. Sister is with them.

As we's working a feeling of dread creep into my stomach like cold water into your shoes. We is slaves! And between the mad one Cummings and the brutes Mandeville and Penzance, they plan to keep us as slaves in this place that I hear the other slaves calling Belvedere.

But we is Yenkunkun, and Yenkunkun cannot be slaves!

As I's working, I feel the little pouch with my free paper from Major Maxwell touching my chest like a kiss. They took away the bigger pouch I was carrying the first night, the bangles for Georgia Marcy and Elorine must be on other wrists by now. For some reason they don't even ask about the pouch round my neck. Maybe because a lot of the slaves have something hanging on a string around their necks.

When the Cummings one was calling me Billy I thought to take out the paper and show him who I am, and what. He can read, I see lots of books around his house. But something tell me not to. "Wise as a serpent, cunning as a fox," Da like to say sometimes.

Baddu and me is Yenkunkun. We will not be slaves forever, neither in our hearts or in our body.

93

Elorine: Mawga Dawg, Wednesday, December 21

THE DAY AFTER, PAPPI BACK STILL raw meat, and who should turn up but the one who call himself Duncan. To tell truth, with all the palampam happening in these parts I forget about him long time. But as he show his face at the foot of the kitchen steps I know him.

The way he show me his teeth make me think of dawg. "Howdy, Missus," he say when Jassy call me into the kitchen. He is standing in the yard but about to come up into the house. As if anybody invite him. Cyrus is behind him watching my face and his back. I remember right away how he look at me the first time he come here with Uncle Teo, like I'm a piece of paper. I bristle. He show me more teeth.

I don't have any time for him. I hardly have time for myself. Pappi is inside resting on his belly, a poultice of bitter aloe across his back that I have to change at lunchtime, and again suppertime. Plus Christmas is four days hence and I have orders for people and little clothes to make for the pickni of Zion. And Jassy, she favour one of those ships in the harbour, she can barely move herself around the house. Any day now she will take-in.

I nod howdy at him, but talk brisk. "I busy, I don't have time to talk to you now."

"Is not you I come to talk to," he say, "is really Deacon."

"Deacon cyaant see you now, he's resting."

"I know," the man grin. "I was in the square. You cyan tell him I'm here, please?"

"No," I say right away. "Go talk to Teo."

"I don't find him."

"Look some more," I say. "Good morning."

I look at Cyrus to make sure he understand that the man is not to remain in the yard any longer than it take the two of them to walk to the gate. Then I go back inside.

Pappi must be hear me, cause as I pass his door to go to my work he call out. The sun fall through the window right onto the poultice on his back. He remind me of one of those vagrants that sleep overnight in the square, a bag of skin and old cloth.

"Who that you talking to?" he croak.

For a moment I think to tell him nobody, but change my mind right away. So I tell him.

"What he want?"

"He want you."

"What he want with me?"

"He was in the square yesterday. So he say."

"So?"

"I didn't let him say anything more. He want to talk to you, not me."

He lift his head and say, "That one is a snake," and wince. The slightest effort burn his skin. And make the hatred flare up in me like yesterday in the square. Holding on to him, I don't know how I didn't burn a hole in Jason's very skin. And now as I see Pappi settle himself down to stop the hurt, everything is looking red again.

Pappi see it in my eyes. "Hush, Puppy." He used to call me that when I was a little pickni, cause I was always falling asleep on top of Ginger's mother. "It don't hurt too bad. And Backra cyaant hurt me inside." He make a gesture to touch his own head but that pain him too, and he let his hand fall back on the bed.

From the doorway I watch him until his eyes shut down, then I go into my workroom. If it wasn't that my feet know where they're going, I would bounce into things and injure myself, sake of the red water in my eye.

94

Jason: Letters, Thursday, December 22

Greencastle, Thursday, December 22

My dearest Carlita,
It is just three days before Christmas morning, when you will be out among the poor, as is your family's long custom. I will be also, in a different manner. Much customary ceremony & largesse attend the first few hours of Christmas & much drinking & jollity afterwards.

When I was a youngster, the slaves had three days for themselves. Now—through the executive wisdom of the Assembled planters in Spanish Town—they are permitted only two.

But this missive will reach you some weeks after the day & things will be different. As I am different now. I feel it. I look different, I know. My skin is burnt, for one thing, darker than you've ever seen it. And all the riding up & down, though not as much as in the beginning because we have a new overseer, has trimmed me down.

The greatest change is within. To the point where sometimes I think I don't know myself, so much have I changed from the man you rashly married. It's as though a shell has been cracked & something new—someone new—has emerged.

I have become coarser. In my language, my behaviour, even in my thoughts. I'm now abstemious in my eating, less so in my drinking. At the same time, I've become more solitary, so that I am in my office (which used to be my childhood bedroom) writing to you as Mathilde & Anna sit on the piazza with a Moravian missionary & his sick wife, to whom we have given shelter & support.

I now find my idiom streaked with slave talk & not only when out in the fields—some of it may even sneak into this letter. Mathilde & Anna are puzzled by the change; myself, less so. Events have conspired to crack the shell I just spoke of. I find even my faith stressed, inasmuch as the foundational injustices of this society continue to escape justice from above—which invariably costs the Negro the most dearly in every case. Even so upright a person as Elorine's father cannot avoid being fed into the maw of prejudice & fear, which here is called justice.

Yourself & Caleb are the only robust lights in this ever-shifting darkness. But you both seem so far away. Your lights seem to waver & at times I cannot summon even your faces. As do I for you, I beg you both to pray for me, that I am led away from the edge of this despair.

Your splintered but loving husband,
Jason

To: Jeremy Cato Esq.,
Courtney Mews,
Mulholland Road,
Croydon

Greencastle,
Bellefields, Jamaica
December 22

My Dear Friend,
I hope you expected better of me, so that at least you can be disappointed by my silence. Then my guilt at breaking my undertaking to write regularly can be assuaged by the hope of forgiveness that accompanies this letter.

I pray it finds you well in body & spirit. I can report myself well in body, perhaps as well as I've ever been. Of necessity I have much daily exercise & going about in the fresh air; I eat heartily but not excessively, though the opportunity presents itself at every meal. As a result I am mercifully free of the various maladies that haunt the land.

But for one. I anticipate your mocking laughter as I tell you that I've caught a dose of the dreaded clap! From a Greencastle slave woman. I was reeled in by the resident fisherwoman whom, I suspect, has been inherited from my half-brother, in whose stead I act as attorney in matters relating to the estate. But I cannot blame the woman, either for the seduction or the clap, which she might, for all I know, have caught from Anthony. It is prevalent here & passed from philandering husband to virtuous wife like the decanter at table. My immediate objective, as you can imagine, is to clear it up before I return to Carla, even as I wonder aloud how you & I managed to escape its net in our younger, profligate days. Perhaps by not frequenting bawdy houses.

I'd given no thought to it before the first signs appeared in my pee. Indeed I'd given no thought to congress with any of the slave women—bar one, to consideration of whom I shall return shortly. My position, in my own eyes at least, was a principled one, much in keeping with those I have espoused, to your cynical but affectionate disdain, since Savernake. That principle was brushed aside by a mere touch—albeit a considered & practised touch—from Lucia.

Other principles have followed. Craving your indulgent silence, I'll tell you alone that I am now a slave-owner. I protested vigorously at my father's bequest of two slaves, "to be determined": it was as though, from the grave, he & Anthony had laid a trap for me. I've fallen into it.

Miranda is her name. She is almost a child, but not one from Prospero's enchanted isle; this island is cursed & your Caliban friend with it!

I am a little frightened by Miranda's effect on me. I behave toward her as I do toward all the many other female slaves in the house: nonchalantly. And I see her less frequently than most of the others, for she works out of sight with her mother the seamstress. She's a secret, one I carry as close as my shirt, hardly daring to confess it even to myself.

But the evidence of her impact is not easily ignored: I desire her. I tell myself it is more than lust, though I cannot parse the condition even to my own satisfaction. It has to do with her youth: she is half my age at most. And while I know from my own early life that concupiscence is rife & easily addressed, Miranda inhabits an aura of purity & innocence. My desire for her is different in some ultimate way from what eventuated & repeated with Lucia. There is no stratagem to Miranda, because she is likely not even aware of my desire. As she is ignorant of my ownership.

Today I claimed her. Not sexually—the thought of which thrills & disgusts me in equal measure. Rather, in a lawyer's office, by inscribing her name on a deed & affixing signatures. She was absent in all but thought. There are processes to be gone through in the courts so, on a technicality, the ambivalent pleasure of ownership is in suspension.

Now, as I write these words to you, old friend, I begin to apprehend the size of the chasms I've traversed in these last weeks. The view from the bank I now occupy is admonitory. The person on the far side, the person left behind, is almost a stranger to me. Almost. But he's also myself, the self that you know well, Jeremy. How I came to cross those chasms, travel those bleak distances, is a matter for conjecture—for discussion over several pots of rum.

That opportunity will arise. I know that. You know the basis on which I left the comfort of England for this place & the reasons. Not a month after landing here I'd decided that I could not remain beyond my pledge to my brother to serve—I see it as service to the family & myself as serving a sentence—for six months. Such is my mental state at the moment, however, that I cannot undertake to present you, upon return, with anyone you would confidently identify as the Jason you've known these thirteen years.

I will end before embarrassing us both by sinking into self-pity. Setting down even the outlines of my self-concern has been salutary. I beg you once again not to share them with anyone, especially with Carla, whom I commend to your always tender mercies. (For obvious reasons I have not shared anything with her relating to Lucia or Miranda.) I will write again soon, I promise.

In the meantime, I remain your diffused but steadfast friend,
Jason

≈ 95 ≈

Elorine: Nakedness, Thursday, December 22

A CRY-OUT WAKE ME. LIKE A PUSS—if we had a puss. I wasn't deep in sleep anyway, and it was close by. So I swing my feet onto the floor and make to stannup, when I hear it again. For certain it's in the house!

Pappi.

Day don't break proper yet and the furniture is like shadows as I move around it quick, to his room. And I give thanks for the nearly darkness cause he is standing there naked as the day he's born. Almost. What make him cry out is trying to put on a shirt, but that is all he have on him, hanging from one hand.

The Good Book say *thou shalt not uncover thy father's nakedness,* but is not me uncover Pappi, is him do it himself. He could've call me and he know I would come to help him dress.

When he see me he turn away quick-quick but the shirt scrape his skin, make him cry out again. And make me see beyond his nakedness to red.

"You going somewhere?" I'm holding his eye tight in mine.

He see the vexness and flare back at me. "I need to ask your permit? Since when?" He shoot a look at me and fling himself into the shirt and then scream out and collapse on the bed, twitching. Both of us frighten. I call out to him and run over and throw the sheet over his legs. Almost I fall on top of him.

And then I notice the blood, making his shirt into bright dots. He's looking at me, his eye bright. But is not anger there, is pain. I feel tears brimming. "Wait," I whisper to him, and then run and get the shears

I sew with, Mama's, and come back and snip off the shirt completely.

I have to make a whole new poultice for his back, and eventually that is done. He is back on his stomach and his breathing settle down. His eye close. Somehow his body is looking smaller.

"Where you was going?" I ask, gentle now. "Out into the shop?"

He move his head *No*. I wait.

"Mary Bees come yesterday. Missa Cavendish say that vestry is meeting tonight. I must apply for a licence." His voice is thick with tiredness.

I notice the jar of honey last night but Jassy was lying down so I couldn't ask her about it.

Like I talking to a pickni I pat his head. "Rest-up, Pappi. Vestry don't meet until afternoon anyway. I will go with you later."

By the time I reach the door I hear a soft snore.

≈ 96 ≈

Jason: Warnings, Thursday, December 22

LINCOLN COME TO ME AFTER DINNER. When I hear the creaking coming up the stairs I thought it might be Lucia, who importune me last night and was vex to be dismissed summarily. But it was Lincoln who push his cannonball head around the door.

"Beg pardon, Missa Jason. A word please."

I was up here in my room, withdrawn from life below, as often I am these recent days.

I suspect Anna and Mathilde think I cloister myself because the goodly reverend and his wife is still here, but that is only part of it. The larger part is within. I don't trust myself to behave properly. White self-satisfaction, which I realize I used to share, never mind my radical ideas, is now like a binding-sheet for me, against which something in me struggles like a poor lunatic on his way to Bedlam.

Lincoln has been a sobering draught. Since getting his freedom, and without toadying, he's been respectful and supportive. When I see him, I wonder if he's come to tell me he's leaving, and need the hundred guineas Lawyer Alberga keeping for him on Squire's behalf. But is not that.

"I know things going bad for you, Missa Jason." He perch on the chair beside this desk, where I usual to leave my clothes overnight for Jack to take them in the morning. "Is a bad thing with Deacon Ishmael," he begins.

I wouldn't have thought Lincoln, a Mohammedan, would know Ishmael or about him.

But Lincoln's been so long in this district he's one of the roots of the nigger grapevine that whites is so fraid for. Ishmael's trials and his punishment would reach him the same evening, I'm sure.

"But Backra right to frighten." I recognize his look into my eyes. As a pickni I'd know a lecture was coming like a cloud on a sunny day. "Trouble on the way," he says.

"From Deacon?" I ask.

Lincoln smiles, indulgent of my foolishness. "No, Missa Jason. He could make trouble if he want, cause Nayga mind what he say. But not from Deacon."

I stay silent so he will read my question.

"From West," he says, all humour gone. "Rickhambone frighten Backra. But Nayga say worse is to come. Everybody vex that they will have only two days to rest after Christmas, instead of the three they custom to from they born."

I'd read it in England, just before departing. A defiant ploy by the Jamaican Assembly, one that served only to harden the battle lines between Abolitionists and the planter faction at Westminster.

Still, I don't say anything. Lincoln is not to be rushed. He leans into me, drop his voice.

"It coming here too, Missa Jason."

So now I feel even more foolish. Because he don't just mean the Bellefields district. He means Greencastle. I been hearing the rumours. From Pompey, Creole Scotty.

"You mean the siddown," I ask him, trying to sound casual and knowledgeable.

"Maybe so." Lincoln shrugs. "But some people want to do more than siddown." His eye isn't letting me go.

"People here?" I ask him.

He shrugs again. "Some," he says, solemn. And then he pushes himself to stannup and give me a little bow. I remember the gesture from Squire's days and feel complimented.

"Tenky, Lincoln," I say, as his sampattas slap the floor on his way to the door.

Listening to him going back down the stairs, a sudden coolness like a vise tightening on my chest, I wish that in truth it'd been Lucia who knocked.

Elorine: It Shall Be Well, Thursday, December 22

WE DON'T REACH INTO THE VESTRY office good before the brown man behind the desk open up his nose-hole wide, like we bring in doo-doo on our shoes.

"Yes?" he say. I don't know his name but the face is familiar at West Street. Afterwards Pappi tell me that man owe him money, but he's respectful as always.

"I have come to apply for a preaching licence," Pappi say. He watch the man, as do I, search his head for a way to make a obstacle. So Pappi put in, quick-quick, "Missa Cavendish supposed to leave some papers for me to sign."

This vex the brown man, whose name is Callender. Like Nayga not supposed to have Missa Cavendish in his mouth. While he's taking his sweet time looking under all the various piles of papers, I am wondering—though I don't really wonder—how he treat those people who come in for a little help from the vestry. I'm truly sorry for them.

Finally—because he can look at Ishmael and know we's not moving—he find it. On the top of the pile right in front of him.

"Sign here," he say, pushing the paper at Ishmael. Pappi take it but otherwise doesn't move.

"I'll trouble you for a quill, Missa Callender," he say, polite, but not really asking.

He couldn't pretend to look for that, it was right by his hand on the desk. So he hand it to Pappi, who tell him tenky. Then Pappi put the paper on the pile closest to him and write his name. It take the Callender-one three breaths to take the paper back from Pappi.

"You're not on the agenda," the brown man say, flaring his nose again. "I don't know when . . ."

"I would count it a favour, Missa Callender, if you take it to Missa Cavendish. Please." Pappi don't raise his voice, but he don't move either, until the man get up. Then we watch him out his office until we hear him going up the steps to the room where vestry is meeting.

On the way back, a dozen people or so stop Ishmael to ask how his back is coming. Some of them is Zion, but not all. People in Bellefields know him, and they don't much like what happen.

Is a long afternoon we spend. The skin is healing good with the aloe, but if he go out to the workshop, which I can feel in his shoulders as I rub, everything will just go back to the start. I tell him another day. I bring his Bible to keep him company, before I go to do my Christmas work. Soon, I hear him snoring.

Later, getting to dark, Missa Cavendish don't send anybody, not even Philadelphia. He come himself to tell Pappi that the vestry turn down his licence. Well, they defer it, he say, but that amount to the same thing cause the Magnus-one will be in charge when it come up again. The custos is still travelling and Missa Cavendish himself resign.

The man embarrass over the whole thing, you could see that from in court. Worse now. Like is him cause it. Which is true in a sense, but Magnus set trap for Pappi with the prosecutor-bwoy, and seem to set trap for Missa Cavendish in the vestry also. You could say that Pappi was the bait.

Pappi it was who had to comfort the whiteman. "Don't fuss yourself, Missa Cavendish," he say. "It shall be well with the righteous, for they shall eat the fruit of their doings."

Backra's response was rough. "The wicked too, I hope."

They standing in the yard next to the horse trough that is between them, Missa Cavendish letting his horse lap. Polite as always, Pappi invite him inside, and in truth he is polite too—some Backra would be insulted—and smile, saying next time. He and Missus Cavendish don't have pickni, so in their house they live entirely amongst Nayga. So they custom.

"We must put ourself in Maasa God hand, Missa Cavendish." He agree with Pappi with a nod. "There is many ways to serve the Lord. He will recompense."

"I hope so, Mr. Livingstone," he say, and catch himself. "How is your back? Shall I send Dr. Fenwell tomorrow morning?"

Ishmael laugh and turn to the kitchen door where I was standing. "I have my own doctor right here, sir." Missa Cavendish notice me for the first time, but men generally don't see women unless is for bed, so he look through me and back to Pappi. "I should be back at work tomorrow."

Missa Cavendish don't leave out the yard any much time before that mongoose Duncan slide in like a whisper in the nearly dark. Pappi recognize him and turn away.

"Daddy," he call out as Pappi step off toward the kitchen.

"I am not your Daddy—find youself back to Deacon Sharpe." Pappi fling the words over his shoulder from the bottom step. "If that is where you come from."

"Is him I come . . ."

He never get a chance to finish. Pappi turn and move back toward him with his right hand high and clenched. "Get thee behind me, Satan," he bellow like a bullcow. "You coming to tempt me into rebellion and darkness. I know that. You serve Beelzebub, prince of darkness. Get out of my sight!"

By this time he's near enough to Duncan to strike him and I am worried that his back is going to break open again. I feel old Ginger slide past my legs and hobble down the steps into the yard, barking. He not custom to hear his master so angry.

The mongoose turn and run out the gate, Ginger chasing on his old legs.

The dawg don't calm down properly when two people come into the yard, one behind the other. Kekeré Bábà, and Philomene, Nana for Francine Beaumarchais that her family bring from Hayti. I know what she come for. Francine trying to rush my hand but she should know I am not to be pushed like that, specially since she bring it to me late. Today is only Thursday, after all, and the parade is not until Monday next, the day after Christmas. So I tell her, gentle, that I will bring it tomorrow evening around this time. That will be a pressure on me still, but Francine is good about money, and I need it. The other people I'm sewing for will take longer to pay, and the Zion people is mostly for charity. But I need to set some aside for Mother Juba—Jassy is almost on her time.

While I'm dealing with Philomene at the bottom step, Pappi and Fergus have their heads together by the trough, talking low. I wait for them, wondering about Adebeh and where he might be. But is not the Scotia man they was talking about.

"That Duncan-one is a serpent in truth," Pappi say to me, also talking over his shoulder to Kekeré Bábà, who is following. "Tell her."

"Deacon is right, Asabi." His voice is stern, and a little sad, as though he's sorry to bring bad news. "I just happen to look toward the underneath of the courthouse as I'm passing on the way here to you, when I see the whiteman Thomas talking to this mawga Naygaman just outside. I don't know the man at all. But the next thing I know he's hurrying past me. I don't know him as being from around these parts, but I don't really think about it until he turn down Church Street and then Water Street and turn along West Street. He don't pay me or anybody else any mind. Missa Cavendish come out of your gate, and I touch my head to him as he pass, and then I see the Naygaman turn into your yard. It was starting to get dark, but my eyes not so old as to mistake where he turn. Well," Fergus laugh, "he wasn't in here a minute before I hear Ishmael shouting and then see him fly out the gate with Ginger rushing after to bite him."

"After Missa Cavendish leave and I come back inside, while you talking to the blacklady—she from Hayti? Her head tie-up like them—Baba give me the story about this man."

"I am not surprise," I say to both of them. "Something wasn't righted about him the first time he come round with Uncle Teo."

"And Teo couldn't tell me anything about him either." Pappi calm down by now and give me a little smile.

"And the day after the punishment, the mongoose was here." I feel the hot water beginning to bubble in my belly.

"That is why I was coming here," Fergus say, "to find out how you is, Baba."

Sometimes I have to laugh at them, but not for them to see. Pappi is the older, and they call each other Baba (father) and Omo (son). And both of them is grey-heads.

"You daughter taking good care of me, Omo." Pappi smile. "And the Lord of Hosts is my fortress, as always."

Kekeré Bábà grunt. I know what he's thinking: The Lord of Hosts don't stop Backra from whipping you to shreds. But he don't say anything. They have too much regard for each other to fight over a few words. Instead, he turn to me with a smile.

"I was coming to beg you some more cloth, Asabi. What you give me is sufficient for my costume, but Quaw decide he want to Jonk-anoo with us so that if I am away at sea next time the band will still have all the character-dem playing."

I take him inside. All the time we's selecting scraps, I'm dying to ask him if he hear anything to do with Adebeh. Which I know is stupid even as I think it. Who but me and Kekeré Bábà know the Scotian? Or care? Adam maybe, but I don't see Adam this long time.

But it's as though Kekeré Bábà read my mind. "Backra Cameron come looking for your friend last week. Sure that I know. He was going haul me off to workhouse." I feel my throat grab me. "Doctor-man talk to him private. And rough. Cause he treating him for the clap, his wife too, he bring it to her from Cassie. Doctor must be tell him he will make his cocky drop-off." Fergus cackle. "He look at me hard when he leaving. Next time, he's telling me."

Kekeré Bábà turn to smile at me, sad. "I really don't know where him is, Asabi. We can only hope that Olofin have him in his eye." Fergus and me don't share those ways, but I know what he is praying for. Me too.

≥ 98 ≤

Adebeh: Billy, Thursday, December 22

WHEN I LEARN SOME MORE ABOUT this Billy that the madman Cummings mistake me for, I's more determined than ever to escape this asylum. Billy was a comfort bwoy for Cummings, who is a sodomite as well. He's probably pronging Petta in her front and her batty. This place is a cesspool. As I remember how his hand felt against my cheek after he box me the first time, my skin crawls all over again.

I asked the woman, Empress, who told me about Billy, about Cubba, supposed to be Billy's woman. Empress took Baddu under her wing when she suddenly appear in the coffee patch, and then me. Empress herself was born a slave at Belvedere, but Cummings and his bullies seem to make a habit of finding people in the bush and dragging them back here to make slaves of them.

"Dem two," Empress say—and spit. Sister and I know exactly who she's talking. "Maasa himself not right in his head. It twiss-up with books he always reading, and de slackness him carry-on with. Man and woman, woman and man. Him even have de lickle pickni-dem playing with him. Mark my words, him going dead bad!"

Empress is a lively old soul, and generous. She took Baddu and me to sleep in her hut the first night. Her man died last year, so she has space. That was when she tell me about Billy, the real one. She cackle softly and say, "You cyan go over and beg a sleep with Cubba, if you like. She not far away." Next morning she showed me Cubba, a big sour-face woman with two pickni holding on to her.

But Empress is a talker, so we don't tell her anything about ourself. Trouble enough that we's in, without looking for more.

And without talking about it, I can see that Baddu is thinking the same thought as me: escape. I can also see, though, that she's including Petta in our thoughts. I's not too fine with that.

≋ 99 ≋

Jason: Preparations, Friday, December 23

MAASA GOD ALWAYS WILLING, THIS WILL be my last Christmas at Green-castle. The first for thirteen years, yes, but my last—ever.

I spend this morning in the fields with Cumberbatch and the drivers, getting the last bit of muscle from the slaves before work stop tomorrow for two days. I overhear the grumbling that Lincoln warn me about, that it won't be the three days they're accustom to from they born. It could make for a lively Christmas.

The crop will start to take off in the first week of January, so everybody is driving toward that like the devil is behind. I can't really argue with Cumberbatch setting harder piece-work—just so long as no whip is involve. I have to tell him that over and over, and I stay out there to watch him and the drivers. The slaves know that with me there nobody will use the whip. Cumberbatch shout and scream at them but they don't pay him much mind. Is the drivers that put some fire under them, with their tongue. "Maas Jason do something for you this lickle while," I hear Scotty shout. "Time for you to do something for Maas Jason." I didn't say anything, but I feel pride.

Is hungry work, though, even for me who is not really doing much. So during the slaves' food break, which I insist on, I go inside for mine. At table Mathilde and Anna was talking about Christmas Day, Anna saying something about sweetie for the pickni-dem, and then look at me. "Remember, Jason?"

I remember, clear as day. But different memories. What Anna remember is when she was little and used to help me give out sweeties and fruit to the pickni-dem. That was the Christmas job Squire gave me after I was brought up to the big house, before England. Squire, and then Squire and Mathilde, would sit in splendour at the top of the stairs just inside the door to the piazza, dispensing largesse to the slaves coming up the steps in a long line out into the yard. Osnaburg cloth and salt meat and fish to the women, rum and fruit wine to the men, and the pickni in a separate line coming to me and Anna for sweeties and orange. Anthony would stand behind his father and stepmother, silent, fuming, glaring at me from time to time. Every year. That was his job when I was in the quarters, his chance to be Lickle Maasa.

That was when his mother Angela was Missus, and I was one of the pickni-dem snaking up the stairs in a cloud of anticipation. I didn't know then that we was brothers, only that he was white—Lickle Maasa. He would throw the sweeties at us for fun. Some wouldn't catch them and would tumble down the steps behind the drops and balls that Constancia make. They would be covered in dust by the time the pickni put them in their mouth, but they were so grateful they would bow to him.

Somehow, small as I was, I know that I had to catch the ones Anthony throw at me, however badly he throw them. When I didn't, I wouldn't bother to pick them up, just walk away and suck my thumb, or maybe get one from Pheba or Jordon, who I thought was my brother and sister. I couldn't understand why he dislike me so much.

It isn't a mystery to me now. The mystery is Squire—why he put me with Anna beside him and Mathilde. Favouring me, yes. But maybe also using me to tell the pickni-slaves that I am all they deserve, not Lickle Maasa.

All of that fly through my head in a few moments, like a cloud of wasps. Still, I manage to smile at Anna. Yes, I say, I remember.

Mathilde remembers too, and chortles. "Wass a goot time," she says. "Ze niggers sooo happy at Crismass. We too."

Anna agrees with a nod and smile.

Nayga was happy cause is the only time in the year he know for certain he will have enough to eat and time for himself. And this year he has one day less than he's custom to.

But I don't say that to them. I don't say anything, just continue eating.

Anthony must've been sitting in Squire's chair last Christmas, handing out the things that everybody knows the slaves are entitled to throughout the year, except for the cloth once a year, and the rum, which in any case only a few slaves accept—they'd rather have food in place of it. Even the more prosperous estates are unable, or sometimes unwilling, to fulfil the requirement. Greencastle can't afford everything they should get, but I tell bookkeeper Simpson to make sure that every man and woman get a sufficiency of meat and fish, salt and fresh. The pigs been hanging in the curing shed from before I come back. The slaughtering of the cows start yesterday.

Day after tomorrow Mathilde and Anna will be dispensing from the top of the stairs.

Lincoln will be behind, handing them the munificence. I'll have to be present, of course, but the Maasa role would choke me. For one thing, the men and women coming up the steps in their best clothes (really, their least holey rags) are the same ones I gave sweetie and orange to those many years gone. Maybe I will decide to give out the sweeties to the present pickni, the ones I don't know too good. But I don't decide that yet.

Sometimes, like when I am up on Knob's Hill, I tell the slaves a silent tenky for not making life more difficult. Is a fine balance they must walk between obedience and brutality: the violence meted out to them and their own, natural response. I come to understand that line and, in a quieter way, to walk it myself: obedience to my promise to Anthony, and a bubbling anger at what I've put myself into.

Lately the bubbling is reaching a boil such as Carla would frown on. I'm afraid for myself, and of myself. Things inside me are splintering, like a piece of glass. I think on Lincoln's word to me last night, about trouble coming from West. A siddown would be bad enough, one foot across that line. But he's warning of more than that. Then the line would disappear altogether. Maybe the worse part for me is that I don't know on which side of which line I would be standing.

While Mathilde and Anna are still chattering about Christmas, I glimpse Lincoln-self, passing like a shadow cross the back of the dining room toward the doorway to the kitchen outside. He's dressing better these days, not just the sampattas, his clothes too. And there's something else different about him as he disappears to go eat his dinner with Constancia.

Is the first time in life I ever see Lincoln with a cutlass at his waist.

Adebeh: Barbeque, Friday, December 23

IT'S TWO DAYS TO CHRISTMAS, AND look where I find myself.

Da doesn't notice Christmas of course. For him and the other stay-behind men, the whole year is a road up to Kojo Day in January, when the first Maroon treaty was signed. But as I's growing, I see little pieces of the whites' practice creeping into the house, like mus-mus. The fruit cake one year, when I was about nine. Da scorned it at first. Then he tasted a morsel from Precious's baby plate and ask Mam for a big slice.

The next year on Christmas morning was church, me carrying Precious and Mam holding Eddie's hand. Da never like that at all. But by then I was in the Reverend Smythe's school, so church wasn't strange to me. Other stay-behind pickni was at the school too. The woman-dem miss Jamaica just like the men, but they's looking at the ground in front of them, not at the ocean or the sky. They want their offspring to improve weself. The women cook for Kojo Day, joyously. But some of them—those lucky enough to find work in whitepeople's houses—is Christian also.

At Christmas here, Empress tell us, a few favoured slaves would custom to getting a ticket to attend service in Montego Bay or Falmouth. But not this year. There's talk of rebellion in those towns, Empress says, and the same Cummings who gives them tickets is cuss-ing the missionaries his slaves go to. The damn fool don't even know which mission his slaves attend, but he's ready to blame. Last week, Empress says, there was a disturbance at a place named Salt Spring, not far from here. The slaves there threaten the attorney for beating a slave girl, and when constables come to arrest the ringleaders, the slaves take away their pistols and their mules and send them walking back to Montego.

"I never see that before," Empress say, with not a little pride in her eyes.

I don't have time to worry about that, though. I's planning my own rebellion. And is Cummings himself who give me the opportunity.

The first roll call, on the morning after they release Sister and me and give us clothes, just contribute to the madhouse feeling. When Mandeville called out "Billy Cummings," I didn't answer. He called it out again. Silence from me. The third time he's looking directly at me and me at him. His fingers play with the whip around his neck, but he can see my hand gripping the digging stick that everybody is carrying to work with. He frown. And move on to the next name.

This morning, he pull me aside and tell me to stand next to a certain tree. He divide-up the gangs, sending Baddu with Penzance, like yesterday. Then he turn to me.

"Maasa want you," he say. "Go up to the house."

Right away I feel ice in my belly. But he's watching me like Penzance's dawg-dem, so I look at Sister going off in one direction and then turn myself in another, toward the big house. Mandeville walk behind me, cause he know if he's within distance I will attack him, whip and pistol or not. We walk in silence. It's a beautiful spot, Belvedere. The mountains are cool blue all around, not like down in Bellefields where they feel like they'll swallow you if you get too close. Is not a place for brutality. But violence grow like the coffee bush-dem. The weeds that Baddu and me was weeding yesterday, in a funny way they come like freedom. Cummings and the other whitepeople spend their whole life digging out those weeds. And they come back, in the same spot and stronger than before.

When we reach just inside the house, Mandeville calls out—quietly, like he don't want to disturb him, "Maas C?"

I understand why when Cummings appears from inside a room, hitching-up his trousers and fastening his shirt. The sun's not properly up yet and he's sweating. It's not as big a house as the doctorman's in Bellefields, so I don't have to strain to hear like a puss mewling. But is not a puss. Petta. Like they have their own mind, my finger-dem tighten around the digging stick. I'm missing my cutlass that Mandeville took away from me when they capture me. And he know. He move around from behind me to stand between Cummings and the room that Petta's inside of, drawing his pistol.

"Billy," Cummings call out to me, like we's friends—which him and the real Billy was, of course—and I's a visitor just arriving. He comes right up to me so I can smell the spunk drying on him, and the coffee beans he's chewing. "You happy to be back? Better than the bush, eh?"

I don't answer him direct.

"You send for me?" I can see that he don't like when my tongue don't tack-on "maasa" or at least "sir".

"I hear that you's working hard, Billy. Good." He pat my face, crawling my flesh down into my belly. I smell pussy on his hand.

"But since you bring me that sweet gyal, Celia, I's feeling kindly toward you." He smile again with his black teeth. He see the query in my eyes—Celia?

"Come, my Celia, let us prove, while we may, the sports of love. Time will not be ours forever." He's throwing the words like birds into the air.

My query is still there, for the madness also, his madness. He doesn't see the second question, but laugh at the first. "You don't remember I used to call you Celia? O rare Ben Johnson, o rare Billy." Before he even think to reach his hand out to touch my face again I draw out of range. He didn't like that, but my eyes, and the digging stick in my hand, quiet him. "No matter," he go on. "Penzance say you work good, you and the woman you bring back." He giggle.

He pull himself up and look over his shoulder at Mandeville. "Take him out to Jackro. Tell him to keep a eye, cause is there he run from the last time. I will make you strip Jackro if Billy run again. Tell him that." And then he spit on the floor and turn back to the bedroom.

Mandeville gesture me toward the front door with his pistol. I walk down the steps and follow his grunts from behind, around to the side of the house and a flat piece of concrete. Five or ten black people is there, raking what I know now to be the coffee beans that other black people reap into bags where I was on the hillside yesterday, with the Penzance-one and his dawg. They pull them off with their hand, or they use a little knife to scrape them into the bag hanging around their neck. I never get a knife, though.

Mandeville take me through the other blacks to a brown man with shoulders on him to lift a ship, and a thin red switch that's smooth from use, I can tell. His eyes, blue and green from a white ancestor, size me up for the switch, I can tell that also.

"Jackro," he say, disapproval in his voice. "Maasa send this one out for you to work him. But watch him too. Maasa say he will strip you if he get away. He like to run." Mandeville chuckle, then turn away, back to his business elsewhere on Belvedere.

"What you name?" Jackro ask, his voice a rasp. There's a long scar under his chin, old and knitted.

"Adebeh."

"What kind of name is that?"

"My name."

"Where it come from?"

"My father."

"You talk funny."

"You talk funny, too."

His arm with the switch had a spasm, and I answer him with a little lifting of my digging stick.

It's the indignity of it, a Yenkunkun being a slave. But it's also how this place make me feel inside: boiling like the sea in Peggy's Cove. I's sheer tired from the controlling of myself. I want to kill too many people. Mam would be shock at my thoughts.

Jackro laugh.

"Mason!" he call out. A bent-over man behind him straightens.

"Yes, sah."

"Give Adebeh here a rake, and show him what he's to do."

The Mason-one, he brings a rake over from a lump of them on the ground in the corner of the barbeque place, which is what they call the flat piece of concrete. It strike me that these people don't care for their tools like they have any value. I don't see anywhere to store them, they probably sleep out on the barbeque. They don't have winter here, or snow, but the evening's cool and misty with water like lace. Sure enough, the tines are rusty, likely brittle. I can see as I follow Mason and get into the line spreading the coffee beans other slaves are bringing from the slopes, that some of the rakes have teeth missing—like some of the people.

But I realize something right away, as I settle my hands round the shaft. The rake is a weapon. And the barbeque is next to the house, which is on the edge of the property. As I's raking, I's glancing at the hills that Mandeville and Penzance captured us in. At the horizon I can see the Cockpits.

The problem is how to get Baddu over here so we can leave together. Petta or no Petta.

Jason: Miranda, Friday, December 23

I WAIT UNTIL THE ALMOST END of the day to call her. I was thinking about it the whole day and decide on that time. She was in the piazza with another girl, sweeping, when I come in from the fields for breakfast. But I didn't want the other one—Griselda I think she name—to hear what I had to say to Miranda. It's private after all. Besides, I didn't know what I was going to say to her.

And I still didn't fully know when I tell Jack to call her. He thinks he knows what I have in mind for her, I could see that on his stupid black face. He knows about Lucia and I can bet thinks to himself, "She'll be more of the same for Maasa." By tomorrow morning plenty other people in the house will think that too. I can't help that.

Not a sound on the creaking stairs and she's into the room like a shadow. I was half turned and saw movement in my eye-corner.

"Yes, Maasa?" She's looking at the floor.

"I tell you already not to call me Maasa," I say sternly to her.

She looks up now. She has grey-green eyes from the white ancestor who gave her buttermilk skin. "So what I am to call you?" She sounds impertinent, until she drops a *sir* into it.

I smile. She smiles and colours, realizing her brush with facetyness; she drops her eyes. I clear my throat and grab my courage.

"I have something to tell you," I begin, "but is something that you cyaant tell anybody, even you mother. You understand?"

Her eyes lift to me and open wider. Her toes grip the floor. She's frightened.

"No," I say to her quickly. "I don't want to do that to you." I smile so that she'll relax. She does, but only a little, still watchful, ready to flee. She remind me of a forest creature, a doe maybe—the same colour—who hear the hunter's horn. The way the candles sit in the room the tips of her bubbies make shadows across her dress, and I feel the worm in my loins move.

"You remember Maasa Squire?" I ask her, gentle like a breeze, to calm her and to calm myself. She nods her head and smiles. And for a flash, like a pinprick, Squire is alive in eyes that don't belong to Prudence her mother, a handsome brownskin woman with dark eyes. Hers are clear as Angel Hole water. Miranda is looking back at me with my own eyes. She doesn't know what I'm going to tell her but she knows who I am. Her smile is almost coy, and I look away, down at the floor. Her feet are flat on the ground.

I seek refuge in the papers on my desk, and pick up one. "You used to belong to Maas Squire," I begin. "And then Maas Anthony." I wave the paper in her direction. "Now you belong to me," I say, and I hear my voice echo in my whole body like it's empty. "Maas Squire leave you to me." I run out of breath, so I stop.

Her eyes stir and her toes curl again. She looks to left and right and touches her own chest. "Me, Maas Jason?"

I nod, forgetting to correct her.

The smile that splits her face dazzles me. "Well," she says, and sighs. Then she looks away. Then she takes half a step forward and drops her voice.

"But I mustn't tell Mama."

I shake my head. And then relent. "Not till I say so," I say. She nods and smiles.

She starts to turn away to leave but I call her back. "You are still a slave," I say, sounding more stern than I intend. "You still have to listen to Miss Anna and Miss Matty when they tell you. And to Balfour when he need you to help out in the house. You understand?"

She nods slowly. Her face closes down, she's not pleased.

I tell her goodnight and she leaves as quiet as she come in. In the doorway before she closes it the lamp in the passage outside my room flashes her nakedness through the thin dress she's wearing. It remains behind like a aftertaste on my tongue.

Her face at the end tell me how much I've changed everything. Not only in myself, by claiming this girl as my chattel. In that face and that eye I see trouble. Is not only my eye I see looking back at me, and not just property.

Miranda is looking through a window that I've opened with all the changes I make at Greencastle. I think back to what Lincoln tell me last night in this very room, and have to wonder if I am the cause of what might happen. Judith, Pompey's woman, Pheba's mother, used to say, "The more you chop down breadfruit, the more him grow." I can hear her dark voice, stern and comforting at the same time. But providing no comfort to me now. Buying Miranda has given her hope. A sort of promise that I don't know how to fulfil.

And at the end of it all, the hardest part: she is almost certainly my sister. My lust—as I now must acknowledge, even as it curdles in my loins—is as inappropriate as it would be for Anna. I squirm inside my skin. We's all three in exactly the same blood relationship, my own blood the most corrupt of all.

Elorine: Christmas Market,
Saturday, December 24

FROM I'M SMALL MAMA SEL USED TO bring me here. I hear her talking about it from days before with Alice, who was the old slave we was renting in those days—and keeping back a little something for her, just like with Jassy, so that they can buy things for themself. Still, since Mama gone, every year when I come here I have mix-up feelings. For one thing, every third person remember Mama Sel, and say how much I favour her. That happen in the weekly market too, but Christmastime bring her back to me stronger.

Christmas market is special. You see the usual things that you see every Saturday or Sunday. But you also see things you only see around this time. Barrels of salt pork and salt beef and salt fish come for Christmas provision for the slaves. Merchants who bring them for the estates bring extra to sell. Backra is suppose to give the slaves these things through the whole year, but when he actually have it, he make the most of it. As if he's doing them a favour, giving them a brawta, when is them doing him the favour, tying-up their bellies through most of the year after the crop done. He feed them enough to keep up strength for crop, but after the hogshead-dem send down to the ships and the rum is seasoning in the barrels, the slave survive on the scraps that fall from Maasa table.

But Nayga not stupid, and riverwater find a way around rockstone. Sometimes Backra have to buy from the slave for his own table, things that Nayga grow in the provision ground back-of-beyond in the furthest corner of the estate, in the worst soil. And they keep chicken and turkey in the slave quarters, and some of them a pig. That is for themselves, and to sell. Same time, some of the same slaves growing them for Backra out on the estate. So sometimes is his own fowl and pig that Nayga sell to Backra.

Christmastime, though, everybody have food enough, eating and selling. Is a happy time and place, the sun hot but a cool Christmas breeze always blowing, people buying and selling so money is like a fragrance in the air, pickni-dem flying up and down like birds, happy. Is the pickni that bring me to myself every time, and make me think of Mama Sel. I was one of them. The rest of the year, sometimes I can hardly remember her face, but at Christmastime she is clear as day, like she's visiting from the other side.

At this time of year when the Christmas pressure is down on her, she ask me to do little things for her, and I'm happy to help out. As the years pass, I get bigger things to do, until both of us working on dresses from the first cut, though she don't make some of the Backra Misses know that is a nearly-pickni make their dress. And then, suddenly, she is gone, and is me-one leave to carry on.

Same time as the dressmaking is going on, all the Christmas activities happening all around us, so I become part of that too. The boiling of the puddings and the sweeties like the ones I see around me at the market, the baking of the different cakes, the endless talk and inspection of the pig-leg and the sausage curing up in the rafters of the foundry in the smoke from the furnace. After Mama die, though, that side of things stop. People come to the house to order this and that, but I couldn't find it in me to continue. Now is more than enough for me to manage the dress-dem, plus those I'm making for the Zion people. I don't have a Elorine to help me.

And I don't have a Jassy either. Last year yes, but this year is me and Christian, Mother Juba's grandpickni—Jassy is like a fat dumpling in her bed, waiting her time. Cyrus, he's a hummingbird hovering around, between frighten and pleased with himself, and totally useless if anything was to happen. Give thanks Mother Juba is just cross the road. I tell her this morning, when I collect Christian, to be ready to move if I am not back from market in time.

I buy a pretty piece of cloth from Chalice, who I can guess tief it from Missa Castleton, her owner, a brown man that import things for the estates and the haberdashers in Bellefields and elsewhere. I don't ask her nothing, is not my business. And I buy a piece of serge to make a Sunday pants for Christian, which please him. What please him even more, though, is the sweeties I buy for him from Little Rachel, a fat brown woman that make the best in the market.

Before I leave I stop near the gate to say howdy to Benneba, a old lady from the time of Mama Sel, who always have the nicest banana and the fattest plantain. Benneba is a Creole, but her face is Guinea, with her mother's marks on it. You can barely see them now, her face have the lines of age creasing it like burnt paper.

She call me over with her finger, and as I'm bending over inspecting the plantains for the ripest, I hear her croaking like a lizard over me, "When you see chicken merry, pickni, you know that hawk is nearby."

Benneba is always talking like that, in riddles and jokes. But I can hear in her voice that is not joke she's making. That stop me.

"Where the chicken?" I ask, turning my head to look around to see if any fowl is running loose—though I know is not fowl she's talking about.

Benneba laugh. "Dem have two foot, but no feathers."

"And who is the hawk?" I look up in the sky.

She laugh again. "Hawk don't fly," she say. "He don't need wing. He have gun."

The Christmas breeze feel cool on my skin, of a sudden, but I don't say anything more. Benneba is a listener, but she don't like too many words.

I buy some overripe banana to make fritters for Pappi, and three plantain to roast tomorrow. As Christian and me is walking home, I'm thinking about Mama, still missing that she's not with me to enjoy the happiness in the market.

But then I hear Benneba's words in my ear, and put them together with other rumours and whispers. Maybe Mama Sel is better off where she is.

Jason: A Wild Idea, Saturday, December 24

A DREAM OF MIRANDA. ALMOST LIKE the one some weeks back but without Victoria this time. And no horse, I was pursuing her on foot. This time I was a man. With a man's lust in my pants and feet. I was almost tripping over it. This time we was running through a town, maybe Bellefields, cause I recognize a few places. Like in the one before, she's fleeing from me but also from time to time over her shoulder flinging laughing eyes. She knows where she's going too, bobbing and weaving through little streets and alleys, round trees and over gullies, pale heels flashing, Nayga-batty jiggling like a promise. She knows here just like she knows the Greencastle trees in the other dream. Little by little I was gaining on her, cocky like wings in my trousers—when she dashes through a bruck-down gate into a yard with a little house to the back.

Ketch you now, I dream as she heads to a door slightly open in the side of the house.

But the door pushes out from inside and a tall woman comes out to stand in the doorway, pushing the girl behind her out of sight. Prudence, Miranda's mother. Threatening me with something held high—a clothes iron, steaming and ready. I'm so frightened I wake up, cock shrivelled.

But in the first minute after I come to my senses, a crazy mad idea grab hold of me: Like how I claim Miranda from Squire's will, I can claim her mother too. And then give them manumission. Could be I'm doing Squire's will. And keeping what's left of my anti-slavery principles intact. A fine present at Christmas, for them and for my conscience.

Still, when the righteousness and sanctimony die away, I feel a worm wriggling in my balls to tell me my true thinking, the real meaning of the dream. Half-sister or no, I want to find my way between those buttermilk thighs.

≈ 104 ≈

Adebeh: Enough, Sunday, December 25

IT MUST BE BABY JESUS HIMSELF who whisper to me this morning: *Enough*. I wake into a brilliant morning, Empress's hut glowing with light. It's late, I know, and as I struggle up into waking I's listening for something. I don't hear anything except birds and I realize why. It's Christmas, so there's no work, today or tomorrow. So there's no conch blowing by Mandeville.

My heart lift a little, but I's still hearing that whisper in my ear: *Enough*. Maybe the babe Jesus on his birthday, maybe the bigi pripri. Either—or both—is telling me to get us away from this place, me and Sister. And today is best day.

I hear her snoring quietly over by Empress, who is also still sleeping. When I look, Sister has a smile on her face. It must be a nice dream.

I go outside to relieve myself. The slave quarters is quiet, just a few chickens and pickni moving around, watching me for the stranger I am. Two women is bent over fires, coaxing them to life. I go past them to where I get to know most of the people in the quarters do their business.

And that is where, as I's peeing, I find the means of our salvation.

105

Narrative: Christmas Morning (1), Sunday, December 25

PRIED OUT OF SLEEP BY THE CREAKING of his room door, Jason opens only one eye, quickly closing it again. It is morning, early, but, facing the wall, that's all he can tell. Then he hears a whispered voice. "Missa Jason." A man, but it isn't Jack. He opens both eyes and turns to the door.

Lincoln is standing in the open doorway, awaiting permission to enter. For a moment Jason is confused: Lincoln, solemn and diffident, is holding a tray with two mugs and a plate. As a boy sleeping downstairs he'd often seen Lincoln carrying just such a tray past his cubicle toward Squire's bedroom. Jason blinks his eyes and shakes his head to clear it.

"Beg pardon, Missa Jason," Lincoln says, his voice quiet so as not to alarm, but firm. "I know is early, sir, but I need to talk to you, and Christmas morning busyness soon start." He lifts the tray a couple inches. "I bring you something to break you fast, sir." A smile flits across his face, gone in a moment. Jason understands his urgency, and his diffidence.

"Thank you," he says, struggles to his feet with a sheet around his semi-nakedness and waddles over to the table he uses also as a desk. Lincoln moves aside Jason's papers and places the tray in front of him, lifting a sheet of folded paper from between the two mugs, one of them steaming coffee, the other a golden circle of juice. On the plate is a toto, a sweet flour cake that Constancia knows he loves. Jason takes a bite and a sip of his coffee. Lincoln is already dressed, in clean clothes and his sampattas.

FREE   455

"Nowadays, Missa Jason," Lincoln begins with a swift smile, "I don't manage to wake up this early myself. I beg pardon again for waking you now, sir, before day even catch itself good."

"Sit down, Lincoln," Jason says, indicating the chair beside his table-desk and taking another sip of coffee. As he chews and sips, saving the orange juice for the last, Jason remembers with chilling clarity the last time the old major domo was in that chair, brought here of his own volition. He waits, noticing Lincoln fiddling with the folded paper.

"What brings you here?"

"I leaving you, Missa Jason," he says simply, seriously.

"Leaving me?" Jason's head is still foggy.

"Greencastle, sir."

Jason looks into the eyes of his oldest friend on Greencastle. Understanding dawns. He sips his coffee and looks out the window at the quarters, where the tendrils of smoke are rising. Fewer figures than usual are moving around. It's Christmas morning, he realizes. With a pang of sadness he imagines Carla and little Caleb trudging through snow—it always seems to snow around Christmas—happily, as they both enjoy snow. He's an aeon away from Greencastle, suddenly chilly, feeling alone. Why is he here?

"Missa Jason." Lincoln's voice gently brings him back. "I need you to sign this for me, sir." Jason's eyes focus on the paper Lincoln has been fiddling with, now flattened on his table beside the tray. "Is for Missa Alberga, sir. He say I must bring it tomorrow."

"Tomorrow?"

"For the money, Missa Jason. That Squire leave for me."

Jason collects his thoughts before speaking. "Why now, Maas Lincoln?" He tries to keep his voice flat above the hollowness in his belly.

"Missa Jason?"

"Why you leaving now?"

"Is time, sir."

"Time?" Jason struggles between a bone-bred habit of deference to the old man and a rising irritation. "It wasn't time yesterday but is time tomorrow? All these weeks since you free, and is only now you decide to leave us? Just before the crop?"

"You don't need me for the crop, Missa Jason. Me not in the field." Lincoln's voice reclaims his historic authority. "Missa Simpson will manage the food when I'm gone. That is fe-him job, and he don't like that you give it to me, so that will make it easier for you, Maas Jason." His voice softens. "I couldn't leave before now, sir. You is lawyer but you don't know how things do out here, you don't have slave in England. My free paper have to register and stamp at courthouse before I can really think meself free. Too many Nayga think them is free and land-up right back in quarters and cane-piece. When they move off the estate, the same Backra who tell them they is free call them runaway, and send Maroon and dawg for them. I not able for that to happen to me."

"I wouldn't send dawg for you, Lincoln. You know that."

"Yes, Maas Jason, I know that and tenky for your regard. But not everybody decent like you, sir."

For a long moment Jason and Lincoln look at each other in silence, Jason wondering, for the first time ever, whether he would find his free paper at Bellefields courthouse.

"So you free paper register now at courthouse?" he asks.

"Yes, sir. During Assizes. Missa Alberga send to tell me yesterday."

For the first time Jason looks at the paper Lincoln has handed him. He recognizes the former slave's handwriting from Squire's letters and the entries in the Greencastle ledgers, which only recently began to show Anna's still childish inscribings. It is authorizing Lawyer Alberga to deliver to Lincoln Pollard "one hundred guineas, an entitlement from former owner (deceased) George Pollard, less expenses related to manumission of the said Lincoln Pollard."

Jason cannot help but smile. "You studying to be lawyer, Maas Lincoln."

"Thank you, sir, but I studying to be free." The old man's face is beginning to crease and sag, Jason notices, around solemn eyes that are looking through the young man in front of him, at a world which Jason cannot begin to imagine.

"Where will you go . . ." he asks quietly, "tomorrow?"

"I make an arrangement with a brown woman in town. She have a room round the back and a tavern in front. I will get to live in the room for working in the bar, fixing the drinks." Another swift smile. "Is something I know I can do." He becomes serious again.

With a sigh that Jason isn't even conscious of making he bends over the paper, dipping his nib in the inkpot. The signature is barely his. He's noticed this before: when he signs documents important to him, his hand stumbles.

"Tenky, Maas Jason." They rest their eyes in each other's, neither trusting himself to speak. Then Lincoln gets to his feet, slowly, almost creaking. He half turns to Jason, bows.

Jason, not trusting himself to respond, turns to stare out onto the estate, seeing nothing. He hears the latch click softly behind him.

106

Narrative: Christmas Morning (2), Sunday, December 25

SHE WAKES FROM DREAMLESS SLEEP SURROUNDED by a feeling of calm like a fragrance in the air. A little gust of breeze through the open louvres teases a smile.

Yesterday, between herself and Christian, she'd made all her deliveries. To Francine Beaumarchais (herself) and to the whitewomen (Christian). A good amount of money is in the strongbox in the floor, tied up in a different colour bag from Ishmael's, which is also plump. It's a good Christmas. The only concern is Jassy, who lies abed, mewing like a puss from time to time. She can only be days—perhaps even hours—away from her time.

Zion people start coming through the gate before the Livingstones have finished breakfast. They pass the house by, going into the chapel to sit down. It's Sunday.

They're expecting words from Deacon Ishmael. Even though they know he's now forbidden to preach, and were lifted up by Brother Teo's preachment last week, they're brought here from habit or compulsion.

It's Christmas, so they've brought food. A lot of food. Some to share and exchange with their fellow Zion members after service, some to take to the sick members and to the very poorest, as well as to people in the workhouse. Zion's Christmas has been so from Elorine can remember.

This year is a little different, though. Backra's shadow hangs over everything.

Normal activities are suddenly tinged with unease. Elorine has already decided that the Sunday morning teaching to read and write will not take place. Backra is suspicious of gatherings at the best of times. Gatherings for such a purpose could be judged seditious if Backra heard of it—and he would almost certainly hear of it, as he heard of Ishmael's preachment.

But the Zion people are waiting in the chapel, the chapel they helped the Livingstones to build plank by plank, bench by bench. For today is more than Christmas: it's the day the Zion community decides who will be baptized in Blue River's mouth next week Sunday morning, to start the new year right. It's a difficult and sometimes contentious process. Baptism is a badge of honour, especially for Zion's slave members. In the process of approval, old injuries and quarrels are reignited and new ones sown. But Ishmael, when he joins his flock in the little chapel, ignores all of that. He pulls the chair that is customarily his next to the lectern down to the floor and into the middle of the benches. He calls the children to him; each receives one of the sweeties Elorine brought back from the market the day before. Then he leads them all in a favourite hymn, his voice cheerfully edging the tune. He calls on Mother Juba's Christian to read the Christmas story from a tattered book. It's a Zion Christmas morning tradition that the youngest fluent reader, chosen by Elorine, reads from the treasured book that is far older than themselves; it's a great honour.

Ishmael leads the applause as Christian concludes his task with a triumphant grin and turns to beam at his teacher in the rear of the chapel. Then Ishmael holds out his hand to Mama Claris sitting beside him. He'd handed his Bible to her when he sat down. The people in the little chapel shuffle their feet and bottoms on the creaking benches, then grow quiet. They're willing Ishmael to the lectern, Elorine knows, but he remains in his chair, riffling the pages of the Bible with such concentration that he might be inside his own house, privately.

Finding his text, he looks around at them, his face radiant.

"My beloved brethren," he reads, his voice tender, "Let every man be swift to hear, slow to speak, slow to wrath. For the wrath of man worketh not the righteousness of God."

He turns to look at Jethro, who belongs to Miss Meyerlink, and whom Elorine has persuaded to let him come to chapel; a faithful and fervent member of Zion for the past year, he's a candidate for baptism. "You hear what James say, Brother Jethro?" His tone is light, provocative.

"James who, Deacon?" Jethro is alert to the possibility of being teased.

"The Apostle James, no? Maasa Jesus brother. He say that anger get in the way of God's work."

"Yes, Deacon," Jethro says quietly, looking away from Ishmael's eyes.

"I know you is angry, Brother." Ishmael's voice is still gentle. "I see you there in the courthouse the other day, and I'm saying tenky to you." He sweeps the little group with his eyes, his voice. "I thank you all for coming, and for the testimony some of you give on my behalf. That is what save me from prison, sure as Maasa God's sun rise in the sky every morning. We is sheep in the midst of wolves. Jesus say we is to be beware of men, cause they will deliver us up to be scourged. You know what is scourging, Miss Abba?"

Abba giggles. A shy old woman who was an incorrigible runaway in her youth, she bears the scars of her several whippings like the Guinea markings on her arms and face. "Yes, Deacon," she says softly with a toothless smile.

"I know, too," Ishmael says, his voice firm, vehement. Then, abruptly, he smiles and looks over to a man sharing Elorine's bench at the back of the chapel, with no one else sitting there. "And I say tenky to you also, Brother Greenwich. You did you duty and you show me the way through my troubles."

Heads turn toward Brother Greenwich, who everybody knows had no choice in the matter of punishing Ishmael. He avoids the eyes trained on him.

"Backra don't finish with me yet, or with Nayga," Ishmael says to the congregation. "That is why we have to be wise as serpent. But Jehovah don't finish with us either. And too besides, He don't finish with Backra."

Amens blow like a soft breeze through the little room. Ishmael sounds more like the Deacon they know. Elorine trembles inside.

Abruptly, he softens his voice. "You all hear about things that suppose to happen hereabouts, when Nayga have to go back to work. You hear about siddown, and rise up, and everything between." His eyes roam over each member of the group as he says urgently, "Beware of man. He will deliver you up to the officials to be scourged in the synagogues. That is what Jesus brother-self tell us. The synagogue is where the Jew-dem worship, they have one in St. Jago, another one in Kingston. It is where they did scourge Jesus before they hang him on the cross. For Backra, courthouse is their synagogue. They worship the law that keep Nayga as chattel. That is where they do their scourging, there and in the workhouse next door."

He straightens in his chair but doesn't stand. "I don't want to hear anything about anybody from Zion involve in any of that. You hear me?"

Yes, Deacon.

"Leave all of that to Maasa God. You understand?"

Yes, Deacon.

For distraction, perhaps, he stands and starts them on another hymn. But before the end of the first verse, their voices are overcome by drums and fifes and singing, sounding at the same time joyful and ominous. Ishmael sings louder but soon abandons the effort and smiles, shaking his head. In a minute a colourful band of costumed dancers and musicians come prancing through the gate, filling the yard with noise and setting off old Ginger and the choir of dogs on West Street.

Jonkanoo. The children in the chapel rush to the doorway and stand quivering between joy and fear. The older ones know what's happening; the younger ones, seeing the commotion in the yard, the restless, gaudy figures with spears and sticks, begin to back away. A brightly coloured house dancing to the music suddenly appears in the doorway, scattering the children like clacking fowls. It's atop a huge figure of indeterminate race and gender, face hidden behind a flour-caked mask and with long blue curls tumbling over broad frock-coated shoulders down to a military belt at the waist. The head and neck move with such sinewy precision that the gloved hands only make an infrequent touch to prevent the whole structure from tumbling to the earth.

Elorine, standing at the window behind her usual place at the back of chapel, recognizes Philadelphia, Missa Cavendish's foreman, dressed in bits and pieces of clothing that no doubt come from his owner's warehouse; the house on his head is a model of his owner's town house, wrought-iron railings and all. Every year Philadelphia, the best dancer of the troupe, plays Jonkanoo. Seductive and mincing in turn, he gestures to the cowering children, inviting them forward, and then takes a mighty leap right up to the bottom step, flinging them back into safety. Elorine, laughing, gathers and shushes them.

Philadelphia dips the house at Elorine, who smiles at him through the window-space. His eyes twinkle at her through the slits in his Backra mask, but then are brushed aside by a pride of feathers. The headdress is attached to Koo-Koo, a white-masked flamboyance who is really Jeffroy the rest of the year and belongs to Antoinette Dellaroux, a Haytian seamstress on the other side of Bellefields. She's not well-beloved among the small group of exiles there—her clientele is mainly white planters and military wives from Fort George, so Elorine doesn't regard her as a competitor. Every Christmas and New Year, however, Jeffroy becomes a prancing advertisement for Miss Dellaroux, part of the band that visits the Livingstone yard, where he gives a particularly exuberant display that begins as soon as Elorine shows herself because it's meant as a provocation.

But the effect on Elorine is laughter, because Jeffroy is almost as big a man as Ishmael and Koo-Koo is dressed in layers of women's clothing, one of them muslin that shows off his muscles, because his mistress works him hard everywhere from her garden to—it is whispered—her boudoir.

Some years Koo-Koo will bow to Elorine and whoever else is there and then launch into a dramatic enactment, complete with lisped dialogue, of a fitting between his owner and one of her white clients, but this year he doesn't get a chance. He's bounced hard out of the way by Pitchy-Patchy, Fergus, who, as Elorine watches him, is a shimmering history of her work over the previous year. Right behind is Quaw, his son, in the band for the first time and delighted. He's bigger than she remembers him, almost a man himself, and augments her scraps with long green grass cut this morning from the mouth of Bamboo River, creating an effect of strangeness, menace, that contrasts with his grinning face, because neither of them, alone among the band, wears a mask.

By this time Ishmael has come to the doorway of the chapel and Fergus acknowledges him with a leather pouch slung over his shoulder that Elorine and Ishmael know to be filled with rum; it is something he brought back from one of his voyages and is very proud of—no one else in Bellefields, Backra or Nayga, has anything like this—quite apart from its contents.

Elorine smiles, not so much at the two Pitchy-Patchies as at her awareness of her father's body beside her, lilting to the music in consort with her own. Mingo, a slave from Greencastle who comes to Zion sometimes, spots Deacon and daughter and comes right up beside Fergus, scraping his donkey jawbone with a smooth lignum vitae stick in rhythm to the gumbay and bass drums behind him, and singing a song in his high tenor, the pride of Zion singing on the Sundays he's in attendance, which winds around the booming drums like a vine. His scraping, the drums, the brilliant yard, lift Ishmael's feet and broaden his smile; every Christmas Jonkanoo reveals to Elorine the young man her father was before she was even conceived. It is a joy to her, and a sadness at the changes.

She wouldn't want another kind of father. He angers her sometimes with his stern face and manner and his Biblical injunctions and exhortations about this, that and the other. But he is a kind man, a fierce loving father, and she knows how to make her will his own decision. And she is content that he is a Christian and not what Ishmael himself contemptuously calls (except for Fergus) a pagan. Her Jonkanoo sadness is perhaps rooted in her own feelings. Watching Mingo and her Kekeré Bábà, and Dukey with his heavy square gumbay drum forcing him to lean backwards to carry it, Pollydore's bass drum balanced on a catta thick enough to cushion his head from the blows he gives it with two hammers that he twirls as prettily as the drummers in the Regiment band—as she watches them, listening to her feet and her heart, she finds herself thinking of Adebeh, vanished into bush as though he never really existed. A balloon of feelings lifts her up into a place beyond memory. Philadelphia and Mingo, Jeffroy close behind, weave themselves through the little group to the bottom of the steps. As if by magic, calabash bowls appear in their hands and are waved insistently at the Zion people in the doorways and windows. Bits of food and sweeties, coins, are deposited in the bowls, tenkys bowed and gestured, and the little group of revellers winds its way back through the gate onto West Street, their music and hubbub lingering like a fragrance.

Ishmael returns to the front of the church but still doesn't mount the little platform or take his accustomed place at the lectern. Resuming the hymn that the band interrupted, his voice now, as slightly off-key as always, is brighter. Led by Uncle Teo in rambling prayers, they remember those who have died during the year. After that, food is eaten, juice drunk, and then the Zion congregation disperses to bring cheer and sustenance to the shut-ins and those in the workhouse.

There will be no formal service this Christmas. And, Ishmael announces, the baptism at Blue River will wait upon the Lord's will. A few grumble under their breaths but not in Deacon's hearing.

It's a perfectly normal Christmas except for one thing.

Jason: Duppies, Sunday, December 25

NOT A MINUTE AFTER LINCOLN LEAVE, Jack pushed the door. He's coming from Mathilde to summon me for worship with Reverend Sultzberger and the family downstairs. Poor Jack. He himself is conflicted. Never mind that he's my body slave, he know that he has to obey Mathilde. And he knows me well enough now to know that I will bristle at his message. As I do.

But I have to go, we both know that. So he helps me dress and precedes me down the stairs. A small semicircle of chairs is arranged in two rows, with plenty space between them. In the front row of four there is one waiting for me; Mathilde, Anna and Mrs. Sultzberger are already seated. The row behind has three chairs. Balfour, Lincoln's son, is sitting behind his protectress, Mathilde, with Gilda, who came with her from Suriname, beside him. Beside her a young man is sitting who don't belong to Greencastle, I think he came with the Sultzbergers. Some ways back from the chairs, against the wall of the room, there's a passel of house slaves like dark panelling.

Reverend is sitting facing everybody, and as I sit down he get up and invite us to stand and start singing, all in a sweep. Is a while, if ever, since hymn singing is heard in Greencastle. Squire's duppy must be churning up the lignum vitae outside. But Mathilde and the Reverend's wife are happy and loud. Anna don't sing out, she have a croaky voice and her father's dead ear. Behind me I hear the Sultzberger man's confident baritone. A few voices float in from the back of the room; when I glance around a few women are singing but most mouths are closed, faces blank. They're only there because

Missus summoned them, like she summon me. I don't know the hymn either.

In any case my mind is far, far away from Greencastle in the meeting house where, this being Sunday, I can easily imagine Carla, with Caleb's sleeping head in her lap. They won't be there so much because is Christmas, but for Sunday, where they custom to sit in silence among their Friends, listening to what Maasa God might have to say through any of them.

When I go to Friends meeting with Carla I don't share, aware that I'm not a cradle Quaker like her, like Caleb and his grandparents. I'm not even a convert, cause they don't believe in those things. Really, I'm a trespasser. They tolerate me for the Gallaghars' sake, pillars of their little community, and because I share their secular ideology against slavery. Should word get back of my present status, I would be shunned.

Perhaps God Himself has shunned me. I don't know who I am any longer. More and more, like now, I find myself sitting up front with Backra while a part of me is back there with the slaves.

As I'm hearing but not really listening to the Reverend preaching in his German accent, I'm wondering what Balfour and Gilda and the other slaves behind me are making of it all. The missionaries always preach and say that all of us is equal in God's love. But the slaves, even the converts who go to church and get baptized, they must be questioning the truth of it. Jesus and John the Baptist don't save them from the whip or the bilboes or the treadmill, and plenty of them get punishment because they convert. Evangelist John and the missionaries might tell them that Jesus make them free, but Backra don't get that news.

Squire, to his credit—but really because he didn't care—allowed them as wanted to go to the various chapels, and Anthony, as Pheba explained, don't stop them either. A few planters allow a chapel or meeting house on the estate, even in the face of scathing attacks by other planters, but Squire wasn't about to go that far.

Reverend finish preaching, we sing one more hymn—even I know it this time—and we say the Lord's prayer. The slaves disappear like a breeze blows them.

Constancia sends in some coffee and tea and juice and pork skin to nibble on. The big food will come later, but first the Christmas morning ritual must perform itself. Anna and Mathilde give out the cloth and food and rum and sweeties, Balfour and Gilda behind handing them the stuff from piles and buckets and pails inside the piazza. Thankfully Mathilde don't ask me to be part of her ceremony. Perhaps because I told her quietly about Lincoln leaving, though not where he's going. She didn't know to smile or frown.

I stand in the doorway and match eyes with some of the slaves as they come up the stairs, feeling like a duppy hovering between the two worlds. The ones I know from old or from the field, some nod at me, a few smile. But their mind is really on their part in this ceremonial, which begin when they was in the pickni line, some of them with me. A few of them will wonder how I come to be up here when I born down there, but only the younger ones. Older slaves will know from their years and trials that Maasa God's wind bloweth where it listeth, and in all directions. So they give their own thanks for the food and clothes—to Backra, to Maasa God, to Ogun, to whoever—and go on their ways, giving further thanks that for the next two days at least their backs can be straight and not bent over a cane row.

Still, at the back of my head I'm hearing Lincoln rumbling at me earlier about trouble after Christmas. I find myself looking at some of them closely, without staring, but wondering. If I was them I would be in the siddown if it happen, and maybe in the worse too. But I am also Backra, responsible for Greencastle. Duppy.

And then I hear it. I realize that that is what I've been listening for from I was singing hymns inside. Listening for Kwesi's Christmas. Is a whistle on the air like a bird, but is not a bird. It come and go like a bird flying, and dragging sounds behind it on a string. The same time I realize what it is, the same time I find tears in my eyes, closing them as I turn away from the slaves coming up the stairs.

Jonkanoo. And what bring the eyewater is not the whistle of the fifes so much as the drums under it. They bring everything back in a flood.

At school at Savernake, every May Day a travelling fair would set up in the town. Jeremy and I went down every year to see the jugglers and the freaks and barkers who would sell their own mothers to a likely buyer. My own favourite was the Jack-in-the-Green, a huge terrifying figure on stilts, a moving forest, everything but the masked face covered with leaves and branches.

Nobody would get close to him cause from time to time he twirl around and send everything on the ground and nearby flying. It was my Jonkanoo, in the middle of my England life. I would feel eye-water then too, though not so Jeremy would notice. And the eyewater this Christmas morning, miles and years away from Savernake, is for Carpenter John, Tombo, who in the Jonkanoo of my childhood was the gumbay drummer. Whole then as I'd left him, the old John would come alive among the drummers, prancing in memory like the prideful Negro he always was, the father of Bristol, my remembered childhood friend. Duppies both.

Blind to the line of bodies trudging up the stairs I turn to look down the path leading from the quarters. I'm looking for Tombo, even the gnarled twisted figure that I found upon return. His absence is as powerful as it would've been to see him. Instead, a Guinea named Strap, a sub-driver on Breadfruit Tree, is dancing his way forward out of the shimmering mid-morning sunlight as the Jonkanoo dancers appear on the path. A few at first, and then multiplying like butterflies—dancers, musicians, all men—and two sets of women at the back—Creoles, the born-ya, and Guineas, children of the last slave purchase before the trade was ended, some of them still clinging to the old ways and dress.

It's a fierce competition every year, and big politics for weeks after Christmas as to who wins and why. I'm hoping Mathilde and Anna don't involve me in the deciding.

As they come closer the mid-morning yard fills like a basin with colours and movement. Is not a big band of Jonkanoo, about ten including the musicians, but all of them in costume of one sort or another, many with masks too. And the other slaves are in Christmas make-best clothes, cause even though they're coming to get their allotment of cloth for the next year they not going to show Backra their everyday tatters. They wearing clothes they make from cloth they buy with money they get from food they sell, some of it to the big house, from their provision ground. That keeps shame from their eye. And maybe anger too.

A towering figure I recognize right away breaks loose from the milling and dances, prances, in the direction of the big house. Pompey. He is Jonkanoo, or House as some call it. He's wearing a mask, black and white and terrible, but I can't mistake Pompey. When I was a bwoy Pompey was always Jonkanoo. By and by, after I leave for England, I hear from Anna that he cease to be head driver so maybe somebody else was Jonkanoo, perhaps even Hector last Christmas. Now, though, nobody would dare argue with Pompey's right. And he find his young self this Christmas morning, frisking like a colt to the drums behind him, as though the thing on his head is a feather. It's a model of Greencastle's big house in every detail, and looking prettier than the real thing, which I have it in mind to touch up before Anthony come back.

Pompey prances right up the steps, scattering the few people still in line, the pickni tumbling back down the steps. Pompey don't care. He comes for his puncheon, though you have to wonder whether he have some inside him already. He gets a big jug from Mathilde, cause it have to share with the band, and the others is watching him. He bows to her, still sprightly, and then turns to me and bows again, which I return. He jigs back down into the yard and hands the jug to a young boy who is there for that purpose alone, cause he peels away from the group and heads back down to the quarters, to hide and guard the precious brew. The sharing will be done when all the collecting—of rum and coins—is done.

Pompey gives a few twirl-arounds at the bottom of the steps and dances off into the small crowd still in the yard, who widen to give him room. The yard is a bustle of colour and movement, old and young, with Pompey and the dress-up girls at the centre. I spot old Tanti Glory from the hothouse, clutching her Osnaburg in one hand and a small puncheon in the other. She probably tells Mathilde she's taking the rum for the men that help her but I don't know how much will leave by the time she gets back there.

And here comes Dollybwoy heading up from the gate for his Christmas share. He's not paying the pickni any more mind than usual, but for a moment it looks as though Dollybwoy, with his funny walking, is really been dancing to Jonkanoo music all his life. I couldn't help but smile.

A fantastical figure detaches himself from the crowd and approaches the bottom of the steps, walking in a stately manner like I see lords in London doing at a Season ball. Dressed like a lord too, but also like a lady. He's wearing britches and a dress, colourful both, with a rainbow of a waistcoat above, and a long dress in layers and frills below. But his glory is his head, a concoction of feathers like the peacocks I see in Hampton Court, and long blonde locks, if you please, curled and styled straight from the Regency. A dead-white mask and white gloves, one holding a fan, complete the masquerade of Backra. From my perch at the top of the steps it seems the headdress is as tall as the figure wearing it. I dredge memory to find the character commanding all our eyes. Nothing comes.

But I hear Mathilde and Anna beside me asking themselves and each other, "Who is Koo-Koo?" over and over.

"Is a girl or a bwoy?" Anna asks.

"I has to remind you? A boy," says her mother. "Girls don't do Jonkanoo, except the sets."

Koo-Koo mounts two steps and strikes a pose with his headdress, pausing for the effect. His audience in the yard gives him a round of clapping just for that; his audience above waits, expectant.

"People of Greencastle, give me you ears," Koo-Koo begins. The voice, despite what Mathilde says, could be bwoy or girl, just like the costume; the mumming of proper English speech is as rich too, like the clothing. "I am far away in Virgin Virginia," he continues, "and you, Mr. Jason, think you is in charge, you and Missus and Lickle Missus." He makes a broad gesture with his gloved hand that includes all of us at the top of the stairs.

And I notice a strange thing happening, eerie as if, like Nayga say, puss walk over your grave. Koo-Koo's voice is transforming itself the more words it utters, like something else is feeding on them. "I, Anthony, is still the Maasa of this kingdom. Greencastle is here, in my heart!" He thumps his chest hard, shaking his very self, at the same time striking another pose, which gets some claps from the gallery below.

The voice is Anthony's, whatever its source. He could've been standing beside me, among us, at the top of the stairs. Mathilde and Anna, after a moment of frozen horror, cackle like fowls. At that Koo-Koo bows deeply, and lift his mask with a flourish that is almost defiance.

And my questions about him are answered. Koo-Koo is Achilles, the light-skin green-eyed slave whom I'm always aware of in the corner of sight, or who makes himself noticeable in some way out in the field. Achilles is Anthony's son. And the few seconds he allows for a glimpse of his face tell me his mother: Lucia.

⇒ 108 ⇐

Adebeh: Escape, Sunday, December 25

MAM IS ALWAYS TELLING THE THREE of us pickni that we's smart. When she know we's going into some difficult situation, especially when it concerns whitepeople, she say we must play fool to ketch wise. Today, Baddu and me do like Mam say, even though Baddu don't know Mam yet.

Middle morning, after we put together some bickle to break the fast, Empress change into what she call her go-to-town clothes, the tidiest I's ever seen her, and tell us to follow her up to the big house. "You will get something to dress in up there," she say, looking at our hang-pon-nail garments with a smile. "And some provisions."

We'll need the provisions, whatever they are. I follow Sister outside when she goes to do her morning business, and wait for her at the edge of the hillside, brushing the big fat flies from my face. As we's walking back to Empress, I tell her my determination to leave this place of bondage and madness—today! She agree.

Without telling her the story I show her the piece of metal, like a short post, that I found as I was peeing in the grass, part of what-left of a bruck-down fence grown over by grass and weeds.

Maybe long ago was a enclosure for animals, small animals like chickens or piglets, on that piece of ground. I extracted two posts from the wire, one for Sister, and put them carefully under Empress's hut as I went back inside.

Baddu smile, and finger Delphis's necklace. Inside, we lie back down on the pallets that Empress give us, not speaking unless Empress direct a word to us. But if Empress was watching, she would see that we's talking to each other with our eyes.

Outside, following Empress, we find we's at the back of a line. Everybody that we ever see on Belvedere is either waiting ahead of us, or pass us on their way back to the quarters.

Everybody coming back is carrying something, man and woman: bundles of cloth like the flour sacks Mr. Bernard sell from in his shop in Boydville, some of them with writing on them, just like his. The woman-dem have chunks of meat bare in their hands, dripping into the cloth, and strips of dried fish tucked in their armpit. I suddenly remember the *Eagle*, the ship that bring me here in the first place. Fergus told me that some of the cargo was dried cod from New-foundland. Maybe these women I's watching is carrying some. I's watching them to see how much food they's carrying. It's not a lot, but is the same for everybody. That give me heart. Sister and me will have enough in the bush.

Cummings is sitting at the top of the stone steps, in the doorway of the house. He's in a fancy chair and dress-up like a prince, with even something like a turban on his head. Behind him is Mandeville, wearing what reminds me of a page bwoy at one of those fancy dinners of Major Maxwell and his Missus in Halifax, when I look after the horses. Except that Mandeville, who is handing his owner the cloth and the food with his bare hands, is busting out of his clothes and looks like a ridiculous rag doll.

Empress is leading the three of us up the steps. Cummings's eyes shine at her. "My Afric Empress," he pronounce, "dark widow of my darker Hercules." His voice is like those thespians I's heard outside the Bowater Theatre in Dartmouth while holding the carriage that brought the Maxwells there. Dealing with me, at least, he sounds local, but now he's in the world he creates from his books and his rum and his coffee beans. His world of madness that Baddu and me is caught in.

Empress take the cloth and provisions from him and bob a little curtsy as she turn down the steps. No tenky pass her lips, no fawning smile as I've seen on other faces.

Sister is next. "Who you?" Cummings ask, rough, local again.

"Baddu," she answer, not rude but not giving him "sir" or "maasa" either, like the others did.

"I don't know you," he say, and turn his head. "Mandy. You know this nigger bitch?"

"Yes, Maasa. Billy bring her back with him." He's looking at me as he speak, challenging me to deny "Billy".

Cummings push the cloth and provisions at Sister. "Here," he say.

"Tenky," is all Sister say to him, and turn away.

But my eye catch on a slash of yellow through the window-slats to the other side of the doorway into the house. Petta. Must be that she heard Baddu's voice.

Cause it's Christmas—and part of Cummings's madness—that's why she's in drapery like those statues in the public gardens in Halifax that Georgia Marcy and me go to sometimes, on a Sunday afternoon. Poor thing, she could as well be naked, her bubbies is plain as fruit under the cloth.

She's looking straight into me, and her eyes is a pool of water. It's as though she know what we's planning, Baddu and me, and she want to come.

But I have to look away, cause Cummings is staring at me. "Billy-bwoy," he say. His voice soften, and I make sure I's standing far enough away so he can't touch me, face or other parts. "You come back for Christmas bickle, eh? You think I don't know you?" He giggle, like he's scolding a favourite child. I don't move. "Here, Billy-bwoy," he say, handing on the cloth and food from Mandeville. "Come show me the clothes when you make them. And maybe I'll let you back in the house."

"Tenky." I say, and turn away, knowing he's waiting with a frown for a "sir". I step past the few people behind me, who I don't know and don't expect to see again.

In the yard I find myself thinking like a hunter. The day is still brilliant, and it's cool, good for travel. But rain would be better in a way, because up here rain brings the mist. Mist can be the enemy of hunters and a friend of the hunted. We'll be hunted. Maybe Penzance and his dawg-dem. I say a prayer to Baby Jesus and the bigi pripri that nobody won't know we's gone until tomorrow, or even the day after. We should be far away by then.

But that was not to be.

Back at the hut, we both give Empress our food, except the cod—that don't need cooking like the salt pork and beef. To stop and cook would be time-wasting, dangerous. We give her the cloth too, except a little piece that Sister's already tied into a pouch for the cod.

"Tenky, Empress," I say, holding her old hand in mine, Sister beside me.

"You going somewhere?" Her eye is bright with curiosity.

Sister take her other hand. "Shhh," she whisper, finger to lip.

The old woman cackle softly. "Go over the top part," she say, looking at me. "Where you was working before the barbeque. Watch out for the Penzance-one. Dem dawg will kill you like rat."

We put our hands together on her old head, in blessing.

Outside, as I's taking the two iron sticks from under the hut I hear Baddu above me. "What about Petta?"

Her name drop like a big stone into Walford Pond behind our house in Boydville. Eddie and me used to lay down on our bellies in the ancient oak tree over it and drop stones, scattering the duck-dem that float in it. Right now, though, what's scattered is my thoughts. I have many thoughts about Petta, and maybe one of them is jealousy. I stand to look Sister serious in the eye, like Petta look at me from through the slats in the big house awhile ago.

"I don't know how we would get her out of there," I say.

"The man is a animal," Sister say, spitting right beside me. "He will kill her from fucking."

I draw breath and let it out. "If we go back up there," I say, calm as I can as I toss my head toward the big house, "they will kill us."

"I will go," she say suddenly, reminding me of Mam when she's vex with Da and maybe would hurt him if she don't walk away.

I haven't yet give her the other metal stick I have for her, so she goes off with her empty hands and the pouch with the cod tied around her waist. The rags she was wearing as clothes when they capture us is even more threaded now, just like mine. And no doubt Petta's, before this crazy man drape her up in that whisper of cloth.

I sit down to wait on a stone next to Empress's hut. I don't go inside to Empress—the less she know the better. Once they know we's gone they'll press her for knowledge, and she'll suffer for what she knows.

Anyways, I expect Sister to be coming back in a short time, as she give thought on the way to what I say. Her face I's expecting to see long to the ground, cause I know the Petta-one is dear to her. So I'm trying to breathe in and out against the wriggling in my belly that's telling me I have to do something, though I can't hardly think what.

It's longer than I expected but she do come back, and her face is almost on the ground. "You right," she grunt. "The one Mandeville see me and point his gun at me. But I not leaving her. Come."

She turn back the way she'd just come. I catch up and give her the metal stick, glad she didn't have it the first time or maybe she'd challenge the head driver and be dead now. I send another word in the direction of the Baby Jesus.

The giving-out is done by now, the steps empty of Cummings and slaves. I spot Mandeville, though, watching through the slats on the other side of the door where Petta was. When he see us his pistol push out through them and follow us. Don't ask me how she would, but it's as if Baddu know where she's going, cause without pause she go close-up to the steps and then go left, looking up the wall of the house. I notice she has her necklace from One-Eye Sarah in one hand and the metal stick in the other.

And don't ask me how I know—maybe the bigi pripri—to go right, round the other side of the house. But I do that, and Mandeville's gun is confused. It wave from left to right, and down, but the slats too close together so he don't have much play. The house has a cellar, which I'd notice before, and I duck into there. It's dark and chill and musty, and Sister is there before me. I see her backside bend over, and she hear my feet. She turn and shush me with a finger to her mouth, but she needn't bother, cause I hear Mandeville on the floorboards above, crossing from the front of the house to the back. Looking for us.

Bend-over, Baddu creep toward the edge of the house and I realize where she's headed. Under the room where Petta stays. It's where Cummings came out of when Mandeville took me to him before I got sent to the barbeque. The wall of which is blocking that end of the cellar. So, as it turn out, the barbeque is right below that room.

I send a big prayer up that Cummings is somewhere else in the house.

Baddu tap her stick against the floorboards in a rhythm that sounds like a signal to Petta above. And it's answered. Three thuds. A whispering comes from the floorboards, then silence, then, in a little gap between the wall of the barbeque and the wall of the house, Petta's face appear. She's lying on the barbeque, looking through at Baddu, me right behind her, with a big grin.

Baddu must be realize, the same time as me, that we can hardly get out over the top, as Empress advised us. To walk out from under here and across the open space toward the high groves would bring big trouble. Especially since, as she show herself, Petta is still wearing that piece of statue cloth. She's wrapped it more decently around herself now, but out in the open she would be a moving flame.

We come out from the cellar by the side, into bush and straggly little trees, stony ground underfoot sloping down. Making haste here will be difficult and dangerous. But we can't go slow either.

"You!" The voice comes from behind. "Where you think you going?" I know it, and turn. The Monkey Man who tormented us on the way here. Still with his stick. Now with a small wiry brown dawg on a piece of thin rope. I know from home to watch out for the small ones. They's always hungry, and fierce like ferrets.

"I ask you a question, bwoy." He's looking straight at me, don't even notice Baddu and Petta.

"I's not a bwoy," I answer him, my voice flat.

"But you's a nigger, yes?" He lift his stick slightly.

I raise my own stick enough to make sure he notices it. And I look down at the dawg.

"I's not a nigger," I say in the same even voice.

"Then what you is?" His eye is aglitter with mischievous violence.

"I's going about my business," I respond. "Is Christmas."

"You have a ticket?"

I'm about to respond that I have one when I hear Baddu behind me. "I have one," she say, and come to stand beside me, Petta just behind.

"Show me."

Sister hold up her necklace from Delphis, which she's still carrying in her hand, and step right up to Monkey Man.

"Dis is my ticket, Monkey Man." Her voice snarl at him. "You see my ticket? You cyan read my ticket, Monkey Man? It say I'm a obe-ahwoman, and you an you lickle mawga dawg is like insect to mash with my foot." She twist her heel into the rocky ground.

I's listening to Sister, but I's watching the Monkey Man. He seem, the closer she get, to be smaller, shrinking into the ground. The rattle of the necklace beads in his face turn his eye almost inside out. And the little dawg, him turn right over onto his back and stick his legs straight up, and tremble. The two of them making the same sound—a squealing in the back of their throats.

Myself, I's a little frighten too. I remember Sister's story about the whiteman on her estate who just drop into the sugar cauldron, but I didn't want to believe. Now I know. For some reason I glance at Petta. She's smiling.

"Somerset!" I hear Mandeville's voice from the house behind us. "What is going on down there?"

But Somerset cannot do more than snivel, him and the little dawg sounding the same. I turn myself and look up at Mandeville. His pistol is steady on the slat, pointing straight down at us, his finger snuggled into the trigger. Eyes bright with malice, he's looking for a reason to pull it.

Is the dawg who gives him that. I feel a explosion in my ankle and jump in the air. The dawg is there like I'm wearing it, but I still have the metal stick in my hand and I slash at this wriggling brown thing, wild but careful not to slash myself.

And then I hear two sounds. A pop and a sigh, one close behind the other. Petta is down on the ground between Baddu and me, screaming.

109

Elorine: Birth, Monday, December 26

AT LEAST THE BABY WAIT UNTIL MORNING, and it didn't catch us by surprise. From yesterday afternoon, Jassy was mewling like baby puss. Thanks to Mother Juba, I get almost everything beforehand, between the market and Missa Cavendish, through Philadelphia.

A month now Jassy's been haunting my workroom when I finish for the day, begging me for this piece and that piece of cloth from the floor to put in a basket in the corner of her room, for when her time come. Some of those cloths had to use up yesterday, when Mother Juba instruct her to purge herself with castor oil. It'll make it easier for the baby, Juba tell her, and for she, Jassy.

Jassy herself, and Cyrus, is a picture. One breath the two of them is bright like new money, so pleased with themself like is them alone can make baby. The next breath pull in silence, the two of them looking everywhere but at each other, frighten like they see duppy.

Still, Cyrus don't have to be here at all. Like how it's Christmas he could be out carousing with his friends. He wanted to stay and sleep the night on the floor, but I send him home, tell him to come back early morning. On the way, I tell him, stop and tell Mother Juba I will surely need her tomorrow, which is today.

I go to sleep a little nervous, but I leave time and circumstance in Maasa God hands. I turn a couple times during the night, and I listen out for Jassy, but I only hear the night noises I'm custom to, so I go back to sleep. Good thing too, cause with the first break of day the excitement begin. Jassy bawl out like when you pass the slaughterhouse on Pinchon Street and they cut a pig throat. Pig can sound like a person. Like Jassy this morning.

Cyrus take my advice about early. Him and me nearly collide in the kitchen, him coming to fetch me, me going out to Jassy. His eye-dem big as plum seed, and he stuttering my name, teeth clacking. I brush past him into the room to see Jassy in a arch, only heels and shoulders touching on the pallet. Then she collapse and start to groan as if she's fighting with something bigger than her inside herself. The contractions that Juba warn me about straighten her body stiff as board, her fingers and toes like spikes. Next minute she crumple like paper.

Two, three times she bunch-up and then flatten-out, bunch-up, flatten, all the while sweat pearling on her skin in beads, damping the sheet. A big fraid grab hold of Cyrus and is shaking him like puss with a mus-mus. And I smell something—shit.

I send Cyrus to get Mother Juba.

While I'm waiting, telling Jassy meantime not to mind, not to mind, soon done, soon done, water start to stream out from between her legs. Juba tell me to expect it but it still shake me up, cause Juba say that is when the baby ready to come. Suppose the baby come before Juba!

But Maasa God was kind. As I was wiping up Jassy, I hear Juba in the yard outside. When she come through the door she don't give Jassy more than a glance. Right away she set to sweeping the room with a broom she bring herself, the handle smooth from longtime use, the palmleaf brush with old and new fronds. She sweep the dust into the corner by the door, but not into the yard. I wonder if is obeah, but I don't say a word. And Jassy quiet down as soon as Juba come in and get busy.

"The water come?" Juba ask her. Me and Jassy both nod, but she wasn't seeing me, she was pulling Jassy to sit up. Another cramp take Jassy and fling her back down. Juba bend over and hold down her legs, easing them apart. When she relax Juba pull her up again, and this time, quick-quick, she take off the flimsy dress that Jassy is wearing and throw it aside. Juba reach into a little goatskin bag she's carrying over her shoulder for a bottle and pour something on Jassy and rub her all over, slow and easy, paying no attention to the twitching limbs and the moaning, which is softer now.

As I'm watching Mother Juba rubbing Jassy, it's like she's creating a completely new person, like her hands belong to Jesus who can make cripples walk and the blind to see. Naked as the baby that will soon appear from inside her, Jassy come to my eye like a lamp that is filling the room with light even like the sun that is just now filling the day.

And the Jassy who been dragging herself around here these past months like a poor thing appear to me now like a offering that the prophets talk about, as a gift to Maasa God, to honour and praise Him. Cyrus plant the seed, but is Jehovah who grow it to this time when it will burst forth. And a strange opposing set of things come to me as I'm watching. I feel like Juba have her hand on my belly, which is flat and dry. I feel my own pumpum, feel it from inside of me. I want to be a offering to someone, a lamp to fill a room and a life. I never feel that way before. I know who it is that cause both the dryness and the light. I know who is to anoint me.

I'm following these strange thoughts round and round in my head when I notice the rhythm between the two of them change. Jassy stiffen, but not as violent as before, and Juba lift her legs from behind the knee and turn to me. "Come hold her foot," she say, gruff. "You have cloth?" I bring the basket of pieces that Jassy collect over to Juba and then take hold of Jassy by her ankle.

Juba, she move up to Jassy head and put it in her lap. Same time she take a piece of cloth from the basket, roll it up and put it in Jassy mouth like a bridle. Then with the same slow and easy motion Juba start to push her hands and Jassy belly toward me. My eye seem to fill-up with her pumpum. It seem to come alive, like a face trying to smile and frown at the same time. And then it open wider, and wider, and Juba say, "Push, pickni," and she is easing Jassy belly down toward me. Jassy is biting the cloth, stifling the scream that's pulling her body tighter and tighter.

All this time I'm watching her pumpum as it widens and the baby headtop appears like a pink ball. Same time dribbles of watery shit is coming out below the baby and I'm worrying that the head will fall into it. I promise myself that if that look like happening I will let go Jassy foot-dem and grab the baby.

And that is what I had to do. In two-twos the head and then the shoulders come out, the face down and headed straight for the little puddle of shitty water.

"Grab him," Juba cry out, and that is what I do. Jassy two foot drop back onto the pallet but she barely notice cause the pain that was jukking her from inside is gone now. Is a girl. She favour a big rat, with a tail and all, from her navel back into Jassy pumpum.

"You member the knife?" Juba bark at me, and give thanks I remember. I hide it under Jassy palette from yesterday when the mewling begin, so I reach under now and hand it to Juba, pleased with myself.

"Pass the basket," she say, and take the baby from me and pull out a piece of cloth. Same time she wrap the baby in it and slice the red-and-purple rope that is keeping the baby joined to Jassy. Juba do all of that in one moment, one movement, with one thought. The baby is wriggling in my hands like a fish; I fraid I'll drop it and I fraid in case, so as not to drop it, I hold it too tight. Meantime Juba take a deep draw of the piece of jackass rope that is always in her mouth, and she blow the smoke gentle into the face of the baby, who cough fit to break her little body and then let out a big yelling.

Juba lift back her head and laugh.

Then she turn to Jassy. "Push still, pickni," she instruct her, "more to come out." What come out is like tripe and liver mix-up together, and Juba and me is busy taking cloth out of the basket between us to soak it up. The baby is lying beside Jassy to keep it out of the mess, but she is still not paying the baby or anything else good mind. Her eyes is quietly looking up into the roof as though what is happening around her is concerning someone else.

I cyaant judge her. She must be tired and frighten. I can understand that even though I never give birth yet. But I know what is in my own mind: Revelations. *A great wonder in the heaven, a woman clothed with the sun, and upon her head a crown of stars. She is with child and travailing in birth. And another wonder appeareth. A great dragon with seven heads and crowns. And the dragon stands before the woman that is ready to be delivered, to devour the child as soon as it is born.*

Is not something that Ishmael give any preachment on, though I know he know it. I come to understanding of it from Mama Selina, who read it to me a few times when she's talking with me about Adam and her life on Cascade. For her the dragon is slavery. And maybe that is what Jassy, who may not even know the scripture, is seeing up in the dark ceiling. Her baby girl that she birth with such travail and pain is not hers, or Cyrus's. It belong to Missus Procter, the brown woman in town who own Jassy, and to who we send rent money for her every month-end.

110

Narrative: Tenky, Monday, December 26

"MAAS JASON?"

He'd been dreaming of her in half-submerged reveries. Her voice sprung his eyes open.

Guilty as charged.

"You awake, Maas Jason?"

She'd been measuring him for trousers, both of them trying to ignore his tremulous cock. Her hoarse voice—like a child with a cold—bores into his doughy thoughts. It's almost dark, her face floats above him. He smiles.

She doesn't. "Mama want to talk to you," she says crisply and moves out of his sight.

Jason raises himself as though drawn-up, throwing his legs over the side of the bed where he's been sleeping off Constancia's Christmas feast. Drowsy, he sees the door close behind a woman who must have just entered. Prudence the seamstress, Miranda's mother. In real life she does the measuring.

"Beg pardon, Maas Jason," she begins, with a quick curtsy, but he abruptly tells her not to call him that. She bobs again, momentarily confused, thinks of fleeing after her daughter through the door.

"I'm not Maasa, Prudence," he says, gently. "I don't own you." He stands up, as if to make the point.

"No, sir. Yes, sir." She smiles and frowns. Pleased that he remembers her name though they've had little to do with each other beyond a few fittings. Confused as to how to address him.

He ventures a smile meant to reassure. "What is it?"

"I come to tell you tenky, sir."

"For what?"

"Mirry tell me Maas—Sir." Her smile is sly, challenging.

"I told her not . . ."

"Yes, sir, and she hear you. She never tell nobody! I had was to beat it out of her. She come back from you room so please with herself, and so frighten at the same time, I think to meself . . ."

"Think what?"

She answers his rough question with another smile.

"You think I tumble her, not so?" He feels the beginning of anger and shame. Her smile doesn't change. "You ask her?" Her smile is blasted away by his anger.

"No, Maas . . ."

"I don't put a finger on her."

"Something wrong with she, sir?"

"She is a pickni."

Prudence makes a soft squawk and shrugs. "She see her blood two Christmas gone, sir."

He's silenced by the challenge. Then he says, "She is Maas Squire pickni, don't it? Like me? Unless is Maas Anthony?"

Her response is brisk, dismissive. "No, sir, not the Anthony-one. Him did try a few times, with Mirry too, but I tell Miss Anna and beg her talk to him. And now him gone." The relief lifts her voice for a moment, but she continues earnestly. "I wasn't any older than Mirry now, with Maas Squire. And it was just the one time, when I was measuring him for trousers. Just the one time, Missa Jason. Imagine that. Just the once." A little smile flits through her eyes.

"And you think I going to do that to Miranda? Breed her?" His anger has been softened by her story, but he keeps his tone stern.

"I can't know what you have in mind for Mirry, Missa Jason, she belong to you now. Is that why I come to you this evening, sir. To tell you tenky, and to ask."

He cannot answer her. He doesn't know the reason himself, why he decided to translate Squire's bequest into actual ownership of another person, any person. It wasn't really a decision, even, not one he could explain to anyone, even his friend Jeremy Cato. And he certainly cannot find words to explain to this woman, a concerned mother, his feelings for her daughter, his half-sister.

"You will take her with you, sir? When you go back to England? I hear they don't keep slave in England, sir."

He has not thought that far. He takes refuge in honesty. "I don't know, Miss Prudence. Whatever I do she will be well taken care of."

As he listens to his own words, made in the clipped voice he brought back from England, a tumble of ideas about the future assaults him. Elorine: Miranda as an assistant seamstress. Tomorrow he'll make a Christmas visit to West Street and broach it.

Or he could take her back to England where, as Lord Mansfield declared, slavery cannot exist (though bondage and exploitation are permitted). He could introduce her to Carla as his sister, and to Caleb as his island cousin. Within a couple winters they'd be as light-skinned and curly-haired as each other. But then what? And what will he do with his desire?

Prudence is watching him keenly, picking through his words, his ominous silences, for a grain of assurance.

"She will not come to harm, Prudence," he intones. "Not from me. I promise you that."

"I hope so, Maasa," she says, anxious.

Abruptly, she drops a little curtsy and fades through the door.

Jason, immensely relieved, falls into the chair by the desk and looks out at the darkness that fell while he was mouthing senseless words to Prudence. A few points of light flicker out there, like closer stars. There are voices, white voices, filtering up from downstairs, but he has no desire to join them. Lincoln would give him sage advice. But he left before luncheon, quietly.

Tasting, smelling his clotted breath, Jason contemplates the endless night ahead.

III

Adebeh: Darkness, Monday, December 26

"I GOING BACK THERE," BADDU SAY, fierce as the pruning knife she stole. She mean Belvedere. "I going deal with that bitch." She mean Mandeville.

I point out to her that we don't even know where we are. In case Mandeville and Penzance think we's going back home to Kojo Town, we walked in the opposite direction from where they found us. The terrain is up and down but mostly barren, with few big trees as markers to guide us. We's listening all the while for dawg sounds, but don't hear any. Baddu's necklace must be frighten them bad!

"I can find me way," she say, folding me into her angriness like a cloth.

"Go on, then," I say, as if I don't care.

But I do. I's missing Petta too. I barely get to know her, but she and Sister were so dear to each other that she come to me as family. Last night she invade my spirit. I could feel her body on my back as I carried her down the slope from the barbeque. Still warm, and the blood running down me is warm. She's whimpering like a just-born puppy. But by the time Baddu say, "I'll carry her," and I transfer Petta, I notice that she's been quiet a while, and that less blood is flowing.

We walked as much as we could in water, but there isn't a lot of that.

We buried Petta in the sand by a little river that we found just as it was dusking. The river looks no different to me than the one we crossed after we set out from Kojo Town to go to Bryden. That seems a year ago. We dig the grave with our two metal sticks, Baddu's hands and shoulders furious, like a hungry dawg digging for bones. All the while eyewater dropping in blessing on the body that she loves. I's digging, but also I's listening for sounds from behind us.

Dark sail down like a big bird coming in to land, cooling the air.

"We shoulda keep some of the cloth," Baddu say as we settle down behind a outcrop of rock. I know what cloth she mean, the one we left as tenky with Empress. It's so cool, if we wasn't brother and sister we could hug-up. Which put me in mind of Elorine. In my head she's as far away as Georgia Marcy is.

We get through the night as best we can. Sister found some leaves that we crush and rub on our body, even our face. The mosquito-dem sing all night, but we wasn't too bitten in the morning.

And now here she is, ready to go straight back into the jaws of trouble that we just escaped. I's still getting used to having a big sister. As the Bible say, *What was hidden is now revealed, and I have joy in the revelation.* But maybe because it's One-Eye Sarah who raised her, Baddu can be wild in her thoughts. I's the little brother, and I will defend her with my life, if needs be. But I's not putting myself into the jaws of death alongside her. Or allow her to do it by herself. If I was to arrive back in Scotia to tell Da that I find his daughter, and then lose her for a foolishness, he would skin me alive, and Mam would cook me for soup.

Sister is wrap-up in her anger, but one ear of mine is still listening for dawg. We have the metal fence-sticks close by, and Sister is not letting go of her pruning knife. I find that I have a stone in my hand—I don't even know where or when I picked it up.

"We's not going to Bryden again." I's casual, playing fool to ketch wise, hoping to distract her from Belvedere. "You know that, yes?" "I know," she say. Her soft voice splinter on the word. I hear a snuffle, and then a sobbing. We's only maybe fifty yards from where we bury Petta, and miles and ages away from anything we know. I put my arm round her shoulder and hold her.

I take a breath, for it's a hard thing to say. "I want to live. I want to go back to Mam and Da."

"So whabout me?" Her voice flash anger and pain.

"You too," I say, soothing. "I going back with you."

"How?"

Her question is simple but the answer is not. I have no idea. My mind hasn't reached there yet.

"The ancestors will find us a way." My words are more confident than my thoughts, and Sister hear that.

"How?" Her voice is soft, but firm in doubt.

I make a desperate lunge. "They bring me here, don't they?" I get a smile for that. "I don't want to dead before I take you back to them. You neither."

"Alright," she whisper in the dawning day.

112

Jason: Is Christmas, Tuesday, December 27

THE VIXEN LUCIA MUST KNOW THAT I wake early—she slips into the room like a shadow. I thought it was Jack, who sometimes brings a mug of coffee or juice from the kitchen. I'm sitting at my table desk looking out at the pearl-coloured waking-up world when I feel something soft on my both shoulders.

I know right away is not Jack, he would never be so familiar. I smell the rank sweet smell of sleep and rosewater. For a moment, a wisp of hope, it's Miranda.

"Mornin, Maasa." Voice soft and with a smile she comes around into view. The nights are cool now, so she's decently covered. But there's nothing underneath and she's standing close. I recognize the look in her eye.

"You give me a dose." My tone is Maasa's.

Her eyes open wide. "No, Maasa!" But she's fraid too. So frighten she drop into the chair beside the desk. In my eye she sees the field, the ultimate punishment for a house slave like her.

"Then who?" I ask, still Maasa.

"Somebody else, Maasa. Me clean."

I don't know how long she was Anthony's; she must be a young gyal when Achilles was born. She's still attractive, the pock marks barely showing. But right then she turns my stomach. I dismiss her with a wave, and she knows she's to go as silent as she come.

Like a revenge, though, I have to piss. The house quiet, but I'm listening for the slightest movement outside my door as I sit there with the chimmey in my hands, cock drooping into it, watching for a trickle. I'm trying to relax cause I know it will ease the piss. But my body isn't paying any mind. Expecting the pain, I clench inside. Which stops the piss, of course. And when it comes, finally, it's pale yellow and red. Pus and blood. But it's not like thin soup, like it was last week.

Which reminds me. As I'm watching my poor cock struggle, I remember that I need more silver solution. I didn't need it then, but in England you pick up bits and pieces of information about the treatment for clap from just listening in public houses and clubs. They take it as nothing, a rite of passage. I counted myself fortunate that I'd never paid for sex, and, without ever formulating it to myself, morally a little superior to the sons of gentry.

Experience teaches you, though. I'm embarrassed and ashamed. Part of the anger at Lucia this morning is toward myself.

But I still have to go into Bellefields, to Missa Benjamin, a brown man who in London would be apothecary, and here is simply a medicine man. Is he who tells me, the first time, to eat plenty fruit and drink as much juices as I can.

"And this," he say, giving me a brown bottle with a stopper. "Shake it good," he say, "and then put five drops in the juice or water. Three times a day."

I remember hearing his name. Anybody sick in the big house and Dr. Fenwell isn't due, Israel is sent to Missa Benjamin for medicine. Israel can't read but his memory is good, so he remembers every little thing the medicine man tell him.

By-and-by I get myself up and, with Jack's help, dressed. Downstairs there's few people around, no whites. Cherry is waiting at the bottom of the steps, a red-eyed Israel holding her. He reeks of stale rum. Usually good for several minutes of conversation, I get only a growled "mawning" today. I reply civilly, but remember as I'm mounting that he is Lucia's poopa.

The riding isn't as painful as last week, for which my balls is thankful. Castaways from the Christmas merriment litter the pathway between the big house and Hope Come Over, where the empty fields begin. And from the left, the quarters, I hear drumming and singing. Any other time this would be worrisome. Slaves know the law better than lawyers—they have to in order to oil around it. Against drumming especially. Backra frighten for drum. But for the few days of Christmas each estate is its own law, and there isn't many rules.

One Christmas at Greencastle—the year I leave for England, I think—the next day after, while we was at lunch, a tree of a man, October, come bursting into the sitting room from the front steps, beating a tube drum around his neck and with two gyal prancing after him. Without a by-your-leave they circle the table, making a infernal racket. Squire, who don't like his meal to interrupt, laugh and clap his hands with the drum, and slap the gyal bottom-dem as they pass him by. Mathilde didn't even mind, she laugh too. Some of the gyal-dem from the kitchen come inside and join the line, and I glimpse Constancia, fat as she always was, standing in the doorway, jigging, a big smile on her face.

Is Christmas.

This year, though, the celebration is all outside and in the quarters. Is the first without Squire. Is a big set of changes, cause Lincoln isn't there neither. Yesterday, though Balfour was doing his father's duties with the things to be handed out, I catch Anna looking around him a few times. She looking for Lincoln.

And—as it turn out—is me see him first.

As I'm riding into Bellefields I remember that Lawyer Alberga send a note last week to invite me to a open house he always have around Christmas, for Hanukkah. I remember Squire going, and doubtless Anthony last year, cause Squire was bedridden by then.

I'm late. So I take Cherry past Missa Benjamin's little lean-down shop to Alberga's place. I ignore the Christmas detritus in the mud on Charles Street from yesterday's Set Girls' parade.

There's hardly any front yard for such a large house, and four or five horses tied on the rails on either side of the entranceway. One of his boys takes Cherry's reins and shows me the way in to where I hear voices and laughter.

And who should I see first—Lincoln! For a minute I'm at Green-castle. He's holding a tray of drinks, just like he did there. But he's better dressed, and decked-out in his sampattas. And smiling. Glad to see me. Not a Lincoln I'm accustomed to.

"I hoping you was coming, Missa Jason. How you is?"

His voice is different today. Softer in some way, and darker. Himself, I find myself thinking.

"I'm good," I tell him, though my clapped cock is nibbling at me. "How you do? You turn lawyer in truth? You working for Missa Alberga now?"

Lincoln laughs. "No, Missa Jason. The lady I working for make the food for him, so I come to help serve it."

I look over Lincoln's head and see my host—not exactly frowning, but clearly wondering why I'm chattering and smiling with a servant. I ignore him, enjoying the pleasure of Lincoln's regard. I take a jar from his tray and go inside.

Alberga manages a smile. "Catching up with old friends," he says, and I nod while taking his proffered hand. "That other matter will be back with you the end of the week," he says quietly. He means Miranda.

There are only men in the lawyer's living room, about fifteen of them. If Alberga had a wife there would be women too, but I never know him with a Missus. I don't know many of the men, but as I'm walking toward two I do recognize—Arthur Hollyoak and Joel Meyerlink, neither of who I see since Anthony is gone—I suddenly realize why I'm here: we is all slave owners. In all likelihood, Alberga would invite me anyway—I'm his old friend's son. But now he figure that with Miranda's transfer to myself I will fit into society better, never mind the strange work practices on Greencastle he must be hearing about.

Hollyoak and Meyerlink hear about them too, I can see it in their eyes. They don't hear about Miranda—yet. Nothing can stay secret for long in this place, though; is too small. And what make me really think about it is that them won't find it strange. Them will hear that she's a pretty brown gyal, and them will know why I buy her. Them talking about the parade of Set Girls in the town yesterday, and I get to understand that Hollyoak's mistress was leading the Blues. While I'm listening to the two brown men about this and that, in my head I'm thinking about my life. My whole life. Son of a slave, owning a slave. So blind in my putrid cock, I never really put those words in my head before. What will I do with the pickni—cause she's still something of that, never mind she see her blood Christmas before last. And she's almost, like Anna, my sister!

A theatrically cleared throat from the other side of the room disturbs my musing, and the conversation around. Everybody falls quiet. Old Ralston Penninger—who I don't see since Anthony's dinner party, and didn't notice was here at Alberga's—come out of a group of white men like he's stepping onto a stage. He has a sheet of paper in his hand that he waves at us.

"I've just got this from Governor Belmore, with a request that it be given as much broadcast as possible hereabouts." He clears his throat again and starts to read. "Whereas it has been represented to us that the slaves in some of our West Indian colonies, and of our possessions on the continent of South America have been erroneously led to believe . . ."

Right away I realize what he's reading. The proclamation that King William issued in the summer, just before I get Anthony's letter about Squire that trick me back to this cursed place.

". . . that orders have been sent out by us for their emancipation, and whereas such belief has produced acts of insubordination that have excited our highest displeasure . . ."

I'm wondering why the governor in Spanish Town is suddenly sending out this King's proclamation six months after it issue. But I don't have to wonder far. All the man-dem in this room already know about the proclamation, starting with Penninger. Himself and Hollyoak and Meyerlink talk about it at the same dinner party we was all at for Anthony's departure. The slaves would know of it too, the ones that can read. It was in all the papers in England, and I'm sure the same thing here. But they don't want to believe the King could be so wicked.

". . . the slave population in our said colonies and possessions will forfeit all claim to our protection if they shall fail to render entire submission to the laws, as well as dutiful obedience to their masters . . ."

The goodly governor in Spanish Town is giving new life to the old proclamation because of circumstance. The King in England—their friend, as a good many of them believe—set them free already. Plenty slaves believe that, even some on Greencastle, and despite what I tell them. There's disturbances in places out West despite this, as Lincoln tell me.

". . . to enforce by all the legal means in their power the punishment of those who may disturb the tranquility and peace of our said colonies and possessions."

Penninger harrumphs like a horse and looks around the room, rolling up his paper. His eye catches on mine and sharpens. I know what he's thinking. Is people like you and you friends that bring this about. I keep my face a slate until he looks away.

As though it's intermission at Drury Lane Theatre, Lincoln and his helpers start circulating with food and drink.

Beside me Hollyoak, who is attorney for a estate in West, says to Meyerlink, "The governor wait too long to warn the niggers. Trouble start already."

"The soldiers will take care of things," Meyerlink says, chirpy and confident.

Lincoln approaches us, and as I'm exchanging jars he looks over his tray up at me and gives a tiny nod, his old eyes solemn.

Penninger steps forward again, raising his voice. "Governor Belmore want each of us to read the proclamation to their slaves. Copies is on a table over there," and he points.

I cannot but think, in echo of Hollyoak, and interpreting Lincoln's sign, this won't make any difference.

113

Adebeh: New World, Tuesday, December 27

WE WAKE SLOW, IN COOL SHADOW. I know we's facing west, cause the sun, who just get up himself not too long, is on my back. Baddu and me find different trees to do our morning business behind, and then find ourself, without even a nod at each other, beside the trickle of a stream where we buried Petta yesterday. Plenty tracks in the river sand from overnight, but not from anything big enough to move the stones we put over her.

We's hungry. We study the water like it's the book of life. Nothing moves in it except the dancing light and the bush and trees reflected. Sister disappear into the bush and comes back with a handful of berries. "They sweet," she say, "but drink plenty water with them." We do, lapping straight from the river like dawg. Still, it's something to hold the two sides of your belly apart.

From habit, though, I's listening behind me for sounds, animal or human. I don't know which I'd prefer, cause a human sound might bring danger. A animal might bring danger too but it might also be something to eat. All we hear is birds.

Our eyes follow the water until it disappear between two big rocks, and then we hear it laughing down a steep hillside. Behind us is something like the country we's accustom to, especially Baddu, around Kojo Town. But what is ahead as we look down the hillside below is a new world.

I turn myself away from it. "Come," I say to Sister, setting off back up the stream to Petta's grave. There's tracks there that I get to know from Henry belong to wild pig. Maybe even more than one. They cross the stream and go back into the bush we came through. My belly is telling me to follow them there in the hope. But my head hold me back. Between us we have the two pieces of metal post from Belvedere, and Sister's pruning knife and digging stick. The knife would help with skinning and cleaning the pig, if we catch it, but the only other thing with a point is the digging stick.

So I take her piece of metal from Sister and go back to the two big rocks that the water leap over, leaving her beside Petta, which I know is hard, but may be a kind of comfort too. I don't know, nobody that close ever dead for me.

Getting energy from my hungry stomach, I start rubbing the metal against one of the rocks. The posts is old and crusted, and it's not too long before I'm handing Baddu a weapon that can jook or slash. Can kill anything, man or pig. Looking tenky at me, her eyes and cheeks is wet. She's not really seeing me. But I can't afford that, so I take her hand and we set off where the pig tracks lead. I figure that will take her thoughts off her friend, cause if we come upon anything, I need Baddu in full mind.

And not thirty yards into the bush we hear them. Grunting and snorting and squealing. A grown-up pig. And piglets. My stomach remembers from the Preston Kojo feasts that the babies have the sweetest flesh. If the grown-up is a mama we will have to get past her to the pickni. If he's a daddy pig, he will have tusks to tear us to pieces. No way to know, we can't see them. So we do the only thing that make sense. We rush them, where the sounds is coming from, screaming and yelling to high heaven. And it work! They was settled down in a hollow for the morning, three piglets and the mama feeding them. They wasn't expecting a disturbance. I almost feel sorry for them as they scamper away from us further into the bush, the little piglets dribbling milk. Almost.

Sister grab the nearest one and I grab the next. The little paws beat a tattoo of fury against we chest, but we don't even feel it, cause we wasn't letting go.

A while later, a hour or so, we's back on the other side of Petta's stream, Baddu gutting and skinning the piglets, me burying the entrails in the sand, deep as I can reach, so as not to bring any animals here to go after Petta. Then I set about getting a fire going. As I's gathering dry leaves and twigs as catchling, I's cursing Penzance and Mandeville for taking away my leather pouch with my flint. From Boydville, really, cause no Scotian living in the bush would leave home without something in his pack to make fire.

I ask Sister to throw me her digging stick, and I commence to rubbing it between my hands into a dry branch within the nest of leaves in the hope of getting a spark. The sweat is breaking out on my forehead and my jaws is cursing the two niggers back at Belvedere. When Sister sees what I's trying to do I hear her laugh, and then she's beside me on the other side of the stream. She ease me out of the way and fumble around under her skirts, still laughing.

A flint appear in her hand! She's lived in this bush longer than me, ranging all about. She know what to prepare herself for. And she wear plenty more clothes than me. I recognize the flint from Kojo Town, when she and Petta would cook whatever meat I managed to scrounge from the bush. So in two-twos we have a fire going, and two little pigs roasting above it on a spit.

I leave Sister to tend it and go back into the bush to find a little grove of plantain that we passed yesterday. I's listening out for the mama pig, in case she want to settle the score, but the ancestors is with me. My stomach was hoping I'd find a few ripe plantains to throw into the ashes under the spit and roast. They's all green, however, so I slice off five leaves from the tree and go back to find Sister with a big smile on her face. The pig is ready.

The first thing she do is slice a chunk of the pig's haunch, the sweetest part, and put it among the stones over Petta. For the bigi pripri to feed her with on the journey over. We take both pigs to the big rocks downstream, and sit down. As we's filling ourselves, hardly talking, we's thinking and looking about somewhere to hide the second pig. For tomorrow.

Because we can't turn back. Maybe by now Mandeville and Penzance get over their fear of Baddu's obeah, and have the dawg-dem sniffing and snarling their way after us. Now we's armed, that is true. But they will be also, and you never know with dawg.

So we's looking below into this place we's come to the edge of, trying to find a sign from the ancestors for what to do next. Below is the greenest place I ever see, even in this green island. With the most sugar cane. Is a valley with a decent-size river. And a big sugar works. But after Belvedere, we's fraid to go anywhere near a estate.

Belvedere change something in me, maybe Sister also. I's the same person, but it's like when you move something in a room, a piece of furniture or a painting. Just a little bit, and the whole place can look different. That's me. Yenkunkun is the same as every other black-people. But still, we's not exactly the same. We's different from the Loyalists in Scotia, we and they know that. And I's different from the blackpeople here—even the Yenkunkun-dem.

When I was a slave, though, even for just those few days, I realize that I's not so different after all. Just another nigger, as Mandeville like to call us. You have to hold on to youself tight, or they will make you think you's a animal. Cause when you find youself without any choice, you *is* a animal. And when they drop a switch on your skin, or make dawg growl at you like you's vermin, the way you feel come from the part of you inside that's ugly and raw.

We settle down where we find weself. Belly being full, we's soon drowsy. Before we let ourself sleep, though, Sister wrap the other pig in plantain leaves and bind a piece of vine around and shove it into a cleft in a sturdy tree nearby. For tomorrow. You couldn't do that in Scotia; squirrels would get it. But I don't see anything in the trees here except birds and some lizards.

It is so quiet and cool that we sleep-off easy. The sun wake us from the west, almost going down into sleep behind some soft hillsides. Below us, the valley is like a huge animal resting, the cane moving in the breeze a pelt of golden light.

We nibble some more of the first pig and watch the sun go down. We's thinking about what to do tomorrow, but we don't talk. "Dat's tomorrow's trial"—I hear Mam's voice. As the estate chimneys melt into the dusk we see two of the hillsides on the other side of the river bloom flames. Same time I feel Baddu quicken beside me.

She say something to herself that I have to ask her to repeat.

"Today is the day."

"What day?" I ask her.

"Judgement Day," she say. I hear a smile in her voice. I's thinking to myself, I never before hear a Christian word in Baddu mouth.

114

Narrative: Siddown, Wednesday, December 28

EARLY MORNING, BEFORE TIME BEGINS, is Jason's favourite time of the day. Even when it's raining; perhaps especially then, when he'd remember the pickni Kwesi, newly elevated to the big house from the leaking quarters.

And even when, like now, Pompey is standing in the doorway to the piazza, soaked to the skin and scowling. The few spectres drifting about the shadowy house behind Jason, far from the full complement usually getting the house up and running, ignore both men.

"Beg pardon, Missa Jason," the driver says, nodding, raising his hat. His voice is tight. "You haffe come."

Jason doesn't move. "What happen?"

"You haffe come, Missa Jason." Pompey's wet face and shoulders are streaked with red and green and blue from the Jonkanoo House, giving his presence a surreal urgency. "Trouble in the quarters, sah."

"What kind of trouble?" Jason is still sitting, his coffee mug on an arm of the chair he has made his own over the weeks.

"Come, Missa Jason, begging you pardon." Pompey, not at all apologetic, hooks his head, turns and starts down the steps.

"Where Busha is?" Jason calls out.

"At the quarters, sah."

This pulls Jason to his feet.

Often he shares this dawn hour with Mathilde, also an early riser. He brings her up to date on what is happening on the estate, since he knows she writes to Anthony. This morning, however, she sleeps late, for which Jason is grateful. It's the morning when the break for Christmas ends and the slaves go back to work. There'll be a day-off on Sunday for the new year but the drive to take off the crop begins today. Jason is uncertain how his piece-work scheme will help or hinder that process, and knows Cumberbatch and Simpson will want to revert to the old ways, with long days driven by the whip. The trouble Pompey speaks about likely has to do with that.

Jason isn't fully dressed, but nowadays he puts on his boots and carries Squire's hat as he leaves his room for the morning. He is glad for both today. The rain is insistent and cold, shrouding the world, but, hatless and purposeful, Pompey strides ahead to the quarters, silent. Jason is mystified. Lincoln's pre-Christmas warning is in mind, but he sees Teckford on his donkey leading a line of people, slow-moving through the rain but walking without fuss toward Breadfruit Tree field. Hope Come Over, where Pompey used to be driver, and Sambo Ireland now rules, is bristling with activity within its dense rows of cane. The third field, Tankwell, Creole Scotty's domain, Jason cannot see yet.

As they round the sugarhouse, Jason sees ahead to the big guango tree, Old Man, under which the slaves muster for the morning roll call. There's a small crowd there. A few sitting, most standing quietly under the spread of branches for shelter. All are watching the approach of Pompey and himself.

But from their other side two figures, Cumberbatch and Simpson, come galloping fast.

Jason stops and waits for them.

"Mr. Pollard!" Cumberbatch shouts from several yards away, and throws himself off his horse. He stumbles, propelled by his obvious anger to within feet of Jason. Who notices two things right away. The overseer is not carrying his customary riding crop; and he stinks, of morning breath untempered by chewstick, and of rum-soaked clothes in which he obviously slept. Simpson, still on horseback over the overseer's shoulder, is trying to look as fierce.

"Yes, Mr. Cumberbatch."

"The niggers are in rebellion!" He blasts Jason with foul air.

Jason, despite an abrupt awareness of a cold breath that chills more than his skin, looks around with a theatrical nonchalance. "I see Negroes, Mr. Cumberbatch, but none of them seem to be in rebellion."

"They won't work!" Another blast from the cesspool that forces Jason back a step, but only one. Cumberbatch is pointing at the group of slaves under the tree.

"They're just standing there, Mr. Cumberbatch. That doesn't look like rebellion."

"They say they're free," Simpson chimes in, his own reddened eyes summing up his Christmas break.

"They took away my whip!" Cumberbatch shouts. "And laid hands on me!"

Jason tries not to smile at the Biblical turn of phrase from this stale-drunk backslider.

And notices, behind Cumberbatch and Simpson, two people detach themselves from the group under the tree to join Pompey: Creole Scotty, the sub-driver for Tankwell, and Pheba. They circle around the white men and approach from Jason's left side.

"Begging pardon, Busha," Pompey says, raising his hat as he nods to Cumberbatch, and then addressing Jason. "You also, Missa Jason."

"This one too!" the overseer shouted suddenly, stepping toward Pompey. "I tell him to beat that other one"—here pointing to Creole Scotty—"and he don't do a thing!"

"Missa Jason."

"And he have his whip right there in his hand."

"Missa Jason."

"Be quiet, Cumberbatch," Jason snaps, before the overseer can interrupt again. "Yes, Pompey."

"I did have the whip, yes, Missa Jason. But if I did make after Scotty with it him woulda kill me, sah." Jason looks at Creole Scotty in time to catch the last wisp of an apologetic smile: he would have.

"And him"—Cumberbatch's finger is a quivering arrow at the sub-driver—"take away my whip. Imagine!"

"He lick me with it, sah," Creole Scotty said calmly to Jason, ignoring the others. "You say no whip is to use on Greencastle, don't it, Missa Jason?"

Jason nods distractedly. Whips are still carried in the field by all those in authority, even the sub-drivers. But since the incident in the first days of Cumberbatch's incumbency they have not been used. Until, apparently, this morning.

Jason turns to the overseer. "Did you?"

"He refused to go into the field."

"Did you hit him?"

"Yes, he refused . . ."

"He was going hit me again, sah." Creole Scotty's voice is quiet but firm.

Pheba speaks for the first time. "Scotty never hit Busha back, Jason." Her voice is crisp in its contained bitterness. "He only tek way Busha whip and give it to me. See it here."

She holds it out to Jason, which drives Cumberbatch close to apoplexy. "You hear that? 'Jason'! I don't call you 'Jason'. They warn me . . ."

"They warn you what, Cumberbatch?" Jason, voice curt, sighs inwardly. He knows the answer to his question.

"That is the niggers who run this estate."

"Cause I'm a nigger myself. Did they warn you of that?"

The overseer's outrage shatters, and through the opaque screen of hangover bluster, he glimpses a likely fate that reduces him to a stutter.

Jason takes the whip from Pheba and turns to Creole Scotty. "So why you not in the field, Scotty?"

"We tired to be cattle, Missa Jason, sah."

The calm directness of the man momentarily disarms Jason. "You isn't cattle, Scotty. None of you." His own voice sounds like a gourd.

"But we's not free, Missa Jason."

The lawyer is on the verge of correcting the driver on choice of pronoun but catches himself. "No, Scotty, you not free. One day maybe, in God's good time."

Cumberbatch comes back to life, drawing ostentatious breath, but Jason cuts him off. "It will happen, Mr. Overseer, and neither you nor I can stop it."

"They will kill us," says Simpson, speaking for the first time, almost a squeak.

"Quite possible, Simpson. In fact, very possible."

The rain has stopped by then, and shafts of weak sunlight—Maasa God's finger, the slaves call it—silver the trees and the sugar-cane spears. It'll be a hot day.

"We want to be free now, Missa Jason." Pheba is as businesslike as before, but her tone is civil.

"We cannot serve two Maasa, sir," Creole Scotty says. "Maasa God himself say so in the book of Matthew."

Jason smiles. "I didn't know you was a Christian, Scotty."

The burly driver's reddish skin brightens with discomfort and pride. "Yes, sah." He looks shyly at Pheba beside him.

"I take him to my chapel, Missa Jason, but he don't too like it. Then he follow Mingo to Zion in town. Miss Elorine teach him to read and write. He go there almost every Sunday now, even without Mingo. He will soon baptize." Her pleasure is a personal one.

Pompey chuckles. The streaks colouring his skin, relics of the model of Greencastle he carried as his emblem for Jonkanoo two days before, are fading. "Him change him ways, Missa Jason. Since Pheba ketch hold of him. Him hold prayer meeting every week in fe-dem yard." The head driver's soft laughter is not entirely mocking.

Creole Scotty is likely the father of at least one of the children Jason saw with Pheba on their first encounter after return. He is struck yet again by his distance from the quarters. The Greencastle landscape, so familiar and almost comforting one moment, is utterly strange the next. He's brought back to himself by the overseer climbing onto his horse and galloping off, followed like a tail by the bookkeeper. They could be going to the fields or to the big house.

The trio of slaves, hats in hand, wait for Jason's next word.

"I cyaant free you," he says, his lawyer's mind at least partially relieved. "You belong to Maas Anthony, not to me."

Lawyer or not, he's not entirely surprised by Creole Scotty's next statement. "We will wait for him, Missa Jason."

The three nod respectfully, replace their hats. Pompey retrieves his mule tied to a Seville orange tree nearby and rides toward Breadfruit Tree. Pheba and her babyfather turn and walk away, back toward the group under the guango tree.

Jason takes a final look at the cluster around the tree and turns toward the big house.

115

Jason: Doing Something, Wednesday, December 28

BY TIME I REACH BACK TO the big house everybody is up and doing. And they know what is happening in the quarters and the fields. That knowledge is plain in the faces of Mathilde and Anna, who is having first morning bickle in the piazza. I want only to go upstairs and shed my damp clothes, but before I can shout for Jack, Mathilde beckons me.

"You has trouble, Jason." No twinkle in her eye today. "Ze slaves rebelling, eh." It's not a question.

"They's striking," I say. "Some of them. Not all." I'm trying to sound nonchalant but not succeeding.

"Striking?"

"Striking what?" asks Anna, as puzzled as her mother. "Who? You mean they fighting each other?"

I realize the very word is foreign to them. I'm searching for a simple explanation when Mathilde interrupts.

"Cumberbatch say ze niggers is uprising. Simpson tell us you turn Greencastle over to ze niggers. Iss true Jason?"

"That is not true," I say, angry at the two white men who know their best audience.

"I did know it would come to this," Anna says, scathing, dismissive.

I feel my control fracturing. Behind their slate eyes I sense their thoughts: the same as Cumberbatch. One of them. Useful in a emergency. But not dependable. Blood will out. Blood indeed! Bile rise up in my craw. I'm thinking, theirs! But I keep my eyes hooded, and don't allow them to leave Mathilde's.

"So what you going to do, Jason?"

"I going to change my clothes, have some more coffee, and then go back to the fields." I keep my voice civil, though I'm not feeling so at all. I turn my head and shout, "Jack!" By the time I turn it back, Mathilde is standing, stiff with fear and hostility.

"What you going do? When you get to the field."

"Get them back to work."

"How?" Anna demands.

"Not with that drunken pair and their whips, I can promise you that."

"So how?" they chorus.

I couldn't resist the laugh rising through the bile. "I'll talk them back to work." I didn't believe it myself but I'd be damned if I'd let them see inside me.

Mathilde didn't laugh. "Well, we will has to do something. Something not a joke."

To contain the rising tide of furious words within, I could only walk away into the house, calling again for Jack. As I'm walking up the stairs with him I hear Anna call-out for Malachai, who goes with her when she's off the estate.

But when I come back down, after I wipe myself dry and get into the clothes Jack set out, I hear Anna's voice in the room where Prudence and Miranda work, quarrelling. I don't hear Mathilde. Maybe she's gone out somewhere. Though I didn't hear her carriage from upstairs, I hear a horse. However, Mathilde would not ride a horse, and there would be another horse in such an unlikely case—a male slave would certainly ride with her.

But I don't think too much about that. Jack is waiting with a big mug of coffee in one hand and a cloth with some warm journey cakes in the other.

As I take them he whispers to me, "Miss Delphis say to have a word with her, Maas Jason. Please."

So I walk out to the kitchen, stepping light and listening carefully for Mathilde out there. Generally she calls Constancia into the house to give instructions for the day, but every now and then she goes outside herself. But all the voices I hear is black, so I go into the kitchen.

Constancia is sitting by one of the two window in the place, catching a little ease before the day's hard work begin. Two young gyal whose names I forget standing over the stove fixing breakfast for later. The salt herring and tomatis and onion tickle my tongue, so I bite into a journey cake to quench the hunger.

Constancia call out to me, "You hungry, Missa Jason? Food nearly ready." I tell her no, the dumplings will do me for now.

From I know her Constancia always have a little piece of stick chewing on. I don't know what bush it is but her breath is always sweet. Mixed-up with her cooking smells, she is the one part of Greencastle I sometimes stumbled over in England, in dreams or when I step into a tavern.

She takes the little stick out of her mouth and calls me over.

"Lincoln say to tell you he gone. Yesterday."

"He tell me when he was going, Miss Delphis." Her eye is wet, both the blue-blind one and the normal. "I miss him too," I say.

A thought flames in me that I could claim Constancia as my second inheritance from Squire's will, but it dies just as quick. She has served as long and as faithfully as Lincoln, and deserves freedom. But this would disrupt the household too much. There's no alternative in the kitchen. It would be spiteful of me, and would damage, perhaps irreparably, all relations with the Pollard family.

She turns to look through the window into the little courtyard that she and Lincoln share and says something. When I don't respond, because I don't hear clearly, she says it again. I draw closer and put my own head through the window.

"Miss Anna send that facety red-bwoy with a letter Missus write." Her tone is caustic.

I understand right away that she talking about Anna's Malachai, who indeed thinks himself a big cut above even the other house slaves.

Before I can say anything she continues, "I don't know what is in the letter but the gyal-pickni who sew the clothes for you, Prudence daughter, she come out here for some tea for Miss Anna and say Miss Anna send the red-bwoy riding to Cascade to get the soldier-dem. The gyal-pickni say I must tell you that. I hardly have anything to do with Prudence, much less her daughter. So when the pickni say I must make sure and tell you, is important."

My head is spinning. A child-like pleasure that Miranda would think to warn me.

Uncertain over what she's warning me about, and about what I'm about to do out in the field, I mumble a tenky.

Constancia puts the piece of stick back in her mouth and resumes chewing on it as she speaks out the window, knowing I'm listening. "Me just a old Guinea Nayga, Missa Jason. But me know Backra. And me know Nayga. You have to watch both of them, eh, Missa Jason? Both." She points a crooked black finger at me. "You have to watch dem, specially."

She's said what she called me here to say. Maybe she's remembering Lincoln and the days when they would sit out there in the evening and talk about the world.

"I will watch meself, Miss Delphy," I say to her. "Tenky." I squeeze her nearest shoulder.

"You sure you don't want some bickle? Is a hard road today, Missa Jason."

So she knows too. Everybody knows. By now, maybe even Magnus Douglas knows.

≋ 116 ≋

Elorine: Navel Tree, Wednesday, December 28

SAKE OF JASSY I MISS THE EXCITEMENT in town yesterday. I did plan to go and see Francine parade in her queen frock that I make for her, but I don't think she miss me. Me, I only miss the seeing of the parade on Charles Street. By the time Courtney Waterman finish telling me about it last evening, after all the excitement of Jassy pickni is over and Mother Juba gone home, I feel like I was there myself. Francine will rule over the other brown gyal-dem for the next year, and Backra Pennington can boast that he have the prettiest one in his bed. Everybody happy.

I'm happy too. People will ask her and she will tell them who make her dress and crown. Business will come. More troubles too, but that is part of business.

Trouble is part of life. Courtney come back today around lunchtime, to warn me not to go into town even if I have to. The militia is mustering, he say. And his friend Royston Morris, who is a guard at the courthouse, say that they send message to Fort George for the soldier-dem to be ready to march into town. Royston cyaant tell him the reason, what happen. Backra always nervous at Christmas time, and maybe something happen in truth. Either on a estate or in town itself.

I send Courtney to the workshop to tell Pappi. If there is a muster it could bring plenty worries for him. This time, with almighty Magnus Douglas so big in the militia and the vestry, and watching Pappi like a chickenhawk, they might force him to march up and down with them.

Courtney don't come back to me, but I don't hear any change in what Cyrus and Ishmael doing outside. Whatever that might mean, I take his uniform out of his cupboard and hang it in my room where I put the dresses waiting for collection or delivery. Near the window so it will smell fresh.

My nose catch a whiff of the cloths Juba and me use yesterday on Jassy. First thing as he come this morning to start the furnace I give them to Cyrus to burn. Ishmael could barely get his breakfast down, the way the air stink, but it faded by midday, except every now and then when the wind change. The little pong remind me to go outside and put some water on the baby navel tree in the yard.

Yesterday, after the baby was born, I show Cyrus where to dig the hole, close to the chapel. Near to mine. While he's holding the sapling I coil the navel cord from Juba around it, and we push the earth back into the hole with our feet and tamp it down.

I notice, as I'm about to pour a little water from the jar on the plant, that it's damp. Cyrus when he come this morning, must be. Which make me smile. Cyrus is so proud of himself he can hardly fit into his clothes. And never mind if she live and die a slave, Jassy's baby will always have a tree, and some civil orange from it, that belong only to her.

Even if she don't know it, Cyrus and me will know it.

117

Adebeh: On the Edge, Wednesday, December 28

WE HARDLY SLEEP LAST NIGHT FROM watching the fires. We count six in different parts of the valley.

And Sister, as we's watching, finally give up some of what she knows. Today the Christmas break come to a end. As she says, "Everybody in a bad mood today. Everybody. Backra Maasa, some of them been drunk for the three days and wake up vex, cause they head as heavy as jackfruit. Nayga don't drink much, most of dem. But dem vex to be going into the cane to bruck dem back."

Only this time, she say, some of the slaves will not be going into the field. A siddown, they call it here. We have strikes in Scotia, every now and then, in the little factories and workshops. Those employ mostly whitepeople, who generally want more money. A few blacks too, but they know better than to stop working, for any reason. Plenty other blacks is lining up outside to step into their place. When you have plenty of nothing, any little something is gold.

But the slaves here is not striking for wages. They don't get any! According to Sister, what they want is their freedom. Then they will want wages for their labour. And they will get it. They's no other labour around for the whitepeople to call in, like they do in Scotia.

But the slaves will have to get their freedom first. And they will have to take it by force. No whitepeople—neither in England, or Scotia, or here—will hand it to them just so. The King in England made that plain as water. A month or so before I get work on the *Eagle* a royal proclamation appear in the *Gazette* telling the slaves that they's definitely not free, whatever rumours they might be hearing. The King tell them to submit to their masters and the law. Here, like in Scotia, the master is the law.

From where Sister and me sat watching them, last night's fires seemed like torches held up by black giants. Maybe too, they's a sign from the bigi pripri. About what me and Sister is to do next.

"Stannup and deliver," we hear from behind us. Is a croak of a voice, could be man or woman.

We spring up and turn. A burnt stick of a man in tatters of clothing appear through the leaves as though they's forming him in our eyes. But he's pointing a long digging stick like a spear in our general direction, and a cutlass is in his other hand. Baddu bust a laugh before I could.

"Old man?" she say, cackling. "Me alone could draw the little blood you have leave in you, much less the two of we. Who you is?"

But Baddu isn't laughing now. Her own digging stick is in one hand and her pruning knife in the other.

The old man try a little smile like his lips just melted. "Cho, lady," he whine. "You don't have to go on like dat."

"How I must go on then?" Baddu is quietly moving closer to the intruder, holding her weapons up. My fence post is at the ready too.

The old brute laugh softly, showing all his six or so teeth. "Me passing and smell food, Missus," he say, "and me hungry."

Scrawny as he is, he's probably been hungry all his life.

"Puddown you things," Baddu say, stern. The old man obey. Sister open the plantain leaf we's been nibbling from, but she's holding her pruning knife alongside it. The old man take a few halting steps forward, looking from me to Sister to figure if it's a trap.

She break off a few ribs and hand them to him. He take them with a shy little bow and then retreat to a little mound of grass. In two-twos the ribs are clean. Sister give him a couple more. Same thing.

He belch like a bark. "Tenky, Missus." Then he smile, showing us his few teeth again. "You is Maroon, yes?"

Baddu couldn't help but smile back. "How you know?"

"The way you hold youself," he say, looking between Baddu and me. "But how come you don't grab-on to me to take me to Backra?"

His eyes are crafty, perhaps regretting the easy surrender of his weapons.

"We's not like that," I find myself saying.

"And you is Guinea," Sister say. His face has markings like some of the very old Loyalists in Nova Scotia have. And some of the black-people here.

"Mi poopa," he say. "I born ya-so. Kensington."

"What you name, old man?" she ask. Her voice is softer.

"Mi poopa name me Akeen," he say. "He tell me it mean brave. On Kensington they call me Morris, cause that is Maasa name."

"You's far from home, Fahder," Baddu say. "Kensington is near to where we come from. Kojo Town. What you doing this side?"

"I come to join the regiment," he say.

"What regiment, old man?" I's asking him.

"Backra-Maasa have regiment," he reply, calm as you please. "Him have militia too. Nayga need to have regiment too. You don't think?"

He's looking straight at me. In my head I can't help but remember the stories that Da tells, the stories that the leave-behind old-timers tell from deep in their cups of screech when they's full of juicy pig. Stories of ambush and hand-to-hand. That is the Yenkunkun way. Not marching and saluting and moving in formation, like the white soldiers in Halifax on the Citadel square. That is their way to make war, not blackpeople's.

So I ask him, "You have a regiment, old man?" I find my voice gentler also.

A candle in his eyes tells me there's a lot of faith in a regiment that don't even exist.

"Not yet," he say. "Is there I was heading."

"Where?" I ask.

"Great River," he say. "Here."

"Here name is Great River?" Is a stupid question in a way, cause apart from Bellefields and Kojo Town, and some of the places I pass through, I don't know anywhere in this island.

Akeen point over our shoulders. "Down there."

"Nayga have a regiment down there?" This is Baddu, voice rough again. She look out over the valley, her body stiff. She don't really expect to see anything—she's making a point at the old man. "Where?"

"You will see," Akeen say, the light back in his eye and his voice. "Daddy will be there, and his captains."

"Daddy?" I ask.

"Captains?" ask Baddu.

"Daddy Sam Sharpe." He say it as though he expect everyone to know Daddy Sharpe.

"I hear bout him," say Baddu, and glance at me. "A preacher man in Montego, don't it?"

Again, I's wondering how she can stay in Kojo Town and know so much about what is happening in Montego, two days away.

"Daddy Sharpe tell you to come here to him?"

Akeen bless us with a pitying smile. "Not exactly. He tell us first to siddown."

"So you siddown, old man?" I ask.

"Some of us harken to Daddy and siddown," he say, nodding.

Baddu: "When?"

"Yestiday. When me was a bwoy Maas Johnny fahder would give us three days clear after Christmas to enjoy weself and rest. But young Maasa don't believe in more than one day after Christmas. Him is wicked, worse dan him poopa."

"So you siddown yesterday?"

He nod. "Daddy say we shouldn't work for free. Not any more. We walk on two foot, not four like the beast-dem."

When you's black in Scotia you get to learn that some of us is slaves. Not a big number like here, but enough for me to know that the same whitepeople who own slaves pretend that slaves only live in the States. Enough for me to know that the paper in the pouch around my neck is worth more than frankincense and myrrh. And to know that, as old Akeen says, slaves in Scotia believe they walk on two feet, not four.

"What happen when you siddown?" I ask Akeen.

He laugh again. "They bring whip to we. Whip and dawg. Daddy say that if they do that, if they bring violence, then we's justify to smite dem hip and thigh. So we smite dem. We that siddown chop-up the dawg-dem. When the odder slaves to go out into the field see that we's serious, dem stop work too.

"Dat evening some of them go and burn down the trash house. Busha Overseer find himself lock-up in his own house. And when Maas Johnny go to look for his gun-dem where he always keep them, to shoot us, he find dem gone." Akeen cackle. "We's tired to be beast of the field. Maasa God mek de beast-dem on the fifth day. He make us on the sixth day, and give we dominion over de beast-dem."

He's not laughing now, and I see the anger and pain leeching into his old face like a stain. It make him suddenly younger.

And I's thinking that even Empress, a kindly old soul, would slit Cummings's throat if she was to get the chance. Mandeville and Penzance maybe not, cause without their pistols and dawg they's just another set of Nayga, like the rest. Empress, she know she's not chattel, even though born and grow a slave. I don't know who she worship, but she knows that she stannup on two feet, not four.

Others too. Some of the lowliest you could find, they's tired of being like the puss and dawg around the place, and treated worse than some of those. Even Billy, Cummings's cushion. Maybe that's why Billy ran into the bush in the first place. To be free.

Baddu: "So how you not still at Kensington, Fahder?"

He cackle again. "Big confusion when the trash house go up. The slaves from the big house running one way to help put it out, the sid-down slaves running anodder way to help it along, the Backra-dem on de property trying to whip everybody into line. Some guns firing, and everybody shouting and screaming. Me? Me just take myself careful out of all dat. Nobody even notice. Them won't miss me even today. Me just another Nayga wid a cutlass in the cane. But me remember what me hear from all about, that Daddy and his captains is in Great River with a regiment. So me find meself here."

Baddu chuckle at him. "Maybe you come to the right place, Fahder."

"How you mean?"

She explain about the fires last night, and we look into the valley. There's spirals of smoke down there, but there's new fires too, dancing.

Akeen clap his hands. "Hip and thigh, Daddy clap them. Yes." He get to his feet and goes back to collect his digging spear and cutlass. He's preparing now to find his regiment.

Sister and me look at each other, thinking the same thoughts. This is more than a siddown and a few fires.

"Missus," the old man say as he stand above us, ready to set off. "I can beg you a little bickle for de journey?"

Without hesitation Baddu hand him the plantain leaf with the rest of the first piglet. "Walk good, Fahder."

"You too, Missus. And sir." He show us his few teeth in a smile as wide as a ripe plantain, and heads off down the slope leading into the valley.

Sister wouldn't know about this, but I'm remembering the news on the Halifax docks as I'm looking for a ship coming to this island. In the Iron Dog drinking house where they gather, the blacks who work on the ships coming north from the slave states is raising a glass to someone name Nat Turner, who led a rebellion in Virginia that kill plenty whitepeople, and frighten the shit out of the rest of them.

Maybe that's what Sister and me find ourself on the edge of. So far we's just on the edge, but we have a decision to make. We could turn back and try getting back to Kojo Town by a way that avoids Belvedere and the dawg-dem. We could just go on there, minding we own sweet business until the ancestors find a way for us to go back to Scotia.

Or we could follow old bag-o-bones warrior.

118

Narrative: Soldier, Wednesday, December 28

IT'S AS THOUGH CHERRY KNOWS WHERE Jason wants to go without him directing her: to Old Man, where the edges of the three fields meet and the slaves assemble for roll call after the conch.

Or maybe Cherry smelled her friend, on whose large grey back Cumberbatch is perched, turned away from their approach. It's his horse, turning, that alerts the overseer. He's been contemplating the group of Negroes under the tree—fewer of them now, it seems to Jason.

Cumberbatch nudges his mount toward Jason, his face bright red under his hat. Jason remembers that he's left the man's whip, which Pheba presented to him, on his desk.

Cumberbatch is about to say something when Jason pre-empts him.

"I came to say to you, Mr. Overseer," his voice low, scathing, "that if there's any trouble on Greencastle today, I'll hold you and Simpson the cause of it."

"Me? Simpson?"

"Yes. The two of you."

"What kind of trouble?" His voice rises with his colour. "You have trouble already," and flings his hand behind him.

"You know the kind of trouble."

"How? I didn't refuse to . . ."

"If it come,"—Jason cuts him off, firm—"the two of you'll be sharing a table at Mrs. Grenville's, where I found you."

Cumberbatch is non-plussed, his mouth open. Without saying

anything more Jason brings Cherry around and rides off, ignoring the words he hears like fading birds behind him.

Under the guango tree most of the slaves, perhaps fifteen now, are sitting on the ground. Creole Scotty and Pheba lean against the trunk, looking like roots grown overnight. Pheba is patting Scotty's donkey. It's an almost domestic scene.

Jason approaches them with a smile. "You not out in the field yet, Scotty?"

"No, Missa Jason."

"But some of the gang is at Tankwell."

"Yes, sah. Jupiter watching them."

"Well, you better send tell him to watch out for soldier. And watch for them youself."

The driver's singular calm is shifted. He looks quickly at Pheba and then back at Jason's serious face.

"Soldier?" They are one voice. The men and women on the ground stand up and cluster restlessly behind Scotty.

It's his turn to be calm, though inside he is anything but. "I hear say—I don't know it for certain—but I hear up at the house say Missus send for soldier. Say you is rebelling."

Pheba recovers her composure, throws a sly smile. "Soldier far away in Fort George." Childhood lives uneasily behind the authority of the adult Jason. Pheba, older by a year, was often the saving intermediary between Jason and the peremptory, casual brutality of Pompey, and occasionally of Judith. In the field now, he doesn't show favour in word or deed, but is ever aware of their ties; so is she.

So he is firm, but gentle. "Is not the fort they will be coming from, Pheba," he says. "Missus send message to Cascade. Missa Douglas."

This information commands everyone's attention. They know Missa Douglas. Missa Douglas and Maas Anthony are good friends all their lives, they visit with each other quite often. And the slaves know about life on Cascade. Hector told them about it, where he'd been first just a slave, then a sub-driver for one of the fields, before being sold by one friend to another and ending up on Greencastle and inflicting Cascade ways on Greencastle slaves.

The slaves also know that Missa Douglas is a big Backra in the militia that musters once a month in Bellefields and marches with the soldiers when trouble breaks out. Like now. As magistrate and now, as vice-chairman of vestry, he is even more powerful in the district.

The men and women shift as through an invisible current. A few draw closer to Creole Scotty and Pheba; several move further away.

"Missa Douglas won't come alone," Jason says, looking directly at the driver. "He might not bring the soldier-dem, but he won't be by himself."

Scotty's eyes break from Jason's to glance at Pheba. Hers have been on Jason all the time, as he's aware.

She speaks evenly, placing her words like stones on the ground. "Maasa Jesus say, no man who put him hand to the plough and draw it back is fit to enter the kingdom of Heaven." She wraps her hand around the rope on the donkey's neck.

"You know what will happen to you," Jason says, hearing his voice rise as his eyes sweep the small group. He fights the impulse to dismount from Cherry and go over to Scotty and Pheba and—what? Drive them back to work? How? He doesn't even have the riding crop he usually carries, more from habit than for use on Cherry, who often follows her own path anyway. Besides, as Scotty himself had indicated, Christian or no, he'd as easily kill Jason as Pompey.

He remains on his horse, feeling as though the giant tree under which they are all standing might topple at any moment.

119

Adebeh: Decision, Wednesday, December 28

WE DIDN'T TALK LONG ABOUT IT. "Now for sure they have poster up in The Bay and Falmouth for me," Sister say, looking fierce. "We's free here," she say, tapping her own head, "but what happen to us week before last musn happen a next time."

I finger the pouch with my free paper around my neck. Baddu doesn't have any papers at all, she's only free to herself. So if one of the whitepeople was to stop us she would be arrested, and maybe me too, despite my papers with Major Maxwell's stamps. I wouldn't be so lucky as with the whiteman Cameron when I landed in Bellefields, who just happen to know Major Maxwell. If he didn't, I'd be still on the ship. That puts me in mind of Fergus. The *Eagle* must be sailed by now and me not on it. I make a quick prayer to the ancestors to keep Fergus from any harm on my account.

But before we do anything about finding this black regiment that Akeen tell us about, we study the valley from the little rise we's been on since Belvedere. Just as well. A troop of whitemen on horses and in uniform—militia, Baddu tell me—come splashing across the river from a place that look like a cattle pasture, and turn onto the road that we watched the old man take when he left us, in the direction that I figure to be south. The man leading them on a big chestnut horse he can barely control is wearing a blue tunic that look new, and his scabbard is glinting in the sun. They's galloping hard.

I wonder if they's setting off after the black regiment. Which mean that Sister and me should go in the other direction. Whether or not we do find the regiment is another matter, but it will have to be by a different way. In any case, we's both fidgety after so long in one place. So when the militia-men's dust settle back we go down into the valley.

I feel naked. The clothes I's wearing cover me, but they belong to a dead man, who used to be with Empress. With her permission I take the best of them when we's leaving Belvedere. He was bigger than me, but not by much.

They fit Sister better. She look like Mam but she don't inherit Mam's bubbies, so it's easy for her to bind them to her chest. And me, with her pruning knife, cut off her hair. Anybody passing would think she's a man. That is what we want.

We don't know what is waiting for us, but we decide that if it come to fighting, a woman soldier would draw attention. We's going among people who maybe know each other, and will know us as outsiders. Just like Akeen, somebody might recognize us as Yenkunkun. And they won't wait to find out if we's going to try and put hand on them to take them to the magistrate. They'll kill us first.

Once we's on the road, though, hardly anybody notice us. We know that we want to find this black regiment that Akeen was talking about, but we don't really know where even to start looking. All he said was Great River, and this is a big valley.

The road we's on, running between canefields with borders and ditches, is as wide as a public road. Smaller roads is coming from almost every direction through the cane. Is like eeny meeny miney mo . . . This time, though, is not a children's game. The niggers that get catch by their toe might be Sister and me.

We encounter quite a few blackpeople on the move, only a few working in the fields. So the siddown must be reach here also. The ones that pass us—mostly going in the same direction as the militia, which is curious—they's not sneaking through the bush. These Negroes walk about like they own the air. Every now and then one of them is carrying a gun. I know that some slaves is hunters for their master's table, but these isn't looking for birds. And a few of them is wearing uniforms that look somewhat like those the militia-men we watched have on.

"Dey tief dem from Backra," Sister whisper to me in a giggle after we pass a particularly splendid specimen, accoutered in a new red coat and, instead of a sword like the militia leader, a wicked-looking cutlass, its blade silver-shine, hanging naked from a leather loop around his waist. He stepping smart like he's marching in a parade. He not as old as Akeen, but he not off by more than a few years.

As I look into the hopeful, determined eyes of the faces passing us, some of whom give us a howdy, I say a prayer—to Baby Jesus this time—that this Daddy Sharpe is a honourable man and not another black trickster. That he leading these pious, brave, believing-in-freedom men out of their own darkness. Not deeper into it.

120

Jason: Rebel, Wednesday, December 28

BETTER SCOTTY AND PHEBA HAD GOT UP this morning and decided to be rebels outright. Fire the fields, or the sugarhouse like that fool at Richambeau, or even fire the big house itself. And then run off into the mountains. That is how rebellion is supposed to go, that is what Backra understand.

They don't understand siddown. Something like siddown frightens the shit out of them. And when Backra gets frighten, Nayga have to watch out for himself.

Scotty and Pheba supposed to know that. But they is Christians. They's looking up in the sky, waiting for Jehovah's truth and justice to descend on them, or take them up to the angels, or something. Truth and justice did descend. But it was Backra's Truth, and Backra's Justice, and it fall on them like the old guango they's still standing under when Magnus arrived just before lunchtime.

As I warned them, he isn't alone. He's dress-up in his militia uniform, epaulettes and braid and a sword. Behind him is four white men in old red coats that is clean and recently pressed but threadbare and streaked with sweat from riding in the midday sun. Magnus's sword is slapping against his leg and the over-weighted horse, but the others have guns strapped across their chests.

All this I am seeing from behind them, riding back from Tankwell, Scotty's field, where the other men and women are working. Not the full gang and no one apparently in charge, but they know what to do anyway. I'm trying to decide what to tell Cumberbatch and Pompey—whether to drive full day from now until crop-over, without the whip, or stay with the piecework—when I see Magnus and his troop ahead of me. They're coming from the direction of the house and they know where they're going, of course. Magnus is very familiar with Greencastle.

There is no way to warn Scotty and his small group but I dig my heels into Cherry with unaccustomed vigour and ride her as hard as I can. Not to warn Scotty and his little cohort, now down to four, but to reach them ahead of Magnus. Which I do, just barely. As I pass them, one of the men is untangling a whip from his rifle strap. Scotty and Pheba see me coming and is looking from Magnus to me, waiting to see the excitement. Still, they show no sign of moving from under the tree.

I swing Cherry to come between Magnus and the slaves, forcing them to stop. He didn't see or hear me, and wouldn't have bothered watching the slaves' eyes. So he's surprised. And irritated. His frog jowls puff out, almost swallowing his eyes.

"What are you doing here?" I ask him, careful not to be belligerent.

"I was sent for," he says, growling like a watchdog.

"By who?" I keep my tone civil.

"That's none of you business, Pollard."

I look him up and down and glance at this four companions. "The militia is mustered? No one came to tell us."

"It will be," he yaps. "As soon as I get to town."

"Well, continue your way there," I say. "You have no right here until then."

"The owner invited me. There's rebellion."

I'm so tight inside, I'm grateful for his jibe. I allow myself a mocking laugh while looking over to the tree at Scotty and his pathetic little band, one of them a pickni. With the same exaggerated glance I take in the fancy-dress-up men with him. Two of them have their guns at the ready, resting across their saddles, the other two with whips in hand.

"I don't see rebellion, Douglas. I don't see the owner either." Magnus make to say something but I don't give him a chance. "We don't use whip on Greencastle again, and we only use gun to shoot bird and wild pig."

The slaves are behind me but I can feel them. Magnus is facing them, and what he sees make him vex.

"What they doing here? Is middle day. They should be cutting cane. Is . . ."

Vex catch-up in me like a blaze, and I let it out at him. "I don't tell you how to run your estate so don't tell me how to run mine."

"Is not your estate." He is Backra magistrate johncrow, now, speaking to a coloured.

"For now it's as good as mine. And I'm telling you that you and you friends is not welcome here. Please leave." I realize from glancing at them that they are probably his employees on Cascade, so I've made another four enemies.

But after a moment they wheel their horses around. Magnus, the last to turn, fires a parting shot, whetted with a sly insidious grin. "The higher you climb up the tree, Pollard, the more I can see you ass."

He spurs his horse before I can even think to say anything. In any case my anger at him is already fading. I turn Cherry the other way. They could be a single lump of flesh with five heads and ten eyes, all fixed on me. I recognize Mingo, a member of Ishmael's chapel, who is doing his best in the sugarhouse since Tombo's gone. And Pheba's friend from that long-ago Sunday, who I come to know as Christian Eddie. Clinging to her is a gyal-pickni of about ten; she should be in the pickni gang.

There's a moment of sympathy as I look at them dwarfed by the massive guango. But it's swept away by a stronger urge.

"Missa Douglas not gone far. You know that." My voice is raucous. Scotty and Pheba nod. "He mark you face." They nod again. "And those he don't mark, he will get from Backra Cumberbatch. You know that." Another nod, all of them now, even the pickni.

"You is rebels," I say. "They will hang you."

But perhaps they see my fear. Scotty says, "We cyan runway, Missa Jason. But that is not free. Maroon, an Backra dawg-dem, an every Nayga out there in bush would be hunting we like we is wild pig."

"Better we dead here," Pheba says.

And Eddie adds, pulling her daughter closer, "We don't fraid to dead, Maas Jason. Missa Douglas haffe dead too, by-and-by."

I have no answer for that.

More quietly I say to her, to them, "If you's still here when he come back next time, you will dead long before him, Eddie."

Pheba steps forward and comes right up to Cherry's flank. "Missa Douglas will try to take you with him too, Kwesi. For Backra, you is rebel too. Just like us."

She speaks privately, beyond the ears of her comrades, to put into words the worm that's been wriggling in my intestines all morning, from Pompey first summoned me.

121

Narrative: A Reckoning, Wednesday, December 28

MATHILDE: Magnus say you send him away, Jason.

JASON: I did.

ANNA: Why?

JASON: He was trying to tell me how to run the estate.

MATHILDE: Somebody need to tell you. You iss doing foolishness.

JASON: Maybe so, Mathilde. If you want Douglas to run Greencastle, I'm sure Alberga can arrange it. I'll go tell him myself.

ANNA: He make my skin crawl.

JASON: You same one send for him.

MATHILDE: I tell her to zend for him.

JASON: To do what?

MATHILDE: To get ze slaves back to work.

JASON: He was ready to shoot them. Dead people cannot work. Besides, there's only four of them now. And a pickni.

MATHILDE: Ze rest iss working?

ANNA: Everybody must work. Is crop time.

JASON: They know is crop time.

MATHILDE: So zey must work. Everybody.

JASON: Only four people is not working. The crop will be taken off.

ANNA: Not if you keep up with you piecework foolishness. Dem will disappear to get out of the hard work.

JASON: If you had to cut cane for twelve hours every day in the sun you would disappear too. Or drop dead from it.

MATHILDE: Jason! Zat is very rude.

JASON: But it's true.

ANNA: You might as well give all the slave-dem free paper.

JASON: If they was mine, I would. Tomorrow.

MATHILDE: And vhat vould happen here? Zey would leave.

JASON: Maybe some of them. Most don't have nowhere to go. They would stay. But you'd have to pay them.

MATHILDE: But zey's slaves!

JASON: Not if I give them their free paper.

ANNA: And dem would sleep all day.

JASON: Maybe. Them is very tired.

MATHILDE: I vish Anthony vas here.

JASON: Me too.

ANNA: Dis wouldn happen.

JASON: You right. Him and Magnus would shoot Scotty and them.

MATHILDE: And everybody vould be working every day.

JASON: Except Scotty and them. And the others.

ANNA: What others?

JASON: If anybody shoot anybody, you would have a uprising. Not only at Greencastle.

MATHILDE: Zat is foolishness. Ze militia and ze soldiers vould stop that foolishness.

JASON: Maybe. Maybe not. Some time, by-an-by, a uprising will come that can't be stopped.

MATHILDE: You vant Hayti here?

JASON: No. But slavery is doomed.

ANNA: But you same one have a slave, Maasa Jason. Is that you don't feel anybody else must have slave?

MATHILDE: Vhat you iss talking about, Anna?

ANNA: Him must tell you. Him buy a pumpum for himself.

JASON: I didn't buy her. And—

MATHILDE: Who?

ANNA: Prudence daughter. The Miranda-one.

JASON: Is not for that, Mathilde. Anna is bad-minded.

MATHILDE: So, Jason. You iss not as goot and holy as you think, eh? You iss not the saint you make yousself. Eh?

JASON: I never say I'm a saint.

MATHILDE: Never say so, no. But you look at us so.

ANNA: Like we is Nayga, and you alone white.

JASON: That is not true. How I could be white? Tell me that.

ANNA: You think you white. Poppa send you to England and you mix-up with whitepeople till you think you is one of dem.

MATHILDE: And you come back here wit your foolish ideas.

JASON: I come back here because you all entice me back here. You all did know Anthony was going to Virginia when he write to tell me Poppa was calling for me. You all know that would bring me.

ANNA: He was calling for you.

JASON: Maybe. But maybe you should've give Greencastle to Magnus to run. From then. You would be happy now.

MATHILDE: Magnus iss a beast.

JASON: So you send for a beast to kill-off the other beast-dem.

MATHILDE: You hass become a beast youself, Jason.

JASON: I was born a beast, remember? A slave. The one who think him is white enough to have slave?

ANNA: What you going to do with her? Tek her back to England with you?

MATHILDE: Mek her free? Like all de odders you want to mek free?

JASON: Maybe.

ANNA: Well, you better do one or the other with her.

JASON: Why?

ANNA: De gyal facety-off to me this morning. I tell her to sew up something for me this morning and she tell me right back that she don't have to do anything anybody but you tell her. Is you tell her that?

JASON: No. I tell her the opposite. That she must continue to obey you. Both of you. Even Balfour.

ANNA: Well, she gone well past that now. Her mother-self cyan hardly control her.

JASON: I will speak to her.

ANNA: You better do more than that.

MATHILDE: Whip her.

JASON: I will not whip her.

MATHILDE: Iss de only ting dey understand.

ANNA: Generally she do what I tell her, I don't have to beat her yet. I box her this morning, though. She too rude. I send her to the kitchen to get me tea. To show her who is who. She go, but she tek a long-long time to come back.

JASON: I will speak to her. But please don't box her again.

MATHILDE: So what iss we to do with her, Jason?

JASON: Talk to her.

ANNA: You fucking her in true.

JASON: I am not. But I will speak to her. There will be no more trouble.

MATHILDE: You want no more trouble, Jason, you better fuck her.

122

Elorine: Born fe Dead, Wednesday, December 28

MOSTLY, NAYGA GLAD FOR A BABY when it come. But they fraid for it too. Baby is coming from the world beyond the flesh, the world we all go back to when we die. That world have good and bad spirits, just like this one. Nobody knows which one the baby is, cause the journey from that world to this don't finish when it's born. So they leave the mother and the baby by themself for a week. Plenty babies don't even make it all the way into this world beyond a day or two. They's so flimsy, like breeze could blow them away, or two fingers could snap them like a dry branch.

Mother Juba tell me, when she go home after Jassy born her baby, that she will come back in seven days, when the baby form itself, as she call it. "Then we can give it a name and drink some rum and roast some corn and plantain and yam. Jassy bubbies have plenty milk for the baby," she say.

But I remember the stories Mama Sel tell me more than once. Adam is a strapping man now, almost as big as Pappi. But when he was just born and the Nana tell everybody to leave them alone for seven days, Adam nearly dead, Mama too. The day they name Adam was the day they nearly had to bury him. They both needed food, she tell me, the mother most of all. Then she always looked at me and laugh. "You was a hungry baby and I was a hungry mother. But I make sure that I get food from Alice, who was here then." She laugh some more. "Dem Guinea ways will kill you."

I remember those stories. So, I make sure Jassy always have food. I boil a big yabba of soup, with beef bones Christian get from Setty at the market (I tell him to tell his mother I'm sending him to deliver clothes). Twice every day, lunchtime and dinner, I take some out to her. Most times I see the baby latch-on to her bubby like the vise out in the workshop. It is finding something to eat there, that's for certain. And Jassy eat like one of the horse-dem that Pappi sometimes keep overnight.

Despite that, though, her baby sicken and die. Not from hungry, cause it wasn't sicky-sicky. And no matter what Nayga have it to say, it wasn't a bad spirit. Is mostly a quiet baby, only crying when is hungry.

This time, though, the baby didn't wait till it was convenient.

Jassy come at me out of the night like a spirit herself, frighten me near to death. "Baby dead, Miss Elly," she whisper at me, two-three times as she is shaking me awake. She'll soon be wailing, I know, and wake up Pappi and everybody on the street, so I sit up quick and hold on to her.

"You sure?"

She could only nod. Poor thing, she frighten till she can't find words. Jassy can be scatterbrain sometimes, but she surprise me with how much attention she give the little baby. So I know she is very likely right.

I light a candle and we make our way to her room outside. The night air chill my skin. The baby is lying naked on the floor. It look like one of those dollies I have when I was a little girl. Still. No part of it is moving.

"What you do to it?" Right away I realize I ask the wrong question in the wrong voice.

"Nothing, Miss Elly. Nothing." The girl start to cry. "I never do it anything, Miss Elly."

I tell her sorry, that I wasn't saying she do the baby anything, and ask her how she come to know it was dead.

"I was sleeping, Miss Elly. And I kinda wake up and don't hear it like I'm custom to, making little noise like Ginger sometimes. I stretch out me hand to touch it face and it was cold like a stone. I frighten and jump up and take off all it clothes and put me head down on it.

I don't feel or hear a thing, Miss Elly, it only cold like a stone." She start to bawl now, and I have to put the candle down and hold her and tell her hush to make her keep it down.

It was moonlight outside, so with the candle the room seem bright, and the baby is just lying there on the little pile of cloth that Jassy keep it on beside her palette. I look around. Somehow it seem that the room should look different now, from when I see it this afternoon. But the same little pile of dust and scraps is in one corner that Juba sweep-up when she come first, and tell me not to throw out till the baby have a name. The pile of cloth that Jassy get from me is smaller now, but is still in the same place under a window. The room even smell the same, of piss and doo-doo and sour milk.

But the baby is not the same.

A big fraid suddenly take me by the throat and won't let me breathe. Maasa God must know why the baby dead, but still and all dead is bad luck and worse. And is the middle night, so we cyaant do anything for it now, even bury it. I force two-three breaths down my throat and say to Jassy, "Come inside with me. You cyaant stay out here by youself."

I feel her stiffen. She's frighten at what happen, but she really don't want to leave her baby out here by itself. Still, she don't want to stay out here either. I'm by the door with the candle when I hear her call at me. "Look, Miss Elly."

A piece of moonlight fall through the window onto the floor like a blanket on the child. A blessing, as I see it, Jassy too. We latch the door behind, and find our way back to my room.

But at least the baby is not all by itself. That is a comfort to both of us.

≈ 123 ≈

Jason: Talking to, Thursday, December 29

I DON'T HAVE A CHOICE. Being as I promise Anna and Mathilde that I would, I send Jack for Miranda.

And it's while I'm sitting at my table waiting for him to bring her back that it occur to me that is him, Jack himself, not Miranda, who tell them downstairs. He must be listen at the door when I was talking to her the other night. He belong to Mathilde, not to me. She tell her mother, yes, I couldn't really expect otherwise. But I don't think is Miranda herself that throw her situation in Anna's face. The change in the girl is because of the change in her position. Poor girl, maybe she think I would be able to protect her.

That is why I need to talk to her. Like a owner, God help me!

When she and Jack come in, right away, before I say a word to Miranda I send him off.

"Go look and see if Scotty and Pheba is still under Old Man," I tell him. "Even if they back at the quarters, tell them I want to see them at the steps. Right away."

He look at me with his little smile. He think I'm sending him far because I want time to fuck the girl, like he thought the first time I send him for her. But I don't care what he's thinking. I nod my head curtly and he disappear through the door.

I'm trying, as I turn it to her, to keep the sternness in my voice that I speak to Jack with. But it's like water running off me when I look at her. Poor thing, she look like a wet puss, hair plastered to her head. She seem to just finish bathe, and never have time to dry herself properly before Jack came to fetch her. That is what one eye see. The other eye, though, see a flower.

The room downstairs where I slept before England catch the sun as it first comes over Flambeau, even before it reach down like a hand into the fields. When I was a bwoy, sometimes I would wake up before everybody and go outside in the foreday.

Anthony's mother had flower beds planted right around the house and Squire had somebody keeping them up after she dead. Them is gone back to rubble now, but I remember them. That time of day, the dew is still on whatever's blooming, and if you look close at the drops of water you see the veins on the leaves and the flowers magnified. That is how my eye is looking at Miranda. Or maybe is really the eye in my cock.

I try to reassemble the frown on my face as I beckon her over from the door. She stop a yard or so away. Sitting at my desk, I'm only looking up a few inches into her eyes. My own eyes looking back at me.

I clear my throat, toughen my voice.

"Didn I tell you you was to obey Miss Anna? And even Balfour?"

I'm talking rough to her but what I'm seeing is the littlest drops of water like dew on her cheeks and forehead, and some tiny beads caught in her eyelashes that I didn't notice before how long they are. Caleb have long lashes, I don't know where they come from. But to think of Caleb makes me think of Carla, and this girl before me is shrouding that.

"Yes, Maasa," she say, a whisper.

I don't even bother with my usual business about calling me Maasa.

"So why you facety to Miss Anna?" I coarsen my voice again, but my hands resting on my legs want to lift like birds and perch on her little bubbies nestling in her damp shift.

"She two-face, Maasa." Her voice is suddenly emphatic. "An she pick directly on me, though it wasn my fault."

"What wasn't your fault?"

"She put down her tea careless on the table and it turn over. Splash up a dress I was working on for Miss Matty. She blaze-up at me, say is my fault it turn over. It wasn't my fault, Maas Jason, is she put it down careless."

Miranda starts to whimper, the drops on her cheeks joined by eyewater.

"But she say you facety-off to her. What you say to her?" I'm keeping my voice quiet.

She's sobbing in earnest now.

"I tell her is she careless, Maas Jason, not me, I talking the truth, and she know it too, I cyan see in her face. But she box me. Hard, nearly throw me back onto the table with the needle and pin and scissors. I know I shouldn't talk like that to Miss Anna, and I won't do it again, Maas Jason."

Words and tears are tumbling out of her like a stream that will never stop. Is the easiest thing to simply reach my hands the couple feet between us, meaning to comfort her. And she come, without reluctance. My face find itself in her shoulder blade, bony as a bird but smelling of soapwood and rosewater. All by itself my tongue reach out and taste her butter skin, and I am lost.

I hear and feel her mouth mumbling and sobbing on my own shoulder, I feel a wetness from her eyewater seeping into my shirt, but the nearness of her is blinding me to everything else but the smell and the taste of her butter skin. I'm looking through the dewdrop lens with my tongue and seeing the rosewood of her little nipples harden as I suck them like sweetie through her dress, and is not my tongue that's the lens any longer but my cock, which is snaking down my leg that's touching hers. I feel her feeling it against her, and she draw back. Just a little. Enough to bring me to some sort of sense, but not my cock. Everything inside me squeeze together like a fist and then it explode with a kinda pain into stars and flowers, and I feel something trickling down my leg that is no longer touching hers, thank God, and saliva is filling my mouth that is remembering her bubby.

She don't run away. Only step back to where she was before and look at me, frighten. I frighten too. I never know myself like this before. As I feel the seed-juice cooling into a crust on my skin, I feel my whole self crumble like dry bread.

I want to tell Miranda sorry, but my tongue is as dead as my cock. Is she save me.

"You get the message from Miss Delphy?" She speaks quiet.

"Yes. Tenky."

She take her hand and wipe her face dry. Her face is darker than before, but her eyes seem brighter.

"I will behave, Maasa," she say, soft-soft as I'm smelling her still on my top lip.

She whisper through the door just as Jack come through it to tell me that Mathilde is calling me downstairs.

"Missa Douglas come back," he says.

He pays not the slightest attention to Miranda. His eyes is seeing what he imagines awaits me downstairs.

➣ 124 ⬿

Narrative: Whip, Wednesday, December 28

JASON HEARS MAGNUS BEFORE SEEING HIM. Coming down the stairs with Jack as a shadow he hears Mathilde first. Just her voice, irritated—maybe at him. He doesn't care. But Magnus he hears clear as a bell.

"According to what the governor say, I can muster even *him* if I want to. Is a general emergency for the whole island."

Jason steps down into the room at that point. Magnus, still in his militia gear, including the sword, turns and smiles at him like a cat seeing his bowl of cream.

"Your three months are up," he says. "Get your uniform and your gun." He flicks his head as though dismissing Jason upstairs to his room.

"Not quite," Jason replies. "Another week."

"Well, there's a general emergency proclaim. The whole island."

"Have you seen the proclamation? Spanish Town is a long ride away." Jason's voice is casual, almost friendly.

"I don't have to see it. I know what it say."

"What it say?" asks Jason.

"It say you must get you gun and come and fight with us."

"I don't have a gun, Douglas." His voice has hardened. "And I don't want to fight anybody. Besides . . ." Jason laughs. "No proclamation from Spanish Town would say that."

He hears Mathilde behind him start to speak, but she doesn't get the chance. A well-built white man in dirty white drill comes noisily through the door, through the piazza and then into the living room.

Jason is amazed to recognize Cumberbatch, the overseer, to whom he has given scant thought, and who ignores him as he comes to attention in front of Magnus and salutes.

"We've found the ringleaders, Colonel," he reports.

Magnus lifts a casual salute to the overseer and turns to Jason. He grins. "Harbouring rebels, Pollard?"

Jason laughs, sees the face of Douglas darken as he asks, "Ringleaders of what?"

"The rebellion," Cumberbatch cries, turning in appeal to Magnus and noticing Jason for the first time.

"What rebellion?"

"They refuse to work." Cumberbatch's eyes open wide in astonishment and appeal to Magnus. "And they lay hands on me."

"No one lay hands on you, Cumberbatch. You whipped him. He took your whip away to stop you. You got it back."

Magnus Douglas is watching the exchange with growing incredulity. "Taking away whips?"

"Zey refuse to go into ze field this morning. Somesing about a strike, Jason say." Mathilde's smile includes Jason in its mocking tilt.

"Where you did find these rebels?" Jason asks the overseer.

"Under the big tree," he says.

"Which is exactly where you leave them this morning. And where I leave them too. How many of them?"

"Four." Cumberbatch's answer is surly; he's almost pouting.

Jason turns to Magnus. "You can only harbour someone who's running away. No one run away from Greencastle lately. Cumberbatch himself can tell you."

"Refuse to work?" Magnus's voice is tangled with disbelief. He points at Jason. "And you didn't whip them?"

"He don't allow whips on the niggers," says Mathilde from the side.

Jason looks cold at her. "I cyan speak for myself, Mathilde. No, Douglas, I don't allow whips to be used on Greencastle. The slaves is not animals."

"What they is?"

"They're the engines of our survival. For the moment."

Jason can see only Douglas and Cumberbatch, who scowl at him as with one face; he hears Mathilde draw a sharp breath behind him. Anna is silent.

"This place is a madhouse," Magnus bellows and stamps away to the door at the top of the steps. He pauses, looking down into the yard.

"These the ringleaders?"

"Yes, Colonel," says Cumberbatch.

They're looking down at the group at the bottom of the big house steps, four blacks surrounded by four whites with guns pointed at them, Simpson with a pistol at Scotty's head.

"The ones that refuse to work?"

"Yes, sir."

"The man is the one that hit you?"

Before the overseer can answer, Jason, right behind them, says, "He didn't hit him."

"You was there?" Magnus's spittle flies.

"No, I come just after. But I believe Scotty."

"You believe a slave. Before a white man?" He is almost choking on his exasperation.

"This slave, yes."

"Is you brother or something?" His eyes and lips are radiant with the taunt.

"No, Douglas. Not me brother. Only a honest man, that's all."

"What he is is a nigger," Magnus shouts. "A rebel." And he turns to suddenly rush down the steps, a riding crop raised high like a flag. His colonel's jacket flares as his sword clatters down each step. He rushes at Creole Scotty screaming "Get back to work!" and slashes repeatedly at Scotty's face, driving the slave, arms protecting his head, further back into the yard and the barren embrace of the whipping tree. There, no further retreat possible, Scotty steps forward to pin his attacker's arms to his side. The two men's faces are inches apart, the white man still bellowing, the black man silent, his face streaming with sweat and spit.

Jason is only yards behind, ignored by both. Surprised by Magnus's eruption of fury and Scotty's reaction, the four white men are undecided as to protecting their colonel and protecting their captives. Their guns swivel here and here, useless and frightening. Jason is aware of Simpson close beside him, pistol wavering in the direction of the two struggling men. Scotty is holding on to Magnus for his life, trying to keep them in one spot. Simpson in the corner of his eye, Jason hears again Christian Eddie's calm voice: *Missa Douglas haffe dead too, by-and-by.*

"Shoot him!" Magnus shrieks, his spittle caught in the golden light of sunset. "Shoot!"

An explosion close-by deafens Jason. A few seconds later another, further away. He hears women crying out like birds—Mathilde, Anna, perhaps Pheba.

Jason rushes up to the embracing men, separates them. His back to Scotty, he snatches Magnus's crop and pushes him away. "I tell you already. No whipping on Greencastle."

Douglas, wiping his lips with the back of his hand, reaches for his sword. Without a thought Jason hits at his hand. He's holding the tip so it's the handle of the riding crop, a wooden core braided with leather, that strikes Magnus on the knuckles. Magnus spins away and rushes up to Simpson, grabs his pistol. His crippled right hand cannot grasp it, and when Simpson says, whining, "It empty, sir," Magnus throws the weapon at him and rushes over to the other white men at the bottom of the steps.

Jason, riding crop properly held now, stalks a few yards behind Magnus, noting what might be relief on the bookkeeper's face as he passes.

"Shoot him!" Magnus shouts at them, flinging an arm behind and almost striking Jason. "He assault me. You is witness." He points at Mathilde and Anna halfway down the stairs. He turns back to the men. "Arrest him. For assault."

"I was defending myself, Douglas."

"I didn't hit you," Magnus says, as though surprised by the comeback.

Jason points at Scotty and, as calmly as he can manage, says, "You assaulted my property."

Magnus, hand momentarily forgotten, laughs. "He's not yours, Pollard. You don't own any niggers here. They're Anthony's."

"I'm in locum, Douglas. I explained that to you all earlier." He includes the other white men, Simpson and Cumberbatch who have joined them as well, in his explanation, and then turns back to Magnus. "You is a magistrate."

Jason's patronizing tone is not lost on Magnus, whose eyes flare at him. But just for a moment, as he again points his swelling hand at Jason. "You will wish you did stay in England, Pollard. With you saints." Magnus turns his back and then gestures in Scotty's direction. "But I taking him with me. Property or no property, locum or no locum, him is a rebel. And I will heng him."

Jason watches, silent and helpless, as the whites encircle Scotty and entrap him with pieces of rope. Staring elsewhere, Scotty makes no resistance. A Greencastle slave whom Jason recognizes as from the house but doesn't know leads several horses from behind the big house and stands, as the white men claim them and mount. Last is Cumberbatch, who knots Scotty to his pommel and, with a mocking look at Jason, kicks his horse forward, flinging Scotty's trussed body to the ground.

Magnus, having difficulty mounting without his right hand, shouts at Cumberbatch. "I don't want to hang a dead man. No fun in that. Take you time."

Jason watches the procession disappear in the direction of the road to Bellefields, highlighted in the slanting rays of sunset. He looks around for Jack, who will have to find torches for them to go into town, back to the jail once again. Pheba, Eddie and her daughter seem to have melted into the darkening air.

Righteous anger drains to lead in his feet.

≈ 125 ≈

Elorine: Prayers, Wednesday, December 28

SOMETIMES ON A WEDNESDAY PEOPLE COME to Zion after dark, them who can. Is not a regular thing, and Pappi usually tell us whether or not at the end of Sunday service. Since there wasn't any real service Christmas Day, nobody think to ask about it. They start coming, though, as soon as it get dark. Mingo is first.

Mingo don't usually come mid-week. Since Magnus and the mongoose-one Thomas hang Carpenter John, Mingo have a lot of responsibility in the sugarhouse. So when he turn up tonight, and before everybody else, I wonder if something happen up at Greencastle, cause Mingo know that Jason is a familiar down here. He come to the back door and call out to me, not loud but to make sure I hear him. Jassy don't leave her room since we bury her baby, and Pappi is still outside with Cyrus. So is me in the quiet house.

Mingo is hopping on his feet like the ground, even though is almost dark, is hot. As I greet him he begin. "Trouble, Miss Elly."

"Where?"

"Greencastle, Miss Elly."

"What kind of trouble?"

"Dem going to hang Scotty."

"Tonight?" I feel my foot-dem get heavy on the steps looking down on the yard.

"I don't think is tonight, Miss Elly. But when they tek away Scotty, Missa Douglas face was set."

As I hear the name I feel cold.

"Jason mek dem tek Scotty?" I feel a flame at him inside.

"The only thing Maas Jason could do, Miss Elly, is to help Scotty upright when Backra was going to drag him on the ground all the way back to town. Like him is wild pig." Mingo spit on the ground beside him.

Scotty was at Christmas chapel to hear Pappi tell Zion people they must not involve themself in any of the palampam that might happen. In myself, though, I can't blame him entirely. Sometimes you have to take you life into you own hands for it to mean anything. And now that life is in the hands of Magnus.

"So you was with Scotty in the siddown?" I ask Mingo.

"Yes and no, Miss Elly." He look away from me.

"What that mean?" I set my voice firm. Mingo can be girlish sometimes, like to carry news and talk in riddles.

"Maybe he tell Pheba in the night, and she tell Christian Eddie, but nobody never tell me what was going to happen." Mingo sound sulky. "But is my bredda from Zion, is me bring him here. So when we answer the conch this morning and assemble at Old Man, and Scotty announce that he not going back to work, I stannup with him. Rahder, I siddown."

But I know Mingo. There's more to come.

"Scotty declare that he's not working any more until he is free, or until they pay him, and all the slave-dem pon Greencastle. You shudda see Busha face, Miss Elly, you would think it was a garden egg with hair pon it." I couldn't help but smile.

"When Maas Jason come and tell us that Missus send for militia, though, and that Maasa Douglas is coming with them, I figure is time to make myself scarce, Miss Elly. Coward man keep good bone, eh?"

I couldn't blame Mingo for that neither.

While Mingo and me is talking, other people come through the gate. From the corner of my eye, I see Lissy and Mama Claris, and behind them Uncle Teo, who was out fishing Christmas Day. He turn to the workshop, but as the others going to the chapel at the back Lissy call out, "Mingo, come raise a hymn with us, nuh?"

"Soon come," he call to her.

But when we finish he tell me, "Another time, Miss Elly," and I give him tenky for coming to tell me what happen. Is dark by then, and probably he don't have a paper in case a constable stop him on the road through town, so he walk brisk through the gate.

Lissy see him and call out. Mingo hear her but he keep going. By-and-by Ishmael finish for the day, wash himself and change his clothes inside. Cyrus disappear into Jassy room. While Pappi and Uncle Teo is having a little evening bickle I sit down and tell them what happen up at Greencastle. I can see Ishmael is vex with Scotty, but he understand also.

In between the hymn-singing, Lissy leading us, he ask for prayers for our brother. I'm singing with them but I'm not listening, even to myself. I'm praying for Jason. I don't have words to say to Maasa God, I'm just praying that Jason will catch up with himself and behave sensible.

126

Narrative: Black Regiment, Thursday, December 29

ADEBEH AND BADDU SPEND THE MOST comfortable night since Belvedere in the abandoned slave quarters of a small estate. The big house is a smoking ruin; only the stone foundations remain, which they do not approach. On the front steps of the skeleton of what must have been the overseer's house, they see a figure sprawled on the porch. The canefields through which they passed yesterday to reach their sanctuary are mostly intact, just here and there patches of burn that didn't properly catch before an early-evening cloudburst doused them.

The man was spread out on the wooden porch like how Adebeh and Baddu had seen drunken men of every colour everywhere. They are most accustomed to black men like that, but this man is white. He's dead. Someone has done to his face and shoulders what Baddu did to the piglets two days before in the bush. There's as much blood splashed on the porch floor as Adebeh remembers on the ground beside the stream.

Adebeh cannot quell his rising stomach, and vomits.

The watchfulness that could have saved them from capture and slavery is a third presence in the hut they choose, at the section of the quarters furthest from two bodies, a man and a woman, found on the ground at the end nearer the big house. They'd been shot in the face and chest. Their cutlasses lie on the ground nearby; Adebeh and Sister claim them.

They inspect some of the other huts and find a few utensils, and a flint, to cook the plantains and yams they took from the provision grounds. But that was luck: it's clear the huts were abandoned after almost everything valuable and useful had been prepared for flight.

As they make a fire in the cooking spot in front of their hut, they're less cautious than they have been about smoke. They spent much of yesterday with the stain of it in their nostrils from the destruction they walked through, wiping dust and ashes from their sweating faces and arms.

They eat well: plantain and yam and some of the second piglet from up the hill. They sleep well, hands resting lightly on the cutlass handles, and wake refreshed. They bundle the remaining food for the day ahead, which they know must not be spent here.

They're retracing their steps through the canefields to the roadway they travelled yesterday—unsure of where they'll be going next—when they hear a shot, then, right afterwards, a confusion of horses and men crying out, and then more gunfire, from several guns. They dive into the cane and keep their heads down. People crash through the cane around them, some of the legs bare and dark, some uniformed, and the attached hands, holding rifles or pistols, pale.

"You two!" they hear a voice above them. "Stannup."

Adebeh turns his head to look up. There's a light-skinned militia man waving a rifle between Baddu's head and his own.

And then the man's mouth opens on a shriek as he pivots on one leg and collapses, clutching his other leg. Baddu springs upright wiping her cutlass through fingers as she grabs Adebeh's arm and sets off through the cane. Adebeh follows as best he can until the man's screams die away in the cane they're dodging through.

They burst into a shady space between three or four big trees, from behind which twenty or so men appear and move toward them from all directions. Their weapons—digging spears, cutlasses, two guns—are alert.

"Who you is?" The man demanding has a gun pointed at Sister. Standing as though on parade, he's wearing a crimson uniform jacket. They're in a clearing of bare hard-packed earth created between canefields and around a large tree. Adebeh senses more eyes watching them from within the cane.

"What you doing here?" another man shouts. His raised cutlass glints.

With great deliberation they both put their cutlasses on the ground next to their feet. But they don't step away from them.

"We come to join you," Adebeh hears Sister say, deepening her voice and looking directly at the man holding the gun.

"Join who?"

"The regiment."

"What regiment?" This from the man with the cutlass.

"You's not the black regiment I hear bout?" Sister's voice is challenging.

"Hear from who?"

"Nayga," she answers with a wave. "All over."

Adebeh notices the leader man with the gun relax a little. "Where you come from?" he asks.

"Lima."

"I never hear bout Lima," he says, flexing the gun again.

"Near Palmyra."

He relaxes again. "You cyan fight?"

Baddu pats her shirt. "This is blood," she says, smiling with pride. "Militia man." As carefully as she put it down, and without another word, Baddu bends and picks up her cutlass.

Adebeh, whose shirt is clean, mimics her.

They haven't seen Akeen, whose eyes, Adebeh thinks, may well be among those in the cane. But he's confident they've found his black regiment.

127

Adebeh: Waiting, Thursday, December 29

THE PLAN IS TO ATTACK THE big estate where Sister and me find weself. Montpelier. The whitepeople who own it own most of what we was looking at from on top. The militia have barracks here, the troop that went haring off south. They'll come back in due course.

Meantime, Sister and me find weself marching up and down on a piece of road between the canefields. The road snakes between hillocks, and Dove, the man with the gun who challenged us first, puts lookouts on rises in front and behind us. We's part of the regiment now. Nobody around us know, or even suspect, that we's Yenkunkun, or that Sister is not a man.

A few of them have guns, like Dove, who stand to the side of the road with his rifle on his shoulder and shout us to and fro. But most is like us, with cutlass and digging stick, long and short. Some of them is barefoot, but they's marching up and down with the rest, eyes bright and hopeful. As we's marching, kicking up dust to choke on, I's finding a trickle of brightness, of hope, seeping into my own self. Maybe is because we's part of a big group, about sixty of us. Just the marching make you feel strong.

Blackpeople have a way to look at people with lighter skins like they's omnipotent. And sometimes they's right, especially if you's a slave and belong to them like a shoe or a cow. Yenkunkun don't think like that, but the longer I stay in this island, the better I understand how these blackpeople allow themself to get beat-down into the ground. Especially the ones that born and grow here. Belvedere teach me a lot about slaves. And about hope.

And now they's rising up at last. And on the open road! Where every puss and dawg can see them, and every white puss and dawg can challenge them or shoot them down.

As we's marching I hear the men talking to each other. There's another slave regiment coming up from the south, and maybe one more from across the river nearby, from the west. Still, I can't help but think the thoughts I had when Akeen first tell us about the black regiment. The militia men I see all have guns, some of them, like the one Baddu chop down, and pistol as well. And every man of them have a horse. We's barefoot soldiers. Infantry, if you want to give us a fancy name. And the men is grumbling against Dove already. I hear one next to me saying that no one elect him Maasa God Almighty, to be ordering Nayga to march in the hot sun.

I feel to box the fellow and tell him that if Dove was white, him would not be complaining. Still, I holding on to hope. And to the prayers I make about Daddy Sharpe, whose name I hear tossed about like a ball by the marchers. After half an hour of drilling, Dove call a rest. Me and Sister find a big stone by the side of the road and siddown on it, the two of us. We's not there long when a shadow fall on us.

"Don't I know you?" A man's voice, old. I recognize it but he's pointing at Baddu.

"Somebody else, old man." Baddu's voice is deeper and harsher.

To distract him I get up and pull him a few yards. "So you find you regiment," I say to Akeen, smiling.

"You don't believe me when I tell you," he laugh. "But see it here!"

His scrawny neck is turning back every now and then to look back at Sister. "What happen to the woman that was with you?"

"She still up there," I say, waving at the hills behind us. I lead him toward a group of about ten men sitting down on the verge. I don't know them, nor them me. The only people I know here is Sister—who answer to the name Bryden—and now old man Akeen. I plug myself into a space in the circle and immediately realize why the space is there in the first place. The next man on my left stink!

But then I realize the smell. Horse. I turn and smile at him. "I name Adebeh," I say as friendly as I can. "May I ask you yours?"

"I name Kofi," the man say. His voice is dark chocolate, and private.

A pistol on the grass between his feet, a plaited leather riding crop next to it. His left hand rest on a lance. Not a long digging stick as I see some of them carrying but a gnarly piece of polished tree branch with a fitted iron tip made in a foundry. Also—and most unusual of all—his feet live in leather shoes that enclose them, and have soles. This is not a field hand like most of the others in the regiment.

I put down my cutlass and offer my hand. From working on the coffee slopes and at Kojo Town, mine isn't any longer but I recognize his. Working with horses and leather makes your hands soft.

"You look after horse," I say. He nods and looks hard at me. "Me too."

"Where?"

I don't know a thing about it, how many horses or otherwise it has, but I answer, quick-quick, "Lima."

"Where dat?"

I give Kofi what Baddu gave Dove on the first go-round. "Near to Adelphi and Content. Is a small place, not big like here," I say, waving at the canes around. "You know St. James Parish?"

"Only the town," he say. "Montego Bay. Busha send me there sometime, to hire out."

"Horses?"

"I do other things," he reply. "Mason work, and carpenter." He flick a prideful smile at me. "I make plenty money for Shettlewood."

"And now you planning to make plenty for youself," I suggest to him. He smile, broader, nod his head.

I find myself liking this Kofi. His Guinea markings are different to Akeen's, and not as deep. He could have a slave name as well, but I don't ask him. I like his quietness, and the way he look you in the eye. You know he's not a man to mess with. Besides, he look after horses.

Everybody is relaxing in the afternoon breeze, glad for the sun's cooling down toward darkness, when we hear two abengs, one from each side of us. Everybody jump up. A voice shout, "Disappear!" We all just melt into the cane, me worrying where Baddu is.

128

Elorine: Distant Drums, Thursday, December 29

COURTNEY COME BY THIS MORNING, plenty earlier than he usually come to clean the chapel. I can tell from I see him that he have news.

Good news and bad news, as it turn out.

The good news is that his friend Royston had it wrong the other day. The Bellefields militia is not mustering. Not yet anyways. So the soldiers at Fort George is not marching into Bellefields. Instead, they sailing West, in some ships coming from Port Royal today. Real trouble is out there, just as people been promising for the longest while. But is not a siddown, as the snake Duncan would have us think. Is a rebellion. Courtney call it a uprising, though I don't know the difference, and Backra wouldn't even bother to figure it. To Backra, anything disturbing the peace, their peace, is rebellion.

West is not like Rickhambone that happen on just one estate. Plenty estates is burning, according to Ralston, and more than one Backra get himself dead, a whitelady too. Backra running from them estate into Montego and Falmouth, getting themself onto ship in the harbour, wanting to sail away for safety. Governor and general in Spanish Town getting on a ship, and soldier is sending from all parts to Montego. Militias in West is marching up and down. Big excitement!

Still, that is far from us. For now.

Courtney come just as we finish burying Jassy baby, just the four of us. I went myself to tell Mother Juba what happen but she wouldn't come. "Dat one born fe dead," she say with her pipe in her mouth. "Duppy come back fe duppy, me no business." She don't even stop sweeping her yard.

As soon as day break I did wake up Pappi and tell him. He grunt, that's all. I feel a little vex with him. But later he come outside to us, and take the shovel that Cyrus was using to widen the hole with the civil orange tree sapling and the baby navel string already. Pappi dig a deep hole. When he finish he stand back and look at me. I couldn't ask Cyrus or Jassy to do it, so I go myself to the room and gather up the bundle of cloth. It feel like it have a big yam inside. I bring it outside to Pappi. He turn and hand it to Cyrus.

Cyrus don't have any expression on his face as he bend down and put the bundle at the bottom of the hole. Pappi by that time gather some good-size stones and put them in. To stop the dawg-dem, even old Ginger, from digging. Then Cyrus take back the shovel and cover it in. Pappi put more stones atop.

Now the tree will grow around the baby, and the two of them will be one. By the time the tree come to bear, the baby won't matter so much, maybe even to Jassy and Cyrus.

129

Narrative: Montpelier, Thursday, December 29

THEY WAIT SOME MORE, Adebeh and Kofi and Baddu, who eventually finds her brother.

Standing as still as they can among the canes, there's nothing else to do but talk, softly. The whispering around them, cane leaves and voices, seems palpable. Listening, Adebeh learns a lot.

"You know this Daddy Sharpe?" he asks his new friend.

KOFI: I hear him preach.

BADDU: Where?

KOFI: I explain to you bredda already that Busha send me into the Bay from time to time. Is there I hear Daddy first. But I hear him later at prayer meeting also. In Retrieve and Belvedere. Is Belvedere Dove come from. Johnson come from Retrieve.

BADDU: Which Belvedere is that? Cane or coffee?

KOFI: Sugar.

ADEBEH: I thought Daddy Sharpe was from near to Montego.

KOFI: Yes. But him Maasa give him ticket to go up and down. That is how him reach down this side.

BADDU: So you's Christian.

KOFI: You could say that. When I baptize they give me the name John, and at prayer meeting they call me John. On Shettlewood, Busha-dem call me Sippio, I don't know why. But my poopa name me Kofi. That is what I call meself.

BADDU: So is Daddy why you find youself here?

KOFI: Yes and no. Is not a simple story.

ADEBEH: But he's a part of the story?

KOFI: Yes and no.

BADDU: What is the yes part?

KOFI: If you did ever hear him preach you would understand. You would believe say him could talk the bird-dem right down into his hand.

BADDU: What him say?

KOFI: That we's not horse or mule like the way Busha feel free to lash we when he please. We's Maasa God pickni too, just like Busha and Maasa. But is not him bring me here.

BADDU: Who then?

KOFI: Captain Dove.

ADEBEH: You mean . . .?

KOFI: Yes, him same one. Maasa don't allow a chapel to build on Shettlewood, but he allow us to go to the one at Belvedere—is not far. Dove is deacon for there. Dove don't tell us so himself, but I get to learn that Daddy make a set of the deacon-dem hereabouts put their hand on the Bible and swear a blood oath.

BADDU: What kind of oath?

KOFI: That they will tell the slaves not to come out after Christmas. To siddown until Maasa agree to pay us. And if they don't pay us, or if they bring violence, then we is to fight. And if it come to that, he make certain people officer in the regiment. The black regiment. Dove is captain. Johnson is colonel, Campbell too.

BADDU: This Daddy Sharpe maybe talk good, Kofi. But if he think Backra going to pay we to work, he dreaming.

ADEBEH: The white man not paying any slave wages.

KOFI: We won't be slave much longer. Johnson bringing another regiment up from the south.

"How many?" Adebeh asks Kofi, who shrugs.

"Could be a thousand," he says. "Could be fifty."

"Militia have more than fifty," Baddu says. "And then there's the soldier-dem. Dem is more than a thousand."

"The soldier-dem not going attack us," Kofi says with a confident smile.

"Why?" asks Adebeh.

"Dem is the King soldier. And the King sending we free paper with Reverend Burchell, who is coming on the ship from England. Him leave some time past to go and collect it for us. Moreso, Backra is making a secret plan to transport all the man-dem to dem cousin in America, who have slave. They will keep the woman-dem to fuck and breed and make more slave. So that Nayga will never be free in this life."

"Who tell you so?" Baddu, standing close to Kofi, leans back to look into his face. "Daddy?"

"That is what I hear around." Adebeh watches his eyes darken with the first doubt.

Neither of them press him further. But Adebeh, knowing more about the King's soldiers than their new friend, and recalling the terms of the King's proclamation while he was still in Scotia, begins to wonder what he and Sister are in for among people who probably share Kofi's views. The day before yesterday they were complete strangers. They still don't know even their names.

"We have to free weself," Adebeh offers, softly, more talking to himself.

"We can't wait for the King." Baddu's voice is sandpaper. "Him is far away. And him soldiers is here."

From the edge of the canes they can see the militia barracks for the troop that startled them on the road, the King's Road, as Kofi calls it, that leads through ornate gates into the property. They're encamped in tents of various sizes on pastures that lie beyond the wall that separates the canefields from the sugar works and great house. The horses are gathered under a spreading tree, tended by blacks.

It's a prosperous settlement. Adebeh can see that right away. The house and the sugar works are substantial. And, in the slanting light of late afternoon, lovely. A stream meanders beside the King's Road and slips onto the property under a bridge built into the wall. It waters the pastures on which cows browse amid the clusters of militiamen before wandering through the sugar works. Behind everything the mountains glow, receding in golden-blue waves into the darkening sky.

Suddenly, there's a flurry of men scrambling for horses under the tree. And then, led by the man in the blue frock coat and the sword, a horde of them carrying guns across their backs gallops furiously through the gates and toward them. The canefield blacks, almost invisible at this point from the gathering dusk, shrink further into the canes, convinced their presence and purpose are known. But the men gallop past them, lashing their horses toward an inflamed sky. Adebeh smells the now familiar whiff of burning cane.

"Little Britches," Kofi says with a scornful smile as the troop gallops past.

"Who he be?" Adebeh asks.

"He name Grignon," Kofi says. "From the other side of the Bay. A big Backra in these parts. He in charge of militia for St. James."

"Why you call him Little Britches?"

"Everybody know him by that." Kofi shrugs.

From the dark distance they can hear shots and an uproar of voices.

"Maybe dem fire the trash house at the new works," Kofi cackles. Adebeh presumes he means another estate nearby.

Dove is not far off, straddling the edges of the cane and the King's Road. But they're not close enough to him to hear his discussion with two men who have appeared close behind each other. They're new to Adebeh and Baddu, but not to Kofi.

"The big one is Johnson," he whispers to them, his cheeks touching theirs on both sides. "The uniform is Campbell." Campbell, the smaller man, is wearing a military coat whose every cut is as fine as that worn by Little Britches. "They must be bring their people here." Kofi's voice quivers with excitement. "I did tell you. We ready for them now."

Campbell and Johnson are not by themselves; three or four men cluster each of them. Johnson's are all as powerfully built as him, two of them with rifles. Campbell's acolytes are as fancy as their leader, with jackets of various colours whose buttons gleam in the soft light. Then they merge into the cane with Dove's group.

Horses. More militia, brown men this time. In the middle of the troop Adebeh recognizes the man who Sister chopped, his leg heavily bandaged. Wincing with every jolt, he's sharing a mount with another man. Baddu touches her brother's arm.

"Reinforcement," Kofi whispers. He points with his chin. "See Maasa there."

But there are too many men moving past too quickly for them to identify Kofi's Maasa. It occurs to Adebeh that this conflict, as well as being a general fight for freedom, concerns any number of very personal matters that are in play between the men in the canes and those in the barracks. And the time for settlement is come. The men are restless, anxious for the fight.

And then Little Britches and his troops come back, some of them hooting as they ride past. Bad news for blacks, Adebeh figures. Johnson and Campbell and their men have disappeared. Easy in this near dark. Dove holds his hand up, first finger pointing. Be ready.

Adebeh, a small knot of unease forming like foam in his stomach, leans his shoulder against Sister. She presses back. For all he knows Lima's Maasa is here too. Or Cummings from the coffee mountainside.

A few cook fires dot the darkness beyond the wall of the estate as the militia men settle in for the night. Two sets of them: those mostly white, who'd ridden with Little Britches, and the brown troop that came later, the encampments separated by a few yards. The white line stretches all the way up to the great house.

Almost invisible figures appear, a man and a boy, and drive the cows into a pen on the edge of the pasture; they probably do this every evening at this time. Above them the birds gurgle as though burrowing themselves into the night.

At the moment Dove signals them out onto the roadway, Adebeh hears a sound that seems to be swelling out of the ground. It reminds him of the swarm of bees he remembers from a hive that he'd kicked over on Mr. Gregory's property in Hammonds Plain, near to Boydville where, aged sixteen, he had his first job.

Slowly the cacophony separates into conch shells and abengs and bugles being blown, pots beaten with metal sticks or flat cutlass blades, and wordless human shouts and screams. In the dark there's the sound of marching men, and of singing, as though accompanying the commotion.

As he and Sister and Kofi get closer, it becomes for Adebeh a carnival of duppies. Everything is shadows and dark movements distorted by distance. Dozens of ghostly rebels are inside the wall, and some of the noise is coming from them, but some also from the road, where a column of black men appears—only those in light clothing visible—heading for the open gate and the guardhouse. The first few ranks have rifles and pistols, those behind wave their cutlasses and digging sticks. Campbell leads them, seated on a big dark horse and flanked by two torchbearers. Close around him are several armed rebels, three of whom Adebeh recognizes from the consultation with Dove.

The ones inside the wall surge toward the white militia line, who seem immobilized by the dark turmoil. Three of the attacking rebels stumble, wounded. One gets up and staggers forward, cutlass aloft. Adebeh sees him illuminated in his death by the flash of the pistol that fells him a yard before he would reach his target.

Dove's men pick up speed and run toward the wall, beginning their own shouting. Beside him Adebeh hears Sister's bellow of rage, and remembers her mourning for Petta. His own voice catches in his throat like a trapped bird, but as he runs he's thinking of Mam and Da, of the violence and cruelty he's witnessed and endured in this place, of the banished and leave-behind Trelawnys in Scotia hemmed in by whites. A roar fills his head, quickening his feet.

He trips over a man who stumbles in front of him. Kofi grabs his arm to steady him, and the three of them, behind Dove waving his pistol in the air, run on toward the property wall. They aim for the gatehouse, a sturdy hut with six or so militiamen on guard. The tumult of attack engulfs them.

But there's a strange silence beyond the boundary wall, Adebeh observes. The line of white militiamen clusters around the grand staircase leading into the great house. The brown militiamen are moving their guns around, searching for targets. They've formed themselves into an untidy square, having no idea where an attack might come from. The few shots heard must be from Campbell's rebels rushing the wall or from those already inside. Adebeh finds comfort in the darkness that renders them—and himself—almost invisible. But the calm of the militia is ominous.

Beyond the wall in the last of the sun's light a figure in a pale shirt that he thinks is Johnson emerges from what Adebeh concludes are the slave quarters. He runs toward the militia followed by several shadows who have regrouped from the earlier rush. He's waving a torch in one hand and a pistol in the other. Fifty yards from the militia line Adebeh sees the figure disappear.

Johnson—if it is Johnson—has been shot. The light shirt rests on the ground, unmoving. The men running behind him rush to the body but are driven back by a cascade of shots. Some sprint back where they came from, others frantically scrape at the ground with their hands to appear flat. The volley sends Dove diving against the wall. He rests against it, Kofi and Adebeh and Baddu huddling together beside him.

"Johnson look dead," Dove says. His composure tells Adebeh that perhaps he expects the same fate. Neither he nor Kofi has fired yet. "We won't get to bury him neither."

Campbell is urging his men forward, sword aloft and boots digging into his horse's flanks. And then, as they stream through the gate, he's tumbled from it, grabbing his left shoulder and landing heavily with the shriek of a slaughtered pig. In a moment he's on his feet, screaming obscenities at his armed guards. They fire at the militia guards around the gate. Fire is returned and one of Campbell's guards holds his stomach and folds over. Campbell himself collapses. The other guards quickly surround their colonel and lift him back into the canes where Dove's troop hid.

And then a building near to the militia line bursts into flame. There's a big whoosh of sound and leaping fire. And then a torrent of shot, like heavy rain or light thunder. The duppies become real; the kneeling militiamen now have targets they can see.

Adebeh, peering over the wall with Baddu and Kofi on either side, watches those who can, flee in every direction, leaving behind those who can't.

"See the brute there!" Baddu exclaims, pointing her cutlass at a man riding a horse behind the militiamen. The figure is maybe a hundred yards away, and the dancing flames won't allow Adebeh any certainty. But Baddu is sure.

She's clambering onto the wall. Adebeh and Kofi grasp her shirt but she wrenches herself away and stands up on the narrow ledge. A moment later she's fallen back into Adebeh's arms that had just released her. Her shirt is second skin, pasted with blood that pumps all over her brother. Kofi hovers over them, whimpering prayers.

Adebeh uses the same pruning knife from Belvedere that he'd cut Baddu's hair with yesterday to slice the binding cloth over her breasts; that's where the blood is coming from.

Kofi gasps. "Lord Jesus!"

Baddu gasps too, looking into her brother's eyes with a longing he'd seen with Petta.

And then the gleam dissolves, and Sister is a log in Adebeh's weak arms.

The three of them are a stillness unto themselves, a pool of sorrow. Around them noise and flames and people billow in a storm. One of whom overshadows them and takes shape as a gun pointed at Kofi.

"Sippio," the man says. "I find you."

Before he can think, Adebeh drops Baddu and grabs Kofi's lance from the ground beside her. With an upward sweep he impales the militiaman looming above them. He slides down the crooked handle of the weapon, gurgling with surprise.

Kofi steps over the man and pulls his lance out from behind. Then he rests his pistol on the man's head and pulls the cocked trigger.

130

Elorine: More Prayers, Thursday, December 29

JASON SLEEP HERE LAST NIGHT. He send his bwoy Jack back to Green-castle, and was getting ready to bed down next to the dining table, just like when he was a bwoy himself. But I tell him I couldn't allow that, and clear a space in my workroom.

He arrive here after dark in a fury at the Magnus-one, who have Creole Scotty in jail, planning to hang him this morning for rebellion.

"Scotty coulda kill him," Jason say, more vex than I ever see him. "Kill him. But he just hold onto the fat fool. And he going heng for that!"

He come after we finish with prayers, just when Pappi was settling down to read. Pappi was not well pleased when he hear Ginger bark-ing, so is a good thing is only Jason. Who say sorry for visiting so late, and then launch himself into a cussing of Magnus that woulda include plenty badword if I wasn't there. He put me in mind of the Adebeh-one. I never heard a badword fall from his lips yet, and I know is because he have respect for me. Other man-dem cuss like I'm a duppy, not there.

When he finish telling the whole story, some of which I know already from Mingo, Pappi say to him with a grunt, "Is better Scotty did run way. Or kill him. Is the same difference to Magnus and them."

"I agree with you, Missa Livingstone. But Scotty don't kill anybody." He puff up himself like he's a bwoy playing at man. "He not going to hang Scotty so easy. Not like he do with Tombo."

"Is emergency," Pappi say, solemn as stone. "Backra can do anything him feel like in a emergency."

Jason suddenly get smaller. He know Pappi is talking truth.

"I have to try, Missa Livingstone," he say, lifting himself. He glance at me as if for backing. I had to stop from smiling. Is like Jason, for all the things he see and that happen to him in his life, still don't understand how things go in this place.

"How?" Pappi ask him. "You going to force Magnus to give him to you?" His face is serious and he's not mocking at Jason. Jason get smaller still.

"I can only try, sir. I owe Scotty that. Meself too." That's when he ask if he cyan sleep here.

This morning he tell me he sleep like a tree, and to tell truth I didn't hear him the whole night. He was luckier than me—I didn't sleep good at all. Every little sound, even Ginger clearing his throat, get me wondering whether is something in the yard, something in West Street, or something in town. If it was in town it would mean something big, something to do with the emergency. The vestry don't send for Pappi yet, cause he's working to get Backra ready. But we expect somebody to come today.

As I hear Jason stir I am up and through to the kitchen. Jassy is snoring, poor thing, so I catch-up the fire and get busy with the cornmeal and flour so at least he will have something in his belly to go and deal with Magnus.

He smile when I put the platter and mug in front of him. "Thank you, Elzie. I was going into town for something to eat, I don't want to be a trouble."

My chest flare-up to cuss him but I bite my tongue and just give him a look.

"So what you going to do?" I ask him.

"Get to the courthouse before Magnus have his way with Scotty."

"I will pray for you." It was all I could think to say.

"Thank you."

131

Adebeh: Through the Night,
Friday, December 30

"I COULDA NEVER EVEN WONDER THAT Bryden was a woman." This is Kofi, as he's taking me to Montego for me to send a letter to Mam about Sister.

I's thinking I maybe would find a boat to Halifax there—is a port, after all. A boat for myself, I mean. But I don't decide yet about that. The bitterness and rage that took Sister over the wall to go for Cummings, never mind he was so far away she didn't have much chance of reaching him, it transfer itself to me now. And it don't relieve itself even after I shoot the man. I was looking over the wall along with Kofi and Baddu, but I never see where the shot came from that killed her. But after she died between us, I take Kofi's pistol out of his hand and look over the wall again. I see a militia uniform about twenty yards away wrestling with a rebel, like the two of them is dancing. I steady Kofi's gun on the wall and wait. When the black man managed to push the other one away from him, I fire. The militiaman grab his throat and tumble. The black man swing a mighty swing with his cutlass into the other's shoulder and then disappear.

I see that as revenge for Sister. I don't see what colour the militia-man is, and it don't matter, only that he's dead. But so is Sister. I realize my angriness don't ease one little bit. I want to go on kill-ing—anybody, white or brown, who have to do with slavery. When the simple thought come into my head that Kofi and I are headed to a place full-up of white and brown people who must have slaves, I throw that over the fence and follow him.

I count myself blessed by the ancestors. They always put somebody in my way that can help when I most need it. They send Henry to help me find Sister. And now Kofi to lead me to Montego Bay. And they send a good night for it. Bright and clear moonlight. If the moon was up when the Regiment make their attack, the whole thing would be worse. Our black skin protect us.

My head is not as clear as the moonlight, though. The words to tell Mam about Sister is jumbling in my head like ants in a sweetie jar, but there's nothing sweet about any of them. And when she tell Da what is in the letter, it will be worse. But I figure the ancestors, or Baby Jesus who just born, will put the words on the paper for me.

I ask Kofi about that when we start out, where I will get the paper and things to write with. He smile a little secret smile and tell me don't worry about that. About three times in the night as we's picking our way through the bush, up hillside and down gully, across stream, he tell me tenky for saving his life, as he call it.

"You know him?" I ask.

"Him is attorney for the pen next to Shettlewood. I do some work over there sometimes. Him is a brute—plenty Nayga at Montpelier was looking for him. They will thank you. And if you didn't stick him first, him woulda kill you too, even though he don't know who you is from Adam." Kofi squawk with delight and relief.

Mention of Adam bring the Elorine-one into my mind. And Fergus. I feel bad about Fergus. His owner seem a decent man, but my experience in Scotia and the few months I spend in this place tell me that, as Mam says sometimes, *Outta street and inna yard is different place.* Whiteman Cameron maybe is sober long enough to remember me and what he give Fergus charge to ensure about me and the *Eagle.*

I just hope he's not in the workhouse, or that place under the courthouse that the other damn fool whiteman was trying to send me into for walking past with Trojan. All of that was working in me yesterday at Montpelier. Pastor Gilliam in Scotia is always reminding us that Jesus say you must love your enemy. Jesus was a brown man, from what I figure. But he wasn't black, and he wasn't a slave.

I don't know if I could live with leaving before I find out what happen to Fergus. And the person to ask is Elorine. She will know. And will listen.

"Lookya!" I hear from Kofi up ahead. We's on top of a rise, and he's pointing ahead in the general direction we's been going. A fire.

"Reading," he say. "The wharf. They must be burning the ships." I can tell from his voice he's pleased about this. Christian though he be, Kofi is not for turning the other cheek. The sky is a red-gold platter fanning out from the flames, like a offering. On the edge the stars twinkle like decorations for the feast.

When we're finished watching, though, Kofi head off again, and doesn't change direction or hesitate in where he's leading me. A hour or so later we's on the flat, and the sky behind the fires is brightening at the edge of the horizon. There's a lot of blackpeople on the road Kofi leads us onto. Like us, they's heading for Montego, or the Bay, as Kofi call it.

But as the road touch the seashore he pulls me to one side. "You have clothes?" I nod. I have Sister's bag with what leave back of the gift from Empress.

"Good," he say. "Sufficient people know me in the Bay. They don't know you, though. Like how you have blood on you clothes and you face, you favour rebel. Them will shoot you like bird as soon as spit on you."

He point to the sea, a small cove with yellow sand glowing in first light. "Give me Bryden bag," he instruct. "Then wash off." He's still having difficulty with Bryden being a woman. But his main problem now is me, even with saving his life. Nobody know who I be, and nobody much care. Is how it is, and I have to understand that. I can't get my friend into trouble sake of me.

So I go quiet into the sea, which is still warm from last night and wash off myself as Kofi instruct. I give him my bloody clothes and he take his cutlass and dig a hole in the sand to bury them. I pull up some seaweed from under my feet to scrub my body. Then I put on the dead man's clothes, figuring they'll be dry by the time we reach into town.

Kofi smile at me as we set off toward a church steeple he point at.

132

Jason: Mercy and Revenge, Friday, December 30

I THOUGHT I WAS GETTING TO courthouse early, but Magnus was there before me, watching my approach from atop the courthouse steps with a grin that grow bigger the closer I get.

When I reach the bottom of the steps he comes down a few, waving the bandage on his right hand at me. His jacket sleeve is slit to allow the enlarged hand and wrist.

"I tell Dr. Phillpot to send the bill to you."

I nod. "I will pay it."

He pauses, as if waiting for me to say something else, perhaps an apology. His uniform, without sword, looks like he's slept in it.

"You can take you nigger home," he says eventually.

"He's not mine," I say again.

Magnus shrugs. "If he was yours, I woulda heng him, like I say last night." He throws me a bleak smile. "But he belong to my friend. He woulda cuss me."

I keep my face blank, but behind it I'm wondering what Magnus is up to. He's watching my face closely. His unexpected magnanimity is almost certain to cost somebody else.

"What I have to do?" I ask, polite, formal.

He waves his hand again. "I tell Thomas already. Just go sign for him and take him home." He points at me. "But make sure you go back home. Straight. I might change my mind."

"You make the right decision," I tell him.

His eyes get small and hard. "Don't talk down to me, Pollard, remember you place. And you don't know what decision I make."

The last remark set my ears to tingling. There's a price that *some-body* will pay. Likely me, but it could be somebody else. Still, I busy myself into the jail and say "Morning" to Thomas, who look like he don't move from the last time I was here.

By-and-by a guard bring Scotty. As he comes toward me from the dark hole of the jail, he don't look like the man I know. Not his face anyway. And he's holding one arm with the other. And he's limping. When he smiles at me, I see only crusted lips. He says something to me but I couldn't hear words.

"Take him," Thomas says, like he's handing me a piece of dead meat.

When we step out from under the arch into the square, Scotty flinches from the light, and throws up an arm as though somebody might hit him.

Magnus is not on the steps, or anywhere else I can see. But as Scotty and me are walking over to Cherry under the big shade tree, I hear a clatter of horses, and when I look around I see Magnus followed by Cumberbatch and Thomas, and one of the men he bring to Greencastle yesterday. Behind them six or seven black men are marching, three of them with rifles.

They're not looking anywhere but straight ahead, and they're going in the direction I just come from. A cold hand grips my heart.

I find myself up on Cherry and saying to Scotty, urgent, "Get youself back to Greencastle. I will find myself there later."

I dig Cherry with my heels and follow the troop. When I'm sure of their destination, I kick Cherry again and gallop past them, leaving Magnus shouting behind me, and into the Livingstone's yard. Ishmael and his apprentice are just opening up, busy with starting the furnace.

"Trouble coming, Mr. Livingstone," I say to him, tripping up my legs and my tongue. "Right behind me."

I was correct. Magnus and the other white men file into the yard. The whites fan out, the guards surround myself and Ishmael.

"What is this about, Missa Douglas?" Ishmael, calm and polite, doesn't move from just inside the shed where he's met me.

"I don't have to tell you, Livingstone," Magnus says, scraping Ishmael and me with his voice and eyes. "But I will." His lips slit into a smile. "You been preaching rebellion. I have a real witness this time."

"Who you have, Missa Douglas?" He's behind me so I cyaant see his face but I know the tone of voice. He vex.

Asking the same question in my head, I look at Magnus for an answer. And see that he realizes he shouldn't have impressed upon me the importance of taking Creole Scotty straight back to Greencastle. I also understand why Scotty looked the way he did. Either Thomas had a guard beat a report out of Scotty, or he was beaten because he wouldn't report Ishmael as the preacher of rebellion.

"I don't have to tell you that either, Livingstone. This is a emergency. You will do as I tell you to do." Magnus is puffing-up himself to cover his foolishness and give courage to his henchmen.

"I know that. But I have to remind you that Backra court dismiss the charge of rebellion against me last week. You was there, Missa Douglas. And I get lashes to tell me not to preach any more without a licence. With Maasa God as my witness, I don't preach one single word since last week Tuesday."

"Quiet, nigger." That is Cumberbatch barking, from his horse next to Magnus. And something jook me, call it revelation.

I turn to look at him. "Is *you* that beat-up Scotty, eh, Cumberbatch? You. Bruck his hand and mash-up his face."

The knowledge must be come from on high but is a true word, I know that in a instant. Cumberbatch start to swell himself to answer me, but he think better of it and try to knife me with his eyes. I look back at him like he is a new wall.

"Boynton?" Magnus says, formal and cold. "Arrest them. Both of them."

The same angel that bring revelation on its wings snap something inside me. As if I'm looking down from high-up, like from my room at Greencastle, I see myself set off between two guards for Magnus, something in my throat like a animal cornered.

And then I hear somebody scream-out "Jaze!"

I stop. Elorine. My hand drops to my side before I even realize I was holding a piece of iron above my head that I must-be pick up from the workshop. I have no memory.

Through the bubbling in my head, as my eyes focus on Elorine at the bottom of the kitchen steps, I hear Magnus.

"Little Missus Livingstone." Slime is on his tongue, and in his eyes as he looks from me to Elorine. "Come to rescue you boyfriend. You too late. You father, too. Go back inside."

Elorine draws back into herself a moment. But just a moment. Then I see something ignite in her shoulder and blaze-up into her eyes.

"You don't give me orders in my yard, Missa Douglas." She slaps her chest. "In your yard, but not in mine. Only me poopa."

Magnus is not expecting anything like that; none of the white men either. The guards look nervous. Then Magnus recovers.

"You want orders?" He yelp, "Boynton! Arrest that bitch as well."

"You call me bitch one time, Missa Douglas. I was a gyal then. I not a gyal now. I wasn a bitch then and I not a bitch now. Don't call me bitch."

The slimy smile appears on his face again as he croaks, "You remember."

Elorine clears her throat and spits in the dirt between herself and Magnus's horse, who skitters.

I feel a tingling inside me, and a sudden stillness in Ishmael behind me. None of us know what is happening. Except Elorine. And Magnus.

133

Elorine: Old Story, Friday, December 30

HOW COULD I EVEN *IMAGINE*, this morning when I get up early-early to fix bickle for Jason, that the day would turn out like this? And is not even lunchtime yet.

I hear the horse-dem come into the yard, and voices I know belong to Backra. But I'm thinking is people come to get their gear ready for muster, now that a emergency call, as I get to understand. Because of that I'm not paying any attention. Until I hear Jason. And then I hear the Magnus-one.

I drop the dress I'm sewing and fly out in time to see Jason with a piece of iron in his hand heading for Magnus. I so frighten that when I scream out his name, I didn't even hear myself. Give thanks, Jason hear, and stop. Which bring Magnus into everything.

I didn't know everything that was going on when I reach outside, I just see some guards in their blue uniform standing around Jason and Pappi. One of them is that worm Boynton, who come here with Thomas to arrest Ishmael last week, and I see Brother Greenwich, from Zion, the one who whip Pappi and then come that same night to beg his pardon. All the Nayga look uncomfortable, even Boynton.

But once Magnus open his mouth I don't see anybody else, or hear anybody else. To tell truth I frighten myself with how I talk back to him. I never talk to Backra like that before. I think it, but I know better than to say what is in my mind. But once I make up my mind you cyan only dead one time, at the same moment I decide that is Maasa God deliver him here. And once I start to facety-back to him I realize why. He been a canker on my soul since I was sixteen years old. I feel dirty as shit to remember his hands under the frock I was wearing the day, that I can still remember even though I burn it the same evening, that cock inside me like a snail, that smell of him swaddling me like a dutty blood-cloth that need to burn.

Until I decide this morning that I don't care, this is the work of Maasa God, and open my mouth back at Magnus. As I'm listening to my own voice, I feel the bitterness that been inside me all these years like a sour orange squeezing a little sweetness into me. The more I talk back is the more sweetness easing itself into me. So by the time he call me bitch, I was free of him. And when I can see in his fat sweaty face that he know exactly who he is talking to, I was ready.

"Yes," I say. "I remember. I can remember every piece of doo-doo that splash on me."

As I say, I don't see or hear anybody else in the yard, not even Jason or Pappi. I don't know where the words coming from but I know I have to say them, get them out of me. Like the spit I spit into the dirt in front of him.

He still trying to keep that lizard smile, but I see that he's surprise. No Nayga bitch ever talk to him like that before.

"Boynton," he shout at the poor man. "I tell you to arrest her. You want me to shoot you? You disobeying orders?"

"What?" I hear myself say. "You going to arrest me cause you fuck me? Is me should arrest you, Missa Douglas."

And then I hear Pappi. "You do something to me daughter, Missa Douglas?" His voice coil around the words like a whip. "When she was a pickni?"

Magnus slide his smile from me onto Pappi. "You daughter . . ."

But he never get any further. Pappi chop right across him like he bring down a hammer in his shop. "You is the abomination of desolation," he shout at Magnus, not moving from where he stand inside the circle of guards. "You is a whited wall sitting in judgement when you youself is full of uncleanness."

I give a glance to Jason, almost next to me. He watching Magnus like you would watch a mad dawg you buck-up out in the street, and he still holding the piece of iron. But he don't say anything.

"You fool me father, Livingstone. He think you is a good nigger.

That fool Cavendish, too. But you don't fool me. You is a trouble-maker, and I going hang you for it."

That is when Jason move. Quick as sight he's over at Magnus, making sounds I never hear from a human before. Before anybody else could move he leap up on the horse and him and Magnus go over the other side onto the ground, landing in a tangle of bodies and horse legs. Jason raise his hand with the iron and Pappi shout-out "Jason!" but it was too late. His hand come down once with full force, and I hear two sounds—the blow, and Magnus shoulder as it shatter. I see the other Backra-dem start to move their horse around as they searching in their waist for pistol and I find myself in the middle of them waving my hand in front the horse face so that they frighten and jump around. Backra shouting at me but I don't pay them any mind. Ishmael run over to Jason, who have the iron in the air again, and lift him up like a sack of cornmeal off of Magnus. He put him down on his feet and hold him from behind to keep him from getting back to Magnus.

Pappi never mean it to happen, of course, but that was the worst thing he could do for Jason. It give one whiteman—I hear after-wards he name Cumberbatch—a clear shot at Jason. He fire one bullet into Jason chest and kill him dead on the spot. Jason sag in Pappi hands like a dolly. Pappi himself don't understand what happen for a moment.

A silence like stone descend. The sun is bright overhead but every-thing in the yard is dark. Jason shirt turn red and is when the blood touch Pappi hands, still holding Jason, that he lower him to the ground.

134

Adebeh: Sister! Friday, December 30

Montego, Jamaica
December 30, 1831

Dear Mam,
I hope this finds you and Da well, and the little ones. Please say howdy to all for me. Especially to you, Eddie, since you will be reading this to Mam.

I am writing from the place all Trelawnys' troubles began, to bring you more trouble. I am sorry to say this letter is bringing bad news. You and Da send me here to find Baddu, and I find her. I remember all the stories that you told me, and I find her. She was in Kojo Town, so I got to see the places I been hearing about since I was small.

But I cannot bring her back with me to Boydville. There is no other way to tell you why but to tell you. She is dead.

By and by you will come to hear about the uprising by slaves in Jamaica. It is still going on as I's writing to you. Baddu and me was part of it. It would take too long to tell you how, but I will tell you, in the goodness of time, when I see you and Da and the little ones.

She didn't die a slave; she died a Maroon, in battle. And I took a revenge on the people who shoot her. I also killed another militiaman who was going to shoot my friend. It's cause of that friend why I's writing to you now. You could say that he save my life, because I didn't have any idea how I was going to let you know the sad news. I know somebody who can help, he said, and I feel better right away. He is not Maroon, but has been a true friend. I will tell him thanks from you and Da.

But if Kofi and me had remained long enough to bury Baddu in the right and proper manner, I would not be here to write to you because that battle was lost. So say words and drink some rum for Sister's spirit.

I have to go now, to find some way to get this into your hands. Maybe there's a boat going to Halifax. If there is, the ancestors will lead me there.

Your loving but sad son,
Adebeh

135

Elorine: Rachel Weeping, Friday, December 30

BULLFROG MAGNUS MUST UNDERSTAND BY NOW that Pappi save his life. It would scorch his tongue to say so, much less to say tenky, but he *must* know. He don't even try to take Pappi with him when they leave. You could see the brute thinking about it, but his shoulder is swelling every minute, leaking blood on his tunic, and between that and the hand that have a bandage already from Jason, and which he fall down on top of from the horse, it was as much as he could do to not bawl eyewater from the pain. You could see that too. And he wouldn't notice, or any of the other Backra-dem, but if Jason didn't kill him, one of the guards with a gun would do it. I see that in their face, even though none of them know Jason. The way they look at Magnus, and the one name Cumberbatch, their life didn't worth much to Nayga.

Pappi stand over Jason and look around him with a terrible anger in his eyes. But his voice is like sandpaper, weary. "Enough blood spill here today, Missa Douglas. Yours, too." He looking only at Magnus but he talking to all the Backra-dem, and to everybody in the yard. "Leave us, please, to bury we dead."

Magnus horse move under him and I see him wince.

When they leave, Pappi bring Jason inside. I run and find a set of cloth to put under him on the dining table so that the board is not too hard for him—poor me, to worry about stupidness like that. I send Jassy, eye big like a bowl, to fetch a basin of water with rum and orange and rosebush in it. While she's doing that, I cut off his shirt completely. The hole in his chest bring bile to my mouth but I force it back down—Jason would laugh at me if I bring up my bickle all over him.

When Jassy come back, I wipe him off like the baby I will never have. Pappi appear with some aloe vera from the yard, peeled and ready. He lift and I tear the cloth under him to bind the aloe over the wound. It's bitter, but he cyaant feel that now.

Then Pappi go back outside, as if he know I need to be alone with my friend. And as I look at him, his face is at peace like a flower; I couldn't help but remark to myself on his skin, and remember when we was young pickni before either of us grow hair, splashing naked in the sea at the end of West Street. I am black, of course, so nothing on me look different even now. But Jason always look as if he's wearing shirt and pants, his face and hands so dark and the rest so fair. Now too, in his chest.

As I look down on his face, I feel my eyes prickling like onion juice get into them. Is cause of me why Jason is dead. Is all well and good for Jesus to give up his life for his friends, but that is no comfort to me now. He know he was coming back. Jason not coming back. He gone from me forever and ever amen. Cause of my sin of pride. Thinking that is Maasa God deliver the Magnus-brute into my hands for me to cuss him and feel good. Instead He deliver Jason up like a offering for Backra to sacrifice. Cause of me. I will take that knowledge to my grave, and all the tears I feel building up like a river behind my eyeball will not wash that stain away.

I find myself sitting in Pappi chair to one side of the table, and reach under it for his Bible. Flies are buzzing around, even with the bitter aloe and sour orange, so I send Jassy for a piece of lignum vitae bush to brush them away from him.

I don't rightly know whether is my fingers or my mind but I find myself in the Psalm by the rivers of Babylon, weeping. The tears start silent, dropping one-one onto Pappi Bible. When I see that I shut the book, and it's as though that open the doors behind my eyes. My voice rise up into my throat and spill out into the room like water. Rachel weeping for her children because they are not.

Mercifully, after a long time I fall into a drowse. I don't really sleep, cause every time I hear a fly my hand with the bush sweep out by itself over Jason. But between times I sink back into David's Psalm, carried away captive but still having to sing a song of Zion. The song don't have any words, and is about Jason the sacrifice, pickni and man. Every time I doze off, I feel more tears running down on my cheeks and then drying to salt.

So my eye-dem was red when Anna come for him.

Pappi send a letter to Greencastle with Juba's Christian, soon after Backra leave, telling him to find himself there fast-fast. But is almost dark by the time Anna reach here. Her face is as pale as Jason chest. I don't know what Pappi letter say but it must be enough, cause she don't ask me anything, and I thank Jehovah for that. Anna is the closest I have to a white friend, but as things stand, I don't know if I could control myself. Her eyes red like the freckles on her face, but all I am seeing is skin. She is white. She is weeping for Jason her brother, yes, but she is white.

The same Jesus say you must forgive your enemy seventy times seven. I'm not good with sums except for money, but Nayga have plenty more than that to forgive whitepeople. That is a sea I know in my belly I can't cross right now. Maybe Jason cross it in England, but look what happen to him when he come back.

Two strapping Nayga come into the house behind Anna, one of them the yellow bwoy that always come with her into town. When she sign to them, they lift Jason off the table, the cloths too. They do it careful, showing some respect.

As I follow them down the steps with him, his chest and bandage bare to all eyes, I call out to them to wait.

I run inside and find the wedding cloth that Kekeré Bábà bring for me from Africa. When I reach back outside they have him lying on the back of a cart on a heap of cane leaf, though it is fresh-cut.

I fling the cloth over him, face and all.

"You can go on now," I say to Anna.

ACKNOWLEDGEMENTS

First, I'm very grateful to the taxpayers of Canada, whom, unbeknownst to most of them, contributed greatly to the writing of this book through timely grants from the Canada Council for the Arts, the Ontario Arts Council and the Toronto Arts Council.

Special thanks again to my late sister, Jean Pollard, who paid for writing lessons when I was just a teenager: trees from acorns. Special thanks also to the historians—in particular, Kamau Brathwaite. I'm privileged to call many my friends. Without their books and articles, this book would not exist. My nephew, Julian Cresser, a historian himself, provided research material, sometimes at short notice, when I needed it. He was also kind enough to drive me through the Great Valley so I could justify my flights of historical fancy. God bless him!

Our daughter Rachel, who has read the book in various forms and formats several times and possibly knows it as well as I do, is thanked for yeoperson service to her father. I am indebted to Jean D'Costa for her invaluable feedback, especially on linguistic aspects of the text.

Margaret Hart, my former agent, whom I dragged out of retirement, for the purpose of selling "her old friend", is thanked bounteously.

Several people contributed critical support of different kinds at different times in the long gestation of this project. Some of them, alphabetically: Marlene Bourdon-King, David Findlay, J. Fitzgerald Ford, Nalo Hopkinson, Hiromi Goto, Larissa Lai, Maureen Radlein, Olive Senior, Jennifer Stevenson. Many others also provided insight and sustenance; you know who you are.

I have derived much inspiration and encouragement from our children, David, Rachel and Daniel Mordecai, who, not generally patient otherwise, have waited most of their lives to see this book, cheering their Papa along the way with opinions (generally correct) and suggestions (not always taken).

My wife, Pamela Mordecai has been the most patient, most supportive and most enthusiastic. What more can one ask in a life partner? One who writes so wonderfully to boot.

The errors are, of course, all mine

Give thanks and praises!